Frank Lee Benedict

John Worthington's Name

A Novel

Frank Lee Benedict

John Worthington's Name
A Novel

ISBN/EAN: 9783337000653

Printed in Europe, USA, Canada, Australia, Japan

Cover: Foto ©Andreas Hilbeck / pixelio.de

More available books at **www.hansebooks.com**

Anthony Trollope's Works.

Anthony Trollope's position grows more secure with every new work which comes from his pen. He is one of the most prolific of writers, yet his stories improve with time instead of growing weaker, and each is as finished and as forcible as though it were the sole production of the author.—*N. Y. Sun.*

Mr. Trollope's characters are drawn with an outline firm, bold, strong. His side-thrusts at some of the lies which pass current in society are very keen.—*Congregationalist,* Boston.

BROWN, JONES, AND ROBINSON. 8vo, Paper, 50 cents

CAN YOU FORGIVE HER? Illustrations. 8vo, Cloth, $2 00; Paper, $1 50.

CASTLE RICHMOND. 12mo, Cloth, $1 50.

DOCTOR THORNE. 12mo, Cloth, $1 50.

FRAMLEY PARSONAGE. Illustrations. 12mo, Cloth, $1 75.

HARRY HEATHCOTE OF GANGOIL. Illustrations. 8vo, Paper, 25 cents.

HE KNEW HE WAS RIGHT. Illustrations. 8vo, Cloth, $1 50; Paper, $1 00.

LADY ANNA. 8vo, Paper, 50 cents.

MISS MACKENZIE. 8vo, Paper, 50 cents.

NORTH AMERICA. 12mo, Cloth, $1 50.

ORLEY FARM. Illustrations. 8vo, Cloth, $2 00; Paper, $1 50.

PHINEAS FINN, THE IRISH MEMBER. Illustrations. 8vo, Cloth, $1 75; Paper, $1 25.

PHINEAS REDUX. Illustrations. 8vo, Paper, $1 25; Cloth, $1 75.

RACHEL RAY. 8vo, Paper, 50 cents.

RALPH THE HEIR. Illustrations. 8vo, Cloth, $1 75; Paper, $1 25.

SIR HARRY HOTSPUR OF HUMBLETHWAITE. Illustrations. 8vo, Paper, 50 cents.

THE BELTON ESTATE. 8vo, Paper, 50 cents.

THE BERTRAMS. 12mo, Cloth, $1 50.

THE CLAVERINGS. Illustrations. 8vo, Cloth, $1 00; Paper, 50 cents.

THE EUSTACE DIAMONDS. 8vo, Cloth, $1 75; Paper, $1 25.

THE GOLDEN LION OF GRANPERE. Illustrations. 8vo, Paper, 75 cents; Cloth, $1 25.

THE LAST CHRONICLE OF BARSET. Illustrations. 8vo, Cloth, $2 00. Paper, $1 50.

THE SMALL HOUSE AT ALLINGTON. Illustrations. 8vo, Cloth, $2 00. Paper, $1 50.

THE THREE CLERKS. 12mo, Cloth, $1 50.

THE VICAR OF BULLHAMPTON. Illustrations. 8vo, Cloth, $1 75; Paper, $1 25.

THE WARDEN AND BARCHESTER TOWERS. Complete in One Volume. 8vo, Paper, 75 cents.

WEST INDIES AND THE SPANISH MAIN. 12mo, Cloth, $1 50.

Published by HARPER & BROTHERS, New York.

Sent by mail, postage prepaid, to any part of the United States, on receipt of the price.

JOHN WORTHINGTON'S NAME.

A Novel.

By FRANK LEE BENEDICT,

AUTHOR OF

"MY DAUGHTER ELINOR," "MISS VAN KORTLAND," "MISS DOROTHY'S CHARGE," &c.

NEW YORK:

HARPER & BROTHERS, PUBLISHERS,

FRANKLIN SQUARE.

1874.

BY FRANK LEE BENEDICT.

MY DAUGHTER ELINOR.   8vo, Paper, $1 25; Cloth, $1 75.

MISS VAN KORTLAND.   8vo, Paper, $1 00; Cloth, $1 50.

MISS DOROTHY'S CHARGE.   8vo, Paper, $1 00; Cloth, $1 50.

JOHN WORTHINGTON'S NAME.   8vo, Paper, $1 00; Cloth, $1 50.

PUBLISHED BY HARPER & BROTHERS, NEW YORK.

Sent by mail, postage prepaid, to any part of the United States, on receipt of the price.

TO MY DEAR FRIEND AND RELATIVE,

MRS. A. S. CHURCHILL.

FLORENCE, ITALY, 1874.

JOHN WORTHINGTON'S NAME.

CHAPTER I.

ROUGE-ET-NOIR.

THE music swelled joyously out again, and the dancers began their dizzy rounds with the fresh energy inspired by Strauss's most bewitching waltz. The bright toilets of the women, as usual, presented so odd a contrast to the sombre garb in which custom arrays the masculine race on festive occasions, that a fanciful person might have compared the scene to a troop of gaudy butterflies entangled in the embrace of wicked black wasps, from which no effort of the filmy-winged creatures could set them free.

It was the ball-room at Baden Baden, so I need attempt no description; the generality of people in this age of pilgrimages are as familiar with it as with their own libraries—a good many of them more at home there, perhaps; and those to whom fate has denied the privilege of absolutely standing within the enchanted precincts, know it nearly as well from photographs, and the endless summer tours wherewith travelers insist upon inflicting the public, in spite of loud and prolonged remonstrances from that much-suffering body.

Milly Crofton sat in the shadow of plump Mrs. Lawrence's voluminous draperies, and, with the enviable faculty of eighteen, was able to admire the brilliant spectacle, though she was only there for a short time as a looker-on. It was fortunate that she had youth enough to find amusement so easily, otherwise the last half hour might have dragged rather heavily; for Mrs. Lawrence had stumbled on an old acquaintance, and the two were so deep in conversation about matters which dated at least twenty years back, that neither the good-natured lady nor the antiquated beau—long resigned to flesh and lumbago—remembered that they were scarcely doing their duty by the young woman. But Milly bore the forgetfulness patiently, in spite of the fact that patience did not rank among her chief virtues, and that she belonged to a nation whereof the youth of both sexes are popularly supposed to enforce their wishes and whims upon their elders without compunction, and to find a ready submission on the part of the antiquated generation.

Milly was a charming specimen of the prettiest type of American girl; dazzling in complexion, with a profusion of soft blonde hair, eager blue eyes like a child's, a mouth which could pout or smile, perfect as to hands and feet, and with that indescribable elegance which is a more fortunate gift even than beauty. I think she is not exactly my heroine—certain dyspeptic critics insinuate that I have a bad habit of not contenting myself with one—but I am very fond of her, and could not resist these few words of personal description.

There she sat, listening absently to the unwearied hum of Mrs. Lawrence's voice, and the stuffy tones of the ancient beau, which sounded as if he spoke through layers of turtle steak, and watching the dancers while her tiny feet unconsciously kept time to the music. Presently two men paused by chance near the spot, and continued an audible conversation in French, which roused another train of thought in Milly's mind. One of the mustached creatures had just come from the gaming-tables, a winner, it appeared, and his companion was endeavoring to persuade him not to tempt Fate further on this occasion, but rest contented with the brief favor she had shown.

I am sorry to confess it, but straightway the Devil put a horrible idea into Milly's soul—I wish I could say a new one, but the Devil had whispered that thought on the first evening she set foot in the place, and during the last three days had never grown tired of presenting it to her. Heretofore Conscience had driven the tempter away without difficulty, but now, though a very well brought-up young person, Milly grew a little tired of Conscience and her admonitions—you know our best friends, unfortunately, are often somewhat wearisome! The ill-regulated and improper longing to try her luck at the tables rose once more in Milly's heart, growing stronger as she remembered—still the work of the imp, of course—that to-night would be her final opportunity. In the morning she was to return to the dullness of Vichy and the charge of her rightful chaperon, and the gayety of Baden would appear like a dream.

Milly did her best to struggle against the temptation, but most of us have occasionally discovered that a prolonged combat with desires leaves us so weakened, that in the end we are as bad off as if we had not fought at all—unless our guardian angels are kind enough, in spite of the failure, to count the effort in our favor. This was Milly's case; she began to feel really desperate. If she persevered in crucifying her own inclinations, she should certainly go frantic with regret when too late. She tried to be shocked at her own wickedness, but did not succeed very well. She remembered her dignified aunt away off in New York, by whom she had been intrusted to the care of some distant connections for these four months of wandering. The very idea of Mrs. Remsen's horror, if she could see her at this moment, and know what was in her mind, sent Milly into a fit of silent, nervous laughter. The Devil and Conscience strove awhile longer, and once Conscience was near gaining an ally. The ancient beau made an effort to depart—Milly saw it, and was half glad in the midst of her disappointment, as she thought that now she should be put beyond the reach of temptation. But Mrs. Lawrence unintentionally aided the Devil by detaining the decrepit beau.

"Don't leave us," she said, "we want to sit here; Milly enjoys watching the dancers—don't you, Milly?"

"Oh yes," Milly answered; then Conscience pricked her, and she added, "but don't stay a moment on my account." This was a triumph, but a brief one, for her monitor, because straightway the tempter offered Milly a hurried picture of the green tables, the eager players, the flash of the gold pieces, while the tones of the croupier rang in her ears, and the chink of the napoleons as they fell on the board, and she said, breathlessly, "though I like being here, I could stay all night."

Conscience retired in disgust, probably feeling that nothing further could be done to aid a young woman so hopelessly fascinated by the snares of the enemy.

"Dear little Milly," Mrs. Lawrence said, patting the girl's shoulder with one hand, while she held the beau fast with the other. "And so the story was true, Mr. Noyse?"

The antique sat down again. The pair plunged into a fresh torrent of talk, the more absorbing because it was the raking up of an old scandal about some mutual friend, and had to be whispered in order that it might not reach Milly's maiden ears. They were good for half an hour—the young lady was certain of that. She caught words enough to know of what they were talking: it was a fearfully long story; she remembered having heard it whispered by cronies of her aunt's while she was supposed to be busy with her drawing. Children hear every thing nowadays; the mercy is that they do not comprehend; though the freedom with which they discuss all sorts of subjects causes ill-natured people to give them credit for knowledge which they are far from possessing.

Now or never! If she slipped away at once, she could make her venture and get back by the time the history ended. If she hesitated,

this grand opportunity of doing something preposterous and appalling was not likely to recur. She was quitting Baden—almost on the eve of quitting Europe, and a return was not probable. It was a misdemeanor so out of the common, and so fearful, that, now the instant for decision had arrived, it looked perfectly irresistible. What a horribly delightful secret to confide to her intimate friends when she reached home! They might be able to tell of stolen interviews—mysterious flirtations—astute dupings of maternal guardians—but how tame the records would sound in comparison to her own exploit! Actually to have gambled at Baden and to have won—for she should win, she knew that! She decided at once that, with the improper gains, she would purchase a bracelet which she had lately admired—a marvelous beast with more legs than a centipede, and as many eyes as Argus, only composed of rubies, and turquoises, and various other stones, and no two eyes made of the same gems. What were insipid flirtations, no matter how forbidden, to a wickedness like this?

Oh, she must go—she should get wild if she waited another instant—that idea of overwhelming her girlish friends by the confession of her enormity had been the tempter's crowning stroke! She rose from her seat—whispered to Mrs. Lawrence that she must seek the dressing-room because there was something wrong about her multitudinous tresses. "Don't stir," she added; "it is only a step; I can get there and back without any body's noticing me."

The color flamed into her cheeks, and the words nearly choked her; for she was a truthful little thing, and had not yet acquired the habit—only too common among her elders—of acting lies. Mrs. Lawrence nodded, without pausing in her rapid whispers, rather glad to have the girl absent for a time, because she had arrived at the most exciting point of her narrative, and it required a great effort to keep her voice sufficiently subdued, so that no syllable should reach her young companion.

Milly fled into the dressing-room first, because she knew that from thence she could escape unperceived. I suppose that, at this juncture, conscience flew off with a shriek from the contaminated purlieus of Baden. It is not probable there could chance to be, at the same moment, two persons worth worrying over in that home of dangerous delights; so, after this dismal failure, there was nothing left for Conscience but to fly away to her celestial home, and weep over the downfall of humanity

Milly allowed herself no leisure to think; she drew her white opera-cloak more closely over her shoulders, and sped on so eager to gain the goal of what she considered her diabolical desires, that each room seemed a thousand miles long, and the green tables a whole world away. Poor little Milly—I mean, wicked little Milly—it was very wrong; but, at the risk of appearing to encourage the younger generation in impropriety, for the life of me, I can not help laughing at the importance which the transgression assumed in her eyes. Nor was the freak in the least in keeping with her usual conduct. She had a genuine dislike, growing out of her thorough delicacy, to any thing that looked "fast," or sensational. She had led the quietest possible life, under the care of a relative far stricter in her ideas than modern guardians in general. She had read few of the romances which are only too much in vogue; daily newspapers—those curses of American homes—she had been taught to avoid; indiscriminate intimacies with girls of her own age were even unknown to her. In numberless ways, she was fresher and more child-like than most damsels of eighteen. Even her heart had never, in the slightest degree, awakened, and so helped her on toward the tumultuous season of womanhood. She had never had experience of a single flirtation; never found a temporary hero, except in books; and, usually, her heroes were evolved out of the wise histories Aunt Eliza had obliged her to read. I am quite aware that she will appear a very tame, uninteresting animal to young ladies learned in the lessons acquired out of hours, in boarding-schools, familiar with dramatic novels, and accustomed to criticise plays from the Gymnase. But I must write down the facts as they really were, even at the risk of depriving this one instance of depravity, on Milly's part, of all interest in the minds of the youth of to-day.

This very visit to Europe had been made under circumstances which would have denuded the idea of any charm, to most girls, and rendered the reality an unendurable penance. The Crittendons were distant connections of Mrs. Remsen's; and, the previous winter, Mrs. Crittendon had suffered from a tedious illness, during which Milly had so often cheered the invalid by her bright presence, that when, in the spring, the physicians ordered a sea-voyage, and a sojourn of two months at Vichy, Milly's society had been begged as a great favor. It would be a dull, stupid undertaking, old Mr. Crittendon confessed; but he pleaded so earnestly, that Milly could not have refused had the stupidity presented itself ever so strongly to her imagination.

She had a week's sojourn in Paris, a little wandering about Germany, then Mrs. Crittendon was seized with an acute return of her malady, and they hastened at once to the Baths. The time had not hung heavily on Milly's hands; she had no excitement, made few acquaintances; but every thing was so new and strange, that the quiet sojourn did not fill her with the weariness and disgust which they would have roused in the bosoms of many of her sex.

It was the first week in August now; only a fortnight before, Mrs. Lawrence, having indulged in one of her frequent visits to Europe, strayed into Vichy, and proposed taking Milly, for a few days, to Baden. Mrs. Crittendon was much better; and both she and her husband insisted that the invitation should be ac-

cepted. Milly had private doubts of her aunt's approval—if that lady could know she was to be trusted to the care of Minerva Lawrence—for, in spite of her wise baptismal appellation, and her forty-five years; in spite, too, of her having been, from childhood, Mrs. Remsen's friend, that dignified person had a very slight opinion of Minerva's wisdom and prudence. However, it was not a case for Milly's decision, and she submitted with a good grace to that of her elders, wild with delight at the idea of seeing the famous place, and certain that Mrs. Lawrence would prove an agreeable companion, if not a trustworthy chaperon.

And this was the result! In her most insane visions—if a mind so well regulated could be supposed to indulge in such—Mrs. Remsen would never have dreamed of Milly's sinking into so deep a pit, even under Minerva Lawrence's guardianship. It is difficult to see how the good soul could be blamed; but this would not have saved her from condemnation, could the appalling scene have been made visible to Eliza Remsen.

Milly Crofton hurried through what seemed the endless suite of rooms, and at last found herself at the entrance of the apartment down which the *rouge-et-noir* table stretched its sinuous length. It appeared to her that she had taken so much time to reach the spot, that she should already be missed; but this thought gave her no inclination to go back. Many girls, more capable of mad freaks than Milly, would have hesitated on the threshold; but she was rather an odd compound; childish as everybody thought her, there was a force of will at the bottom of her character which kept her determined and unshaken, now that she had fairly yielded to the temptation.

It was already late, and the room was crowded to excess. Of all places in the world where she could have ventured, perhaps there was none in which her appearance, unaccompanied, would have attracted so slight notice. The whole vast throng was too eager and engrossed to give her a single glance. People were either trying to push their way toward the tables, surrounded by rows three and four deep, or they were coming away with faces flushed by success, or hurrying out of sight of the spell which, in many instances, had lured them on to ruin and despair.

Men and women from every civilized nation under the sun were gathered there; the nearest realization possible to the scene the Tower of Babel must have presented might be gained as one listened to the subdued hum of conversation, subsiding into a complete silence near the tables; for even the spectators were too much occupied for speech, and only the croupier's voice, or the quick chink of gold pieces, interrupted the stillness.

Nobody appeared to see Milly; and she was equally oblivious of the crowd. To get to the board—to throw her stake upon it—that was the only thought in her mind. She had put her purse in her pocket while dressing—not with a premeditated intention to play; but she chanced to see it on her table, where she had carelessly left it—her boxes were locked, and she ready to go—so she seized the purse and hurried off in obedience to Mrs. Lawrence's impatient summons; for the good soul was the most restless woman alive, and never could bear to wait an instant.

Every thing seemed to favor Milly's wrongdoing. As she got near one end of the tables, the circle was broken momentarily by a man pushing his way rudely out of the press, with a muttered curse upon his luck. Milly was too busy to look at him, or she might have started back in horror at the white face, the rigid, set features, and the anguish of the dilated eyes.

The next morning, when the chill, gray dawn broke over Baden, the guardians of the night found a prostrate body lying in a lonely part of the grounds—a pistol by the white hand which still clutched at the turf it had torn up in final agony—a stream of blood oozing slowly from the left temple, and staining the grass. But the tragedy has nothing to do with my story, and it was not a sufficiently uncommon one to cause more than brief wonderment.

Milly only saw the broken *cordon* of human beings through which, by a quick movement, she could reach the tables. Another second, and she stood so close, that her hands touched the fatal board. She held her purse in her fingers—poured the gold it contained into her palm. There was not a large store—only five or six napoleons—but as Milly was far from rich, she knew too well the value of money to have regarded it, at a cooler moment, as a small sum. She was acquainted with the manner of playing; the morning she arrived, the ancient beau Noyse had shown her the gambling-rooms, and explained the mysteries of the game—that is, as well as he was able.

Milly had no space to reflect, or grow frightened; she was elbowed and pushed; no one seemed to regard whether she was old or young; then out rang the hoarse voice of the croupier, "*Faites votre jeu, messieurs!*"

Milly flung a napoleon upon the red—she had won. She was too sorely agitated to remove her winnings—to think at all—and, somehow, the sight of the gold gave her a sensation of terror, for the first time since she entered the room. A few seconds more, and her stake had doubled—trebled—quite a pile of yellow pieces lay before her. She became conscious now that those close about her were watching—some voice advised her, in French, to retire her gains—she could not do it—she was too much alarmed—she only wanted to get away—but the crowd had closed too thickly for any possibility of retreat.

A few added instants of indecision, while the table swam before her eyes—then she heard the cry, "Black wins," and saw her hoard swept away. She uttered a little exclamation —it was a kind of rage that took possession of her. If, an hour previous, any body had told her that anywhere in her life she could feel such emotions as beset her now, she would have laughed in scornful unbelief.

She dashed another napoleon upon the board —lost! Still another followed—lost! I am ashamed to write it—she had two left in her hand; she flung them both down—saw them both swept away!

As she raised her eyes she saw a man—a young man—standing opposite, and regarding her with a cold glance of wonder and disapproval. It only needed this to make her humiliation complete. How she got out of the throng she could not tell; but she was free, and trying, with tear-blinded eyes, to find her way back to the ball-room—tears of bitter shame, such as it was right she should shed, but—as I fear would have been the case with any of us— tears of anger, too.

She took the wrong turn—found herself in an apartment that she did not recognize; and before she could flee, a tall, black-mustached man was bending over her, and saying in French,

"Don't be afraid; we never eat pretty girls; I'll take care of you, my little one."

He actually touched her arm; she neither shrieked nor ran—simply waved him off, and said, in a voice which was calm in spite of her terror,

"Let me pass."

He was making an effort to detain her; before she could realize any thing, a strong hand pushed him violently back against the wall; and when Milly could see clearly again, his face was quite black under that iron gripe which had seized him.

"Don't, please, don't!" she cried.

The chevalier released the Frenchman, pointed to the door, and, after an instant's hesitation, the animal retreated, probably not caring to risk a second embrace from his antagonist.

In the midst of her alarm, Milly could see distinctly enough to know that the gentleman who had protected her was young, and evidently either English or American. She was trembling from head to foot; past tears now—but she said, piteously,

"I want to get back to the ball-room; I have lost my way."

"Allow me to show it you," he said, offering his arm with grave courtesy.

He led her through the chambers in silence. Half dead as she was, a new fear broke over Milly's mind. She stole a second glance at his face—it was the countenance she had seen watching her as she fled from the tables. What must he think—but she was too cold and lifeless to care much. She was filled with horror and remorse as disproportionate to the magnitude of her offense as could well be perceived; besides this, she was sane enough to remember that she had lost the sum put by for the purchase of a present for Aunt Eliza.

Milly felt that there was nothing left but to

die—she certainly had disgraced herself to all eternity—she would have liked to confess to somebody, any body—tell just what had led her on—it seemed as if there would be a kind of relief in putting her dismal secret into words. Again she stole a look at the handsome, grave face beside her—perhaps with some wild, childish thought of telling her story then and there, stranger as he was. But, fortunately, they had reached the ball-room—Milly saw Mrs. Lawrence and the beau, evidently seeking her. She pointed to them, half whispering,

"Oh, what will they think! I—I ran away into the other rooms—first—first—I thought I could get back before they missed me."

The gentleman smiled, half compassionately, half in amusement: looking at her more closely than he had before done, he saw how young she was.

"Is that the lady you were with?" he asked.

"Yes—I—"

"Mrs. Lawrence is an old friend of mine," he continued; "I don't think she will scold."

"But—but—I wouldn't like her to know about—that I was—spoken to— Oh dear, I want to go home."

She was half sobbing now, and the stranger appeared a little afraid of a scene. At this instant the beau perceived Milly, and hurried up with Mrs. Lawrence; and the two began to exclaim and question.

"Why, Milly Crofton, you frightened me half to death—where on earth have you been?" cried the lady; while the beau nodded and gurgled, and grew scarlet with excitement. "Good gracious, Mr. Halford, I didn't know you were in Baden! Where did you come from—it is —ages— And you joined Milly—"

"Miss Crofton lost her way, and I had the good fortune to meet her," he answered, speaking Milly's name as composedly as if he had been familiar with it for the last ten years.

"Why, however did you manage, Milly! Oh mercy, I know—you turned out of the wrong door —you poor dear! Never mind, we'll go home —there, there, don't mind," said Mrs. Lawrence, too busy soothing the girl's agitation to wonder how or when she could have known Mr. Halford. Milly was horribly angry at her own childishness; but she could scarcely keep her tears from falling, and words were an utter impossibility.

"She'll be glad to get away," pursued Mrs. Lawrence, putting her hand on Milly's arm, "And when did you come to Baden, Mr. Halford?"

"Only yesterday, and am off early in the morning. I came to spend a day with some friends, but am returning to Paris at once."

He glanced so meaningly toward Milly, who was shaking from head to foot, that even Mrs. Lawrence discovered he thought it her duty to take the poor child away immediately; so she hurried the ancient Noyse off, only stopping six separate times, according to her habit, for more last words with Mr. Halford.

Milly caught a bow from the stranger, a grave, kindly smile, and the next thing she could remember, though she walked on steadily enough, was finding herself in the carriage and hearing Mrs. Lawrence and the antique still in animated conversation.

"But goodness me!" cried the chaperon, rushing back into Milly's chamber that night, after getting partially undressed, "I forgot to ask—how on earth did you happen to know Kenneth Halford? He hasn't been in America these ten years."

"I didn't know him; he—he—"

Here Milly's latest shred of composure gave way, and she sobbed until Mrs. Lawrence forgot every thing in the necessity of quieting and putting her to bed.

CHAPTER II.

MILLY'S ADVENTURE.

Two days later, Milly was safe under Mrs. Crittendon's guardianship; and the visit to Baden seemed a dream—one of those horribly fascinating dreams which are half nightmare, and the more interesting from that touch of the terrible. Milly could not dismiss that last evening's exploit from her mind; it filled her with shame and remorse; and she would have given a great deal had there been some one to whom she could reveal her fault, and from whom she might receive the severe lecture and penance due to so enormous a transgression.

But she kept her own counsel; to attempt a confession to her friends was a simple impossibility; her exaggerated view of the case made her dread their pronouncing it unpardonable. She knew that they were rather strict in their ideas, and had visions of being deserted on the spot—at least of their telling Aunt Eliza—and what would befall her then was too awful to contemplate. The next winter was to witness her presentation in society; if Mrs. Remsen were to learn what she had done, there would be an end to that hope. The mildest retribution she could imagine as likely to happen was banishment to a convent; and straightway there rose before Milly a picture of herself with her pretty hair cut short, her face half hidden under an unbecoming coif, and the chanting of dreary psalms the chief occupation of her life. Not that the vision had the slightest show of reason for a basis—Milly knew that well enough—but she had just been reading an old novel where a similar fate befell the heroine; and the convent imprisonment suggested itself to her mind as the method of punishment her relative would adopt, though it is probable that even to fancy a good church-woman capable of such Papistical wickedness would have offended Aunt Eliza more than the original fault which Milly deplored so bitterly.

She might in safety have eased her conscience by an avowal to Mrs. Lawrence; but, in her most tragic moments, Milly could not help feeling confident that the frivolous Minerva would laugh and treat the whole affair as an excellent joke. So she kept her own counsel; but the secret preyed upon her night and day till she felt like a woman in a romance going about with a history and a mystery which made an invisible ban between herself and others of her age; and it was all inexpressibly horrible, though with a certain sensational interest about it which was painfully agreeable.

It frightened her sometimes to remember that her secret was not wholly in her own keeping. Mr. Halford had seen her at the tables—she was sure of that—the recollection of his grave face watching her was clear in her mind, though, at the moment, she had thought as little of him as she did of the crowd around her. If she should ever meet him again! the idea was too dreadful, and she always got away from it as fast as possible, though it would return with sullen persistency, and she often dreamed of him sitting on a throne, in the traditional stage-dress of Richard III.—only the effect was slightly marred by his always wearing a smoking-cap on his head, instead of a crown—and Aunt Eliza dragging her up to the foot of the judgment-seat, to receive sentence. Here, again, the grotesque mixed itself up with tragedy; for Aunt Eliza invariably appeared with Joan of Arc's mailed coat over her crinoline; and Milly would be conscious, in the midst of her own agony, that her feet were bare, and that her only garment was an old yellow-flannel dressing-gown, which had belonged to her nurse, and which she had not recollected for years until it thus thrust itself into her visions.

She seemed so dull and languid, that the Crittendons reproached themselves for having allowed her to stay so much confined, and, as Mrs. Crittendon's health was fully restored, decided to make a journey to Geneva. Mrs. Lawrence—always glad of society and change—accompanied them; and Milly enjoyed the expedition so thoroughly, that her remorse ceased to torment her so constantly. It was somewhat late for a visit to Chamouni, but Mrs. Crittendon insisted that the rest of the party should go, while she remained comfortably in the quiet city; and her husband yielded to her wishes, after the commendable habit customary with American husbands.

They reached Chamouni in the evening; and the next morning, at the first peep of dawn, Milly was up, and out, to catch a glimpse of Mont Blanc, and repeat Coleridge's poem, as any girl barely eighteen ought to do—an innocent enthusiasm we wise older people would give the world to be capable of, however much we may laugh at it.

The day after, they mounted on mules, and rode off to the Mer de Glace; and Milly was in such extravagantly high spirits that her companions caught the infection; and if Mrs. Remsen could have heard Minerva Lawrence's shrieks of laughter and nonsensical talk, she would have regarded that plump body with more pitying contempt than of old. Milly never once remembered her dismal secret, and the day was one of unclouded enjoyment until the return, during which her unusual excitement made her a little reckless; and, encouraged by Minerva's approval, she insisted on urging her mule forward more rapidly than was prudent, in spite of the expostulations of the guides.

Of course, I brought her out to Chamouni on purpose to meet with an adventure: conscious that my story is not likely to prove very romantic, I am glad to crowd all the incidents I can into these opening chapters, consoling myself for their lack of novelty by the fact that they actually occurred. So Milly urged on her mule, and Minerva laughed and applauded; the guides spluttered admonitions in French and German; and good Mr. Crittendon was too much engaged in keeping himself secure in the saddle, and wondering what could have tempted a man of his years, weight, and tender flesh, to trust himself upon such an instrument of torture, to pay much attention.

On went the willful girl; and at length the mule, roused out of her customary staid behavior, either became infected with something of her rider's excitement, or else determined to give the young woman a lesson which should serve as a warning for the future. Two of the guides were occupied with Minerva, who, however much she admired Milly's courage, was far from imitating it, and shrieked dolefully each time either of the men tried to quit her side. The third was busy assisting Mr. Crittendon; the fourth hurried after Milly, uttering counsels and prayers in French, and breaking them, at intervals, with awful German oaths, each of which was at least a yard long. Away dashed the mule—she owned the poetic name of "The Morning Star"—and, though she did not attempt to sing, seemed inclined to emulate the swift motion of that planet. Milly would have checked her course now, but it was too late; the Morning Star had taken the bit between her teeth, and pranced on down the narrow path. Milly did not shriek: she was frightened, but glancing back, saw that her guide was in hot pursuit, and tried to believe that he would overtake them in time to prevent danger. The path made a sharp turn—the mule stumbled—a shriek broke from Minerva's lips, echoed by the guide, which roused Mr. Crittendon to a sense of Milly's peril. It was only the work of a moment, long as it takes in the description. Milly was conscious of a lightning-like thought that this was death—her dazzled vision caught the immeasurable depth, with only a few feet of the path between her and it, and that so steep that, once over the side, nothing could stop her swift descent into the chasm. Every thing slid before her eyes as if she had already commenced that terrible fall; she could not cry out—could only remember that there was no help—watching always the shining snow, while a thousand sights from the old life in her far-off home rose, like phantoms, between her and the great white depth.

The mule struggled—recovered herself—dashed on—a second turn—a quick curve—the abyss frowned below, without even a ravine to break the immeasurable distance! Then new shouts and cries—blind, sick, and faint, Milly became aware of a party approaching up the path—another instant, and she knew that the animal's speed was checked, and she lifted from the saddle. When her senses came back, she was lying on the ground, her head supported in Minerva's lap; Mr. Crittendon was fairly wringing his hands; Minerva in hysterics; the guides performing a sort of red-Indian dance of craze and fright: the only quiet object that met her eyes was the sad, grave face which bent toward her—the face of the man who had witnessed her crazy exploit at the gaming-table.

The girl's first connected thought was that it would have been better to go with Morning Star straight over the precipice than be saved by this man, and forced to remember the secret which he shared. But a second glance at the countenance showed it so full of anxiety, that she rather forgot her longing for death, and was able to laugh, soothe Minerva's hysterics and Mr. Crittendon's distress, and utter a few broken expressions of regret.

"And where on earth did you come from, Mr. Halford? Oh, Milly, Milly! I believe my hair has turned gray with fright!" moaned Mrs. Lawrence, coming out of her hysterics to gratify one of the strongest instincts of her nature—curiosity. "The first thing I saw was you holding that dreadful beast's bridle, as if you had flown up the precipice."

"Not exactly," he replied. "I reached Chamouni just after you had started this morning, and proposed to these gentlemen to overtake you. We should have done so, but one of our party was indisposed, and we had to leave him at the last chalet; but, after all, we reached you at the right moment."

Milly, lying with her head on Minerva's lap, listened to the explanation, glancing long enough at the other men to perceive that they were three young Englishmen, evidently fresh from the University, and, of course, too youthful to possess the slightest interest to the eyes of eighteen.

"There never was any thing so fortunate, Halford!" said Mr. Crittendon, shaking his hand warmly. "If our little girl had—I mean, if it hadn't ended as it has— Bless me, that brute of a mule ought to be killed at once!" he added, finding that to finish the sentence he had begun caused a suspicious gurgling in his throat, and anxious, like most people, to avoid dramatics.

"At all events, there is no harm done," Halford said, cheerfully. "The next thing is to get Miss Crofton back to the inn."

"I am not in the least hurt," Milly answered, trying to raise her head, but feeling so dizzy and odd still that she decided to relinquish the effort. "I can ride easily enough. Don't be anxious, Mr. Crittendon. Oh, I am so sorry to have frightened you all!"

"We are very glad to be quits for the fright, Milly," he replied. "But how can we manage, Halford? We ought to have a litter, or something."

"Mercy, no!" cried Milly, rather impatiently, raising herself this time, while the color came back to her cheeks; and the three youths, huddled together at a little distance, like a covey of frightened partridges, wondered that any thing human could look so pretty, and straightway became her victims for the moment. "I can ride perfectly well; poor old Morning Star was not to blame for stumbling."

"You sha'n't ride her!" squeaked Minerva. "The awfullest brute—why those guides ought to be hanged for keeping an animal of the sort. She's fitter for a menagerie of wild beasts than any thing else."

Poor Morning Star stood with her bridle held by one of the guides, her ears drooping, her head down, with so ludicrous an expression of shame and wonder on her visage, that Milly began to laugh—then stopped quickly, lest she should cry also.

"Miss Crofton can take my mule," Halford said; "a wooden one couldn't be safer. I'll ride Morning Star."

He ordered the guides to change the saddles, talked cheerfully with Minerva and Mr. Crittendon, tried to put his three youthful companions at their ease, and distracted the general attention from Milly with a kindly tact which she fully appreciated.

"But you were going on up," Mr. Crittendon said.

"No, our friend's little illness hindered us so long that we decided to put off our expedition until another day, and only came on to meet you."

"We shall be uncommonly glad of your company down," Mr. Crittendon replied. "I'm rather old and heavy for these sort of expeditions—especially when it comes to taking charge of young ladies."

"Please—" began Milly, thinking that his words implied a slight reproach; but he interrupted her.

"My dear, it was not your fault; and if it had been, I'm too happy to see you safe to lecture. All the same, I shall be very glad if these gentlemen will go back with us."

The three youths came sufficiently out of the bewilderment into which they had been thrown by Milly's pretty face, added to their constitutional shyness, to express a proper delight at the privilege.

By this time Milly could stand and walk about, and announced herself quite ready to continue the descent. She did not speak often to Halford, though she was longing to thank him for his kindness; but she grew afraid and ashamed whenever she recollected their first meeting, and was anxious to depart.

The ride down passed in the most common-place manner. Halford did not even beg the happiness of walking beside Milly, as a man would have done in a novel; and it was certain that he could scarcely have taken as good care of her as did the chief guide, who stalked stern-ly along at the mule's head, and made a move-ment to catch the bridle if Milly so much as looked up, apparently suspecting her of an in-tention to attempt a second escapade. Mr. Crittendon and Halford kept near each other; and the youths were able to talk to Minerva, since she was not that (to them) most formida-ble of created beings—a young girl. So Milly had a rather silent ride, and ample time for nu-merous reflections—so absorbing, that she for-got to admire, as diligently as she ought, the wonderful panorama spread out before her eyes. On reaching the chalet, they found that the in-valid had entirely recovered from his indispo-sition, and had returned to Chamouni without waiting for his companions. Scarcely a word was exchanged between Milly and Halford dur-ing the whole ride; and before they reached the inn, the feeling of restraint and shyness had arrived at such a pitch that she only sought to escape from his presence. There was a strong probability that, with the usual inconsistency of human nature, she would proceed to hate him because she had placed herself in a somewhat questionable position in his thoughts—that is, if he was inclined to pass harsh judgments on a girl of her age.

Finding that Mr. Crittendon had invited the party of gentlemen to dine with them, Milly in-formed Mrs. Lawrence that she was too weary to sit up another moment, and retired to her room. She was at once punished for her half fib; Minerva would not leave her till she had forced several infallible remedies on her, and given orders to her maid to look in upon Miss Crofton every fifteen minutes, lest she should be taken with a fainting-fit, or spasms, or some other feminine malady requiring attention.

"Spasms!" cried Milly, ungratefully, in great scorn. "As for fainting, I never did such a thing in my life—really—and I am not likely to begin now."

She spoke as if she were at least three-score-and-ten, according to the habit of her age.

"Oh dear me, you were as white and limp as that handkerchief, when they laid your head in my lap," moaned Minerva. "Oh, Elise!" —this to the maid—"you never saw any thing so dreadful in your whole life! Did I tell you exactly how it all happened?"

She had—at least fifteen times since they got up stairs—but the well-trained attendant was ready to listen again, and express suitable alarm in voluble French, and such English as she could muster.

"Of course, you've told her," said Milly, ir-ritably; for her nerves were too sorely disor-dered for her to emulate the Parisian's pa-tience.

"You are trembling this moment; you must have some red lavender," pronounced Minerva, rushing to the little medicine-chest which she always carried with her, and which was the horror of her friends.

"I can't swallow another thing," pleaded Milly. "I only want to get to bed—I'll have some tea later."

"Oh, but the lavender would set you up at once," urged Minerva. "You're all of a shiv-er; just like a—a—what is the word? Elise, what is it shakes and shakes always?"

"I did not forget for the moment," returned Elise, staring at her mistress as if she thought it was a conundrum proposed for her solution. "There is the—how you say in English—*gelée des prids de veau*—that shake and shake ever."

"No, no, how stupid!" said her mistress. "Dear me, the word is on the end of my tongue."

Elise looked helpless, but stared at the lady as if trying to get a glimpse of her lingual adornment, in the hope of seeing the desired word. "I was never good at the calembours," she said, meekly.

"The woman's mad!" cried Minerva, spread-ing out her plump hands and laughing hearti-ly, then breaking off to add, "Hush, hush, Elise! you mustn't make a noise; Miss Crof-ton's nerves won't bear it."

The Frenchwoman, who always moved like a cat, and spoke in the lowest of monotones, stood aghast at this undeserved charge; and the whole thing was so ridiculous that Milly began to laugh and sob and shake more vio-lently. Minerva flew about in great agitation, knocked over every light object within her reach, upset her medicine-case, and created the confusion that well-meaning people usually do in the presence of an emergency.

"If you'll only leave me alone for a while," sobbed Milly, throwing herself on the bed. "Please—please—just for half an hour. I shall be perfectly well then."

"Why, of course, of course," said Minerva. "Elise, don't worry the poor thing; how can you? Now here's the lavender, Milly; I'll set it on the table; here's a spoon: don't tease her, Elise."

Milly was ready to promise to swallow the whole medicine-chest, if her friend would only leave her alone; and having exhausted every means of good-natured torment that suggest-ed itself to her mind, Mrs. Lawrence departed, driving Elise out before her as if the docile woman had been some mischievous animal not to be trusted for an instant.

The door closed, Milly turned her head on her pillow with a long sigh of relief; but in an instant the rusty hinges creaked again. Mrs. Lawrence put her head into the room and ex-claimed, in an unearthly whisper,

"Milly, Milly, I've found the word—aspen! Of course; I said it was just on the tip of my tongue—aspen, to be sure! Now, Elise, don't make a noise; step softly; you don't know what weak nerves are."

This time she absolutely departed, and for a long hour Milly was left to herself, and, having finished her cry, could go comfortably to sleep. Then Elise, the light-footed, brought her a delicious dish of tea and a tiny bird; and Milly felt much better, though she instructed the maid to tell Mrs. Lawrence that she meant to go to bed at once, and sent her good-night, that she need not be disturbed by a second visit.

Milly sat at her window, looking out over the narrow valley, and watched the gray twilight settle into the gloom of evening. The last faint glow died from the highest mountain peaks—a few stars shot up into the sky—a soft, velvety darkness settled about—the murmur of unseen water-falls came up through the distance, and there Milly sat, and wondered, and dreamed, sorely perplexed between her gratitude to Kenneth Halford for this day's deliverance and her irritated recollection of the night at Baden, which really seemed to make it her duty to detest him with great energy; it was the only means of escape from that overwhelming sense of shame.

However, fatigue subdued her at length; she was forced to put by both remorse and her unsettled feelings, where Halford was concerned, until another season, for she was so sleepy that she could scarcely see to undress.

At her age, and with her perfect health, a night's quiet sleep was sufficient to remove every trace of the weariness left by her previous day's excitement. She rose early, had a cup of coffee in her room, and went out for a long walk, before the substantial breakfast which Mr. Crittendon always expected to have at precisely half-past eight o'clock.

In this world Fate seems to have a special pleasure in confronting us with the very persons whom we could most wish to avoid; and the truth of the remark was proved in Milly's case this morning. She walked about the hamlet for a while, returned toward the hotel, and took the path up to the field from whence she had once watched Mont Blanc in the gray dawn. Some one had reached the best point of observation before her; a single glance showed who it was, and she would have retreated; but, in her reverie, she had walked so close to the spot that the sound of her footsteps roused Kenneth Halford, and he turned toward her with a pleasant-enough smile, though, polite as he was, Milly fancied she saw in his face that he would have preferred his solitary musings to any companionship.

"I hope you are quite recovered from yesterday's fatigue, Miss Crofton," he said, "and have had a good night's rest."

"Thanks, yes," she answered.

"At your age one does not require long to get over fatigue, and sleep comes very easily."

"Bless me," thought Milly; "he talks as if I was about ten years old, and he Methuselah, at least."

"You leave for Geneva this afternoon, Mr. Crittendon tells me," he went on, evidently thinking her silence rose from shyness, and wishing to put her at ease.

That idea made Milly more vexed than ever; she only bowed carelessly, by way of answer, and turned to study the king of mountains, glorious in the early morning light, with his robe of clouds and diadem of snow.

"I suppose you have already quoted,

"'Hast thou a spell to stay the morning star
On her swift course, O bald and sovran Blanc!'

he said, with what seemed to her a sort of superior smile.

He had not given the words exactly—there was a slight satisfaction in this, as it gave her an opportunity to smile in her turn.

"I have made a mistake, I suppose," he added. "You see it is a long time since I studied Coleridge."

"And why did you suppose him fresh in my mind?" Milly asked, unadvisedly, still rather in the mood for warfare.

"Because he is usually a favorite with very young people," he replied; "not but what he ought to be with us older ones, only, as we get on through the world, there's less leisure for poetry-studying."

"You speak as if you were old enough to be Mr. Crittendon's grandfather," said she, conscious that the words sounded almost rude, and, worse, that her evident irritation was a convincing proof of extreme youthfulness, but not able to check either.

"I am not sure that, at least, I mightn't almost be yours," he answered, with a pleasant laugh.

"Do you think me about ten?" she asked, with a small violence which she felt to be very undignified, but could not repress.

"Perhaps one might add ten or eleven years to it," he said; and it was plain that he had a certain satisfaction in her vehemence, which made her look prettier than she knew.

"I am eighteen," exclaimed Milly, trying to speak disdainfully, but succeeding poorly. "At least, I shall be next week," she added, forced on to the concluding confession by a prick of her uncomfortable conscience, that would never let her alone.

"It's a very nice thing to be eighteen," he said, gravely.

Milly hesitated whether to reproach him with looking old, or sneering at his claims. She decided in favor of the latter, as he was a handsome man.

"I should scarcely suppose it was long enough since you passed that season to have any great regret," said she.

He laughed outright—a slow, musical laugh, but it irritated Milly's nerves sorely.

"What age should you give me?" he asked.

"Really, we have fallen upon a very American train of conversation," returned she, with another attempt at disdainfulness. "English people say we can never talk two minutes without bringing up that subject."

"Mayn't we claim our little peculiarities as well as other nations?" demanded he, in the same teasing way. "But you've not answered my question! Perhaps you are afraid of hurting my feelings, by putting on too many years."

"You may be twenty-six," said Milly, regardless of conscience now.

"What a nice bit of flattery that would be, if I were only fifty, instead of three-and-thirty," he replied, laughing again.

Thirty-three was exactly Milly's pet age for her heroes; she felt a little softened toward the man; besides, though the face was rather sad and worn, it showed no lack of youth; and, much as Milly detested boys, she hated wrinkles worse.

"And you are going back to America soon," he said, dismissing the subject of years so suddenly, that Milly, given to fancies, wondered if their conversation had roused some sad thought in his mind. "It is almost ten years since I came away."

"It must be delightful to travel as you have done," Milly said; for she knew that he had held a diplomatic appointment in Egypt, and written a rather wise book, which, naturally, she had not read.

"Still, I should be very glad to see home again," he replied. "I say home, though I have nobody left who could make it such."

These words, quietly as they were spoken, touched Milly; she was a sympathetic little soul, and any thing in the shape of sorrow or sadness appealed to her at once.

"You live with your aunt, Mrs. Remsen, Mr. Crittendon tells me—I used to know her years ago, and her eldest daughter—I believe she is Mrs. Ramsay now."

"My cousin Adelaide—oh yes," Milly said, rather indifferently; for it was difficult to attempt interest where that lady was concerned.

"Didn't you like my aunt very much? She is so good!"

"A woman to respect and admire greatly," he said. "I believe I used to be rather a favorite with her as a boy. I wonder I never chanced to see you in my visits."

"Oh, aunt never allowed the children in the drawing-room—that was her law—then, while Adelaide reigned—" Milly stopped, remembering that it would not be nice to find fault with her cousin to a stranger. "Don't you mean to go back to America?" she asked.

"Some time—I have thoughts of returning to Egypt—I don't know that there is any thing to take me to my old home."

Milly was conscious of a vague feeling of disappointment, though, for the life of her, she could not have told why; but the feeling rose, and her perception of it, in some odd way, reminded her that she had meant to hate this man. On the heels of that thought came the recollection of their first meeting. The color flamed into her cheeks, a startled expression crept into her eyes. She glanced quickly about, and some wild desire to run away and hide herself started up in her mind. While playing with a pretty Alpine weed he had plucked, Kenneth Halford watched her furtively. He was a peculiar man in many respects, and his intuitions were almost as quick and unerring as a woman's. He knew as well as if she had put it in words, what the reflection was that disturbed her. He began to talk—of his travels—of a Nile journey—of Greece. Milly grew interested, and showed that books had made her perfectly familiar with the scenes of which he spoke. The conversation glided naturally to other subjects—pictures—the new novels—certain old and beloved poets, whom the startling geniuses of the past ten years have not wholly banished from men's memories.

They strolled slowly along, talking in the most animated manner; and when they approached the hotel, Halford was astonished to find how quickly the time had fled, and what a sympathetic, intelligent companion Milly proved; for, like many men between thirty and thirty-five, he was given to regarding girls as only a superior sort of dolls, incapable of any thing beyond an interest in their toilets, and a weak attempt at flirtation. One exception to this sweeping condemnation he always made—that is, when he allowed himself to recall the solitary instance—but that was as seldom as possible; for stern, old, and practical as he considered himself, these ten long years of absence had not wholly obliterated the memory of a bitter pain and wrong received at the hands of the one girl whom he had weakly believed so different from the generality of her sex.

While he was mentally wondering at the rapidity with which this last hour had flown, Milly was indulging in a second's reflection too, but a less pleasant one than his. Again the gambling-room at Baden rose before her eyes—herself standing by the green table—clutching her little store of gold with one hand—the rush, the whirl, the dizziness—and this man's grave face watching her. She felt no anger now; she only remembered that they must part in a few hours, perhaps never to meet again; and she could not bear to let him go without attempting, if not an excuse for her conduct, at least an expression of her shame. What must he think of her—composed and careless as she had been this past hour—unconcerned as though their first meeting had been under the most decorous circumstances! She was ready again to run away and hide herself; but she would not yield to such cowardice—she would do what was right without delay. If she could not change his opinion of her terrible act, at least he should see plainly how bitterly she regretted it.

"Mr. Halford!" she exclaimed, stopping short, as they neared the house.

Her voice sounded so odd and labored, that he turned toward her in surprise. She had grown pale, and her changeful eyes were unnaturally bright with pain.

"You are not well," he said, anxiously;

"you have walked too far! How careless of me to forget that you were not strong just now."

"No, no," she said, eagerly; "it's not that—it's— Oh, there's something I want to say, and I don't know how to begin."

"Come sit down on that bench," he said; "you must not stand any longer."

"No—I'd rather walk about—it's easier," she replied, in the same breathless fashion, though never for an instant faltering in her resolve. "I want to tell you—I want to say—"

"Take time, Miss Crofton," returned he, smiling kindly. "I am not a very formidable person—"

"I'm a fool," broke in Milly; "but I will not be so silly! I— Oh, it's too late—see! they are coming."

Halford followed the direction of her eyes; as usual, an interruption had arrived at a critical moment. The three young Englishmen were close upon them, and Halford had to engage the trio in conversation, and afford Milly an opportunity to escape.

CHAPTER III.

THE EXPLANATION.

MR. CRITTENDON came down to breakfast somewhat tired, and indisposed for exertion, after the unusual fatigues of the previous day; and Mrs. Lawrence, who delighted in nothing so much as having a friend at hand with some slight ailment, upon which she could exercise her medicinal skill, insisted on their remaining at Chamouni until the next morning.

"Your wife will not really expect us before," she said, "and I don't like the idea of your undertaking the tedious drive until you are thoroughly rested. I'll look out some remedies—I've just the thing for you, I am sure."

He hesitated somewhat—perhaps as much from a dread of Minerva's doctoring as any thing else; but just then, from her seat in the window, she saw Milly conversing with Halford and the young Englishmen, and pointed out the group to the old gentleman.

"She would enjoy the day, I know," said Mrs. Lawrence; "and she's such a dear little thing, that one likes to give her pleasure."

"The best child in the world," pronounced Mr. Crittendon; "as unlike modern young ladies in general, as if she had been brought up in another planet."

"Oh, that comes of Eliza Remsen's absurd ideas," returned Mrs. Lawrence, impatiently; "she always was the most crotchetty woman that ever lived. But I'm very fond of Milly, and it would be a kindness to her to stay. The young people can go off on some expedition, and I'll go too; and you can rest comfortably."

The restless body was as eager as a girl for amusement, and enjoyed the idea of remaining, on her own account; though it is only justice to add, that she would have staid as willingly in any case, if it could have obliged one whom she liked.

"We'll call it settled," said she, triumphantly.

"Yes, if Milly wishes."

"Oh, put it on that ground, and she'll say go. You must tell her you need rest, and indeed you do. Let me see—Sepia—no, scarcely;" and she put her head on one side, and contemplated him with an air of as profound wisdom as if she had received her degree at the Sorbonne. "Perhaps Ignatia—what do you think?"

"Thanks—I dare say that would answer as well as the other," he replied, secretly indulging in an old-fashioned contempt for every thing in the shape of homœopathic remedies.

"Oh, good gracious, don't speak like that! It's very important to choose the exact— But I'll watch you," she added, leaving her first sentence unfinished, after a confusing habit she had. "By the time breakfast is over, I can decide. No sense of fullness in your head—"

"Bless me, no!"

"Ah, so much the better—that might mean apoplexy, you know," said Minerva, cheerfully. "No numbness in your right knee?"

"Never had any sensation of the sort in my life," returned the old gentleman, with indignation.

"Good!" pronounced Minerva, still in her doctorial tone. "No danger of paralysis—"

"I wonder if they ever mean to allow us any breakfast," interrupted Mr. Crittendon, giving the bell-rope a vigorous pull, as a slight relief to his ruffled feelings.

"Phosphor," muttered Minerva," eying him meditatively.

"Perhaps—or camomilla—though, in case of slow digestion—"

"If those wretches below stairs will only give me some food, I'll engage to digest it," he broke in again, unable, in spite of his momentary irritation at Minerva's awful hints in regard to possible maladies, to repress a smile at her look and attitude.

The breakfast-tray fortunately appeared just then; and Milly's entrance, a moment later, put a stop to the conversation; though, every now and then, the old gentleman felt Minerva's professional eye upon him, and knew that she did not mean to release her prey.

"Milly," said Mrs. Lawrence, as the young lady came in, "we're not going back to Geneva until to-morrow."

"That is, if you would like to stay," added Mr. Crittendon, as he held out his hand, by way of a morning salutation.

"But you must not do it on my account," Milly answered.

"No, no, my dear; I'm a little tired after yesterday's jaunt," he said; "and our good friend there has persuaded me I need rest."

"Aurum!" cried Mrs. Lawrence, in a sort of Eureka tone, looking up at the ceiling as if

2

in consultation with some invisible spirit. "No—I think not! Hyoscyamus—maybe."

"It sounds as if she were calling up ghosts by their names," Milly wickedly whispered in Mr. Crittendon's ear; and the old gentleman was delighted to laugh at his friend's follies as a return for the unpleasant suggestions she had thrown out.

"Milly's scoffing at my skill," cried Mrs. Lawrence. "Never mind—she can't deny that my medicines always do her good. Now come and pour out the coffee, like a good child."

Milly was pleased at the idea of remaining another day: now that she had made up her mind to speak to Mr. Halford about her transgression, she longed to have the opportunity before leaving, and his conversation during their walk had banished the feeling of irritation toward him. He entered the room while they were at breakfast, and Mrs. Lawrence hastened to inform him of their change of plans.

"So you must propose something to amuse Milly and me," she said.

"I am quite ready," he answered. "There are several places to visit—you'd not mind inviting my friends?"

"Delighted, of course! The more the merrier! Milly, Eliza Remsen vows that all proverbs and old sayings are vulgar; but she can't hear me; so, no matter."

Milly paid no attention; she was accustomed to Mrs. Lawrence's little flings at her aunt, and Mrs. Remsen's open condemnation of Minerva's follies. She knew that neither would let anybody else abuse the other—it was a privilege of friendship only to be shared between themselves.

Halford gave the ladies a choice of several expeditions; but Mr. Crittendon insisted that Milly must not attempt too much.

"You look a little pale, my dear," he added.

The color rushed into Milly's cheeks as she remembered the agitation at the close of her morning's interview with Halford, which had brought her into the house so tired and pallid; but he carefully averted his eyes, and went on talking with Mrs. Lawrence, apparently unconscious of Mr. Crittendon's remark.

With much discussion, and numerous impossible proposals from the namesake of the goddess of wisdom, it was decided that, after an early luncheon, they should ride to a beautiful water-fall several miles from the village. Halford departed in search of his friends, to delight and terrify them by the news that they were to be again thrown into feminine society; and Milly sat down to read the latest newspaper to Mr. Crittendon. Mrs. Lawrence disturbed the old gentleman frequently by breaking in with exclamations of pleasure at having found the precise remedy to suit his case, and invariably adding, in the same breath, that it would not answer Finally, she rose to go up to her room and search her beloved medicine-chest and consult her favorite authority, pausing at the door to ask, abruptly,

"Your feet are not cold, Mr. Crittendon?"

"Never, ma'am," said he, with the severest glance over his spectacles that his kind old eyes could manage.

"I wish they were," sighed Minerva; "then I'd say aconite."

"Try it all the same," returned he, curtly.

"Mercy on us—the idea!" shrieked Minerva. "It's by just such carelessness people do harm—I'm prudence itself." Then, with a fresh relapse into her professional voice—"Your heart is all right."

"So my wife says," answered he, resignedly.

"Oh now, don't jest—these are always serious matters!" said Minerva, with ludicrous earnestness. "Just answer me one question—you never had a touch of rheumatic gout in the chest?"

Mr. Crittendon did not even look up; he signed Milly to go on with her reading; and Minerva, perceiving that her old friend's patience was worn threadbare, wisely took refuge in flight.

"I've known her, girl and woman," said Mr. Crittendon, slowly, tapping his fingers on the table, to emphasize his remark, "ever since she was years younger than you, Milly! She was always the best creature in the world, and the greatest fool—my dear, she hasn't changed an iota in all that time."

He refreshed himself with a pinch of snuff, and recovered his good-humor; while Milly, as soon as she could check her laughter, continued her perusal of the newspaper.

Luckily for Minerva's peace of mind, before the hour of their departure arrived, she was enabled to make her decision in regard to the remedies Mr. Crittendon required. She covered his table with tumblers containing a few drops of liquid medicines in water, tiny bottles of infinitesimal pills, and gave him scores of numerous and contradictory directions in regard to taking them. He promised whatever she wished—people always did promise Minerva any thing and every thing where her medicines were concerned—and she set off in high spirits. The expedition proved a complete success. The two ladies rode, and the men walked beside them; and there was any quantity of chatter and gayety. Even the shy University men came out in a surprising manner; and the most venturesome of the three actually perpetrated a compliment to Milly; but it was afterward agreed between his friends that he had taken too much bottled ale before leaving the inn; and, indeed, at the time, they did not hesitate to whisper in his ear sundry cautions about exposing his natural imbecility more than he could help. However, he set all that down to the score of envy, and always looked back upon that afternoon as the crowning success of his youth, confidently believing that he had made an impression on the mind of the young American girl which could never be effaced.

Masculine vanity is almost without limits;

but the vanity of a shy man invariably surpasses that of any other.

There were several parties of tourists at the inn, and among them young people of Mrs. Lawrence's acquaintance, whom she invited to join the expedition; so that they mustered a tolerable company at the moment of departure.

It was a glorious day, and the water-fall—like the scenery through which they passed to reach it—so beautiful that no human words could convey the least idea of its loveliness and grandeur.

Halford's manner to Milly was simply perfect. She was able, at times, to forget that she had any confession to offer, and, in her enjoyment, blossomed into such beauty, that even he, unimpressionable as he considered himself in these days, was absolutely astounded. It was an afternoon that Milly would never forget to her dying day, though, at the time, she had no perception that it was more to her than a thousand other seasons of pleasure. Long after, when she was so changed from the blithe, childish Milly of this period that she scarcely recognized herself as the same person, she used to look across the bleak stretch of storm and tempest which swept between her and that season, and marvel why Fate should have been cruel enough to lead her blindly out into the glory of that vanished morning. But no premonition disturbed her now; she rode on, merry, happy, infecting the others with her gayety, until Kenneth Halford forgot that he had long cherished a cynical contempt for unreasoning and unreasonable enjoyment, and yielded to the spell of the hour as entirely as if he had been a boy of eighteen, instead of a stoic of three-and-thirty. He regarded her as a mere child; but it was that very childishness which made her society so agreeable, since, as far as cultivation by study was concerned, she was superior to girls in general.

A pleasant, idle, unprofitable day; but it fled only too quickly; and through the gorgeous sunset they journeyed back to the inn, with Mont Blanc flaming in the distance, and the changing hues of the mountain ranges fairly making the eyes ache with a sense of beauty. They lingered so long, that the last marvelous rose-tint had faded and the soft twilight lay about as they approached the inn. Milly and Halford were a goodly distance behind the others. Some slight mishap to her saddle—the undoing of a buckle or other trifle—necessitated her dismounting while he arranged it, and he had called to the others to go on, they would not be many moments late.

He had walked by her side during the whole homeward journey, and their talk had strayed so far from Milly's dreary thoughts of the previous night, that no recollection of them remained in her mind. It had been a rare pleasure to Halford, this whiling her into conversation; an agreeable surprise that she had ideas—strong, vigorous ones, too—and her very simplicity and Utopian fancies rendered the discovery more delightful. He smiled sometimes,

compassionating her childish ignorance; yet he liked to see it, and thought to himself what a pity that she could not always remain thus—that the years must change her till she became like the rest of dull mortality; till her eyes lost their mistful innocence, her voice its joyous ring; till, saddest of all, she would live to laugh in bitter scorn at the beautiful fancies which were sacred truths to her now.

While lifting her into her saddle again, he chanced to say,

"So you really go to-morrow."

He was about, man-like, to add some nonsensical words of regret; but the change in her face checked him. His remark had recalled the dark secret—she shivered, and grew pale—looking at him so like a frightened child, that he longed to comfort her.

"What is it?" he asked.

"I had forgotten," she said, nervously. "To-morrow—we are going to-morrow—I shall not have another opportunity to tell you—"

"I don't think you need to tell me any thing," he answered, kindly. "Perhaps I can imagine what it is—I assure you there is no need."

"I must," she said, hurriedly; and he appreciated and admired the courage with which she fought down her terror in that determination to do what she considered right. "You—you— Oh, Mr. Halford—that night at Baden!"

"Don't think I mean an idle compliment, Miss Crofton—it was a very pleasant night to me, since it gave me your acquaintance."

"You're very good," she said, with a piteous quiver of her lips, and a trembling in her voice which showed how difficult it was to repress her tears. "I don't deserve it—I thank you so much!"

"Then there's an end," he replied, anxious to spare her pain.

"No—not till I have told you—I may never see you again—and I couldn't bear to remember always that you thought ill of me—"

"I am not likely to do that," he interrupted.

"But you must—you can't help it," she continued, struggling hard to keep her voice firm. "I don't know what I can say to set myself right—only I didn't think—I—"

She could get no further; she had to turn her head away for a little, and he saw her clench her hands in rage and disgust at her own weakness—that very weakness which he found so bewitching. He still hoped to spare her somewhat; so he said,

"But you were not to blame for missing your way, or for the rudeness of that brute."

"Oh, it's not that—you know—that is just because you are kind-hearted, and want me to believe you didn't see me. But you did—afterward I remembered your face so distinctly—looking at me in such a grave, disapproving way. Oh, it makes me so ashamed!" she cried, covering her face with her hands.

He kept his hold of the mule's bridle, and walked slowly on, saying, in a soft, kind voice,

"You exaggerate the whole thing so much,

Miss Crofton! I don't think I looked any serious disapproval—at least, I did not feel it."

"Oh, don't try to treat it as a joke—don't," she said; "that makes me feel worse than any thing."

He saw that the only kindness he could show was to speak seriously of the matter, and allow her to ease her mind by full avowal.

"I have no inclination to do so," he replied. "I am sure you would never have gone to the tables, had you thought how it might appear."

"Indeed, indeed, I would not! I don't know how it came about—I was bored in the ball-room, because there was nobody I knew, and I thought about playing—it seemed to me I should go wild if I didn't! I never thought about the people—or the wickedness—it seemed such a mere trifle! It wasn't till I had played, and was going away—just as I saw you—that I came to my senses; for I do think I was crazy —I really do."

"Now is that all?" he asked.

"Yes—you see it's no excuse! I might talk a week, and I could not make you understand why I did it—I don't know! But oh, I have suffered so—it's not the being found out—do believe that, though it's awful to appear bold and fast—but to have done it!"

"Your trouble is quite punishment enough," he said; "the harshest judge could not wish you more. Now let me tell you—and I mean it— you have brooded over the thing until it looks much more important in your eyes than it really is."

She shook her head.

"You want to comfort me!"

"I mean to tell you the exact truth—I shall not try to palliate your conduct—that would be a false kindness, in your present state of mind."

"I feel so wicked!" sighed Milly.

"My dear Miss Crofton, very few people ever go to Baden without throwing a napoleon on the board once—your feeling in regard to the matter was what everybody has. I have many a time seen men let their daughters tease them into permitting one trial. I don't think you did right—"

"It was awful!" parenthesised Milly.

"If you had told Mrs. Lawrence, she would have gone with you; and old Noyse would have played for you—it was very wrong to go alone—but, fortunately, nobody recognized you except myself; and I am glad I was there, since it will be better for you to have told some one, instead of brooding longer over your secret."

"What must you have thought!"

"I will tell you frankly. I am a rather censorious person—not fond of young ladies, and given to harsh judgments in regard to them— admit that my opinion was likely to be as severe as possible."

"Tell me," she said; "I'd rather know."

"My first thought, when I saw your face— how oblivious you were of the crowd—was just this: That little girl deserves to have her ears boxed; but she has not the slightest idea what

she is doing; she is neither bold nor fast; she's just a child, and has escaped from her friends for a minute to play, they are the ones to blame, in point of fact. There—is that very dreadful?"

"And are you really in earnest?" demanded Milly, looking up at him with searching eyes.

"On my honor," he replied; "and those are words I never use lightly."

There were a few sudden tears on Milly's cheek, but her face lost its troubled, frightened expression.

"I know it was very wrong," she said, humbly; "but it's a good deal to think that it didn't make me look so degraded and wicked as I thought."

He could not repress a smile; she uttered the exaggerated expressions without thinking in the least what they implied.

"It did not," he said; "and if it didn't sound like lecturing, I would tell you that you may be glad to have done it: the remembrance of that night may often keep you from real imprudences, such as so many of us have to regret."

"Oh dear, I'll never be bad again!" cried Milly. "Why, it isn't nice a bit."

"A very happy conclusion to have arrived at so easily," said he, laughing. "Now you don't mean to sit in sackcloth and ashes any longer, I hope!"

"Indeed, telling you has done me a world of good. Do you think Aunt Eliza ought to know?"

"I should say not, decidedly," he replied. "It was an act that can have no consequences; so, having spoken of it to the one person who was a witness, there is an end."

He had to look aside to conceal the smile of amusement at his own grandiloquent phrases; but Milly received them seriously, and drew a deep sigh of relief.

"I have so dreaded to speak of it," she said.

"I am very glad you have, since I am able to clear up your ideas a little about the enormity of the affair."

"I shall always be ashamed," continued Milly; "but I needn't think about it all the time —I really felt I ought, by way of punishment."

Halford, remembering how humanity in general get away from all recollection of wrongdoing, drown it, bury it in any way, could but wonder afresh at the childish creature so ready to accept the penance she considered her due.

"You have had punishment enough," he answered. "Promise me that you will forget the whole thing. Come, as I have been your judge, I have a right to insist upon that."

"If I may—if I ought!"

"You ought, I assure you; there is nothing so hurtful as to grow morbid by dwelling on errors that have been fully expiated."

She smiled, dried her eyes, and stretched out her hand impulsively. "I thank you very, very much," she said; "and I don't mean ever to be wicked again."

Somehow, in looking at her, there rose before

his mental vision that image which it had been for years the study of his life to shut out—the face of a girl not much older than Milly at this moment, but very unlike—more matured, more beautiful—already, in many things, a thorough woman. But he had loved her—believed in her—and the end had been that her conduct sent him a wanderer over the earth for a long season, almost depriving him of any possibility of faith.

Why did that ghost rise now out of his buried past? For years that season had been only a memory—why should Alice Berners's face haunt him now? Unconsciously, he called her by the old name, then remembered that she had not borne it since her girlhood—only a few brief months after listening to his vows, she had exchanged it for another, that ought to have been, he considered, a badge of shame, since she had sold herself, her truth, all that renders womanhood pure and noble, for wealth.

Milly's voice roused him from his reverie. They were nearing the hotel, and once more she uttered her thanks for his kindness. His mood had changed; he was glad the day had come to an end; why should he interest himself in this child, who, innocent as she seemed, would probably live to wring some honest man's heart?

"You have given me a very pleasant day, Mr. Halford," Milly said; "I am so, so much obliged."

He bowed silently; his face looked rather grave and stern.

"I'm afraid you are tired," she said, a little timidly. "I have wearied you with all my chatter."

There was no resisting the shy glance, the fleeting smile. Halford came resolutely out of his dark thoughts, and thrust those troublesome memories aside, the more vexed at their resurrection because he knew they were only memories. The old love was dead as Pharaoh—if to-morrow he were to stand face to face with the woman Alice Berners had become, she would have no more connection with that past dream and pain than the first stranger he met.

"It is for me to thank you, Miss Crofton," he said; "I have not enjoyed any thing so much in ages as our expedition."

"Do you stay here long?" she asked, as they approached the inn.

"Perhaps a week yet. I am rather an idle man just at present, and it is a pretty place to be lazy in—unless the recollection of this afternoon makes it seem dull."

"It has been very nice," she said; and he saw that she did not even notice the little old complimentary speech. "How fortunate you are, to be able to travel."

"You would like to stay longer in Europe?"

"Oh yes, and see Italy and Greece! Still, I shall be glad to get home—it seems a long time—and next winter will be my first in society," she added, with kindling eyes.

"I am sure it will be a pleasant one," he

said. "I wish there was a probability of my being there to witness your triumphs—I don't believe they will spoil you."

"I should think not," replied she, gayly; "I shall get rid of this childishness every body laughs at."

"I hope not," he replied, seriously; "keep it as long as you can."

"So you don't think of going back?" she asked.

"My plans are very undecided—at present I can not tell. Will you promise not to have forgotten me, if I should come?" demanded he, with a certain mock earnestness he might have shown had she been in years the child she seemed.

"Indeed I shall not," she answered, frankly.

"Ah, but will you be glad to see me?" he persisted.

"Very glad," she said, as frankly as before—and there was not a tinge of added color in her cheeks—repeating her words with so much earnestness, that she quite forgot even to be shy.

"I shall recollect that," returned he, still with the playful voice and smile wherewith he would have listened to and answered a child. "Here we are at the inn—our pleasant day is over."

"It has seemed very short," sighed Milly.

"Say good-bye now," he urged, holding out his hand before helping her to descend. "The other good-bye will be before all those people, and not count. Remember, you have promised not to forget me, and to be glad if I do appear."

"I shall remember," she replied; and for the first time her eyes sank under his, and a deepened pink tinged her cheek.

She slipped past him as he lifted her from the saddle, and ran into the house—the bright day had come to an end.

CHAPTER IV.

THE HAUNTED CHAMBER.

THE sun stole through the parted curtains, and lighted the room cheerfully; it quite put the fire out of countenance by its rays, roused sweeter odors from the blossoming exotics, and excited the cardinal bird to a loud, triumphant burst of song.

It was the brightest possible American winter's day; a sufficient suspicion of snow had fallen during the night to bring out the sledges of half the youth of New York, and the tones of the bells rang gayly up to the chamber as the fanciful equipages dashed on toward the Park with their joyous occupants. It was the prettiest room of the prettiest house that Murray Hill could boast — charming and luxurious enough to be the home of a fairy princess; and within its quiet sat the owner and designer of this elegance—a woman so beautiful, that, for

several years, her name had been in two con-
tinents a synonym for loveliness and grace.
There she was, leaning back in a low, easy-chair,
her violet dress enhancing the delicacy of her
complexion; the luxuriant masses of bronze-
tinted hair, banded back from her forehead,
catching golden gleams in the sunlight; her
great brown eyes gazing absently before her,
and the glorious face, which had worked such
havoc in countless hearts, a graver and sadder
one than those who were only familiar with it
as it looked in the world's sight would believe
it could ever become.

The last room, and the last presence, to be
haunted by a skeleton; yet there was one there
—a grim, pertinacious skeleton, which had
dogged Mrs. Marchmont's footsteps for weeks;
grown so familiar to her vision, that sometimes
she wondered how it was possible he could have
escaped the observation of others. He followed
her home from last night's ball—haunted her
troubled dreams; and this morning, when she
left her chamber, and came out into this sunny
apartment, half dressing-room, half boudoir,
there he was, awaiting her, more lively and animated than ever. He grinned among the
scarlet and white flowers, danced about the
pure statue of Innocence which some Italian
sculptor had sent as a homage to her beauty,
and was so jubilant and ubiquitous, that she
almost thought he must have hunted up half a
dozen of his bony brethren to disturb her. His
companionship transformed the regal chamber
into a sepulchre—made the sunshine hideous,
and the bird's notes a shriek of despair to her
ears. She rose at last, and swept the velvet
draperies down over the casements, that the
softened gloom might leave his society a little
less odious than it was in the full daylight.

The bronze clock on the mantel struck twelve.
She had risen earlier than usual this morning,
to be ready for the visitor whom she expected;
but he had not appeared—no summons had
come—no one had intruded upon her since the
model French maid stole quietly out, wondering a little, in her dull fashion, what could have
made her lady so very matinal after the fatigues
of the previous night, which she knew had comprised a dinner, the opera, two balls, and a supper at Delmonico's.

No visit—not even a letter—and the clock
struck twelve! This woman had been all her
life so petted and worshiped, that a crowned
queen could not have been more indignantly
surprised that any mortal should venture on
keeping her waiting; and, of all persons in the
world, that Richard Faulkner should be guilty
of this presumption. She had told him the
evening before that she should expect him;
actually motioned him to her side in the face
and eyes of the whole ball-room to whisper her
commands; hating herself and him because
the order had to be half an entreaty; shivering inwardly, as she had learned to do within
the past month, at the smile on his false mouth,
and the mockery which she perceived, or fan-

cied at least, under his affectation of respect.
Every thing about him was so hateful—the very
scent of hyacinths which always clung to his
dress, rendered the beautiful flowers abhorrent
to her. She could tell the sound of his footsteps among a hundred, and no matter how
crowded the room, how much occupied she
might be, was sure that she felt his odious
presence the moment he entered, long before
he could bring his bold looks and fulsome flatteries within her reach. How she hated the
man! she acknowledged the sentiment to herself, and it was the first time such feelings had
ever been wakened in her soul toward any human being—she had not believed her nature
capable of them. But she did hate him, with
that most active form of repulsion born out of
distrust and dread. She admitted this, too, at
last—she was afraid; and the very vagueness
of her fears rendered them the more unendurable to her impatient temperament.

As if for the express purpose of allowing that
dread to assume a tangible shape and increase,
he neglected this morning to obey her imperi-
ous request. This was his reason—she felt
certain of it—and the fears deepened, and the
skeleton danced until the suspense and inaction
became worse to bear than the blackest news
his deceitful lips could have uttered.

It was an odd secret which gave those two a
certain community of interests during this season. People had marveled somewhat that she,
coquette as she was, could have taken leisure
from the scores of her victims to subjugate Dick
Faulkner, in spite of the fact that his successes
in Wall Street made him, to a certain extent, a
power in these days. Naturally, they attributed
her conduct to her boundless love of power—
her unwillingness that any man, however doubtful his position or morals, should escape her
thralldom; but even when she knew him better
than now, Alice Marchmont would as soon have
dreamed of flirting with a cobra as this monarch
of the Gold-room and share-market. Her most
intimate friend had no perception of the truth.
That she, with her reputation for vast wealth,
could be troubled by business embarrassments,
did not occur to any one, though her name was
a by-word even in Paris for extravagance;
and Worth averred, during the last days of the
Empire, that when Madame Metternich herself
turned ruefully away at the price set on some
fresh emanation of his genius, the famous
American beauty was ready to seize it, and add
a still larger bribe to prevent any sister-woman
obtaining a duplicate of the costume.

She had been running a mad race ever since
the days when she threw off her widow's weeds.
She had dashed along the road to ruin in a tri-
umphal chariot, stimulated to increased speed
by the plaudits of the crowd that bowed in adoration about her course. There was no one
to exercise the slightest restraint over her actions; no one to offer advice; and she had the
most delightful ignorance in regard to money,
beyond spending it lavishly so long as it could

be obtained. Now when a person's ordinary expenses are nearly double that person's income, and there are a thousand extraordinary expenses weekly indulged, it is not surprising that the unfortunate should at length be brought to understand the fact that there is an end to all things. Mrs. Marchmont found herself overwhelmed with debts; absolutely badgered and bothered by the trades-people who had been, at first, so happy to do whatever lay in their power to minister to the petted, luxurious life which was regal indeed in its triumphs and glitter. She only knew that she could borrow money, and she did, of course paying exorbitant rates of interest, and adding more and more to the reckoning which loomed beyond. Actually, she did not think of the future. To queen it in society—to be noted for her lavish expenditure—to have every man she met at her feet—to make prudent people's hair stand on end with horror, yet force the whole world to admit that whatever she did was charming—she had thought very little beyond these determinations. Very little, save when something in her soul fretted and moaned, and she grew dissatisfied and wretched over the emptiness of existence, and thought how different her destiny might be if she had only grown up under other teachings than those of her girlhood—had been left her youth and love, and all that was gone forever.

But such regrets only rendered her more imprudent. Like the rest of us, she contented herself with blaming her relatives—fate—anything and any body—instead of trying, so far as in her lay, to set straight the thwarted life even then. She hurried on and on—or allowed herself to be carried blindly forward—until, during the past summer, she reached the consummation of her folly. She was at Newport, and Dick Faulkner and his wife were there—Dick Faulkner, grown famous of late through his successes in Wall Street, and so notorious for his vices, that one could not easily understand how husbands and fathers were able to tolerate his presence near their womenkind. But, unfortunately, many of the male guardians aforesaid were so deeply interested in Dick's bubbles and speculations, that it was not possible to offer him the cold shoulder in a social way. Mrs. Marchmont disliked the man, and would perhaps have set the example of treating him as he deserved, had not his wife been foolish enough to oppose her on several occasions; and Mrs. Marchmont could not resist amusing herself at the vicious creature's expense. She tormented her by graciousness to Dick; and though that was bad enough, no harm need have come of her unworthy caprice, had she not been seized with the idea of making the man useful.

Several times she had—like most people during the past ten years—indulged in a little gambling, done under the pretty and respectable name of speculation in stocks. Some Wall Street broker had taken "flyers" for her, and she had called the pleasant gains fairy gold, and, before she was aware, developed a finely-grown taste for the excitement. Knowing less than nothing of business, she had only vague ideas that, if she bought certain stocks, or allowed Faulkner to buy them for her, and he turned them over—whatever that mysterious process might mean—she should be certain to win thousands, and all in a moment; no tiresome waiting—that was the most satisfactory part of the alluring vision.

Any terms which placed him on a familiar and confidential footing with Alice Marchmont were pleasant ones to Faulkner. He divined her wishes at the first hint, and entered into her plans with great eagerness. Positively, while still at Newport, he handed her an amount which put her mind at ease for the rest of her stay, by settling a modiste's account that was nearly as long as one of Mademoiselle de Scudery's romances, and showed more imagination in embroidering plain facts. And all Alice had done was to give him an inconsiderable sum. Oh, at this rate, she should soon not only be free from worry, but there was no end to the delightful possibilities which might occur. Dick Faulkner certainly was not an agreeable person to admit into her circle; but in those days he was respectful, almost shy in his manners; and a doubt that the time might come when she should find it difficult to keep him in order, never occurred to her; for Alice prided herself, like so many women, on the fact that no man had ever dared to utter a word—however plainly he might betray his feelings in his face—which could cause her annoyance. She prided herself on this always, during her married days, as if it presented an excuse for her flirtations. She forgot, as women do in their love of adulation, that to go near enough the verge of propriety for a man to have an opportunity of entertaining wrong wishes, was a degradation, and a stain upon her soul, as real and ineffaceable as if she had listened to vows which ought never to reach her ears. But she did not think of Dick Faulkner in any other light than as a person who might be useful—whom she repaid sufficiently by the honor of leading her to her carriage, or holding her bouquet while she danced.

Of course, she began the season's campaign in the maddest fashion, on the strength of her successes and brilliant visions. Winter was more than half over now, and she discovered that not only were her debts doubled, but loss after loss had followed, until she owed Faulkner a sum so large that she dared not reckon it, and had no more idea how he was to be repaid than she had what was to become of her after the rumbling in every direction burst in one grand earthquake.

But dreadful as such reflections were, there was a worse fear in her mind, roused by the change in Faulkner's manner as the weeks went on, and day by day she found herself more deeply involved in the web of his countless schemes. This man, once so respectful, almost timid, had dared to treat her in a way which forced her to contemplate the possibility of reaching a crisis when the charmed atmosphere which had hitherto enveloped her life should be sullied by the disclosure of a disgraceful secret.

So far she got in her thoughts this morning; then could endure her solitary vigil no longer. The skeleton leaped higher in his hideous dance, and grinned with more appalling malice. She rose quickly and rang the bell—Pauline the patient appeared in an instant.

"Are there no letters?" her mistress asked. No letters whatever; but if madame pleased, it was one o'clock, and Miss Livermore and her sister were below.

"That is nothing to me; they are Miss Portman's friends," Mrs. Marchmont replied.

But if madame pleased, Mrs. Townley's carriage had just driven to the door, and Miss James was with her. Evidently it did not please madame, for she said, impatiently,

"I don't know why they come at this unholy hour; it is not my day—I don't think I'll see any body."

"But madame has forgotten — I beg madame's pardon—they were all invited to luncheon," returned Pauline in a deprecating voice, which was an annoyance of itself.

"So they were—I did not remember it; very well, I will go down. And no letters—you are sure?"

"Ah, madame!" cried Pauline. If she had talked a week, she could not so eloquently have expressed her sense of injury at the doubt implied of her faithfulness by this repetition.

"Yes—you would have brought them at once —you never forget any thing," her mistress said, kindly.

The very depth of darkness to which her fancies had plunged during the last hour brought a reaction. Faulkner's silence was a good sign —this very morning the long-delayed rise in that wonderful stock of which she had hoped so much, might take place. It had been only a matter of time—Peep-of-Day was sure to succeed—it had glittered too famously to be a mere bubble! At this moment, perhaps, Dick Faulkner was bidding it up in the Board—too busy to recollect her note. Before night she should have news; good news; for if only the expected rise took place she should gain thousands upon thousands. Her debt to Faulkner would appear the veriest trifle; not only that, but her other embarrassments could be cleared away. She would take her fairy gold and rest content —nothing should ever tempt her into another speculation. Faulkner would slip naturally back into his rightful place—a man to be cavalierly smiled upon—invited, perhaps, to her general parties—but in no way to have a closer connection with her life.

She was too variable in her moods for the Frenchwoman to feel the slightest surprise at the sudden change which came over her face; though, familiar as she was with its beauty, she could not help wondering at the loveliness of the smile that beamed upon her.

"I'll go down to the people, Pauline—I hope I'm not hideous this morning?"

The Parisian could only lift her hands again —language was too inexpressive just now. Mrs. Marchmont laughed, and passed down into the room where her guests waited, as charming in words and manner as if they had been a group of men to be subjugated, instead of members of her own sex.

"This has been the longest morning I ever spent!" she exclaimed; and there was such sincerity in her tone that they believed her, females though they were, and actually thought she had been anxiously anticipating their arrival. "Now who has any news—I am famished for something in the way of novelty."

"There's a great stir in Congress over Hamilton's Bill," said the elder of the two old maids, who prided herself on reading the political journals, and liked to present the opinions she gleaned therefrom.

Mrs. Townley and Miss James looked distressed at once—if the ancient cat got off on that theme, there was an end to all enjoyment.

"Is there, indeed?" demanded Mrs. Marchmont in the most interested voice, as she gave her two despairing friends a mischievous glance. "You must tell us about it—I never find time to read the newspapers."

The two butterflies showed their trouble still more plainly, and the antique virgin at once assumed her oracular attitude, and prepared to pour forth a flood of eloquence; but Mrs. Marchmont had no intention of permitting that.

"Yes, you must tell us," she continued, quickly; "your views on political matters are always so lucid and correct, dear Miss Livermore; but we'll save them for luncheon. I'm only a silly, frivolous creature, though I do admire wisdom — at a respectful distance — and what I want first is gossip—I always mean gossip when I ask for news—I'm insatiable in that line."

The butterflies brightened into smiles of relief—the present demand was quite within the scope of their powers, and more than a recreation—the serious business of their lives. But before they could commence either of the half-dozen stories which they always had on hand, Miss Portman, seldom as she spoke, felt it her duty to defend her relative from that self-imposed injustice.

"My dear," she quavered, "how can you say such things!"

"Oh, I adore gossip—it's of no use for me to deny it! Do you think I am willing to believe people are so much better than I know I am? It's such a relief to hear of all sorts of weaknesses and lapses on the part of one's friends."

"I'm sure every body's friends give sufficient opportunity," said Mrs. Townley, laughing.

"Oh, you feel malicious this morning," returned Alice; "now that's delightful! Among us, we'll not leave a human creature a shred of character by the time luncheon is over — apropos, there's Ferguson to announce it."

They followed her into the breakfast-room, and she continued—

"Now Miss Portman is just as crazy for news as I, though she does pretend to be virtuous—you know you are, Adeliza."

The meek, elderly lady was a distant connection of the late Mr. Marchmont's, who lived with the beautiful widow and played propriety —a creature so quiet and inoffensive, that I must describe her at once, lest I forget the fact of her existence. Alice was kind to her pale shadow of decorum, and tried often to give her a share in conversation; but Miss Portman invariably waved off the opportunity with a little nervous gesture, and had nothing beyond a weak smile, and faint ejaculations to offer. She was one of those persons born never to be of any consequence — not even recollected; still, she evidently had a use in the world, since dashing young women without natural protectors require a show of companionship.

She was as mild and timid as a mouse; and indeed she rather looked like one—a Chinese mouse at that, if the small animals there follow the example of Celestial humans, in having their eyes turn up at the corners. Her voice, too, assisted the resemblance—a sort of quavering, hesitating squeak, all the odder from the fact that she was tall and straight, and so stiff that strangers often mistook her shyness for dignity, and were afraid of her. I have nothing for her to say or do, because she never said or did any thing; and perhaps the best idea I can give of her is to repeat an anecdote with which Mrs. Marchmont once convulsed her friend John Worthington. The poor woman had vexed her one evening by sitting a little party through where every body else talked— just a little knot of Alice's agreeables—upright and patient as a ghost, smiling painfully at intervals, but not so much as uttering a strangled squeak when caught in the trap of other people's conversation.

"Dear Miss Portman," said Alice, "I wish you could help play the hostess rather more— it would relieve me a great deal."

"My love," returned she, in a deprecating tone, "what more could I do?"

"You best of old souls! Look energetic; go about among the tiresome creatures, and talk to them."

"My dear," she answered, in a voice which began to quaver ominously, for she was sensitive to a shadow of reproach, "I am sure I smiled whenever any body told a story! I said excellent to Mr. Worthington's anecdote, though I did not understand it—for I have the highest respect for him — and I changed my position twice."

"So," said Alice, in repeating the conversation, "I kissed her, and told her she was a duck, and that her positions were both beautiful."

After that, it was a standing joke among Mrs. Marchmont's intimates to ask her if she had changed her position lately; and dear Miss Portman always smiled when she heard the question addressed to her relative, because she saw that there was a jest intended, though it had no special signification to the placid pool she called her mind. So now, when Alice appealed to her, Miss Portman gave the requisite smile, and changed her position immediately. Mrs. Marchmont had done her duty, and could leave the poor soul at peace for a time.

"The last news I have heard," said Mrs. Townley, "is that you are to marry your French baron."

"Bless me, that's stale," returned Alice; "people have said it now for ten days; I must give them something new! I always feel injured if the reports about me don't change at least twice a week."

The idle stream of chatter went on; but though she played her part admirably, Mrs. Marchmont had leisure to think of other things. Her morning's uneasiness occasionally recurred; each time she heard the door-bell, she fancied that it might be the expected letter; but it did not come. The baron's name, too, suggested fresh thoughts; for once flung into the conversation, it was bandied about for several moments. The creature had fallen helplessly, dazed at the first sight of her—there might be worse fates than becoming a baroness —she had never before contemplated the possibility except in jest; but with this new fear of Dick Faulkner in her mind, any chance which would take her completely out of her present life possessed a certain charm.

When she could listen again, a new name had come up—she caught it—a name no one had mentioned in her hearing for years. How it carried her thoughts back into the past—into the days of her girlhood, when she had been full of hopes and dreams rudely dashed out of existence by hands stronger than her youthful will.

"Is is possible!" the elder Miss Livermore exclaimed. "Kenneth Halford back—I wonder I had not heard of it."

"Oh, he only landed yesterday; I dare say, though, Mrs. Granger has already secured him for her ball—she's the most inveterate lion-hunter, that woman," returned Mrs. Townley.

"So Kenneth Halford has come home," pursued Miss Livermore.

"How old!" added her sister. "Did you hear, Mrs. Marchmont?" she continued, with a meaning inflection of voice.

Mrs. Marchmont had been busy giving some whispered direction to Ferguson; she turned now, and said,

"I beg your pardon! There's a new plat on my mind that I begged the chef to try! Who has come back?"

The virgin sisters replied together, one in a voice that squeaked, the other in a deep barytone.

"Kenneth Halford."

"What a resurrection!" laughed Mrs. March-mont.

"I don't remember him," said Miss James.

"Oh, he was rather before your time," observed Mrs. Townley, "and mine too; for I lived in Albany in those days; but I recollect all about him; yes, indeed—oh, Mrs. Marchmont?"

"He is a very old friend of mine," she said, as composedly as if the significant tone had been lost upon her.

The ancient virgins laughed, and Miss Portman looked distressed. "Dear me, what is it?" cried Miss James, nearly wild with curiosity at once. "There's some mystery, I'm sure!"

"None that I know of," returned Mrs. Marchmont. "I said he was an old friend; I shall be glad to see him again."

"Shall you, really?" demanded the younger sister, while the elder chuckled.

"Oh yes! a very old friend; I think we all remember."

Mrs. Marchmont never allowed any human being to attack her without making the reckless person sorry. She paid a few compliments to the man of whom they had spoken, as calmly as if he had been an indifferent acquaintance, instead of the one love of her girlhood; then she asked Miss Livermore, "Is it true that your cousin, Mrs. Grayson, is coming home?"

The old maid colored, well tanned as nearly sixty years had left her complexion, and stammered out such answer as she could find, while her sister choked herself with a glass of water, and Mrs. Townley and Helen James enjoyed their distress. Mrs. Grayson had not set foot in her native country for more than five years; and this story of her return, which had lately spread about, was misery to every body connected with her; for she had long before gone so far over the pale of propriety, that her memoirs would have filled three volumes.

It was a cruel thrust, and Alice felt ashamed a moment after it was dealt. She tried to atone by overwhelming Miss Livermore with attentions, and actually forced the others to endure a long recital of the spinster's views in regard to the political state of the country. Once mounted on her hobby, it was difficult to unseat her. She pranced over into England—descended upon humiliated France—pointed out the duty of Victor Emanuel—and even penetrated into Russia, and galloped a little about Poland, before she could be checked.

Two or three men called while they were at the table, and were allowed to enter; the reunion was as pleasant and gay as any festivity always was in Alice Marchmont's house, and the morning wore on. It was a terribly long one; she fervently wished her guests at least in the frozen regions over which Miss Livermore had pranced on her hobby-horse; but there was no trace of fatigue or preoccupation in features or manner. She laughed and talked, dazzled and flattered men and women alike, able as ever to make either friend or foe admit that she was the loveliest and wittiest of her sex.

The day drifted on; but no message came from Faulkner. At one moment she was able to believe it a good omen; at the next, her dark forebodings would start up with new force, and it seemed impossible to wait in this passive inactivity So many other thoughts, too, in her mind—this new idea in regard to the baron; and as she contemplated it, his studied manner, his long-winded compliments, appeared more wearisome than ever. And Kenneth Halford back—it seemed strange that he should have returned at this precise juncture. But he was nothing to her; it could only be a pain to see any ghost rise out of that dead past which often—when she had leisure to look back—seemed so beautiful through the mists of distance.

No message—no letter! The day got on—at least she should find Dick Faulkner at Mrs. Granger's ball. There were other duties to be performed before she got there; a dinner—a reception by one of the stateliest of the old Knickerbocker families, people who despised such mushrooms as Mrs. Granger and her set. It was a long time to wait before she could get within the man's reach—his detested, odious presence; and to wait with even a show of patience was a lesson Alice Marchmont had never learned.

CHAPTER V.

AT A BALL.

MRS. GRANGER gave her ball that night; and it was one of the most brilliant of the whole season. Among all the faces there, Milly Crofton's was the freshest and the fairest girl-face to be seen, and her enjoyment of the evening something for older people to marvel at, it was so unalloyed. It had been altogether a bright, charming winter, though perhaps misanthropic sages would have pronounced it a somewhat unprofitable one; but Milly was troubled by no such doubts. Very charming it had been, with its balls, its operas, its pretty new dresses, and the pleasant success which her introduction into society proved. Mrs. Remsen was too wise to allow her to rush about until she wore the first freshness off her face and thoughts, as so many girls do, before their opening season is half over, and the experienced lady understood, too, the wisdom of making her charge a little difficult to get at—among the earliest to leave places of amusement, and to be carefully guarded from detrimentals who only meant flirtation, instead of serious business.

Milly had returned from Europe early in the autumn, and brought with her the prettiest possible wardrobe, which wise Aunt Eliza had instructed Mrs. Crittendon to purchase in Paris, and to which that lady had made many charming additions on her own account. The elderly couple were sorry to give the girl up, but it was decided that they must go to Havana for the winter, and Mrs. Remsen would not hear of Milly's accompanying them. She found her niece so much improved and beautified by her foreign travel, that she was anxious to exhibit her to society, and her old love of managing and match-making rose with new keenness in her mind.

She was a born match-maker, this smooth, plausible lady: it is a firm belief of mine that all women have a genius for something; and match-making was Mrs. Remsen's specialty. She had been at the business for years, yet always managed so artfully that nobody ever thought of calling her by the odious name which less astute feminines receive with much less reason.

She had married off numberless relatives and friends long before; two of her daughters were already provided for—brilliantly, so far as wealth and position went, and fortunate, besides, in the personal character of their husbands. One of the pair had been intellectual, and almost strong-minded; oddly enough, she was the pretty daughter. The other—Adelaide Ramsay—was ugly, and not over-furnished with brains. Things ought to have been differently arranged; the intellectual young lady should have given up the pretty face to the dunce; but Mrs. Remsen made the best of matters. The discrepancies between looks and tastes only amused her, and rendered her more determined to outgeneral destiny. She succeeded, and people considered her the most fortunate woman in the world, and held her opinions in the highest respect.

She had still three daughters on her hands; but two of them were children yet, and Maud, the elder, a year younger than Milly Crofton, and doomed to retirement for the present—a fate against which the young lady stoutly rebelled; for she was the most unpromising charge that Mrs. Remsen had ever possessed. Indeed, the mother confessed to herself that Maud was an idiot; but she promised to be a pretty one, and there was still the hope left that another year might soften her asperities of character somewhat, or, at least, teach her to conceal them under a polish of manner which Mrs. Remsen felt to be sadly wanting. But at present her mind was occupied with Milly Crofton. Milly was the only child of Mrs. Remsen's best-beloved sister, and had been treated with the same affection and interest that the lady bestowed upon her own daughters; indeed, she was fonder of Milly, at the bottom of her heart, than she was of the elder members of her own brood. She had a habit of always looking things straight in the face, and did not try to disguise from herself the fact that Milly, childish as she was, possessed more head and heart than her two put together; and she was glad to see that the little ones resembled their cousin much more than they did their sisters.

She had done her best to make Milly's winter successful; and it had proved so, though Mrs. Remsen began to fear that the season would end without the girl's being engaged and settled, and she had not looked forward to giving her a second chance. Maud's turn must come next year, and she could not afford the expense of two young women to dress and take out. However, she had not opened her lips to Milly. If nothing better offered, the child must accept an elderly man, as each of her own daughters had done, or else resign herself to Charley Thorne, a young fellow with any quantity of money and no brains to mention. But the idea was a disappointment to Mrs. Remsen; cold and worldly as she was, she would have been glad to see Milly live the girlish romance suitable to her age—but a wise one, with a rich man—if possible, a famous one—for the hero. She felt a little vexed with destiny for not having thrown any such in the way, and sometimes wished that she had been rich enough to take Milly back to Europe for a year. She knew, of course, of the acquaintance with Kenneth Halford; Mrs. Lawrence had told her how much he appeared struck with Milly; and it seemed a pity that fate, after commencing the acquaintance between the two in a sensational and poetic manner, should have provided no materials for a closing act. Halford had not a vast fortune, but he was rich; and, added to that, had already acquired an enviable reputation, both as a diplomatist and as a man of letters. Mrs. Remsen felt that destiny had treated her ill, and chafed accordingly. But the very morning of Mrs. Granger's ball, she discovered that she had been hasty in blaming the much-abused old dame—Kenneth Halford had actually returned—fate had once more brought him within the sphere of Milly's influence; and before she returned home, Mrs. Remsen had arranged the finale of the romance to suit herself. She did not mention the news that had reached her; she only made sure that Milly wore her prettiest Parisian dress—which had been saved for some especially grand occasion—and saw that the girl was looking more lovely than ever.

"Will I do, aunty?" Milly asked, as she entered Mrs. Remsen's room for inspection, after her toilet was finished.

Then it was that Mrs. Remsen surveyed her critically, and decided that, so far as young girls were concerned, not one who might be at the ball would compare with Milly.

"I never saw you look so well—I am content," she said, with a low sigh of satisfaction, which Milly perfectly understood. Mrs. Remsen must have been in a high state of contentment when she gave that peculiar sigh.

Maud the rebellious happened to be in her mother's chamber, and, though not particularly acute, she comprehended the meaning of the long-drawn breath; and that sign of approval, added to Milly's beaming loveliness, was more than the rebellious could endure.

"Any body could look pretty in a dress like that!" cried she, with an acrimony that made her mother shudder to think what an awful old maid she would be if some unfortunate man did not prevent the catastrophe. "When I come out, mamma, I shall remember all the things you let Milly get in Paris; Adelaide says that it's more than you ever did for her."

"I hope, at least, that Adelaide said it in a more lady-like voice," replied Mrs. Remsen, calmly "I beg, Maud, that you will not touch my powder—you will ruin your complexion."

"Oh, I'm of no consequence," cried Maud, spitefully; "nobody is, except Milly."

"You are cross to-night, Maud," said Milly, laughing, too happy to pay much attention to her cousin's ill humor.

"I'm nothing of the sort," asserted Maud.

"If you must contradict, at least do it in a lower tone, I beg," said her mother, resignedly, quite aware that a little quiet contempt was a more effectual way of subduing the young woman than any assertion of authority. "Also, let me set you right in one particular, and Mrs. Ramsay, too—Milly's own money paid for her winter's wardrobe; we had saved a good while for that express purpose. When your day for ball-dresses comes, I hope you will receive a little of the attention Milly gets so freely on all sides, and I should like to think that it would not turn your head any more than it does hers."

Maud gave the footstool at her feet a vicious kick; she pretended that it was accidental; but her mother and cousin knew that if ever a kick was given with malice prepense, this was the time.

"We will say good-night to you, Maud," said Mrs. Remsen, with awful courtesy; and Maud departed.

That silly little Milly could not bear to have her in an ill temper, so kept her aunt waiting while she sought Maud and coaxed her back to amiability—a state of affairs only to be arrived at by a present of a large packet of bonbons and a neck-ribbon; and then Maud grew radiant, only assuring her cousin that the new French dress was not nearly so becoming as mamma pretended to believe.

Mrs. Remsen and Milly set off for the ball; and as soon as she entered the rooms, the girl was so beset by partners and flatterers, that the aunt's anticipations of triumph were fully realized. Kenneth Halford was not present; but before she had been five minutes there, Mrs. Remsen contrived, without asking a question, to learn that he was expected. Mrs. Granger had heard of his arrival, and immediately pounced upon him on the strength of an old acquaintanceship, that she might be the first to exhibit him since his return to his former friends, possessed of the twofold advantages of wealth and position.

Mrs. Remsen was as kind as ever to Charley Thorne; but as he hovered about Milly, teasing her for more dances than she had a right to give to one man, talking a great deal of nonsense in a merry, happy fashion, that lady allowed herself to think what a poor, weak, frivolous boy he was, and how much better it would be if he were compelled to work, instead of being led into numberless follies by his great fortune.

Milly danced and enjoyed herself greatly; and at the end of a galop, as her partner led her back to her seat, she saw a gentleman conversing with her aunt; and though his back was toward her, and she had no idea that the person of whom he reminded her was within a thousand leagues and more of the spot, her heart beat fast, and she did not venture to look again lest she should be convinced of her mistake. It was very natural that Kenneth Halford should have been often in her mind, from the peculiar circumstances of their acquaintance; but she was unconscious how persistently her thoughts had dwelt upon that season, or of how much consequence it was in her life.

But in another moment the well-remembered face was bending toward her, and the low, soft voice said,

"Miss Crofton promised not to forget me; I hope she has not forgotten her pledge."

"I am so very, very glad to see you," Milly answered, through her blushes and smiles. "I saw you as I came up, but thought that I must be mistaken."

"And I saw you, too, while you were dancing," he said; "but I knew that I made no mistake."

Mrs. Remsen smiled amiably, and joined just enough in the conversation, until some friend sat down beside her and began to talk, and she was able to leave the pair to themselves for a little, having made sure that Milly was looking and behaving just as she ought.

"I had been renewing my acquaintance with your aunt," he went on; "she was good enough to remember me."

"Oh yes; when I spoke about you to her, she said that she always liked you very much."

"Then you did remember to speak of me?"

"I should be very ungrateful if I had not," Milly said.

"Oh, I'll not be remembered out of gratitude," returned he, gayly. "But you promised to be glad to see me if I came home."

"When did you get here?" Milly asked, instead of replying to the words, though her face rendered an answer unnecessary.

"Only the day before yesterday. We had a passage as smooth and pleasant as if it had been June. Now tell me what you have been doing—have you enjoyed your winter?"

"Yes; it has been very nice indeed."

"I am glad of that! I imagined that it had; for I met Mrs. Lawrence this morning, and she told me so much about the admiration you received, that I was half afraid I might find you altered."

"What a very weak head you must give me credit for possessing," Milly said, laughing.

"I don't know if that would be a sign, only I liked to think I should find you the same."

"And I am," she replied; "I'm not very nice, but I don't think the winter has done me any hurt; I have been very happy, and they say happiness is good for people."

"I am sure it is—at least for you."

"Have you come back to America to stay?" she asked.

"My movements are uncertain; I shall be here until spring, at least. I must see how I am treated by you and the rest of my friends, before I decide to stay longer."

Milly thought how pleasant it would be to meet him at balls and parties—to have him visit at the house; but her reflections did not go beyond those simple details.

"I have not danced in a long time," he said; "would you dare try this redowa with me? I may be very awkward, I warn you in advance."

But Milly was not afraid, and he led her off, while Charley Thorne, once more trying to get into her neighborhood, watched the proceeding in silent wrath, and decided that, of all prigs with an immense opinion of themselves, this man was the worst.

"And he must be no end of an age, too," thought Charley, with the natural scorn of an American youth of one-and-twenty for any body who had gone a decade beyond that season. "The idea of his dancing—why he's old enough to have the gout! I can remember seeing him when I wore petticoats; and he was old then."

But the fossil, as Charley wished to believe him, certainly had not forgotten how to dance; and when the music ceased, he stood by Milly and talked until somebody came to claim her according to promise, and Charley found no opportunity of getting near. Halford conversed with Mrs. Remsen for a few moments, and then sauntered away through the rooms; but he did not dance, except that once with Milly.

Charley Thorne felt it his duty to watch this man, about whom he was inclined to fancy something dark and mysterious; and whether dancing or uttering the little remarks which he fondly believed conversation, he always had an eye upon Halford. He saw him approach Milly several times in the intervals of the dances; and at last, when it came Charley's turn to have another waltz with her, this fellow positively kept near and chatted with her each time they stopped to rest, and, to make matters worse, was civil and good-natured to Charley himself, which the boy felt was more than he could endure.

"I don't see what he's here for," Thorne grumbled to Milly, as they were whirling about again like two Dervishes; "he's old enough to have seen the folly of such amusements, you know—why, he might have danced with your aunt when she was young."

"Who—old Mr. Edmonds?" asked Milly, innocently.

"No; that Halford! I say, I don't see that he's so very stunning, that they need all make such a row about him."

"Oh, I don't know; I haven't thought," replied Milly, with half-unconscious deceit. "But you are cross to-night; you don't dance half so well as usual"—this last remark a little

feminine scratch, which she could not resist the pleasure of giving him, as a punishment for his impertinence in regard to Halford.

Poor Charley had but three strong points—dancing, skating, and billiards; it was rather hard to be accused of falling off in the very one of the brief list upon which he most prided himself.

"Why, Miss Jones said she thought I was a better stepper each time I took her out," he said, pathetically.

"Very well; if you think Miss Jones's opinion more likely to be correct than mine—" began Milly; but he interrupted her with an indignant gurgle and moan.

"You know I don't; I think nobody's opinion of so much importance as yours."

"But when it comes to hearing Miss Jones quoted in defiance to me!" cried Milly, laughing; for it was all play to her, and she really had no idea that the poor fellow was as wretched as his limited capacities would permit. "I really can not allow that; Miss Jones is the bitterest enemy I have in the world."

"Oh, by Jove, that's strong, you know!"

"But true! Didn't she, the night of Mrs. Lawrence's tableaux, try to spoil my pale blue dress by wearing a bright blue, and ruin my poor little seed pearls—or the effect of them—with her great monstrous things, that look like so many blisters? Of course she's my enemy; I'm astonished that you should ever dance with her or look at her."

"I won't," gasped Charley, "if you tell me not."

"Don't be a goose," said Milly; "of course, I was only laughing at you."

She had known Charley Thorne all her life, and considered herself much the elder, though he had three years the advantage, in point of fact. It was nice to have him an obedient slave; but it never occurred to Milly that he could be foolish enough to get in earnest, or expect her to regard him as other than an old playmate and friend.

"You laugh at me a great deal," sighed Charley.

"Of course I do; it's good for you! But don't you see that the people are all stopping, and the music, too? We can't hop about here with no accompaniment, for the general amusement!"

Fate was not kind to Charley Thorne to-night. They had not taken ten steps, when they met Mrs. Granger and Kenneth Halford; and that lady said,

"Oh, Milly, do show Mr. Halford the conservatory; I want him to decide about the Egyptian thing."

Charley Thorne wished her dead and embalmed along with the Pharaohs; but, as if not content with having stabbed him to the heart, she turned the knife round and round with fiendish pleasure.

"I want you too, Mr. Thorne," she said; "you have not been presented to my little cousin from Washington, and I wish you to know her."

Charley could only bow and grind his teeth.

"You know what Mrs. Faulkner said, Milly," pursued the lady, "about it's not being Egyptian —we can easily settle the question now."

She sailed away, bearing the unfortunate youth with her, who cast one last backward glance for the express purpose of driving himself to despair by seeing that Milly did not even notice his departure.

"By Jove," thought Charley, "I feel like one of Owen Meredith's poems! I'd like to set my bull terrier on this old woman."

"You are to show me the conservatory and the Egyptian thing; it's not a mummy, is it?" asked Halford.

"No; it's a plant with a dreadfully long name; but it's very pretty," Milly said.

So they walked out of the ball-room, through a salon, and entered the conservatory, talking gayly as they went.

The arrivals had long been over. Most persons who danced had already worn the freshness of their enjoyment; and the greater portion of those who had not, had probably grown as weary as people do, night after night, in the performance of their duty toward society. It was, therefore, vexatious to hear a name announced with great energy by the domestic guardians outside, and to see Mrs. Marchmont enter, in the full splendor of her beauty. The perfection of her dress though, was the greatest injury—a satin robe that matched, in hue, her amber ornaments, covered with floating tulle draperies of the same tint, caught up here and there by diamond sprays, which sparkled like dew-drops among the fleecy folds of lace—the whole effect so airy and light, that the costume looked rather as if woven out of sunset-colored clouds, than composed of materials within the reach of ordinary mortals.

Naturally, nine out of ten of the women could have strangled her with serene satisfaction, including the hostess, who received the tardy guest with such sweet smiles and rapturous greetings. Straightway there was a crowd of men about her; for, whatever female nature might think of such wiles and "affectations," it was not to be expected that any masculine fancy could resist this incarnation of freshness and grace, appearing so unexpectedly in the midst of the heat and turmoil.

Mrs. Granger's house was large; at the end of the suite of drawing-rooms there was an apartment extending the whole breadth of the mansion, which, like a sensible person, she called a ball-room—forcing the word down her acquaintances' throats at the point of the bayonet—thereby pleasing the young people and saving the expense of a carpet. I did not give you this bit of information with any idea of filling in a page of upholstery items—only to show you just where Mrs. Marchmont found her hostess, so that you might understand the position. She stood in fair sight of the dancing world and the throng moving about the salons; there chanced to be a pause in the music as she entered, so that nothing of the effect was lost.

Of course, the women knew that the late arrival had been a premeditated business; but I think that each feminine heart must have bowed in wondering consciousness of defeat and a secret acknowledgment of a superior power, when she had the audacity to avow it. Mrs. Granger said, in the sweetest possible way,

"What makes you so late, dear? I had entirely given you up, and was dreadfully disappointed."

"It was quite like an entrance in a play," added Mrs. Faulkner, who chanced to be standing close by, with as near approach to a sneer as she ventured to indulge.

"That was what I wanted," returned Mrs. Marchmont, coolly, and in a voice audible to those about. "I had a new dress just from Paris, and knew it would double the effect if I came in when every body was warm and tired."

She said it with such arch malice, made her greetings right and left, to women and men, so pleasant, that no masculine at least but would have scouted the idea of her confession being serious; and, as I said, her own sex had to acknowledge her profound generalship, and admire, however much they might detest, her on account of it.

So there she stood, in that marvelous dress, with a group of the best men in the rooms about her, in the very zenith of her beauty and grace, and her witty and terribly heedless tongue more unmanageable than usual. She would not dance yet—after a while, perhaps; really, she would not promise! She never kept a list, and promises always led her into trouble! But as she swept away on somebody's arm, for what she called a tour of inspection, she could not resist giving Mrs. Faulkner a needle-thrust in payment for her impertinent speech.

"Is your husband here?" she asked.

"No; he is coming, though—at least he told me he would," Mrs. Faulkner was obliged to answer, as amiably as she might, though succeeding so poorly in hiding her annoyance, that the by-standers smiled.

"I am so glad—I think he will come—I came on purpose to see him," retorted Mrs. Marchmont, with a cool deliberation which caused the fingers of her discomfited adversary to tingle with an unlady-like desire to attack her then and there.

Having punished her antagonist—a bad habit of hers—Mrs. Marchmont floated off; really, what with the dress and all, it is the most applicable word. Mrs. Faulkner solaced herself by whispering to their hostess,

"She is the most outrageous flirt I ever saw."

"Oh, I don't know," the other replied, of course having hugely enjoyed the defeat of her sharp-nosed ally. "People say that; but she is so frank and open—still, I can't make her out."

Neither could Mrs. Faulkner; for all that, she was excessively jealous of her husband, and had every reason to be; but though Mrs. Granger could not exactly say it to the wife, she was thinking that Alice Marchmont, at the culminating point of her popularity and success, would be little inclined to go any great lengths on account of a man like Dick Faulkner.

The music burst out again, the whirl recommenced, and Mrs. Marchmont was a star of such magnitude that the freshest face of the season paled before her splendor. Perhaps that belonged to little Milly Crofton, who returned to the ball-room on Kenneth Halford's arm, at the summons of the dashing galop. They had not witnessed Mrs. Marchmont's entrance; for it was just before she appeared that Mrs. Granger had asked Milly to take Mr. Halford into the conservatory, that he might decide whether the abomination in the way of a huge water-plant was really Egyptian, as asserted by the florist, to whom she had paid "shekels of gold" for the unsightly thing. Mrs. Faulkner had declared her friend cheated, and there had been several warm arguments between them, conducted with such ill-nature on the part of naughty Dick's wife that the remembrance afforded an addition zest to Mrs. Granger's enjoyment of the scene wherein Alice Marchmont had so effectually worsted the jealous lady.

Milly and Halford had staid in the conservatory much longer than was necessary, so far as their errand was concerned. Had any body peeped in, the pretty picture they presented, standing among the flowering vines, might have suggested a flirtation; yet nothing could have been farther removed from such dangerous trifling than their talk. Halford was telling her of his first voyage up the Nile, of a visit to the Pyramids, and other expeditions, which scores of books rendered stale years ago, though, coming from his lips, the account sounded so new and interesting to Milly that she drew him on to such lengthened details that he was forced to smile at his own egotism.

The sound of the music floating into the quiet of their retreat reminded Milly that she should inevitably receive a lecture, if Aunt Eliza noticed her prolonged absence.

"We must go back," she said, with a little sigh. "I wanted to hear how the day ended."

"Indeed, I beg your pardon for making my story so long," he answered.

"I think it's ever so much nicer than any thing in your book," she said, heedlessly.

"Have you actually done me the honor to peep into that heavy volume?"

"I read every word of it," returned Milly, pouting. "Did you think I was too great a baby to understand it?"

"By no means; but what with statistics and all, I fancy it must be very tiresome work to wade through it."

They were in the ball-room now, and Milly did not answer; she had no mind to tell him with what eagerness she had perused the book,

not even skipping the figures, though she never stopped to wonder what gave her so unusual an interest in a work of the sort.

"Am I to have the galop?" he asked.

"Oh no; it is promised; besides, Aunt Eliza never likes me to dance twice in succession with the same person," she answered, with a little accent of regret which Halford, man-like, appreciated, though he did consider her a mere child.

"That is a very wise regulation of Mrs. Remsen's, though it might admit of occasional exceptions," he said.

"Do look!" exclaimed Milly, suddenly, instead of replying. "There is the most beautiful woman in New York—in the world, I believe—Mrs. Marchmont! Did you ever know her?"

Kenneth Halford turned rather quickly, and glanced down the room; but before he could speak, Mrs. Granger loomed upon them from one side, and Charley Thorne, to whom Milly had promised the galop, rushed up on the other, and carried her off with an air of injured and jealous proprietorship which would have amused Halford in a less occupied moment. But he had no opportunity to pursue his scrutiny of the lovely woman Milly had pointed out. Mrs. Granger was eager to hear his decision, and fairly shook his arm in her anxiety to have her twice-repeated question answered.

"It is Egyptian, isn't it, Mr. Halford?"

He recovered a proper sense of decorum—actually turned his back upon the glittering vision which had startled him, and said, quietly enough,

"The most Egyptian thing possible—Cleopatra herself was not more so."

"Come and tell Mrs. Faulkner," cried she, in delight. "I knew it was; but she's always so positive, and so ill-natured."

She hurried him away in search of that lady, and announced her triumph in eager phrases.

"Egyptian be it," returned Mrs. Faulkner, with a provoking yawn behind her fan. "It is ugly enough to be any thing. My dearest Clara, you really ought to have supper—people are saying the most ill-natured things because it is so late—old Mr. Yates was just wondering if you had forgotten to order any."

"After two more dances," said Mrs. Granger, feeling that, since her victory, she could afford to be oblivious of her friend's malice. "This is the young people's night, and they'd rather dance than eat."

Halford drew their hostess away; he disliked feminine squabbles; besides, he wished her countenance in renewing an old acquaintance-ship which his pride would not allow him to postpone, because, to his secret self, any hesitation would have appeared a confession of a weakness which for years he had disavowed.

Alice Marchmont had been dancing, with due precaution in regard to the marvelous dress, which, as usual in her case, escaped the accidents that befall other women's diaphanous raiment on such occasions. She had walked about, and made her presence duly felt everywhere; and now sat in a sort of recess at the side of the middle drawing-room, holding her little court, and queening it with that royalty of an hour which we are all obliged to confess is so absolute, however loudly, out of the profundity of our virtue and wisdom, we pronounce it not worth possessing.

There she sat, and looked down the crowded rooms, wishing herself a world away, while her conversation and repartees dazzled the group about her; wondering, too, why the person whom, of all others, she wished to see, much as she had grown to fear and detest him during the past weeks, did not make his appearance. Suddenly even her weariness, her impatience, faded from her mind; even the dread which the thought of Dick Faulkner roused, went too. She saw her hostess approach, leaning on the arm of a man the sight of whom took her as suddenly back into her vanished girlhood as if some enchanter's wand had caused the room, the crowd, and all surroundings, to disappear like a scene at the theatre, and brought the lost life up in its place.

She knew him in an instant. She was standing in the wood, back of the old country house where they parted on that autumn day. It was the strangest possible mingling of effects. She could see so plainly each incident of that far-off scene—the blue smoke curling lazily up from the trusted chimneys—the golden haze that beautified the landscape—the carpet of gorgeous-tinted leaves beneath their feet—the wild, eager eyes gazing into her own. She could catch the voice of the low breeze as it murmured past, scented with the breath of the late blossoms—hear the crows calling idly in the field below—the querulous complaints of the thrushes in the trees overhead, loud in contention over their southward flight: the stillness and peace, making itself so distinctly felt, in such painful contrast to the agitation of her companion, and the dizzy whirl in her own brain, the mad voice crying out in her soul, which she so ruthlessly silenced. Across it all came the present—the throng, the gay music, and Mrs. Granger's voice, saying,

"Dear Mrs. Marchmont, I have brought you an old acquaintance, who fears that you may have forgotten him."

Half-mechanically, she extended her hand—still with the odd inability to tell where reality' began or ended—and answered,

"How do you do, Mr. Halford? Mrs. Granger excels in pleasant surprises."

He replied; a brief, laughing conversation followed; then Mrs. Granger carried off several of the dandies to attend to their duty, as she told them; and the others, one by one, dropped out of the talk, and departed to find partners, or any occupation they pleased, as men are forced to do on such occasions. There the two sat; and it was like a bit of Alice's girlhood come back, only, all the while, she was looking down the room, and wondering why that man did not bring his disagreeable presence and his news, whatever it might be. Bad enough it would prove, she had horrible fears; but nothing could be worse than the suspense which she had endured during the whole of this dreadful day.

"I feel as if I must be dreaming," Halford said. "That it can be you and I sitting here seems impossible."

Did he mean to be tender in the very outset? If so, what was she to do or say? That was another question—in her peculiar position, one that startled her. Before she could answer either interrogatory he spoke again, in the low tone that was like the well-remembered voice, only with a difference. You shall often hear that, and be disturbed thereby, in meeting unexpectedly some person who belongs to your past, and, ten to one, for your sake and his, never ought to have intruded into the present. The change which has come over the voice! the familiar tones sometimes making your heart throb like a strain of old music, then dying out and the other voice becoming audible—the slow, indifferent voice that the world knows; sounding, as all our voices do as the years go on, as though the dust had got into them and spoiled their ring.

But Halford's next speech, following, in spite of my digression, so close upon his first words that it seemed like a continuation to Mrs. Marchmont, only interrupted by her quick thought, showed that, whatever his feelings might be—if indeed the lapse of time had left him any—he did not mean to indulge in tenderness or sentimental retrospection.

"Am I to begin by congratulating you on your triumphs?" he asked.

"Do you think it necessary?" returned she.

"How can I tell? Certainly, you have achieved enough to offer the opportunity. Well, triumphs and successes are pleasant things; and I know of none pleasanter than those of a successful woman."

Did she want him to be tender? She could not have told. At all events, she was not pleased with that utter obliviousness of the season when he had warned her that their separation would blight his whole life. Perhaps the sensation, which there was not leisure to analyze, scarcely to avow, rendered her voice somewhat satirical, as she said,

"Do you wish to remind me that I have also to compliment you, and on real success and worthy achievements?"

"It did sound a little like it," he answered, quietly; "but it was not what I meant."

"Still, there is every reason," she continued. "You have been climbing all sorts of difficult heights—"

"Nothing worse than Mount Etna."

"It was ill-natured of you to spoil my pretty speech," she said, laughing, but a good deal irritated. "Besides, as a diplomatist, you ought to know that it is unwise, as well as rude, not to hear people out."

"Then I beg your pardon for crushing your intended compliments under Mount Etna—may I hear them now?"

"Too late! Indeed, though, I would have read the book you wrote while in Egypt, only I came on a lot of horrid figures in the beginning, and they frightened me. Why didn't you write a novel?"

"You must remember that the work was written at the request of an archæological society. I suppose a novel would scarcely have been as satisfactory to them, though you might have found it more entertaining."

"And did you like living in Egypt—blooming into a Consul-General at last?"

"Neither was particularly agreeable."

"But the reputation—the—"

"Yes, I know; but this is an odd world, and we are such unaccountable beings! Is anybody satisfied?"

"You should know better than to ask that question of a woman."

"I thought women easily found contentment. Pleasure—admiration—"

"Don't finish, please! You thought, and think, as most men do, that we are children, to be pleased with any bauble which life may see fit to offer us."

"Are you reading me so easily, after all these years?"

"Only judging you by your sex in general."

They were drifting into a style of conversation which he felt unsuited to the perfect amiability and self-control he had meant to exhibit, knowing that at the bottom of his heart there was no real emotion to disturb either his good-nature or calmness, though it was natural enough that the old memories should flutter a little. He hastened to speak, but, the moment the words were out of his mouth, perceived that they were any thing rather than what he wished to say.

"All these years," Mrs. Marchmont had half-whispered to herself; the repetition was part involuntary, part because she had grown so consummate an actress that she never could resist indulging in a dramatic point.

"Some of them have been very dreary ones to me," he said, and immediately became conscious that it was a silly thing to say to this woman, who was nothing to him, whatever the girl she once was might have been to the boy he had long outlived.

But whether it was or was not an allusion to their buried past, Mrs. Marchmont had no leisure to discover; their conversation was interrupted by a brace of men, each of whom claimed her hand for a dance; half a score of others followed, and Halford stood aside, and could watch what the world was ready to give in the way of triumphs, if she thought them worth accepting. Perhaps he did wonder what she thought, for he had loved this woman, loved her with the intensity of a first passion, and, end how it may, that is always a serious matter—at least, for the time.

He had loved her, and life seemed at an end when they parted; he had gone through the usual round of rage, anguish, contempt, studied indifference; and had finally settled down into a philosophical view of the whole business; but he had not forgotten. I beg you will not imagine that he had been pining and moaning during these long years; people have not leisure for such amusements in this busy century. Besides, she became a married woman soon after his departure, and, according to his somewhat old-fashioned creed, he had no right to think about her, only as he might of any other beautiful dream which had gone wholly out of his life. It had been a memory for ages, as we count time nowadays, and nothing more. Still, he was moved at the sight of her, and he could not help marveling if her heart retained any recollection of the summer idyl, or, indeed, if she had a heart left to be touched.

There had never been any thing original in the story, though in its season it seemed wonderfully fresh and new to them. They had loved each other as boy and girl, and Alice was not much beyond eighteen when he was swept out of her horizon by the stern decree of her sage relatives, who very possibly knew the beauty of life's young dream, but knew the value of discretion and common sense, and shillings and pence, still better. He had not known the whole truth until long after; then it came to him by accident; but though it could change nothing, it was at least a satisfaction to learn that she had not been so false and cold-hearted as she appeared. Her mother and stepfather had actually employed threats to induce her to give him up; besides, they appealed to her affection for her weak little shadow of a maternal parent, and, into the bargain, she had tasted just enough of the excitements of society to be influenced thereby, and had been reared with a horror of poverty, in an atmosphere so artificial and false that the wonder was she had any youth left, even at eighteen.

So they parted her from her lover, and the rest followed naturally enough; but the bargain was a more fortunate one for her, in many respects, than often happens. Her husband proved good and kind; and though, while he lived, she never appreciated him at his just value, she could look back now and see that she might have made a good deal out of those wedded years, had she been wiser and less selfish—less vitiated by the false creeds taught by her former pastors and masters—less eager for excitement and adulation, and the thousand miserable intoxications which make up a society life.

But though Mrs. Marchmont occasionally glanced toward Halford, she could not tell whether he watched her. He was a new arrival, and a lion of considerable growth, and his hostess expected him to shake his mane and roar a little for the delectation of her guests. He would not do that; but he was unable to avoid her importunities, or the absurd flatteries

3

of the wild-beast hunters in general; so he strayed back into the ball-room where the youthful
generation reigned, and a "good stepper" was
of more consequence than the greatest hero or
sage that the world could boast.

He came face to face with Milly Crofton
again—pretty Milly, beaming with smiles and
girlish enjoyment, so unconscious yet of her
own feelings that she received him with the
same child-like frankness which had pleased
him during their brief acquaintance in Europe.
She had seated herself to rest for a few moments by her aunt's side; Charley Thorne still
hovered about, and rather glared at Halford—
that is, as nearly as his cheerful boy's countenance could manage to do; for the state of
his mind where Milly was concerned, rendered
him as clear-sighted in regard to the danger of
having this elder man intrude, as if he had been
the wisest of his sex.

Mrs. Remsen—a perfect Napoleon in a small
way—was quite alive to the triumph of having
the new lion distinguish Milly by attentions on
this first evening of his appearance, and cruelly
sent poor Charley off on some errand to the
dressing-room; and Charley turned into a melancholy misanthrope at once, but could not
avoid going. Milly was too much occupied in
listening to Halford even to notice the reproachful glance Charley darted at her as he turned
away, but Halford saw it and smiled, though he
was rather sorry for the boy, all the same;—
there is nothing so aggravating as the half-
contemptuous pity men of thirty always bestow on
youths ten years younger than themselves.

"Did I blunder so atrociously that you are
afraid to give me another dance?" he asked
Milly.

"You dance beautifully," she said. "But
please don't ask me just because you think I
can't sit still."

"I ask you as a great pleasure to myself.
Don't you remember, I told you I never indulged
in fibs?"

Mrs. Remsen had returned to her conversation with a sister dowager: she never made the
mistake of interfering and trying to aid, as so
many chaperons do when desirous that their
charges shall produce a favorable impression;
she knew that, with a man like Kenneth Halford, just Milly's natural manner, her enthusiasm and childishness, would be more successful
than the art and worldly wisdom of a score of
ordinary women.

So, when luckless Charley got back from his
mission, he saw Milly whirling about, encircled
by Halford's arm, to the tones of the very waltz
she had often saved for himself; and the gay
scene became a howling wilderness at once, and
the troop of dancers more ridiculous than a
band of maniacs; and he would have liked to
have been Samson, that he might drag down
the pillars and crush the whole throng.

By the time the music ceased, people were
making toward the supper-room, and Halford
conducted Milly. Mrs. Marchmont was there,

but so far off that he only caught occasional
glimpses of her through the crowd. Mrs. Remsen forbore to damp Milly's spirits by speaking
until they were ready to leave the apartment;
but then she said, in her smiling way, that they
must go home; and Halford's laughing suppli-
cations only made her the more determined.
She saw, what Milly did not, what he had
scarcely thought about yet himself, that the
girl had produced an impression; the surest
means of heightening it was to take her away.
Milly, who knew that, in spite of Aunt Eliza's
pleasant manner, her laws were as unchange-
able as those of the Medes and Persians, did
not rebel, even forbore to plead for one more
dance—a self-restraint so unusual in a young
lady that Halford was filled with astonishment,
and admired her the more, as shrewd Mrs.
Remsen perceived.

"I like my little girl to enjoy herself," she
said, in an undertone, to the gentleman, "but
she will not if I allow her to make balls hard
work, and I can't bear her to grow like young
women in general."

"You are quite right," he answered.
"Please don't forget that you have given me
permission to come and renew my old acquaintance."

"We shall be very glad to see you," she
said, cordially; and the smile with which he
turned toward Milly at the words consoled the
girl somewhat for her banishment.

CHAPTER VI.

"PEEP OF DAY."

AND all this time there had been but one
thought in Alice Marchmont's mind—that
man, Dick Faulkner, did not appear. She ar-
gued hopefully from his dilatoriness; if he
could have brought her bad news, he would
certainly have come long before. If the doubts
and fears which had been growing each day
stronger in her mind during the past month
should prove mere fancies! If there should be
a favorable turn, and she found herself free—
above all, free in every way from him!

The bare idea sent her spirits up to fever
heat, and she looked more beautiful than ever.
It was just at this moment that Kenneth Halford approached her again, and she unscrupu-
lously deserted her most faithful adherents to
bestow her indescribable witcheries upon him.

"Do you remember that?" she asked, suddenly, as the music burst out anew.

"Perfectly," he replied. "Such an old, old
air—it is like a strain coming straight up out
of the past."

"And you still think it pretty?"

"I remember once hearing it played by
some street musicians in Naples," he said; "I
shall never forget how oddly it sounded."

It had been their pet melody in the far-off
dances; the waltz she had always kept espe-

cially for him. There are the merest trifles connected with every body's past, which never cease to move us, however completely important events may have been blotted out of our minds. Certain sights and sounds—the scent of a particular flower—an ancient proverb—the strains of a simple song—will stir a chord deep in our souls, so long after the memories with which they are connected have died, that we are forced to search our minds to recall the association.

"Come dance with me," he said, quickly.

"I thought you had grown too wise for such follies," returned she, laughing, yet an instant after she sighed.

He had been watching her, so brilliant and courted, till, between her present glory and the recollection of the time when those white hands had lain freely in his own, when those proud lips had trembled under his kisses, his head fairly swam, though how much was real feeling and how much that vague sentiment born somewhere between brain and heart, he could not have told. So they whirled round and round to the bewildering music that possessed such hosts of reminiscences for both, till it was natural enough that, when it ceased, they felt drawn near together again, as if, in some mysterious fashion, the events of the intervening years, which had worn channels in either soul that could never be effaced, had been only a long, dark nightmare.

"So like the old, old time," he said, as he led her to a seat. "I did not think I had such capabilities of enjoyment left."

He had not forgotten; the thought was very pleasant to her for the moment—whether because her heart was really softened toward him, or the sense of power regained intoxicating, she did not ask. A mingling of both feelings, probably. It is difficult enough to tell what really moves other people and inspires their actions, but to discover the motives by which we are ourselves actuated is, I think, a problem beyond the skill of the greatest philosopher.

"You have not told me yet that you are glad to see me," he said, as they sat down to rest.

"Have I not?" returned she. "Then I will now! I am very, very glad to see you."

She said it with a candor that was charming, and dangerous, too; and, as she spoke, she was glad. He began to talk of the former days, not with any distinct reference to feelings or events, but with the recollection of all that had been hanging about each sentence. Mrs. Marchmont listened till the weary present faded out of mind; the troubles and cares which beset her—the waste of time and talents in the mad rush wherein she had lived, which looked so petty and despicable since the clouds began to thicken—all vanished utterly under the spell of his voice. Nor was he less moved; for it is perilous amusement, the going back over past days, the wandering in buried paths side by side with the woman who ought to have been your fate, and was snatched from you.

"After all," he said, "life has nothing to offer like our first youth."

Had any body told him, the hour previous, that he would make such an avowal to Alice Marchmont, he would have scouted the idea with scorn.

"But a man scarcely feels that," she answered; "life has so much to give him. It is we poor women, who have nothing but our youth, that may well mourn over its loss."

"They told me always you were very gay and happy," he said. "I often heard your name, but never except in company with those words."

"Did you believe them?" she asked, almost in a whisper.

She had not meant to utter the question; it escaped her involuntarily; she was strangely softened by this meeting, and coquetry came as naturally to her as breathing.

"It was best to believe it," he replied; "there were seasons, at first, when I could not have staid away had I believed otherwise."

He had said more than he intended—more than he ought—for words were serious things with him. He checked himself immediately; there had been no space to think, in the suddenness of this encounter; yet he knew that it was the memory of the dead dream, not an emotion growing out of the present, which moved him. Still, having gone so far, it was difficult to retreat, especially as she sat silent, and he could see the color deepen a little on her cheek. He did not recover himself so well, or with so much ease, as a less honest man could have done, but said, abruptly,

"I did not intend to stray into all this Old-World talk; I think I am dazed yet with seeing you."

The first part of the remark was enough to allow the quick-witted woman to understand his feelings as plainly as if he had put them into words, and she was offended, as any one of her sex would have been. The close of his sentence might be a slight salve to her vanity, unless it was a mere figure of speech—she did wish to know whether it was; she would not go away and end the conversation, as she had three minds to do—he should say more.

"Not dazed enough to come to harm," said she, laughing. "I think you have prudence and discretion sufficient to meet any emergency."

No man likes to be told that he is prudent, particularly by a woman; indeed, nine times out of ten, when a woman says it, you may consider it equivalent to a blow if she loves you—as a taunt to draw you on, if she does not. Halford felt a sudden rage which fairly lighted the old memories at his heart into a momentary blaze of passion.

"Would you be better satisfied if I made a fool of myself?" he exclaimed, hotly. "I did not think you would have wished that! If you are doubtful about my having suffered, be at rest—I did suffer, and I am not ashamed to acknowledge it."

"Poor Kenneth!" she said, softly. "And I have suffered too—don't you believe it, Kenneth?"

"The old voice and the old name," returned he, in a more quiet tone, as if soothed by it as he had often been in former times when some trouble arose. "I like to hear you call me that—it sounds very sweet."

"It makes me feel young again to say it," she said; "there are so few people left now whom I call by their given names—so few to speak mine. Heigh-ho! how the years fly and drag, both at once. Do you know I am almost eight-and-twenty?"

"And I three-and-thirty."

"But that is young for a man."

"And you certainly have a decade to live before you will look even your present age."

"It is pleasant, at least, to be told so."

"And you know that I never told you what was not true."

"No; on you I could depend—the only person, almost, on whom I ever could. Oh, the world is very false and hollow! The worst thing about living in it is that one grows so too—perhaps in sheer disgust of wasting truth so uselessly."

She looked very beautiful as she spoke, with that mournful smile on her lips, and her eyes full of regret for something better and nobler than life had left within her reach.

"Very young people have a very different world," he said; "and we had ours in our day."

Truly, the words, and the possibilities they might imply, were sweet; it was like a new feeling of rest to hear them. But Alice chanced to raise her eyes, glanced down the room, and saw the man whom she had been so anxiously expecting. There he was—handsome, bold, bad-looking Dick Faulkner, with a reputation which accorded with the latter part of my description of his appearance. The sight of him brought Mrs. Marchmont back to the present with a breathless sensation, as if she had suddenly fallen out of a balloon from a vast height. What had she been doing? Whither had they two wandered? They must come down to reality, to stern, hard prose. She could not stop now to play with old feelings. If he were in earnest, so much the more reason why they should pause where they were. As for her own emotions—well, they were so confused that she could not pretend to answer for herself. One thing was certain, she could neither listen, or be in love, or do parlor-comedy, just then; the harsh exigencies of the present had returned. If Faulkner should bring her good news—oh, who could tell what might happen in that case—if she might only find herself free!

She realized her madness more than ever during that instant of rapid, bewildered thought; it was the only thing clear to her. Yes, one thing besides; she must speak with Faulkner—must hear what he had to say—news of some sort was at hand. So, in a breath, at sight of this odious wretch, she passed leagues out from the phantom likeness of the glorious world in whose reality she had once dwelt with this man by her side.

She was very glad that an interruption came at the same moment. A quadrille was over, people were seeking places to rest, and the recess was invaded. Almost before she had done wishing for him, Dick Faulkner was leaning over her shoulder, and talking in a way that seemed horribly impertinent, with these new fears in her mind, though, in truth, it was his usual manner with all women. It displeased Halford, with his fastidious taste, that she should appear even on friendly terms with a creature like that. He could imagine no reason beyond her boundless love of coquetry and dominion, and thought somewhat ruefully of the sentiment he had talked, and began to regard her with a certain bitterness because she had proved sufficiently fascinating to betray him into such weakness. He sauntered off, joined a group of old friends, but for the life of him could not help watching her, though now he was thinking what an idiot he had shown himself, and comparing her tutored, guarded face with the innocent girl-loveliness of Milly Crofton.

"You will break my fan, Mr. Faulkner," Mrs. Marchmont said, irritably, as Halford moved away.

"Who is that man?" he asked.

"A very old friend of mine."

"An old lover, you mean, I suppose," returned he, with his harsh laugh. "Nobody wants him."

"I meant just what I said," she retorted; "and perhaps you will allow me to choose my own society."

"Oh yes, if you choose me," he said, with that laugh again, which made her shiver, and a glance from his cruel black eyes that filled her with such indignation she longed to strike him.

"Have the kindness to give back my fan before you break it."

"I was trying to," he said, "that I might have the pleasure of presenting you with a new one."

"Thanks; I will keep this instead. You are very late in making your appearance to-night."

"Then you did think of me?" he asked, dropping his voice, and trying to render the conversation confidential.

"I saw your wife," she replied, audibly; "naturally, I thought of you."

Two or three people heard the retort, and smiled; for Dick Faulkner and his spouse led an existence, as all the world knew, to which purgatory would have seemed agreeable in comparison. His eyes flashed, and Mrs. Marchmont remembered that she could not affront him with impunity. She gazed in his face with her sweetest smile and played carelessly with her fan—the slender, nervous fingers looked so frail and white, as they closed over the ivory bars. She was thinking—and it was not unnatural—that if it had pleased Heaven to make her a South Sea Island queen, and Dick Faulkner had chanced to be shipwrecked on her domain, and she had her fingers about his throat, just as she had them twisted over that pretty toy—

Well, it was only a second's wickedness, and she did not even finish the thought; and if you have ever felt yourself in the power of a person whom you knew to be utterly faithless and base, I think it is possible that a likeness to Alice's South Sea Island dream has flitted across your imagination.

"You promised to dance with me," he said, his countenance clearing under her smile, as any man's must have done.

"Did I? Then I will; partly because I am a woman of my word, partly because—"

Whatever the end of the sentence might be, it was lost to the by-standers; for he led her away.

"Partly because?" he repeated. "Will you finish?"

"I don't want to talk nonsense," returned she. "Tell me how I stand—I could make nothing out of your note—I have waited all day."

"I can't tell you yet," he said, carelessly, "because I don't know myself."

She uttered an exclamation of anger. It was too much, after her dreadful morning, after this long night of anxious waiting.

"Why can't you answer me?" she urged.

"Because the market has not cleared! Don't be so impatient—one thing at a time—what heavenly music!"

He seized her in his arms; they were flying up the room to the merriest galop, and more than one person was echoing Kenneth Halford's wonder that she could be on terms of intimacy with that man, only they said it aloud, and added divers other remarks, which would have stung her to the quick had she heard them.

"What do you mean by the market not clearing?" she persisted.

"Oh, I can't explain—the commonest term!"

"I saw myself that Cumberland was up—"

"Yes, and gold down! My dear Mrs. Marchmont, you are the most delightful woman in the world, but I never can make you understand the intricacies of the stock-market."

She was furious. She had tried, during her whole acquaintance with him, to be careful—had avoided places where he visited; and here, in the face and eyes of the whole world, he had deluded her into dancing with him. Nothing but her belief that he had news to give, and her own mad anxiety to hear it, could have induced her to consent; and not one serious word would he speak—her head whirled with anger and fright. To have his arm about her, straining her so close that it was more like an embrace than any thing else;

to feel his breath, heated with wine, burn her cheek; to see his bold eyes fastened with a coarse smile upon her neck—oh, she should do something desperate, if he did not set her free on the instant—astonish the crowd by a shriek, or fairly attack him with teeth and hands, like a raving Bedlamite.

"I want to sit down!" she cried. "I tell you to stop—I'm tired—I will sit down!"

He knew very well why she had consented to dance with him, and that she stopped because there was nothing to be gained by going on, and he cursed her in his heart; while sharp-nosed Mrs. Faulkner looked on from a distance, and longed, in her turn, to make a scene. There was nothing for it but to lead her to a seat, and she paid no attention when he said,

"Is it because you are dancing with me that you get so easily tired?"

"Mr. Faulkner," she exclaimed, "I came to-night on purpose to see you—"

"That repays me for every thing!"

She gave him one glance of contempt which sent the blood to his face, callous as he was; then she remembered—growing sick and faint to remember—that she dared not treat him as he deserved.

"I must know just how and where I stand," she went on. "This uncertainty is more than I can bear! I have been reckless—crazy! I meant to buy a few shares—just to gratify a whim—"

"But you see you developed the taste," he broke in; "it was natural. Bless me, you needn't be shocked at yourself; plenty of people indulge in such speculations."

"I am not talking about that. I have gone on losing here—gaining there—borrowing on this—paying off something else—"

"That Peep of Day proves such an awful sell," he said, with a careless shrug of his shoulders, as she paused, from pure inability to articulate. "An awful sell," he repeated; and it seemed to her that he had a pleasure in adding to her torment.

The anxiety that had preyed upon her for so many hours culminated now in an emotion which threatened to overcome even her wonderful self-control. There had been a belief that certain stocks—this poetically named one among them—were doing wonders; he had led her to think so; and she had soothed her wildest fears by the hope that to-night she might find all well ended.

"You have not sold the shares?" she asked.

"Oh, bless you, every thing fell back so flat at noon—nothing to be done! But don't get discouraged—a few days—"

She stopped him with a motion of her fan.

"I would as soon you talked about a few centuries," she said, with a kind of sullen desperation upon her.

He laughed outright, as if she had uttered the best jest imaginable.

"Are you trying to annoy me?" demanded she, with a haughty anger in her face which warned him that, if he went too far, she would risk any thing to free herself from his toils.

"How can you think it—how can you misunderstand me so? I am as sorry and anxious as a man can be; but I know that it will end all right if you can only have patience."

"I am sick of the word!" she replied.

"I assure you that the quality must be acquired, if you mean to have any thing to do with Wall Street."

"Only let me get out this time—"

She did not finish; she would control herself. Dick Faulkner whispered the incomplete sentence to himself, and added, in his thoughts, "Let you get out—ah, my pretty lady-bird, you're in a web one doesn't break so easily!"

"When do you think the other stock will take a turn?" she asked.

"Oh, any moment; it's only that Locksley has cornered it, and the Walton men want to drive him to the wall."

The experience of the past months rendered the jargon intelligible enough to her. She opened and shut her fan two or three times—one of the ivory sticks snapped—it was a sort of satisfaction to break something!

"Ah, ha, you'll have to let me buy the new one, after all," said he.

"My first dividends will do that—if your belief is true," she replied.

"I wish you would believe me, and so not work yourself up to such a pitch of excitement; you will certainly be ill! Surely, you know how much I have your interest at heart—that I would give my right hand, any day, to oblige you."

This was the style of conversation in which he had indulged more and more of late; it made her more afraid than any thing else that their business schemes were a failure—this coarse, insolent flattery was so different from the respectful manner of their first intercourse, when she had believed that he could be kept without trouble at a proper distance. She could not endure it another instant! If she sat there while his watch could tick once, she should inevitably astonish the crowd by some mad attempt to strangle him. She took advantage of the first available man's arm to escape, and left Dick Faulkner muttering some energetic words between his shut teeth which would scarcely have helped to compose her had she heard them.

She did not go home; late as it was, the throng had lessened little, and Mrs. Marchmont seemed in her gayest mood. People called her mildest manners flirting, but to-night she really did flirt with any man worth it, or in any quarter where there was a sister-woman to be annoyed, until those who knew her best were appalled by her genius in that line, and her recklessness in exhibiting it.

In spite of himself, Kenneth Halford hovered about her; and, with her fears and troubles biting like a nest of scorpions, it was torture to look in his face and recollect all that lay between her and the time of which his eyes reminded her—to look farther on, and see Dick Faulkner scowling at her, and recognize him as a fate standing between her and any possibility of happiness which might ever offer. She succeeded, at least, in rousing that latter individual to a pitch of fury, if she did nothing else. But she had become too desperate to care—nothing could make any difference now. She was in the state of mind which business anxieties are liable to produce upon a person who understands little of its mysteries, and has become involved in plans which glittered famously at first, and shrunk, one by one, like pricked soap-bubbles, when first within the grasp. Added to that were these other emotions—her fear of Faulkner—her disturbed feelings at meeting Halford; either excitement, by itself, would have been enough to unnerve most of her sex.

She was a woman, too, and must get rid of her agitation in some way. In her position, certain of her sisters would have been at home tearing their locks, shrieking in hysterical spasms, and making themselves odious in the eyes of any unfortunates doomed, by destiny, to take care of them. Other women might have been able to look the whole matter in the face, already reaching forward to oases of refuge, in the possibility of pecuniary and social ruin coming closer than was agreeable. Mrs. Marchmont's way of enduring the suspense was different from either. She had an odd feeling—ridiculous as she knew it to be—that this was her last night in such scenes, and she would at least make it one for the world to remember.

The consequence was, that she waxed fascinating and imprudent beyond description or belief up to the last moment; and if the elderly cats who appear to frequent such scenes for the express pleasure of being horrified by coquetry and similar performances—in which, since the memory of man there has been no possibility of indulgence on their part—had never found reasons enough for belaboring Alice Marchmont to their heart's content, she certainly gave them ample cause this evening.

But it came at length—a sudden, staggering blow. She had been certain that some crisis was at hand; the presentiment had never left her during the whole day; it was fulfilled as unexpectedly as if she had not believed herself, to a certain extent, prepared. She was on her way out of the drawing-rooms; people were talking to her on her passage; she encountered a fresh group near the door, and it was all to go over again. She was saying the wittiest things imaginable, still with the odd feeling that it was her closing triumph, and determined to dazzle to the last. Dick Faulkner was hovering about her, Halford coldly regarding her from a distance, scores of women whom she had roused to mutiny by her reckless poaching on their manors eying her with bitter feminine malice, new admirers rushing up, more chatter, more laughter; and in the midst of it fell the awful shock.

Just behind her stood two elderly men, holding snatches of conversation not intended for any ears besides their own; but Mrs. Marchmont's senses were in a state of such nervous exaltation that she was able to see and hear every thing going on about her, though talking all the time. She distinctly heard one of the pair say to his neighbor,

"If she was in for Peep of Day like poor Trevor, she wouldn't be quite so full of life and spirits."

"No, I rather think not! They say the whole thing has caved in," returned the other, in the delightfully unconcerned tone in which people usually discuss misfortunes that can in no way affect themselves.

"Gone down as flat as your hand," was the answer; "and, what's more, it will never come up—stock and company were both a humbug."

"I said so from the first, but people would not listen! I'd not have touched a share of it as a gift," said the first speaker, in a voice of conscious and satisfied wisdom.

Mrs. Marchmont knew that she kept on her way into the passage, but she was dizzy and blind, and as she reached the foot of the staircase, Dick Faulkner whispered in her ear,

"I am sorry you heard that—two old fools; but don't you mind in the least."

He was glad in his heart, glad and exultant, for he was in a frightful rage with her. She knew that he was glad; her quick perceptions caught the savage ring of triumph through the attempted solicitude of his voice. She turned and faced him; the rest of her courtiers had dropped a little back; they stood quite alone.

"Is it true?" she asked.

He hesitated; his features assumed an expression of regret and sympathy very tolerably; but she saw the devilish smile that shone in his eyes.

"Will you answer? Is it true?" she repeated; and there was more haughty impatience than fear in the tone.

"Yes—perfectly true," he replied, slowly.

She stood still; the floor heaved and swayed so unsteadily to her sight that she dared not stir.

"I am so sorry," he continued. "I did not mean you to hear to-night. Don't you know, I would rather have cut my right hand off than for this trouble to have reached you?"

The woman's mettle asserted itself—just then, at this crisis wherein even a strong man might have been utterly overwhelmed. She looked Faulkner full in the face; not a muscle of her own quivered.

"Will you tell me how much I have lost?"

Again he hesitated—not, she was certain, from any kindly feeling—just from the sort of instinct which leads feline animals to worry their prey before killing it. She made a quick gesture: exaggerated as the comparison sounds, I can only liken it to the threatening command

some Eastern monarch might have given a rebellious slave.

"Ten thousand dollars, if you will know."

He had dropped his sentimental tone; and though he spoke necessarily almost in a whisper, the fierce rage her haughty assurance caused him sounded through it distinctly enough.

"That is, over and above the other?" she asked, still with her dilated eyes full upon him.

He bowed his head.

She passed on up stairs without another word —without allowing him the satisfaction of seeing the change which she knew had suddenly come over her face—the terror and despair that at length forced themselves through the defiant composure she had maintained. There were women in the dressing-room pausing for a last interchange of scandals; they chattered and poured out a torrent of questions and bittersweet compliments, and she answered at random, till able to collect her wraps and flee beyond the sound of their odious frivolity. They, naturally supposing that her only reason for haste was because they belonged to her own sex, abused her with additional virulence, and did it well. If there ever is a surgical operation neatly and thoroughly performed, it is the flaying of a sister by those gentle proficients.

Mrs. Marchmont hurried into the corridor, and at the head of the stairs met Kenneth Halford.

"I am just in time to see you down," he said, offering his arm. "I am sure you must be tired to death."

His voice sounded a little cold. He had not been so much charmed with her during the latter part of the evening. Very beautiful and brilliant she might be; but this woman with the crowd about her, saying careless things, with smiles for any body that came near; worse than all the rest, with more than one man about her whom he knew ought never to be tolerated by any good woman, was not the Alice of the old time—had no connection whatever with the innocent girl of that season.

Had he looked at her now, the pallor and dread in her face might have softened him; but he kept his eyes averted as they walked on, and she continued a fire of witticisms and nonsensical talk which sounded too much like the bonmots of a modern novel to be agreeable to his hypercritical taste.

"You may come and see me," she said, as they reached the lower floor. "You may come to-morrow, if you like."

He thanked her. She felt, rather than heard, the restraint and disapproval in his tones. Through all her misery and nervous agitation, her temper flamed up. This man was venturing to sit in judgment; he dared to blame her. In her best moments, Mrs. Marchmont could not have borne that consciousness patiently; just now it irritated her till she longed to do or say something that would shock him more completely.

"No, not to-morrow," she added; "I re-

member, I am going out. The day after—no;
what is it I have to do? Never mind; we
shall meet somewhere in the crowd, sooner or
later. Good-bye till then, Mr. Halford; you
needn't take me out to the carriage; I want to
speak with Mr. Duval; he is one of my favorite knights."

She knew he said something—she could not
tell what—and drew aside. She had succeeded
in her wish of rousing his censure to a higher
pitch, for the man whom she beckoned toward
her was of Dick Faulkner's stamp, and nothing
but her insane desire to be as reckless as she
could manage would have induced her to accept his arm. But he led her out in triumph
—apparently, that is; for in reality she never
addressed a single word to him, or paid the
least attention to his remarks. As he placed
her in the carriage, and turned away discomfited, Dick Faulkner looked in at the window,
smiling still.

"I will come to-morrow," he whispered.
"Don't worry yourself; there is no reason. I
have been cross to-night; you tormented me
beyond endurance. Don't think about the
money; it is only to me; we can arrange it
easily enough."

The carriage was off; she thought—her
senses were so bewildered and stunned that she
could not be certain—but it seemed to her that
he had tried to kiss her hand. She was shivering from head to foot, burning with fever at
the same time, body and mind alike threatening to yield under the awful crisis which had
overtaken her; yet, woman-like, all the way
home she was not thinking so much of the evil
tidings she had heard, of the probable ruin
which menaced her, as of the humiliating idea
that the lips of that horrible man had brushed
her hand.

CHAPTER VII.
SHOWING HIS HAND.

MRS. MARCHMONT sat the next morning,
waiting for her visitor—waiting beset by a host
of reflections and fears which were by no means
pleasant companions for a solitary hour.

She knew well enough that Faulkner would
come; to refuse him an interview would only
be to put off the evil day, and perhaps render
any peaceable understanding more difficult by
rousing his evil temper and obstinacy. Besides, she could bear any thing under heaven
more easily than suspense; no words that he
could speak would prove half so terrible as her
anticipations of the scene. She had contemplated the worst possibilities so often during
the past night, her restless fancy had tormented
her with so many different aspects of the tête-
à-tête, that to face the reality, no matter what,
would be a relief. If he were insolent, she
could rise and leave the room; if he— Oh,
what folly to indulge in such thoughts! She
owed him thousands of dollars, and for the

present there was no means of raising them in
her power. He could not be quite so vile as
her fears during three weeks had caused her to
dread; there must be some trace of humanity
in his nature! Whatever his intentions were,
she should be able by her tact to keep him
from breaking through the ordinary rules of
decorum.

That she should have lived to hold such reflections in regard to any man!—oh, no wonder
she clenched her hands and stamped her feet
on the carpet, and wished that she had died a
year before! But she controlled herself, and,
when he was announced, was able to receive
him without varying from her usual manner.
Skilled in seizing the slightest advantage in
the fencing-match of a difficult conversation,
she had seated herself with her back to the
light; and both attitude and costume were as
perfect as if she had set her heart upon fascinating the man who, her intuitions told her,
would force her to an open declaration of war
before the interview ended.

"Ah, good-morning, Mr. Faulkner," she said,
laying down her pen as if his entrance had interrupted a real occupation, and pushing the
gilded writing-table a little away. "You are
still alive after last night's fatigues, I see."

"Oh, I can bear a good deal," he answered.
"But you—I declare you women work harder
going to balls evening after evening—"

By this time the door had closed—the stern
domestic guardian was out of hearing. She
did not wait for the reasonable politeness of
letting him conclude his speech.

"I have been waiting anxiously for you,"
she said.

"That is a little consolation at least," returned he, with the smile which always made her
blood tingle. "I was afraid that my visit was
unconscionably early."

"I asked you to come," she said, calmly,
ignoring the insolent freedom of his first sentence.

"Yes, and I made haste, for fear that you
had been worrying yourself all night over the
talk of those two fools."

"I always reserve my powers in that line until it is absolutely necessary to exercise them,"
she replied; and all the while she was thinking
—loathing herself for the thought—how natural
subterfuges and falsehoods had grown to her.

"That's right," said he; "but you are the
one woman I have ever seen who really had a
head! So you slept comfortably?"

She caught his smile; she knew perfectly
well that he was not deceived by her manner—
that he exulted inwardly at his ability to pierce
through all her pretty pretense of composure.

"You have brought the papers—accounts—
or whatever is the proper name, I suppose,"
she said, carelessly.

"Upon my word," retorted he, with an irritated laugh, "you speak as if I were the family
solicitor, or an agent, or some cad of that sort."

"I hope the ball has not left you in a bad

temper," she answered, hating him the more that she dared not persevere in her tone of insolent superiority.

"If it had, seeing you would have dissipated it," he said.

"Ah, that is very pretty; but it is too early in the day for compliments; like jewels and perfumes, they ought to be reserved for full dress."

"How neatly you always put things!" he exclaimed, with a coarse admiration that made her shudder.

"Then let me try to put my first question, which you seemed to think offensive, a little more neatly, too," she said, leaning back in her chair and playing idly with the bronze paper-cutter she had taken from the table. "Have you come prepared to give me an exact statement of my affairs?"

"How fearfully business-like you are this morning; I hardly recognize you," he replied, laughing again.

"It is time for me to be so," she said, quietly, though her fingers closed over the hilt of the toy she held till the sharp ornaments cut cruel red creases in her hands. "So there is nothing to hope from our brilliant scheme, Mr. Faulkner; Peep of Day has vanished?"

"There's no good in trying to deceive you, or to smooth matters—"

"The plain truth will be the greatest kindness you can show; that is, if the plain truth can be got at in our century," she added, unable, in spite of her dread, to resist this little thrust.

"I was completely taken in and duped," he said; "it's almost the first time such a thing has happened to me since I commenced business."

"Then you were not one of the originators of the scheme?" returned she, in a voice nicely modulated between question and assertion.

"I should think not; why, I explained that at first. They have let me in finely; I shall have great difficulty to— But that's no matter! Your affairs are the important thing just now."

"I am sorry to appear selfish; but they are so to me, unfortunately, Mr. Faulkner, at this moment. I have lost ten thousand dollars—"

"But only to me; do understand."

"Before that I had lost—what was it—five thousand?"

"The exact amount is of no consequence—"

"Excuse me; it is of the greatest consequence! Please to answer me; was it five?"

"And a few hundreds over," he said, peevishly. "But it is only to me; you have no doings with any body else; your name does not appear! Why on earth will you torment yourself about such a trifle?"

"In your vast schemes fifteen thousand dollars may seem a trifle," she replied, laughing a little, though her lips were dry and parched; "but it looks a large sum to me."

"I never want you to think about it," he averred.

"That is very kind of you; but you must know it would be impossible. From the first, I only meant to go so far as I could give you a margin in safety; I mean, put securities in your hands—"

"Yes, yes; it's all right!" he broke in, drumming with both hands on the table in a nervous, excited way, new to her in her knowledge of him.

"Unfortunately, during these last weeks I forgot my resolution—that scheme showed so fair—I have been drawn on and on, till now—" she stopped to steady her voice, which had begun to tremble—"I find myself deeply in your debt."

"No debt at all," cried he. "I was duped —sold. I'll pay them for it before I'm six months older, as sure as my name is Dick Faulkner!" he exclaimed, striking the table with energy.

But though he did annoyance and a desire for revenge well enough, Mrs. Marchmont was not deceived. That gleam of infernal exultation was in his eyes still; her woman's intuitions told her that he had a hand in this failure —whether to serve some purpose where she was concerned, she should soon know.

"What I want to do this morning," she continued, with her voice once more under proper control, "is to see what arrangement we can arrive at in regard to my debt to you."

"The easiest in the world," he said, eagerly.

"You mean you will be satisfied with a mortgage—"

"I don't mean any thing of the sort," he broke in rudely. "Put the money out of your mind; call the thing canceled. I'll give you a receipt this moment, if you like."

She half started forward in her chair; the proposal sounded so generous, that though she did not dream of accepting it, she almost felt that she had misjudged him. Again she caught the expression in his bold eyes, and knew that some insult lay beneath this offer.

"You are very kind," she said, regarding him full in the face now; "but in your desire to spare me uneasiness, you go beyond what you know yourself to be possible."

"Not a bit," said he. "Come, call it ended!"

He rose quickly from his seat; his face frightened her; but she leaned languidly back, saying, in the gayest way,

"Sit down, sit down; you are too impulsive by half for a business man, Mr. Faulkner. Good gracious, if you treat all your creditors in this Quixotic fashion, you will be ruined in a year."

"Other people must shift for themselves; I am talking about what I am ready to do for you," said he, doggedly.

"And I thank you sincerely for your generous intentions, but must refuse them distinctly," she answered. "Now, that point settled —only do understand how much obliged, how grateful, I am—let us consider the best means of acquitting my debt."

She had a vague hope that, by appealing to his better self—if he had one—at least, by this appearance of believing in his sincerity and good faith, she might be able to keep the interview within the bounds where she had, with such difficulty, managed to retain their intercourse during the past fortnight, in which the business troubles had drawn her further and further into the net.

"I don't want your gratitude," he said, quickly, almost roughly. She might have thought him eager to escape the expression of her thanks, had not the light in those bold eyes burned into her very soul, bringing a sense of humiliation and dread which nearly overpowered her desperate courage.

"But you must have it—sit down, please; you make me nervous twirling your chair—and you must have your money, too."

"Confound the money!"

"Not in my presence, if you please," she said, with that haughty movement of her head which had so often awed him in spite of his effrontery. But he did not mean to be awed now; he had come to the house with a settled purpose in his mind; neither her graces nor her histrionics should keep him from revealing it. He sat down, though, as she had bidden him, more at a loss just how to act or speak than he had ever been in his whole life.

"Well?" he asked, anathematizing himself mentally for his own hesitation.

"I want to explain. I have not the money to pay you now; you know that; for the present, I could not raise the sum—"

She stopped; she thought, she was almost sure, that he smothered a laugh. Her first impulse was to rise and leave the room; but a second's reflection showed her the uselessness of any such show of indignation. She was in his power; she must submit to an interview, in order to arrange some means of freeing herself.

"Why don't you go on?" he asked.

"I am thinking what security I could best give you," she answered; and her voice did not tremble, though the real thought in her mind was that she had none to offer.

"Finish what you have to say," said he, sullenly; "then I have something to say in my turn."

"The last few weeks have made you tolerably well acquainted with my affairs—"

"Yes; tolerably," he said, as she hesitated; and there was no mistaking the sneer on his face now.

"But what you do not know is that I have a hope of—"

She stopped again. What she had begun to say was, that she hoped to dispose of certain Virginia lands she owned to a company—a tract of coal, lead, and oil lands, which one day would be immensely valuable. There was a probability of her disposing of them—retaining percentages—becoming really a rich woman; but, with this new fear of him in her mind, she hesitated to trust him with the secret. If her

vague dread of his evil intentions—the bare thought of which, in spite of the vagueness, made her abhor herself to think that she had lived to give place to such ideas in her mind—were correct, he might find some method of hindering the sale, invent lies to prejudice the company—no, she would not trust him.

"You don't tell me what hope you have," he said.

"I will; I want—"

"Oh, now, let's have an end of this!" he cried, springing up from his chair again. "I'll not have you distress yourself any longer about this silly business! Look here, Mrs. Marchmont—Alice—cut my heart out, and stamp on it, if it will do you any good—I love you—I love you!"

He was close beside her, his eyes blinding her with their glow; and all her tact, all her pride, did not save her from the unutterable humiliation of having Dick Faulkner hold her two hands fast while he told her over and over that he loved her; that for months he had thought of nothing else; that he must speak now, or he should go mad! Alice felt sick and faint with terror and abhorrence. To flirt to the extremest verge of prudence was one thing; to make some sister-woman insanely wretched by bewitching her husband before her very eyes, was a recreation full of delight. But a scene like this was very different, and something undreamed of in Mrs. Marchmont's experience—as repulsive, indeed, to her whole nature as it could have been to the most rigid puritan that ever lived. As I have said, she had always so prided herself on the fact that during her wedded days no man ever ventured to whisper a single word that could be construed into a liberty. Since that, during this season of her widowhood, no married man among the many with whose fancies she had chosen to play havoc had ever dared, even by a look, to express any thing beyond knightly courtesy and entire devotion to her slightest wish. Knowing this, she had never reflected that to receive such attentions was in itself a degradation; but she would hereafter, forced by this insult to regard flirtation truthfully. She had never dreamed how often the world had harshly judged her, or that, as will frequently happen, among the numerous votaries at her shrine, there had been more than one wretch base enough to atone for his lack of courage and success by meaning smiles and dastardly insinuations.

It is strange, but you can seldom persuade women that such reports, such cowardly malice on the part of many men, are to be expected. Nor does the inability to believe proceed from the fact that women are so truthful themselves; it is only that to each woman it seems impossible that such slanders should come near her.

But there Dick Faulkner was at Mrs. Marchmont's feet; and his eyes looked straight into hers till they seemed to scorch every pure feeling, every sense of feminine delicacy, with their glance. Her first impulse was one of pure terror; her second, a mingled horror and rage that disgrace should have ventured so near her petted life. She forgot what she had done to help on this unpleasant position; forgot the scenes through which she had gone this very morning with unfortunate trades-people; forgot the debts that overwhelmed her on all sides; forgot that she owed this reptile a sum which she was powerless to pay, and that her reputation was at his mercy; forgot every thing in a burst of wrath and disgust, which, of itself, proved that, in spite of her follies and wickedness—for extravagance is wickedness—she had kept her soul womanly and pure.

"Be good enough to let my hands go, Mr. Faulkner. We are not rehearsing for a French comedy."

These were the first words she spoke in return to the insane tirade which he poured out, and they stung him worse than blows. She might have burst into ejaculations of virtuous rage; he would only have considered them employed to lure him on. She might have treated him to tears and piteous laments that he should insult her weakness; they would have been a poorer and still more ineffectual refuge. But to meet that cool, quiet contempt; to hear the indolent voice, as if he really were not worth a scene—ah, she had touched him as scarcely another woman in the world could have done. He dropped her hands, and was on his feet in an instant.

"Now sit down," she said, quietly, "and let me think what is to be done. Well—I suppose you want your money, Mr. Faulkner?"

She asked the question as indifferently as if there were nothing but the merest business matters to arrange between them—as if she were not half out of her senses with shame and passion, thinking that there was no act too terrible to commit, if it could only free her for all time to come from the sight of this man.

"Do you mean to insult me?" he cried. "Have you the heart to talk about money, after what I have said?"

He was trying hard to control his rage, to keep back the threats and imprecations very near his lips, and essay the magnanimous and injured—that is, according to his conception of the character.

"I conclude the money must have been somewhat in your thoughts," she answered, with a contemptuous smile. "It has been, and is, a good deal in mine, I assure you."

"I came to beg you not to think of it—to say that if the sum you owe me were ten times the amount, I should be only too happy to be your creditor."

"Yes, you told me that; I thanked you. It was very pretty and gallant on your part," she said, laughing cheerfully, while her head spun round and round, and the bare effort to think was like having a sharp knife thrust into her brain.

"It came as my love does—from my heart!"

"Stop, stop! We are in Wall Street this morning, talking over a purely business affair. Wall Street knows nothing about hearts."

"I was not aware that Mrs. Marchmont did me the honor to regard me as her commission broker," he said, with an ugly sneer.

"I considered you my friend," she replied, eagerly. "As such I have trusted you, presumed upon your good-nature beyond all limits" (here she smiled again), "till I dare say you have many times wished me and my small ventures at the bottom of the Dead Sea."

Her heart gave a little bound of hope, though she did not fully comprehend his baseness; but she had been so accustomed to intercourse with gentlemen, that she could not resist the idea of yet touching his generosity, since he must see that the love-making was a failure.

"I think I have shown myself your friend," he said.

"Yes, yes; no doubt you meant for the best—"

"Ah, you take to reproaches!"

"No, Mr. Faulkner; but I do think you might have warned me—held me back—kept me from being so overconfident."

"I was afraid of your thinking that I wanted to save myself trouble; indeed, I did not think at all, except about pleasing you."

She had not expected this speech, after his conduct; perhaps she had been a little unjust in her thoughts concerning him; he might not have pushed her on to her present position to hold her in his power; at all events, so long as he kept to the ground upon which he had shifted she was perfectly at home, and mistress of the position.

"I am sure of that," she said; "and it was very kind of you. But you remember that, in the beginning, I told you I wanted to be business-like, if you would only show me how. I wanted to try no ventures except such as I put money in your hands to make a basis for."

"But that you were only able to do while you confined yourself to little windfalls for pocket-money. So purely a business arrangement as you contemplated—"

"Ah, now you are angry; and indeed I had no intention of being rude. I only meant that I did not wish to place myself under pecuniary obligations to any body; the kindness and friendship I appreciated—you know I did—at a high value."

What to make of this woman was more than he could decide. For years he had not given any human being credit for possessing honesty or principle. He had looked upon her as a woman hard to win—never to be won by him unless he paid very dearly for the conquest. That in spite of her coquetry she could be pure and innocent, so far as there was any possibility of wrong in her actions; that all this while she had really believed he would content himself with doing her work and receiving a few smiles and pretty words for payment, had never occurred to him."

"I am sure you know this," she urged, when he did not speak, busy studying her, and thinking the words I have set down. "Please say you did, Mr. Faulkner."

She gave him one of her most dazzling smiles, and she looked very beautiful. The instant's wonder and doubt left Dick Faulkner's mind. Was he to be done by this artfulness, and laughed at for a fool—worse still, fail signally in what he had believed would be his hour of triumph, in the very sight of the loveliness which moved him as no beauty had ever before done? He had scarcely a decent impulse left in his nature, and he loved this woman: I must use the word; it was his sort of love, the strongest and fiercest he had ever felt or could feel, and a passion hot enough to have tempted him to any extreme.

"This is of no use," he exclaimed. "I love you, Alice! I'll do any thing you want; only give me a kind word. My life is such a lonely one; I want to be loved! I have purgatory at home; I—"

She rose from her chair pale as death, her great eyes black with indignation; she made a gesture which is indescribable unless you can remember Rachel, as Virginia, ordering away the man sent to outrage her by insulting offers.

"Leave the room!" was all she said; but she fairly hissed the words from between her shut teeth. Her voice was little more than a whisper, but it would have been impossible for human tones to have expressed more loathing and contempt.

"Take care!" cried he, rushing into one of his furies; for, once excited, the man's temper fell little short of insanity. "You have chosen to place yourself in my power; you must take the consequences."

"Oh, you coward!" she answered, in the same tone as before.

"Don't you use one more such word! You told me in the beginning that you couldn't raise this money. You are crippled with debts; I know more than you think. It would be a pretty story that I helped you. Do you suppose any body is going to believe the truth?"

"You will know it," she replied; "and your knowing the falsehood would be my bitterest revenge, where you are concerned."

"You have chosen to defy me—"

"Mr. Faulkner, I bade you leave this room! I knew you were base and despicable; how utterly so it remained for you to prove."

He caught the loose sleeve of her dress as she turned away, she was so beautiful in her scorn. At that moment he would have gone straight down to purgatory for one kindly glance.

"I'd sell my soul for you," he exclaimed, huskily, "if you'd only let me love you; I'd ask nothing, if you'll only give me one sweet word—"

"Oh, this is worse than your threats," she interrupted.

"I was mad to speak so. You know I would not harm you. No woman ever had the power over me that you have; it is the blindest, the craziest infatuation—"

"I can't put you out of my house," she broke in, feeling that unless she could end this scene she must become a raving lunatic; "but I can leave you!"

She had read of desperate creatures of her own sex committing deeds of violence, and wondered if such things were possible; but at this moment Dick Faulkner's life would not have been worth the purchase, if her hands could have laid hold of any weapon with death in it.

"Only listen to me," he pleaded. "I'll not stay; I'll not make you angry; but I must speak just a word."

"Let go my sleeve, then. I don't care to be addressed as if I were taken by a policeman."

She sat down again; her limbs were trembling so that she could not stand.

"You are so pale; you—"

"Finish what you had to say," said she, with cold contempt.

It certainly was not easy to utter tender declarations, or dramatic remorse, under such circumstances. He grew furiously angry again, and it had been many a day since any thing so honest burst from his heart as the curse with which he cursed her through his teeth. She caught the words, though in his rage he had not known that they were more than a thought.

"I think not," she said. "I am not a good woman, but I don't believe that I shall have any thing so bad as a dwelling-place where your society would be inevitable."

"So you mean war!" he cried. "You want a battle, do you?"

"There will be no occasion, Mr. Faulkner; you shall have your money."

"That sounds well, but you know you couldn't raise one quarter of the sum to save your immortal soul."

She did know it, but something kept whispering to her that she could and should—to set the time, even, when the payment should be ready.

"In ten days you shall have your money," she said, slowly. "In the mean time, for your own sake, if not for mine, you will be silent."

"Do you think I am likely to tell—do you suppose me capable—"

"In ten days you shall have your money," she repeated—still, as it seemed to her in her frenzy, uttering words put into her mouth by some invisible power extraneous to her will. "I—I am very tired now. Will you have the goodness to go away?"

"Shall I come here for it?" he asked, sullenly.

"I want a written statement of every thing —you understand what I mean; I don't know your business words—and I want a receipt. Yes, I suppose you will have to come here."

"And you mean that is the last time I ever shall, Mrs. Marchmont?" he demanded, while an uglier frown darkened his face.

"It is very possible, Mr. Faulkner," she answered, struggling back to her usual indolent voice and manner, and sweeping him a slow courtesy. "Permit me to wish you good-morning."

There was nothing for it but to go quietly away; and Dick Faulkner yielded to the necessity, not trying to add another word. He was gone, and Mrs. Marchmont had not even leisure to yield to the hysterical spasms which were trying to overcome her—the natural consequence of this prolonged suffering and excitement. She was obliged to dress and go out; and it was not a pleasant part of town into which her business led her, though during the past months she had grown only too familiar with its appearance.

The money—she must have the money; there was no other thought in her mind; the money, the money!

But it was not easy to impress upon her Israelitish friend whom she went to visit, and in whose escritoire lay so much stamped paper with her dashing signature attached, the necessity of lending it. Indeed, he pointed out with charming candor, while putting a long ruler in and out of his sleeve, as if doing conjuring tricks on a small scale, the utter impossibility of such a procedure on his part under existing circumstances. He was so very quiet about the matter, so smilingly persistent in his refusals, that his manner seemed only the last straw needed to turn her brain.

Sitting there in the dusty upper office where every thing she touched left its impress on her delicate gray gloves and the small fortune, in the way of lace, that decorated her dress, Mrs. Marchmont was brought face to face with the startling fact that, as matters stood, she had even nothing available left to mortgage, since the negotiations in regard to the Virginia lands had proceeded so far that she could not incumber them at this moment. Nothing but somebody else's very good name would assist her with her Hebrew, as he frankly, but mildly, asserted. And the money to be raised within ten days; and, apparently, the only way out of her difficulties to go quietly home and make a last investment in a sufficient quantity of laudanum to send her out of Dick Faulkner's reach, at least.

It was not strange that some such dreadful thought flitted across her mind—if she could be said to have a thought in the chaotic whirl of her senses. She was so near mad, too, that she caught herself laughing at the horror of her maid when her dead body was discovered; or perhaps the old relative who lived with her—prosaic Miss Portman—would be the one to stumble over the cold carcass; and she would shriek so dolefully; and people would talk and marvel. She knew she was laughing, and her child of Israel looking a little oddly at her, but she could not restrain herself. Yet all the while she was listening to his words, and saying over and over, below her breath, the exclamation that had been the one conscious reflection in her mind during her drive.

The money—the money! She must have the money.

She was capable of nothing beyond that weary repetition till across her dazed brain struck the meaning of the sole hope held out by her Israelitish counselor. Another name added after hers to the little bill—"the leedle pill," Moses's descendant called it—might prove the "open sesame" required to free her from the terrible dilemma.

"A—what do you call it—an indorsement?" she demanded, sitting, suddenly, upright in her chair.

The Hebrew nodded.

"If I can get that, you will give me the money?"

"Why not, if the dame is edough?" he questioned in his turn, his peculiarities of pronunciation rendered more remarkable than usual by an acute attack of catarrh.

"Somebody to indorse it—somebody to indorse it," she muttered.

"Just so! Very leedle; then we have no troubles wid the pill."

She left the office, and all the way home her thoughts roamed out among her friends in search of some one who would possibly aid her in this emergency, and fell back as wearily and helplessly as most persons must under such circumstances.

In all the world, among her hosts of acquaintances, she could only think of one man who would assist her; but she felt that she could easier die than go to John Worthington and make the confession which would be necessary.

CHAPTER VIII.

A HASTY WORD.

THE season had been an unusually gay one, and from its opening Alice Marchmont had allowed herself no repose, the leader of every species of fashionable dissipation, till, had there been any person with the right to remonstrate, she must have endured, in addition to her restlessness, the annoyance of expostulations and reproaches in regard to her reckless conduct. Sometimes her old friend, John Worthington—the only creature who ever ventured to scold her—did say a few warning or sarcastic words; but he was not a society man, and at this period his professional duties were so engrossing that he had little leisure to bestow even upon her.

And this week was worse than all the uncertainty that had gone before. The days passed with frightful rapidity, filling her with horror and anxiety at their swift flight, though they seemed endless as she looked back across their length. She had herself set the term of probation—ten days—and six of them had already vanished, and she was no more prepared to meet Dick Faulkner than in the hour when she had so haughtily assured him he should have his money.

How could she stay at home with the horrible phantoms which crowded about in her loneliness growing more tangible each day! It was bad enough in a crowd; even then she never knew when a sudden fear might check her laughter and blanch her face—when some chance story or allusion might bring the horror of her position to her mind. Worse than any thing, Dick Faulkner haunted her steps with his silky smile, always watching her, she thought, with a certainty of triumph in his wicked face which often made her so wild with dread that the ball-room floor would heave like a sea under her feet, and the lights rock to and fro in a mist. No wonder that even in those few days she altered rapidly in appearance, growing thin, with deep, shadowy lines tracing themselves under her eyes, that only increased their brilliancy. She was more beautiful than ever, but it was a beauty which would have caused sharp anxiety to any body who loved her well enough to notice the change.

One man did observe it, and that was Kenneth Halford. Since the first meeting with Mrs. Marchmont his feelings in regard to her had undergone many changes, most of which were so inexplicable that he was often enraged with what seemed his own weakness and fickle nature. Whenever the memory of the old days came up, he found himself greatly touched by their influence; but he so utterly disapproved of her rush after excitement, he so thoroughly despised half the men by whom she was surrounded, and his strict sense of decorum was so deeply outraged by the gossip which her careless conduct caused, that the woman herself was, at times, almost an object of dislike. Often he thought that she wished—perhaps out of mere coquetry—to subdue him by the power of those old associations; and then he grew very bitter and hard toward her. Fortunately, just now, Milly Crofton was kept a good deal at home by the illness of her cousin, so that Halford ran no risk of being tempted into attentions which could disturb her peace of mind. The pleasure of meeting the child again had been so great, that he was genuinely astonished. Sometimes it fairly seemed as if she were the innocent creature whose love had made his youth beautiful—that this dashing woman, with her ceaseless, painful brilliancy, hard and cold and bright as the diamonds blazing in her hair, could have nothing in common with the girl whose image had been so deeply impressed upon his heart. Yet, perhaps an hour after indulging in such reflections, he would meet Mrs. Marchmont, and the weariness and trouble his quick eyes read in her face, some chance quiver of her voice, some frank appeal to his judgment, or pathetic deprecation of his censures, would bring up—not the old love—but a feeling of tender compassion which caused him for the time to believe she was not really false and cold.

He was in a singular state of mind; yet it was a phase which many a man of his age must pronounce natural. Mrs. Marchmont's manner toward him was the perfection of caprice, and it was not possible to have the slightest clue to her conduct. If this woman had indeed loved him through all these years; if, in spite of her worldly life, the renewal of their acquaintance had brought the youthful dream back in its freshness, and his conduct the first night they met had helped to do it—must he not try to forget the past—to have faith in her? If not—if he could become convinced that she was the heartless coquette he had striven in the bitterness of his anger to believe—why, then, to love Milly Crofton would only be like going back years and years, and taking up his broken hopes just where they were brightest; and this woman would have no connection in his mind with that season—Milly would be the realization of his boyish ideal.

Little wonder that Mrs. Marchmont puzzled him. He could not know how his presence at one instant gave her a feeling of protection, by bringing up the old days; how in the next some softened look in his eyes, some familiar smile brightening his lips, forced into her mind a recollection of the terrors which surrounded her; and the bare thought that she dared not love any man filled her with rage and pain. She could not bear to have him leave her, because, in her desolation, he was the one link that connected her with the innocent past; and yet she could not allow him to love her, because, even if she lived beyond these days of peril, the memory of their secret would always remain, and leave her afraid of him. She could not endure to lose his respect; if she had loved him better than in her girlish days, it would have been easier to part than to run the risk of living till the hour when some chance might make her reckless conduct known to him, and kill his affection outright and forever. And even a knowledge of half the truth would do it —she knew him so well—so firm, and with such rooted principles of honor; hard, too, toward his own weaknesses and those of others.

Let him love her? She dared not! With the stain of Dick Faulkner's insulting kiss upon her hand; with the remembrance that, in her mad extravagance, her craving for social distinction, she had bartered with this wretch smiles and coquettish words in return for a share in his Wall Street bubbles, until he actually presumed to believe that he was at liberty to present his passion to her eyes; that she had expected—that— Oh, Alice could never go further in her thoughts! She so hated and abhorred herself that she would strike the hand he had polluted with his kiss fierce blows, overwhelmed by a sense of actual degradation and guilt. Besides all this, the fact that her name was attached to scores of bills lying in the money-lender's safe—that she was covered with debts, and, worse than any thing, only a few days to elapse before she must raise the money to pay Faulkner.

She love and be loved! The words would

utter themselves in spite of her—not connected especially with Kenneth Halford—rousing her to such misery, wrath, and self-contempt, that she would fairly moan in her agony, wrestle the night through, wonder if she should go mad before the dawn—lying, perhaps, on the floor just as she had returned from some ball, blazing with jewels and costly raiment.

One night, as she entered her opera-box, Halford chanced to sit where he had a full view of her face; and the change was very plain to him. She returned his salutation with a slow, difficult smile, and shrunk back into the shadow of the curtains. Not obliged for the moment to talk, her countenance had not lost the expression which she had brought out of her solitary chamber.

Kenneth Halford was not that meanest of created beings, a man given to fancying that women were in love with him. But it was not strange, considering the past, and the manner in which she had treated him since his return, that, now perceiving the sudden trouble in her face as she looked at him, he should wonder whether he had any share in the pain which he read there. The idea brought him no pleasure; it did not gratify his vanity, as would have been the case with many men; but his strict sense of honor and justice made it impossible to put the thought aside. He had committed a score of follies on that first evening they met; he must atone for them, if necessary; he could not retreat from the position which he had then assumed. On the instant up rose a vision of Milly Crofton's girlish prettiness and innocence; he asked himself why, and found no satisfactory answer, since he still regarded her as a mere child to be petted and amused, without any capability of rousing a stronger sentiment in a heart so worn as his. He wished heartily just then that he had remained in Europe; wondered testily if he should always be a fool; but turned to glance again toward the box, and met Mrs. Marchmont's eyes as she once more leaned forward from among the curtains. It seemed a sort of invitation to join her—one that he could not refuse. He left his seat and made his way through the lobbies to her loge, with his mind in a state of confusion very humiliating to a person who prided himself, during these latter years, on having arrived at such entire self-control that he was never to be shaken out of it, able always to analyze his own emotions, know exactly what they meant, and how much they were worth.

With his hand upon the door-knob, he had three minds to turn back; but that stern inward monitor of his asserted its power again, and held him fast. It was too late to retreat, he must go in; if events justified his suspicions, he must continue in the course he had begun. That she had once been false through weakness would offer no excuse for trifling on his part; it would appear like an unworthy revenge for the pain she had caused him in the old days; she had suffered enough without having this humiliating idea added

"I thought you must have gone to the moon for wonderful discoveries, till I saw you down yonder," she said, as he entered. "Indeed, you look a little as if you had been, and had just returned, and were still dazed by your lunar expedition."

As he took her hand he could feel, even through her glove, how icy cold it was, how suddenly its pulses leaped under his touch, and could see the quick rush of color which tinged her cheeks. Certainly he could not be accused of vanity for thinking that his appearance, the pressure of his fingers upon her own, had caused this emotion; it was true, too. But how could he understand, or dream, what the feelings really were which gave rise to her trouble? He could not imagine that, when he came in obedience to her glance, and she felt that he had not been able to resist her influence, there rushed upon her, like a flash of lightning, the thought of all which kept her so far apart from him—that this possible awakening of the faded dream must be subdued, crushed, rooted out, just as those terrible recollections quelled it in her own heart. But she could not think; she would have a little rest, talk of the pleasant things of her youth, and forget the present, and the awful possibilities of the future.

"Why hasn't one met you for several nights?" she asked.

"I think I have had my share of balls," he replied; "and society here seems to mean dancing insanely from one week's end to another."

"Now don't be misanthropical or wise; you will have to wait several years yet before you do either well," laughed she. "But why have you not been to see me?"

"Are you ever at home?"

"What an unpardonable Yankeeism in a man who has lived so long abroad, to answer one question by another. Come, we will have a course of interrogations, since they please you! Have you been to ask whether I was or not?"

"It is not very—"

"Take care! Reply as if you were in the Palace of Truth—always supposing that any thing masculine could enter."

"I have not been to-day," he said, finding it difficult, in his present mood, to smile and jest.

"Yesterday, then?"

"Not since the day before."

She looked troubled again. Her first thought was, did he suspect—could any whisper have crept out—or had Faulkner in his rage already begun to hint the scandals with which he had threatened her? This was always her first dread now, when she perceived, or fancied, the slightest change in any body's manner toward her.

"I believe I have been busy," he continued; "at least, I have made a great pretense of work."

"And so satisfied your conscience," she replied, growing animated again just from remembering how ridiculous her fear was. "Make

an ample confession, and perhaps we will forgive you—eh, Miss Portman?"

She remembered that she had forgotten to
give the spinster any opportunity of waving the
conversation away from herself, in her usual shy
manner, and it was a matter of conscience with
Alice to do that once or twice in the course of
an evening.

So now, hearing her name, the virgin turned
from her contemplation of the stage with her customary flutter and nervous gasping for breath.
"I beg your pardon; did you speak, my
dear?" she asked.

"Yes; I'm always talking, you know, though,
luckily, it does not amount to much."

"Oh, my love!" quavered the spinster, who
never could bear that Mrs. Marchmont should
speak slightingly of herself.

"I suppose that means you regret my folly,"
laughed she.

"Oh, my love!" quavered the virgin anew,
raising her voice half a note higher, so that it
sounded more than ever like the squeak of a
mouse caught in a trap.

"But where was I?" pursued Mrs. Marchmont. "I was asking somebody something—
Oh, it was you, Adeliza."

"Asking me— Oh! yes, you were—I
mean I heard you pronounce my name," returned the old maid, struggling, after her habit, to be perfectly truthful and correct in her
assertions.

"I was asking you if you thought we had
better forgive Mr. Halford his numerous sins
and enormities."

The spinster began to wave off the conversation with more than ordinary haste; this
style of talk was completely beyond her comprehension. She waved, and gurgled, and
looked so awfully stately, in the height of her
embarrassment, that a stranger would have believed her the most formidable old woman one
could possibly encounter.

"I fear that Miss Portman thinks my enormities beyond the reach of pardon," observed
Halford, unable for the life of him to resist
laughing, and desirous of affording himself a
decent pretext.

"Oh, Mr. Halford!" was now the squeak of
the poor mouse.

"Never mind," said Alice; "you can't
think too ill of him; but you are not bound to
put your opinion in words."

"Oh, my love—my love! When you know
how highly I respect Mr. Halford—you are
jesting—pray, pray state that you are jesting."

"I really can not jest on a subject so serious," returned Alice; "but, to relieve your
mind, I will admit that you like this wretched
man very much; does that content you?"

The spinster sat up straighter than ever, and
heaved a sigh of relief.

"I'm sure I thank you exceedingly, Miss
Portman," said Halford. "I wish you could
teach your cousin a little of your universal charity."

Poor Miss Portman grew frightened and bewildered again, and waved and shook, to keep
from becoming entangled in the web of talk.

"Don't abuse me to my relations, if you
please; that's shabbier than any thing, Mr.
Halford," said Alice, good-naturedly coming to
the old maid's rescue.

Miss Portman took advantage of the inter-
position to lean forward and study the stage
attentively, wondering why she could not be
let alone. But just as she was composing her
mind to be tranquilly deafened by the crash of
the instruments, Halford, fearing that his teasing remark might have annoyed her, felt it his
duty to address her once more.

"They've almost reached the famous duet,
haven't they, Miss Portman?"

She looked back helplessly; she had seen
the opera at least twelve separate times, but
had no more idea to what he referred than if
he had asked her to explain a page of Sanscrit.

"I am sorry—I—"

"Don't let him disturb your enjoyment,"
said Alice; "go back to your beloved music;
he only wants to get rid of my searching questions."

Miss Portman changed her attitude. Really, this was likely to prove a very fatiguing
night—these young people were so thoughtless!
"I wish I could be certain," she faltered,
consulting the libretto.

"It is of no consequence," Halford said, sorry now that he had disturbed her again.

He spoke to Mrs. Marchmont about some
other subject; and this time the spinster was
allowed to resume her listening attitude, and
retain it till her head buzzed between the roar
of the orchestra and her efforts to discover the
hidden meaning which she felt the music ought
to possess.

"Will you confess?" Alice asked Halford,
anxious to keep their talk down to the idle
nonsense where she felt safest. "Only don't
imitate 'Topsy,' and, for fear of punishment,
'fess by inventing something."

"I believe I have been cross," he said.

"Bravo! That sounds more probable than
men's confessions often do: with the world in
general—not with yourself, of course—because
no man ever admits that there could be any
reason."

He was vexed with her trifling. If she really cared for him, and was glad to have him
once more at her side, why did she treat him
as she would have done any dandy who chanced
to be drawn into her orbit?

"Do you always mean to tease me with per-
siflage?" he asked, in a tone that sounded almost ill-natured.

"By which pretty French word you intend
to tell me that I talk nothing but nonsense."

"Not that; but is one never to be serious,
nor in earnest?"

"Better not," she said; "much better not."

"And yet one grows very weary of this surface life."

"Only experience teaches us that it is dangerous to go below it," she replied. "Very young people can afford to be in earnest—or what they believe so—but who would have the courage for a second trial?"

"That would depend on how much one had at heart the object to be gained. I don't like to believe there is no possibility of happiness after one's past youth—"

"Ah, don't let us talk about happiness," she interrupted. "One has dreams, delusions—what you will—until the power of dreaming is lost; but where are we straying to? Tell me what you are doing, Mr. Halford! Do you propose to give us a new book this season?"

Miss Portman was temporarily deaf and blind by this time; so this little dialogue was lost upon her. She was a conscientious old soul, and, though she did not know one note of music from another, always listened diligently to orchestra and voices with an attention which people who considered themselves real lovers of harmony would have done well to imitate. It was the good woman's creed that one ought always to be gaining knowledge; so night after night she listened to Verdi or Donizetti, gaining nothing apparently beyond a severe headache; but she had constantly the hope of finding out what it all meant, and so did not regard the time or pain as wasted.

Halford looked eagerly at Alice again. Was she indeed afraid to talk seriously with him? Was there that left in her heart which she feared to betray, dreading lest it should meet with no return in his? Was she conscious that, in spite of her worldliness, her nature still held capabilities of feeling and love, and was not willing to risk trouble for herself a second time? He gazed so earnestly at her while propounding these mental queries that she began to laugh.

"Are you about to tell my fortune?" she asked. "Some old Frenchman, the other night, professed his ability of reading the future by the lines on one's face. The best of it was, he said it to Mrs. Stuyvesant."

"I never saw any lines on her face except those made by India ink and rouge," he answered, trying to do his part in the nonsense.

"Now you are malicious! I left every thing to the imagination; but so few people really know how to say ill-natured things well."

She was too nervous this evening to be quiet; she chatted and laughed until, vexed by the contrast between her light talk and the shadows in her face, he said, abruptly,

"I wonder—I do wonder if you are happy!"

Mrs. Marchmont gave him a glance of keen reproach—not from wounded sentiment—only it seemed so bitter a mockery for any human being to talk to her of happiness, that, coming from his lips, it sounded like an absolute taunt; for she forgot that he could possess no knowledge of the troubles which made her restless and miserable.

"I would change places with the first beggar I met in the street!" she exclaimed, passionate-ly. "I, happy! What do you mock me with such questions for? Oh, if only men and women could have their lives back—if there were ever any possibility of bridging the gulf that sweeps between them and their youth!"

She stopped, and looked away across the house, wondering at her own madness in speaking like this. She was not thinking, when she spoke, of any connection between her past and his—not even remembering that he was the man who had loved her in that youth which she lamented—only thinking of the dreariness, the desolation, the horrors, which surrounded her at this moment. But what could he imagine? He saw her grow deathly pale; saw the pain darken her eyes; perceived her stung by his careless words into an utter forgetfulness of the artificiality with which, in general, she so successfully covered her real feelings. It was natural enough that he should be hurried by his regret and sympathy—his Quixotic ideas, where women were concerned—into uttering an avowal which he had not meant to speak—an avowal for which he knew perfectly well he should, in a calmer moment, find no warrant whatever in his heart.

"It is never too late to bring the past back when hearts remain unchanged," he whispered. "Alice, do you remember—is the recollection of the old dream sweet to you?"

She gave him one startled look, suddenly recalled to a consciousness of the dangerous ground upon which her outburst had led her. But before she could answer, there was an invasion into the box, and Halford was forced to resign his place to the new-comers. Among the men came Mrs. Marchmont's French baron, and she proceeded to turn his poor head more completely by her smiles and words—a hot rage and bitterness took possession of her—there was a horrible pleasure in tormenting somebody in her present mood.

The baron was exceedingly fluttered and charmed by the beautiful woman's marked consideration, till, between his sentimental mood and the thought of the enormous fortune for which report gave her credit, he regretted that there was no opportunity of securing the prize then and there.

Alice rushed from her maddening reflections back to the safeguards of folly; and at length, sickened by the nonsense in which she apparently took her part with such enjoyment, Halford made his bow and went away. She was glad to see him go; any body who reminded her of the past—of all that she had sacrificed and lost in her insane chase after excitement and distinction—was odious to her at this moment. The dandies' absurd compliments—the baron's broken English, whispered words of laborious flattery in his own tongue, his glances and sighs—were more acceptable than any thing else. The whole was poor and miserable, empty as her life; but it was safest and best. She could gratify her irritated temper by laughing at his tenderness; and if there was nothing

4

amusing in the dandies' jests, at least there was the satisfaction of helping them to be ridiculous. She did not want such men as Halford or John Worthington about her now; they were too clear-sighted; they talked of things which frenzied her, by rousing thought and reminding her what a wreck she had made of her life. The baron was better than that; he talked as if she were a beautiful doll, without an idea beyond her toilet, or an ability to appreciate a chapter of doubtful morality in a French novel. The dandies were better with their stereotyped dress and appearance, their back-hair elaborately parted, their attitudes so precisely alike, each bending slightly forward, hanging to his hat with one hand, the other fingering his watch-chain—all uttering the same interjections, and built so completely on one model that she felt as if there were a puppet before her, which her dizzy eyes magnified into half a dozen. Even young Bramwell's well-known remark, which she induced him to repeat, was better than Halford's talk.

"What a beautiful buff rose, Mr. Bramwell!"

"Yaas; I always insist on that color; it is so difficult to dress a blonde, Mrs. Marchmont!"

So Halford left her, remembering, as he walked homeward, with a sensation of anger and dread, that he had gone a step too far. Other men might have considered the words which he had spoken the idlest possible figure of speech. Not so in his creed—spoken to a woman whom he had once wooed. So he went home, thoroughly dispirited and disgusted, recollecting Alice as she looked surrounded by her butterfly admirers, and forgetting the change in her appearance which had lured him on, as he ruefully recalled that whispered question. Besides, Milly Crofton's image came up like a vision of rest, and he could not drive it away. Altogether, Halford retired with an uncomfortable feeling that the world was out of joint, and that he had been doing his best to put his portion of it in a still more uncomfortable predicament.

CHAPTER IX.

CLOSER AND CLOSER.

HALFORD did not go in sight of Mrs. Marchmont the next day, nor the next; but he by no means forgot the words which he had spoken, and was wondering how he ought to act. It might have been a relief to him to know that Alice had forgotten ever hearing his whispered question. She was too busy to give him, or any other possible or past admirer, a moment's thought in any way.

Busy with the graver matters of her life; and stern enough they were. There was the worry of arranging a new influx of bills—holding consultations in regard to the sale of her lands, from which she hoped so much, and growing sick with horror at the new delays, as she remembered how the time was fleeting away.

Besides these affairs, rushing about in a vain attempt to raise the money she had promised to pay Dick Faulkner, circumscribed in her efforts by the fact that she dared make no trials in quarters where a suspicion could intrude into her world. Two days passed, in which she lived through mental anguish enough to have lasted a lifetime. Indeed, the second evening she was ill; she came home only in season for dinner, having been again to her Jewish friend, with no better result than on the first occasion, having tried to soften the hearts of sundry of his fraternity with whom the experiences of the last year had made her acquainted, but failing as signally as she had done with him. No effort was of any use; she had turned in every direction, and was fairly brought to bay. Even to raise the sum required upon her jewels was out of the question; her Israelite already had a lien upon them, and twice a week made himself certain that such as he left in her possession were safe, and the original stones. She had seen him, and his petticoated associate—who good-naturedly allowed herself, in her visits, to be supposed, among the domestics, a worthy widow in deep distress—so often examine the gems and settings—touch them with their tongues, or attempt other tests familiar to the initiated—that she fairly loathed the sight of the glittering baubles, and would never have put them on only she feared that to appear without them would occasion remark; and she had grown so afraid of rousing the least suspicion, that it was almost a monomania with her.

Kenneth Halford need not have feared that she spent the time dreaming of his imprudent words. Her reflections would have been as prosaic as those of the most determined money-worshiper in Wall Street, had not the dreadful skeleton dogged her footsteps all day, and kept watch over her pillow through the whole night. No hope, no gleam of light, and the time she had set for Dick Faulkner to claim his money drawing closer and closer, and she helpless as a blind man bound in a dungeon! Three days more, three short days; if at their expiration she had not the sum in her hands, what would follow? It was the persistent iteration of that question in her ears as she drove home, while the skeleton grinned beside her on the seat of her clarence, which overwhelmed her so completely that she had to throw herself on her bed and admit the plea of illness.

Poor Miss Portman was terribly alarmed, and forced numberless potions upon her, which, in her bewilderment, the old lady offered rather indiscriminately from any bottle she chanced to lay hands upon. Suffering as she was—so near nervous spasms that she dared not attempt to speak—Alice was conscious of tasting red lavender, cologne, sherry, Miss Portman's favorite Mohawk bitters, not to mention tea, sal volatile and various other remedies, in quick succession. For an hour Mrs. Marchmont herself almost believed the illness a warning that a speedy means of relief out of her troubles was at hand, and endured the agonies which only diseased nerves can produce—agonies of which no human being sound in body and mind can form the least conception. But the utter collapse of force and will did not last long. The instant she could rise, it became impossible for her to lie there, and wait even for death; and with the return of volition came the sense of her own absurdity in believing that such a boon would be granted. The mere physical restlessness induced by her state would have made it a relief to run, dance, scream, until she fell blind and insensible.

Toward midnight she got up, and, in spite of Miss Portman's tears, her maid's expostulations, she insisted on dressing and going to Mrs. Lawrence's party.

"I will go, my best of women," she said to her friend; "so you needn't waste your breath in words."

"You will kill yourself," moaned Miss Portman; and Alice burst into a fit of hysterical laughter which increased the good soul's distress.

"You shall stay at home," Mrs. Marchmont said; "I'll not drag you out, but go I must; it is the best thing for me; I am not ill, only nervous—no reason for it, either."

"Not ill!" squeaked the poor Chinese mouse. "Look at yourself in the glass."

"Oh, my dear, a little rice-powder will hide that! Now don't tease me; that's a darling! Pauline, I am awfully pale to-night; so we'll intensify it; then people will think I did it on purpose. Get out that new dress from Paris—the black one—and I'll wear a few diamonds; I'll get those myself. You are always calling me careless, my Portman; admire my attempts at improvement—I don't even let that faithful Pauline keep the key of the safe where I have my ornaments and papers."

She laughed and jested while her toilet went on, and, in less than an hour from the time when she lay writhing on her bed in the last of those nervous spasms, entered Mrs. Lawrence's drawing-rooms, more peculiar-looking and beautiful than ever, though with a face to have excited any body's pity who had time or discernment to read it. Her dress added to the effect—of black lace, heavily trimmed with jet ornaments; no trace of color except a broad green scarf; bands of black velvet about her neck, and arms upon which blazed diamonds of great value—it was odd and striking as possible, but utterly beyond criticism, even to feminine eyes.

One man at least noticed and read her countenance aright—that was John Worthington, the man whom, of all the world, she most respected, and whose judgment she most feared. He considered the gravity of his forty years somewhat out of place in such scenes as the present, but he had come to-night to gratify his niece. When he saw Mrs. Marchmont, he looked straight through the glitter and the brilliant smiles, and knew that she was either suffering mentally or was very very ill. He went up to her, and the first words he spoke were,

"In the name of Heaven, what have you been doing to yourself?"

"Putting on my prettiest new dress, and marking under my eyes with India ink," she answered.

"India ink never made those lines," retorted he; "nothing but sleepless nights and hard pain ever did it."

"That is all the gratitude one gets for frankness in this wicked world! I don't suppose there is another woman here who would have made the confession."

"Will you tell me what you have been doing?"

"I thought I had just done you that honor."

"Nonsense! I have not seen you for nearly a fortnight, and I never saw any body so altered."

"Very well; you have always told me I was the most capricious creature in the world; what do you expect?"

"I believe you would jest in your coffin," he said, rather severely.

"After I had seen whether my shroud was becoming," she answered, unmoved by his gravity, and laughing in a way which caused his stout nerves to quiver with anxiety.

"Have you had a doctor?"

"No; and I'm not going to make my will, so I don't want a lawyer. Keep your horrid questions for the court-room, and tell me why I have not seen you for an age."

"I wish I had taken time to go and see you," he said, regretfully. "I would have made sure that you did something for yourself."

"I have done my best to-night in the way of dressing, and it's wicked of you to destroy my confidence by abusing my appearance as soon as I arrive. But how on earth does it happen that you are here?"

"Partly to oblige Constance, partly that I remembered I had not seen you for some time, and I wanted to know what you were doing. I felt certain of finding you in this Babel."

"Don't come to people's houses and call them bad names; it's not polite! Doing? nothing, as usual."

"Then it is time you did something, if this is the effect that a lack of occupation has upon you."

"Ah, now, let my looks alone," she pleaded, with a smile that it was difficult to resist; "please be amiable."

But though he smiled, he would not relinquish the subject, and said, with gravity,

"I thought you would treat me differently; I thought you would be frank and honest—"

"Don't go taking away my character! Yes, you may, on second thoughts; like most people, I'd be glad to get rid of it."

"Alice," he said; calling her by the familiar name, as he had been in the habit of doing from her childhood, "there is something the matter! Either you are ill, or some trouble has come upon you."

"Trouble! Always the first thought with a lawyer! I have neither near relations nor a mother-in-law. May I ask, what trouble would be likely to have the impertinence to assail me?"

"Then you are ill!"

"How you do ring the changes! Oh, John Worthington, John Worthington, you've buried yourself among your law-books till you are almost daft."

He would have been vexed with her, only his anxiety prevented any such feeling.

"Alice," he said, "I thought you considered me your friend."

"Dear soul, don't get sentimental! The baron gave me his arm up stairs, and he has exhausted that style for the evening. You know my baron, don't you?"

"Yes, I know him, and he's an ass! But don't you feel alarmed about my growing sentimental."

"He resents the bare idea as a slanderous aspersion upon his legal character; what a delightful collection of long words!"

"I do think that a friendship which dates back to your childhood—"

"There's no such word!" she interrupted, for an instant breaking down in her part, and giving vent to the bitterness in her soul. "Who has any friends—what does friendship mean? Pleasant words—an exchange of dinners! Suppose trouble came—nonsense, Mr. Worthington; I am not a girl to believe in romances; I am a woman—a coquette—I have no heart, no ability to feel."

"Yes, you have," he answered. "Ah, child—I may call you child—tell me if you have any real anxiety or care?"

"Yes; my bracelet is too tight! Didn't I do my bit of tragedy well?"

She could not tease him into anger or drive him away.

"You shall not vex me," he said.

"Wouldn't do it for the world; I should have to beg your pardon. But now tell me—I've a question to ask—a grave, legal question."

He almost thought her serious for an instant, her face and eyes grew so earnest.

"Ask it," he said; "I will answer."

She hesitated a second longer; the half-formed determination to speak freely which he had seen in her countenance gave place to a provoking smile.

"Shall I become a baroness? That's the question! Bless me, I do believe I'm talking Shakspeare."

"I thought you never boasted of your conquests," said he, sternly.

"For shame, as if I were likely to! But it is my creed that a woman may marry whom she wishes; so I might be a baroness."

"Very well, be one, if you can, and the idea pleases you."

"I declare, he is downright crabbed about it! After wanting me to ask advice, and all."

"I'll not be vexed," he said.

"But I shall," laughed she, certain that he was about to speak seriously, and longing to prevent it.

"When I promised to be your friend—when I promised your husband that I would be—I was in earnest. I should poorly prove my claim to the title, if I did not expostulate with you upon your conduct."

"I don't want a friend," she cried, her nerves exasperated to a pitch where she could no longer control herself. Her haunting fear that some whisper had crept out returned, and drove her so nearly wild that she hardly knew what she said. "What do you mean, Mr. Worthington, by questioning and watching me like this? What do you want to accuse me of?"

"Questioning and watching, Alice!"

"Oh, I beg your pardon; I did not mean it! I do believe I am mad. Please let me alone! You are the only friend I ever had; don't hate me."

"What an exaggerated word! As if I could lose my interest in you—my liking, which dates so far back."

"You might; nobody can answer for himself; you might."

"Alice, you have some trouble; don't deny it."

"No, no. Come away; we are too near the conservatory; the flowers make me ill. Yes, that's it; I am ill—I mean I was! Mr. Worthington, I thought a while ago that I was dying."

He gave a sort of groan.

"Don't be frightened! It was pure nervousness—hysterics—but it was like dying. It's the life I lead; why, I work harder than a factory-girl."

"You must be quiet; you are completely worn out, and can not go on as you have been doing."

"Yes, I know. I will be quiet, but not yet; I can't yet. There comes the baron for his redowa— Oh dear! Where is Constance? Oh, I see her yonder; how pretty she looks."

Her partner came up, and she floated away. Mr. Worthington saw her dancing with a smile on her lips, and the fools staring at her.

When Mrs. Marchmont was able to think, she remembered how wildly she had talked to her friend, making an idiot of herself, as she called it in her thoughts. To have him, of all people in the world, watching and suspecting her; and she to give him added grounds for believing that she had some trouble, by talking in that crazy fashion. She could only comfort herself by thinking that what she had said would not sound as it might have done from another person's lips. She was so much in the habit of indulging in every extravagance in the way of language, appearing as whimsical and capricious as she saw fit, that perhaps the painful impression would speedily leave his mind.

The baron was talking to her, inclined to be tender and pathetic, and she had great difficulty to keep him from a downright declaration; and she did not want that, at least now. Whom could she tell what might happen? Every possible or impossible way out of her dilemma occurred to her. If stories did get abroad; if Faulkner did sully her name with his vile aspersions, so as to make a residence among her old friends unpleasant, then she might marry the baron at once—always supposing she sold her lands and recovered her fortune—and get away forever. But if she did not? And in two days more the period for redeeming her pledge to Faulkner would arrive. Good heavens! she should be a raving lunatic before then. At least that would settle matters; and she laughed again, till the baron asked what amused her.

"Only Mrs. Stuyvesant's turban," said she; "what a flamingo she looks!"

"I do not know the flamingo," he answered, in his hesitating English. "But you are of a great gayety to-night."

"Yes; I never was in better spirits."

"Hélas! and you have not the pity for me, and I sigh;" and here he did it elaborately.

"I wouldn't; it's bad for digestion! There, the music is stopping; take me to a seat."

She caught sight of herself in a mirror as they passed down the room: her cheeks were flushed, and she looked quite a different creature from what she had on entering. She could endure scrutiny now, even that of John Worthington; only for the present she would avoid him, if possible. She was so near mad to-night that there was no telling what she might do or say to rouse fresh wonder in his mind. A group of men gathered about her, and rather crowded the disconsolate baron into the background. Looking out from the circle, Alice perceived Kenneth Halford at a distance, talking with Milly Crofton and her particular friend, John Worthington's niece. A sharp envy of the youth and innocence of the two girls filled Mrs. Marchmont's soul; she could have shrieked in agony as she reflected upon all which lay between her and the season when she had been like them.

Presently Dick Faulkner thrust himself in among the group about her, and she thought,

"You are the cause of every thing—oh, you reptile! How I do lie to myself; it was not his work; just my own recklessness, my own wickedness, has done the whole."

Undeterred by her cool obliviousness of his presence, he got closer to her, joined in the conversation, and at last absolutely asked her to dance. He knew that she would refuse; still he could not resist working himself into a passion by running the risk of being snubbed, as he called it. He was obliged to repeat his question before she vouchsafed any consciousness of his having addressed her.

"Won't you dance with me? You never did but once."

"And once was quite enough," she replied, indifferent to the fact that there were a number of people listening. "I heard the other day that your wife said I flirted with you."

"Oh, I think not," said Dick, looking rather sheepish.

"Yes, she did; and it was ill-natured of her —very! Why, good gracious! I never said she flirted last summer, when she danced every night with Howard Conyers."

Now every body knew that Howard Conyers was the only man ever known to get an advantage of Faulkner in a bargain; but he did let Dick in for a large amount of money, and then failed; and people said that Dick had been friends with him in the hope that Mrs. Faulkner would flirt until she compromised herself enough to render a divorce possible. Mrs. Faulkner said it louder than any one else, and of course the world was ready to believe it; consequently, Mrs. Marchmont's little retort caused Dick nearly to burst a blood-vessel with rage.

Mrs. Marchmont turned, and saw Kenneth Halford standing near, and looking at her very gravely. It was the style of speech to offend his sense of delicacy. John Worthington would have said that she had served the scoundrel right, and have liked her the better for her unmanageable tongue.

"I suppose he is disgusted," she thought; "so much the better." Then she remembered that he was the last link which connected her with her youth—to the beautiful past; and with her usual inconsistency, her heart cried out, "I can't let him go; I can't have him hate me; I can't!"

She smiled at him, and made him come nearer; then she said,

"I promised to promenade with you while they are doing the quadrille; we will go now."

So she took his arm and got away from her admirers, the baron sighing dolefully to the last, and Dick Faulkner treating her to a parting menace from his black eyes which made her shiver, desperate as she was.

"You are thinking me the rudest woman you ever saw," she said, abruptly, as they passed on.

"Not that," he answered; "you could never be that."

"And a story-teller into the bargain."

"But since just now it was in my favor!"

"I was dying to get away, and I knew those tiresome wretches would hang about unless I said I had promised to promenade with you. One has to tell so many falsehoods—it is loathsome! Ah me, what are you thinking? That I am not like the Alice you remember?"

He had been thinking that, and as he hesitated, she went on—

"Oh, very unlike her. So that was your thought, Kenneth? Well, well, Heaven knows you were right."

It always softened him when she spoke the old name; and she knew it. Just then, her wish was not to lose her power over this man —the one living memory of her vanished life.

"Sometimes I wonder if you are as much changed in reality as you seem," he said.

"Then I seem changed?"

"You must feel it, I think."

"Do I not? Sometimes I wonder too! Oh, Kenneth, life hasn't been kind to me—it hasn't been kind."

The familiar pathetic voice, the same mournful droop of the head—how it brought the old time back! But even as he remembered, he chanced to glance toward the spot where Milly Crofton was seated—looking the fresher for her brief seclusion—and she seemed more like the dream he had lost, than this woman with all her witcheries. Then he recollected somewhat ruefully the words which he had spoken two nights before; and even with Mrs. Marchmont's hand resting on his arm, her wonderful eyes fixed upon his face, he acknowledged to himself that if it were not for those hasty words, he would go straight to Milly and rest in the peaceful influence she cast about her, and so make amends to his fancy for the stern manner in which he had forced himself to be only civil and polite on this first meeting after her temporary retirement.

But Mrs. Marchmont was speaking again; she had seen his attention wander, and she wanted to fix his thoughts upon herself. It was partly because, in her excited state, she felt a wild yearning for some human sympathy—partly that peculiar dramatic talent, which often rendered it difficult, even for her, to decide how much she felt or how far she was really in earnest.

"Living is dreary work, Kenneth—oh, such dreary work! I am so tired sometimes! Do you ever feel like that—I mean, feel that you would like to lie down and sleep forever, without a dream to trouble you?"

Here was an opportunity to say pretty things —serious ones too; conscience told him that he ought to say them, considering what had passed on that night in the opera-box. But he could not do it; whenever he saw Milly's girlish face, he knew that the faded dream could never be taken up again by his heart, though he did not really believe that it was Milly who stood in the way; only that to look at her, and then look back at the woman by his side, was like comparing her present self with the bright creature whom he had loved, and showing how little she now had in common with his ideal. Still, the words he had spoken held him fast; they could not be recalled; and never in his whole life had he broken even an implied pledge.

"You don't answer me, Kenneth! Do you think it is silly—did you never have such a fancy?"

"Sometimes, perhaps," he replied, and was ashamed to think how commonplace and practical both voice and speech sounded, but, for the life of him, could do no better. "But one is never well when one feels in that misanthropic mood. You have been exerting yourself too much; you need rest."

"Are you going to deliver a discourse on medicine for my benefit?" she asked, laughing almost harshly. "Mr. Worthington has already given me one. What a nice girl his niece is—I saw you talking with her and that pretty Milly Crofton. Ah, there is a lovely, happy child."

"She seems very happy and fresh."

"And lovely?" she persisted.

"Very pretty, at least," he answered; and the tone was so studiously careless that Mrs. Marchmont perceived the effort.

He was going from her too; she could not keep him; she was to have nothing of her old life left. She knew perfectly well that, in the present chaos she had made of her fate, she dared not claim even his friendship—she could not stop to think whether, if her life had held no secret, she could have loved him, had he come back with the old look in his eyes; but to lose him, the last tie to the broken past—to be utterly alone in the darkness which had closed so hopelessly about her—that was the pang! Her heart ached so keenly for an instant that, could he have seen its workings, he might reasonably have thought that it was absolute tenderness and love which moved her; but she knew well enough that it was nothing of the sort. She wanted comfort, sympathy, and could ask neither; besides, her illness and agitation gave her fresh craving for excitement, and these dramatics had just sufficient foundation in reality to give them an interest.

"You don't want to talk to me," she said, in a pretty way she had, when it pleased her—almost as childish as Milly Crofton's, and not all acting either. "You may go away, Kenneth; you don't care about me to-night."

"You have not been like yourself," he replied. "I don't know the brilliant, witty Mrs. Marchmont, you must remember."

"Ah, you hesitated over the adjectives; you had a mind to apply harsher ones," she said, piteously.

"Indeed, I had not; don't misjudge me."

"And be as forbearing with me, Kenneth."

"I will; I promise."

"That is good and kind—like yourself. So you don't know me as I am? Oh, there's little wonder; sometimes I don't know myself. And Alice is dead, you think—poor Alice! Do you believe she is quite dead, Kenneth!"

"Heaven help me, I can't tell," he fairly groaned, in his bewilderment and distress, unable to decide what was acting and what real—whether she loved him or was coquetting—but remembering always the words which he had spoken, and that they held him fast.

"And I can not always tell," she replied.

She was herself too much excited to remark any thing peculiar in his manner. Her nerves had been so strained during these past days, that the wildest ravings of tragedy would have sounded like natural conversation to her.

"Why don't you speak, Kenneth?" she went on.

"I think I was waiting for you to finish," he said.

"What was I saying? One forgets so. Well, never mind! Something about myself—always a tiresome subject."

"Ah, that little attempt at humility will not succeed," returned he, trying to get back to the safe ground of jests and badinage. "The world too long since accorded you your rightful place."

"The world—why do you speak to me about that? How I hate it! and what nonsense I am talking," she added, making an effort to appear less exalted and odd. "You are cold and stiff to-night; I suppose you are vexed with me."

"No; why should I be?"

"But you are," she persisted still, with the absurd desire—she told herself it was absurd—to make him feel, when, if she were to succeed, she knew perfectly well that she should flee in terror. "You are not the old friend to-night—and we can be friends, can't we, Kenneth?"

"I trust that we are so."

"Only the other evening you were so good and gentle!"

She did remember what he had said—she expected further explanation; then he could not go back! And all the time she without the slightest recollection that he had uttered more than words of the commonest compliment! If he had followed the dictates of his conscience, and tried to speak, she would have stopped her ears and run away, afraid to hear somebody cry out the exact truth in regard to her position, just as she heard voices do in her dreams. This was neither a fit time nor place for the question which he must ask—a question against which his soul rose in rebellion—at this moment; but it was too late to think of that. He was about to inquire if she would be at home the next day, when she spoke again suddenly—

"I have just been thinking, Kenneth! Do you know, I believe that sweet little Milly Crofton is more like the ideal you made of me than I was, even in the old time. Were you thinking that—do you know what I mean?"

"I don't find your sentence very clear," he answered, annoyed by the pertinacity with which she brought the girl's name into the conversation, but trying to treat her words as a jest.

"Don't laugh!" she exclaimed. "Yes, do—on second thoughts. I want to dance. Will you dance with me?"

He looked at her in utter astonishment, and asked,

"What ails you to-night? You are a perfect chameleon." Then he perceived how deathly white her face was, its pallor only broken by a scarlet spot on either cheek. "You are certainly ill," he added.

"Ill? Nonsense! I am only making you acquainted with Mrs. Marchmont—you said that you did not know her. Don't you mean

to dance with me—after my asking you, too? Have you forgotten that it is leap-year, Mr. Halford?"

Then she sat down, for the simple reason that she could not stand another instant; and he wondered if she were really offended with him. Not strange if she were, he thought, after his cowardly hesitation to follow up his half-avowal; and he tried to think how he might set matters straight. As for Mrs. Marchmont, she was only thinking that, if she remained there quiet any longer, she should inevitably scream, or indulge in a nervous spasm. When Halford raised his head, after that moment's preoccupation, she had left her seat, and was taking the arm of some man who had come up to claim a dance.

"Good-bye, Mr. Halford," she said, with a light laugh. "Let me know when you come back from the moon."

She was angry, he thought; he must speak at the first opportunity. He went and stood near the dancers, to wait until she should be at liberty again, and found himself beside Mr. Worthington.

"Come and dine with me to-morrow," that gentleman said; "I have asked a few people. I am so busy in these days that I have scarcely seen you since your arrival."

Halford absently accepted the invitation, still watching Alice Marchmont; and though he did not perceive it, Mr. Worthington's eyes were fixed upon her too. She and her partner paused for an instant's rest. Dick Faulkner seized that occasion to approach; he wanted a little revenge for the blow she had dealt him earlier in the evening.

"It seems an age since I have seen you," he whispered, while her partner was answering a question addressed to him by some person standing near. "This has been the longest week I ever spent."

She never turned her head or vouchsafed the slightest consciousness of his neighborhood; not a line of her face changed, not an eyelash quivered—a marble woman could not have been more utterly regardless of his presence. Her calm contempt enraged him to an extent that the harshest words could not have done.

"At least I have not much longer to wait," he continued; "the day after to-morrow will give me the pleasure of an interview. I shall be able then to see you without all these tiresome people about."

Her partner turned to her at this instant; she made a sign that they were to join the dancers, and left Faulkner uncertain whether his taunt had produced the slightest effect.

Another moment, and Mrs. Marchmont and her partner whirled past the spot where the two men stood watching her, and they heard her say, in a broken voice,

"Stop; I am faint—stop!"

Just as she was slipping slowly from the young man's hold, John Worthington caught her in his arms.

"It is nothing," she said; "let me sit down."

Then, with one long, shuddering sigh, she fainted completely away, for almost the first time in her life.

CHAPTER X.

THE OLD QUESTION.

THE next morning early Halford sent to inquire after Mrs. Marchmont's health, knowing the Chinese mouse was always visible at the most preposterous hours. Miss Portman sent back a string of old-fashioned compliments and thanks, and the information that her cousin was quite well. The good soul had not even been told of the fainting-fit.

A message from John Worthington also reached Mrs. Marchmont before she had left her chamber; but he was himself waiting below, having called on the way down to his office. She scribbled a pretty little billet, promising to dine at his house that night, and giving him an opportunity to see with his own eyes that she was entirely recovered, though only a few moments before his name had been taken up stairs she lay on her bed staring out at the streaks of light which crept through the silken curtains, loathing the sight of the new day, and wondering where she was to find strength to rise and recommence her wild chase in search of means to free herself from Faulkner's toils.

Kenneth Halford had not spent a tranquil night, but never once during the long hours had he wavered from his resolution. He was going to-day to ask Mrs. Marchmont to become his wife. Argue as he would, he could not feel himself at liberty to do otherwise, whatever another man might have felt under the circumstances, though there was no glamour before his eyes which could help him to believe that her consent could afford him a moment's happiness. This woman of society, eager for adulation, with all freshness of feeling worn out of her heart—this woman, who had been the idol of scores of men; who had smiled at them, listened to their flatteries, allowed them to love her just for a gratification to her desire for power; whose name, he had learned, even in the brief season which had elapsed since his return, was a by-word for coquetry and extravagance—this was not the wife he wanted. He detested society—could he hope that she would be satisfied without its plaudits? Why, in her girlish days had she allowed herself to be separated from him because she adored this hollow world—could he expect her now to relinquish the excitements on which she had fed for years? There might be moments when her fascinations would carry him back into the past, but they would be brief ones, and their pleasure marred by the recollection that his ideal of that season existed, though possessing no connection with her.

This idea brought Milly Crofton again before his mind; and the position in which he found himself in regard to Mrs. Marchmont showed him plainly what his feelings were toward the young girl, child as he had tried to consider her. He thanked Heaven the time had been so short—that he had kept aloof from Milly; so neither by word or look could he have troubled her youthful peace. Pretty Milly! what an image of rest her memory seemed! He went over and over each incident of their acquaintance in Europe—recalled her child-like frankness and innocence; and they appeared more beautiful than the charms of the most elegant woman that ever lived. It would have been so sweet to teach her to love him—to watch that pure nature develop in the sunshine of a first dream—and by his own folly, by a few hurried, unworthy words, he had put that happiness out of his reach.

He would go and see her first this morning. It was a silly thing to do—weak and boyish; but after his long season of faith in himself, he found his confidence so misplaced that he might as well admit his own shallowness, and be done. He had never paid but one visit to the house; he would allow himself that pleasure a second time. It would be a sort of righteous penance to torment his soul by the sight of the peace and rest which he might have gained had he been true to his own manly dignity and self-control.

He found Milly seated at her embroidery, in the morning-room, the prettiest object in all Mrs. Remsen's belongings—a little surprised at his appearance, but all the more pleased on that account—with the softest blush on her cheek as she gave him a quiet greeting, doubled in warmth by the sudden brightness in her eyes. Aunt Eliza was just going out, and, as a friend was waiting, she could not linger.

"I must leave Milly to entertain you," she said. "I've only time to say that I hope you will not be such a stranger as you have been since you got back; one never sees you except at parties."

He bowed and thanked her, but, as he replied in some fitting words, remembered, sadly, that his visits could not be made more frequent; no gradual gliding into familiar intercourse, no pleasant study of Milly's mind and character, would be possible now.

He gave Mrs. Remsen his arm out to the carriage, and she said, very graciously,

"It is not my habit to allow my girls the American liberty of receiving visits without my presence; but you are so old a friend, and I am so glad to see you in my house, that I can't remember rules."

Again he thanked her, and wished that he had gone straight on to his duty, instead of coming hither to torment himself by a picture of contentment which could never be realized. The carriage drove away, and he returned to Milly, fully determined to be staid and sage, and leave her with the feeling that he was very elderly indeed.

"I am an idle man just now," he said; "so I thought I might allow myself the pleasure of seeing you here in the quiet, where you look most at home."

"Where I am most at home, too," she answered, with her sunny smile; "though I like going out very much. But I can't get over feeling a little shy and awkward."

"Those are not just the words I should have used," he said, in a gentle, caressing voice he had—if I may employ the expression—it is the only one that serves; and, somehow, that voice made common words sound sweeter than the elaborate compliments of most men.

"My aunt laughs at me," Milly continued, with the blush a little deepened on her cheeks. "She says that another season will quite cure me of the shyness, at least."

"It will not change you much, I fancy," he replied, and then remembered that these implied flatteries did not agree well with the reputation for wisdom wherewith he meant to impress her. "Your cousin is quite well again?" he asked.

"Yes; it was only a severe cold; but Maud is so seldom ill that aunty and I were frightened; and Maud can't bear to be left alone when she is out of sorts."

He looked about, and he looked at her. The room was very pretty, and suited to her appearance; and she gave it an air so home-like! sitting there with her work-basket and her book, sharing the footstool with her pet cat. Halford felt that it would be dangerous for him to sit long in silent contemplation. He began to talk of whatever came uppermost and easiest—of the story she had been reading—her stand of flowers—the veriest trifles which make up ordinary conversation. But gradually, in her pretty way—wholly different from the artful tact of a practiced woman—she drew him on to talk of such things as she liked to hear about: his travels—the strange countries of which she dreamed—forgetting the restraint she sometimes felt in his presence, and unconsciously revealing her simple tastes and pure fancies to the world-worn man.

He gazed into her stainless soul until he had the sentiment of reverence come over him such as one sometimes feels in a foreign land, when stepping suddenly from the crowded, bustling street into the shadowy recesses of a cathedral, with the voices of unseen choristers, and the veiled tones of the organ, stealing through the stillness. It was a brief hour of rest to Kenneth Halford; then she herself uttered the words which brought him back to the reality, and its cares.

"I think you must be quite worn out with my ceaseless talk," he had said, suddenly.

"I like it so much! Nobody ever talks at all in that way—unless sometimes—but no; she is so restless, and her wit blinds me like lightning—"

"Who is that?"

"Oh, Mrs. Marchmont; she comes to see us occasionally. I think I admire her more than any woman in the world, and so does Constance—that is my dearest friend—Mr. Worthington's niece, you know."

"Yes, and a very lovely girl," he said, preferring to lead the conversation away toward her. "So she is your special friend?"

"Yes, indeed. We so often wonder if we shall ever learn to be in the least like Mrs. Marchmont. Mr. Worthington says she has talent enough to write books or paint pictures, if she would only have used it, but that she makes herself charming instead, by bringing all her gifts into conversation."

She had brought him back! He must not sit there any longer—above all, he must not hear her talk about Alice Marchmont.

"I have to thank you for a very pleasant morning," he said; "but I ought to apologize for my unconscionable visit."

His face looked gray and changed; Milly gazed at him with her eyes full of innocent pity and wonder; then a sudden pang crossed her, which, if she had been older and wiser, would have shown her at once how it was with her heart. Was it the mention of Mrs. Marchmont's name which had caused this alteration in him? Did he, too, care for this woman, who had the whole world at her feet—who seemed able, by a single smile, to bring any man under her spells? Somehow, the idea struck Milly unpleasantly; her lips retained only a very pale reflection of the smiles with which she had listened to his conversation. Something, that almost approached haughtiness, gave a new piquancy to her manner: with the inward question in regard to Mrs. Marchmont had come the sudden knowledge that he only considered herself a pretty child; and just at this moment Milly was not in the mood for such treatment.

It was not possible that, after her two romantic meetings with Kenneth Halford, he should have occupied the same place in her mind that other men did. She had dreamed a great deal about that last pleasant day at Chamouni, though she had scarcely spoken his name—even to Constance. She was perfectly unconscious how frequently his image had been in her thoughts. Fluttered and pleased as she was when he so unexpectedly appeared again in her life, she had not been disturbed by any idea of the truth; but it would only require a few annoyances like this to teach her.

"I hope you will forgive me for interrupting your quiet morning," he added, before she had finished her swift reflections.

"Oh yes; it has saved me the trouble of reading that tiresome book I had begun. You have given me the cream of it without the tediousness."

Was she trying to make speeches and indulge in epigrams, like the woman whom she admired—to be satirical and witty? Halford would have liked to ask her not to do it—to be always her simple, natural self. Then he remembered that he had no right to ask any thing of her—no right to give himself in any way a prominent thought in her mind. He had risen, but still lingered, though he knew that he ought to be gone.

"What beautiful weather we are having," he said; "it reminds me of Italy. Do you recollect how lovely the sunshine was at Chamouni?"

The words—uttered from sheer idleness—recalled to Milly's mind all his kindness upon their first meeting—the debt of gratitude which she owed him for what followed in Switzerland. She felt ashamed of her momentary, vague irritation, and wanted to make amends.

"That was the pleasantest day I ever spent in my whole life," she said, with a return of her pretty frankness. "I have not forgotten how kind you were to me, Mr. Halford."

"I wish it could have deserved the name," he answered, smiling to see how the brightness and animation came back to her face.

So they talked a little longer; then he went sadly away, and, as he descended the steps, bethought him of his self-appointed duty. He would not go to Mrs. Marchmont's house yet; he wanted an hour's solitude, and a brisk walk. He had done a foolish thing in venturing into Milly's presence; but he had grown idiotic of late: there could be no doubt of that.

He walked on, thinking what a disappointment and failure life was—thinking that he had no aim in view which would make the world's choicest honors worth winning: all vain, morbid reflections; but they are common enough to all of us, after the first glitter has rubbed off existence, and we see in their full barrenness the rocks over which our pathway must lead—the path which years before showed bright and glorious under the beautiful mists of youthful illusions.

It was late in the day before Halford found himself at Mrs. Marchmont's house; but he received the information that she was out. Her absence seemed a sort of reprieve. He felt that the sensation was an added weakness, but could not repress it. Fate, however, had no intention of indulging him in his desire to procrastinate. By the time he reached the street, Mrs. Marchmont's carriage stopped in front of him. He stepped forward, helped her out, and said,

"I had just been sent away with the news that it was only known that you were absent—the time of your return was beyond the foreknowledge of your Mercury."

"My movements are always uncertain," she replied, languidly; for it was not easy to speak at all. "You may come in now, if you choose to endure the society of a very stupid woman."

She did not want to be left alone; she felt like a child forced into the dark—any companionship was better than solitude; even the effort to control herself would do her good, for when the carriage stopped she was very near past the possibility. Since early morning she had been out on the errand in which she had wasted so much time during the past week. To-day's efforts had proved as useless as those which went before, and there was no more space left for her to struggle.

To-morrow Faulkner would present himself—to-morrow! On her way home she had actually counted, watch in hand, the hours which lay between her and the crisis of her fate; it had become an affair of hours! One faint hope left still wherewith, until evening, she could keep her brain somewhat steady—that of receiving news that an agent had succeeded in procuring the money. He had not been sanguine—in her heart she knew that it was the merest, the most improbable chance—but she held fast to it as the one slight barrier which kept despair aloof.

So she was glad to meet any mortal visage at this moment; it was only half-past four now, and she could not have an answer from her business man until six. It was better that Halford should think her ill or crazy, than be left face to face with her own soul.

She preceded him into the library and sat down—tossed her bonnet on the console; and the one glance into the mirror which she must have taken had she been called to listen to her death-sentence, showed that her hair was not disarranged, nor her features any paler than she had grown accustomed to seeing them.

"Are you quite recovered from last night's attack?" he asked. "It seems a little imprudent to have gone out."

"I am perfectly well; I can't imagine what made me faint—indigestion, perhaps. One always has dyspepsia at this season."

"Miss Portman sent me word that you were better."

"Yes, she told me of your message; it was very nice of you. My poor old cousin is a tender-hearted goose, who thinks that the wind mustn't blow over me."

"You look very pale yet," he urged; "I am sure you can not be well."

"Never mind my looks," returned she, impatiently, "I am not ill." Then hearing the irritation in her voice, she added, with one of her magical smiles, "What a temper you will think I have grown! Never mind; I mean to give up my caprices. Admit that you find me dreadfully gater—excuse the French word—it softens it a little to my vanity."

"Would you be satisfied, if I made the admission?"

"No; don't say it, if you do think so. Please don't find me changed; I like to be remembered just as I once was," she answered, rushing, in spite of herself, straight to the verge of a dramatic scene.

"But are you the same?" he asked.

"Oh, don't ask me! Is any body the same? They talk of a physical change once in seven years, that makes new creatures of us; why not a mental, moral, or immoral, as you please? There's a question for the doctors! When I get leisure I shall study the matter, and write a magazine paper on it."

He laughed a little; but there was no lightness in his thoughts. He could not decide whether she was all sparkle and hardness, like the diamonds for which she had allowed herself to be sold years before, or had learned completely to smother her feelings, because it was her only chance of peace and safety.

"And talking of magazine papers," she continued; "do you mean to give us something else—scientific, and learned, and awful?"

"Indeed, I do not know; I am growing fairly ashamed of my own indolence and waste of time."

"Take care! I'll not have you give me covert thrusts under the guise of reproaches to yourself. Wasting time—what is that line about rendering an account for each idle word and hour? Ciel! what a list there must be! Oh, that sounds irreverent."

"And that you would not be."

"I hope not; it is doubly odious in a woman. But one gets in the habit of laughing at everything, just to make people stare, or to be thought witty. It's a dreadful habit."

"It is, indeed," he said; and knew that his voice sounded priggish and sententious, but could not change it.

"I'll not be lectured," cried she. "If I abuse myself, it is with the expectation that you will contradict me."

"I fancy it will be necessary for you often to give me a hint, that I may be sure what you really do mean."

She did not notice his words, saying, suddenly,

"Do you know what our talk about right and wrong brings up? The country-place where we were that last summer. Don't you remember the little church down in the village? Oh, Kenneth, Kenneth, how pleasant it was to go there!—don't you remember?"

How often during the first years of separation, while remembrance was still a bitter pain, he had thought of those visits to the quiet chapel, and repeated Longfellow's pretty lines about the lost girl who looked like gleaning Ruth—repeated them, and stamped his feet on the hot Egyptian sands in rage and anguish. But the reality to which he had returned was not the old dream; he could not speak of those recollections to this woman with the flashing, restless eyes, so unlike the light which they poured on him once—this chameleon, vexing him by her quick changes and brief glimpses of the girlish creature whom he had loved.

"But, somehow, I hate our churches in town," she was saying, when he got his thoughts back from that mental view of himself, gazing off at the pyramids through the white distance, and moaning his grief out in poetry. "Besides, one is always too tired to go! Just think, those Spanish people next door always dance on Sunday night; and I have been to them sometimes—how I hated

myself for doing what I thought wicked; but one does so many hateful things! Dear me, don't sit looking so grave."

"Was I looking grave?"

"A perfect monument of reproach; and I don't liked to be reproached."

"I have never done it," he answered, slowly—"never."

"You had no right—no reason!" she cried, with sudden passion. "I could not help myself; you know that. Every relative I had in the world setting at me! Oh, you never can understand what I endured!"

His face had looked so like the old time, that she could not forbear crying out, in the quick rush of memory, without thinking how her words might sound.

"I always knew," he replied, in a kind voice. "Even in the height of my anger, I always pitied you as much as I did myself."

"That was like you—such a good, patient Kenneth! Perhaps I might have behaved differently; but I was always a coward. I could not bear to be frowned at; and you will never know half the means they used—even my own mother against me! Oh, my mother, my mother! if she had only been another sort of woman! I never cease to be thankful that I have no children; at least, I can not make their existence such a curse as she did mine."

"Hush, hush!" he said, inexpressibly pained by her wild looks and words. "You don't know what you are saying."

"Let us talk of something else," she cried; "it is not well to think. Have you heard the new opera they are to give next week, for the first time here? One can always talk about the opera— Oh, Kenneth, don't watch me like that! I know I am frivolous and wicked; but don't look so disappointed!"

She could not help it; all sorts of insane speeches would force an utterance, in spite of her. She could not lose this friend—she did not think about his making love to her—she did not want it—only, in her misery, she could not bear to see disapproval in any countenance; her own thoughts and condemnation were enough. Perhaps a little longer, and even her good name must go; she would hold fast to every precious thing while she could. For the present, the scorn and contempt must lie between her and her own soul; she could not support even disapproval from him.

"Don't look disappointed, Kenneth," she repeated. "Wait a few weeks; who knows—perhaps I shall be less restless and changeable—"

She stopped short. A few weeks—she might as well ask him to wait and see what she would be like in eternity! She to talk of weeks, when only brief hours hung between her and ruin! She could fairly hear Dick Faulkner's odious step, that she knew so well—those firm, quick footfalls, the sound of which had so often sickened her during the weeks which led to this awful moment. She could absolutely see his loathed face peering into her own, with its smile of triumph! and she had nothing to propose—just as unprepared as the day he was last there; and yet she must meet him. The picture her vivid fancy drew so completely overpowered her that, before she was aware, she had cried out bitterly,

"Oh, pity me, Kenneth, pity me!"

It was spoken! She had broken down at last; her whole secret had nearly escaped in that appeal. She was close to a burst of frenzied sobs, and an hysterical scene that would have appeared like insanity or play-acting to a well-regulated person.

What could he think? Only that this woman loved him—that she feared, in spite of his previous words, he did not mean to take up the thread of their destinies from the point where stronger hands had torn it out of their grasp. It was impossible to think any thing else, and not to believe, also, that she suffered so horribly at the dread of his not forgiving her, that it overcame even her pride and feminine reticence. Yet, even as he admitted it to himself, some perception struck him that this was not the conduct of a woman who loved. It did not, it could not, occur to his mind that any terrible secret burdened her soul, and made her long for sympathy; he could only believe that, if she did not care for him, she was leading him on from an impulse of fiendish coquetry; but in either case he must speak. He must speak, though he, too, was haunted by a quick vision—of the pretty room where he had that morning sat with Milly Crofton, her pure girl's face gazing at him, so free from worldly emotion—even from the common cares which must leave their impress upon any countenance after twenty-five.

"I came here to-day to talk seriously with you," he said, and knew that his voice sounded hard and cold.

She thought he was about to remonstrate upon the folly of her life—to reproach her for wasting it—perhaps, to tell her of vague rumors which might have fallen from Dick Faulkner's venomous lips.

"No, no," she exclaimed, trying to smile; "don't talk seriously; we are safest on the surface."

"You and I can not stay there," he continued. "Do you remember what I said to you the other night?"

She shook her head, making a vain effort to recall any special words that he might have spoken. What could they have been about? Had he heard vaguely of her difficulties, and come to help her? Oh, if he could—if he would! She might better tell him the whole; even if it cost her his friendship and esteem, she could, at least, have her life free from Dick Faulkner. It was only a second's wild thought—she remembered that he was powerless. He was not rich enough at so short notice to raise the amount she required. If he could, if he were able to borrow it, she must not ask the favor; ten to one, she should not be able to repay it in time, if ever, and he might be ruined. So that quick hope died out like those which had gone before. She sat looking straight at him, yet not seeing a line of his features in the blinding pain which made her head reel till sparks of fire danced before her eyes.

He could not tell from her words—what he believed her pretended forgetfulness—whether she was afraid of betraying herself, or was only coquetting with him. He grew very angry at that suspicion—there was a bitter pang at his heart all the while—but he must go on.

"You can not, I think, have forgotten what I said," he began again.

"Oh, I dare say—" She stopped short, conscious that she was making some irrelevant reply, though not certain what he had said. "I beg your pardon—did I interrupt you?"

"I said you had not forgotten," he repeated, rather sternly.

"I wish I could," she muttered, too low for him to catch the bitter complaint; "I wish I could!"

"We were talking of the past—"

"Then we had better have let it alone," she broke in, passionately. "I want neither to look forward or back; let me rest where I am, while it is possible."

"I must finish; I must tell you what is in my mind," he persisted, more and more convinced that she was trifling, and feeling his heart harden toward her.

"Oh, tell me then," she said, impatiently, throwing herself back in her chair, and trying to fasten her attention upon his words, though the effort made her head ache worse than ever, and she still dreaded reproaches or remonstrances upon her wasted life. "You want to scold me—no wonder; but I wish you wouldn't! You couldn't say any thing half so bad as I have said to myself—not a thousandth part so bad as I deserve."

"I did not dream of doing any thing of the kind," he answered. "I only wanted you to remember our conversation in the opera-box the other evening."

"Then I can't—do believe me. I am not always false—what object could I have?" cried she, angrily—not because she felt in a rage; it was pure nervousness that rendered her voice sharp.

"I said that it would still be possible to bridge over the gulf which separates us from our youth—"

"Never, never!" she interrupted, dimly comprehending now what errand had brought him, yet not trusting her own intuitions. "We could not do that; it is impossible."

"Not if you will be my wife," he said, slowly, conscious that never was woman wooed in such a cast-iron sort of fashion, but not able to make either tone or manner one whit warmer.

"Your wife!" she repeated, in a bewildered way. "I be your wife?"

"I came here this morning to ask you," he continued.

"You don't mean that," she exclaimed, still too much confused to believe him in earnest. "That is carrying nonsense too far, even for amusement. Don't say such things."

"I am speaking seriously," he said; and a second glance showed her, blind as she was, that he meant it.

"Oh, Kenneth!" she faltered.

"I come with the old question, Alice," he said, for the first time calling her by the familiar name, and painfully aware, as he uttered it, that it no longer possessed the slightest music to his ear. "Will you marry me?"

"I marry you?" she echoed.

"I said I came with the old question," returned he, not perceiving until he had spoken that he was only repeating himself—to her whose presence had once been a spell to rouse him easily into eloquent speech—into the passionate utterance which ought to come natural to a lover.

"But do you come with the old heart?" cried she, suddenly. "Oh, Kenneth, Kenneth, why do you talk like this! It can not be—it can never be—you feel, you know, that it ought not."

"Tell me why, Alice?"

"Even if you came with the old love warm in your heart, it could not! We are worlds and worlds apart; I would not dare let you approach nearer. But you don't, Kenneth; it is only the memory of the dead dream—the dear, sweet dream."

"Not dead—"

"Yes, and the girl you loved dead with it! It is only that you are attracted to me by the occasional likeness I have to her; but I am not she—O Heaven, how different!"

"Alice," he said, "I come to you in earnest; I don't understand your words or manner; this is a serious moment. Surely you would not coquet with me now; you can not be so changed as that."

"Changed in every way," she cried. "I am not the Alice you knew; do understand that! But I would not coquet or trifle; you are right there; try to comprehend."

"Surely, you are not surprised—"

"Yes, yes!"

"But you must have expected me to speak."

"Never; indeed I did not. I thought you liked to recollect the pretty dream—that it pleased you to stray toward the old time—that there might be occasional vague regrets over the vanished hope; but not this—nothing like this."

"You might have known me better."

"And that is what it is," she went on—"just an unreal sentiment born out of old memories; nothing else."

"And—and you have felt so, too?"

He could scarcely have put a question so misplaced, or in a more awkward fashion; but it was all he could say.

"What have my feelings to do with it?" she asked.

"If you remembered—if you cared—"

"Why, you thought I loved you!" she broke in.

"Don't accuse me of being vain and unmanly," he exclaimed. "At least, you know that I am not mean and base."

She started from her chair, then as quickly resumed her seat: a sweet, womanly smile came across the trouble in her face.

"I don't think so; you know I could not. It all comes to me now; I understand every thing. You thought I loved you—don't say a word! Kenneth, you are a good man—a noble heart. You came to me because you thought that some idle words you had spoken made it your duty; but you don't love me."

"Have you not believed that I did?"

"No; it was impossible."

"But after what I said—"

"I did not even remember it. If I noticed it at the time, I only supposed it a mere compliment—I am so used to sentimental talk! Stop, Kenneth; don't interrupt; don't try for pretty words; we must be perfectly frank and honest now."

"Yes, whatever comes."

"Dear old friend, if you loved me ever so well, I would not marry you; yet you are good and noble to have come. I could hate or laugh at another man who fancied that I cared for him, and so offered me his hand; but it was generous of you."

"Then my—my loving you would make no difference?"

"None! Nothing could make any difference—nothing under heaven. Kenneth, Kenneth, if we were in different worlds, we could not be more completely separated; if I were dead and buried, we could not. Yes, that's it—think of Alice as dead; think of her kindly, and pity me. I could bear your pity; and oh, Kenneth, I am the most miserable woman alive!"

She buried her face on the arm of her chair, and for an instant sobbed uncontrollably, though she shed no tears.

"You drive me wild!" he exclaimed. "You say that we are separated forever, yet in the same breath you talk of your misery."

"Yes," she said, raising her head and forcing herself back to a sort of composure. "I forgot how it would sound; it seems as if I meant that I cared for you. Then I must tell you this—you have no part in my trouble."

"Is there in your mind some scruple, some fancy, that, because my heart is not the boy's heart, you must refuse it?" he questioned, determined, at least, to be sure that he had done no wrong.

"Not that. Oh, it is impossible to explain —not where you are concerned, though. I don't mean to speak rudely, but I have scarcely had time to think about you since you returned. I was glad to see you—I am glad—

but it has no reference to the past; I couldn't think of you in that way—you're not vexed?"

"No, no; speak your thought out."

"You can listen, because your heart is not touched either. Why, if I had that added to all I bear, I should go mad. I caused you trouble enough in the old days; thank Heaven! I am powerless now. As for the rest, what worries me I can not tell you—only so much; and believe me now—it has nothing in common with thoughts of you. Don't ask me any questions; only be my friend. Promise that."

"I do—always your friend; nothing could ever happen which would make me otherwise."

She felt herself growing very faint; his words roused anew the thought of what dire mischance tarried just beyond. Her lips were so dry and parched that she could with difficulty articulate, yet she went on speaking; any thing was better than to sit silent with that horrible dread in her soul—the skeleton grinning between her and this generous-hearted man, who, in spite of his kindness, was as powerless to aid her as if he had been an indifferent stranger.

"Some time you will really love, and marry," she said—"perhaps some pretty creature like Milly Crofton. I often watch her, and think she is like the girl you used to know—the heart they killed, Kenneth."

"My poor Alice!" he murmured, involuntarily giving voice to the great pity which stirred his soul; for he knew that, whatever might be the secret of her suffering, it was real.

"Yes, call me that; think of me so," she said; then the faintness against which she had been struggling for many moments grew so strong, so like the chill of death, that she was forced to add, "I think you must go away now, I am so tired."

He saw that her very lips were blue-white; the face leaning back against the cushions of the chair was so ghastly that he could scarcely repress a cry of alarm. He hurried to a table where there sat a carafe of water, poured out a glass, brought it, and obliged her to drink. In a few moments she was better, could sit up, smile and speak.

"I ought not to have worried you when you were ill," he said, remorsefully.

"No, no; I am glad you came. We shall be friends, Kenneth—always friends?"

"Always, Alice."

"Yes, whatever comes. I believe you would pity me— Don't look at me so, Kenneth; are you thinking that I am half mad? Sometimes I think so. It's only my absurd life; I have had no rest for weeks; but it will soon be over now—very soon."

"What, Alice?"

She was thinking of the one way out which presented itself—the one hope of freedom; the horrible thought which had been growing stronger in her mind as these last awful days drifted by. Nothing else left—but she could die! She had tried to put it from her, this crowning wicked impulse, but it would not go; and as she glanced at the clock, saw that the hour was near when her last vague chance of relief must prove vain as the rest, it started up in her soul so like a full-formed resolution that it broke through her words.

"What will be soon over—what do you mean?" she heard him ask.

"Why, all the trouble—I mean the season will end, spring come, and I shall go into the country. Indeed, I am so worn out that I don't know what I say."

"I shall go, that you may lie down and sleep," he said, extending his hand.

She caught it, and held it fast in her cold fingers; it was dreadful to be left alone! Then, with her usual inconsistency, her ability to think a dozen things at once, came the idea that she might have had his support; he would never have gone back, once pledged. Nothing could have induced her to drag him down in her fall; his love, if she could have had it, would have proved an added terror; yet her heart grew bitter to think that she had lost it. More than all, she could not bear to part with him because he was connected with her lost past.

"You will think of me at my best," she said. "You'll not see me like this again. Will you remember me sometimes when you are happy with pretty little Milly?"

"Why do you talk so much of her? I scarcely know the child."

"But you love her—I mean you will; I feel it. She will make you happy; oh, I am glad of that. She will be like the old dream to you—as if these years had not come between. But no; I can't have that. You must not forget me. Think of the Alice you knew as dead. I must have my place."

"You torture me!" he cried. "I can't understand you! If you could love me, let me try to make you happy. We will go back together to the old dream, away from this weary bustle, and look for our lost happiness."

"We couldn't find it, Kenneth! Don't be vexed with me; no wonder I puzzle you. I can't tell, myself, how much of me is real. But, indeed, I don't want your love. You may believe that."

"But you will have my friendship?"

"So thankfully! There, go now, before I say something else silly or insane."

He took her hand again with a feeling of profound pity, and was raising it to his lips. She snatched it away, startling him anew by her vehemence—it was the hand Dick Faulkner had kissed!

"Not that!" she exclaimed; "not that, for the world!"

Then, even in this moment of acute suffering, with the consciousness full upon her that soon she must make a choice between disgrace and death, the coquetry ingrained in her nature came up. At least, it seemed such to herself, only she was in a sort of earnest all the while, giving way to the emotion only excitable people can understand, which is neither exactly of the head nor heart, yet belongs to both.

"You shall kiss the other," she said, and held it up with a gesture and glance which made her a very Circe.

He kissed it gravely: this was not the kind of spell to fascinate him, because it was not like the Alice of former days.

"The last kiss," she added; "but your golden-haired ideal need never be jealous, though no other men's lips shall blot out the touch of yours, Kenneth."

So he went away, conscious that he left behind him forever the latest memory of the old dream. He was naturally enough a little saddened for the time, but could not resist a feeling of self-gratulation that he had proved true to his own sense of honor. How hard the struggle to go to that woman with his question, he fully now appreciated by the sense of relief which came over his mind. He was sorry for her; he saw that she suffered; yet he could not decide whether she was the most consummate actress that ever lived, the creature of some passing impulse, or indeed oppressed by a secret trouble under the excitement and brightness of her life.

As the door closed, Alice Marchmont sank back in her chair, and sat with her eyes fixed upon the clock. The room was quite dark now, except where the bright fire-light illuminated it, reflected upon the face of the pretty pendule so that she could see where the hands pointed.

Twenty minutes to six — twenty minutes! She sat still and waited, counting the seconds as they dragged by, yet with scores of varying thoughts in her mind all the while. At last the bell-like chime sounded the hour; a moment after, the door-bell rang. She did not stir; she had a feeling as if she were dead and cold, and must sit there staring out through the darkness till the Last Judgment.

The door opened—a servant with a salver in his hand.

"I beg madame's pardon; I only just learned that she was here, else I should have lighted the candles; I was out on madame's service."

It was a caprice of hers never to burn gas in her rooms: there was no possible expense, great or small, she had failed to incur.

"Who rang, Ferguson?"

"Only a person with this letter, madame. Shall I light the room?"

"No; go away, please."

The model domestic departed; she tore open the envelope—only another failure; but it was the last!

She sat still for a few moments longer—not faint—not suffering acutely—her powers seemed deadened; then she rose and walked quietly away to her chamber.

CHAPTER XI.

THE POTENT NAME.

ALL that had happened, and was still to happen, did not alter the fact that Mrs. Marchmont must dress and go out to dine; for, at all events, she had not yet left the world. To send a refusal and remain at home was out of the question. She would have rushed into the society of a coterie of ghosts beckoning with spectral fingers to worse than the horrors of a German romance, rather than keep herself company.

She dared not stay at home, that dreadful idea of self-destruction so pursued her. It might come to this; she expected now that it would; but it was not time yet, and solitude would drive her so mad that she might attempt her own life before she knew really what she was doing.

As she entered her dressing-room Pauline the faithful gave her one glance, and uttered a little cry of alarm.

"Are you growing hysterical?" asked her mistress, coldly.

"I beg madame's pardon," apologized the woman; "but if madame could see how pale she is she would be herself startled."

"I am not so easily alarmed," she replied. "But I suppose you can make my cheeks red; you have something that you put on your own."

"Oh, pardon; I could do it beautifully, if madame permits, just by rubbing the cheeks with a peculiar red ribbon. Nobody could ever suspect."

"I don't care how you do it, or who suspects," she answered, sitting down in a chair by her dressing-table, though not glancing toward the glass. "I am very cross, Pauline, but don't mind."

"Never; madame is never that! She is not well just now; but cross? she is like the angels."

"Very like," returned Mrs. Marchmont, with a bitter laugh, and added, to herself, "there are two sorts."

"Madame shall dine out?" questioned Pauline.

"Yes; where is Miss Portman?"

"She have gone to her old friend's, Miss Livingston's."

"Yes, I know. What time is it?"

"Not quite seven, if madame pleases."

"Dress me, Pauline. Don't ask me what I will put on; pull my chair away from the glass. Be sure you make me handsome, very handsome; I have a special reason."

If it should be the last night any human being connected with her society world ever saw her among them again; if, on coming from John Worthington's house, she knew that nothing remained for her but death, at least let them remember this evening. Ah, he would be sorry, that good, tried friend; and Kenneth too: there was nobody else to get beyond horror or wonder. And she had come to this!

she, Alice Marchmont; and the time had been, in her girlish days, when, in spite of worldly influences, in spite of a frivolous mother's example, she had said her prayers and read her Bible, and allowed the one sensible woman who ever approached her at that season—a governess, of whom Mrs. Bemers got rid of as soon as possible—to teach her the blessed doctrines of the Catholic faith; when the Church services were familiar to her, and the thought of Confirmation a pleasant one, and no shadow troubled her soul of the season when she, in her turn, should crucify the Christ anew by willful departure from his teachings.

She sat motionless as a stone image under Pauline's skillful hands, till at length an exclamation from the French woman, who could not longer support the silence, made her look up.

"Well?" she asked.

"Madame is so beautiful! if madame would only take one little peep in the miroir."

Mrs. Marchmont rose, walked to the cheval-glass at the end of the room, and surveyed her full-length image. The dress was some marvelous tint of green, so pale as to look almost white, with long hanging sleeves, showing the white arms; precious old cameos encircling her neck, spots of vivid rose-color tinting her cheeks, and the great brown eyes almost black with the pain which cut, like icicles, across her heart—a sharp, physical pain, added to her mental distress.

"I shall not leave the house till eight," she said, turning away after one glance. "How much time yet?"

"Twenty minutes," replied Pauline, in a tone of mortal injury which struck the other's ear.

"You have done wonders," she said; "I thank you very much. Come and tell me when it is eight o'clock."

Pauline went softly out; there was something very odd about her mistress to-night, something which she could not understand; but she was a silent creature, and did not even express her thoughts to the band below stairs.

Mrs. Marchmont walked slowly up and down the room several times, her hands crossed behind her back, her head drooped. At length she unlocked the safe where she kept such of her jewels as were in her possession, and took out a tiny phial. It contained opium. It had lain there since an illness she had in the autumn. Why she kept it she had never known. As she held up the flacon to the light, shaking it slowly, she felt that now she did understand. An instant after, she asked herself was she capable of doing the deed? Of physical pain she had a great dread; but the death that this dark liquid would bring was so easy! And she had come to this! she, who even a month before would have said that she believed in God, and trusted him, believed in the Bible too, reckless as she was, page for page and word for word, weak and superstitious as the faith might appear to modern philosophy.

This was the point to which life had brought her, the life she had willfully, determinedly chosen, as she thought now, though, in reality, once drawn into the vortex, she had been whirled on and on without space for reflection. The bitterest remembrance in her mind was the reason which obliged her to contemplate this last step, this irremediable sin. Dick Faulkner's kiss still burned upon her hand; his shameful words yet rang in her ear. She had lived to have an avowal of degrading affection forced upon her: worse than that, she had arrived at a crisis where her good name must be utterly ruined by the slanders of this wretch, or she end her mortal career with a dose of the poison she held in her hand. Yes, one other way out—she had to repeat it to herself—dishonor!

And now she saw what had really brought her to this strait: it was rather what the world calls flirtation, permits and approves, than the business exigencies of the case. Had her conduct been always circumspect and guarded, Faulkner's power to harm her would be confined to their moneyed relations; but pecuniary ruin was the least misfortune which menaced her now. She had allowed herself to be drawn into receiving his attentions; she had gone on and on, as scores of women have done before, and now she stood face to face with the loathsome, abhorrent truth, stripped of the disguises in which she had so enveloped it that she had never perceived its real shape.

There is an old-fashioned, almost an antiquated, Book wherein are set down these words, from the lips of the one Preacher whose every syllable is truth: "The man who looketh upon a woman to lust after her hath already committed adultery in his heart." The married woman who indulges in flirtation, the woman who receives tender looks and whispers from a married man, is a woman who has been sullied by such thoughts in the man's mind. This sounds coarse; but this is a coarse world, and ours a coarse century, in spite of the fine names under which we clothe our vices and our crimes. These things look very differently set down in the language they deserve, instead of dressed up in the glowing paragraphs of sensation novels or French plays; but we have trifled with the glittering exterior long enough; it is time to make ourselves see the blackness and the rottenness under.

In this hour Alice Marchmont saw it plainly enough, and felt that nothing could ever free her soul from the degradation of all that she had brought upon it. If she could be liberated to-morrow, the horrible fact would remain that she had rendered it possible for a bad man to speak vile words; she could never wash that memory out, and there could be no punishment equal to it.

A rap at the door roused her from her maddening reflections. She hid the phial, and when Pauline entered was throwing her opera-cloak about her shoulders. It was eight o'clock, and the carriage had been waiting some time. She went her way.

Among the circle of guests gathered in Mr. Worthington's library, until such time as Mrs. Marchmont's arrival should enable them to eat their dinner, were Halford and Milly Crofton.

"I supposed you would be late," her host said, hurrying forward to the door to meet her.

"Of course you thought something bad of me," she replied, gayly; "you always have—a liberty that comes of old acquaintance."

"You like it," said he; "you know you do! You get fed with so much sugar that it suits you to come, now and then, and let me say sharp things to you."

"They keep my mind in tone," she answered. "But really, I think you look more wicked than usual to-night."

"And you—are you well again?"

"Look at me," she said, smiling.

"Oh, this is your company face; I'll study it later."

He laughed, and passed her on to his niece, a pretty girl of about Milly Crofton's age, to whom Mrs. Marchmont said a dozen charming things in a breath, and thought,

"I dare say you think what would you give to be like me. Ah, if we could change. 'Oh, my youth, my youth!"

But neither despair nor sentiment could be indulged just then; she had only time for a word with Halford, a flattering greeting to Milly, who had forgotten her momentary annoyance of the morning, and was as enthusiastic as ever in her admiration of the beautiful woman. Dinner was announced, the guests marshaled in their proper order, and Mrs. Marchmont was led away by her host.

It was a delightful party; there were not more than a dozen people, but chosen with the tact Mr. Worthington displayed on such occasions—a dinner to be remembered by any quiet person, who had leisure to think and to recollect. Mrs. Marchmont as far outshone her ordinary self as, in her mildest moments, she outshone ordinary women; and all the while she was marveling whether it was only a dream, every thing seemed so far off and unreal.

She saw Kenneth Halford seated by pretty Milly at the other end of the table, looking at her occasionally in a kind of wonder, then turning back to his neighbor with an expression of rest on his face. She saw how it would be—he might not think it now—but he would marry that young girl. It did not matter, so far as she was herself concerned; nothing mattered. There was no man living whom she would dare to wed. Oh Heaven! in all her list of adorers and friends, not one but would shrink away in horror at a perception of the truth.

The money—the money!

Somebody else's name—some help!

All these wild thoughts in her mind while the conversation went on, while she was talking and laughing, wondering vaguely if she should lose her last gleam of reason, scream

suddenly, stab herself with the carving-knife by Mr. Worthington's plate, and make an end of it—and in the midst scenes from the old days rising whenever she looked at Kenneth Halford. The gray autumn afternoon in its quiet; the blue smoke curling up among the trees; the countenance which she saw across the lights, so calm and grave, gazing into that young girl's eyes—she could see it as it looked on that still afternoon when he had said farewell to that other girl, as much a stranger now to Alice Marchmont as the pretty, innocent creature before her. The recollection, too, of what awaited her return home—that came in the jumble of her thoughts also. She could see the phial of nauseous black liquid where she had hidden it, and catch the sickening odor of the poison, growing faint and weak as if the fatal draught already stupefied her senses.

There was nothing spared her, for somebody began to talk of a recent venture in stocks which had astonished Wall Street—some bold outsider who had accumulated a vast fortune in a few weeks.

"To lose it, probably, in as short a time," John Worthington said, when the story ended. "The taste for gambling, once formed, is not easily subdued; the man will go back."

"Gambling is a rather harsh word," some woman said.

"I don't know of any other that applies," he answered; "do you?"

"Please to recollect that my husband is a Wall Street man," laughed she.

"Your husband is a regular commission-broker, doing a legitimate business, and never by any chance going outside of it. That is one thing—an honest, honorable occupation. The man who goes into Wall Street to throw his money upon some stock is a gambler as much as the man who sits down at the green table and risks his substance."

"I don't think those would be very popular doctrines in our day," Kenneth Halford said.

"Is the truth ever popular?" demanded Worthington.

"And what do you call the woman who 'dabbles in stocks?'" asked the lady who had just spoken, only too familiar, like the rest of us, with the cant phrases used to express such transactions.

"I call her a very unwise person," Mr. Worthington answered, laughing, unwilling to be drawn into a serious argument upon the subject at his own table.

"He shall not get out of it in that way—shall he, Mrs. Marchmont?" persisted Mrs. Townley.

"No, indeed," returned she, feeling herself shiver from head to foot. "We will know just how bad things he dares think of us in his bachelor mind."

"The queen has spoken," some man said. "Out with it, Worthington."

"I call her a gambler too, if you will have plain words," he replied, trying to speak jest-

5

ingly, though it was difficult upon a matter where he felt so keenly—"a gambler, and with less excuse than a man, because she forsakes her sphere to reach the temptation."

A chorus of laughing expostulations greeted the remark; then Mrs. Marchmont said, gayly,

"Please to remember how much woman's sphere has widened; it takes in every thing, even to Wall Street."

"I'll not jest upon the subject," he said, pleasantly. "Suppose we talk of something else, for I have a bad habit of calling a spade by its name."

"Oh, I insist on knowing what makes you severe," continued Alice. "Upon my word, Mrs. Townley, I believe he has been wandering from the path of rectitude, and has suffered for it."

"I ?" he exclaimed, with a genuine horror which made them all laugh again. "I would as soon put my hand in the fire."

"We all know that a burned child dreads it," cried she, teasingly.

He laughed, and attempted to change the conversation; but some reckless impulse, which she could not resist, forced her to annoy him by persisting in the discussion, and Mrs. Townley joined her from mere frivolity. The dinner had lasted an unconscionable length of time. It seemed to Mrs. Marchmont that the morrow must have come, it appeared so long since they sat down at the table, glittering with plate and delicate Sèvres, and odorous with flowers born in warm Southern lands.

"We insist on having the truth; don't we, Mrs. Marchmont?" cried Mrs. Townley, in her affected way.

"Yes; either he shall make a full confession, and admit that he learned his scruples from a severe lesson, else he shall give his reasons for flying in the face of popular opinion in this savage fashion," she said.

"There is no way out, Worthington," laughed a male guest.

At this instant a message was brought Miss Constance by one of the servants.

"Oh, uncle," she said, in the deep distress which trifles cause at her age, "we are so late with dinner that some friends I invited for the evening have already come."

"What a terrible catastrophe," he replied, smiling. "Very well, dear, you and my little Milly shall run away to them; we will all come presently."

Halford rose to open the door for the two girls. Milly gave him a shy, inquiring glance, which caused him to follow them out, wondering a little at such folly on his part; and Mrs. Marchmont observed him go.

"If you will promise not to make me argue, and will leave the subject after," Worthington said, "I'll tell you a story, now that those two children are gone. Perhaps, then, none of you will marvel at my severity."

"Is it very sensational and exciting?" demanded Mrs. Marchmont, with a pretty eagerness, while it was all she could do to keep from springing up and running away, to escape this new torture.

"Yes; and the best, or the worst, of it is, that it is true."

"How delightful!" cooed Mrs. Townley.

"Fill my glass with Champagne first," laughed Alice; "I'm an impressionable young person, and may faint before you finish."

"It was only a year ago," John Worthington said, trying to keep his voice quiet and unmoved, "that I went home to dine with a friend who had been at my office on business. It was very late: when we got to the house, the servant told us that his mistress had started for Albany an hour before; a telegram had come announcing her mother's illness. He gave his master a letter, and went out. I stood and looked at my friend as he opened it and began to read; before he had finished the page, he fell at my feet in a sort of fit—"

"Oh, go on!" pleaded Mrs. Townley, while Alice Marchmont leaned back in her chair, smiling still.

"This man had been enduring terrible business anxieties for months," he continued; "I had succeeded this very day in assisting him; we had gone to the house together to gratify his wife by the news, for he loved her."

"She was not to blame for her mother's illness; relations are always committing some indiscretion," said Mrs. Marchmont, with a flippancy so out of place that it shocked her own delicate sense of tact, though she could not keep silent.

"This letter was to tell her husband that for the past year she had allowed a man of their acquaintance to buy stocks for her," pursued Worthington, slowly. "He had led her on and on, deceived her, lied to her—at last came with the news that she owed him a large sum—either she must run away with him or he would expose the whole affair, and prosecute her husband: she had gone."

There was an instant's silence, broken by expressions of horror.

"But he could not have been a man of business or respectability, since he was willing to ruin his own future," Mrs. Townley said.

"Both; that is, he was received in society; every body knew him for a bad man," Worthington said.

"Go on," Mrs. Marchmont urged, in a low voice.

"Yes; what did the husband do?" asked Mrs. Townley. "Left the creature to the fate she deserved, I suppose."

"He found the route his wife had taken; she was to meet this man in a Southern city, and go to Cuba—from there to South America. He reached the rendezvous before the villain who had helped her to this, and he took her home with him."

"What! he forgave her?"

"Yes, he forgave her—paid the debt, and was ruined."

"And did he kill the man?" demanded some one.

"No; because that would have disgraced his wife," Worthington replied, playing with his fork in an absent way.

"No wonder you have a horror of stock speculations," said Mrs. Townley, with a shudder.

"Mr. Worthington!"

It was Alice Marchmont who spoke his name. He looked up at her, and waited for her to go on.

"Would you have forgiven the woman?"

The answer rang out slow and ominously firm.

"No."

Mrs. Marchmont arranged the lace upon her bosom, and looked already a little weary of the subject.

"Oh, you hard-hearted man!" cried Mrs. Townley; and the men added one thing, most of the women another.

"I might forgive a woman who was unfortunate enough to love where she ought not," John Worthington said. "I would never forgive one who placed herself in the position this woman did, from coquetry, or a cold-blooded design to make a merchandise of her smiles, and go to the extremest verge of decency and dishonor without going over."

As he ceased speaking there was a movement to rise. It was so difficult for Alice Marchmont to get out of her chair, it seemed to her that her limbs were half paralyzed; but she struggled to her feet, took Mr. Worthington's arm, and her laugh rang out gay and unconcerned.

They went up to the drawing-room. She was still the centre of attraction; they made her talk, they forced her to sing; and each instant she grew more brilliant and beautiful, as the fever in her veins drove her nearer and nearer absolute insanity. Then there was a brief space of quiet for her; she knew that Halford had come to her side while she sung, at somebody's request, a song of the old, old days. She glanced down the room, and saw pretty Milly looking at them, and thought, drearily,

"She loves him; let him go to her. I can not give him the girl he lost, but this pure creature is more like her than I; let him go. I dare not even have his friendship, which he promised; I can keep nothing; I am alone."

All the while there was a sharp pain beyond her bitterness, beyond the insane whirl of her thoughts. A year before she might have taught this man to love her anew; she might have had her girlhood back; but now? Oh, now she regarded the possibility as a lost soul in the depths of purgatory might look back over the records of its earthly existence, and see where sin avoided would have led it far from the present agony.

"You must go and talk to those young girls," she said. "I have been looking at Milly to-night; she reminds me more than ever of the girl we used to know. Go to her, Kenneth;

pray God that she may never change so that she shall look back on herself as she is now, and wonder if she can be the same."

"Your voice sounds so mournful," he said; "I am sure you are ill."

"Ill? I have no time to be! Don't you know that I am a star-actress? I never forget that I am before the foot-lights."

The interview of the morning left no trouble or constraint in either of their minds. He was glad that he had spoken — glad that it was over; but his sympathy was profound, and she would always possess for him an interest peculiarly her own—occupy a place in his thoughts which no other woman could usurp. Her laugh jarred upon his ear; after what he had seen that day it sounded forced and unnatural. He glanced, too, at Milly sitting there in her girlish innocence—truly, an image of rest. He was worn and weary—glad to be done with worldly women and their ways. At this moment Mr. Worthington came up, and Halford moved to Milly's side; it was pleasant to see the smile which lighted her eyes, and to think that it might be possible to win her love and be ministered to by her tenderness—somewhat selfish in his fancies—after the habit of men who have reached his age.

"I want you to come and see the alterations I have made in my study," John Worthington said. "You abused it for a den the last time you were here. I consulted Constance's taste, and now I suppose you will say that it is much too fine for a crabbed old bachelor."

"I shall certainly find fault because you consulted any feminine authority besides mine," she said.

He smiled at her pleasantly; she had no idea of a certain secret which had lain in his heart for years.

"I did remember the color you said I ought to have, but I was afraid of boring you by asking your advice."

"The excuse is worse than the offense," she replied. "But, indeed, to-night you seem determined to add enormously to your catalogue of faults."

"Why don't you say crimes, and be done with it?" laughed he.

"Don't use such a horrible word," she exclaimed, quickly, and as quickly forced her voice back to the indolent quiet proper to the occasion. "You've not said a single complimentary thing to me this evening."

"But I never do."

"Then it is time you began. Your education has been dreadfully neglected; I really must take you in hand."

"Very well; I promise to prove a docile, if not an intelligent pupil."

"Oh, don't be so horribly correct even in your language; at least, show your claim to humanity by making a few lapses there."

"I make them often enough, in every way; you don't think I set myself up as a criterion, or a judge?"

"You are hard on people's failings—don't deny it. Because you can be stately and determined, don't blame weaker mortals for not attaining to your pitch of perfection."

"Upon my word, you are downright ill-natured! What a disagreeable old fossil you make me out."

"I think you the best man in the world, but I am horribly afraid of you," she replied, lightly, yet with a certain earnestness in her voice.

It was dangerous, but she found a relief in going as near the truth as she dared.

"Afraid of me, indeed; you were the most impertinent critic I ever had, even as a child."

"Was I? Tell me; was I a nice child?"

"The most spoiled little monkey—"

"But nice?"

"Well, one couldn't help loving you, and giving way to your whims; you made every body do that."

"And as a girl?"

"Why, you know I was absent for two years —my one holiday, nearly. You were married when I got back."

"Oh yes; I remember."

She took his arm, several people followed, and they passed down stairs to the ground-floor, and entered the pretty apartment of which he had spoken. They all stood there chatting for a few moments; then two of the men —elderly bachelors—took that opportunity to steal away into Worthington's snug smoking-room, and enjoy a surreptitious cigar. The other pair, being birds of opposite sex, and having a very interesting flirtation well under way, chose to walk up and down the passage for a few moments. In John Worthington's house people were really at liberty to enjoy themselves, and it was his habit, in general, only to invite people with brains enough to know how to do it in a sensible fashion. So he and Mrs. Marchmont stood chatting by his great table, loaded with books and papers.

"Such frightful disorder," she said, beginning to toss over the volumes.

"May I write a note?" he asked. "I have just remembered one that I promised to answer."

"Write, and don't apologize," she said, seating herself in his favorite chair. "You have been persistently rude to me for ten years; it is only cruel now to attempt an affectation of ceremony."

"And you must get a little tired, occasionally, of always wearing state robes, and playing queen," he replied, searching among the piles of manuscript for the letter he needed.

"I'll not have you laugh at me and my poor little life, just because you happen to be a distinguished man, and as wise as all those books up yonder," she said, pointing to the well-filled shelves which lined the walls. "I wonder if you really read them!"

"So, after all, you doubt my claims to the wisdom you just complimented me on possessing."

"I believe the man wants another compliment!"

"Yes; I retain my innocent tastes; I rather like bonbons."

"Then you'll not get them; write your note."

"Time enough: one does not often catch you alone. I wonder sometimes if each of these years that slip so rapidly away finds you a happier woman."

She shivered at his words, but laughed out, partly from the recklessness grown natural to her, partly to hide her emotion.

"Don't wonder about such things, you dreadful book-man! Don't you know that civilized people keep such wonderings for their own private delectation?"

"But I don't pretend to belong to civilized people."

"Oh dear, I wish we did not, any of us. How nice, if we could only live on an island in the Indian Ocean—wherever that may be—and care for nothing, but pick our enemies' bones in peace behind the doors of our—well, whatever one uses there in place of a house."

"I have been thinking of reading you a lecture," he said; "it has troubled my mind for a good while."

"Don't then, please; I hate to be lectured."

He looked grave, in spite of returning the smile with which she strove to soften him.

"We are such very old friends," he said.

"You are very rude to remind me of my age."

"You used to come and talk freely to me," he went on, notwithstanding her efforts to shake his gravity; "but you are always in the world now. Don't be angry—your extravagance, of which I hear so much, is your own business, so is your flirting—but don't flirt with Dick Faulkner. There, it is off my mind at last."

"I hate that man!" she exclaimed.

"So you ought," he answered. "But they tell me he visits you—that he boasts of your acquaintance."

"I meet him—I—" She stopped short in the prevarication.

"I suppose you wanted to tease his wife," he continued, beginning anew his search for the letter. "But just let that man alone altogether; I know him."

A wild longing came over her to tell him the whole story—to go on her knees and beg him to save her. But to lose his respect and affection—she had such a craving for both—to hear words of reproach, read her condemnation in his face, in the first sound of his voice—how could she do it? What would life be worth when she had lost these from him, and the admiration of her world! better die and be done, than confess, or live deprived of them. Perhaps she might have tried though, might have yielded to the voice of the good angel that pleaded with her—Heaven only knows—but his next words rendered it impossible, by reminding her of the verdict he had passed upon a weak woman only an hour before.

"One other thing; I must say it, even if you never forgive my impertinence; long ago you gave me the right to meddle — about stock speculations, which we were talking of at dinner. Only yesterday I heard that fool of a Mrs. Doane boast that her brother let her take ventures; don't you ever be deluded into such schemes."

"But Mrs. Doane did make a lot of money."

"Never you mind; so much the worse, if she did. Gambling is gambling; nothing can make wrong right. It is sure to end ill for a woman — particularly a woman alone in the world. Ten to one she gives some rascal power over her which he is not slow to use in any way. You are not angry?"

"No, no!"

"I see you hate the bare idea connected with yourself: no wonder. I vow, if I caught my niece at such performances, I would disown her; it would be the one thing I never would forgive."

No hope! She could not appeal to him — could not tell him even a portion of the truth. Before she left home she had told herself that every thing was at an end; still it seemed as if there had been a door partially open whereby she might escape, and he had just shut it in her face. She was away off in the blackness again; the night was deeper, more impenetrable, than ever — no guide, no help, no loop-hole; his stern words had flung her off the last halting-place where she had clung; she was sinking down — down!

"There," he said; "I believe I have finished my lecture and my cautions. I wish you would be more quiet, give yourself a little rest; but I have not the heart to scold further; you always disarm me by your patience."

"It is very good of you to care—"

"I do care; I always shall. Now, then, I will write my note, and will go back to the people. So you like my room?"

"It is very pretty," she answered, quietly; a strange composure had succeeded the whirl in her brain.

Mr. Worthington seated himself at the table and wrote a few lines—held up the paper so that she could see the signature, in the great, sprawling, irregular hand.

"I don't improve in my writing," he said. "Do you remember the summer we were all at Lake George, when you used to amuse us by imitating my signature?"

"Did I? One forgets so."

She felt so dizzy that she had to grasp the arms of her chair for support. Just as if the devil had whispered it audibly in her ear, came the first intimation of the one possible way out of Faulkner's power.

"Oh yes; Marchmont said you must have been meant for a forger, you were so successful. Indeed, it was wonderful; I couldn't tell it from my own; I always promised not to prosecute you when you forged my name in earnest," he added, laughingly.

She shrunk back in mortal terror; that dreadful word seemed to snatch her from the precipice where she had stood for an instant. She saw him look up in surprise at her sudden movement. She knew that she must speak, must say something.

"One forgets so," she repeated. "It seems ages ago."

"It was a very pleasant summer: I remember it distinctly," he said.

There was no further opportunity for conversation; more people entered the room, and the stream of idle talk and laughter went on until Mrs. Marchmont could endure it no longer. She ordered her carriage and made her adieus, sparkling to the last, and left them wondering at her spirits, speaking of her as one of the few persons in the world really to be envied.

She was at home, up in her room, and there on her dressing-table lay a note directed in a hand with which she had grown only too familiar during the past weeks.

She tore it open; it contained but a few words.

"Have you forgotten that to-morrow makes the tenth day? Admire my patience; I have not even been near you. It has seemed an age, but you will let me come in the morning; you will let me arrange the affair without trouble to yourself.   DICK."

Oh the insolence—the cool sense of power! it drove her, for the time, beyond the verge of reason upon which her brain had tottered so long; she went wholly mad.

She could not die—she dared not; she told herself that. Then she knew what lay before her—disgrace, in one form or another. Only one way out—one! He had pointed it to her himself; John Worthington had shown her the one way. She must seize it—she could not die —she must! She would be free at any cost— be able, when the morrow came, to fling that wretch's money in his face, and have done with him forever.

Are you pronouncing it unnatural? Think a little of the circumstances—the awful strait which she had reached—and see if there would have been no temptation for you. I do not mean to palliate her sin, yet I aver that she was not a bad woman. I can at least say that she did not realize what she was about to do; never stopped to think of the consequences in case of discovery; thought of nothing only to free herself from that man.

I can not make a sensational scene; I can only describe exactly what this woman did. She believed afterward that she was mad; in many instances crime and insanity are so closely connected that it is difficult for human judgment to separate them; but no metaphysical discussions could change the matter—this was what she did.

She had been sitting in the chair where she threw herself on entering the room, going over the events of the last few days, her utter failure in every quarter to obtain assistance bringing the review up to the words John Worthington had this night spoken. The scene that must take place on the morrow rose in her mind; she could see Faulkner's devilish smile again. Ruin—disgrace! Either the ruin of her womanhood and her soul, or disgrace and exposure before the world. If she could die! if she were not so utterly weak and despicable! She actually held the poison in her hand, and tried to raise it to her lips; she could not do it. Her hand fell to her side as suddenly and powerless as though some invisible strength grasped it and would not let her go. She thrust the bottle out of sight; it was useless to struggle with her own cowardice.

She ran to the safe, unlocked it, and took out a paper—came back to the light, and studied it—the paper which she had twice presented in vain to her Hebrew friend. It was a bill for the amount needed, with her signature attached—worthless! It only required another person's name—an indorsement on the back; that was all—and her Jewish friend would be happy to further her wishes.

She searched among her letters for specimens of John Worthington's writing. There were numerous notes from him; he was always inviting her to his house, or sending her rare flowers, with notes scribbled in his trenchant, amusing vein. She sat down at the table again, and began to copy the name—John Worthington. She covered a whole page with those two words; you could not have told the signature from the original before her.

She drew toward her the paper which she had offered to the Israelite. There was an instant's pause; her white face glared upward and about; her wild eyes seemed, at that last moment, searching some refuge, some aid. She made a movement to fling the pen away—her hand touched Dick Faulkner's note; she gave a low moan, more painful than a shriek of the keenest agony.

Again she seized the pen; this time there was no hesitation. The potent name—John Worthington's name—was on the paper when she laid it aside.

CHAPTER XII.

THE FIRST WALK.

THE next morning Milly Crofton went out for an early walk. A former servant of Mrs. Remsen's was dying of lingering consumption, and Milly always found leisure to go and see her once or twice a week, though it never occurred to her that she was doing a meritorious work, and she had not the slightest idea how much pleasure her bright presence afforded the desolate woman.

She turned into Fifth Avenue, almost deserted at that time, and walked rapidly on; for the invalid lived in a narrow street so far up among the sixties that it was quite beyond the pale of civilization, and required a good hour's march to reach. It had been an effort for Milly to go out this morning; but she had some money to give their protégée—her own and Constance's savings, largely increased by a donation from Mr. Worthington—and she was anxious that poor old Abigail should have it at once. This sacrifice of her own inclinations met with a very unexpected reward—all the pleasanter, for that reason. As she stopped at a crossing until a butcher's cart, which threatened instant destruction to the unwary, dashed past, followed by the butcher's dog, looking so fierce that Milly felt grateful he had not time to pause in his chase, Kenneth Halford appeared up the side street, and was close to her before she perceived him.

"Miss Crofton! is it possible?" said he. "I did not suppose you had wakened yet, after last night's fatigues."

"Wakened and out, as you see," she replied, with the quick blush and the smile—rather of the eyes than lips—which he thought so pretty.

"You are as energetic as an English girl," he said.

"Oh dear!" returned Milly; "all the slanders about American girls' indolence and ill health may have been true of the past generation, but we can walk as far and wear as thick shoes as any of the English women, I assure you."

"I really believe you must have run away," said he, jestingly; "I think it will be my duty to take you in charge."

"Have you lived so long abroad that you consider it improper for a young lady to walk out alone?" she asked, pouting.

"Not a bit of it; I am proud to think that my young countrywomen don't need watching."

"Indeed, aunty doesn't let me go by myself during promenade hours; but so early as this one doesn't expect to meet any human being but the brick-layers, and they are always civil."

"I will promise to be as civil as a brick-layer," laughed he, "if you will let me accompany you; I had set out for an early walk too."

"But I am going ever so far, and over to the east side of town," she replied, naming the locality to which she was bound; but he had been so long absent that he knew nothing about the neighborhood.

"And I want to walk ever so far," he said; "so, unless you will find it a bore, pray let me go with you."

Milly wisely said nothing except, "It won't bore me."

He caught a glimpse of her face, however, and it spoke as eloquently as the most exigeant person could have desired. She looked like an English robin, in her simple brown dress, with a bit of bright scarlet at her throat; and her step was as springy and light as if she trod in time to music inaudible to other ears.

He walked on beside her, having first offered his arm; but that Milly refused with another blush and a laugh.

"Is it improper?" he asked.

"No—but—I mustn't take it," she said, unhesitatingly, though he could see that it was an effort for her to be courageous enough to speak. "Here, no young lady takes a man's arm in the day-time unless he is her brother, or she is engaged to him."

"I did not remember that," he replied, too delicate to disturb her by a jest, as many men would have done.

So they went on through the bright sunshine; for it was a beautiful morning, the weather almost unseasonably mild, though with a sufficient sharpness in the soft air to keep it from being heavy or oppressive. They were at no loss for subjects of conversation, and Halford had the art of making people talk; indeed, afterward Milly was rather startled to remember how freely she had spoken her thoughts out, only consoling herself by the reflection that, though she had not known him long, the circumstances of their first acquaintance prevented her regarding him as a stranger.

The church clocks were striking nine as they passed Mrs. Marchmont's elegant house, and they both looked in astonishment at the unexpected sight of her brougham before her door.

"I didn't know that she ever stirred out till noon," Milly said.

"I think the coachman must have fallen asleep there after bringing his mistress home last night, and forgotten to drive to the stables," replied Halford.

Then they both forgot the circumstance in a renewal of the conversation which the sight of the carriage had momentarily interrupted. Bright and pleasant as the winter had been to Milly, this early ramble seemed the brightest and pleasantest occurrence of the whole season; she remembered it long after, when between her and that time swept a tempest of pain, wrath, and trouble, such as yet her young life held no perception of.

When they reached old Abigail's house, Milly said,

"I shall have to stay here a little while; so I must bid you good-morning;" and there was a shadow on her face, bravely as she fancied herself speaking.

"Why must you?" he asked.

"Because you will want to walk farther, or go back."

"I have promised myself to see you safe home to your aunt," he replied; "so I shall wait for you. Don't think to escape in that way."

"Oh, that is very good of you; but Abigail always keeps me so; and I shall be uncomfortable to remember that you are waiting."

"Unless you really want me to go, I shall wait. I see a little open square yonder; I shall find a bench, and smoke my morning's cigar while you are doing the amiable to your old woman. But don't let me stay, if you would rather have me away," he added, for the express pleasure of seeing her face grow earnest in her protestations.

But she disappointed him; her head was turned, so that he could not see it as she answered, demurely,

"I shall like to have you wait very much, if you don't mind."

Then she ran into the house, and Halford strolled on to the square decorated with two trees and a hideous pretense of a fountain, and sat down to smoke. About as unfavorable a spot for day-dreaming as one could well conceive, but he managed to lose himself, nevertheless, in a reverie more agreeable than any that had visited him for a long time.

It was not more than half an hour before the green door opened again, and his unfashionably far sight perceived Milly descending the steps. He hurried forward to meet her, saying,

"I am afraid I forgot myself, and smoked more than my regulation cigar; now will that small sin lie at your door, or Mrs. Abigail's?"

"Neither," said Milly; "you can't shift your sins off on other people in that fashion, Mr. Halford."

"You are discouraging, with your straightforward, uncompromising orthodoxy," he answered. "I thought you would quiet my conscience by at least offering to share the blame."

So they walked back, chatting gayly, and Halford rather wondered at himself for the pleasure he found in this child's talk; but it was so different, in its artlessness, from that of old women, it possessed all the more charm.

They found themselves within reach of civilized regions again, and turned once more into the Avenue. As they went by Minerva Lawrence's mansion, that namesake of the Athenian goddess chanced to be standing at a window of her breakfast-room, and, as soon as she saw them, thumped vigorously on the glass, regardless of etiquette, or the risk she ran of having a glazier's bill to pay.

"Let's pretend not to see her or to hear," said Halford; but Milly shook her head.

"She's always so good to me," she urged; "and I half promised to go out with her yesterday, but Aunt Eliza wanted me."

"Then we will be conscientious, and go in," said Halford, "especially as I see the man already opening the door; it is as well to do right, when you can't help it."

Milly ran up the steps, laughing at his remark of doubtful morality, and he followed. Mrs. Lawrence met them in the passage, voluble in her astonishment and pleasure.

"Where on earth have you been? why, you must have started at daylight. I had just come down to breakfast, and one never has any appetite alone. Oh, you naughty Milly, not to have remembered yesterday! But come into the breakfast-room, and have some coffee.

Dear me, Mr. Halford, you aren't running away with the child, I hope."

"I am taking her safely home; or was, when you stopped us, Mrs. Lawrence. Coffee indeed! why it is almost luncheon-time," he added, as they entered the breakfast-room, and then began to ask her numerous questions, lest she should disturb Milly by some attempts at raillery; and her efforts in that line were not always discreet.

"I am late," she said; "but I was at Mrs. Philips's last night, and not a soul of you there; it was a failure: poor thing, it's too bad, when she works so hard to get people to notice her. And, Milly, why didn't you come to me yesterday as you promised, you bad child?"

"I said if I could, but Aunt Eliza wanted me."

"She always wants you if you are coming to me," grumbled Mrs. Lawrence, in a comfortable way; she could not even grumble in earnest. "That's just like Eliza; she must rule, or she's not happy; but I'm very fond of her, for all that. Here's chocolate, if you won't have coffee, Mr. Halford; or they can make tea."

He chose the chocolate, in order to get rid of her persuasions, and she forced a cup upon Milly: nothing made her so happy as to have an opportunity of gratifying her hospitable instincts.

"I've not seen you since my ball, Mr. Halford, though I found your card. How Mrs. Marchmont frightened me! I never knew her to faint before in my life."

"I can scarcely fancy it being any body's favorite recreation," said Halford.

"But she is quite well again; I had a little note from her yesterday," pursued Mrs. Lawrence.

"Oh, I saw her at Mr. Worthington's last night," added Milly; "we had such a charming dinner; I like her so much."

"Dear me!" cried heedless Mrs. Lawrence; "and only last week I heard Eliza Remsen say, with my own ears, that Mrs. Marchmont was so careless in her conduct—no, she said reckless—"

"Ah! you see," interrupted Milly, mischievously, "Mrs. Marchmont has rather forgotten us all winter, except for her large parties; and after all, aunty is only human; but she does admire Mrs. Marchmont; who could help it?"

"Nobody, of course; but la, my dear, the way people talk! But then, they would talk about an angel; and the whole world is ready to lie down and let her walk over them."

"How nicely your flowers look," Milly said, not having yet developed any taste for scandal or gossip. "The bigonia you gave me is in full blossom; you can't think how lovely it is. And now I really must go home; I promised Aunt Eliza not to be gone any longer than I could help."

"She's the sweetest child in the world," Minerva declared, pointing her plump hand at Milly, and addressing Halford. "I'd give half I'm worth for a niece like her. Come straight here and kiss me this instant, you little witch; you've no business to be so pretty."

She allowed them to go away, at length, and they walked on past Mrs. Marchmont's house, and soon turned down the street in which Mrs. Remsen resided.

"You must not forget to ask me in," Halford said, not above artifices to prolong this pleasant morning; "you know I promised myself to see you safe in your aunt's guardianship."

"She will be very glad to see you," Milly answered.

"As far as you are personally concerned, I dare say I have wasted as much of your time as you can bear for one day."

"Indeed, I have enjoyed my walk so much!"

"Then may I ask the aunt if the experiment may not sometimes be repeated?" he inquired.

Milly gave him one of her demure little answers as the door opened; but this time he did catch the expression of her face, and saw that it was much more enthusiastic than her words. She conducted him at once to the morning-room, certain that Aunt Eliza would be there, and as well prepared to receive visitors as if the hour were a reasonable one; for Mrs. Remsen never indulged in careless costumes, or allowed her young people to acquire the bad habit either.

She received Halford cordially, but there was no sign, in voice or manner, of the satisfaction which the sight of the two together afforded her.

"You see I have brought this young lady safely home, Mrs. Remsen," he said. "I chanced to be setting out for an early walk too, and was rewarded for my good habits."

"It certainly was very nice for Milly," she answered, quietly. "How was poor old Abigail, dear?"

"About as usual; she had passed a very comfortable night," Milly said, sitting down, her face so animated and her color so bright that her aunt saw with delight that she was looking her very best.

"Are you given to early walks, Mr. Halford?" she asked.

"Yes, as spring comes on. Miss Crofton tells me that it is her habit too; will you let me join her sometimes? She has promised not to refuse, provided you permit."

"Oh, of course; indeed, I don't like her going out much alone; but I am always busy of a morning, and my daughter Maud still has her lessons to occupy her."

"Then, Miss Crofton, you will not forget, I hope, that I am always at your service," he said.

Milly had risen, and was busy about the pagoda in which her birds lived; so, again, she only said,

"Oh no," and went on with her task. "Aunty, I think Maud has forgotten the fresh water: she said she would put some in."

"Oh, my dear, if you trust to Maud!" returned Mrs. Remsen, lifting her hands to signify the vanity of any hope where that young lady was concerned.

The aunt and Halford talked for a few moments, while Milly flitted about her bird-cage, joining in the conversation occasionally; and at length Halford rose to go, feeling that he really could not decently intrude any longer at this hour. Mrs. Remsen was just cordial enough in her manner, said exactly the right words, and he went away thinking her a very agreeable woman, and a very wise guardian for a young girl.

Once in the street, he remembered a magazine paper that he had promised an editor to send to him this morning, and turned his steps homeward to attend to the forgotten duty. As he neared Mrs. Marchmont's house, he saw her carriage again in front of the door, and the lady herself just descending from it. Before he reached the spot she had entered her dwelling, and he went on, wondering anew, as he and Milly had done, at such matutinal exertion on her part.

It was odd enough; but Alice Marchmont had gone to bed and soundly to sleep after her work of the previous night—so completely worn out by the fears and emotions of the past days that not even a dream disturbed her repose. She woke early, and at first could not realize what had happened. Gradually the whole truth came back; but with it came, also, the recollection that by noon Dick Faulkner would seek her presence; she must be ready to meet him; she must complete the task she had begun.

She did not falter; she positively did not think. She was burning up with inward fever; her head ached and swam so that she could scarcely get out of bed; but she must rise; she must go in search of the Jew as early as possible. She kept in her room to avoid meeting Miss Portman, replying so coldly to Pauline's first expressions of wonder at finding her up at so unusual an hour, and partially dressed, without assistance, that the polite Frenchwoman did not venture to add another word.

"Bring me my coffee and order the carriage," she said; "I must go out at nine o'clock. I have to meet some people on business down town."

"Madame is overwhelmed with affairs," the Frenchwoman said, sympathizingly.

"Yes; but I am through now; I shall settle every thing this morning," returned Mrs. Marchmont.

She was astounded at her own calmness; she could not reflect upon what she had done, or was about to do; it literally conveyed no meaning to her mind for the time; she could only remember that she was free of Dick Faulkner—free to draw her life back from the horrible shame which had menaced it.

She drove away to the dirty, crowded portion of the city where the small Hebrew had his den. On the ground-floor was a shop in which were displayed the wares that comprised his ostensible business. There was a huge collection of rococo things, tempting enough in this day, when there is a rage for impossible old traps in the way of ancient cabinets, uneasy chairs, insane-looking ornaments of all sorts; so that she ran no particular risk of exciting surprise in the mind of any body who chanced to see her in this neighborhood.

The little Hebrew was visible, as innocent as ever of clean linen or acquaintance with soap-and-water. He received her in his usual wooden manner, showed her a marvel of ugliness in the way of a carved table that had lately come into his possession, and finally conducted her up stairs, that she might see some wonderful vases which had only just been unpacked, and not yet exhibited to any customer. It was doubtful if this bit of acting imposed upon the shrewd Hebrew clerks, as greasy and soiled as their master; but he knew that it would be a consolation to the lady to go through the pretense, and he was always willing to oblige his clients, even to the keeping up of appearances, provided he was paid for it.

The fat, untidy wife, who made regular visits to Mrs. Marchmont's house, in the character of a distressed, but virtuous, widow woman, was as careful as her husband to preserve the demeanor suited to the occasion. She was busy at a lofty desk, with huge account-books, seated upon a high stool, with her legs hanging down, and displaying an extent of black stocking and an amount of yellow garter which was really astounding. There was not even speculation in her fishy eyes, as she looked at Mrs. Marchmont—not the remotest gleam of acquaintance with that lady's private affairs, or her diamonds.

Once safely up stairs and seated in the den of an office, oppressive with a stale smell of smoke and Bologna sausage, a sudden faintness came over the desperate woman, but she did not lose her self-control; the dire exigencies of the moment nerved her.

"I wish you would open the window," she said; "it is very close here."

The little Hebrew obeyed, though now there was an expression of surprise in his face; that any human creature could desire fresh air filled him with astonishment.

The cool rush of wind steadied Mrs. Marchmont's reeling brain a little. She leaned back in her chair, looking languid and careless, and stately all at once. The little Hebrew was watching her keenly enough from under his bushy eyebrows; but there was nothing in her appearance to excite either wonder or suspicion.

"I have arranged my little affair," she said; "I think even to you the paper I offered the other day will be perfectly satisfactory."

"But if you please not to say 'even,'" returned the Hebrew. "Surely, the madam never found me hard to deal with;" and he looked quite a picture of injured innocence.

"I did not only ask a name; that is not much; and the lady knows business is business to a poor man."

"And I have the name," she said. "Of course, I could have obtained it in the beginning; but I hated to expose the state of my affairs even to so dear a friend as Mr. Worthington; however, you obliged me to do so by your obstinacy."

"That is a good name—a very good name," replied the Jew, rubbing his hands softly together.

Mrs. Marchmont took the bill from her pocket and laid it on the table. He examined it, but with no show of suspicion, though the momentary delay was more than she could endure.

"Have you some new scruple to satisfy?" she asked, impatiently.

"No, no. A good name; I know it very well; many a time he has give me a check for the things he bought here."

"Very well; then that is all you want, I suppose."

"Yes; yes. Now I have to think if I can raise the moneys—next week would not be soon enough?"

It was not a wish to annoy her which caused him to speak, only the magpie fondness for hoarding which made him hate to give up his treasures, or admit that he had them, as long as he could avoid it.

"Give me back that paper," said she, rising angrily. "You know very well that I have a large payment to make at noon; it is simply impertinent to ask if I can wait."

"If the lady will not be impatient," he said, in a deprecatory manner, holding fast to the bill. "This morning? then she must have it."

Mrs. Marchmont sat down again.

"Now understand," she said, "this bill is not to leave your desk—not to be seen by any body till I take it up. Mr. Worthington has no idea that it is to go into your hands; he would be furious at my putting myself in such a position. He thinks it is to be in the hands of my agent; he does not dream that I know you."

"Just so; just so; I know how to keep a secret: the lady can certify to that. I am not hard, like some beobles."

"I shall be ready to take it up before the three months are over—"

"The ninety days," corrected the Hebrew.

"Very well. This is the last of my business annoyances. You will have your other money too, and I shall take my jewels."

"As the lady wishes."

"Come, don't keep me; that's a good soul. I have a great deal to do."

"I count the interest; we must take that out."

"Oh, I shall not dispute over the amount; it is terrible, the usury you demand; but I can't help myself."

The Jew made his calculations upon a bit of dirty paper, and showed them to her."

"That is it."

"You told me the other day; I drew the bill for a sufficient amount to cover it and leave me what I want."

"It is a large sum—"

"Are you hesitating? If you haven't the money, after all, say so, and let me go elsewhere," she cried.

"My bank is the Shoe and Leather, in the Bowery," he said.

"What do I care about your bank? Am I likely to go there, or anywhere, and present a check with your name attached?" she asked, haughtily. "I could have had the money from Mr. Worthington, but I would not take it; I can't bear to borrow from my friends. I know that he runs no risk in lending me his name; I need only a few weeks to get all my matters arranged."

"Just so; just so," he answered, in his monotonous voice, which irritated her beyond endurance.

"Do you mean to give the money?"

"Why not, with a good name? but if the lady will not take a check I must go to the bank; a poor man like me doesn't have such sums in his safe."

"How long will it take you?"

"I am back in ten, fifteen minutes. Will the lady wait here?"

"No; can't you send it to my house? Yes, I'll wait; only be quick—that is, I'll wait down in my carriage; one can't breathe here. I'll drive to the corner of the street. No—the coachman—I'll look at the things down stairs."

"And the vases; I am sure the lady would like the vases, if she will only take a peep at them."

"You can't delude me into a purchase this morning, Mr. Herman," she said. "Do go and get the money; I don't wish to be kept here all day. Where are the vases? I'll look at them while you are away."

"I shall call Mrs. Herman to show them," he said, hurrying off.

He disappeared, and presently the jointed wooden doll of a woman came up, wiping her nose on a red silk handkerchief. She was a taciturn body, and scarcely spoke as she conducted Mrs. Marchmont into the chamber where the vases stood.

They were old enough, ugly enough, rare enough; but all Alice Marchmont saw, as she looked at them, was a vision of Rome, which she had visited when a very young girl. Somehow the vases brought it all back, and there she stood, lost in her memories, while the wooden woman stared at her furtively, perhaps wondering, in her dull way, if it was possible that they belonged to the same species and sex.

The quarter of an hour passed; the Hebrew returned panting—the package of bank-notes was in Mrs. Marchmont's hand.

CHAPTER XIII.

BAFFLED.

THE deed was done, and could not be undone; for the note lay hidden among the mysterious documents in the desk of the bland but unimpressionable Hebrew, and the money had soiled Alice Marchmont's hand.

It was done, and could not be undone; and from that hour the real torture and suffering began. For the morning she put thought resolutely by, with a brief return of the ability so to do which had of late deserted her. There was great triumph in her heart when she reflected that she was out of Faulkner's power; but even under the first gladness a sense of self-abhorrence, a consciousness of guilt, coiled about her soul, and stung it with a nameless pain, which must increase to an agony beyond any thing she had yet endured.

They came, and said that Mr. Faulkner was waiting to see her; and she went down stairs to go through this interview—the last, she kept thinking, which he would ever have with her, except in the eyes of the whole world. Back came the reflection of all from which she had been saved; her vivid fancy pictured the contrast to her present feelings, supposing the required sum were not in her possession; and again she was glad, horribly glad of what she had done. She would have rejoiced to enter and overwhelm him with a burst of indignation and scorn, to tell him exactly the sort of man he was, and how thoroughly she understood and despised him; but the restraints of her life were too strong upon her to render that possible. She did so love her position, the verdict of the world was so much to her, that she could not afford to indulge in the truth even now; she must still keep on terms of civility with Dick Faulkner, and with Dick Faulkner's wife. She could not allow a marked change in her conduct to lead any body to suppose that he had been on terms with her where he could have a possibility of giving offense.

"How I hate it," she thought, as she descended the stairs—"all the deceit, the lying. I don't believe that I was naturally artful. Oh, if they had only left me alone ten years ago, what a different woman I should be to-day! I can hear him walking up and down; if I could only go in and trample him under my feet! I wish the man lived who loved me well enough to hear the whole truth, and—"

She did not finish her reflection, called herself a fool for raving in that absurd fashion, and walked on into the morning-room, so calm and self-possessed, receiving Faulkner with so entire a forgetfulness of their last interview in this very apartment, that he was absolutely embarrassed for an instant. She had freed herself—he understood that; how, he could not imagine; but his prey had slipped through the toils which he had so cautiously woven during the past months. She saw the confusion and

wrath in his face, and exulted, though her manner was very quiet, and her voice delightfully languid and disdainful.

"Business is the order of the day," said she, without giving him time for more than such greetings as he could utter in the first instant of his disappointment. "I will not detain you; I am growing business-like, you see."

She motioned him to a seat, sat down herself opposite, with a table between them, whereon she laid the great pocket-book which he had noticed in her hand as she entered. He did not speak; he was watching her, with that murderous frown on his face, wondering, while he cursed her in his heart, how she had managed to compass her deliverance. She took out the packet of crisp, new bank-notes, each of them for a thousand dollars, and, as she touched them, shuddered to see what a pile there was, remembering how she had stained her soul to obtain them.

"I suppose you did not think a check would serve the same purpose," he said, speaking for the first time since his confused salutations.

"I did not," she replied. "I believe you will find the amount correct. Now, if you will give me those troublesome papers I asked for, I think the matter will be arranged."

She pushed the pile of notes toward him, but still kept her hand upon them until he tossed rudely down the receipts, at which she glanced for an instant.

"Are they satisfactory?" he sneered.

"Perfectly," she answered, with a courteous bow, and signed to him to take up the money.

He crumpled the package into his pocket, and sat irresolute.

"Now," thought Mrs. Marchmont, "if he is not an utter idiot, he will say a few commonplaces and go. There's not the slightest necessity for a scene; I don't want to be obliged to turn him out. Good gracious, I couldn't live to own that Dick Faulkner had insulted me!"

But he was an utter idiot—that is to say, a man; and he must needs air his penitence and remorse, really supposing it necessary in order to have any hope of her ever speaking to him again. If he could only have gone away without the slightest allusion to what had happened, she would at least have been forced to admire his tact and coolness.

"I don't know what to say to you," he began.

"Better say 'good-morning,'" she replied, laughing. "I know these are business hours, and you want to be gone. A thousand thanks for having taken the time to come up to-day."

"I think I must have been mad that last time—"

"And one never notices the ravings of delirium," she interrupted, gayly, and thought, "Oh, will he have it?"

Yes, he undoubtedly would; his next words convinced her of that.

"I want to know if you have forgiven me,"

he continued, awkwardly—"if we may be friends still."

He would have it out; well, perhaps it was better; at all events, since he forced her to speak, she would treat him to as much plain truth as might leave civility in future possible.

"I can at least forget, Mr. Faulkner," she answered; "and as long as I am not obliged to remember, there will be nothing to forgive."

"You don't know how much I thank you," he exclaimed. "Indeed, I am not so bad a fellow as people say! If you could only know what my life is; if you could understand half its wretchedness—but why should you be troubled."

He had recovered his wits sufficiently to try what he imagined would be the most effective way of softening her. He was a handsome man—in a bad style—and he looked particularly picturesque and interesting then, flinging his curls impatiently back from his forehead, copying an attitude of a favorite *jeune premier* at the French theatre, and speaking in the same monotonous tone, with a little quiver in the voice which is popularly supposed to give strong evidence of repressed emotion. The attitude and the tremulous accents might have been very telling with many women, but, unfortunately, Mrs. Marchmont had studied the *jeune premier* quite as closely as he, and was too much in the habit of essaying private theatricals herself to be in the slightest degree moved. She was so much an actress, knew every dramatic trick so well, and had studied men so thoroughly, that the most awkward bluntness would have been more effective, and stood a better chance of deceiving her.

"Absolutely, he is posing," she thought, "as if I were a girl of sixteen. Ugh, you great silly, ugly, black spider! does the woman live idiot enough to be duped by your borrowed airs and graces?" But when he had finished his little speech, she said, sweetly, "I suppose everybody's life has its trials, and we must each bear our own; mine to-day must be a struggle with my modiste, for I need a new dress, in a great hurry, for Mrs. Rosevelt's ball."

How Dick Faulkner would have liked to strangle her! He fairly hated her as he looked covetously at her disdainful loveliness, all the while a fierce passion glowing in his heart. Still, he must cling to the sentimental rôle; he knew no medium between that and attempts to frighten her; and those were useless now.

"So you will not be friends?" he sighed.

"With all the pleasure in life," she answered, "as one has friends in this busy Vanity Fair."

"I don't understand you," he said, with a studied gloom which made her long to tell him she could herself get up a much more truthful imitation of the admired *jeune premier*.

She began to grow irritated at his determination to be sentimental; since she could not deal him one honest blow full in the handsome face which she had last seen so insolent and wicked, she would punish him by making plain her appreciation of his histrionics.

"Then you shall understand me, Mr. Faulkner!" she said; "and we will have done, if you please, with this foolish talk, which is pretty enough on the stage or in novels, but very tiresome in real life."

She had the best of him every way; she had slipped out of his clutches just as he believed her hopelessly in his power; it was hard work to keep the devil under.

"I am sorry if I have been tiresome."

"That is good of you, at all events," said she. "You remember what the clergyman said to Canning? But I suppose you don't know much about clergymen."

"As much, perhaps, as my neighbors," he retorted, allowing his natural voice to be audible.

"That is not pretty of you. But this particular clergyman said to the statesman, in speaking of his own sermon, 'I tried not to be tedious.'"

"And Canning?"

"Answered mildly, but with a sense of injury, 'And yet you were.'"

Dick Faulkner showed his white teeth in a grimace which he believed a smile, but the devil did so break out in his face that Mrs. Marchmont's blood ran cold as she remembered what she had escaped.

"Now let us put sentiment aside; it is dreadfully antiquated in our century," she continued, gayly. "I shall be glad to see you and your wife at my parties, Mr. Faulkner—glad to meet you in society; and more I could not say to any one. The life I lead leaves me no leisure for any closer acquaintance."

He returned to the monotone and the repressed agitation.

"But you will forgive—"

"Don't remind me! I said that I had forgotten—you may believe that; but never trust to a woman's forgiveness."

"Can one trust to a woman at all?"

"Oh, that is the grand question with poets, from Byron down. I was to be trusted, you perceive—in business matters. Let me thank you again for worrying yourself with my little affairs."

"If you would allow me to do more—I have something on foot now that is sure to be successful."

"No; thanks. I will take my little losses and—my little lesson."

Was there no way in which he could sting or hurt her—leave her with a certain dread in her mind that the affair might not be so completely ended as she believed? He would have sold his soul at that instant to give such threats a foundation.

"You are quite sure that I shall never mention your having made ventures in crooked Wall Street?" he asked, meaningly.

"Perfectly," she answered, with composure, and a softly ironical ring in her voice. "You don't suppose that I could accuse you of any thing so ungentlemanly? What an unmitigated villain a man would be considered on all sides who betrayed a confidence of the sort! Don't be astonished, though, if I tell the story to your wife some day, when I am bored or cross."

That would be pleasant! His wife—happily for her—had money that Dick Faulkner wanted, and always hoped to obtain; and besides this, he had no wish that their quarrels should come to an open outbreak. He had trouble enough now at home—trouble enough to keep his place in society; and a hint of this business might drive the jealous woman to extremities. "And this one would do it," he thought. "What a born devil she is! I do believe she'd tell my wife just for the fun of the row, however much she suffered by it."

Mrs. Marchmont perceived that her final shot had told; and it so lightened her spirits, under the rage and disgust which she felt for the man, that she bowed him out of her presence with the utmost graciousness.

Dick Faulkner went away thinking, "The woman has done me; what an ass I have been! I might have drawn her on—got her to invest in some stock company till she hadn't a penny—she was crazy enough over it—and then—"

He ground his teeth with rage, to think how he had defeated his own game by his inability to wait.

"How ever did she raise this money? She is dreadfully crippled. Never mind, madam! The game is yours this time; but if ever I do get a chance to turn the tables—! I don't know whether I love her or hate her. I know I'd like to carry her off in the face of the whole world, and let every thing go to the devil together."

He was gone, and Alice had leisure to think—I should have said, she could no longer keep thought at bay. It came like an audible voice, crying out to her what she was—a criminal—a forger!

She ran up and down the room like a wild animal in a cage; the full horror and degradation burst upon her. It seemed to her that before the day was gone she should be discovered, her guilt published, and she dragged out to face it. Where? To prison? Yes, to prison, along with thieves and murderers, and horrible women, such as she had read of, and never been able to realize as absolutely belonging to the same sex with herself. This was where her life had ended. It must be a dream; it was impossible that she could have committed a crime: she did not believe it; she would not. Women committed sins, but not of that sort. There was Sybil Ansley, who ran away from her husband with the lover of her girlish days. Only a short time before, she read of a woman who shot the man that had deceived her, and killed herself afterward. Such sins women were guilty of sometimes. But a crime that could lead to arrest, a trial, imprisonment! No, it was not possible.

She had seen the Tombs once; a party of country friends had persuaded her to go there with them. She saw all its dreary horrors anew at this moment—the dark corridors, the narrow whitewashed cells; she scented even the indescribably loathsome prison odor; and worse than all, the women's faces looking out at her from between the bars—the dreadful, dreadful faces! Now she was akin to them. It grew too horrible; she buried her face in the cushions of her chair, and sobbed and shook in an hysterical spasm which made her almost believe that she was dying.

When that was over, other thoughts came; she began trying to cheat herself, to lie to herself. She had not meant to commit a crime; it was not one in reality. Before the three months were over she could return the money; that long-delayed sale of her Virginia lands might any day be concluded; she should be a rich woman then. There would be the dividends from those railway stocks; and she had property to sell—oh, a hundred things, with a little time—she was not ruined. Oh, she was sick of it—the hollow life, the foolish whirl! It would not have been worth even the time she had lost upon it. Just to be petted, and flattered, and wondered at; and there was no one she cared about, after all. Where were her friends? Women hated her, in spite of their smiles. There was John Worthington—yes, he had been her friend; and he was the very man against whom she had sinned.

But it was not a crime! If he could only have known the strait she was in, he would have helped her; only she could not tell him. She could more easily have died than meet his look of reproval and contempt. She tried to think how she could have wasted so much money; and one extravagance after another came before her mind to reproach her. The parties she had given, the unheard-of expense and luxury—oh, she could not think about it; she would not. Every thing should be right again; she would take up the note, and no one need ever know. She must not think of it in that light, or she should go mad. She must not think about it at all; she must put it aside like a horrid dream. And just as she had reached the refuge of her chamber, and was looking in silent dismay at the haggard face which stared at her in return from the mirror, they came to tell her that Constance Worthington was below.

She, of all persons! The very name made her heart stop beating. She was afraid of falling on the floor, or doing something unheard of and ridiculous, before the servant could get out of the room. Then she remembered how necessary it was that there should be no change in her manner. She must see the pretty girl often, as had been her habit—see John Worthington, and learn to hide her remorse while listening to his friendly words. Oh, existence had been hard enough upon her, but nothing like this!

"When they obliged me to give up Kenneth, I believed I should die," was her thought. "During that short season of my married life, I fretted and moaned, and it seemed very dreary; and these past weeks—but now—Oh, there was nothing so bad as this!"

She wrung her hands, she beat her face, she did a variety of insane things, at which we laugh in romances and call stage effects; yet sometimes, in each of our lives, we have, perhaps, committed the same insanities when trouble met us and drove our poor wits before it. At last she got her senses back; bathed her face, and looked to see that the puffs of her hair were properly arranged; wet her eyes with soothing liquids, to do away the redness left by her tears, and rubbed her face with numerous other things, hoping to hide the traces of emotion. By this time she was herself again. She rang for Pauline, and made a lovely carriage toilet; for she meant to take Constance out-of-doors; there would be a certain relief in escaping from the house. She was ready, at length, to go down and behave decorously, and utter her polite falsehoods, as one must, whatever crisis may wait beyond. Constance found her more bewitching to-day than ever, and was herself as pleasant and cheerful as possible.

She meant to be agreeable, even when speaking of her uncle, she said, "He is busy over the Gordon case—the forged will, you remember."

Alice had reason to rejoice that, trusting to the shelter of her veil, she had touched her pale lips with a little red for the second time in her life.

"The—what?"

"The will case they were talking of last night—oh, it was after dinner. Well, you must have read about it; uncle is on the nephew's side; he thinks there is no doubt of Jordan's guilt."

"No doubt—oh! And your uncle is against him? And he'll go to prison for years and years?"

"Oh, don't pity him!" cried Miss Constance, with the fierce decision of youth that has never suffered or been tempted. "Such a wicked man, to cheat that poor brother and sister!"

Alice felt as if she must scream, or throw herself under the carriage wheels, or do any thing to get beyond the sound of that young voice.

"Uncle says that crimes of the sort seem to increase of late; and then he scolds about the wicked extravagance of the age, and—"

A sudden fright that the horses took at the instant fortunately so distracted Constance's attention that she never remembered to finish her sentence, and did not notice Mrs. Marchmont's face. A huge van, piled with furniture, dashed across the street, appearing so unexpectedly close to the animals' heads that they forgot their customary good behavior, and

bounded into the air in a way that would have been becoming enough in a pair of unicorns, but was not a satisfactory performance on the part of two well-trained carriage steeds. Constance was not strong-minded, and uttered a little cry of terror, catching her companion's arm; but Mrs. Marchmont did not stir, or attempt to re-assure her. The disturbance only lasted a moment: she was conscious of wishing that it might end in death.

"Oh, weren't you frightened?" cried the girl, as John succeeded in soothing the horses so that they decided to forsake their statuesque attitudes, and plant their fore-feet on the ground; "I am sure you were; you look pale."

"Oh, frightened out of my senses," returned she. "Let me see—what was I going to tell you when those wretched animals began doing circus? Oh, I know! I'll not be cheated out of my witticism."

She took the conversation into her own hands, and sparkled so bravely that Constance laughed until Mrs. Marchmont marveled if the time had ever been when she, too, could laugh like that.

"I want you and your uncle to go with me to the opera to-night," she said. "You may tell him that he promised last evening."

"No, I'll not tell him that; for he hates fibs, even in fun," said Constance; then began to look remorseful, for fear her speech was rude.

But Mrs. Marchmont patted her hand re-assuringly, as she said, "A lawyer with a tender conscience—what an anomaly!" Then she wondered to herself if she would be different had there been any body in her girlish days to reprove her kindly, as this good man did his niece, and added, "He is right, Constance! And women do lie so—don't let yourself get the habit; besides, it does no good. Where was I? Oh, you are to go and have supper at my house after, with such available spirits as we chance to lay hands on."

"That will be delightful! Uncle always says that your impromptu suppers are enchanting."

"Then he shall be enchanted," said Mrs. Marchmont.

It was not that she wanted them, or any body, near her; but somehow she should have a sensation of safety to-night, if she could only bring John Worthington within the spell of her smiles. Would she ever feel safe in any other way during this season of suspense which must ensue? Three months to pass before the money need be returned—this was the manner in which she phrased it in her thoughts—and her only hope was that at the expiration of half the period she should have it in her power to retrieve her sin.

Retrieve her sin could she ever do that?

Thus she went thinking again! Was she never to get her mind away from the dreadful subject?

"I'll tell you what we will do, Constance," she said, suddenly. "I have owed Mrs. Remsen a visit for an age : we'll drive there, and ask her to let your pretty little friend, Milly, join us to-night : we don't care about the elder lady, but Milly is very nice—next to you the nicest girl I know."

"Oh, she is lovely !" cried Constance. "She will be delighted ; for she admires you so much."

"Very well ; then we will go and ask her. But your uncle must come ; I will take no refusal, remember."

The more she thought, the more anxious she grew. It seemed of vital importance that she should have John Worthington in her sight during these first hours of unfamiliarity with her present self.

"He will be sure to come," Constance said. "You can depend on him. For that matter, he never refuses your invitations, though he hardly ever finds time to go anywhere else, unless as a kindness to me."

"Yes, he is always kind," Mrs. Marchmont said, slowly.

"But he likes to go to you, and he is always delighted when you come to our house," continued thoughtless Constance. "He is never so particular about every trifle as then, and he talks about it for days afterward."

It was odd that these unconscious revelations, by no means uncommon on the girl's part, never helped Alice Marchmont toward a perception of the man's secret, quick as she usually was to perceive her full power over those about her. But John Worthington had always held a place in her mind quite apart from other people : that he could possibly care for her other than in a friendly, elder-brother spirit had never entered her mind. Now, Constance's artless words only filled her with fresh horror, as she remembered how unworthy she had proved of this friend's confidence— how basely she had repaid his trust. The recollection of his unvarying goodness was too keen a torture, in these first hours of remorse : she must get away from it—away from the solitary companionship of this happy creature.

She gave the order to drive to Mrs. Remsen's house—a commodious dwelling in a fashionable quarter of the town. Though not rich, Mrs. Remsen never did things by halves, nor committed blunders. When she had a young lady to present in society she allowed no neglect of appearances to interfere with success.

She was at home this morning, and more flattered by Alice Marchmont's visit than she would have cared to acknowledge. Milly was in the room, and Hortense Maynard—the second daughter—chanced to be honoring her mother and cousin by a half-hour's utterance of wisdom and philosophy.

"This is as unexpected as June weather in midwinter," Mrs. Remsen said, as she came forward to meet her guests ; and she had a very nice manner of doing and saying things, though she was liable to attacks of overdignity.

"Now that sounds a little like a reproach,

pretty as it is," returned Mrs. Marchmont, prepared to try as hard for the general approbation as if there had been a man present. People always said that she flirted as desperately with women as she did with the opposite sex. "But if you could know how busy I am, you would not wonder at my finding little leisure for morning visits. I hope you are quite well, Mrs. Maynard ; I've not forgiven you for not coming to my last party ! Ah, small Miss Rosebud, I needn't ask how you are. Where on earth does she find such color, Mrs. Remsen ? Bless me, child, you needn't make yourself prettier by blushing like that !"

"I have wanted to see you and offer my excuse," Hortense Maynard said, in her voluble fashion. "I always hate to miss your evenings, but I was engaged every night that week. I had three lectures, a meeting at Professor Drivler's, the new somnambulist, the society for the universal language, the—"

"And you are still alive !" said Mrs. Marchmont, in a wondering voice, that convulsed the two young girls with silent laughter.

"I shall live, I trust, while I have a duty still left unperformed," replied Hortense ; and there was something *piquant*, absurd as it was, in the contrast between her pretty face, elegant dress, and the sort of conversation in which she indulged. "Dear Mrs. Marchmont, I want to interest you in the new hospital."

"I can't be interested, but I'll give all I can."

"Now, Hortense," cried her mother, "I'll not have you make a trap of my drawing-room to catch people in and frighten them out of their money."

"Mamma can't understand," sighed Hortense, resignedly ; "Adelaide can't—even Milly does not really, though she is better than the others."

"Thanks," laughed Milly.

"What I want you to do, Mrs. Marchmont, is to take an actual, personal interest in these things ; it would do you good, ennoble your life, lend a fresh enjoyment to existence—"

"Hortense, do you know what you are saying ?" interrupted her mother.

"I am obliged to come to this house to have that question asked," said Hortense, addressing Mrs. Marchmont, with sad patience. "Do I know what I am saying ? And only last night Professor Driver said that the expression of my ideas was something so precise and exact that each sentence was ready to stand in a book as I uttered it."

"But you know we poor ordinary women have so few ideas," said Alice ; "and mine, at least, are always in a sad jumble. It's of no use, Mrs. Maynard ; we have each our mission, and must fulfill it."

"And yours is to be charming," said Mrs. Remsen, with a severe glance at her daughter.

"That's very nice. But, indeed, I reproach myself for not doing a host of things ; but, besides the society work, I have a good deal outside. You know I am a solitary female, and must attend to my own business ; Mrs. Maynard is spared such worries."

Hortense shook her head, and looked unutterable things. It really was useless to waste her wisdom ; these butterflies would not be lifted out of their frivolous ways either by persuasion or example. At the same time she was wondering if Mrs. Marchmont's elegant costume was from Worth, and what it cost.

"I came partly to beg a favor of you, Mrs. Remsen," Alice said, taking advantage of Hortense's momentary silence.

"It is granted in advance, I assure you."

"I want to beg your Rosebud for the evening. Miss Constance and her uncle are going with me to the opera, and home to supper afterward ; they will call for your niece, and bring her back."

"Milly will be delighted, I am sure," said Mrs. Remsen, secretly flattered by this attention on the courted woman's part, though only the day before she had told an intimate friend that she did not and could not approve of the way in which Alice Marchmont "went on"— that vague term of condemnation so much in vogue with women.

"And it's the first night of 'Favorita,' and I never saw it but twice !" cried Milly, ecstatically. "Oh, Mrs. Marchmont, how good of you to think of me !"

"How good of you to like to go with me, you mean !" said Alice. "Mrs. Remsen, you'll not be afraid to trust her ? Mr. Worthington's presence will be a surety that I shall have none of my ineligibles about."

Mrs. Remsen agitated herself with protestations and assurances that no guardianship for her niece could be more acceptable than that of the lady whom she addressed ; and Alice smiled graciously, and thanked her, and said sweet things in return, perfectly well aware of every word of censure the speaker had ever uttered in regard to her.

"I wish you could be persuaded to come to one of the meetings of the Earnest Workers for Japan, Mrs. Marchmont," said Hortense, dashing into the conversation again. "The other night we had a speech from a real Japanese. It was so interesting."

"Highly lacquered, I suppose," said Alice ; but Mrs. Maynard was too busy talking to notice.

"Just now I am greatly occupied with the society for the promotion of a universal language," she continued. "When one thinks of the benefit to civilization ; when one reflects upon the countless myriads in heathen lands talking an incomprehensible jargon, which renders it impossible for the sun of knowledge to illuminate their darkness—"

She held up her hands to express the weakness of words where such reflections were concerned, and added, in the same voice as before,

"You have every thing over from Paris, don't you ?"

"Usually ; I find it cheaper in the end, and so much less trouble."

Mrs. Remsen plunged eagerly into *chiffons*, in the hope of getting Hortense off the pedestal which she had mounted ; and indeed the wise lady showed as much excitement in the discussion as if she had been the weakest of her sex.

At length Mrs. Marchmont rose to go. Much as all the idle talk wearied and irritated her, it had helped another half-hour to pass ; she was, at least, a little nearer the end of this dismal day. It seemed so strange to be sitting there among innocent women, talking of the petty affairs which interested them, with this new ban which separated her life from theirs rising before her mind. Often, in reading novels, she had wondered how people felt when some secret crime haunted their thoughts, and they were obliged to go calmly through the details of existence, repressing every evidence of care. And now she knew ; she was like them—an outcast—a criminal ! She thought this while taking her part in the conversation, while the idle talk went on, and the laughter of the two girls rang in her ear ; they laughed so easily, the joyous creatures !

"You will come and see me soon, Mrs. Remsen ?" she said, rising. "And don't give up my next evening in favor of the Japanese, Mrs. Maynard, else I shall throw my influence in the opposite scale, and vote for leaving them heathens."

"My life has so little leisure for the amusements of society," sighed Hortense. "Sometimes I wonder myself how I get through all I have to do."

"Weren't you at Mrs. Morford's dance last night ?" asked her mother, rather given to pulling her off her pedestal.

"Yes ; she fairly insisted ; but my mind was far away," returned Hortense, with unshaken dignity.

"One can dance very well without it," said Alice. "So next time send your mind to do duty among the Workers for Japan, and let me have your bodily presence. Come, Constance, we are making an unconscionable visit."

So she went away, left Constance at her own door, and drove on home, sitting face to face with the terrible secret which had usurped the place of the skeleton, and was a more awful sentinel still.

CHAPTER XIV.

UNDER THE YOKE.

Looking across the "glittering horseshoe," Mrs. Marchmont saw Dick Faulkner in his wife's box, nearly opposite ; and when she remembered that the time had gone by for her to shiver at the sight of him, her excitable nature found its first feeling of relief since her solitary communion of the morning. She was glad, horribly glad ; she had been right to free herself from him. She would never think about the matter again; and the sensation of rest and security grew stronger as she turned and met John Worthington's smile.

"It was very good of you to give up two nights in succession to folly and idleness," she said.

"I have got in the way of yielding to your caprices," he replied. "Now, Constance, I could have put off easily enough; but when she said that you wanted me, I resigned myself at once."

"You knew that I would be capable of coming to capture you?"

"Quite; even the sight of my law-books would not have driven you away. You lack reverence."

"And you have humored my caprices so long!"

"For which I ought to be ashamed. Everybody spoils you, but I don't wish to help, I assure you."

"Your conscience may be at ease; at least you have done your duty in the way of reproval. You are the only person who has ever ventured to scold me; admit that I always listen patiently."

John Worthington was forty, and one of the most famous lawyers of the day; but such geese are men up to the last, that I think to hear this queen of society make such acknowledgments was pleasanter in his ears than the loudest plaudits he had ever received in a court-room.

They were seated at one side of the box, quite by themselves; Miss Portman, as usual, was conscientiously following the scene, libretto in hand, and resigning herself to the invariable headache produced by the crash of the instruments; the two girls were holding a whispered conversation about some trifle which they considered of vast moment; and none of Mrs. Marchmont's satellites had as yet appeared upon the horizon: so the friends were able to converse unrestrainedly.

"I scold you," Worthington went on, "because I really think you have a little mind and soul at the bottom of your nonsense and waywardness."

"Your gallantry is overpowering! But had you finished?"

"No; you interrupted me, as usual."

"Then don't make periods in your voice till your sentence is finished. What comes after waywardness?"

"And most women have neither mind nor soul, I meant to say."

"Such a stale libel—such an old, worn-out charge! But after all, I am no better than the rest."

"I should think not, indeed! I hold you worse, a great deal."

She gave him an odd, frightened glance.

"Now I don't know what you mean."

"Because they are not accountable beings—a set of dolls—while you, pushed to extremities, could show character enough of some sort."

The talk was drifting in the direction of all others most terrifying to her; but she could not resist an impulse to continue it.

"Upon my word, Mr. Worthington, one would suppose you thought me capable of murder."

"Under certain circumstances, possibly," he replied, coolly. "The truth is, Alice, you have more brains than heart—"

"Now I take that as a compliment!"

"Because your heart has never had fair play; at the same time, you are as impulsive and irrational as a child."

"Always remember that!" she exclaimed, with a feverish earnestness under the laughter in her voice. "Promise me always to think it!"

"I can safely do so."

"And would, even if I committed the murder?"

He grew suddenly grave; her reckless words jarred upon him somewhat.

"Don't talk in such extremes," he said.

She laughed, gave him one of her quick, bewildering glances, and added,

"You will always like me? I need not feel afraid of losing you?"

I think I have said somewhere that for years John Worthington had guarded a certain secret, and it was one which he meant never to betray. He believed that it would be only folly to break the silence so long preserved; to do it might even bring to an end the pleasant, intimate intercourse that brightened his life in a way of which no one dreamed. But the desire to speak rose powerfully in his soul as she asked that question; it was quickly repressed, however, and he said,

"It is too late to try making you afraid. But see, the girls have ended their talk, and Constance is looking reproachfully at us for not paying any attention to her favorite duet."

"Ah yes, it is all new to them both," sighed Mrs. Marchmont. "Only think of being still in one's first season!"

She could not keep quiet; she wanted to talk, and drown the tones of the thrilling music which wakened strange echoes in her soul.

"I hope I frightened you the other night when I fainted," she said.

"Indeed you did."

"I am so glad; that was what I wanted."

"I suppose you fainted on purpose?"

"Of course—just to make a scene. I had done every thing else that evening to astonish you; so I tried that. Was it effective—did I do it well? You caught me, I believe—gallant man! But you couldn't call me a heavyweight."

"Now take breath and begin again," he said, rather grimly, disturbed by the recollection of her singular manner and illness.

"Thank you—no, I'll not speak at all; you may listen to the music."

"That is your gratitude, I conclude, for my caring whether you are ill or well, alive or dead!"

6

"Oh, I am grateful; I make you my best courtesy, metaphorically. Laura Keene was the only woman I ever saw who could courtesy like an angel and not step on her train. I declare, if I was Madame Rothschild, or the Princess Marguerite, or somebody who could afford it, I would give her a fortune if she could teach me to act off the stage half as naturally as she does on."

"I never thought you could be improved."

"In the way of acting?"

"Of acting, certainly."

"But do you know, Mr. Worthington, I am very weary of it! I am glad Lent is near. I wish it was time to go into the country. I want to get away. I don't believe I'll come back into the world any more."

"You are not well yet; don't let me be so unpardonably rude as to remind you of the old proverb."

"I would not prevent your being rude for the world;" and she laughed heartily. "'When the demon was ill,' et cetera. I read once in a book on good-breeding and morals that it was unlady-like to say devil."

But her face had grown too haggard and worn for her fun to be agreeable to the man.

"Are you sure that you are quite well yet?" he asked.

"As well as I shall ever be."

"What do you mean?" he asked, anxiously. "There is not really any thing serious the matter? You are not hiding some illness from—from your friends?"

She looked at him in surprise for an instant, and the tears rose in her eyes.

"I believe you would actually care!" she said, wonderingly.

"Care?" he repeated; and words which he did not choose to utter started to his lips.

"I didn't know there was any body left who would think twice about it," she said. "No, there is nothing the matter—unless my mind has a crook in it; but I think it always had."

"And something has been troubling your mind; of that I am sure."

If she could tell him! The insane thought presented itself—if she could reveal, word for word, what she had done!

"I was thinking, after you went away last night, that I ought to have told you, if there was any thing I could do, you had only to speak; but I think you know that."

"You would do it?"

"Yes," he said, very quietly; "if it were to go against my creed, my principles—no matter what—I should do it, if necessary."

Great Heaven, and she had doubted this man's friendship—had preferred guilt to trusting him!

"Dear friend," she said, "I need no help. I beg you to believe that. I am in no difficulty, except the one that troubles most people—the inability to get away from myself."

"You would tell me?"

"I think so—if you could help me. Mr. Worthington, I believe I never understood you before; I wish—"

"What, Alice?"

"That was not what I meant to say. We have been on familiar terms from habit; after all, we have seen little of each other's real selves."

It was so difficult to keep back what he would fain have said, that any made words sounded poor and weak.

"I mean what I say. I am your friend; I shall always be. It is not only that I admire you more than any woman I ever saw—pshaw, I needn't be stagy!"

If he had only spoken like this last night! Yet no; she knew that her lips would have remained sealed. The more he showed his fondness, his admiration, his faith, the less possibility there would have been of destroying them by her avowal.

"No, no," she replied, hastily; "we'll not indulge in a scene. Hereafter, I don't mean to have bothers of any sort. I want to try and be less frivolous and absurd."

"You have never been either the one or the other."

"Such an empty, aimless life, with no thought beyond the little worthless success of an hour."

"I don't agree with you, nor with all the things wise people say and write about such matters. I don't consider it a poor ambition for a woman to make herself a leader in her world —a power in society."

"It isn't worth the trouble one takes."

"It isn't worth rushing into such follies as women do," he said—"extravagance, debt, and that kind of thing."

"My days of extravagance end with this season," she replied. "My debts I mean to pay; so I'll not take your axioms to myself."

"I should be sorry to think you had any real cause."

"Don't you ever be sorry for me in any way, Mr. Worthington! I'll not tell you all my frivolity. I'll not confess my sins to you, because I can't live without the respect of the few whom I really esteem; but don't be sorry."

"And don't you use such strong words."

She laughed—if he could know the truth!

"I was speaking as if you were my conscience," she said; "I always try to coax that."

"Not if there were real reason why it should condemn you; then you would never try. I should pity you very much if there had been any possibility in your life of meeting—as so many unfortunates do—a place where to go wrong was easy, and the right so hard that you yielded."

"You think I would suffer?"

"Suffer! You would make each day an eternity of torture! You have great capabilities for suffering in that high-strung nature of yours; don't ever give them an opportunity to have the upper hand."

"But no troubles come to women except

through their hearts; and I have none, you know."

"I suppose you had once."

"I can't tell—only a flirting machine, I think. But do you know that is more like the real thing than people imagine? It can ache, and be in earnest, and simulate all sorts of feelings."

"You must be somewhat tired of that?"

"So tired! I tell you, I'd like to be a shepherdess and tend sheep. Heigh-ho! I wish I was in the forest of Ardennes."

"And very miserable you would be in a week."

"I suppose so, unless I found such a satirical old Jaques as you are somewhere about."

"You'll marry—"

"So people have said for quite a number of years! No, Mr. Worthington, I would not let a good man marry me—a bad one I would not take."

"What do you mean by saying that you would not let a good man marry you?" he asked.

"Because I am not worth such a man's love. There, I'm not acting—it is the honest truth."

He turned and faced her.

"What will you say when Kenneth Halford asks you to marry him?"

"I never shall be obliged to say any thing, for he'll not ask me."

"I thought he had been in love with you once."

"Nonsense; I have arranged his destiny in my own mind;" and she glanced toward Milly, who was eagerly watching the stage.

"Indeed! And what shall you say?"

"Congratulate them."

"And what shall you think?"

"Mr. Worthington, nothing could induce me to marry Kenneth Halford, if he wanted me; and he does not. He will worship an ideal all his life, and moan because no woman fulfills it."

"Oh, if he wants an angel, he must go where most people won't go in a hurry; and I don't know that he deserves so much better than his neighbors."

She noticed the tone of relief in which he spoke, but did not attach any particular meaning to it; for not the slightest perception of his real sentiments had ever reached her, keensighted as she usually was to discover when a man's heart or fancy was touched.

"Now we have settled every thing," she said. "Just in time, too; for here come some tiresome men. Ah me!"

There was no further opportunity for uninterrupted conversation; the curtain had fallen, and there was a constant succession of dandies fluttering in and out of the loge. Mrs. Marchmont called the girls to her side, and found a pleasure in making them talk, looking at them the while with a sharp pang of regret rather than envy. John Worthington leaned back in his seat, and allowed the stream of idle chat to flow on, without discomfiting any body by sharp, quizzical speeches, such as he sometimes permitted himself, and which were not easily parried by people in general.

So the evening wore on, and Mrs. Marchmont made the two or three additions necessary to fill up her supper-table. They were all for the benefit of the young ladies, however, as she intended to keep herself free to engross Mr. Worthington.

Dick Faulkner irritated his wife by his persistent staring at the opposite box, and the pair managed to get up one of their fierce quarrels before the opera was half over. Faulkner did not venture to intrude into the loge; for he knew that if he did Mrs. Marchmont would make him repent severely; and he cursed her anew at the thought, as he had done many times since the morning. And Alice, reading his discomfiture in his face, knowing that he dared not come, exulted from the bottom of her heart, and again, in her delight at feeling once more free from the nightmare of his influence, almost forgot the price which she had paid for this liberty. Under the circumstances, Dick could do nothing but abuse his wife; and he made her suffer not only on her own account, but vicariously for Alice Marchmont's contempt. However, she was quite able to take her own part, and the presence of other people did not in the least interfere with the energy of the matrimonial battle.

At length Kenneth Halford came and paid his salutations, after a long season of furtive watching of the two—the elegant woman and the rose-bud of a girl by her side. At first Mrs. Marchmont was gratified by the complete ignoring, in word or manner, of any remembrance of their conversation of yesterday; but suddenly there rose in her mind the recollection of what had happened since—the memory of the past night's work—and her mood changed. It was utterly unreasonable and unfounded, and she knew it, but she was ready to blame him in a measure for what she had done. If he had been true to his early dream—if he had ever really loved her—he might have saved her in those closing hours. And now where did she stand? What had she become?

She was ready to spring from her chair and rush out of the box, as the dreadful answer hissed through her soul. Then she reproached herself for being so miserable and weak a fool that she was not able to bear quietly even the first hours of acquaintance with her sin. She must conquer this absurdity, at any rate; she could not take to making a high tragedy of herself, and discomposing people by sudden starts and suppressed moans at any chance word which touched her secret, or each pang of remorse that stung her.

She consoled herself by saying several intensely disagreeable things to Halford, as most women—or men, for that matter—would have found a consolation in doing. He looked, not hurt, but as if he were pitying her; and then she fell in a hot rage. Of all the old passion, the old love, there was only this sentiment left—pity! It was more than she could endure, just then, and she as nearly turned her back on him as was lady-like.

He went and leaned over Milly's chair, and she was frankly glad to see him, and talked in her girlish way, though not after the fashion of ordinary girls; and once more Halford thought what a rest and quiet her society gave. Mrs. Marchmont saw it; if he had put his feelings into words for her benefit, she could not have understood them more clearly; and to-night, in her new mood, she did not approve. She had of her own accord sent him away—had herself pointed out Milly as capable of offering the love which he craved and needed, and had felt willing to aid them both, instead of trying to bewilder his fancy by her own smiles and arts.

She had thought so, and, remembering who and what she was, had sent him away hurriedly, frightened at the bare idea of loving and being loved. But to-night she was not pleased when she saw him bending over the girl and talking, with such a quiet, rested look on his countenance. Her heart was very bitter and sad; she wanted to be truly loved. She had scores of adorers, and adulation enough lavished upon her to satisfy a dozen women; but she had never been loved but once, and then it had not been her present self, but the girl she used to be, and of whom she had thought for years with such regretful pity; and it was Kenneth Halford who had loved her.

She felt a sudden rage at Milly's youth and Milly's face, with its beautiful promise of development when her heart should be fully awake, and her mind in the maturity of womanhood. She called Kenneth Halford to her; she could not sit there just then, with others, and see him placid and content in Milly's presence, while she had such an ache at her heart and such a troop of confused and conflicting thoughts in her mind. Not aching for love of him, this heart. Let me see if I can make plain the feeling by which she was possessed. Alice knew that the woman she had become was a world away from Kenneth Halford; she could not have dared let him approach nearer; but she pitied the girl that she once was—the girl they had sacrificed so remorselessly to their Moloch, the world—and she could not bear to see him bending over this other young creature, as if able to forget every past dream or suffering in that calm presence.

Mrs. Marchmont called him to her, and sent the dandies over to Milly, for which neither she nor they were thankful. John Worthington had left the box to speak with some friend; so Alice had an opportunity to talk with Kenneth Halford. But, in spite of her efforts, she felt impelled to say the precise things which she knew would annoy him, and so hurt herself, by reading disapproval in his eyes. In a few moments, however, as other people came and went, she allowed him to pass from her, and paid him no further attention. Indeed, when he took his leave, she was so much occupied in listening to some man's nonsense that she could scarcely accord him a parting smile. Her first intention had been to ask him to accompany them home, but she had not done so, and she was not too much engrossed to notice Milly's look of disappointment as he was allowed to go away. Mrs. Marchmont noticed it, and for an instant almost hated the girl. Then a feeling of regret crossed her mind—of shame, too, for her own pettiness.

She called herself hard names, and would have made any atonement to Milly, even to uniting her and Halford, whether they desired it or not, and attempting any number of sacrifices and expiations for her own part. Indeed, she sent in search of him; he should come to supper; pretty little Milly should be gratified. But her good resolutions awoke too late; Halford was not to be found by her messenger, having gone straight out of the house on leaving her box.

Before long the curtain fell on the last act: the two girls had wished to see the closing scene, and they were gratified. Passing through the lobby on John Worthington's arm, Mrs. Marchmont encountered Dick Faulkner, so close that her white mantle brushed him as she passed. She had to bow and smile, shivering inwardly because so much as the folds of her garments had touched him, loathing the sight of the handsome face, whose wickedness was so plain to her now under its smiles, and shuddering again as she remembered how hopeless her fate were it possible that she should ever be put a second time in his power.

"I do so cordially abhor that man," Worthington said, as they moved on, regardless whether or not his words were audible. "I can not understand how it is that decent people tolerate him."

"I'll not have you abhor any body just now," she answered; for it gave her a sensation of fear to listen to his words. "I want you to be agreeable; the man is nothing to you or me."

"Thank Heaven for that!" he said.

In the depths of her heart Mrs. Marchmont fervently repeated the thanksgiving. She was free—at least she was free! She cast one glance back through the crowd; Dick Faulkner was leaning against a projection of the wall, and looking after her with an expression which made her shiver afresh, till Mr. Worthington asked if she were cold, thereby bringing her down to the necessities of the moment.

The supper was very gay and pleasant; even Miss Portman warmed so much under the wit and merriment, or the Champagne which Worthington persuaded her to drink, that she positively laughed aloud, changed her position three times, and twice volunteered a remark, so astonishing those who knew her best by this unprecedented display of animation that they absolutely forgot to answer. Constance and Milly found the evening delightful, though the latter had leisure to miss Halford; yet at the same time she was glad—not attempting to account for the feeling—that he and Mrs. Marchmont were not on such intimate terms as she had at first fancied, for Alice had said,

"I only ask my very, very special friends on occasions like these; so you see I have adopted you into my heart, Miss Milly."

She was in a charming mood, which lasted almost up to the time that they were ready to leave the table; then something Worthington said, some chance words which struck close upon her secret, gave her again the desire to escape—to get away from every one of these familiar faces—above all, from the man whose friendship she had returned by such awful treachery.

"You will have an opportunity to find out whether you miss me," she said, suddenly, addressing him, but speaking aloud.

"Do you mean to go into retreat for Lent?" he asked.

"The next thing to it—I am going to Washington."

"Now please to explain this freak," said he, while the other men uttered exclamations of horror, and Miss Portman turned into a statue of astonishment at once.

"No freak whatever," replied she, as decidedly as if the idea had been a long time in her mind, instead of having just entered it, born of her sudden dread of the constant dissimulation needed in his presence. "I have business there, and I must go."

"Are you going to settle the affairs of the nation?" he asked, smiling.

"To settle my own, at least," returned she. "I have developed a fine taste for business, I assure you."

"Now I believe this is as new to you as to the rest of us," said he.

"She says it to frighten us all," added some man.

"Not I," she answered. "If I must give reasons, every body knows that I own a tract of land away off somewhere—I don't exactly know where. Is West Virginia near China?"

"Oh no, my dear! surely you know better," said poor Miss Portman, with a sad earnestness which made every body shriek.

"Very well; I'll not expose my ignorance by trying to tell where it is," said she. "At all events, I am going—"

"Not in search of it?" asked Worthington.

"No; to Washington, because—"

She stopped again, remembering her fear that Faulkner might learn something of her plans, and attempt to balk them.

"I intend to delude Congress into making it an independent county for me," she added. "Now this is a profound secret; so all of you rush off and tell it as soon as you can."

"I've no doubt you'll succeed," said Worthington.

"I assure you I am perfectly serious—"

"Have we doubted it?"

"At least about going. I leave the day after to-morrow."

"Is this news to you, also, Miss Portman?" asked John Worthington.

"Oh yes; and so sudden; really, Alice, it is very confusing," groaned the old maid.

"My dear, you adore Washington; you worship the President, and regard Congress as an immaculate body, that ought to be immortalized in statues of brass."

"And Congress could easily furnish the material," said Worthington.

"It is entirely on your account that I am going, Adeliza; so don't be ungrateful," pursued Alice. "You know you have been sighing all winter for a sight of—well, I'll be merciful, and not give the Senator's name."

"Oh, my dear!" squeaked Miss Portman, in deep distress.

"If it is a case of attending to Miss Portman's happiness, there is nothing to be said," observed Worthington.

"And it is," Alice averred.

"Oh, my dear!" repeated Miss Portman, on an ascending scale, and looking more like a Chinese mouse than ever.

"And you really are going?" Worthington asked, as soon as the laughter had again subsided.

"I really am, and for a long visit," she replied, rising from the table. "Mr. Worthington, set the example of going home. Remember that I am an unprotected widow, and it is past one o'clock. What will my neighbors say of such dissipation?"

"Going to Washington!" murmured Miss Portman, despairingly—not that she objected to the journey, but any sudden proposal always filled her with confusion and dismay.

"I am so glad to have had you here this evening," Mrs. Marchmont said to Milly, passing her arm about the girl's waist for an instant, and speaking in a low tone. "You're a dear little thing, and I fancy that I shall grow very fond of you. Be sure to like me."

"Indeed I do," said Milly; and meant what she said.

Mrs. Marchmont gazed earnestly, regretfully, in her face for a little; then let her go.

"I wonder if I was ever like that," she said to herself.

John Worthington did not catch the words, but he read in her countenance the fancies called up by Milly's youthful happiness, and drew close to Mrs. Marchmont's side.

"Will you write to me sometimes?" he asked.

"Yes. Don't I always when I am away?"

"And if you want me—if there is any thing I can do—only send, and I will come at once."

She took his hand, dropped it as quickly, and said,

"Good-bye, every body. Miss Crofton, Mr. Worthington and Constance are to take you safe home."

She detained them all still for a few last

words—gay, laughing to the last. Worthington left the room behind the others. As he reached the threshold she ran forward, seized his hand again, shook it warmly, saying,

"You promised always to like me; don't forget."

He turned and looked at her, his grave features stirred into unusual emotion.

"God bless you!" he said. "Good-bye."

As the outer doors closed behind her guests, Mrs. Marchmont flew off to her chamber before Miss Portman could utter a syllable. Human companionship was not to be borne an instant longer.

CHAPTER XV.

ELF-LAND PATHS.

THERE commenced for Milly Crofton a succession of weeks, in the very beginning of which her feet strayed into elf-land, and each day only led her further along the mazes of that enchanted realm. Her dreams heightened the commonest objects and the commonest incidents into absolute beauty and perfection. Never was there such sunlight before as played about her way—never such music as she listened to at balls or opera. Oh, it was the old, old story, but always new, always sweet, and will remain so while this world holds fresh young hearts like hers in the midst of its dreariness.

Alice Marchmont departed on the day she had named, and the season hurried toward the soberness and quiet of Lent. People seemed determined to crowd all the gayety possible into the short weeks before Ash-Wednesday should usher in its period of penitence and reflection.

Milly enjoyed the festivities more and more, and wherever she went she met Kenneth Halford; and his presence brought the charm which brought this new brightness over her life. She did not think much in these days; she did not question her heart—indeed had grown terribly shy of herself—but she did know that she seemed lifted above the common earth, and wondered if such sunshine had ever been granted any other mortal.

Halford was a great deal at the house, and he did not forget Mrs. Remsen's permission in regard to morning walks with Milly. That lady watched the progress of events with the most unconscious air, and never troubled Milly by word or look. She knew the man with whom they had to deal, and was perfectly certain that these attentions to the girl were neither idle nor unmeant. He was not a man to retreat from any position that he had assumed, or amuse himself at the expense of any woman's happiness. So she waited composedly, certain that an agreeable *denouement* to Milly's pretty romance would come, sooner or later.

Fortunately, Adelaide Ramsay was absent all this month; otherwise she would certainly have found some means of troubling Milly's peace, as her envious dislike of her cousin had reached a tolerable pitch of hatred in these days of the latter's little triumphs. The old story of the engagement which once existed between Halford and Alice Berners was not generally known among their present acquaintances; so not even a whisper in regard to the past intruded to cast a shadow over Milly's way. It was a season of unalloyed happiness; but she was too young and too undisciplined to know how seldom it is that a long season of uninterrupted contentment is granted to any mortal. No romance or poem ever pictured an idyl half so beautiful as Milly's life during those charmed days, though the details would be slight enough if put into words.

So the beautiful days floated on, and each successive one lured Milly farther and farther into the Eden from whence a return to the old life became always more impossible. The golden dream must either widen into realization, or, when it faded, leave her wounded and faint upon the bleak rocks of the desolate desert in which so many hearts like hers have wakened after a brief wandering in that fairy-land of youth.

The pleasant walks, the daily visits, took their course; there were frequent invitations to the opera, with only Aunt Eliza besides themselves in the box, when the music was, in Milly's ears, a joyous pæan that no instruments of mortal invention ever played, the passionate arias and duets thrilling her soul with melodies which no human voice ever expressed; there were evenings at the French theatre, which were hours of such enchantment as no dramatist's eloquence or actor's passion could ever evoke; occasionally quiet hours at home, when no visitors were admitted, and Aunt Eliza read her newspaper, or made a pretense of embroidery, or wrote letters, while Milly sat at the piano and sung old ballads, often interrupted by long, low-voiced conversations, not containing a word which would merit to be set down, but deeply engraven in her heart, as if they held all this world's wisdom in their length.

So little to tell—a story so old, so worn out; yet I would gladly linger over it; and you who should read, though you might pretend to smile in scorn, would feel your own hearts stirred to their inmost depths—not by my poor words—but by the spell of memory carrying you back to the enchanted realm where each has wandered in his turn. But let the details go; there is no need to picture them; and sneer as we may, not one of us ever grows hard enough or worldly enough to forget, when we watch the progress of a romance like my pretty Milly's.

"Do you think I am wearing out my welcome?" Halford asked, one day, as he returned to the house with Milly, from an expedition to a private picture-gallery.

Mrs. Remsen had accompanied them; but on leaving the gallery Halford had begged that Milly might be allowed to walk back with him, as she had taken no exercise that day. He had assumed a great deal of responsibility about similar matters so naturally that nobody thought of questioning it.

"You must ask aunty about that," Milly answered; "she has not hinted to me that she was tired of your visits."

"So I will; that gives me an excuse for going in," he said. "I was wondering what one I could manage; now I can enter boldly; indeed, it really is my duty to know at once if she is weary of the sight of me."

It had been four o'clock when Mrs. Remsen left the pair at the entrance of the picture-gallery, and it was somewhat past five, and nearly dark, when they entered the room where she sat. But she did not ask how they had managed to consume a whole hour and more in a walk which a tortoise would have accomplished in less than half the time; nor did she make any remark when, later, some chance words of Milly's revealed the fact of their having come round by Madison Square—to accomplish which feat they must have gone at least a mile out of their way.

"Mr. Halford has come in on purpose to ask you a question, aunty," said her niece, as the two appeared before the matron, and interrupted a little vision in which she had been indulging as freely as if she had not lived long past the period when such weakness is permissible.

"What is this important question, Mr. Halford?" she inquired, suavely.

"But you are not to hesitate just for the sake of politeness, aunty!" cried Milly, before he could explain. "Aunty does sometimes, Mr. Halford. She hates to tell fibs; but she has very stately ideas in regard to civility and hospitality."

"Now you are throwing out base insinuations," he said, gayly. "You want me to think that, if she denies being tired, it is only because she is too kind to mortify me."

"Has Milly been hinting that?" asked Mrs. Remsen, entering into the badinage gracefully enough, thinking the while, as she glanced at Kenneth Halford, how much these quiet weeks had changed him. He looked younger, more restful and content; and it was pleasant to her to see it, and then turn to the radiant brightness that grew each day more lovely in Milly's face. "Has she been slandering me, Mr. Halford? But you and I are too old friends for her wicked little tongue to make mischief between us."

"I did not say a word; it was his own conscience that accused him," Milly averred, in laughing self-defense.

"What have you done, Mr. Halford, that your inward monitor has become troublesome?" demanded Mrs. Remsen.

"Upon my word, I am afraid that even in this statement Miss Crofton is not correct," he replied. "My conscience refuses to blame me as it ought—"

"It must be made of gutta-percha," put in Milly, parenthetically.

"I only asked her if you were tired of the sight of me. I have bored you so constantly of late that it occurred to me that I might wear out my welcome."

"I am always glad to see you," she replied. "As a proof, I was meaning, when you came in, to ask you to stay to dinner—a very unceremonious one; for Maud has gone to her sisters; so Milly and I must dine alone, unless you will give us your company."

"But his conscience!" said Milly, mischievously."

"I shall reward it by staying," Halford declared. "Thanks, a thousand times, Mrs. Remsen; for I should have been doomed to a solitary dinner at my club."

"A meal prepared for feminine tastes may not be very tempting, I warn you," she said. "But at least I have always a very tolerable glass of claret to offer my male visitors. Mr. Crittendon brought me a huge case from France."

"I shall prove the innocence of my taste by hugely enjoying the dinner prepared to suit feminine palates," he answered.

In truth, Mrs. Remsen was not in the least troubled about the dinner. She had foreseen that Halford would enter the house, and had already instructed the cook as to the changes and additions which were to be made in the repast.

Milly went away to get rid of her out-door garments. There was to be no dressing, her aunt had said; but she could not resist induing herself in a white cashmere, with a blue over-skirt, which was as becoming a thing as she could have put on; and Aunt Eliza did not remark the change.

The dinner was a complete success—even to the venison which had been sent by an acquaintance gone to the Adirondacks for a week's winter sport; and the claret was beyond reproach.

"The chef at the club couldn't equal this," Halford averred; and Mrs. Remsen did not think it necessary to admit that she neither possessed one of those troublesome French treasures, nor even a cordon bleu, though, indeed, her wonderful old black woman, who had lived with her mother before her, deserved the latter badge if ever a female did.

The evening was not quite so pleasant as the dinner, because Hortense Maynard was seized with the idea of visiting her parent on the way to some learned reunion; and poor Charley Thorne and a brace of other youths strayed in likewise. But Milly was too happy to feel annoyance at the interruption, and greeted luckless Charley with so much kindness that for an instant he brightened out of the gloom into which he had been thrown by the sight of Halford so comfortably established by the young lady's side.

These had been troubled weeks to Master Charley, and he really suffered in his little way, since it was to the full extent of his capabilities. I suppose he found it just as hard to bear as people of a different calibre do their miseries. He was a perfect model of the youth of New York; the parting of his back hair was always irreproachable, his neck-tie a marvel, and his trowsers real works of art. He had not much more to say for himself than his species in general; but at least he was free from affectations and vices, and Mrs. Remsen was already precipitating her soul into futurity, and regarding the possibility of Maud, some months later, catching his poor little heart at a rebound.

"I never see you any more," he began, as soon as he could get near to Milly and make his small moan, Hortense Maynard having unconsciously afforded him the desired opportunity by taking instant possession of Mr. Halford. "I might as well be off in the—the desert of Sahara, or up with those fellows in the Adirondacks."

"I saw you only night before last, at Mrs. Morrison's concert. If you forget as easily as that, I don't think much of your friendship," returned Milly, cruelly, though she did not mean to be unkind. "And I wonder you did not go up to the Woods. I should think an expedition there in the winter must be delightful."

Charley went down into the depths of black despair at once. Even Mrs. Maynard was making a grand display of her acquirements and the incessant duties of her life for Halford's benefit; and at last she got upon one of her favorite hobbies—the praiseworthy efforts of a band called "The Earnest Workers for Japan," among whom she ranked as chief; and she did not leave the subject until she had deluded Halford into putting his name on her subscription-book.

"You are incorrigible, Hortense," said her mother, coming up at the moment. "Don't pay any attention to Japan, Mr. Halford. It is too far off for sympathy."

"Oh, that is its chief charm," returned he; but Mrs. Maynard was too serious to notice the raillery.

"I wish you could persuade mamma and Milly to take some interest in the good work," she said. "Now Milly is a nice, dear little thing, but so childish; and mamma only encourages her."

"I hear you, Hortense," said her mother, laughing. "Say what you like of me, but don't ask for any change in my Milly. Besides, we can afford to be lazy and selfish. You are so determined to do good till people hate you that you leave us no chance."

"You always turn serious conversation off with a jest, mamma," sighed Hortense. "I have ceased to hope for any impression on you or Milly either."

"So much the better for us all," returned Mrs. Remsen, gayly. "You will not need to distress yourself, and will leave us to our frivolity in peace."

Hortense shook her head and lifted her hands —such pretty hands! She was altogether so elegant and fine-ladyish, so totally unlike the received ideas concerning strong-minded women, that Halford could not avoid a smile at the contrast between her appearance and her much-vaunted pursuits.

"I wonder you don't wear yourself out," he said. "You never give yourself a moment's rest."

"At least I should exhaust myself in the cause of duty," she replied, with a reproachful glance at her mother.

"I see the look, Hortense, but I am too thoroughly hardened to be affected," that lady said. She always consoled herself, when Hortense talked stilted trash to any man, by the fact that the creature was pretty enough to make any sort of conversation endurable to masculine ears.

"You were at Professor Drivler's lecture the other night?" asked Halford.

"Yes; I would not have missed it for the world. The crowd was frightful, and the heat beyond description; but it was suffering in a good cause. Mamma, my new velvet polonaise was absolutely ruined; the lace was in rags."

"Now that does touch me," said her mother. "If you must run the risk of suffocation or being trodden to death by a learned mob, you might at least wear something plainer."

"It was a marvelous effort of genius," pursued Hortense. "I never listened to such fervid eloquence. He spoke for two hours and a half, and it seemed only a few moments."

"It tires me to think of it," said Mrs. Remsen.

"I confess to running away," added Halford; "the heat was unendurable."

"Take care," said Mrs. Remsen. "Hortense will accuse you of encouraging Milly and me in our frivolity."

"If my efforts everywhere were as useless as they are among my own relations, I should call my life a wasted one indeed," she said, playing with her bracelets, and looking very handsome in her melancholy.

"Fortunately, your constant exertions are too fully crowned with success for you to become discouraged," Halford said.

"You are very good; I hope they are not quite thrown away," she replied, with a sweet self-complacency. "I have always wished that mamma had left Milly more to me since my marriage; I am growing a grave old woman—"

"At twenty-six," interrupted her mother "Hortense, it's lucky Adelaide does not hear you, and I don't mean to be made out quite as ancient as the Pyramids, either."

"Age does not count by years," returned Hortense. "But you do fly about so—"

"Naturally, being a frivolous young thing," again broke in Mrs. Remsen; for her spirits had been unusually high all the evening.

"I would have taken Milly with me in my studies," pursued Hortense. "At this moment I am deep in Sanskrit—"

Here there was a general outbreak. Milly gave a little shriek of horror; Charley Thorne groaned; and Halford could not keep from laughter at the idea of poor little Milly doomed to Sanskrit. But Hortense pursued her theme composedly, and Halford drew a pencil and paper toward him, and made a sketch of Milly trying to study a Sanskrit manuscript, which delighted Mrs. Remsen beyond measure.

"You have studied the Eastern languages, Mr. Halford?" continued Mrs. Maynard. "You know how delightful the labor is—a positive recreation to a well-disciplined mind."

"I have battered my head a little against Arabic," he replied; "but I am afraid that my mind is not in a proper state of discipline, for I found it terrible work."

Milly laughed, and Hortense shook her head again.

"Why will all men, even wise ones, students like yourself, encourage the frivolity of the women of this age by such remarks!" sighed she.

"You speak as if you belonged to some other century," said her mother.

"I feel sometimes as if I did, mamma; at least, I am glad that I find something in this to occupy my powers."

At this juncture Charley Thorne managed to get near Milly again; and, as Mrs. Remsen had no mind that he should distress the child at present by an untimely disclosure of his passion, she was obliged to leave Halford to Hortense's tender mercies, while she went to protect her niece. The two youths, who had been undergoing a voluntary and embarrassed banishment at the piano ever since Milly deserted it, were called out by the hostess, and she assisted Milly to keep the conversation general among their group. All Charley Thorne could do was to sigh prodigiously, and nibble so recklessly at the fingers of his gloves that Mrs. Remsen longed to tell him he would bring on an attack of indigestion. Milly was really and truly quite unconscious of his deplorable state, and teased him, as she had always been in the habit of doing, until he turned misanthropical, and took refuge in "Owen Meredith." He announced, suddenly, that the Queen of the Serpents was a truthful picture of woman, and only frowned and tried to look as much as possible like Lester Wallack in "The Stranger," when Milly laughed, and his two male friends followed her example.

"It must be dyspepsia," Milly said; and Charley half rose to his feet, meaning to depart; but the idea of leaving Halford master of the field was more than he could endure, so down he sat again. Even the sight of his gorgeous new shirt-studs, that shook under the tremendous sigh he gave, did not console him.

"You don't treat me well," he moaned; "and it's too bad when I've known you all my life; and to slight me without any reason."

"You always quarrel with me nowadays," replied Milly; "and you're not half so nice as you were once. It all comes of that set of young men you go with so much. But there's Cæsar offering you tea. Will you have a cup?"

But Charley waved off the elegant coffee-colored servant and his tray with a tragic gesture.

"I'd take some if it was poison," he said, dolefully.

"It's good Orange Pekoe," returned Milly; "and I wish you would give me a cup. Put but one lump of sugar in it, and—oh, you've ruined it with milk!"

For Charley had seized the jug and transformed the dish of tea into a white pool, with one reckless dash.

"I never can do any thing right!" he sighed.

"Now you must drink it," said Milly, severely; "we can't have cups of tea wasted in these expensive days."

"But I don't like tea; I never touch it," pleaded the poor boy.

"So much the more reason why you should drink every drop. I dare say it will be your first attempt at penance. Now don't hesitate; it will only get cold and taste the worse."

"And I hate it with milk," urged Charley.

"I am very glad of it," replied pitiless Milly; "another time you'll not deluge my cup when I don't like it, either. Now drink it at once, without any more words. Aunty is looking at you! She is very peculiar about certain things, and nothing vexes her so much as to see people waste her Orange Pekoe."

Halford, sitting near enough to catch the dialogue through the monotonous hum of Mrs. Maynard's voice, smiled at Milly's nonsense, and the unconscious way in which she displayed the feline instincts of her sex by tormenting her victim. Luckily, he thought, she was still a kitten, and the velvet paws gave no vicious scratches.

"I'll not have you tease Charley Thorne," Mrs. Remsen said, coming up at the instant that Milly was sternly ordering him to swallow the nauseous draught. "Mr. Carrolton wants you to sing, Milly. I shall stay here and protect you, Charley, from such treatment," she added, by her frank manner making the miserable youth feel younger and more helpless than ever.

"I doubt my having a suspicion of a voice," Milly said, rising, as the Carrolton youth ambled up. There is no other word which expresses the peculiar style of 'locomotion' which the youth of Gotham invariably affect. "I will do my best, though. What shall it be?"

She looked at Halford rather than at the person whom she addressed; and as Mr. Carrolton seemed incapable of any thing beyond twirling his watch-chain and swaying gracefully back and forth on his heels and toes, that gentleman begged for "The King of Thule." Milly sang it exquisitely. Her voice was not very powerful, but thoroughly cultivated, and her taste perfect; and there was, too, that pathetic ring which one often hears and wonders at in the voices of young girls — sometimes almost saddening one by the thought that it is like a premonition of experiences still undreamed of, which shall yet render that piteous tremor a settled and ordinary tone.

Some such fancy occurred to Halford as he listened; but he said to himself that in Milly's case the fear should never be realized; it should be his care to prevent this; for though, when these weeks began, he had no thought how far they would lead him, he had no mind to regret their course as he looked back. This child possessed an absolute fascination for him. There was a rest and peace in the idea of winning her love sweeter than any sentiment which had touched him for many a day.' He did not perceive the leaven of masculine arrogance and selfishness in his reflections.' That any trouble could ever come to her through him did not occur to his mind. That this very love which it pleased him to see so unconsciously taking a deeper hold upon her heart might transform her from a child into a woman, was a fact which he forgot likewise, as the wisest of us overlook truths which concern ourselves, though they would be plain enough to us in the case of another.

Charley Thorne looked and listened too, and indulged in his own little attempts at sentiment and reflection; but his mood was by no means so tranquil as Halford's. He had three minds to make a *confidante* of Mrs. Remsen on the spot; but that astute lady perceived his desire, and took measures to prevent its expression. When the time came that Milly was actually engaged, she would play the part of consoler to Charley with great satisfaction, and do her best to teach Maud to help in the charitable work of soothing his wounds; but at present any confession would be an embarrassment, since she could not positively affirm that Milly was out of his reach. So she kept up an animated conversation upon such subjects as he could best talk about—his wonderful breed of dogs—his horses—his genius for billiards—his athletic feats at the gymnasium. And even after Milly had left the piano, she contrived artfully to keep the wretched boy from the *tête-à-tête* he desired.

Except to him, the evening was not an unpleasant one, for Hortense Maynard was obliged to leave before she had utterly reduced Halford to a state of coma by her long words and eloquent periods. One of the youths accompanied her for the express pleasure of attending on a pretty woman. But he was sorely punished for the weakness by what he endured at the learned party. Charley Thorne told Milly afterward that the unfortunate wretch was ill for a week in consequence of the sufferings of that night, and he vowed to Charley that henceforth, to the day of his death, he would never so much as read a newspaper, and had burned everything he owned in the shape of books as soon as he reached home, while the memory of his wrongs was fresh in his mind.

It was soon time for every body to go, and Halford set the younger men the example by rising to take leave. Charley Thorne would have sat there till daylight—at least, he told himself that he would—sooner than leave Halford to profit by his departure; but under present circumstances he could do nothing but follow in the wake of the others. He made his farewells lugubrious in the extreme; but his misery, deep as it was, would have been increased tenfold had he dreamed that Milly did not hear a word that he said, in the pleasant confusion which Halford's parting sentences created in her mind.

Poor Charley was any thing but an agreeable companion to his friend after Halford left them: he loathed the idea of billiards, treated with contempt the proposal of broiled oysters and a bird at Delmonico's, and scouted with still more scorn the idea of lounging into the club and finding out what the other fellows were at.

"No, no, Jack," cried he; "there's a—a what-you-call-it between us—a gulf—a desert, you know!"

"I don't know," retorted Jack, naturally a little nettled in spite of his good temper by the contempt which his friendly proposals had met with from his chosen comrade. "I've crossed the Desert of Sahara, and I've been up the Archipelago—no, the Bosporus; but never mind—and I'm blessed if I understand what you're driving at, old man, or what's huffed you."

"I'm not huffed," moaned Charley. "I'm—but never mind, Jack; you wouldn't understand."

"Now see here, Charley," returned the other, "you've been regularly knocked off your perch lately. You just come along with me to Delmonico's, and let's have it out over a bottle of Rudesheim and a broiled bone or something. Now we've been pals too long for us to fight shy of each other; so come along."

The youth's brain was not immense, nor his slang very intelligible, but he meant, perhaps, more kindly than a superior animal would have done. Charley allowed himself to be persuaded, though he did not disclose his secret—even to the faithful Jack he could not do that—but he managed to 'pick a bone,' and 'get outside' of a flask of wine—to employ the elegant expressions of the youth of our day, and felt relieved, momentarily, by the performance.

The Lenten weeks drifted on, and Easter came—the most beautiful Easter, Milly thought, that had ever gladdened the earth. Two or three days afterward there was a little break in her dream—Kenneth Halford was obliged to go to Baltimore for a time. But Milly was not unhappy or restless; only, instead of being an affair of each moment, her happiness was made up of memory and anticipation.

The night before his departure Halford was at the house. There was no opportunity to have much private talk with Milly, for there were two or three people present. But he was not sorry for that; he meant fully to speak the words which he had promised himself to utter; but he was, unconsciously, somewhat selfish in his new contentment, and had no mind to break the silence until his return. He wanted Milly to miss him; she was not half enough aware of the secret which he read so plainly in her face. This week of loneliness would show her plainly whither her heart had strayed, and her joy at seeing him again add to the pleasure of the avowal he should then utter.

Milly was sorry to have him go, but she had not thought enough to expect a declaration; and his manner was too kind and tender up to the last for any feeling of disappointment to trouble her.

"You will be sure to miss me?" he said, as he stood beside her at the piano during the latter part of the evening. She had been singing, and he thought that he had never heard any thing half so sweet as the ringing tones of her fresh young voice. "You will be sure to miss me?"

"Oh yes; I shall have to walk alone or with Maud," she said, woman enough to try for any subterfuge that should keep her words from becoming too earnest.

"What a selfish little Miss Milly!" he whispered.

"Indeed, indeed, I am not," she said, eagerly, so moved by his laughing reproach that she forgot her evasions. "I shall miss you very much—you have been so kind."

"To myself," he replied. "And you'll be glad to have me come back—promise!"

"I do promise," she said, rather unsteadily, letting her fingers stray softly over the keys.

"Say it in so many words—you will be glad," he urged.

"I shall be very glad," she answered, almost inaudibly.

"The week will seem a thousand years long to me," he said.

Just then some wretch approached the instrument, and there was no opportunity for further conversation. Halford perceived that these weeks had drawn him on further and more rapidly than he had meant so soon to go; but he could not be sorry. Life could offer nothing brighter than the love of this beautiful child—no higher pleasure than to watch the development of her mind and heart. He was more satisfied with existence than he had been in years, and rather wondered at his own capabilities for enjoyment as he looked back over the past month.

Presently Mrs. Remsen came up and spoke to him. He had promised to attend to some business for her in Baltimore, and she wanted to give him the necessary papers and directions.

"I am ashamed to bother you," she said; "but as you kindly offered to save me the trouble, perhaps, of a journey—"

"It will be a pleasure to oblige you," he answered, as she left her speech unfinished, as people do about half their sentences in real life.

"I have written out plainly all that is necessary to do," she continued, "and will send you the letter and papers to-morrow."

"But I leave by the early train," he replied. "You must give them to me to-night."

"Then, as there is no one here with whom I need stand on ceremony, if you will come into the other room, you shall have them," she said.

So he followed her; and, after the business matter was arranged, they still stood talking for a few moments.

"You will only be gone a week?" she asked.

"Not longer," he answered, rather absently. He was thinking that, though he could afford to please himself where Milly was concerned by not putting his intentions into words till after his return, he had no right to exercise the same reticence toward Mrs. Remsen. To speak—even vaguely—would settle his fate at once; but the thought was not unpleasant. He said to himself again that life had nothing pleasanter or brighter than the chance of taking into his own guardianship this girl-heart, and teaching it to throb and glow into a woman's power of affection, while still preserving all the freshness and innocence that it possessed in this season of girlish dreams.

"We shall be glad to have you back," Mrs. Remsen said, graciously, breaking in upon his thought.

"Thanks; you are very good. I hope, though it is not very long since we renewed our acquaintance, you have learned to consider me an old friend and to like me a little?"

"Indeed I have, Mr. Halford."

"And to trust me?" he asked, smiling.

"I have proved it," she replied, with an answering smile, which told him she had been by no means blind or unobservant during these weeks which had been allowed to take their course unchecked.

"And I shall try to be worthy of it," he said, earnestly.

"You don't need to tell me that, Mr. Halford."

"When I come back, I shall have a favor to ask of you. I think you know what it will be!"

"I will tell you when you come to ask it," she replied, pleasantly.

"I want to steal the very prettiest of your treasures," he said. "I want you to give me your little Rose-bud."

"But the favor will not be for me to grant; you will have to ask in another quarter," she said, not affecting the slightest surprise, for she knew the man well enough to be certain that any such common feminine artifice would annoy him, and, perhaps, rouse suspicions in his mind that he had been angled for and led on to this moment.

"I have not spoken; you may be sure I would not until I had your permission," he replied.

"At least you have that," she said; and her heart swelled high with gratified vanity and pride, though, to do her justice, there was a better feeling mingled—she rejoiced honestly in the prospect of Milly's happiness.

"Of course, I can't be certain what my fate will be," he continued; "and I have a fancy to leave it undecided till my return."

"You must choose for yourself; I've nothing

to do with the time or reasons," she said. "I don't think I need to tell you, Mr. Halford, that no word of explanation has passed between Milly and myself. I really believe she is not conscious what it is has made her so happy during these weeks. She's an odd compound—artless as a child, but with a heart that any man might be proud to win."

"And if I find I have won it, she shall be a happy woman," he answered, with the self-confidence only too common with all of us.

"I am certain of it. You shall have her without a scruple or fear on my part, Mr. Halford."

"Then we will leave every thing just as it is until my return," he said. "I want her to find out that she misses me; I do think she will."

"I fancy there is little doubt of it, you have been making such a little princess of her all these weeks. Certainly I shall give her no hint of this conversation; I have left her to herself, and shall continue to. I did it because I knew the man with whom I had to deal, not because I am a careless or unobservant guardian."

"And I thank you for your confidence in me."

"So this ends all we need say about the matter at present. I suppose I must go back to those people."

He put into his breast pocket the papers which she had laid on the table, and followed her back to the drawing-room. Mrs. Remsen was a proud and triumphant woman, but she gave no sign; she was too acute for any such weakness. Perhaps there was an added cordiality in her manner to every body; she really felt amicably disposed toward the whole world.

The time for leave-takings arrived, and Halford had only space for a few whispered words to Milly.

"You will not forget your promise?"

"I shall not forget."

"It is not good-bye, you know, though it seems a long time."

He held her hand for an instant in his own, made her heart throb tumultuously by the earnest look in his eyes—then he was gone.

As soon as she could, Milly ran away to her own room, that she might be alone with her delicious fancies, free to listen to the voice in her soul, which sounded more sweet than the song of a Southern bird.

CHAPTER XVI.

"INTO THE MAGIC REALM."

THE week of Kenneth Halford's absence got by, but the waiting had not seemed very long to Milly, for constant reminders came to assure her that he by no means forgot their *acquaintance*—Milly called it that to herself, and had grown conscious enough to blush a little as she did so—in the engrossing cares of the business which had caused his departure. Bouquets of choice flowers, for which he had left an unlimited order, reached her daily; he sent such books as he chanced to read and like, and there were occasionally marginal notes on the pages in his writing. Even a few tiny billets came, also, inclosed in certain epistles to her aunt, which were rendered necessary by the affairs he was arranging for her. All these things were trifles, perhaps, but they served to keep up the brightness of her dream undisturbed.

The week ended, but he was not able to return on the day he had appointed; forty-eight hours more absolutely went by, and their length roused Milly at last to a full perception of the new world into which her heart had strayed. She was almost frightened at first, ready to reproach herself as unfeminine and bold, and shed a few tears in the solitude of her chamber. Finally, she opened the box in which she treasured his notes, read them again, went back in fancy over the events of those charming weeks, and by the time her reverie ended, the fear, the sense of shame, were forgotten in the delicious thrill which stirred her soul to its inmost depths.

The night after was Mrs. Lawrence's ball, the very last of the season; for on the next day but one Lent would begin. Halford wrote Mrs. Remsen that he should certainly be back for that occasion, and begged, as the greatest possible favor, that Milly would keep her first redowa for him—he deserved so much show of consideration after his banishment. Mrs. Remsen gave the letter to Milly without any remark, apparently unconscious that the half-jesting lines were more than a bit of ordinary gallantry. In all this time, never, by word or look, had the wily matron betrayed the least knowledge that Halford's attentions to her niece had any special meaning; and though she talked of him frequently, and landed him to the skies, she appeared to consider his friendship as belonging to her rather than Milly.

Mrs. Remsen and her niece were very late in arriving at the ball; in fact, Milly began to despair of ever getting there; and, though she said not a word, Mrs. Remsen was almost as impatient as her niece of the delay. But one of the children chose this opportunity to indulge in an attack of earache just as they were dressing, and could not, of course, be left until remedies had been found to soothe her pain. She must have Milly by her, too; lay her poor little head on Milly's lap, and be coaxed and comforted by her alone. The girl bore the waiting wonderfully well, not evincing the least show of impatience, even sitting by the child after the pain had ceased, and lulling her to sleep with the strains of a quaint old melody made doubly sweet by her fresh young voice. Mrs. Remsen—more than ever inclined to be fond of her niece during these days—said to herself that this certainly was the most charming creature that ever existed, and was delighted to find that she looked prettier than ever in the new dress which had been prepared for this important occasion.

But late as it was when they entered Mrs. Lawrence's rooms, Halford had not appeared, and Mrs. Remsen half feared that the new gown would prove a useless expense. Somehow, disappointed as she was, Milly could not help feeling certain that he would arrive before the night was over; and this inward assurance kept her in a state of pleasurable restlessness which only heightened the bloom on her cheeks, and added a new brilliancy to her eyes. She was beset by partners, poor Charley Thorne the most persistent, of course; but, though she gave him and others galops, and even stupid quadrilles, in abundance, nothing could induce her to a redowa, even Strauss's loveliest waltzes; and at last her cruel refusals quickened Charley's jealous mind into a suspicion of the cause.

"I know," he whispered, going up to her at the close of a dance during which he had watched her from a distance with a bitter envy of the man who happened to have the bliss of supporting her, "I know why you have refused every *valse.*"

"Do you?" returned Milly, fanning herself, anxious to make it appear that it was the heat, and not his question, which deepened her color. "Well, why shouldn't I be capricious the same as other people?"

"You've promised not to *valse* with any body while that man is gone," asserted Charley; and his angry tone made the innocent appellation sound more like an opprobrious epithet than the general term applied to the male species of humanity.

"I remember giving you at least half a dozen *valses* last week," said Milly; "and I think you are very rude."

"I didn't mean to be," replied Charley, growing humble at once, not so much from honest contrition as because he feared that, if he did not attempt a show of it, she would treat him to cold looks for the rest of the night. "But it's awful to think that's the reason, and it makes me wretched."

"Then I would advise you not to think of it," said Milly, with a dignity quite overwhelming. "You always quarrel with me nowadays, and I shall end by not liking you a bit unless you stop this absurd way of talking."

"Oh!" gasped Charley, catching the lapels of his coat in both hands, as if to hold himself up.

"Yes, indeed. Now don't talk any more nonsense, and I'll walk the next quadrille with you. I am sure I don't know why you are so ill-tempered all the time, and it annoys me very much; so I wish you would stop it."

"If you'd only be as you used!" sighed Charley.

"Oh dear, you have told me that so often—as if I had lately turned into a Gorgon, or something else dreadful!" said Milly.

"I don't mean your looks," Charley began; but she would not listen.

"I shall send you away if you don't stop this instant; my aunt would be angry if she heard you," menaced Milly; so he had to content himself with looking as gloomy as his youthful face could manage.

The evening flew on, supper-time came and passed, and still Halford did not appear. Milly's pleasant anticipations began to fade; she was vexed at herself for having expected him. The ball, after having been so agreeable, suddenly appeared tiresome, and she almost wished that her aunt would signify her desire to depart. She had just finished a tedious quadrille with an elderly beau who still ranked himself among the dancing men; he was leading her back to her aunt, when, as Milly raised her eyes, she saw Kenneth Halford standing by that lady. She was near the doors into the passage—she did not wait to think that Halford might have seen her—she made some rapid excuse to her partner, and darted away up the stairs, anxious only to escape for a few moments before meeting him.

Mrs. Lawrence's house was an immense one, divided in the middle by a great corridor, and besides the suite of drawing-rooms (situated on the ground-floor, after the arrangement in most New York houses) there was a succession of pretty apartments on the upper story, always thrown open for the convenience of such elderly people as preferred whist or conversation to dancing, and ending in the prettiest little boudoir imaginable. Milly passed through the first card-room, where turbaned dowagers and ancient masculines squabbled over the card-tables, and on into the second, which chanced to be empty. She sank down into a seat in the corner, and, catching sight of her face in a mirror, was startled by its color; but, before she had time to confuse herself with further thought, the draperies were flung back from the doorway, and Kenneth Halford entered, looked eagerly about, and, catching a glimpse of her in her retreat, hurried forward with words of delight, which caused poor Milly's heart to flutter more helplessly than ever.

"I have been looking everywhere for you," he said. "Didn't you see me? Why did you run away?"

"I—I was tired; I came up here to rest for a moment," Milly said.

"And aren't you in the least glad to see me?" he asked, though to a man of his years and experience the question was unnecessary. "Won't you say a single word?"

"Oh yes, I am glad," returned Milly, trying to speak carelessly. "We had given you up, it is so very late; but I suppose you forgot about the ball—dining with friends or something."

"I have only just had time to dress and get here," he replied. "Late as it was, I determined to come; but, if you are not glad to see me, I might as well have staid away."

Milly had risen as if to go down stairs, but he drew her hand through his arm, feeling it tremble under his touch, and led her on into the little boudoir, letting the draperies fall back over the entrance, so that they were concealed from the view of any person entering the outer rooms.

"Do come in and sit down," he said. "It is cool and pleasant here, and you must need a breath of fresh air after the heat down stairs."

"No, I am not in the least tired," she answered, forgetful of the declaration she had made a moment before. "Besides, I remember now, I promised the next dance to Mr. Thorne, and I must not hide myself."

"Sit down just for one minute," pleaded Halford.

Milly still hesitated. She was so troubled by the inexplicable nature of her own feelings that she felt almost afraid of him, and her very agitation annoyed her into a sort of vexation toward herself and him.

"Just one moment; it's not much, when I have been away so long," he said.

She allowed him to lead her to a seat, turned half pettishly, half timidly away, and began pulling her bouquet to pieces as carelessly as if the violets had been found under a hedge for the picking, instead of having drawn a large bank-note out of poor Charley Thorne's pocket, unaware, as he was, in his youthful inexperience, that his offering gifts and attentions, and showing himself ready to play Sir Walter Raleigh, if necessary, that she might keep her little feet unsullied, would never win from her more than a few capricious smiles when there was no more important person at hand.

Kenneth Halford stood watching her, thinking how pretty she looked, how useless it was for her to attempt this show of indifference, and how bewitching she was altogether, with her whole face gaining a new depth of expression under these first struggles of her girlish heart.

"Won't you speak at all to me?" he asked. "I had been flattering myself that you would be pleased to see me come back, and now you receive me as if I was your deadliest foe. At least, if you are angry, tell me what I have done."

"I am not angry," she said, flinging away half a dozen more violets. "But—but I came up to rest, and you came in so suddenly!"

"When I hurried back on purpose to see you to-night! What a silly animal I was—I actually thought you in earnest when you asked me to be here for this ball! But you show plainly that I might as well be at the North Pole, for any thing you would care!"

"I said I was glad," she replied.

"Oh yes; but you'll not talk; you'll not look at me!"

"I am talking now, and I am looking at you," returned she, attempting that last effort as she spoke; but the little coquettish effort at composure which would have been easy enough to an older woman was a pretty failure. Milly's voice faltered, and her eyes sank shyly beneath his, while her dainty fingers again worked sad havoc among the odorous blossoms they held.

"Did Charley Thorne send you that bouquet?" he asked.

"It doesn't make any difference who sent it," said she, so near crying outright from her varied emotions—anger at her own absurd behavior among them—that she was obliged to take refuge in rather sharp speeches. "Any way, I have three more lovely ones at home."

"What an overflow of wasted adoration that implies," said Halford, smiling; for her shyness, her little attempts at dignity, her pettish voice, were all incense to his masculine vanity. "Poor flowers, luckless swains! But really, my dear child, if you don't stop tearing this to pieces so recklessly, you will have to send home for one of the neglected offerings."

"I wish you wouldn't call me child, Mr. Halford," returned Milly, gladly rushing into any pretense for anger. "Because you know my aunt so well is not a reason for addressing me like that; and I don't like it. I'm sure you're quite acquainted with my name."

"I know your first name best of any," he answered, his voice sinking lower; "I ought, indeed—Milly! Why, it has been the last thought in my mind each night of this cruel absence—like a prayer! Milly—such a sweet name!"

Milly's devastating hands paused in their cruel work; the lids drooped over the blue eyes, and her head sank a little lower.

"You know what I meant," she said, rather indistinctly.

"Then you'll not let me call you Milly? You'll not be friends?" he asked.

She turned her head still more away; and as he repeated his question, he bent so near, trying to look in her face, the flowers in her hair touched his forehead.

"I thought we were very good friends," she said, managing to keep her voice tolerably steady, and her tell-tale eyes hidden.

"One is good friends with all the world," returned he, in a disappointed, injured tone; "that phrase doesn't mean any thing. But to-night you are not even friendly with me; you don't so much as give me a flower; you'll not say you remembered to keep even one dance for me!"

"Was it my fault that you came so late?" cried Milly, with incautious haste. "And every body teasing me to dance; and I hate to have any body put me in an absurd position!"

"Oh, Milly, Milly, how can you say such dreadful things?"

She had said more than she intended, but not in the sense he meant. She was afraid that she had betrayed the real cause of her agitation—the flutter and dizziness which she had tried to hide under capricious speeches and pettish waywardness—poor little girl! As if the real cause had not been apparent to him from the first!

"Any-way, it is very wrong of me to stay here so long," she added. "I was engaged to Mr. Thorne for the galop; it is perfectly shameful to treat people so rudely! You made me do it, Mr. Halford; you know you did; it is all your fault! But I'll go back this minute, and say how sorry I am."

Kenneth Halford's detaining hand was laid lightly on her little fingers, but, somehow, that gentle touch detained her as effectually as the strongest of fetters could have done.

"You won't go away angry with me, Milly —you won't leave me like this?"

She began to tremble beneath that thrilling whisper; she forgot Charley Thorne and his wrongs, Alice Marchmont's stormy dark eyes, the ball, and every thing connected with it, as completely as if they had all been worlds away. The music surging up into the half-lighted boudoir only sounded like the echo of the melody sounding so loudly in her heart. Then it was that, under the influence of the delicious moment, and the new beauty which her sweet trouble woke in Milly's face, Halford was hurried on to speak the words which carried her away into a new world—words which came from his heart, and were the utterances of real affection, though it was the affection that a man gives to a creature young and childish, finding the sunshine in her eyes a pleasant contrast to the shadows which haunted his older experience and sterner life.

"You know that I love you, Milly," he said; "you know that you are more than all the world to me! Give me your dear little heart to keep; bring your brightness into my dull life; be my wife—will you, Milly? Oh, answer! Don't look away from me, little one—say that you will come to me!"

Milly could not speak; her two hands were clasped in his, her eyes drooped under his eager gaze, and poor Charley Thorne's violets rolled away unheeded over the carpet—just as the incense of his youthful adoration would now pass forever out of her existence, along with the thousand other trifles which had contented her before this bewildering vision came.

"You don't speak—you don't answer me, Milly! Surely you know that I love you? I did not know how dearly myself until now! You will not send me away? You can not dream how desolate and lonely my life has been! Say that you will bring your sunshine into it, and give it a brightness and warmth that, till I knew you, seemed gone out of it forever."

It was certain that he had no need of words. Those quivering hands nestled in his own, the absolute glory of those girlish eyes lifted timidly to his for a moment, was answer enough; but the man's nature could not be content until he should have a complete avowal of his triumph.

"Just one word—do you love me?"

She could whisper it then—just the one word he demanded, faint and low, but fuller of conviction than a whole volume would have been; and Kenneth Halford caught her for an instant to his heart, exclaiming,

"My own darling—all mine now; my charge, my happiness, henceforth. There shall no trouble come near you, Milly; the fairy stories you used to read shall not be brighter than your life, my Milly," he whispered, "my little one—all my own!"

Still the same tone of triumph mingling with his real feelings—the thought that he had gained the treasure which would bring to him the charm now wanting in his existence—a love which would live upon his smile, and grow into worship in return for his tenderness. She was all his, to minister to him alone, to be his songbird, his plaything, content to nestle peacefully among the outer folds of his heart, and have no conception of the inner depths that remained undisturbed.

"Are you happy, Milly? Are you content? Have you loved me—have you dreamed of this dear time?"

Still determined to probe her very soul, and bring out its holiest secrets as an incense at his shrine; and all the while, in spite of his manly sense and true worth, so hopelessly unconscious of his own selfishness. He repeated these words again and again, until he forced an answer from her at last; and out of her bewilderment Milly faltered,

"How could I allow myself to think of such things—how could I know that you cared for me—do any thing but blush at my unwomanliness in—in thinking of you at all?"

"And you loved me, Milly? Don't be afraid of me; surely you can speak openly now; it is only your own heart which hears you—yours, forever, Milly."

"I seem to have been living in a dream," she answered, brokenly. "Oh, don't make me talk of it—I will tell you some time—don't, don't ask me now!"

She hid her face in her hands, and at last he remembered and pitied her confusion, leaving her time to be silent and recover her calmness, while he contented himself with kissing her little cold hands, calling her by every tender, loving name, and promising every thing for the future, as men rashly do at such times. They were so completely out of sight in that bay-window of the boudoir that it was some time before Milly's recollection returned; then, though dizzy still with her great happiness, she could remember that they were not alone in some beautiful world, such as he had been promising to create for her, and had described to her, with an extravagance of metaphor which he would have been the first to laugh at from the lips of another.

"It must be very late," she said. "Please let me go to aunty."

"So soon—you wish to leave me already?"

"My aunt will want to go home."

But he could not let her go yet; he must hold her hands just an instant longer, and exult at the happiness in her face.

"I shall tell your aunt very soon," he said, "but not to-morrow. I must keep our secret a little while—yours and mine, darling—it is so very sweet."

Ah, the heavenly words—their secret! The utterance seemed to make Milly's bliss brighter and greater, if that were possible; he could see it in the sudden tremulousness of her smile.

"It is so delicious to say 'ours,' isn't it, Milly?" he whispered. "Little one, you don't know how happy I am; how my life expands and blossoms under this new content. I did so want to be loved—not as women love who have worn out all their freshness in the world, but wholly, entirely, by a heart that had never stirred at any human voice before."

She paused before him with a sweet gravity which quite took the childishness out of her face—with a purpose and strength that were like a premonition of the womanly soul which love would rouse within her, saying, in a low voice, that had lost its tremor,

"I will so love you—I can so love you; and I thank the Heavenly Father that I am able; yes, I heartily thank him."

Perhaps, for a brief instant, it flashed upon his mind how different a creature this girlish being might become under the influence of his affection—flashed upon him and was forgotten, because he liked best to keep her as she was now, to be his sunbeam, his one flower, which never gave out a tithe of its brightness and sweetness save to him.

"My little Milly—my darling!"

"I can't see all those people again—I can't!" she pleaded, shrinking timidly still from his embrace.

"You shall not," he answered; "they are not worthy to look at the new beauty in your face. I'll take you to the dressing-room; then I'll find your aunt, and see if she is ready to go."

He led her away, but detained her at the door for another farewell.

"I must see you early to-morrow, Milly. You haven't given up your early walks?"

Milly had, since his departure; he saw that in her face.

"My precious child—you'll let me call you that now?"

The words were too sweet for Milly to remember her attempt at dignity when he had first spoken them.

"But you'll go for a walk to-morrow? I shall not even come to the house for you; I shall meet you, and it will be quite like a stolen interview, Milly, since nobody knows our secret."

The little romance made the anticipation doubly pleasant in Milly's mind, but she was so fearful some one might come up that she begged him to go away as soon as it had been arranged in which direction her morning promenade was to lead her. But when he reached the door, he looked back—somehow the brief parting appeared very long—and on her saying that her cloak had been thrown out of sight, he hurried back to search for it, and whisper farewell again.

He was gone at last, and Milly stood there, unable to think, in the delicious whirl of her senses, until she heard her aunt's step, and her aunt's voice conversing with some acquaintance also bent mantle and muffler-ward. They were talking eagerly—probably about somebody's short-comings; people are seldom so earnest about any thing else—and Mrs. Remsen only glanced at Milly in her white wrappings, and said,

"So you are ready? Do just tell them to look for my furs; that's a dear child."

Then she and her companion resumed their talk, continuing it as they passed down stairs, greatly to Milly's relief, for she dreaded questions as to the cause of her disappearance from the dancing-room, and was glad that her aunt's quick eyes did not observe her face, for she felt that it must be telling many things she did not wish to speak.

Kenneth Halford was waiting for them in the passage. Milly hardly dared to look at him. As he helped her into the carriage, he found an opportunity to whisper,

"To-morrow morning, remember."

Mrs. Remsen called, at the same instant,

"You must come and see us soon, Mr. Halford. I have had no time to thank you for your kindness."

As if he were likely to forego any occasion to present himself at the house; at least, that was the way in which Milly interpreted the pressure he gave her little hand while he answered Mrs. Remsen. I dare say that was what he meant, too; entirely forgetting how often he had neglected that privilege, allowing a game of billiards or a dinner to detain him, when he had thought how pleasantly Milly's face always lighted up at the sight of him (what a little darling she was altogether!), and had determined to enjoy her society and pretty songs during the evening.

The carriage drove off. Milly looked out as long as she could see him standing on the steps under the gas-light, then sank back in her seat, only fearing that her aunt would be in a mood for conversation, and so jar upon her dream. But Mrs. Remsen only said,

"I really am too tired to talk; don't expect it, child."

Milly probably did not wish her aunt to suffer from fatigue, but was very glad that any cause kept her silent, though she took half a second, before going back to her vision, to pity Aunt Eliza for having no bewildering reverie to make her forget weariness—nothing to think of but a quantity of troublesome, commonplace ideas—her plans for her children—her expenses—thoughts such worlds away from the girl's dazzling fancies, that she quite pitied the middle-aged lady. Probably Aunt Eliza knew what had happened as well as if ample confession had been made; but there was a nice side to her worldly nature; she could understand Milly's feelings enough to respect them, and would disturb her by no show of consciousness until the proper moment arrived.

As soon as they were safe in the house, Milly ran up to her own room, where she and her dreams would be secure from interruption. I can not put the thoughts of those first hours into words; it would seem a positive sacrilege to analyze and anatomize the emotions of that fresh young heart, half frightened at its own happiness. You can all look back and recall a similar era in your lives; perhaps, in most cases, it proved only a vision, ending in sorrow and darkness, or getting gradually worn away in the hardening contact with the world; but at one time it appeared real and lasting as eternity itself; and you have not forgotten—you can recollect—how every thing shone in the glorious light of its newness, and can picture Milly's dream.

The next morning Milly went out to walk. When she asked permission—for it had never been Milly's habit to announce her will after the bluntness too common with girls of this generation—Aunt Eliza only said,

"It will do you good; stay out in the air for at least two hours."

She smiled to herself after the child had gone, foreseeing just whom Milly would meet as plainly as if she had been endowed with the gift of second-sight. Mrs. Remsen was in high good humor with existence just now, and absolutely enthusiastic in her affection for Milly.

It certainly happened that the young lady had not walked far when she met Kenneth Halford. She saw him long before he reached her side; and, after that first glance, was in a state of such pleasurable agitation that she would have been very glad to sit down. He saw her, too, looking so pretty in her sober walking-dress, with that thorough-bred air which it is permitted to very few young girls to attain; her pure forehead relieved by the masses of soft, luxuriant hair; and he exulted at her loveliness. He hurried on to meet her, glad to find that he still preserved the enthusiasm of the previous evening—well satisfied with himself because he yet possessed the power of loving.

The first transports of the interview had to pass quietly enough; indeed, I fear that it is only in plays any thing out of the common order of affairs often happens; but Halford brought a new color to Milly's cheek by his whispered questions.

"Had she regretted last night? Did it seem a dream still?"

But they soon came down to a safer level of conversation, considering their surroundings, and Milly explained that her aunt had given her a little errand to do.

"Further, perhaps, than you would care to go," she said, with a smile of unbelief at her own words.

"You suspicious, treacherous pigeon!" Halford replied. "You know you only say that for the pleasure of hearing it contradicted."

Already he had invented a variety of non-sensical pet names for her; and, in her ignorance, she was pleased thereat, not perceiving that even in this trifle he showed how young and childish he considered her—a creature to be fondly loved and cherished, no doubt—still, to be looked upon as a child, and not in any way to have a part in the graver emotions of his life.

"Do you remember our first walk, Milly?" he asked. "Had you thought then of the possibility of our ever walking together like this?"

"Oh no, no—how could I?"

"You wouldn't take my arm, and you blushed so beautifully when you explained the reason?"

"And I don't take it now," returned Milly, triumphantly; but she blushed all the same.

"Tell me, when did you first begin to think? Ah, don't shrink away, don't be afraid!"

"I—I haven't thought," Milly said, breathlessly. "Don't ask me questions—please don't!"

"Did you miss me? Just tell me that!"

"Those last days—when you staid away longer than you intended—"

"Then you found out that you cared a little? My precious! And were you disappointed when you thought I should not come to the ball? Oh, Milly, who had my waltz?"

Her indignant glance proved that the promised dance had not been given to any other mortal, though he had felt certain of this without asking.

"We are going to the opera to-night," Milly said, getting away to a safer subject. "We have Mrs. Lawrence's box to ourselves."

"I wish we were to have it to ourselves," returned Halford.

"Now don't say absurd things, because then I look foolish," cried Milly; "and it is not pleasant if one happens to meet people. My aunt said at breakfast that we should want a cavalier, and if she had thought she would have asked you, but now she supposed she must send for Cousin Moulson. I think it's really dreary to be waited on by such a tiresome old man; he always smells of snuff."

"I suppose that is better, though, than the odor of the cigars with which we of the younger generation perfume ourselves," said Halford. "But it would be a shame to confide you to the tender mercies of that venerable party, and have you run the risk of sneezing yourself to death. Do you think, if I chanced to call at—just by accident—"

"Oh, if you only will!" exclaimed Milly, ecstatically. "It's 'Favorita' to-night, and then it would be perfect."

"But you must promise to sit back in the box, so that a whole crowd of your adorers won't see you and rush in."

"As if I had such things!" laughed Milly.

"Oh, don't deny it! I am quite afraid that you are a fearful little coquette!"

"No, Mr. Halford; indeed, indeed I am not."

"Well, well, you needn't be so earnest about it, my little one—as if I could say it seriously! But you called me by a name that is not for your pretty lips."

7

"I am not accustomed to the other," she said, shyly.

"Did you never even whisper it to yourself?" he asked. "Oh, Milly, your name has grown so familiar to me!"

"I am glad you will go," said Milly, becoming a little nervous again at his earnestness, and wishing to avoid the subject.

"Then you'll not answer my question?" he urged.

It was cruel of him to insist on such little revelations while her happiness was so new. It betrayed the selfishness of a man's affection; for he never thought of her trouble in his desire to satisfy that craving of his heart to be idolized and worshiped like a Romney Leigh or a modern Sir Lancelot.

"Please don't talk about it yet," she pleaded. "I feel so strange, so awkward; wait a little—Kenneth!"

He was gratified by her timid utterance of his Christian name, and he saw by her face how sorely she was disturbed, so had magnanimity enough to be quiet for the present. He began to talk of other things, quaintly, pleasantly, as he could talk when he pleased, and Milly soon forgot her embarrassment, and walked on through the bright morning with a step which never once touched the common earth.

They went to the florists to fulfill Aunt Eliza's commission; then made divers détours, so as not to pass down the avenue again—not that there was the slightest reason, but it pleased them to make a mystery of the expedition, turning sharp corners and running away from their acquaintances; and Halford, in spite of his thirty-three years and nonchalant dignity, enjoyed it as much as Milly. They were almost at the street where Mrs. Remsen lived, when Halford said,

"I shall go on to the house with you, and take great pains to relate to your aunt our chance meeting—your casual mention of the opera and Mr. Moulson—and shall say that I have come to offer my services, if she will accept them."

Milly laughed gayly; all their foolish pains to invent a mystery when none was needed pleased her mightily.

"Aunt Eliza will be pleased," she said; "you are a great favorite with her, I know."

"Has she told you that?" Halford asked, quickly, beset by certain thoughts as to the counsels which the experienced matron might have given her youthful charge; for life had rendered him somewhat suspicious, as, alas! it does most of us.

"No," Milly replied, frankly; "I don't think she ever said so; but she is always very friendly with you; and aunty can be haughty enough when she chooses! But once, while you were gone, she did say that you were a man to be honored and trusted."

It was true—he was; a man much more worthy of confidence than the race in general. He felt slightly ashamed of the thought which had sprung up in his mind, though it came from a desire that Milly's love for him should not be mingled with a single worldly feeling. And it was not; he felt certain of this. She had never once remembered his fortune, his position, or any of the advantages which would have been prominent in the minds of so many girls, grown old and calculating before their time.

"To-morrow will be Ash-Wednesday," Milly said. "I have promised Constance Worthington to go to St. Alban's with her."

"And I had meant to go there, too—how very odd! And, little one, we will not tell even Aunt Eliza our secret until three whole days have gone; we will have it all to ourselves until then."

By this time they had reached the house, and he went in, prepared to meet Milly's relative with an accession of kindly feeling. Mrs. Remsen was fully a match for half a dozen Kenneth Halfords, or, indeed, any number of the wisest men, as a shrewd woman always is. From her manner, no one would have supposed that she suspected the young people of having done the very thing she desired—followed the plan she had marked out from the day of Halford's arrival. She was perfectly content to wait and make no sign until they were ready to speak, and could appreciate the feeling which made the pair long to have their happiness, for a little time, entirely to themselves.

Halford presented his petition to be one of the opera party, and it was granted—not a word or look added that could disturb Milly—and, altogether, Halford left the house better satisfied than ever with his future relative, thinking,

"She's a well-bred woman — nothing fussy about her. Upon my word, I don't believe she has talked to Milly about money or position; any way, the little darling is as innocent and undesigning as a wood-thrush—such a comfort!"

He walked rapidly away, so happy and content that he scarcely recognized himself, still with that feeling of self-gratulation at his heart that he yet possessed the ability to love. He thought, too, and more exultantly, how Milly would love him; how pleasant she would make his life with her childish ways; how much better this calm affection on his own part than the restless passion of early youth; how sunny and quiet after the loneliness, the great want, which had troubled these later years. He was more glad than ever that the preceding weeks had lured him more swiftly on than he intended when they began—glad that he had not longer postponed making his contentment complete, though, when he went to the ball, he had not meant to speak the words so soon—it was only that he had been surprised into uttering them by Milly's unconscious betrayal of her feelings and the fascination of the moment. He had purposed to wait—to study her—to consult his own lordly will and pleasure; but he was glad now that he had spoken.

At the opera that night, Milly looked so lovely in her happiness that he was fuller of content than ever. The little supper Halford persuaded Mrs. Remsen into afterward—there being ample time to enjoy it and get home before the midnight bells tolled out the Carnival season—was so gay that really things were growing too pleasant to be real.

The next morning Milly went to service with her friend Constance; but, though she tried hard to be devout and penitent, as suited the day, I am afraid the sight of Kenneth Halford in the adjoining seat sorely disturbed her meditations, though I doubt if her guardian angel set the record against her as a sin.

That evening Halford came to the house; the next day there was another long walk, another visit; and so the three days agreed upon wore by. And such bewildering days they had been to Milly as, I think, come but once to any human being. Later in life there must always be the recollection of certain other days marked with a white stone, to mar the perfection of any happiness life can give; but these were her first—her very first; she had never before strayed into Eden.

CHAPTER XVII.

THE STORY TOLD.

THE morning which succeeded that trio of happy days, Milly Crofton sat alone in the library. She made a lovely picture, curled up in the corner of a sofa, with her blue morning-dress floating over the crimson cushions, and her attitude as graceful as though she had taken more thought in choosing it than was really the case.

The warm yellow sun, which had premonitions of spring in its glow, streamed over her fair hair, gave a new softness to her mouth, and deepened the color of her eyes until they might have caused a careful observer to think that there was an earnestness and strength in her nature which her girlish existence had not yet developed.

Presently she should hear the door-bell ring—hear him go up to Mrs. Remsen's sitting-room—then, after a little, come down again to tell her that all was arranged.

It all happened just as she expected. The ring came—the steps ascended the stairs—then a delicious whirl in Milly's heart and brain left her powerless to take any note of time, or form a single connected thought, until the tread struck her ear anew, the door opened, and a voice cried out,

"Has my bird flown quite out of sight this morning?"

It was so pleasant to crouch behind the window curtains, where she had quickly concealed herself, and watch him looking eagerly about, until the disappointment which came over his face made her forget both her shyness and her desire to tease, and she ran from her hiding-place so quickly that the draperies floated out like banners; and before they had settled to their proper position, she was drawn to his side, his strong arm lifted her from the floor, and his lips rained kisses on her forehead and eyes, by way of punishment.

"Your aunt has given you to me, you naughty white pigeon," he said; "and these are your fetters, my darling, my own heart's darling!"

Then more kisses and many foolish words, until Milly only wondered that she did not die outright from very happiness.

"And aunty was pleased?" she whispered, when they were at last seated, and prepared, as they believed, to hold a sensible conversation. "Was she pleased?"

"As if she were likely to be any thing else, at the prospect of being rid of such a dear little bother?" returned he. "And she consents to our wish, that the engagement should not be announced just yet; so we can still have our secret to ourselves for a while."

"She does not think me a trouble," said Milly, extricating her long curls from his fingers. "Let me tell you, I am not accustomed to have any body tell me so—and you are not to make my hair untidy; suppose some one should come in?"

"But some one can't," replied he. "That coffee-colored man-servant of yours has received orders that there is no one at home this morning."

"So twenty people that one might wish to see may be turned away," cried Milly, mischievously.

"Who is to care? Not you—not I; and your aunt is busy."

Then followed a long talk in the sunlight; and Halford pleased himself with thinking of his good sense in choosing a loving, devoted creature like this to worship him. She had such bewitching ways; and she rested him after his experience of the past—an experience which had left him a little careworn and selfish, in spite of his manly qualities. He asked her again all those questions which he had pressed upon her the night he told his love; and she had more courage now to answer.

"Had you thought of me, Milly—had you, indeed?"

"How could I help it? Had I ever seen any one half so good and noble and handsome?"

"Dear, dear little Milly! And did you wonder if I loved you?" he continued, still eager to feed his vanity with those sweet assurances. "Did you wonder, Milly?"

"Yes," she faltered, but a little sharply; it hurt her pride to have her maiden secrets wrung from her.

He grew tender again, and the morning passed so swiftly that Milly could not believe he had been there twenty minutes, when Mrs. Remsen, thinking he had gone, came into the room to congratulate her niece.

"But I am just going," Halford said; "I have no business to be here; I have oceans to do. Mrs. Remsen, this child makes me forget every thing."

The lady smiled approval, and busied herself good-naturedly at the other end of the room, while he took his farewell—rather a lengthy operation it proved. After he was fairly out of the room, she sat down to talk, expressing her satisfaction with such warmth that Milly was fully content.

"Weren't you surprised, aunty?" Milly asked.

Mrs. Remsen only smiled. She did not feel it to be necessary to tell Milly that this consummation was what she had hoped and labored for; indeed, if she had not seen clearly how matters were going, it was hardly probable that Milly would have been left quite so much to her own devices, or indulged with so many new dresses and pleasant extravagances. It certainly was kind in the aunt; for many a woman with an unmarried daughter would not have relished seeing a niece bear off so valuable a matrimonial prize as Kenneth Halford from one of her own special brood. But, besides loving Milly, Mrs. Remsen was a wise woman. Maud could never have won him—Maud was a fool, and her mother was aware of it. She relinquished the prize to Milly without a groan; better a nephew than no relation. Maud's turn would come now; she should have a clear field and the favor of the married sisters and cousin. Truly, Mrs. Remsen's acquaintance might call her a fortunate woman, and the few who partially understood her admired her sagacity and foresight.

"Now, pussy, you are disposed of," she said; for sometimes she could unbend enough to employ pet names. "I am sure I ought to be satisfied; Adelaide and Hortense settled as they are—you happy as a queen—I should be a wicked woman if I was not."

Milly scouted, incredulously, the idea that any queen whoever sat on a throne was able to compare with her in regard to bliss; but she listened in silence, not choosing to make Aunt Eliza smile by putting her extravagant thoughts into words. So Mrs. Remsen went on to detail her own plans, feeling that in the first part of the conversation she had said all which the poetic and romantic side required.

"Next winter I shall bring Maud out; then you will have a house of your own, and be able to take her a great deal off my hands."

"Indeed, yes, aunty; and you know I would do my best to have her enjoy herself."

"I am sure you would, Milly; you are very young, but, upon my word, I would rather trust her with you than with either Adelaide or Hortense."

Really, such unusual praise was very pleasant, Milly felt; and, as Mrs. Remsen looked at her and saw how pretty she was, and thought what a sensible little creature she had proved herself, and how well every thing was arranged, she was inclined to bestow still higher encomiums. Then her reflections went back to her own special wishes and requirements, and the good which her niece's marriage might work therefor, as was natural, and no more selfish and worldly than it is permitted even good people to be. One does not expect to find at every turn penitent Saint Augustines, and pious, patient Saint Catherines, ready and willing to crucify themselves without any reward whatever.

"I shall depend on you married ones very much where Maud is concerned," she went on. "This bringing out so many girls has thoroughly cramped me; but don't think I regret the trouble you have cost, Milly; you have done exactly what I wished, and are a dear, good girl."

This commonplace fashion of regarding her extreme happiness grated a little on Milly's ear, and she would rather not have heard the gentle reminder which closed the speech; but she bore it very patiently, pleased to see how frank and confidential her own new dignity made Aunt Eliza.

She was evidently not to be treated as a child any longer.

"Mr. Halford will have the sort of people about him that I like," said Mrs. Remsen. "Now Hortense's set are so wise and literary, that Maud would be overlooked; and Adelaide will not give up her liking for admiration; so she has a crowd of men about who are only detrimental to a young lady; for they haven't the least thought of marrying. Your position will be a very enviable one, my dear."

Milly had never once thought of that; it brought a flush to her cheek to hear her aunt speak in so business-like a manner. She would have been glad, in her girlish romance, to attempt some great sacrifice to prove her love. An indistinct vision of toiling for Kenneth, and living in the most modest of cottages, with affection to brighten it, struck her as a thing desirable.

"I never thought about his being rich," she exclaimed, impetuously; "why, Aunt Eliza, it would be the same to me if he had not a penny; he would still be Kenneth Halford."

Mrs. Remsen smiled in tolerance of her folly; she had not interfered with Milly's romantic ideas, because they chanced to take the direction she approved. Had they led her into any undesirable attachment, Milly might have discovered a phase in her relative's character with which she had never yet become acquainted.

Soon Maud came in, and was informed of Milly's prospects; and she dashed frantically at the opening which they left her. She had no great amount of affection for her cousin; she had always looked upon her as an intruder who stood in her, Maud's, light; so now she was divided between envy of Milly's good fortune and self-gratulation that at last she might emerge from the retirement in which she had with great difficulty been kept. She had not the beauty of one sister, nor the tact and style of the other, and she was no more like Milly than a blue jay is like a cardinal-bird. Her face would pass as pretty, and also her figure, with the aid of skillful dressing. She was shallow and ill-tempered; given to talking nonsense, with a strong tendency toward the "rapid" order, so common among the young ladies of the present day. This latter rôle, easy as it seems, requires an unusual share of beauty and wit to make it at all successful, or even creditable. But her mother was not uneasy in regard to her; she could manage Maud's future. There was one good thing: she would never be troubled with any ridiculous ideas of romance and self-sacrifice; these were not in the girl's character—that is, if she could be said to possess such a thing.

"Well, I needn't be buried alive any longer, I suppose!" exclaimed the young lady; "you are out of my moonshine at last, Milly."

"My dear," said her mother, "don't use such expressions!"

"There's no one to hear," retorted Maud, who believed that good manners were to be kept, like fine dresses, for the benefit of society. "I wish it wasn't the end of the season; I could come out now."

"Have a little patience," returned Mrs. Remsen.

"Oh, patience!" repeated Maud, tossing her head indignantly. "I hate the word."

"Next winter you shall have your own way and be introduced," said her mother.

"Next winter!" echoed Maud, in angry dismay. "Am I not going to Newport? You must take me there; I have set my heart upon it. Clara Fay and all the girls of my age this last half at school are to go, and I must go too. All the fellows one cares to know—"

"Maud!" interrupted her mother, in horror. "Where did you learn such dreadful expressions?"

"Goodness, mamma! As if it made any difference here at home—you are so very particular!"

"I detest the habit of slang, and I will not permit it."

"Why, mamma, all the girls at Madame Chonfleur's do it—not, of course, before the teachers. Clara Fay always speaks of her papa as "the Governor," and her mother as "Madame Beck"—it's out of a book—Bulwer, I think; but then he's such a prig!"

"Do be quiet. You talk too much," exclaimed Mrs. Remsen, seeing Maud's follies rather more plainly than usual, in contrast with Milly's good sense.

"Oh, that is what you always say, mamma," returned Maud, in an injured tone; "I believe you think me a fool. What is the good of my going into society, if I'm always to be muzzled like Tom Schuyler's dog?"

Mrs. Remsen held up both hands with such an expression of suffering that Milly had much ado not to laugh.

"Tom Schuyler!" repeated the mother. "A man old enough to be your father, and spoken of in that manner!"

"He pays me a great deal of attention whenever he sees me," said Maud, stoutly; "and I don't care a straw if he is old; he is richer than Mr. Halford."

These last words mollified Mrs. Remsen; her mind rushed forward to future probabilities. After all, these old bachelors often were pleased with such girls; something might come of it; she would not be too severe.

"I have decided upon my first ball-dress—just what it shall be," cried Maud, her mind taking one of its rapid flights toward her favorite subject of thought. "And you mustn't interfere with me, mamma; it will be perfectly lovely."

"The dress, or the non-interference?" asked Milly.

"Oh, you needn't be witty at my expense," said Miss Maud, sharply. "If you are going to be married, it's no reason for putting on such airs. I may be married myself before long! And I don't care a bit if I can't say sharp things. Tom Schuyler says it's no credit to a girl; and he's going to teach me billiards and rowing at Newport."

Mrs. Remsen was obliged to go out on business; so she left the cousins together, reserving her lecture for her daughter until a more convenient opportunity.

"Mamma needn't think I'm going to be kept back any longer," exclaimed Maud, as soon as her mother was gone. "It's a sin and a shame for a girl to be put down as I have been—here I am seventeen! I'll tell you what, Milly, you'll be very mean if you don't give me lots of pretty things when you are once married, to pay me for waiting till you were served."

"I'll do any thing I can to please you, Maud," replied Milly, wishing that her cousin would depart, and leave her to dream in peace.

"There's Hortense snubs me every time I open my mouth, as if I was a—a china poodle," said Maud, casting about for a comparison, and falling upon this somewhat unhappy one from chancing to catch sight of such an ornament upon the étagère.

Milly was wickedly amused, for the china dog had an absurd resemblance to Maud. "She thinks," pursued Maud, "that because she never makes mistakes about the names of books, and can talk about ologies, that she's quite wonderful. I hate ologies, and I can never remember the names of things; but I don't care; I'm not going to set up for a Joan of Arc."

Milly could not see what connection of ideas there was between the heroine of France and a woman who pretended to scientific attainments, and she laughed outright.

"Now, you're laughing at me," said Maud, preparing to go into the sulks without loss of time.

"I was laughing at learned ladies," asserted naughty Milly. "You know I couldn't be one if I tried."

"But you're so bright," said Maud, enviously; "and you know how to say such witty things to men; and mamma says you're so high-principled."

She might have added much more without drawing upon her imagination; but to admit that Milly possessed a reputation for beauty was farther than Maud's magnanimity could go.

"When you have been a little in society these things will come to you," returned Milly, good-naturedly.

"Oh, I don't mind," said Maud, by no means dissatisfied with herself, in spite of envying her cousin. "I think my style will be different altogether from yours."

There could be no doubt of that in the mind of any person who saw the two together.

"I'll go to Newport in spite of mamma," continued Maud. "You won't care to go; you can visit somebody, or perhaps you'll be married before that. I'm going to have just the prettiest lot of new dresses ever seen. Milly, I mean to have one of those new blues, you know—the skirt trimmed with ruchings, and let them run up the side and be caught with poppies. I'll have three—"

Milly leaned back in her chair in resignation; but she was spared the impending avalanche of modes by the entrance of a servant bearing an immense basket of flowers, which he placed on the table before her. Maud looked at the blossoms, remarked that the violets would be lovely in a tulle dress, while Milly was in ecstasies over the beautiful gift, which filled the room with its heavenly fragrance.

"Of course, Halford sent them," said Miss Maud, who had a way of mentioning her male acquaintances with a delightful freedom the reverse of lady-like, usually eschewing any prefix whatever to their names.

Milly was reading a scrap of paper folded among a cluster of rose-buds, and could not listen.

"I say," demanded Maud, in a louder key, "wouldn't you rather he'd sent you a bracelet?"

Milly came back to real life with a glow of indignation.

"Have you no love for beautiful things—no appreciation—"

But she checked herself; where was the good of wasting words!

"Aren't bracelets beautiful things?" retorted Maud. "I saw a pair at Tiffany's yesterday that were perfectly adorable. They were shaped like this—why don't you look, Milly?"

But Milly was reading again the single line written on the slip of paper, and Maud's words fell upon deaf ears. The young lady crept softly behind her cousin and, peeping over her shoulder, read aloud,

"'Sweets to the sweet!' Not a thing else. If that isn't downright silly in Halford!"

Milly turned upon her in extreme wrath. "You are the rudest girl without exception,

Maud, that it was ever my ill fortune to meet. The idea that you could read another person's note!"

"I'm not at all rude, and you need not get a convulsion because I read a little foolish scrap like that. I only did it for the fun of seeing you in a towering rage."

"Very poor fun, Maud, and very unladylike. A sort that I don't appreciate. Be good enough not to attempt it with me again."

"I shall do it whenever it suits me! You are not Miss Pompey the Great if you are going to be married," said Maud, flushing with anger. "You think no one can possibly be engaged but yourself; but I warn you I shall not be put down by your airs and graces. I shall not endure it—there!"

"My dear Maud, you are as foolish as you are rude," said Milly in her loftiest tones, and, feeling that her patience was leaving her, took her huge basket of flowers and went to her own apartment to enjoy them and her tender thoughts of the giver in peace.

"Nasty thing!" muttered the elegant Miss Maud when she found herself alone. "Sweeping out of the room as if she was an English duchess, and I the dust under her feet. I hate her; I'm sure I do. She shall never queen it over me—living dependent upon mamma. I would like to remind her of it when Mr. Halford is here, only mamma is quite on her side, and ought to be ashamed of herself. I hate them all, and wish I had upset the basket and stepped on the flowers—shabby things for a present, any way—I quite hope he's stingy."

She appeared to find a certain consolation in this idea, and went away up stairs to tease a poor seamstress who was making a dress for her; and by way of a vent for her ill humor of the morning, she made that much abused creature take off all the flounces of her robe and place them anew.

CHAPTER XVIII.

MILLY'S DREAM.

THE Lenten days glided on — such sweet, calm, beautiful days to Milly, though she sometimes half reproached herself for not being so grave and sedate as the requirements of the penitential season demanded. But it was very difficult to remember her short-comings in the first ecstasy of her happiness, though she tried hard to be thankful and to recollect whence this great joy came; so, perhaps, she did not put the period to such bad use, after all.

Constance Worthington, having no special dream or unusual cause for elation, flung herself violently into a rigid observance of Lent: never missed a single church service, early or late, and sternly refused bonbons or indulgences of any sort; so that, owing to her state of mind and Milly's constant new calls upon her time, the two girls saw less of each other at this season than they had been in the habit of doing.

At least every other day Milly would find leisure to go up to St. Alban's as well as her friend, and it was very easy for her to pray and be grateful during these weeks; but Halford either accompanied her or else met her on the way; and this was reward enough to make her feel that Lenten observances, so far from being a trouble, were a great pleasure; and she wondered that so many people dreaded the season. The quiet, too, was so delightful: no balls, no rushing about night after night; occasional visits to the theatre or opera, where Halford always sat by her side; now and then tranquil concerts or receptions, at which he could talk to her almost as unrestrainedly as at home; and, better than all, long evenings in Aunt Eliza's drawing-room with her lover, when nobody besides Mrs. Remsen was there, and she careful not to let the young people feel her presence a restraint. Oh, it was a bright, lovely period, and Milly wished that Lent might last until it was time to go into the country. But she only expressed her opinions once to Constance, for that rigid young woman treated her to a severe lecture, mentioning several dry books which she thought Milly had better read; and the very names of them made poor Milly yawn, and Constance's sermon did not prick her conscience so vitally as it ought to have done. But she was not vexed—she could not be angry with any body just now—only she decided to keep her theories to herself, and let Constance go her way. At this time it was Milly's creed—young girls are fond of creeds—that religion was meant to make people happy, and she did not think it had that effect upon her friend; though, in truth, Constance found as much excitement in her new rigidities as Milly did in her dreams; and the two were just a pair of children, with whom any new feeling must necessarily become an enthusiasm.

Milly's wish to have the engagement kept a secret was complied with so far as any actual announcement was concerned; but most people had their own suspicions on the subject, and Minerva Lawrence occasionally teased her to make a frank confession.

"How long do you mean to insist on this impenetrable mystery, little pigeon?" Halford asked her one day. "I invent as many excuses for talking to you in public as if we were surrounded by unheard-of dangers, and when I come here of a morning I double as cautiously as a hunted hare."

Milly laughed at his nonsense, but it pleased her, nevertheless.

"There's no necessity for telling people yet," she said; "we know, and Aunt Eliza knows; the matter doesn't concern any body else."

"One's friends have a way of thinking that it is exactly such affairs which concern them vitally," he replied.

"I don't want them told yet," she pleaded.

"I believe the child is ashamed of her fetters," he exclaimed, laughingly, as he kissed the white hand whereon glittered the sapphire ring he had placed there with words which still made Milly's heart flutter each time she regarded the pretty bauble.

"Oh, Mr. Halford—"

"To whom is she speaking?" interrupted he, addressing a statuette of Apollo on the mantel.

"I mean—Kenneth," said she, slyly.

"Ah, I know him! Very well, sweetheart; what was to be the conclusion of that pathetic appeal?"

"You know that isn't why I don't want people told—you do know it is not, please?"

"I am beginning to have serious doubts," said he, with mock gravity. "Unless you tell me the real reason, I shall be obliged to think you are ashamed of me."

"You are as wicked as you can live!" cried Milly.

He could never be content without making her put each most tender feeling and maiden fancy into words, unconscious that it was positively cruel to insist. She blushed so beautifully in doing it, and the pleasure of reading her guileless soul was so great that he could not resist.

"Now is it because you think I am old?" he continued. "Milly, I saw such dreadful crow's-feet under my eyes this morning!"

"It is a downright fib—the dear eyes—the beautiful eyes!" cried Milly, laying her dainty hand softly over them. "Oh, Kenneth—I can't explain—but somehow I feel as if it was a sort of sacrilege to tell it all out for people to gossip over, as they do every thing."

"Such a sensitive little Milly!"

"I can't make it clear, but I feel it! See, it's like this—the little miniature of my dead mother that I wear always—I couldn't bear to let a stranger touch it, or even look at it—"

"My darling, my precious—I understand!"

So, with her head pillowed on his breast as he folded her to his heart, she could smile and talk more earnestly, though there were tears in her eyes which he was obliged to kiss away, and he felt slightly remorseful for having forced her into an effort to explain her shy emotions.

"Of course every body must know—we must let them be told," she continued; "but there's no hurry—say there isn't, Kenneth!"

"None in the world, little one! There, I only wanted to tease you."

"You bad old thing!"

"I don't believe the news will take any of our friends much by surprise," said he, laughing mischievously again. "You are very wise —I have so much trouble to make you talk when there's any body present that I'm afraid people will think you are a victim; but I'm a foolish old chap, and show my feelings too plainly."

"Nothing of the sort," returned Milly; "if you do care about me, you hide it beautifully! Now the other night, when you talked to Miss Moore, I'm sure every one thought it was she you were in love with."

Of course, she had to be punished for such

wickedness, and the morning seemed to Milly the happiest she had ever spent, though, as each separate one of its predecessors during the last fortnight had appeared thus in turn, perhaps, in summing up and comparing the whole, she would have been at a loss to make a choice among them.

She wasted a great deal of time, undoubtedly, during these days; but though Aunt Eliza was rather a martinet in her ideas of duty and the necessity of occupation, she never reproved Milly now; and, indeed, it was not exactly the girl's fault. Halford was at the house daily, and there were expeditions of all kinds constantly on foot; so that even Mrs. Remsen was forced into idleness frequently, and seemed to enjoy it. Milly did not neglect certain little duties she had long before assumed: each morning she gave the children their music-lessons; and it was a great saving to Aunt Eliza, as it allowed her to get on with an ordinary daily governess for the rest of their small studies. She was never tired of praising Milly, and the wheels of the little household rolled on velvet during those weeks. Prudent and far-sighted as she was, even Mrs. Remsen forgot that the brightest sky can change suddenly; and Kenneth Halford no more remembered that there were such skeletons as disappointment and trouble in the world than if he had been eighteen instead of a man who had lived and suffered till, at one time, he had slight faith left in any quarter. His love for Milly was so totally unlike that early passion which had dazzled his boyhood and left the first years of his manhood desolate that he never thought of comparing the two. Indeed, the past was entirely consigned to oblivion; he had long before outlived it; even his meeting with Alice Marchmont after that lengthened separation had failed to warm the ashes of the old affection into life. He said to himself, and truly, that he was no more the man who had loved her than she was the impulsive girl of whom the dreaming boy had made an ideal. There was not a feeling, not a memory in his heart, which interfered with his loyalty to Milly; yet he had been guilty from the first of a great error. He forgot that in endowing this child with the gift of his love he took her out of her childhood forever. He forgot, too, that in becoming a woman she would have a woman's need and right to share his existence fully—be a part of it, or, rather, allow hers so to mingle with his that the two lives would only form one beautiful whole. There must be no thought which she could not share—no secret left untold which could ever trouble their happiness; there was no aim or care which she would not, through the might of her love, be capable of comprehending. The necessity of none of these things had a place in his mind; she was to be his songbird, his sunbeam, a creature kept apart from the graver interests of his destiny, to rest contented on his heart and warm it by her brightness. He could have seen how fallacious this

idea was had it been the case of another; but, like the rest of us, he was blind when the matter became personal. John Worthington saw the whole truth more clearly, for a warm friendship had sprung up between the two men, commencing in a similarity of tastes, and cemented by the strict integrity which each acknowledged in the other. There had been no confidence on Halford's part in regard to his engagement or love, but as Worthington often saw him with Milly, he could not fail to suspect the truth; and if he had not perceived for himself the state of affairs, Constance's frequent remarks would have pointed it out.

"I wish Milly would tell me, uncle," she said several times, in discussing her suspicions; "I think she might—such good friends as we have always been."

"My dear Con, let Milly alone," was her uncle's reply; "when your turn comes, and you know how nice it is to keep such a pretty secret as long as possible, you'll be glad that you did not tease her."

"My time for such things will never come," she said, with the decision of eighteen, and the amusing contempt with which an unawakened heart regards the weaknesses of others. "I don't mean to leave you."

"Very well; I am glad to keep you—don't forget," he said, laughing.

"There is no danger. Besides, I'm studying German; if Milly would only have taken it up too, as I begged, she wouldn't have had leisure for any nonsense."

"German is a very good thing," said Worthington, with preternatural gravity, though Constance was too much in earnest to observe that it was a little overdone.

"I should think it was," returned she. "But Milly never did have patience to study."

"My dear, I fancy that Milly is busy, too, with a new language, and a more engrossing one than German, though it comes so easy that I dare say she can even think in it without difficulty."

"Oh, now you are laughing!" cried Constance. "Well, I do think it's foolish of her, all the same; and only just before she went to Europe she told me she should never marry—told me so with her own lips," continued Constance, with great energy, as if that method of imparting information was so unusual that it had added solemnity to the declaration.

"Ah, you see somebody else's lips have convinced her that she spoke rashly," he said.

"I don't like it all the same," returned Constance, with an injured air. "I don't think people ought to announce a determination until they have given it so much thought that there is no possibility of their changing."

"Oh, Con, Con!" cried her uncle, with a burst of irrepressible laughter, "I shall have to remind you of this sometime—when you get through with your German."

"Then I shall have something else to occupy me," said Constance, with a little air of superiority too innocent to be disagreeable. "Only yesterday I told Milly one ought always to be busy, and she said she thought it was nice to be lazy—she actually did, uncle!"

"Jupiter Ammon, what a horrible confession!"

"Now you are teasing again; and, indeed, I am in earnest! I am so fond of Milly, and I hardly ever see her now!"

"Be patient, little one, and, above all, unselfish! You've not lost your friend; give her time to get accustomed to her new happiness, and she will love you better than ever."

"And she has such odd ideas about Lent," added Constance, dropping her voice to a solemn whisper.

"What heretical opinion has she expressed? I thought my old friend, Mrs. Remsen, had taught her Church doctrines very carefully."

"Oh, Milly is good—so good—I don't mean that!"

"Then what did she say that troubled you as to the ideas she entertains in regard to Lent?"

"Why, that people ought to be just as happy as possible whenever they could—"

"I agree with Milly, my dear."

"Yes, but that one could show as much gratitude in Lent by being happy as by going to service twice a day. Now, uncle, when Lent means—means—that is, when it is the season for repentance and penance and—"

"And thinking very charitably of our neighbors, my dearest."

"Oh, uncle!" cried Constance, blushing scarlet.

"You would not intentionally do otherwise; but, my child, we can't judge for others."

"Yes, I know, and I don't mean to. But when I wanted her not to touch bonbons or go to the theatre—it was so little to do!"

"Because you wanted it?"

"No; because—oh yes, I'm afraid it was partly for that," she answered, remorsefully.

"My dear, go to church all you can without neglecting other duties — that is right. Give up amusements and indulgences—that is right, too; but it is not a sin for Milly to eat sugar, and I don't believe that sitting through a play will prevent her being thankful."

"I see now—I was judging her! Oh dear, and I was trying so hard to be good!" said Constance, disconsolately.

"Don't try quite so hard; that's all. I mean, don't hunt up all sorts of ideas to prick yourself with, and don't run the risk of paying so scrupulously the tithe of mint and cummin that you forget the weightier matters of the law. I hold to every Church observance—to its full rites and ceremonies; but don't keep Lent so rigidly that you exasperate yourself into uncharitableness toward those who do not feel the necessity to keep it just according to your ideas, or even just to the letter."

"I'll go and tell Milly how wicked I have been; that will punish me," said Constance, feeling herself a terrible sinner.

"I don't think I would use so harsh a word," her uncle replied. "And now put on your bonnet and walk a little way with me, and forget for half an hour that it is Lent."

Constance was happier by the time they returned to the house than she had been for weeks, and her uncle's kind explanations cleared her mind of sundry small doubts, and she ceased to consider herself utterly hardened and lost because she could not help regretting the bonbons—her special weakness—which she had vowed not to touch until Easter Monday.

It chanced that this same evening Worthington encountered Halford at the club, where that gentleman had strayed after his usual visit to Mrs. Remsen's, and the two had a pleasant talk in a quiet corner. The conversation wandered, as the conversation of men of all ages will, toward the opposite sex; and Kenneth Halford's opinions in regard to love and marriage showed Worthington plainly what the feelings were with which he had entered into his engagement—always supposing that matters had gone as far as that.

"I don't understand," Halford said, in answer to a remark of his companion's. "I have always thought that there was a great deal of nonsense in the talk about the danger of disparity of age."

"I don't consider that the danger lies in the disparity of age; it is in the lack of common tastes and sympathies."

"But I hold that a man should teach a wife to acquire his. One could not do this with a woman already formed in mind and thought, accustomed to the world; but suppose a man chose a young girl—a child in heart until his affection awakened it—the case is different."

"Altogether different."

"Don't you believe, then, that a man could train insensibly, and develop mind and soul according to his ideas?"

"He might, assuredly."

"You say it in a doubtful tone."

"Not doubtful as regards the fact."

"How, then?"

"I was thinking of the young girl."

"But if she was loved, cared for, made happy?"

"All right! But suppose she suffered under this training and development—that she learned to chafe at the knowledge that her husband considered her a child?"

"Her very innocence and ignorance would prevent that."

"My dear friend, she would not remain a child."

Halford smiled compassionately, really pitying the old bachelor's lack of knowledge.

"I think," he said, "that one occasionally meets a character which will always retain that happy faculty—not a girl of little mind, either—full of beautiful capabilities which the man she loves may foster without disturbing the child-like spirit which made her chief attraction to him in the beginning."

"I can only say that I think the man would have to go very carefully to work," John Worthington replied.

"Of course," said Halford, confidently.

"I think you mean that this imaginary wife should be kept apart from her husband's actual life—content with that—having, in fact, only a partial love—"

"Fondly loved and cherished."

"I can only say that it seems to me she would probably discover this lack in her life, and either rebel or suffer silently, according to her nature."

"But there would be no lack."

"I beg your pardon; according to my view of marriage, there would. I think that, to have any hope of happiness, husband and wife must be literally one—not even a care left unshared."

"But it is just those annoyances I would keep from her."

"They are not annoyances when they have a place in the mind of the man she loves—she would feel them as she would feel that she was shut out from his inmost self, and the knowledge would make her wretched."

"That might hold good in the case of a woman who had lived and suffered; but the example I am imagining is a very different creature."

"She must grow a woman in her turn."

"Yes, but of another sort from the wordly creatures one meets."

"Humph! A fairy! Well, my dear fellow, I'm afraid that, however carefully you guarded the elf in an enchanted palace, some chill wind from without would sweep in and transform her into an earthly being, with a strong determination to be considered such."

Again Halford smiled compassionately; Worthington saw it, but offered no remark. The conversation was confined to such generalities that his attempt at warning did not strike home; but he perceived that if it had been ever so closely pointed it would have failed to produce any effect.

"I would advise a man to reflect well," he said, quietly. "It is a solemn responsibility to take a human destiny into one's hands—above all, the kind of butterfly creature you mean—a butterfly with a soul; if it was an ordinary one, she might be happy enough."

"But it is the fact of her possessing a soul which would make her charming."

"Just so—and which would give her capabilities for suffering, too."

"I have failed, I see, to make my meaning clear."

"I understand your idea perfectly; and though an ancient bachelor, little skilled in the nature of butterflies with souls, I repeat that I consider such a marriage a great risk."

"You think the man would not be happy?"

"I don't think about him; but I fear that the butterfly-wife would suffer, and her wings droop and fade, and the suddenly awakened soul cry out dismally in wrath and pain." He stopped and laughed a little at his own fanciful imagery, as we all do when conscious of having ventured beyond commonplaces; then felt ashamed of the weakness, and added,

"I don't know why I should laugh; I mean every word."

"It is very pretty, but I should not be afraid. I think I perceive a way of avoiding a single shadow."

"Then you have solved a secret which might have puzzled Solomon; I congratulate you," said Worthington, dryly.

"I'm afraid it did sound conceited," Halford answered, for he was sensitive about laying himself open to any such charge.

"No, but overconfident; I, at my age, should call it a trace of youth, though I suppose you consider yourself years beyond that."

"Upon my word, I think I am growing young nowadays."

"Take care, or I shall believe you have found the fairy."

"And if I had?"

"Then I'd say, heartily, God bless you both! You're a good man, Halford—a very good man! But when you do catch the butterfly, remember my caution about hurting her wings."

"Oh yes; but you see my theory is so clear."

"Heavens and earth!" cried John Worthington, "I'm not likely ever to marry; but if I should, it will not be upon a theory."

Halford laughed, and dismissed the subject; indeed it was idle, he felt, to pursue it; Worthington was a very wise man, but this was a matter outside of his comprehension. So they went into the smoking-room, and on the way Halford said,

"Have you any idea when we shall see Mrs. Marchmont back?"

"Not the slightest—don't think she knows herself. She writes me occasionally; we are very old friends, you know."

"Oh yes; she has an immense esteem for you."

John Worthington smothered a sigh. Esteem—it was all very well so far as it went; he was past forty, and could expect nothing more from any woman, but it seemed very little, and the word sounded very cold. But this was an unmanly bit of weakness; so he hastened to put it by, and say cheerfully,

"I shall be glad to see her back! I always feel that parties at my house are a sad failure without her."

"A charming woman—a remarkable woman—"

"Not like your fairy, eh?" but though he said this, Worthington believed in his heart that Halford would never have relinquished Alice Marchmont if there had been the least hope of winning her—as if any man would! Worthington thought.

"Not a happy woman, I sometimes think," Halford said.

Worthington's fears on this subject grew stronger each day, but he had no mind to acknowledge them even to his friend.

"She is variable and capricious," he said; "but the only wonder is that the adulation she receives has not spoiled her more."

"Nature seemed never to weary of heaping on her the gifts that would bring this about," Halford replied. "I never saw so beautiful a woman, nor so clever a one."

How the pale, proud face rose before John Worthington's fancy! The smile, half mocking, half sad, thrilled across his soul; the passionate light of the great brown eyes lit his imagination into a glow; but the vision must be put aside!

There was a little more idle talk; then he bade Halford farewell, and walked homeward through the still night, thinking that, in spite of fame, of gratified ambition, wealth, all the gauds which had glittered so bravely to his sight in youth, life looked cold and empty; and even his scorn of his own weakness, his stern sense of right, which led him to regard the complaint almost as a sin, could not thrust the disheartening consciousness entirely from his mind.

CHAPTER XIX.

FINDING THE CLUE.

ALL this time people heard of Mrs. Marchmont as brightening the Lenten dullness of Washington by her presence, working sad havoc among foreign diplomats, and creating dire confusion in the minds of stately old senators who ought to have been years past the possibility of such weakness. But they were men; so that period would never arise, if they lived until the age of Methusaleh; and the musty proverb, "No fool like an old one," is as replete with truth as it was on the day of its first utterance.

The French baron had gone on to the capital also, and his name was often mentioned in connection with that of the fascinating widow, and bets were made at the New York and the Union as to the chance of the baron's winning the prize. Of course, in this age there is nothing about which men do not lay wagers, from the truth of the Bible to the probability of some friend's grandmother living the week out.

Richard Faulkner listened to the various reports of Mrs. Marchmont's triumphs, and ground his teeth when they described her as gayer and more fascinating than ever. He was not a man easily to relinquish a well-formed resolution; a certain dogged obstinacy that lay at the bottom of his impulsiveness had been, in a great measure, the secret of his success; and seldom had a stronger emotion found a place in the pandemonium which he called a heart than his passion for Alice Marchmont. It is revolting to write; but, to render my narrative clear, I must set down the exact truth in regard to the people whose characters I wish to make plain to you.

After her hasty departure, he recovered sufficiently from the rage and trouble into which he had been thrown by her outwitting him, and escaping his clutches at the very instant when he believed that his plans were culminating, to get back his usual clear-sightedness and determination to get to the bottom of any affair which puzzled him. How had she raised the money? that was the thought which scarcely left his mind even during his busiest hours in the Gold-room, or while weaving his numberless webs to catch the unwary in the solitude of his private office. He understood exactly the state of her affairs; there was not a detail of her embarrassments with which the past season had not made him familiar; for, after having once trusted him, it had been a great relief to know there was somebody with whom she could talk freely. How had she raised the money? A score of possible devices—several of them founded on that lack of faith in honor and virtue which grew naturally out of his own baseness—suggested themselves in turn; but prone as he was to think evil, each idea had to be rejected in turn because his keen commonsense showed him its impracticability.

The small Hebrew was an old friend of Faulkner's; indeed, he possessed a certain hold over the bulbous-nosed Jew, as he did over most people with whom circumstances rendered him intimate. It was he who had made the Israelite and Mrs. Marchmont acquainted; and he was cognizant of every business arrangement between them, even to the troublesome lien which Herman held upon her jewels. Many a time he had secretly laughed at what the proud woman must suffer from those weekly visits of the distressed but virtuous widow, to make sure that no false play was attempted in regard to the diamonds. The same espionage pursued Mrs. Marchmont during her sojourn in Washington, and Faulkner knew it. The Jew had behaved fairly enough, actally intrusting a larger portion of the gems to her guardianship during her absence, but not running the slightest risk thereby. He possessed a daughter who was the happy and fleshy spouse of a Washington clothes-dealer; and this amiable woman gratified her parent by enacting the part of the distressed widow twice a week, while Mrs. Marchmont dazzled the old senatorial owls by her presence in their city.

With all this knowledge, it was not difficult for Faulkner to discover before a great length of time the precise means whereby Mrs. Marchmont obtained a sufficient sum to repay him, and give herself a temporary relief from other pressing creditors. So much was clear; she had persuaded John Worthington to lend his powerful name to a bit of stamped paper; but the certainty of the method she had employed to release herself from her embarrassments did not materially aid Master Richard in those schemes for revenge which he plotted—not with cold-blooded fiendishness, but animated by a sense of personal injury none the less strong because it was unreal and ridiculous.

He watched; he waited; for, even with the sight of John Worthington's signature to make the affair plain, there was a host of vague suspicions in his mind which would not be allayed. Now I might make a very sensational chapter indeed just here; I might describe Faulkner hunting up a skillful burglar, who, for a sufficient reward, would break into Mrs. Marchmont's house, get possession of a writing-desk which contained a diary wherein she set down each night the day's events, and where the details of the forgery were described as elaborately as if they had been stage directions for acting a drama. Perhaps that *coup* would be a little coarse and vulgar, not exactly suited to the highest rules of dramatic romance; but there are others which would serve: you see, I am unwilling that any body should accuse me of a lack of invention or ability to work out a stirring plot. The Hebrew's spouse, with a genius for histrionics, might have been induced to try a new rôle, or Dick might have known some wronged maiden willing to serve his ends, and overwhelm him by exposure at the close of the volume. This wronged but still interesting maid would, of course, have scarlet hair, green eyes, the pallid complexion of a vampire, not a tinge of color in her face except the coral hue of her lips, with an ophidian head, a serpentine grace and sinuosity in each movement, a strange, subtile fascination which no mortal could resist, and a fondness for soliloquy equal to Hamlet's. She and Faulkner would be discovered in a low, earnest conversation; at the first revelation of his plot she would utter a fierce shriek, changed to a soft moan by a threat from him. More talk—more shrieks. Suddenly Dick would pronounce Alice Marchmont's name; the wronged but interesting maid would spring to her feet with a wild, exultant cry; then immediately turn into a statue for the space of five minutes. After Dick had brought her out of her perpendicular trance by judicious questions, she would howl forth her tale in a paragraph of six pages, in the course of which, by earnest study, one would discover that the man whom she loved and loathed had deserted her for this creature Dick named. She would be ready for revenge—thirsting for a draught of what modern actors term "be-lood"—and would clutch the air wildly with two white hands, make frantic dashes at Dick, ordering him to speak plainly, and talking so fast that she gave him no opportunity to gratify her. The scene would close, leaving the injured maid and Dick in a tragic attitude; and the next one would rise upon Alice Marchmont's bed-chamber, with the wronged female standing in the centre of the room, her costly raiment exchanged for the garb of a domestic, her scarlet hair hidden under a cap; and she would do Hamlet to any extent in order to unfold the plot. Of course, at this particular crisis, Mrs. Marchmont's housekeeper was in need of a chamber-maid; the wronged one knew it—injured feminines always know when their enemies require new servants. Arrayed in fitting guise, she would present herself to the housekeeper; and here would be an opportunity to contrast the homely honesty of the elder woman and the devilish craft of the younger. The avenger would take her place among the band of servitors; after doing Hamlet, she would search wildly—cursing a great deal all the while in blank verse—among Mrs. Marchmont's secret treasures, discover a blotting-book, hold it to the light, pant—gurgle—moan, and finally announce to herself in a confidential voice, distinctly audible in the neighboring square, that she had solved the mystery. The treacherous tissue-paper would have preserved the forged name, and the injured maid would disappear from the mansion, carrying the proofs of guilt away in her mysterious flight.

But nothing so delightfully thrilling occurred; I wish there had, with all my heart. But in real life events have a humiliating way of coming about in a very prosaic fashion, and all sorts of trivial, absurd incidents mix themselves up with the loftiest tragedy.

Some men who belonged to the club of which John Worthington was a member invited Dick to dine there one night, and Dick accepted, though the sight of the place was a severe humiliation, for he had twice been blackballed when seeking admission among the enviable band. He knew very well that he had to thank Worthington for this slight; he had openly said that Dick Faulkner should never be permitted to join a club to which he belonged. Worthington, when they chanced to meet, never vouchsafed him more than a chilling salute or a few brief words, and would not have gone so far as that, only Dick insisted on being elaborately civil; for his desire to keep his somewhat uncertain position in society as steady as possible made him determined to show that he was at least on speaking terms with the honored and influential man.

This evening he met Worthington in the card-room. There happened to be few persons present besides Dick and his host, and the party seated at Worthington's whist-table, which was drawn near a fire-place at one end of the apartment, quite aloof from the other players. There was an empty table close by, and Faulkner and his companion took possession of that to indulge in a game of *écarté*. Before long Dick's Amphitryon was called out for a few moments, and Dick sat listening to a conversation between the four gentlemen, of which he had caught some portion while talking to his companion, and which had by this time grown so animated that it delayed the progress of the card-dealing.

"I tell you that no arguments could affect me," Mr. Worthington said, in that low voice which was at once so gentle and so firm.

"But perhaps I did not state my peculiar example distinctly," returned his partner.

"Yes, you did; but it makes no difference."

I learned my lesson very early in life—by observation though, instead of experience, fortunately for me—but it was one I never forgot."

"How so?"

"Why, you must remember my unfortunate guardian, poor old Longford—the best man in the world, and the weakest. It was nothing but indorsing his friends' bills that ruined him."

"Oh yes; I recollect the whole story now; and a sad one it was."

"You must all three recollect it," returned Worthington. "He was completely ruined, and his good name went too. A better-hearted man never lived. The disgrace killed him; and it was all brought about by the conduct of those he had trusted. The last time I ever saw him, only a few days before his death, he told me the whole story. I was little more than a boy then; and he made me promise that while I lived I would not take the first step which might end in a position like his."

"Keep clear of your neighbors' paper, eh?"

"Yes, and I have remembered it. If ever I felt tempted to yield, that old man's face came up before me and held me firm."

"It must have been deuced difficult sometimes to get rid of doing the thing," observed another of the group.

"So it was," Mr. Worthington replied; "but I've not found the things most necessary to do in this world the easiest, Van Rensslaer."

"No, by George; I should say not."

Then there was a little laughter to get rid of the disagreeable impression left by the memories of old days which Mr. Worthington's words had called up; but he did not join in the merriment: he was looking very grave, and absently playing a silent tune on the table with his fingers.

"You're an awful one for holding firm, Worthington," said his partner. "I don't suppose there's so obstinate a man living, when you have once made up your mind."

"I hope that is not the exact word to apply," returned he, smiling.

"Oh, very well; call it firmness, if you like that name better; but admit that you have the organ wonderfully developed."

"I trust so—not much chance for a man in this life who is so unfortunate as to be lacking in the quality."

"You're right there," assented Van Rensslaer."

"But how to stick always to a resolution like that puzzles me," observed another.

"I would do any thing else for a friend. I hope, if I had only five dollars, I should not refuse to divide with a person whom I called by that name; but put my own to a bill for him —never—nothing would induce me."

"But under the exceptional circumstances I have suggested," observed his partner.

"They would have no such effect," returned Worthington. "If I could raise the money, I would lend it—give it, at any sacrifice, in a case like that of which you spoke—but never indorse a note. No! I am as principled against it as I am against gambling, intoxication—yes, theft, or the lowest vice you can name."

"It's a good rule to lay down, but not always easy to follow, Worthington," observed one of the others.

"I have never swerved from it," he answered; "yet I don't think any friend of mine has ever called me disobliging or mean."

"No, no," was of course the general chorus.

Dick Faulkner leaned over the table by which he sat, and played with the rack of pens.

"It would be a good thing for some of us if we had been as wise as Mr. Worthington," he said, addressing that gentleman's partner in the game—a man engaged in Wall Street, like Faulkner, and not in a position to snub Dick for his free and easy interruption of the conversation.

"Yes, indeed," the other replied; and the two gentlemen at the opposite sides of the card-table addressed some similar words to Dick, not sharing Worthington's prejudice against him, or not caring to take the trouble to be rigid in the cause of virtue if they did.

Emboldened by his success, Faulkner addressed Mr. Worthington, partly because he wished the conversation continued, partly because he wanted the next day to boast that he had enjoyed that gentleman's society.

"And you have been able to keep to your resolution without losing a friend, Mr. Worthington?" he asked, wheeling his chair round so that they sat face to face.

In secret, Worthington anathematized his insolence, but, without being guilty of a deliberate outrage, he could not refuse to answer; and as he never did things by halves, his manner was perfectly courteous as he replied,

"I think I may safely say that I have not lost one in my whole life from that cause."

"And yet you have held firm to your resolution?" persisted Dick.

Mr. Worthington's silent bow would have abashed a brazen image by its awful dignity, but it produced no impression whatever on Faulkner. He had an end to gain, and Worthington should be forced to say more, no matter what slight Dick himself received in the skirmish.

"You never in a single instance varied from your rule?" he asked.

Mr. Worthington gave him a glance of cold surprise, enough to freeze ordinary blood, but said, quietly,

"I never varied from it in a single instance."

"It's the most extraordinary thing I ever heard!" cried Dick, in an admiring voice, appealing to the other men. "I'll lay any wager there's not a man in the house at this moment who could say as much."

"I don't believe there is," averred Worthington's partner; and the remaining pair announced that they did not believe there was, either.

"Even when you were young?" added Dick,

offering the suggestion so apologetically-that it could not give offense—only as any words he might utter — the bare fact of his existence, even—were an offense to John Worthington.

"There is no exception, sir—none," said he, rather sternly.

"I fancy that the rest of us have been guilty of the weakness so often that we should not venture to count the number of times," rejoined Dick, not exactly venturing to put another question.

"Yes, indeed," observed Mr. Worthington's partner—a thin man, with a nose like a trumpet, and eyes that looked sideways, as if they could not see over it—unconsciously aiding Faulkner in his desire to have a cross-examination. "You are perfectly certain you have not forgotten a single lapse?"

"My memory is very good," replied Mr. Worthington, rather stiffly. "I should not have been likely to forget the circumstance."

"You see," said Dick, with a laugh, "we can't bear to think you are so much superior to ordinary humanity; I wish there had been one transgression of your rule."

"Yes, yes, Worthington," added another; "look back—search your memory—was there never one violation?"

"A small one—to oblige some friend—some lady, may be: there's a suppositious case where no ordinary rules would hold good," said Dick, still laughing.

Mr. Worthington treated him to a glance of icy contempt which made Dick wince, and addressed his partner, oblivious of the impertinent remark.

"I never in my whole life put my name to the paper of any human being," he said, with extra distinctness. "So well known is my resolution, that for the past ten years no man—no person—has asked me to do it, or even hinted the wish. I could not express myself more distinctly, so there is nothing else to be said."

"Just so," murmured the trumpet-nosed gentleman; and the other two men uttered the same ejaculation.

But Faulkner did not feel inclined to quit the subject, though Mr. Worthington had partially turned his back upon him.

"Not much use, then, for any body to present a forged indorsement of Mr. Worthington's to a money-lender," said he, "since his rule is so well known."

Mr. Worthington took up a pack of cards that lay by his side and asked the trio generally,

"Is it my deal?"

"Mine," said one of the antagonists.

"I say, any body would have pretty work trying to forge your signature, Worthington," cried the trumpet-nosed man, snorting at his own wit.

"I think so myself," he replied, smiling; "I don't suppose there's a man on Manhattan Island can boast one so bad."

"Never saw it," said the antagonist who had taken up the cards.

"It's a lucky thing to have it peculiar in any way," added Faulkner.

"The 'John' looks like 'gin,'" said the trumpet-nosed, with a fresh snort; "as for the 'Worthington'—well, there's no words! Give us that scrap of paper and the pen off the table back of you, Van Rensslaer," he continued.

"Do you want me to exhibit my chirography?" asked Worthington, as Van Rensslaer placed writing implements before him.

He laughed and scrawled his signature; they all looked at it, Dick leaning directly over his shoulder, and the laughter became general. There were a variety of witty remarks and comparisons, but Dick Faulkner held his peace; he had resumed his seat before Worthington looked up.

"You're safe from the most experienced forger that ever lived," said he of the trumpet.

"I never saw but one person who could imitate my signature," Worthington replied.

"It is to be hoped that was in a quarter where you ran no danger of having it tried," observed Faulkner.

Mr. Worthington did not hear.

"It might place you in an unpleasant box—deuced unpleasant—if it was some friend who possessed the ability," continued Dick, in a louder voice; and, when this remark did not seem likely to be heard any more than the previous one, added, "mightn't it, Mr. Worthington?"

"Really, as the possibility has never entered my mind, I am not prepared to answer your inquiry," was the cold response.

"My suggestion, rather," added Dick, with a bow.

"Indeed, Faulkner's right," said Van Rensslaer. "There might arise a predicament that would pose you awfully."

"My imagination is not sufficiently brilliant to conceive it, my dear fellow," returned Worthington.

"But suppose circumstances—fate, or whatever you please—had put your friend in a tight corner," continued Dick, not to be excluded from the conversation by any reasonable effort on Worthington's part; "he might be tempted to play you a shabby trick."

"By his own wickedness, then; he couldn't lay the blame on what you call fate, and what I am accustomed to calling Providence," replied Worthington, with polite severity.

"All right," said the unabashed Dick. "But suppose the devil took possession of this person, and tempted him to forge your name as the only way out of his scrape—"

Mr. Worthington would not interrupt; but as Faulkner made a slight pause here, he hastened to rejoin,

"Among my whole list of friends there is not one in regard to whom your supposition could ever hold good; so I am relieved from the necessity of contemplating it."

"Now you're going too far!" cried Van

Rensslaer; and his partner, as usual, echoed his words, while Dick waited patiently. "Any body may be tempted, and some fine day you may find that your friend has done your name to a tidy bit of paper, and you will either be obliged to expose him or pocket the loss."

"Just so," said his partner.

Mr. Worthington burst out laughing.

"Upon my word," said the owner of the trumpet, gravely, "I don't think it's a laughing matter, viewed in that light."

"It is the putting it in this light which makes it so laughable," replied Worthington; "and you would say the same if I told you who the person is that succeeds in imitating my scrawl."

"Man or woman?" asked the other, from sheer idleness, and yawning because the subject had lost its interest.

"It is a lady," Mr. Worthington replied.

"Name, name!" cried Van Rensslaer, gayly.

"Nonsense! One would think we were a pack of college boys," said Worthington, contemptuously. "I do wonder, Van, if you will ever remember that it is twice a decade since you were twenty."

"Oh, come, you needn't fling a fellow's age in his teeth," replied Van Rensslaer, in his boyish way. "I insist on your telling now, because it must be a good joke by your laughing."

"Decidedly the best of the season," said Worthington. "I'll tell the lady herself of it before you sometime."

"I know," whispered the trumpet-nosed, bending toward his opposite neighbor. "It is Mrs. Marchmont; she's the only woman in the world he ever takes the trouble to visit."

"Hush!" Worthington said.

Faulkner did not appear to have caught the laughing whisper or Mr. Worthington's grave remonstrance; he was comparing his watch with the clock on the mantle, and looking ruefully at the table he had left, as if regretting his friend's prolonged absence.

"But I was right!" persisted Worthington's partner.

"Yes; and now drop the subject, Livingston. Did you say it was your deal? We'll win this rubber and be done for to-night. Just set the inkstand out of the way, will you, Van?"

As he spoke he crumpled the page whereon he had written his name, and flung it upon the hearth near which he sat. The four returned to the business of the hour; Dick Faulkner rose and sauntered up and down the room till his friend came back, full of excuses for his delay.

"It's no matter," Dick said; "but I must move homeward now; it is getting late."

"I'll walk with you," the other replied.

They left the room together. As Faulkner was going, he took a cigar-case from his pocket, extracted a Havana, went to the fire, and lighted it, picking up for that purpose the paper which Mr. Worthington had thrown on the hearth, twisting the remainder in his hand as he walked on, apparently unconscious that he had retained it.

CHAPTER XX.

THE FIRST SHADOW.

MILLY's bright days remained cloudless until Lent closed, and Easter ushered in its season of rejoicing. Then Mrs. Marchmont returned from Washington as unexpectedly as she went away, not having given any intimation of her plans even in the gay, amusing letters with which she indulged John Worthington during her absence. Back she came, with her gorgeous beauty, the strange glamour in her eyes, and the proud lips that uttered such bitter speeches at one moment, and the next brightened with such bewildering smiles that the gloom seemed only an outward shadow instead of proceeding from trouble within.

Worthington called at her house the day after her arrival, and was shocked and alarmed at the change in her appearance; but she was already surrounded by a group of her friends and admirers, so that he had no opportunity to ask troublesome questions. She had grown thin; but it was not that so much as the expression of her face which caused the alteration. She had not fallen off, so far as beauty was concerned, and her spirits seemed as high as ever; but it was a gayety which jarred upon him, for he felt that it was factitious. She talked a great deal—related a score of anecdotes at the expense of her Washington adorers, and the idiots about her—as John Worthington mentally called them—laughed and applauded, not observant enough to notice the change either in appearance or manner, or, if they did notice, too selfish to think about it, since, whether ill or troubled, she was still able to play her usual part in the tiresome old game.

Mrs. Lawrence had recommenced her weekly receptions as soon as Lent ended; and though this first one, which was to take place the evening after Alice Marchmont's return, was a musical affair, the certainty of a good supper brought the customary crowd.

Halford was there before Milly's arrival; and, after searching for her in vain, he went up stairs into the card-rooms to see whom he could find, as the music had ceased for a little, and the familiar salons looked desolate without the presence of his rose-bud.

"She isn't here yet," Mrs. Lawrence said, chancing to meet him near the foot of the stairs. "I suppose the place seems empty."

"With this crowd?" he asked, not choosing to understand her words.

"That's the comfort of a large house," said she, complacently; "one can invite one's friends without running the risk of their suffocating."

"And I believe you have more friends than any other woman in the world," returned he.

"I ought to have plenty; I like my species! I like you, too, though you're not a bit confidential—it's shabby of you."

"I thought I was frankness itself," said he.

"Oh, indeed! But I'm not blind—not quite," returned Minerva, as if there was a probability of her soon becoming so. "I can see as far as most folk, and you may be silent, and Milly look innocent, and Eliza Remsen purse up her mouth—she always had an ugly mouth, though she doesn't believe it—but I know what is going on."

"Really, your discernment is appalling! You make me afraid," he said, and got away as rapidly as possible.

Up stairs in the chamber next the boudoir where he had told his secret to Milly, he came upon Mrs. Marchmont. She had just left the dressing-room, and stopped there for an instant's solitude before encountering the crowd below. She stood leaning against the window, from which she had pushed the curtains back, gazing out into the garden beneath, where the leafless trees sighed and waved their branches in the night-wind, and the moon, half obscured by clouds, rushed swiftly up the sky as if trying to escape the gloom which threatened utterly to overwhelm her. As Halford saw her, he was as much struck as Worthington had been by the change in her face: it showed very plainly as she stood there unconscious of observation. Such diverse emotions swept like shadows over her countenance, and dimmed the splendor of her eyes, that he was fairly startled. But he moved quickly forward; she caught the sound of his step, and turned to meet the intruder, whosoever it might be, schooling her features into the haughty quiet which had grown their habitual expression.

"How do you do, Mr. Halford?" she said, holding out her hand; but though she smiled, and added pleasant inquiries, it seemed to her listener that she spoke with an effort, as if in reality too listless and weary even to be glad at this meeting with an old friend.

"Are you well?" he asked.

"Perfectly. I have forbidden anybody's asking; it is so humiliating always to be obliged to confess myself in rude health!"

"Upon my word, you don't look it," he said.

"Never mind my looks; those weeks in Washington were enough to make any angel grow plain. But you have been a runaway, too, somebody told me. The idea of your being as near to me as Baltimore, and not coming on to the odious capital!"

"I should have liked it exceedingly," he replied, "but I was too much engaged to spare even a few hours from my business."

"Don't mention the horrid word! I don't allow it uttered in my hearing any longer."

"There seems to be a variety of things that you have forbidden," he said, smiling. "As I have not seen you for some time, you will have to give me a list, so that I may not ignorantly transgress."

"I would forbid every earthly subject, if I could only find new ones—heavenly or otherwise. I have heard every thing discussed till my patience is exhausted," she replied; but, gayly as she spoke, it struck him, as it had John Worthington, that her spirits were more unreal and unnatural than ever. "Who is down stairs—just the old set, I suppose? How nice it must have been to have lived in the Reign of Terror! One had new faces each day in prison; and an hour's flirtation gained a new piquancy by the reflection that a stroke of the guillotine at the end of it would prevent one's admirer ever growing tiresome."

"Washington seems to have had a bad effect on your mind," he said, not half liking the talk.

"On my manners, at least," she replied. "Though I did not bore myself too much; sometimes it was rather pleasant—a change, at all events; and that's the one blessing life offers."

"So the baron followed you?"

"Of course—as you would have done if you had not been the most perfidious and fickle of men. What nonsense I am talking! I really forgot it was you, my good old Kenneth. Have you been here long?"

"No; I only came a few moments ago; everybody that I cared to talk with was busy, so I wandered up stairs to see who was to be found."

"Every body! That always means one body. So she was busy, and could not so much as give you a word—poor man! Did you catch sight of my baron? He has no business to be late, because I expressly ordered him to come early."

"And so waited until near midnight before arriving yourself?"

"Exactly! I thought he would get tired, and go off before I appeared. The poor baron —he really is a nicer creature than one would believe."

"So he is the present victim?"

"Oh, he'll never be a victim to any body or any thing, unless it be tobacco. And you—aren't you a victim yet?"

"I think not—"

He stopped, for at that instant a face glanced in at the door-way—a girl's face, looking very youthful and pretty framed among the silken draperies; but it disappeared before Mrs. Marchmont could remark what attracted his attention. Several people from the inner room entered just then, and Halford took advantage of their appearance to hasten away in search of Milly.

He did not find her, though; and presently Mrs. Marchmont met him in the card-room, and of course he offered his arm down stairs.

Milly had left her aunt for a moment talking to some acquaintance, and had passed through the suite of upper rooms for the express pleasure of glancing into her beloved boudoir. She loved that chamber better than any spot in the whole world; there was no haunt which held a memory so enthralling as that of the night when Kenneth Halford put his heart into words, and led her away into the full glory of the magic land. On her way she fell upon the little tableau—innocent enough, but somehow not a pleasant one to her—Mrs. Marchmont looking full in Halford's face with those speaking eyes, and he bending toward her with a deference and attention which of late Milly had not been accustomed to see him bestow upon any one but herself. She felt a little guilty, too, as if she had intruded upon a scene not meant for her observation—stricken suddenly by the idea that he might think she had watched, or that a hint of their engagement might already have reached Mrs. Marchmont, and she with her careless tongue sting Halford by some such insinuation.

Milly flew off to the dressing-room to have a moment to herself, telling Aunt Eliza a fib as she passed — that she had forgotten her handkerchief, though the fib was unnecessary, for Aunt Eliza was talking comfortably, and ready to wait as long as Milly pleased before entering upon the lofty enjoyment of the classical music which once more surged up from the apartments below. But Milly uttered her little untruth, and fled on to the retirement of the dressing-room. Luckily it was empty —even the maid in attendance had temporarily absented herself; so she had an opportunity to try and calm the agitation caused by the picture she had so unwittingly studied. She remembered her old fears of Mrs. Marchmont, fears so quickly allayed by her departure that they had lain forgotten until now; but they rushed back, and it required some time for Milly to recover the beaming content which had been her portion of late. Presently she could think of the dear words Halford had spoken in that little chamber; of the weeks of happiness which had followed, and was ready to laugh at her own folly—as if any human being could come between her and her bliss, as if any mortal occurrence could ever really disturb it!

She returned to the card-room, and found her aunt; but Mrs. Remsen was so deep in conversation that Milly had to wait, and it was tiresome, now that she was eager to meet Halford and atone for her momentary irritation by increased sweetness and amiability.

"Now I'll go," Mrs. Remsen said, at last. "Are you completely out of patience, Milly?"

"Oh no; but I do like music, you know."

"Exactly," laughed Mrs. Remsen, as she took the girl's arm and led her away; "it is to listen to the music that you are anxious to go down stairs."

"Now, if you tease me my cheeks will get scarlet," pleaded Milly.

"Then I'll do it; for it is very becoming."

"Oh, please—I shall look like a goose!"

"So you are—a dear little goose! But mercy on us, what a crowd there is! I be-

lieve Minerva Lawrence is never satisfied unless she fills her house till one can't breathe."

"But the music is very fine," Milly said.

"I dare say. I'm not musical, further than to like your singing, Puss. If I must have concerts, I prefer them in a room built for the purpose."

Milly was accustomed to hearing her aunt and Mrs. Lawrence indulge in such thrusts at each other's expense; but she knew they were good friends all the same, and neither of them would have allowed any one else the liberty of abusing her old school-companion.

"It's like going into a furnace," sighed Aunt Eliza, as they reached the foot of the stairs. "Oh, Minerva will be a fool if she lives to be a hundred! I never endured any thing like it."

Unfortunately for the good resolutions Milly had so lately been making, the very first sight that met her eyes as she entered the drawing-rooms was Mrs. Marchmont with a crowd about her, from which she was just turning away with her usual ease and indifference, and taking Halford's arm for a promenade between the pieces. Worst of all, he was so much occupied that he did not notice Milly's entrance. She was not a fool, even in her love and her exacting disposition. When she reflected upon the matter, she knew very well that a man was to have a little use of his eyes and ears for old acquaintances, though he might be engaged. Many a time she had laughed at girls for indulging in silly tempers concerning things of the same sort; but that did not remove the sudden chill which struck her when she saw Alice Marchmont leaning on Halford's arm, and glancing up in his face with those wonderful eyes which would look as if they were meaning a great many things that they did not.

It is very well to theorize about such trifles, as Milly herself had often done in the plenitude of her untried wisdom; but a case which appealed directly to her own feelings was a different matter, as you or I might discover under similar circumstances. She followed her aunt with a cold pressure at her heart, a breathless sensation, an inexplicable sickening thrill which made her absolutely faint, and very glad to sink into a seat.

As if her disagreeable thoughts were not annoyance enough, Adelaide Ramsay must needs come up and hiss venomous whispers into Milly's ears under cover of the music, which kept her words from reaching Mrs. Remsen; for Adelaide was not exactly bold enough to run the risk of incurring her mother's wrath by such remarks as her dislike of Milly prompted her to utter. The two cousins never made the pretense of being friends, though it was not Milly's fault. Adelaide had always disliked her, and now, since she suspected that the girl was soon to make a brilliant marriage, fairly hated her. Indeed, she had on several occasions of late been so rude that Mrs. Remsen had advised Milly to keep away from her house, and even

8

threatened her daughter with Mr. Ramsay's displeasure if she did not let Milly alone. Maud had as nearly betrayed the secret of the engagement as she dared, and Mrs. Ramsay could not resist this opportunity of gratifying her spite.

"Do you see Kenneth Halford and Mrs. Marchmont?" she asked, without the slightest preamble or salutation.

"I was busy listening to the music," Milly answered, civilly; "it is very beautiful, isn't it?"

"Oh, you can't put me off that way!" returned Adelaide. "You had better look after Halford, I can tell you, Miss Milly."

"Allow me to beg that you will tell me nothing of the sort," replied Milly, with a good deal of quiet dignity. "It is neither a kind nor polite remark."

"Upon my word, as Maud says, your airs lately are too much for human patience! I shall tell you what I think best. Please to remember I am a married woman, and your cousin."

Milly could easily have exasperated her with a cutting answer, but it was not worth the trouble; besides, she had no wish to quarrel or to dislike Mrs. Ramsay, if the woman would only treat her with a show of decent feeling. So she said,

"I am sorry you and Maud disapprove of me, but I can't help it; and I do not wish you to connect my name with any man's as you did just now."

"I beg your pardon," returned Adelaide, with an insulting laugh; "it was Mrs. Marchmont's name that I connected with Halford's—and with good reason, too."

"One that would not interest me, however important," said Milly.

"Don't be absurd—using words like Hortense!"

"At least Hortense is good-hearted and lady-like. Please to go away, Adelaide; this is no place for a discussion."

"Perhaps you'd better order me out of the rooms, and be done with it! Now I shall say what I like, and when I like. I was speaking in all kindness; but that is the way with you—you never appreciate one's motives."

"I think I do," Milly said; then closed her lips and mentally determined not to be provoked into speaking another word.

"Everybody knows Halford used to be crazy over Mrs. Marchmont years ago, when she was a girl," continued Adelaide. "Dear me! I believe he tried to shoot himself when he heard she was married," she added—this last clause an entire falsehood, of course, born out of her desire to annoy Milly.

"If you don't go away this instant I'll speak to aunty!" she gasped, and Adelaide thought it best to retreat.

Milly began fairly to hate this beautiful Alice, with her picturesque dress, her entrancing ways, her power to sing in a theatrical, passionate fashion, and before the evening was over had

been pettish, and almost rude to her. Mrs. Marchmont annoyed her still more by an amused forbearance, though all the same she felt an inclination to punish her, as one does to punish the freaks of a spoiled child. Poor Milly! Somebody came up to ask her to follow the general example of promenading through the rooms while the musicians exchanged the classics for a slow march. It was Charley Thorne who asked, unfortunate boy!

"You've scarcely spoken to me for a whole week," he said, dolefully; "you never do speak to me nowadays, and I know the reason; but never mind! I wish you would take my arm once more—just once," he added as dismally as if he were to be ordered off to execution immediately after.

Milly's first impulse was to answer the boy sharply; then came a second thought—the biting fear so quick to trouble a woman's mind, however young, that some one might be looking curiously at her, might suspect her secret, notice any change in her manner, and attribute it to its rightful cause. So she made poor Charley—who had flung his young heart at her feet to be trodden upon in the insolent, unconscious pride of her girlhood—happy by taking his arm, and walking up and down the room with him.

Then Kenneth Halford saw her with her cheeks glowing from that fear, and her eyes beautified by the twofold pain in her soul. The course of the promenade brought the couples close together.

"Oh, my pretty little fairy!" said Mrs. Marchmont, holding out her hand. "I am so happy to see you again."

Milly could not bring herself to give more than two fingers and a very cold answer to the lady's greeting, casting one glance toward Halford as she did so; but Mrs. Marchmont intercepted the glance, fleeting as it was, and her wits—sharp as so many polished daggers—comprehended the matter at once as well as if she had received a whole volume of explanations.

"You must come and see me, my blossom," she continued, talking rapidly, while those swift thoughts flitted through her mind, smiling, too, at Milly's stateliness, which was a little like the attempts of a pigeon to imitate a peacock. "Come very soon, you and the dear aunt—is she quite well?"

"Quite well; she is here," Milly replied, not vouchsafing Halford a second look. "I think you may take me back to her, if you please, Mr. Thorne."

Charley led her away. It was a pleasure to get her out of Halford's neighborhood, if only for a few moments.

"I haven't slept for a week," he moaned, suddenly, forgetting the silence under which he had meant to shroud his griefs. Whispers in regard to Milly's engagement had reached his ears, and for days he had been eagerly watching his face in the glass to see if thinness and paleness gave any signs of the speedy death which he believed he wanted. But it was not so easy to die uncomplainingly as he had imagined, and now he turned upon Milly with that peevish confession.

"I should go straight home, then, and go to bed," was her unfeeling answer. "We must not walk any longer. They are beginning that thing of Riesiger's, and every body is expected to sit down."

Milly wanted to go back to her chair. She felt as she had sometimes done under the influence of a bad dream, as if her limbs were half paralyzed and refused to move. Charley Thorne wandered disconsolately away, to watch her from a distance, and think his poor little dismal thoughts, unconscious that any thing was amiss. The look whose language had been so plain to Mrs. Marchmont was lost on him—being only a man!

"I did not see you come in," he whispered, under the cover of the thunder of two violoncellos and a grand piano-forte. "How pretty you look, my little blossom!"

I suppose he could not have stumbled on two more unfortunate speeches! First, so innocently to acknowledge that he had been unaware of her presence. Love was making Milly imaginative and unreasonable enough for the feeling we have each indulged in our turn—the expectation that a beloved is to know by intuition when one approaches or is near. Then to call her by that name! She liked pet names, but this was the appellation that odious woman had just given her in his hearing. It grated on Milly's ear like a harsh word.

"What made you so late?" continued Halford.

"It is not late," replied Milly, fretfully, telling a fib to gratify her vexation; for it was late, and Aunt Eliza's dilatoriness had put her in a fever a full hour before they set out.

The tone was unmistakably cross. Halford looked surprised.

"Aren't you well?" he asked.

"Certainly. Why should you think I am not?"

He smiled; he had never seen her cross before, and it made her so pretty and *piquant* that he rather liked it by way of a change—for a few moments. After awhile another opportunity was given restless people to walk about, and Halford turned from a conversation with Mrs. Remsen to offer Milly his arm. She had three minds to refuse, but could not bring herself to carry her resentment so far. Halford took pleasure in teasing her, and said a dozen things at which she would have laughed in another mood; but she could not laugh now. Mrs. Marchmont passed them on some man's arm, and half whispered a few French words in Halford's ear so rapidly that Milly could not understand them.

"What a pretty lilac," he said, carelessly, pointing to the trimmings on Milly's over-skirt. He was not to blame because her unpracticed

ear had not caught the hurried accents, nor could she quarrel with him outright because the fascinating widow chose to address him in a foreign language; but she could find fault when he gave a wrong name to the tint of her bows.

"They are lavender," she replied. "Something must have made you color-blind to-night."

"My dear child," returned he, bent on teasing her, "I pride myself on the correctness of my eye—lilac, I do assure you."

"Then Aunt Eliza and I and the dressmaker must all be blind," she answered, hotly.

He laughed again at her tone and manner, and was so determined to make her laugh that at last Milly grew amiable in spite of herself. The evening would have passed off tolerably, and Milly need not have felt troubled or cross again had not Mrs. Marchmont chanced to meet her just before supper and utter some innocent remark which turned Milly acid once more. Then it was she committed the folly of being pettish, and almost rude, turning away with a few words so unlike her usual gentleness that Mrs. Marchmont was surprised and offended.

"How cross the little blossom seems!" she said, wonderingly, to John Worthington, who had come in for half an hour just to meet her.

"Perhaps you have been poaching on her manor," he answered, rather wearily; for he was not in good spirits to-night.

"What do you mean?"

"Why, Halford has been very devoted to her all these weeks of your absence, so Constance says; she fancies, too, that they are engaged."

"Engaged—Kenneth Halford to that child?"

"Why not?"

"She is very pretty, to be sure, but a mere baby—and at his age! He must be four-and-thirty!"

"How dreadfully ancient!"

"As most men live, it is. The generality of you are Methusalehs before that—too old and *blasé* for a little innocent creature like her to fancy."

"You will please to remember my age."

"But you don't want to make love to Milly Crofton, I suppose? Mr. Halford engaged to her! Upon my word, it makes me laugh."

Her eyes danced. She was certain that her suspicion, roused earlier in the evening by Milly's manner, was correct.

"And the goose is jealous!" she thought. "She's a pretty young bird, but she musn't hiss at me like a small serpent each time I venture to look toward her idol—that will never do."

There was a confusion of epithets in the lady's mind, but the main thought was very clear under them: if that girl ventured to be impertinent she must be suitably punished.

"Of course she hasn't an idea in her head," Alice went on thinking while she watched Milly. "Well, it's odd how a man of Kenneth

Halford's age will take a fancy to bread-and-butter after ruining his digestion with all manner of forbidden eatables; but I don't really believe in the engagement."

Milly could not tell what was passing in Mrs. Marchmont's mind, or be sufficiently wise to know that in a battle such as she was ready to bring on, a woman like her always has every advantage over a young girl, in spite of love or ties of any sort. She determined that the lady should discover that she did not mean to submit to affectionate patronage, or be called names of extravagant endearment, or be meddled with in any manner. Poor little Milly!

Before the concert was over Mrs. Marchmont had Milly and Halford again brought to her mind by John Worthington.

"Just look at them as they stand there by the piano. Doesn't that look like business?"

"I do believe he is getting into mischief," said she.

"Very pleasant mischief, I've no doubt. She is a bewitching little fairy."

"Just a sweet, undeveloped child! So like a man! and when the child turns into a woman on his hands he'll grow tired of her because she is like the rest of her sex, and reproach her instead of his own folly."

"You speak warmly," said he, rather suspiciously. "I think you prophesied this very thing weeks ago, and I asked how you would like it. Is it less agreeable than you fancied?"

"How cross you are to-night!" she exclaimed. "I think I shall go home to get rid of you."

"But you didn't answer my question!"

"I sha'n't weep over my Kenneth's desertion, if that is what you mean," she answered. "But he's a good man, and she's a sweet baby. I don't like to think of their making each other unhappy; but perhaps they will not."

He felt certain that there was no hidden feeling in her mind. It was a great relief, for he had often feared that Halford's return had something to do with the change this winter had worked in her.

CHAPTER XXI.

CROSS-PURPOSES.

Of course not many days could elapse without Mrs. Marchmont's meeting Dick Faulkner; still she contrived to avoid him a great deal, for though she was free from his power, the sight of him reminded her so forcibly of the insult he had offered—the crime he had forced her to commit—that it was torture to find herself in his presence, even if not compelled to address more than a cold bow or a few chilling words.

Immediately on Alice's arrival, Mrs. Faulkner left her own and her husband's cards, and Mrs. Marchmont returned hers, scrupulously, though she vowed that nothing should tempt

her ever to set foot within the house. She must be civil when they met, lest people should notice and ask the reason of the breach; but she would not go beyond that. Only a few evenings afterward she encountered them at a party, and Mrs. Faulkner fluttered up with her false smiles and honeyed words, doubly distasteful to Alice, because she knew that the spiteful woman only did it at Faulkner's command.

Later in the evening she found Dick himself by her side; he had been annoying her for the last half-hour by standing at a distance and watching her in the old way, so that by the time he approached she was in a state of high nervous exasperation.

"May I compliment you on the restored looks you have brought back from Washington?" he half whispered, in that silky disagreeable voice and the compromising manner he assumed toward all women. "You seemed tired and fagged when you went away, but the old capital has done wonders for you."

There was a covert sneer in his tone which struck her with the old chill of dread, and she knew that the speech was meant for an impertinence; her glass told her plainly how much these weeks had changed her. Fortunately, she was alone for the moment, and could relieve her mind.

"You need not compliment me at all," she replied, not vouchsafing him a single glance. "I have already spoken to your wife; that politeness will serve for you both the whole evening."

"You are not changed, certainly!" he said, trying in vain to keep his voice from quivering with anger; "you come back as haughty and unforgiving as you went."

She did not speak—looked away over his head still, with that same careless contempt which touched him as no display of anger could have done.

"I think you are making a mistake," he said, slowly; "it is Christian-like and womanly to forgive; it is always safer, too, for the patience of the most penitent man may be pushed too far."

"As I am not a Christian, and you any thing rather than penitent, I can make no application of your words," she answered, after a momentary struggle whether to speak, or let him stand there unnoticed till he must leave her for fear some one should observe and smile at his ridiculous position. "The rest of your speech seems a kind of threat; you forget that you are powerless."

He laughed in a low, sneering tone.

"You will think me capable of threats, then? But what folly on my part at this late day!"

"Utter folly!" she said; though, in spite of her, the old fear grew stronger, and she looked at him now—studied his face, to try and discover if there was any hidden meaning to his speech; but features and attitude had assumed the sentimental expression and pose which always exasperated her. "I think it better to be frank," she continued, quickly, under the influence of this emotion; "I shall be obliged to you, Mr. Faulkner, if you will never address a word to me beyond the commonest greeting."

"That is hard," he said; "very hard, when the greatest pleasure I have in life is to converse with you, even if I must endure disdainful looks and cruel speeches."

"This is simply impertinent," she replied. "Have the goodness to go away, or I shall be compelled to leave you standing here."

"No, don't do that," he said; "it would be unwise."

"Another mysterious threat?"

"Only a caution for your own sake; you do not wish people to know that you are offended with me."

"I warn you that I shall not try to hide it, if you venture to annoy me."

"Then you would have to tell the reason. I don't mind; I am not ashamed of loving you."

She half rose—remembered where she was, and controlled herself.

"I think," she said, "there must be some man here who would protect me from your insolence. Will you force me to make sure?"

"But that would only hurt you! Suppose some *preux chevalier* shot me, it would not prevent the world's saying you must have gone very far when I dared say such a thing; you would have to endure something worse than my society."

"Nothing could be so bad as that!"

"Well, well, I don't mean to quarrel—do you know why?"

"No; nor care to hear."

"Simply out of regard for you. I am, what I always have been, the most devoted of your friends. I will not quarrel."

"I think you had better go away," she said, with an ominous pause between each word.

"In a moment; I don't intend to annoy you hereafter, so I must speak clearly now."

"You have nothing to say."

"Yes; this! I want you to remember that I am your friend. When the time arrives that you need my help, recollect what I say now, and send for me at once."

Again the paralyzing fear came back. Had he discovered any thing? did he suspect? was there a real meaning to his words, or were they only an empty insolence for the pleasure of tormenting her? Oh, that last question must contain the rightful answer; yet the bare thought that it might not nerved her anew with the desperation which nowadays served in the place of her old courage.

"When I want you I will send," she answered, with a bitter smile; "perhaps you will have the goodness to wait until then, before approaching me again."

"Yes," he said, gravely; "I will wait."

She would not raise her eyes, anxious as she was to read his face; she feared that they might confirm the dread in her soul.

"And you know that I can wait patiently,"

he went on. "A few weeks ago, when you set a time for me to come to you, I never intruded until the exact day: I shall not now."

"If you will only wait till then, I have nothing more to ask."

"I will wait."

He bowed and turned away, but she felt herself tremble under the triumphant ring in his guarded voice.

A few days afterward she received an invitation to dinner from Mrs. Faulkner it was declined, as were all succeeding invitations from that quarter; Alice avoided the houses where she was likely to meet the husband or wife. In spite of his potency in these days, there were people who refused to allow Dick Faulkner to enter their doors, and as much as possible she confined herself to their society. When she did chance to meet him, he never troubled her further than to speak, as a distant, respectful acquaintance might have done; and as the days went on she put him a great deal out of her mind.

The fears which gathered darkly were not those in which he had a part—she must guard against John Worthington now. The time sped on with such terrible rapidity; the note hidden in the Hebrew's desk haunted her more and more persistently. Twice during her stay in Washington she had thought the bargain for her lands complete, had expected to have the deeds presented for her signature; on each occasion the matter had again fallen through. The company could not agree among themselves, not where her demands were concerned; but there were inward dissensions among them —a change of president, and various troubles, which prevented their having leisure to attend to any purchases as yet.

And the days flew, each bearing her nearer the moment when prompt action would be a necessity. She had no hope of getting a renewal of the note; in the beginning the Jew had allowed her to see that any such clemency was not to be expected. When the fatal day arrived he would appear before her, bill in hand, and at the first word—the first plea for delay—hurry from her to seek John Worthington, and place the forged signature before his eyes. She never got beyond that exposure in her thoughts; when she reached that point she was past forming even the wildest idea of what might follow. Whether he would expose her, allow the law to take its course—oh, she hoped that would prove his choice! A prison—hard labor—life among the vilest convicts, would be easier than to have him come and look in her face, and tell her she was safe from the effects of his righteous anger, so far as betrayal was concerned; but no punishment of the law could equal the agony of meeting his contempt.

She grew more and more capricious in her manner toward him; sometimes seeking his society, sometimes fairly running away, and unable to decide whether she suffered most in listening to his friendly words or in the seasons of solitude when tormented by the idea that before they met again some untoward chance might have revealed to him the truth.

Worthington, troubled by his own secret, placed a construction upon her conduct entirely foreign to the facts. He began to fear that he had not concealed his feelings so carefully as he believed; that she suspected his folly, and was divided between a wish not to break their long friendship, and a dread that he would pain her by putting his insanity into speech. So he visited her less; went less frequently to places where they were likely to meet. Then his absence terrified her, and she would seek him and try to make her manner what it had formerly been, and shudder with remorse at each tone of his voice.

The baron had followed her home from Washington; he was always haunting her steps, seeking an opportunity to lay his title at her feet; and though she knew there was little hope of her daring to accept—the idea, too, of marrying him was a torment—she could not let him speak yet, lest afterward she should regret having thrown away that one chance of escape from her old life.

She had no peace anywhere, but in those weary days Kenneth Halford's companionship was nearer rest than aught else, and she lured him to her side by every art that she could find. He saw more of her real self than others did, and he pitied her profoundly—it was the sore feeling in his heart; but Milly was tormenting him sorely, and Mrs. Marchmont's society was a relief, so he sought it often; and of course there were eyes enough to notice, and tongues enough to hint to Milly of the flirtation that was going on.

The next time she met Mrs. Marchmont after that first evening, Milly carried into execution her plan of showing the haughty beauty that she did not mean to be patronized or treated as a child. It was very like a foolish blossom pitting itself against a diamond star and getting its leaves pierced by a score of the sharp, sparkling points. Again Alice Marchmont smiled sweetly upon her, and held an internal monologue.

"Yes, I'll certainly teach you a lesson, yon dreadful-mannered little girl of the period! If Kenneth Halford is idiot enough to marry you, I shall do him and you a service by aggravating you into common sense. How much you do lack it, my pecked white dove!"

Milly had dealt a dangerous blow to her own peace, poor child! I do not mean to say that Mrs. Marchmont in the least disliked her; but she was accustomed to conquest even among her own sex, and impertinence was a thing she could not endure. Besides, during these horrible days she was hard and cruel; any fancied slight made her long to punish the offender. She would rule absolutely to the last; there was so little time left now—so little!

Had she really known Milly, she was more capable of thoroughly understanding her than any

body had ever done; but meeting her casually in crowds, she only saw the trifling, childish exterior, and believed that Halford—if the story of the engagement proved true—was taking a step that he would bitterly regret when too late. She concluded hastily that Milly's mind was like the minds of so many girls, the best comparison for which is an oak-seedling that the Chinese plant in a vase, and which, under some subtle treatment, speedily shoots into a miniature tree, pretty and quaint, but never to enlarge or grow any higher.

No confidence in regard to the engagement passed between Mrs. Marchmont and Halford, and though Alice heard the reports she did not feel herself obliged to change her manner toward him, since he offered no hint of his new ties. This was, unfortunately, Milly's fault. Only a short time after Mrs. Marchmont came back, he asked his betrothed if he might confide their secret to one of his oldest and dearest friends. She was sure whom he meant, and her budding jealousy prompted her to refuse the request.

"I'll not have it," she said. "You promised me that you would not tell till I gave you leave."

"And I shall keep my word, dear child," he answered, for he was still patient with her; "but in this one case I should like to break through our compact."

"I'll not hear of it," Milly said; "no, I'll not hear of it."

So the conversation ended there, and he did not renew his plea.

The days passed on; it was all the work of a brief season, and the contest thus begun was continued—mere play to the elder woman, but stern, terrible earnest to blind little Milly.

Just her childishness, her sunny laugh, her light heart had won Kenneth Halford's love. Therefore, when she grew fretful, and her temper uncertain, when she took him to task about trifles, not choosing to reveal the real hurt which smarted so keenly, he became impatient, and began to regard her childishness from another point of view. He hoped that he had not been overhasty in entering into this engagement, which was equivalent to fearing that he had gone on too fast. He felt that, at all events and at all risks, she must be subdued and taught that such freaks were silly and ridiculously out of place toward a man so much older and wiser than herself, when that man had honored her with his affection; and I never yet have met one of the sex who would not have felt the same.

Then, out of the mystery of the heart's awakening, Milly's mind developed like an amaryllis bursting suddenly into blossom. She thought of things in a way she had never before done; of life and the world as they really are; of the fact that she could not always be young and pretty. She saw that Halford considered her a child; that he loved her as such; that there were depths in his past which she was not allowed to sound, supposed incapable of compre-hending—experiences which kept them worlds apart in spite of love and vows. She per-ceived clearly that he only allowed her to stand in the pleasant light of the portico, and never dreamed of opening the inner doors of the tem-ple that she might enter and take her rightful place.

Did the awaking of these new faculties, this ability to reason, this clear-sightedness, this struggle into womanhood make her suddenly more patient, better able to set right the tan-gled woof of the present? Ah, never did it so happen in the case of any human being! The wisdom gained by experience does not come until long after the battle is over, the defeat ac-cepted. We look back on our Waterloos, and see how the fight might have been won; but when we have acquired the generalship neces-sary for a victory, the great stakes for which we would struggle are no longer there.

Milly was astonished to find that her temper could be so bad. The children at home fret-ted her; the light duties she had to perform be-came insupportable. Every thing went wrong, and she made herself more wretched each day, without mending matters in the least, and forced her aunt to think her almost wicked, and wonder how it was that her new position could have so changed her nature. Mrs. Marchmont was punishing her for her naughty behavior, without meaning to injure her happiness or be-lieving there was depth enough to her mind to make real suffering possible. Halford was ren-dered colder and sterner by Milly's petulance, and so the clouds loomed swiftly up over the horizon which had been so glorious.

"I want rest, peace," said Kenneth Halford, in his masculine arrogance. "Is this child only to tease and annoy me, instead of proving the cheerful sunbeam that I wooed for my lone-liness?"

No remembrance of the warning John Wor-thington had given recurred to his mind; he was blind as the rest of us are until the time arrives when there is no space for any thing but regret. We can see clearly enough then how we might have averted the tempest. As we look back across the graves of the past we can perceive how patience, self-sacrifice, even quiet endurance of actual wrong, might have been needed to set matters straight, and the sacrifices look very small, haughtily as we should have rejected them while they could have proved of any avail.

Minerva Lawrence struck the crowning blow upon Milly's heart—struck it unintentionally, blindly, without the least idea of her own cru-elty—just as our best friends hurt us, in their desire to meddle with that which is better left alone. She was very fond of Milly, and took it upon herself to be indignant at the gossip concerning Mrs. Marchmont and Halford. But it did not occur to her to believe that it was without foundation—she never stopped to think that he was an honorable man, incapable of proving false. She felt it her duty to caution Milly, to set her on her guard, to rouse in her a proper spirit of resentment; for, though the girl had never admitted her engagement, Mi-nerva, in her wisdom, felt certain that it ex-isted.

So, just when Milly was hottest and most bitter, and her jealousy at its height, Minerva came to make her a visit, and, as Mrs. Remsen was out, had a full opportunity to free her mind of the burden which oppressed it. She felt ir-ritated, too, because Milly had not been frank with her. The more wholly a secret belongs to one's self the more fiercely one's friends resent one's reticence.

"Where were you last night?" she asked.

"Aunty and I had to go to Hortense's," Mil-ly replied, yawning at the bare recollection. "Oh, it was awful!"

"I should think so—I tell Hortense honest-ly I'm not equal to her reunions. She thinks it's because I'm a fool, but I don't care."

"And where were you?" asked Milly, not wishing to be led into fault-finding with her cousin.

"At the opera."

"Many there?" demanded Milly, just to make conversation, for it was hard work to talk.

Halford had gone to Mrs. Maynard's, too, and Milly had managed to get into an alterca-tion. But he would not quarrel; he rose and went away, thereby punishing her more cruelly than if he had scolded.

"Yes, a great crowd," returned Minerva, with unnecessary emphasis. "Mrs. March-mont was in her box, going on as usual—half-undressed—laughing, sighing, rolling up her eyes. I hate her!"

Milly did not reply.

"And you ought to," pursued Minerva. "I can tell you that."

"You have no reason for telling me any thing of the kind," said Milly.

"Yes, I have—don't be snappish, when I'm so fond of you! Kenneth Halford was with her all the last act. I saw her go down stairs on his arm."

He had strolled into the opera-house after leaving Mrs. Maynard's, and seeing Alice Marchmont had gone to her box; but in Mil-ly's state of mind her first thought was that he had promised to do so—had left her with the intention of seeking that woman.

"And what was there improper in the pro-ceeding?" she forced herself to ask, trying to appear languid and bored, as she had seen eld-er feminines do more naturally.

"It's a shame—never mind, I'm supposed not to know—but I'm not a mole, nor an owl!" cried Minerva; and by this time she was in a state of such excitement that she poured out her whole bundle of gossip almost without a pause. "I don't believe you ever heard they were engaged once; but they were! I'd for-gotten it; but when Helen James raked up the story from her old aunts I remembered it. Yes, indeed; and she was always what she is now—the most heartless coquette in the world. She threw him over because he hadn't money in those days, and married Mr. Marchmont, and Halford went off to Egypt. You needn't look unbelieving—it is the truth."

"But it is nothing to me," said Milly.

"So much the better, but it's a fib! You ought to call him to account for the way he goes on;" and she added a long list of enormities which increased Milly's anger, though she would not say a word.

She tried for a little to believe that the story of the engagement was false; but once having set out on her mission, Minerva could not relinquish it until she proved the fact by circumstantial evidence which Milly could not doubt.

At last Aunt Eliza came in, but she appeared too late. Minerva had done all the harm she could, and in Milly's mood it was a great deal. The keeping secret this ancient history seemed, in her exaggerated frame of mind, a deliberate deception on the part of Halford—one that she could not and would not forgive. Worse than any thing, this woman had not lost her old power over him; she was sure of that. But he should learn that she was no baby to be contented with careless smiles and coaxing words! She would have all or nothing; if he was not prepared to give her his full heart, let him go back to Alice Marchmont and his former love, and leave her life free.

Halford perceived that she was jealous of Alice. The idea amused him at first, as her petulance had done. But Milly carried matters too far; it became an insulting suspicion in his eyes, and he was utterly out of patience with her folly. Then Milly began to flirt; she had worn the edge off her other weapons, short as the combat had been; she would go into the fray armed with the two-edged sword of coquetry. But when a young girl attempts to wield that blade out of bitterness and a desire to annoy her lover, she does not handle it with the coolness of an experienced fencer; half her thrusts go astray, and the sharpest blows cut her own heart.

Milly went on foolishly with any body who presented himself; worst of all with poor Charley Thorne, who was as foolish a boy as she was girl, only he had not much mind or soul to develop, so would not get himself so severely hurt as Milly was doing. Still, he loved her to the full extent of his capabilities. We think that a worm is not much to be pitied when wounded, because it can only feel a dull, sluggish pain; but, after all, if it suffers to the full extent of its powers, then it suffers in reality as severely as an angel could.

By this time Halford was really angry. Not that he supposed Milly cared for the youth; but, overlooking the real cause of her conduct, began to fear that she was led on by her love of admiration and flattery, and that she had conceived the idea of taking a leaf out of Mrs. Marchmont's book because she was annoyed with that lady. Milly must learn that such conduct was not to be permitted, and as he compared her with Alice Marchmont, he thought what a pity it was that young girls could not have the experience of worldly women, or that women must give their innocent freshness as the price of their knowledge.

But when you take a simple wild-flower, modest and perfumed with morning dew, and put it in a hot-house to grow double, to deepen in color, and become more gorgeous in every way, the fragrance and simplicity die out of it. You have a beautiful decoration for a *jardinière* or a ball-room, but you have deprived the blossom of the charm it had when odorous of the free air and memories of the pleasant haunts where you played and were happy years and years ago.

CHAPTER XXII.

IN THE DARK.

FROM the moment that Milly admitted to herself the truth of the reports Minerva Lawrence poured into her ears, not a day passed without bringing a host of confirming evidence. She began to find proofs of dissimulation in the slightest thing connected with Halford's conduct toward Mrs. Marchmont, and to indulge more and more in the idea that he felt his engagement a restraint.

"Why didn't he leave me alone?" cried poor Milly, in her passionate monologues. "Why did he come to me, and teach me to love him when he had only half a heart to give? He might have gone back to his old dream, and left me untroubled. Oh, it was cruel, it was wicked! I shall hate him soon!"

At least half their interviews became stormy ones. At times Milly was on the point of telling him that she knew the story of his past—his treachery toward herself, and bidding him leave her forever. But then some effort on his part to pet her back to peace would succeed for the moment, and she would persuade herself that he loved her, until a second meeting with Alice Marchmont roused her jealous fancies to a higher pitch. Had she only told him—bared her whole soul, no matter how harshly, even yet the clouds might have been cleared away. He could have shown how false her fears were; made her understand that his boyish dream had no more connection with his present life, no more hold upon him than the pursuits which pleased her when a little child possessed an interest now. But she did not speak; she kept her secret resolutely, sullenly, and it ate into her heart like a plague-spot, cankering to the very core.

Another week went by, and once again they were all assembled in somebody's house, busy with the old routine of dancing, talking—pitying themselves for being there, and hating their hostess for the invitation as bitterly as she detested them for the necessity of offering it.

Milly was in one of her most violent moods of irritation, and Halford cynical and misanthropical, as he had grown of late. Mrs. Marchmont was there too, and Dick Faulkner watching her, and each time she met his eyes it seemed to her that she read there a triumphant consciousness of the fact that the narrowing circle of days bore her rapidly toward her doom. The sight of him and the dread which his presence roused had its usual effect of putting her in the wildest, most feverish spirits, and prompted her to do and say a thousand things for which she hated herself afterward.

After trying for a while in vain to have a pleasant moment with Milly, Halford went away to make one in the circle about Mrs. Marchmont. They danced together, and finally she complained of the heat, and he led her away into the conservatory.

They fell into a morbid, speculative conversation, sitting alone in the pretty retreat much longer than was in exact accordance with the rules of etiquette, but Mrs. Marchmont had grown reckless of what people said, and Halford, man-like, did not think. Several times a stray couple wandered in, glanced at them, and departed with meaning smiles and whispers; but neither noticed. At length, as usually happened, their talk became personal, and something Halford said roused Mrs. Marchmont into contradiction; but it was a laughing, graceful warfare, very different from poor Milly's sharp speeches and petulant ways.

"I've no patience whatever with you," she said; "not the least. You are like the rest of your sex, Kenneth Halford."

"In allowing myself to be dazzled by your brilliancy?" he asked, laughingly.

"Nonsense!" retorted she. "What is the good of talking in that way? There is nobody to hear."

"Thank you," said Halford, and felt vexed, as the veriest old stager will when a woman says such things, however indifferent he may be to her.

"People say that you are engaged to that pretty little baby, Milly Crofton."

Halford looked up rather angrily at the epithets.

"If I am—she is a darling little thing!"

"Just that," replied she, coolly; "and it was what you wanted to find. Let me see—you are almost four-and-thirty; you have lived ever since you were fifteen—oh yes, I know what men like you want! To be worshiped, adored, made a god of! Innocence and youth for you—very good!"

"Thanks again for your kind opinion so frankly expressed," he replied, amiably enough; "but my vanity is not quite insatiable."

"You don't thank me, and I'm not talking about your vanity. What I want to know is this—since you have seen fit to take a child to bring up, why are you not satisfied?"

"I wonder," said Halford, musingly, "do these children—"

"No, they don't," interrupted Mrs. Marchmont; "they never do grow up, and that is their chief charm—the very reason why they are to be envied. Who would feel if he could help it? You have chosen your wild-flower—sometimes, after the first blossoming, such flowers turn into the most commonplace weeds. I trust it will not be the case in this instance. Still, you must run your chance—you can't have ragout and syllabub in the same dish; excuse the confusion of metaphors. You have grown dreadfully tired of the taste of ragout; I only hope the syllabub will not turn sour."

"How cynical you are!" returned he, in an irritated tone.

"Men always say that when one takes the trouble to tell them truth; verity and cynicism they seem to regard as synonymous terms."

"I wish there was no such thing as truth," cried he, laughing.

"I don't think there will be by the time the next generation gets here," returned she, quietly. "Well, they say we live afresh in our children; with your prospect you can look forward to that poetical delight."

"You sneer, but I know you love children; you would give the world for something to care for as you could for a child."

"I don't deny it," she replied; and for an instant her lip quivered; but the brief emotion passed, and she continued in her former careless voice, "I dare say I shall envy you! I suppose, when a man grows tired of his syllabub, the babies are a great consolation; and our American doves subside very quietly into nurses and upper-servants."

"I don't wish—"

"You needn't interrupt! I have reached the children's chapter, and I am always eloquent thereupon. I say the babies are delightful, but they will grow to men and women; and the first use they make of their serpent teeth is to sting one's dead heart into new life and keener suffering than any thing that went before."

"You are worse than Mephistopheles!" he exclaimed, angrily.

She laughed outright.

"Just because I tell you a few plain, unvarnished facts!"

"I don't believe they are facts."

"So much the better for your peace of mind; don't you believe it until you are forced—the time will come soon enough."

"Upon my word, you are doubt incarnate," said he, laughing too.

"I should be sorry to lead such a tender young Faust astray," returned she, mockingly. "I wish no harm to you or your Marguerite, but I am really afraid for your future. There are acids enough in her composition to make your sweet draught unpalatable whey unless there can something be found to counteract them."

"She is dreadfully exacting and jealous," Halford said, gloomily, with a man's usual lack of generosity.

"Never mind! I am sorry I made that last speech—it was too bad of me; but I have been punishing her lately for sundry little impertinences." Mrs. Marchmont's mood changed; he looked so disturbed that she longed to say something which should ease the pain caused by her words, though she honestly feared that her warnings would prove correct. But it was wicked of her to foster his own feelings of distrust in the future he had chosen! Why should she force doubts more clearly upon him? She was grown too hard and cruel—oh, these last days would leave nothing womanly, nothing even human about her! She was indulging these swift self-reproaches while he spoke again, for he felt ashamed of that weak complaint as soon as it was uttered.

"Milly is only a child yet," he said; "I must be patient. One's theories are fine enough, but it is difficult to reduce them to practice."

"It is the thing of all others, though, which must be done! There I go again! What was it Shakspeare said about the ease of showing other people the road? The idea of my giving advice to any body; why, I haven't even a fine theory left to violate!"

"You never are satisfied without doing yourself injustice."

"It's not of me we were talking," she said, quickly; "it is of you and your hope of happiness—a possibility that interests me more just now than any thing connected with myself. Mr. Halford, listen to me, I am in earnest now: if you go to work aright, I believe that you may be tolerably happy and contented. Go find her, and try to bring back her sunshine. It is a great deal to be loved; don't lose the opportunity."

"If I have found it," he muttered.

"You believed for a time that you had. Why, man, even a pleasant deception is better than a blank! Keep to your illusions, if such they be."

"To tell me that, at my age, when I know how impossible it is to prevent their slipping away!"

"Then don't let this idyl be an illusion! I tell you the future is in your own hands. Take what life offers, and don't fret after the unattainable. You are but a boy. I'll not talk to you any more to-night. I feel bitter—I really envy you the peace that you may have."

She sent him away without the least hesitation or ceremony.

"But I don't want to go," he said.

"No matter—go back to that pretty flower. I don't wish you here; in reality, you don't wish to stay. We are two idiots to stand airing our misanthropy at each other's expense."

She could not trust herself to be grave. She began to say merry, witty things, and sent him off laughing, in spite of his mood.

"I wish the child had brains," she thought, looking after him as he passed out of the conservatory. "But, after all, she is better off as she is. Of course he will get tired—a man!

Bah! the idea of being loved by such a hackneyed heart as his; it would bear comfortably as many crosses as an apple-tart. Still, where will one find a better, or as good? for he is worth infinitely more than any other of his sort, that's certain! My good old John Worthington does not count in the list. Oh, John Worthington!"

She put her hands hastily before her eyes. The thoughts called up by the mental utterance of that name were too terrible to endure. She went to the window, leaned her forehead against the glass, and forgot Halford, Milly, the whole world, but herself and her misery. She gazed up at the moonlit sky: it looked so far off, so cold! There was no comfort, no hope for her even in the future. The forever itself seemed only an empty sound, else a new word of doom.

She heard some one enter the conservatory; she was not alone. Back to reality she came, flashing at the foolish midge who interrupted her reverie a smile so brilliant that it fairly dizzied him.

"Come and say pretty things to me!" cried she; then gave him a second glance, and added, carelessly, "Oh no, you are one of the dancing set. Well, take me among them, Mercury."

I suppose the poor fool was dreadfully puzzled, flattered, and confused all at once. Mrs. Marchmont had a habit of upsetting the brains of the midges, and making them feel horribly uncomfortable and out of place, yet hopelessly fascinated the while. It was a great deal to be seen talking and dancing with a woman who was the rage, and they admired her from the very fact that they could no more understand her than they could decipher an Egyptian hieroglyph, and that her conversation was as unintelligible to them as the complaint of a nightingale would be to a flock of sparrows.

Halford went in search of Milly. She was talking with Charley Thorne, who saw her grow inattentive and deaf and blind, and knew before he looked up that Halford was near. So, with an ache in his poor heart, he took himself out of the way, for fear he should get mercilessly snubbed, as sometimes happened since the Milly of old days had so utterly changed.

"Milly," said Halford, "half our sunshine seems gone. Is it wise to let these shadows come between us?"

Her lips quivered, but she knew that he had just left Mrs. Marchmont. The knowledge did not incline her to accept any share of the blame.

"I have not brought them," she answered, doing her best to look cold and quiet, and to speak with proper indifference.

"No matter who has done it," he said; "they have come, and they will make us very unhappy if they are not swept away."

A fortnight before, Milly would have been softened by those words and that tone; now, out of her new clear-sightedness came the thought,

"He talks to me as if I were a child, to be lectured or coaxed into obedience at his whim. I'll not endure it!"

She did a very silly and unworthy thing, but painfully natural in her state of mind. She gave a little flirt to her fan, and, with a coquetry which no art less than Mrs. Marchmont's could have rendered graceful, said,

"I have not complained of unhappiness! Dear me, where has **Charley Thorne** gone? He asked me to dance."

Of all habits which girls can fall into that of nicknaming their male acquaintances was the most detestable to Halford, and it was a bit of bad taste of which he had never before heard Milly guilty.

"She really has no heart," he thought; "one can neither reason with her nor appeal to her feelings. Am I always to be disappointed and mistaken? is there no rest for me anywhere?"

Milly interpreted the gloom in his face to mean unalloyed censure, and it irritated her into another annoying speech.

"I promised this redowa to Charley Thorne," she said, arranging her bracelet; "how rude he will think me! I hate to be rude, unless people deserve it. Which way did Charley Thorne go, Mr. Halford?"

"Perhaps you would like me to call him," suggested he, coldly.

"Glad to get away," thought Milly. "I'll not let him see that I feel it; I would die first —die—die!" She had learned, out of the experience of the past weeks, to be a tolerable hypocrite, so was able to say, flippantly, "If you would be so good! The room is cold when one sits still, and I promised him this dance faithfully—oh, long ago—yesterday morning, at the concert."

Kenneth Halford stared aghast at this new Milly, who confronted him with those guarded eyes, that icy smile, and found such insolent meaning for her voice. He was at a loss what it would be right and best to say or do; but just then up came Charley Thorne to remind her of her pledge. The boy was frightfully nervous for fear she should refuse, and make him feel boyish before Halford, but could not forego the possible chance of a few moments' happiness.

"Will you—have you forgotten?" he stammered, completely losing the ease of manner for which our New York youths are famous, and which sometimes strikes one in connection with pink cheeks and budding mustaches as ludicrously as it would to hear a lamb growl.

"Oh, I never forget," returned Milly, with a laugh. Up she rose with a flutter, sweeping out her skirts, and speaking more loudly than was agreeable; took the arm which Charley offered, trembling with delight at the idea of taking her away from that man; and Milly smiled defiance at Halford, and floated off.

"Has she neither head nor heart?" thought Kenneth. "Not even good manners! Well, well, that I should live to this age to be a greater fool than I was at twenty! Actually to believe in a girl—a doll! I deserve to be punished for my insanity, my idiotic stupidity."

He fairly ground his teeth, and felt inclined to do melodrama, but, fortunately, remembered where he was, and that it would not be worth while to amuse people by making himself ridiculous. He stood still for a few moments, talked to the first person within reach, then walked quietly out of the room, and went home to smoke many pipes and sulk exceedingly. He sat till near morning, recalling every unpleasant thing which had ever happened to him in the whole course of his life; and when a man past thirty does that, he can speedily reduce himself into a state of sufficient disgust with the world and existence in general to have satisfied Diogenes himself.

Then he brought the record up to this latest disappointment—this child, whom he loved tenderly, mixed with much of a patronizing feeling which was so exasperating to the creature whom his love had quickened into new powers of thought and perception, and he grew still more misanthropical.

After a time the very unreasonableness of his mood brought a reaction. He caught sight of Milly's picture lying on the table. The sweet young face, with its faint shadow of melancholy, like the premonition of a sorrowful destiny which made it different from other girl-faces, looked up at him with a reproach for having indulged in those old memories and raked up the ashes out of the dead past to sully the present. He began to study the picture; to be softened and encouraged by the beautiful capabilities the countenance betrayed, and at last went to bed, determined to make one more grand effort to set Milly right, to bring the sunshine back to her eyes, and secure to himself peace and repose in her simplicity and childishness.

To set Milly right: that was still his thought, erring as sorely now as he had done in the outset. Ah, we men and women going out of our youth—the faded, wasted youth which our own errors or evil fortune has rendered misshapen and distorted till we are glad to be rid of it, to bury it deep, and get away from the lifeless thing which fills us with remorse, such as some wretch might feel in looking at the face of a friend whom he had murdered—how petty and unjust we are toward those still in the springtime of life and heart! We forget to judge them by what we ourselves were at that season; we refuse to acknowledge that they can feel and comprehend mysteries which we know that we felt and comprehended long before we could reason in regard to them. We do this constantly, and so leave ourselves powerless to aid the bewilderment of those young souls, even when we wish in all sincerity to do so. Kenneth Halford was a good man—better than the generality of his kind; but the leaven of conceit and selfishness was there, and by one of those strange, though, unfortunately, frequent contrarieties of our nature, this very love which had come to cheer his heart in the maturity of manhood, roused the perverse qualities which he believed so utterly rooted out that he did not recognize them as evil under the fine guise in which they presented themselves.

Milly, whirling through the dance, saw Halford depart, and straightway her heart went down, down into the black depths, and she would have gladly given her soul to call him back, just for one loving word, one gentle look. Then she detested herself and innocent Charley Thorne, but was borne on and obliged to restrain her tears as best she could. She was a poor, blind, foolish child, with the woman too suddenly wakening in her soul, living a real life, and doomed to suffer its pangs, which are so terribly real mixed up with so much that is small, ludicrous, and absurd, that hurt the more because denuded thereby of half their dignity.

Mrs. Remsen saw that Halford was gone; and before long, feeling a little sleepy and cross (the supper was a failure, so she had her reasons for misanthropy as well as any lover of them all), she insisted on taking Milly home; and though the evening was any thing but an enjoyment, Milly felt that solitude would be worse. Then Alice Marchmont gave the crowning stroke to the girl's multifarious troubles, though actuated by the kindly feeling her conversation with Halford had roused. (I don't know why, but nine times out of ten we do our worst mischief when trying to help people.)

She and Milly chanced to stand side by side in the dressing-room, and nobody very near. Mrs. Marchmont extended her hand impulsively, and half-whispered,

"You don't like me of late. I'm so sorry!"

Milly was not equal to the politeness of seeing the outstretched hand, but she bowed graciously, and answered,

"How very good of you to take so much notice of a child!"

"It is because you are one, my dear," Alice replied, good-humoredly, determined not to be vexed.

"Then excuse me for saying that I find the reason a rudeness," retorted Milly, her cheeks growing scarlet.

"People have accused me of all sorts of things, but I think nobody ever said before that I was rude," returned Mrs. Marchmont, with a smile which goaded Milly into hotter anger. "I wish you would be friends; I learned something to-night which makes me anxious to have you like me."

"I am utterly at a loss to imagine any thing which could give you that amiable anxiety," answered Milly.

"When you speak like that you prevent my explaining," said Alice, rather wondering at her failure in appeasing the pretty blossom.

"So much the better!" cried Milly.

At this moment Mrs. Remsen called,

"Are you ready, Milly? Good-night, Mrs. Marchmont. What a stupid evening it has been!"

When she was shut up in the carriage with her niece the lady fell to fault-finding, and Milly grew flippant, so between them they made matters worse. Mrs. Remsen had her suspicions that things were not going quite smoothly with the betrothed pair, and, though she knew nothing for a certainty, was inclined to blame Milly. She had already delivered sundry lectures to the girl upon her peevishness and variable tempers, and they had produced the effect which lectures offered at the wrong time generally do upon people since the days when Cain was a boy, and Adam scolded him for not liking to hear his brother praised and himself always blamed.

On reaching home, Mrs. Remsen found awaiting her one of the most unpleasant results of our advanced stage of civilization—a telegraphic dispatch. She was obliged, after all, to go to Baltimore in regard to the letting of her houses, and to set off without delay. So she went to bed crosser than ever, which was natural, I am sure.

The next day she departed, taking Maud with her, having decided to remain a week and visit an old friend. She might as well get a little pleasure, if possible, out of the boredom and annoyance. But Milly could not be expected to stay shut up in the house during her absence, nor could she go away on account of the children, so Mrs. Remsen wrote and asked good-natured Minerva Lawrence to play chaperon for her niece's benefit. She could think of nobody else, little as she trusted Minerva's judgment, for Hortense was too busy with her ologies, her hospitals, and her blue-stocking clubs to pay any attention to Milly, and Adelaide Ramsey was too selfish and spiteful even to make a pretense of doing so.

Mrs. Lawrence would have been delighted to take Milly and the children to her house, but that her friend would not permit; all she could be trusted to do was to go out of an evening with the young lady. So Aunt Eliza departed, leaving behind her so many rules and regulations for Milly's conduct that they became, as peoples' rules usually do, a bundle of contradictions.

Hate is a spiteful jade—there is not the slightest doubt of that. When she wants completely to upset any little scheme of happiness that we may have in view, she arranges the most commonplace incidents to suit her nefarious designs; and she was as malignant toward Milly as she has proved to each of us in our time.

CHAPTER XXIII.

THROWN BACK.

THE days passed on; it was late in March now, and the beautiful traces of spring were everywhere visible. The air grew balmy and soft, the trees in the squares had put out their first delicate green, the birds hovered about them just returned from their southward flight, and each morning brought some new miracle in that wondrous resurrection of nature to which we are so accustomed that we scarcely notice its loveliness in our frantic rush after the pleasures and honors of our petty lives.

How fast the time flew—this was Alice Marchmont's constantly haunting thought! Almost a month had gone by since her return from Washington, and there was nothing done, no step taken to relieve herself from the dreadful state of suspense which deepened as each day's swift course reminded her of the necessity for action. And she was powerless; could only wait in that horrible doubt, worse to her impatient soul than any ruinous catastrophe. She watched the days pass, and knew that each left her nearer the crisis which must overthrow her present life as suddenly as an earthquake desolates some tropical land.

She went out constantly, she was more witty and brilliant than ever; but could those of her own sex who envied and reviled her, and would have been glad to see the endless gossip in regard to her grow into tangible truths which should strike her down from her dazzling height, have seen her in solitude, the severest and most malicious among the band might have felt their rancor turned into pity. There was one fancy which haunted her dreams, and in her waking hours seemed the sole comparison that suited the strait in which she found herself. She was like some hapless wretch in a frail boat that swept more and more swiftly down a laughing stream, with bright flowers and graceful trees on its margin, and the roar of an unseen cataract beyond coming always nearer and nearer, and she powerless even to lift her hand or make a movement to turn the light bark out of the fatal current.

No wonder that she grew thinner and paler, her eyes larger and blazing with a brighter light, her wit sharper and keener; yet all her trouble seemed only to increase that beauty which had been her bitterest curse, and she was more admired and courted than ever. Often, in her desperate moments, when she thought of the end stealing closer, she would laugh outright in a horrible merriment to think how the fairy palace in which she dwelt must fall into ruin with one fearful crash, like some enchanted dwelling in an Eastern tale, beneath the stroke of a magician's wand.

The month ended. She had begun to count the days yet to elapse before the forged note fell due, and as the shortening time of grace brought back to her mind the awful dread of madness or death as the only way out, the torture ended. She found herself free! The news came to her early one morning, just when the project for the sale of her lands seemed broken up entirely, owing to the failure of one of the company. But the stock-holders had met again, and this time the bargain was actually concluded with the agent before she knew a word of the matter. Her first thought was that she could deliver herself from peril; her second, that if she had only waited and kept Dick Faulkner from an open *esclandre*, forgetting how impossible that would have been, this stain need not rest upon her soul. And she could never forget. She might render exposure out of the question, she might stand before the world and the friend whom she had betrayed, fearless of suspicion, but in her own soul that gnawing memory and remorse must remain to torture it beyond any hope of peace. She would know herself a guilty woman, and loathe herself for the knowledge. If she had gone to John Worthington and told him the truth, he would have helped her. He could not have left her alone to face that danger; every word and action of his proved that he would have come to her aid. Then she recollected that what hindered her was the certainty of losing his respect and esteem, and each week of this terrible season since had shown her more plainly how dear they were to her. But if, after the note was again in her hands, she could get back to the one hope of quieting her remorse; if she could tell him the whole story and receive his pardon! Tell him what—that she was a forger, a criminal? All courage went out of her heart again as she asked and answered her own dreadful questions, till she forgot that even the surety of keeping her reputation spotless in his eyes and before the world was in her power; and the old scenes of misery and remorse were enacted anew in the silence of her chamber. She had grown fairly to hate this room—the whole house, for that matter. She could scarcely look at an article of furniture which was not in some way connected with hours of insane suffering, or did not stand before her like conscious witnesses of her guilt.

There was the pretty morning-room—she could hardly enter it! There it was that Dick Faulkner had dared to bring his wicked designs clearly before her, put his shameful passion into degrading words. The easy-chair in the window of her dressing-room seemed always reminding her that it was there she had sunk down in the first hours of misery. The very figures on the carpet made her head throb with pain as she remembered how often she had lain, hour after hour, counting them mechanically, following their lines, and trying to hold her reeling senses fast by the childish occupation. And oh, worst of all, the sight of the table on which she had committed that deed—made her bond with the fiend! Why, the very bronze inkstand, with its graceful pattern of a helmet supported by two cupids, had been a present from John Worthington himself! It was a slight comfort that the house had passed out of her possession. She had been obliged to sell it early in the autumn, and must leave it by the first of May. The furniture would go; it was mortgaged to the Jew, and he might have it and welcome.

This sale of the lands would free her from pecuniary difficulties, though she might be in straightened circumstances for a long time, certainly until the company opened the mines and sunk the oil-wells upon whose products she was to have a generous royalty. But if she were obliged to live on bread and water, seek menial employment, it would be better than her life during the past year, viewing only the ordinary difficulties which pursue people in embarrassments. She could silence the ceaseless rings at her door-bell, have done with importunate tradesmen, get back the host of bonds and securities, the jewels and other valuables, which lay in her Jewish friend's possession, and, better than any thing, hold once more that accursed paper and tear it with her own hands. She would go away into the country, cross the ocean, and live quietly in some sober Italian city; oh, it made no difference what she did! Even a prospect of absolute physical suffering and want would be a relief! Go somewhere she must; escape from every thing which reminded her of her guilt—most of all, from the kindly glance of John Worthington's eyes; and, even as she thought that, the sudden pang at her heart warned her for the first time of what he had grown to her during these years.

The tiresome business was settled with very little delay; the deeds were signed, and half the purchase-money in the bank at Mrs. Marchmont's disposal. It was a bright morning—a Tuesday. She was going this very day to her Hebrew confidante, going to make her last visit. It was in her power to reclaim the securities which had gone to help her in her mad schemes, or afford her a temporary tranquillity at the price of frightful discounts and ruinous rates of interest. The thing of which she thought most, of course, was the getting that note in her possession; that done, she would only be obliged to journey forward hand in hand with her remorse. Never to be rid of that, never! It had been the one reflection in her mind since the hour in which she learned that it was in her power to avert danger; it was the sole thought in her soul now as she dressed to go out on her errand.

How these weeks had changed her; five years of ordinary life would not have altered her so much! She stared at the anxious face confronting her in the mirror, and the cruel morning light showed plainly the ravages which this season had wrought. Every body had always prophesied that hers was a beauty which would not soon fade; she had often thought complacently that even her fortieth birthday would not be to her the knell of youth as it was to less favored women. She had been so proud of that loveliness, so fond of it—not from mere vanity, not wholly from love of the power which it gave her, but from a sort of childish pleasure in every thing beautiful, and a childish delight in its effect. Now she was so tired, so worn in heart and soul, so filled with loathing and self-contempt, that she fairly was sorry that her vaunted loveliness had not suffered more severely.

"It's such a hideous farce!" she thought. "Oh, what do I want longer of the world? Let me get away—pay my debts and get away, and at least be honest for the rest of my life. Shall I be able to live quiet and alone? Oh, I don't know! And I might have been so much loved—perhaps Kenneth would have loved me; but I would not have cared for that; I had grown beyond him. But it's too late now to think of such things—too late! Why, what would a crown be in comparison to the happiness of looking in John Worthington's face, and knowing that my soul was free from any wrong to his trust and confidence? Oh, John Worthington! John Worthington! if you could know, if you could only see the whole truth, understand all my misery, you would pity me —I know you would pity me!"

And, as if her mental utterance of his name had been a charm to invoke his presence, some one came to tell her that John Worthington was below.

"But I can't let him keep me," she said to herself. "I must get at least beyond the risk —the danger. I declare, it's harder to meet him now that I have nothing to distract my mind from the sin I committed toward him, than it was when the fear stood between me and remorse. Oh, it's dreadful to think that I don't want to see him—that I am afraid; when I'd rather have his society than the whole world put together! If I dared tell him—if I could speak the truth out! If I think of it another minute, I shall rush up stairs again and hide myself in the dark. Oh, what a fool, what a fool!"

She tortured herself with these reflections as she went down to meet him, paused for an instant at the door of the library, then entered with her usual manner. The old game of dissimulation, which we all play so constantly, must go on. She met him with smiles and fair words, as you must meet the man whom you know you may murder before the week is out; as you must greet the false friend who has betrayed you; the woman for whom you broke your heart ten years before; the relative that believes you inherited grandmother's money by foul play—any body; every body, except in those rare moments in life when the masks fall off each face, and you and your foe or your victim stand grinning at one another in an honest acknowledgment of hatred which ought to ease the soul a little after bearing so long its burden of lies.

"You look better—more like yourself—this morning," were his first words, as he hurried forward and took her hand. "Come, there's some comfort in that. I believe you have actually slept all night."

"Of course I have; what else should I do? And don't talk about my looking better, you rude man, as if my looks were not always the best to be found."

"You are very pale, but—"

"I'll turn you out of the house if you say another word of the sort," she interrupted, sitting down and motioning him to a seat. "By-the-way, what brings you here at this time in the morning? You ought to have been at your office an hour ago. What do you mean by getting into such irregular, dissipated habits?"

"That is your gratitude, I suppose, for my taking the trouble to find out whether you were alive or dead."

He had no intention of telling her the real reason which brought him. It seemed foolish to himself, but he could not pass the house without entering to make sure that all was well with her. The whole night through he had been troubled with evil dreams, in which he saw her menaced by invisible dangers, appealing to him for assistance which he was unable to give; and if the vision changed a little, it was only to see her desperately ill, dying by poison, and a strong hand holding him back when he tried to give her the antidote which might save her yet. Whether these nightmares came from the fact that she was much in his waking thoughts, and he had been sorely troubled about her ever since her return, or whether some strange warning was permitted to startle his soul, are questions in regard to which we need not speculate. These unruly spirits of ours hold strange mysteries, and are subject to odd influences, if only we were not so blind in our shallow wisdom that we refuse to heed them. But the charm of her presence, the sight of her face more tranquil than he had seen it in weeks, so cheered him that his troubled dreams, his anxious forebodings, speedily faded from his mind.

"You are in unusually good spirits," she said, as he talked more rapidly and gayly than was his wont.

"Because it makes me cheerful to see you look so much like yourself."

"There you go again! Pray, like whom have I looked lately?"

"I can't tell—a sort of ghost of your old self."

"Oh, don't talk about ghosts even in broad daylight. There's no knowing how soon you may rouse them," cried she.

"None, I hope, that could torment you much."

"Don't be afraid! You act as if you thought I went about with a secret, like a woman in a romance; but I assure you my existence is a very tame one."

"I don't like your talking in that way," he said, seriously; "you often do it nowadays, as if you suspected me of watching you. Why should I?"

"Why, indeed!"

"I am anxious when I see you look ill or troubled, but I am sure you understand that no other feeling makes me curious."

"You're the best man in the world!" she exclaimed; "I'm not fit to have your friendship. But never mind. When did you hear from Constance?"

"Last night. She is enjoying her visit very much. At her age it needs so little to make one happy."

"Where is she—Albany?"

"No, Cincinnati. She has some cousins there who have begged for a visit these two years, so at last I was obliged to put by my selfishness, and give her up for a few months."

"You must miss her dreadfully; such a dear little thing, and growing so pretty, too!"

"And always honest and true, which is still better."

"Ah! that's a hit at the rest of us poor women," cried she. "You don't give the sex in general much credit for either quality."

"Now you want to quarrel, and I'll not do it. I am contented and amiable this morning, and you shall not tease me into a bad humor."

He sat there for half an hour, enjoying the visit more than he had done any interview with her for a long time. At the last he went hurriedly away, so moved by her gentleness and sweetness that he was afraid to remain lest he should be idiot enough to burst out with the revelation which he meant never to utter, because its utterance would probably cause the loss of the greatest pleasure which his life held —this frank, free intercourse with her.

Alice Marchmont stood there after he had gone, with a line from the Book which she had so long neglected ringing in her ears, "*And some men's sins going before to judgment.*" Truly hers was a case of this retribution; if the sentence had been written especially to point her out, it could not have been more applicable. Twenty times during that interview she had been on the point of revealing the truth. She wished now that she had possessed the courage to do it.

"And then," she thought, "he would despise me; shrink away in horror and disgust, and I should see it. I should be alone! Every thing is lost but his friendship—youth, hope, truth, self-respect—oh, I can't lose that, too! Isn't the remorse punishment enough? Isn't it any expiation, any atonement? Must I lose the regard of my one friend, the one human being I care for? Oh, I can't—God forgive me! I can't do that!"

She sobbed and choked, but no tears came to relieve her, and, suddenly remembering how late it was, rang for Pauline to bring her bonnet and mantle. Of course another person must detain her, just because the anxiety had rushed back, and it seemed that something dreadful would happen before she could reach the Jew's office and obtain that paper. Miss Portman came into the room, and wanted advice upon a dozen trivial domestic matters, concerning which in her most lucid moments Alice would have been as ignorant as a child. Even when she escaped the discussion and reached the door, the spinster called her back.

"Don't forget—I mean, have you forgotten?" —for if conversing with a person who had only five minutes to live she would have hesitated and struggled to make her language strictly correct—"we are engaged to Mrs. Lathrop to-night."

"Yes—what for? Oh, I know—a horrid dinner! I wish dinners were abolished. I wish there might never be material found to get up another."

"My dear Alice," returned the matter-of-fact creature, in horror, "you don't mean that? You don't want the whole human race to starve, I am sure."

"Then I'm not sure if you are! Bother the human race—singly and collectively! Good-bye, you blessed! I'll soon be back. And oh, my Portman, if you don't stop telling people you are anxious about my health I'll do something dreadful to you!"

"But I am anxious, my love."

"That's because you are a dear old goose! But if you ever again hint that I ever was, will, could, or should be ill, I'll—I'll—let me think! I'll make you drive in the Park at five o'clock in the day with a yellow satin gown on and a bird-of-paradise in your bonnet."

She ran off, and left Miss Portman with both hands uplifted and her eyes turned to the ceiling, as if beseeching the crooked-legged cupids depicted there to shield her from so terrible a fate.

As Mrs. Marchmont's carriage made the turn into Broadway at Union Square, she saw Dick Faulkner sauntering along. He saw her, too, and as he lifted his hat she almost fancied that he made a gesture for her to stop. Then she remembered that he was not likely now to be guilty of any such impertinence, and the reflection brought her a feeling of relief.

The carriage rolled on, and she reached her destination at length, solacing herself all the way by the thought that it was the last time she should ever be forced to make the journey. She had her check-book in her pocket—a delightful new volume, sent to her the day before from the bank—and when she left the dusty counting-room she would be a free woman, so far as he was concerned; better still, so far as danger and disgrace were concerned.

The frouzy fat partner of the little Jew's bosom, who was seated as usual at her lofty desk, making her customary display of legs that were not mates and a great deal of black stocking for the delectation of the youths behind the counter, informed Mrs. Marchmont that the Hebrew was in his upper office.

"Then I will go there," Alice replied, cheerfully, beyond the necessity of excuses or subterfuges to delude the Mosaic clerks. "Don't trouble yourself to come with me. I can find the way."

So the frouzy woman mounted again to her perch, but with so utter a disregard of her raiment that the young man nearest was able to see that she had forgotten her garters that morning. Mrs. Marchmont passed on up the narrow staircase, which had certainly never been swept, and entered the counting-room,

which, in addition to its ordinary odor of sausage and leather, had taken to itself several new and indescribable smells since she was last in it. But she was in too great a hurry to be disturbed by trifles. There sat her little Hebrew friend behind his table. Alice thought that in all probability he dined and slept on that stool, and could not be persuaded off it on any less urgent summons than the hope of cheating a customer more effectually than the youths below stairs were capable of doing in their present adolescent state.

It did not take long to explain her business, and her Hebrew looked just as wooden as he did on all occasions.

"I have come to pay every penny I owe you," she repeated, wondering that even the idea of receiving money could not rouse him into a little animation.

"You are the first visitor of the sort I have had to-day," he said, in his wheezy voice, as he laid down his ruler and put his pen behind his ear. "Plenty come to borrow—"

"Yes, I dare say. But I am in great haste this morning; so please don't keep me a minute longer than you can help. I want all the securities—the shares, bonds, my jewels. I'll give you a check for the whole amount—the—the last bill and all."

"Ya'as—so! I heard that madam had sold her Virginia lands to the great company," he answered, composedly.

"I believe you hear every thing," said she. "Come—open your great ugly safe, and reckon your interest, and let me pay you. Please don't keep me waiting. I've a thousand things to do."

"I won't, dear madam, I won't! But give me a little time. I've just had a gentleman here who always does make my poor head so dizzy—Mr. Faulkner."

"Mr. Faulkner here? Why, I met him in Union Square."

"Ya'as—just so. He had been here, but not to borrow. Oh, he's too great a man for that nowadays," replied the Hebrew, and for an instant he did rouse enough out of his impossibility to look resentful; but Mrs. Marchmont was too much troubled by the name he had mentioned to observe his appearance.

"What on earth did Mr. Faulkner want?" she asked, with a sudden fear, which even the thought of the check-book in her pocket could not silence.

"Business—always business," said the Jew, absently, as he rose from his seat and walked toward the iron safe, key in hand. He opened the heavy door, which grated and complained as if unwilling to disgorge its prey, searched among the compartments, and finally returned to the table, carrying a heap of papers which Mrs. Marchmont recognized only too well.

"And the box of jewels!" she demanded.

"Ya'as, presently; as soon as we are through with this," he said.

"Are you afraid I shall seize it, and run off without paying you?" she asked, impatiently.

"The madam knows I never doubt her," he said, unmoved. "She ought to have the diamonds compared with my list, to be sure they are all the same."

"I can trust you, too. I do think you're honest in your way," she said.

"Business is business, though," he answered, taking a soiled bit of sweet flag-root from his pocket, and proceeding to chew it with an air of tranquil satisfaction. He untied the bundle of papers, and spread them out on the table, and she sat down opposite him. "These are the railway bonds, this is the stock; there's the last interest dotted down on this page. I did it last night, for I knew the madam would be here soon, after what I'd heard, and I didn't want to keep her waiting."

Mrs. Marchmont studied the amounts; principal and interest were all noted. The sum was a very large one, but, fortunately, she could pay the whole without difficulty.

"Every thing is here? the amount for the jewels—"

He pointed to the item with his dirty forefinger.

"Oh yes, and the mortgage on the Long Island property— Yes, I see. But the last— the bill?" she asked, looking quickly up.

"The bill?" he repeated, though neither voice nor features expressed any surprise. "The madam is a good business woman, but she forgets sometimes."

"What do you mean?" demanded she. "Where is the note I drew for three months—"

"Ninety days," he parenthesized, as usual.

"Yes, the indorsed note—"

"Indorsed by Mr. John Worthington, of course; that one," returned the Jew, apparently thinking that he recalled to her mind some circumstance she had forgotten.

"But I want to take that up, too," she said, eagerly. "It's not due yet; but no matter— I want to pay every thing."

Probably the Hebrew had not laughed in twenty years at least, but he did laugh now, in a hoarse, creaking tone, as if the muscles of his throat were so unaccustomed to the exercise that they did not know how to behave.

"Now, that is more than I look for," said he, while Mrs. Marchmont sat staring at him with a dismayed wonder, at first the only sensation in her mind. "The madam wants to pay me twice. But once will do."

"Pay you twice?" cried she. "Are you asleep? What on earth do you mean?"

Now his wooden features did show a faint trace of surprise.

"I think I didn't never hear to equal that," said he, shaking his head slowly. "I do believe it has gone out of the madam's mind."

His dull astonishment, the strange mystery of his words, changed the sensation in her mind to one of sudden fear.

"I tell you I want the promissory note I gave you, due in ninety days, indorsed —indorsed—" She could not finish. "Give me

that note! I think you must be a little insane this morning!"

"But I have given it to you," he answered, his face showing that he was still divided between surprise and the idea that she had forgotten certain circumstances in regard to the bill.

She caught up the sheet where the sums were set down—the note was not named. She seized the pile of papers, turned them hastily over—the bill was not among them. The Jew sat perfectly still, and watched her more curiously.

"It's not here!" she exclaimed. "Where— where is that note?"

"But I explain and explain," he said, patiently, spreading out his two hands. "I don't want the madam to pay me twice."

"If you want me to pay you once, you had better be quick," she said, her voice growing cold and haughty. "Are you presuming to attempt a jest? You forget yourself, sir!"

"I don't mean to offend the madam," he said, humbly, "and I don't never joke. I can't understand—she seems to forget, though I try my best to make her remember."

"Remember what?" she asked, forcing herself to sit still and to speak quietly.

"About the note—"

"Mr. Hermans, answer me distinctly—where is that note?" she interrupted, looking sternly at him.

"I gave it up when madam sent me her letter."

She was on her feet now, staring wildly at him, unable to believe the testimony of her own ears. He rose too, perhaps, in spite of his impassibility, somewhat startled by her appearance. She motioned him to sit down; resumed her own seat. The great horror and dread, undefined as it was, which had taken possession of her, made her afraid to demand the close of the explanation which her hasty movement had interrupted.

"When did you receive my letter?" she asked, after a short silence, which he had not ventured to break through fear of displeasing her again, though in what his offense consisted he had not the slightest idea.

"Four weeks ago—nearly five," he replied, determined to confine himself to the simple answer of her questions.

She hesitated again; then inquired,

"How did you receive it?"

"Why, Mr. Faulkner brought it himself," came the response without an instant's delay.

Mrs. Marchmont grew so giddy and faint under the awful shock that her first confused thought was that she had received a physical blow from some unseen hand. As the black, dancing mists cleared a little from before her eyes, she saw the Hebrew looking strangely at her. Very far off and indistinct his features appeared through the shadows.

"The letter—give me the letter!" were her first words.

He opened a drawer of the table, took out a folded sheet of paper, and handed it to her. She was obliged to hold it close to her eyes in order to read; a partial blindness seemed to have seized her. It was her writing, she could distinguish that; after a while could make out the words. They were these:

"Will Mr. Herman please give to Mr. Faulkner the promissory note? Mr. Faulkner will pay the money, and settle the affair."

Her name was at the bottom. She remembered writing the billet; but that was in the autumn. She recollected the whole circumstance, confused as she was. She had borrowed a small amount of the Jew for thirty days; he had accepted her note. The morning it fell due Faulkner chanced to come to her house with a sum of money which he had made for her in a stock speculation. He knew that she had borrowed of the Hebrew, so she had no hesitation in requesting him to stop at the office, pay the sum, and take up the note. That very evening he had sent her the paper, and there was an end. This billet which she held in her hands had no date, but it was the one she had written in November; it was the only time that she had ever empowered Faulkner to arrange any matter with the Hebrew.

"It is all right—madam recollects now," she heard the Jew say, cheerfully, while he rubbed his fat hands together. "Madam was in Washington when she wrote, so busy with her pleasure that she forgot; but it was all settled. Mr. Faulkner came straight here as soon as he heard from madam, paid the thousands, took up the note, and madam must have burned it long ago, and forgotten, as she did all the rest."

She felt no inclination to shriek or faint. She was stupid and numbed by the shock. It had affected her senses for the time exactly as an actual blow on her skull would have done. She could not hear or see distinctly. She spoke, and her voice did not sound like her own; she was conscious of wondering stupidly if it was hers.

"That is off the list, then," she said. "Make up the whole amount of those separate items, and I will write a check."

The Jew began his calculations, and she sat there, regarding him in the same dull, stunned manner. Confused as she was, one reflection gradually separated itself from the chaos of her faculties and started up, like a serpent uncoiling its length. Faulkner held that note! He had discovered the forgery, and she was once more in his power! She held fast to the arms of her chair, griping them hard, for it seemed to her that she was falling down—down an immeasurable height into an awful blackness that stretched below. But she did not lose consciousness, did not cry out. Her face was white and fixed, her great eyes positively looked dead and glazed. She drooped slowly against the chair-back, like a lifeless body; but she could see and hear still.

"That is the amount. Madam can verify it," the Jew said, pushing the paper along the table.

She leaned both elbows on the board, supported her head with her two hands, actually added up the long row of figures—a kind of mental exertion which would not have been easy for her at ordinary moments. Slowly and with difficulty—any physical movement was a labor—she changed her attitude, took the check-book, filled up one of the blanks, and gave it to him. While she wrote he had been to the safe and taken out the box of jewels. It sat on the table by her.

"That finishes every thing," he said. "Madam has all her papers. Here is the list, too, of the stones with the values as near as I could get at it in their settings—she must have it verified. Here is a receipt in full, too, though not needed; but I know ladies are particular. So I thank the madam, and I wish all my customers were as prompt and honorable."

It was a long speech for the small man. She comprehended that her business was ended—that she must go; comprehended, too, that in leaving the place she went forth to meet a danger more deadly, more inevitable than any she had yet known. But she did not faint; made no sign; and the Jew did not trouble himself to study her face.

She took the papers and jewel-box in her hand, and tried to rise. Twice she was obliged to sit down: her limbs refused to support her. The Hebrew was locking his safe, and did not observe her. With the third effort she got out of her chair, walked steadily onward, but in a moment the Jew's voice warned her that, instead of moving toward the door, she had gone in the opposite direction, and was close to the window.

"Madam wants to see if her carriage is waiting. I'll call the man, if he has driven up the street."

She thanked him, knew that she bade him good-morning, passed down the stairs, entered her carriage, and was driven away.

CHAPTER XXIV.

THE POOR BARON.

THE next morning came, and Alice Marchmont rose to meet it with such calmness of desperation as she could find. It was useless to talk about courage now; she had reached a strait where the word possessed no meaning. In Dick Faulkner's power still! That had been her sole tangible thought during the hours of solitude which she had permitted herself after her return from that visit to the Hebrew. She had sent Miss Portman alone to the evening's festivity, glad for once to offer the feminine excuse of illness as a reason for staying at home.

This man, whom she had believed out of her

way forever, held her secret in his hands. Disgrace was before her, after all she had dared; the power to fling it down upon her possessed by the very wretch to escape whom she had soiled her soul with crime. Nothing left now but death—no hope! As well look for mercy from a jungle tiger as from him! It was all over. Truly, her world had fallen in ruins at her feet!

She had decided to wait; she would neither send for him nor write; she would make no sign whatever, as long as there was a day of grace left. It was not from any expectation that her silence would force him into showing the line of conduct he had resolved to pursue. There was no plan in her determination beyond a desire to avoid his presence as long as possible.

Of course, this morning a dozen people came. She had given orders that she was at home to whosoever came. Of all times, she must not at this crisis vary from her usual habits. Besides the visitors, there were calls from creditors whom she had requested to send in their accounts, fancying the delight with which she should pay them. Now, as debt after debt was stricken off the formidable pile, she only remembered that those efforts to preserve appearances, to be honest and straightforward, were in vain. She might pay—struggle; always the skeleton hand kept before her eyes the note which Dick Faulkner owned, the note with John Worthington's signature.

By the time the last of the creditors had gone, reduced to a state of smiling abjectness by the entire satisfaction of their claims, the idle people began to stream in. Helen James, overflowing with gossip; Miss Portman's two old maid friends; half a dozen silly women and sillier men, in pairs or singly, and they buzzed and fluttered. But she bore it all patiently; nothing mattered.

One by one the visitors departed; Miss Portman herself went out, after changing her mind six times as to whether she had better go or stay at home, and insisting that Alice should agree with each separate decision. Mrs. Marchmont sat there alone, wondering if the day would ever come to an end, yet shuddering to see it pass. Presently Ferguson appeared to say that the baron desired an interview. The name roused her to a quickness of reflection which stirred the dullness of her senses into a sudden pain. The baron—why, here was a chance of release, if she should accept him, marry him at once, and go away. True, she was not in possession of the fortune with which report endowed her, but abundance of money was certain to come sooner or later. He was not an extravagant man, nor a mercenary one, though, of course, Frenchman-like, he would not think of marrying a woman who could bring him no *dot*. But his head, if not very wide, was a rather practical one. If she explained exactly the state of her affairs, proved to him that the sale of her lands would make her rich again before five years were over, he would be perfectly satisfied. His income and the ready money which she should have left, after arranging her debts, would enable them to live almost *en prince* in Italy. Rome was not an unpleasant place of sojourn now. The young princess had gone there to hold her court. Since Paris had ceased to be—at least the delightful Paris of the Empire—the Eternal City would rank first on the Continent in the matter of amusements and gayety, thanks to the royal Marguerite's love of dancing and pleasure.

Surely, another escape from the laudanum-bottle was offered. It needed no reflection; the way out lay plain before her. The first idea of a sudden, almost secret, marriage would not answer; Dick Faulkner would discover her plan, appear at the altar, and wave the forged note in the bridegroom's face, if he could stop the nuptials in no other manner. But she might sail at once for Europe, meet the baron in London, wed him there, and let events in America take their course. If John Worthington learned the truth—no, when he learned it, he would not trouble her; he would find means to silence Faulkner. She knew the man; she could be certain that the hour in which Faulkner exposed the secret to him wicked Dick's ability to harm her would be at an end. She should never see Worthington afterward, never be humiliated by the sight of his kind face, dark with loathing and contempt. Faulkner might spread evil stories; they would be powerless in her new life—utterly so. No echo of them could disturb her quiet in the old Roman palace which she and the baron were to choose for their residence.

It takes so many words to describe her reflections, though they arranged themselves clearly in the brief space before the Frenchman could be shown into the room. There was leisure for another thought, too—worse, more degrading than the others. Poor, miserable Alice! mad, guilt-stained Alice! so fallen from the high estate of her glorious womanhood! She need not run away; she could accept the baron, asking only that the engagement should be kept a profound secret until her affairs were entirely arranged. That would give her leisure to outwit Faulkner. She could do it! Smile at him, weep for him, throw herself on his mercy, lie to him, fool him to the top of his bent, meet artifice with artifice, craft with craft. If he believed that he should succeed, that she would listen to the avowal of his shameful love, he would give up the note, take her money—she was free! Only at the cost of a few falsehoods, of a stain upon her soul deeper and darker than that left by her treachery to her friend; the guilt and degradation of smiling on a man whose every thought in regard to her was pollution, whose every smile an insult; by these means she could purchase her release. She felt a glow of exultation at the idea of duping him, of tearing the note before his eyes, and telling him that he had been duped—outwitted; overwhelming him with the full torrent of her passion and scorn, and enjoying his utter confusion and impotent wrath.

Then the very thrill of wicked joy which shook her at the picture of his evil face changing suddenly from anticipated triumph to rage and the humiliation of defeat, roused her to a consciousness of the depth to which her soul had sunk. The self-contempt and abhorrence came back, an unutterable fear of herself, too; but there was no space to moan or cry out. The baron was entering; he was in the room.

There he stood, irreproachable in toilet and attitude, overflowing with pretty speeches, beaming with smiles and delight at finding Mrs. Marchmont alone.

"This is more happiness than I expected," he said, in French, as he finally subsided into a chair near her, after having made himself pink in the face by bows and compliments.

Mrs. Marchmont looked at him, and, stunned and dazed as she was, retained enough hold of her womanly intuitions to understand the errand which had brought him; the baron meant to speak out. It had been very difficult for weeks past to avert the _dénouement_; it would have come in Washington, only that she was always careful never to allow him a private conversation. Let him speak now. He appeared at the right moment; let him speak. She had proved herself a coward; she had tried to die, and lacked the courage to carry out her wish. If she trusted to that means of escape, it would fail her again at the last. She was lost, degraded, sunk below the possibility of recovering her self-respect. But one hold over the world remained, one chance to keep the hollow splendor of her life secure before human eyes. She could accept the baron, and outwit Dick Faulkner!

She had leisure to follow her thoughts so far while the baron chose a more picturesque attitude than his first, arranged the ends of his long mustache, and assured himself that his wristbands showed the proper line of white below his coat sleeves.

"I began to think there was a fate in it," he said. "I haven't succeeded for so long in seeing you alone that I was truly in despair."

"You look very comfortable for a despairing man," she replied, speaking his native language with an accent as perfectly Parisian as his own.

"That is because I am here—with you opposite; no wearisome people to interfere. I am comfortable; I am well."

"But you are not to commence abusing my friends as soon as you come in," she said; "and in such a sweeping fashion?"

"I did not say your friends were tiresome, only that it was pleasant not to have a whole world about us."

"Very well; put in that way, I forgive you! And how does town seem after the dullness of Washington?"

"Oh, it is endurable, because you are here," he said, with a shrug which revealed his slighting opinion of Gotham as plainly as the most violent abuse could have done. "But I can not think why you stay here; you ought to be in Europe. These people do not appreciate you—these dull men of business, with their ledgers always in their minds."

"But Paris is dead—poor Paris!" she answered. "And London is a degree worse than New York."

"Do not mention it!" he shuddered, with a true Gallic horror of every thing English. "I do always remember my one visit there. I staid but a week, and I never can forget!"

"Or forgive," she added.

"Ah! that, yes. One does not hate the poor islanders, one only pities them;" and it was delicious to hear the way in which he said it. If Albion had been situated near the North Pole, and its inhabitants an inoffensive race, doomed to hunt seals and live on train-oil, he could not have expressed more commiseration by his tone.

"I should like to see Italy again," she said; "I have not been there in years. Rome must be very pleasant now."

"Yes; since poor Paris is so changed. I shall go there when I return."

"And you think of deserting us?" she asked. "Are you already tired of our poor country?"

"The country that has the honor to hold you must always be charming," he replied, in the rather ponderous fashion which was due to the slight admixture of Flemish blood in his veins. "But I do go back very soon. I have told you so before."

"Yes, but I hoped you might change your mind. It is tiresome to lose people just as one gets really to know them," she said, and felt it very hard work to sit there and talk commonplaces, and lead the conversation up to the point he desired. But it must be done.

"It is of that I do wish to speak. I came to do so this morning," returned he, fidgeting a little, as the most thorough-bred man will do under the embarrassment of an errand like his.

"Oh, don't talk of any thing so dismal as your going away!" she said, willfully misunderstanding his words, just because coquetry had grown so much a matter of habit that she could not help indulging in it.

"But it is of that I must speak, to give a reason for showing you my whole heart and soul!" he exclaimed, warming to his work.

But the sentence which he thought so neat struck rather heavily on Mrs. Marchmont's ear. She had heard so much glowing talk from really eloquent men, that the baron's poor little periods sounded tame enough. She was not thinking of her own wickedness in allowing him to speak, and making the answer she had decided to give, only wondering how she could ever support life with that unchanging face always opposite her, that measured voice to ring incessantly in her ear, and (it sounds puerile and absurd to write it of her in her state of mind, but I like to show you clearly what an inconsequent, vagrant habit of thought she had allowed herself to cultivate) she wondered if the pointed ends of that mustache would some day put her eyes out when he attempted to kiss her. Then she remembered that he was a Frenchman, and once married. Her face would be of slight consequence; he would be a model husband, visit her occasionally, sometimes breakfast with her. The rest of their two lives would pass free of each other.

He was heavy and tiresome; ..... took him a long while to say very lit... the slowness of his Flemish intellect ...ered him incapable of understandin... ....st; he was the dreariest commonpl.... respectable commonplaces; but a poun...ough gentleman—he would never in any way violate *les convenances.* If he even had small vices, and she almost thought they would make an interesting variety, he would hide them so carefully that they need never come under her notice. But he was speaking again, and she must listen. It would not answer to allow him to propose without hearing it. However, he had not yet reached the important words; he had to go through the business in his own methodical manner. Perhaps he thought that as he should be freed from the necessity of making pretty speeches for the future, in case she became his wife, it was his duty to exhaust the whole vocabulary now.

"I should not have staid in America so long as I have but for the great happiness of finding myself near you," he said.

"A very nice compliment," she replied; "but it does not count for much, since you talk of running away just as we have become good friends."

She had not patience to wait while he sidled and maundered up to the goal through a drizzling shower of flattering words. If he wanted to ask her to marry him, let him do it and be done.

"I like to hear you say that," sighed he; and she thought what a delightful caricature he would make just then, and felt an insane desire to commit some enormity on the instant which would startle him out of his propriety —to dance at him like a maniac, or talk gibberish that he would take for Choctaw, or sing an aria from the "Grand Duchess," but controlled herself. "Ah! yes, they are very sweet words. I would like to hear you say them again."

Positively, this was too much, when every nerve in her body was out of order and her mind a chaos!

"Life is not long enough to repeat things," returned she; "and I am never of the same opinion a sufficient length of time to do it. Take care, or I shall say something savage, by way of a change."

He looked bewildered, and a little hurt.

"You do always confuse and put me off like that," he said, with another tremendous sigh. "It is not right, when I speak earnestly!"

"I had not the least idea you were doing that," she replied. "Come, I will be as serious as an academician."

"Yes; for I came to be serious."

"What an appalling threat! Really, I think I must call Miss Portman. She can deal with such a mood better than I."

"I pray you do not call her; do not rise," he said as usual taking her words literally.

"But I think it must have been she you came to visit. She is a very serious person," replied Alice, for the satisfaction of teasing him, since there was no other relief to be gained.

"It is you whom I wished to see, you only; ah! you do know that—you do see my mind."

"My dear baron, I am the stupidest and blindest of my sex! I need to have any fact clearly pointed out before I can perceive it."

He sighed for the third time. Now it was because she worried him, broke the thread of his prearranged discourse, and ruined his round of compliments. But he was very much in earnest, and though to his slow comprehension it was somewhat like making love to a meteor, he must tell his story.

"You are the most wise as you are the most beautiful of your sex," he said. "See, you do so hurry and confuse me that I can not well choose my words. But I wish to say clearly what is in my mind."

"I am listening," she answered, resignedly.

"I have told you that I staid here because of you. Now I must return to my own land; but I want you to know—"

Evidently the sentence was not the exact one he had meant to put in that particular place; for he broke off and consulted the crown of his hat, as if the proper arrangement of words was noted there. Mrs. Marchmont was thinking over the plan which the announcement of his name had suggested. She could get away—be free from Dick Faulkner; oh, if he would only speak and have it over!

"I am before you this morning," he went on rather more rapidly, as if he had put the sentences in order at last and was encouraged thereby, "as a humble suitor, a poor suppliant upon your bounty; and yet I am to ask that which is priceless, feeling always my own unworthiness."

It was stilted and strained, more so in French even than English, reminding her of a paragraph out of some obsolete romance; yet it was plain that he spoke truthfully. Somehow the idea troubled her; but she did not interrupt him.

"I do come to offer you my hand, my title, though in these days it may be that does not count for much. I do come honestly, gravely, as an honorable man should. I have weighed in my mind well the whole matter. I do think that we might have a happy life if, in your great goodness, you could care for me a little. See, I would not have you accept my offer if you can not do that. I do ask your heart for my heart, because I love you very dearly, and must have your love in return for mine; else I should be most miserable."

Once off, he had spoken more fluently than she ever heard him, and the words and manner filled her with such astonishment that she could not break in upon his speech. This was not what she had expected; she did not want this! Why, the man cared for her! It was not her beauty, her fortune—he cared for her; his slow, dull heart was moved, and cried out for crumbs of comfort. Oh, to accept them would be a wickedness beyond even her! She could not! A quick revulsion shook her mind; the full horror and shame of the project she had contemplated stared her in the face. But he had not finished, he was speaking still; she must interrupt, must tell him that it could not be; and then where was she—what was to become of her, then?

"I could wish you to reflect. I should attend your answer until you have thought well of the matter—"

"Wait, don't say— Let me speak," she faltered.

He bowed, looking at her with a certain troubled surprise.

"I—I can not. Oh, I beg you pardon, baron!" she cried; "I have done very wrong. I did not expect you to speak like this."

He smiled now; her words had evidently restored his self-complacency.

"That does not surprise me," he said. "I am a man with a singular control over my feelings. I willed not to show my sentiments until the fitting moment. You have thought me only an admirer—a friend; but see, now I make plain my secret, and I ask you to consider it."

"But—but when you talk of caring for me —of love !" she exclaimed, involuntarily breaking into English, "oh no, no, I never thought of that!"

"But it is now that you sall sink," he replied, doing his best with the harsh syllables of her native tongue. "Not so soon, peutêtre, but after I my leave take. Zen you sall sink, and I wait till you comment dit—on raflaict."

She did not answer; she did not know what to say. He waited for an instant, then took refuge in his own language once more.

"You may believe me when I say it is all my heart that I bring here. I love you; and I do not lightly speak those words."

"You must not love me," she said, eagerly. "Had you talked to me about respect—no, no"—for the word applied to herself made her shiver—"I mean if you talked of friendship, that would be well enough, but not love, not love."

"I must speak that which I feel; it is love," he answered. "See, I have startled you—I had kept my secret too well. You are moved! Let me go away now. When you have thought, you will send for me to hear your answer."

"No, don't go; we must understand each other fully! Baron, you can't blame me so much as I blame myself."

"But I can not blame you at all; you have not known. I have been so guarded—it is my habit—that you did not perceive."

"I thought—I feared you might accuse me of coquetry."

"No, no," he replied, with a conceit that would have amused her at another time. "I am not a man with whom women coquette. I am too grave, too serious. You have done always what was most charming. But before I go, let me fully explain—"

"I can't have you," she interrupted; "you must not."

"You are nervous only," he said, smiling. "See, I shall tell more about my poor heart; it loves you, and I am a man too sober to speak false you do believe me a other views of the affair; I have looked every side. I am not a rich man—I have my thirty thousand francs a year, but compared with your American fortunes, it is small."

He paused, to be certain that the sentences were following in the proper order, and a delay gave her leisure to see the one way of proving to him the impossibility of any idea of marriage between them.

"You have a right to expect a fortune in return," she said; "a much larger one than your own even, since you have position and title to give."

"Yes," he said, gravely, "that ought to count. Still, once more in the cause of my poor heart, dear lady! Were you less rich, were your fortune smaller than mine, I would ask you just the same to marry me, if you could be brave enough to forego great wealth."

She had laughed at this man, amused her friends at his expense, and here he showed himself kind and noble-minded; and she—but oh, what could she expect of herself—lost, fallen!

"But I have not the great fortune," she said, quickly. "People think me very rich. I must tell you my secret; I know that it is safe with you."

He looked disturbed now, but made one of his low bows as a sign that he waited for her to continue.

"I have spent and lost an immense deal of money. I have been extravagant and wicked. I am trying to free myself from debt."

"That is right; it is like you," he said, his face clearing. "But once your debts paid, all will be well. You do sell your lands—you told me so."

"Yes; but you can form no idea of what my debts are! It will take nearly the whole sum of money I get to pay them. I shall be poor for years, forced to economize in every way possible."

"But after that?"

"Oh, maybe in ten years I shall have a large income again; but it is a chance. Suppose the mines should prove a failure. Don't you see, my fortune will depend on the company's success?"

"But it is sure; it is only a matter of time."

"No, no; it is not sure. There is always a risk in such things."

He sat still for a few seconds, took out his

watch, looked at it steadily for a space, then put it in his pocket.

"I do beg your pardon," he said. "I made myself take those moments to reflect; it is wise always to reflect. Now I shall ask—"

"Don't ask me any thing!" cried she.

"It is the nerves always," he said, in the loftily compassionate tone in which certain people address children, though it was too kindly meant to be offensive — "always the nerves, dear lady. I must finish my question. I had arranged it."

"If he were married and his wife died," thought Mrs. Marchmont, "he'd bury her, if he had made his arrangements, no matter if she came back to life and tried to run away."

"It is this," he pursued, apparently reading it off the crown of his hat. "I have told you what is the amount of my income; could you be content with that and yours, whatever it may be, added? I have reflected—I did not take much time, for I have studied my nature where you are concerned. I always make a study of my nature; but in all that regards you I have done so to a greater degree than ordinary. So I know what I say, I feel what I do offer. I shall be a man very happy if you can accept."

She could not laugh. He might talk in fearfully long sentences, but his proposal was that of a good man, and she felt it—a courageous proposal, too, coming from one brought up under such narrowing influences as he had been, with old creeds in regard to the necessity of wealth to support his title added to the rest.

"I thank you, I do thank you!" she said. "If I were a better woman—I mean if I were not so hopelessly wedded to luxury; if I were able to be reasonable and prudent, it would change matters. But I can not trust myself."

"You have not thought; you must take time. All people do not study their natures closely enough to reply to grave questions without much reflection," he urged.

"No, the matter must be settled here — now," she replied, eagerly; and it was an added humiliation in the midst of her self-abasement to feel how utterly unworthy she was of this man's affection, unconscious that her very inability to carry out the wild plan which had risen in her mind was a proof of how much good still remained in her burdened soul.

"I must tell you plainly, if people knew the real state of my affairs they would call me ruined. I am poor. I must give up my present life, go away where I shall not be tempted into extravagance."

"We could live quietly at Naples, at Florence; even Pisa is not so bad," he said, hopefully.

"I can't marry you; I can't!" she exclaimed. "There! it's out; forgive me! When you came in, I meant to; when you began to speak, I meant to; but I understand you better now, and I will not do you so great a wrong."

"How could it be a wrong to give me my happiness?" he asked, confused again by the energy with which she spoke. "You who are so beautiful, so good—"

"I'm not good," she broke in, then checked herself in time, and continued, more quietly, "let us put the matter solely on pecuniary grounds; you and I are not two children to be blinded by romance. Honestly, I could not marry any but a very wealthy man. I know how mean it sounds; but I should ruin any other. I might try to be prudent; I could not. What would seem ordinary expense to me would be mad extravagance. No, no, baron; it can not be! I thank you for your offer, I honor you, I like you; but I will not be your wife."

She spoke so decidedly that he saw she meant every word, and realized that there was no appeal. He looked troubled and distressed, but conducted himself like a chivalrous knight. Perhaps even the crusaders were a little heavy and stiff.

"You leave me dumb," he answered; "you do not care for me, so I have no hope to offer. Still, I thank you, dear lady. It is something to have loved you. All my life-long I shall feel honored by the thought that I have, though the memory shall bring its little pain, too."

"I hope not, baron! I shall trust some day to see you happy in the affection of a wife more worthy of you than I should have been."

"Madame," said he, with one of his eternal bows, "the day may come—I do not yet see it —when I shall ask some good lady to accept my hand, and I shall try always to make her a good husband; but I feel that whatever the happiness may be that comes, it will not be the happiness your regard could have given, and I shall know that my life held one chance of a great success, and missed it."

Actually she felt the moisture gather under her eyelids—she, who had grown so fierce, so hardened in fighting her terrible battle against the destiny her own recklessness had brought about, that she often thought no tears could ever cool her heart again.

"You will find a better happiness than such a woman as I could give," she said; "and when it comes you must teach the lady to like me a little. She will not need to be jealous."

"No," he answered; "because I shall tell her the whole truth at first. One need have no trouble with those whom one loves, if there is only perfect candor and trust."

He bowed over her hand, uttered his last farewells, and turned to go.

"Not adieu," she said. "You will come to see me again."

"Madame, to-morrow a steamer sails for France. If you look, you shall see my name among the passengers," he replied.

"Oh no! not so suddenly."

"My business here is done," he said, after waiting to be sure that he did not interrupt her. "I shall go back to my own country. I had so arranged it, in case disappointment overwhelmed me this morning. Once more, dear madame, adieu."

"And a prosperous voyage, and many happy days," she said, tremulously.

"My thanks—my best thanks. Adieu!"

He bowed himself out, the door closed, and left her to the reflection that once more an honest heart had been offered for her acceptance, and she forced to let it pass out of reach. Other thoughts came up—thoughts so terrible, so maddening, that she dared not trust herself to their companionship.

The air of the house was stifling; she would suffocate if she sat there a moment longer. She rang the bell, and asked the servant if he knew whether her riding-horse had been brought to the stables, as she had ordered a few days previous. The horse had been sent over from her Long Island farm, and was ready. She never had to repeat a command in her household.

"Tell them I want to ride. I will have James to follow me."

She hurried up stairs; Pauline was not there; she exchanged her dress for a riding-habit, without assistance, doing it all in frantic haste, as if there was some urgent need. Her house was so far up toward the Park, that she could mount at her own door, instead of having to endure the boredom of a carriage on account of crowded streets.

The trees were already fresh and green, the turf verdant, the air balmy and soft, and the bright spring sunshine making all things beautiful. The rapid exercise was a relief. Away she galloped; on through the Park and out on the Bloomingdale Road, regardless of any surprise that her appearance there, with no other escort than a servant, might occasion. She dashed on, heedless of every thing and everybody; and it was only dropping her whip and having to halt, while the faithful James—who thought the end of the world must be near when his mistress obliged him to ride at such a pace—enabled Kenneth Halford to attract her attention. The bright day and his own discontent tempted him into equestrian exercise also, and he was on his way back to the Park when he saw her.

"You were riding so furiously," he said, after his first greetings, "that I almost fancied Irving's headless horseman had strayed down from Sleepy Hollow."

"I hate to crawl," she answered, while he sat marveling at her beauty, familiar as he was with her face. The air and exertion had given a tinge of color to her cheeks, and her great brown eyes were fairly dazzling. "So, you are on your way home? I might have asked you to ride with me, only I am very stupid."

"And I too; but if you will permit, I shall go on with you."

"Why should you be stupid?" she asked; as they passed up the hill. "Haven't you got your strawberries and cream; aren't you satisfied?"

He was not in a mood to be teased; he did not wish the conversation to stray toward Milly, for he had no mind to be guilty of the meanness of complaint in regard to her.

"If you say annoying things, I shall ask after your health," said he. "Let's be civil, and keep to generalities."

"With all my heart, or, better, don't let's talk, just for the sake of novelty. Here's a smooth bit of ground—now for a race. I'll wager six pairs of gloves that Princess and I reach the next mile-stone before your Blueskin."

Away they dashed, and the Princess and her rider won by a length. What might be thought by several stately ladies of her acquaintance whom they passed in the race, Mrs. Marchmont neither reflected nor cared.

"I feel much better," she said, when the goal was reached. "Now we can turn homeward. I feel almost human again."

CHAPTER XXV.

A COSTLY VENGEANCE.

PAUL ANDREWS chose that very week to give one of his delightful dinners, and Mrs. Lawrence was invited. He importuned her to bring Milly; for he had heard rumors of the engagement with Halford, and, having a deep-rooted aversion to that gentleman for declining his acquaintance, he thought that to persuade the girl to accept one of his invitations would be a nice bit of vengeance.

Mrs. Lawrence was a sort of cousin of Paul's, rich, and free to go where she pleased, and having known Andrews in his youthful days, when there was probably some good in him, was ready to believe that he had been injured and maligned, and that very likely he was no worse than other men, only not hypocrite enough to cover up his failings so carefully as they did and keep the varnish of reputation without a crack.

You must remember Paul Andrews? He shot himself not long since, and, so far as this world is concerned, it was the only wise thing he had done in years. He was as bad, and thoroughly *blasé*—the word has become so English, that you can excuse it—as a man could well be. His wife had been a gay, reckless woman. I dare say he ill-treated her, as she said; at all events, something drove her quite mad, and she ran off to Europe with a fellow a shade worse than her husband.

That is a very improper story, told in as few words as I can manage; for it is only as Milly's destiny chanced momentarily to cross his path that I have any thing to do with him. He had returned to New York, after a long absence, having obtained a divorce without difficulty; but the affair had hurt him exceedingly—would have ruined him utterly, had it not been for his high and mighty relations and his money.

Besides his disreputable and delightful masculine suppers, where there was much fun and more high play, he occasionally gave dinner-parties, at which he used to persuade some one of his feminine relatives to preside, and to which many people would go. In our age, people would rush into the mouth of purgatory for an hour's amusement. The dinners certainly were charming, and Paul an angel of an host, however much of a devil he might have been in his private capacity as a man; but I used to think I would rather see a sister or wife of mine dead than sitting at his table, looked at as he looked at all pretty women, and listening to the conversation which went on there, brilliant as it was.

Mrs. Lawrence entered readily enough into Andrews's scheme; the more heartily, perhaps, because, knowing that the best-natured people work better for a reward, he promised her, in case she succeeded, a wonderful carved cabinet he owned, upon which her heart had long been set. It seemed to Mrs. Lawrence the most delightful thing in the world to induce Milly to do something of which her aunt would disapprove. "A regular lark," she called it to Andrews, and set herself diligently to work; for Paul had hitherto been deaf to all entreaties and plans for getting possession of the coveted cabinet.

She failed utterly. Milly would not hear of the thing, and at last grew very indignant, and Mrs. Lawrence could have cried with vexation; she did hate to be thwarted in any project, and the cabinet was such a beauty!

"You're a foolish little kitten," said she. "Why, the Conways go, and Mrs. Dexter, and Helen James. Dear me, you needn't be so particular! Poor old Paul! Why, I met Kenneth Halford there once, and Mrs. Marchmont." She did not add that Halford had accepted the invitation two or three days after his return, before he knew any thing about the character of the man, and had steadily avoided him since; and she could not know that Alice Marchmont had gone, because she was insane to see Faulkner, and he had forced her into the visit as a means of humiliation. Milly felt the fire blaze up in her heart with new strength. Mrs. Lawrence spoke as if they had been at one of the dinners together, and Milly would ask no questions.

This injudicious woman pleaded as long as she dared; but Milly held firm, though it flashed through her mind that it would be a fitting punishment to Halford for her to go, and coolly tell him that, if it was proper for him and Mrs. Marchmont, she concluded there could be no objection to her going likewise. But that was only a passing thought. Consent she would not, and finally reproached Mrs. Lawrence for urging her.

"You know my aunt would not permit it. I think you do very wrong to propose taking me to a place of which she would disapprove."

"Oh, Eliza Remsen was always terribly straight-laced!" returned free-and-easy Mrs. Lawrence, not in the least offended. "I thought you had more love of fun in you, and would like to go, just because you ought not. Poor Paul! he's not so black as he's painted, in spite of what has come and gone. People don't always get their deserts in this world; if they did, I'm afraid that wild-eyed Mrs. Marchmont Kenneth Halford flirts so with would be out of the pale more than Andrews."

Milly listened eagerly, though having the grace to blush at her own unworthiness in consenting to hear the slanders which Mrs. Lawrence poured forth without the slightest scruple. She did not dislike Alice, or believe half the things she repeated, but she was an inveterate gossip, from sheer idleness, and such a woman does more harm than a downright malicious scandal-monger; besides, she was so much vexed at losing the cabinet that it was a relief to abuse somebody.

"I vow Kenneth Halford shouldn't go on as he does, if I were in your place," she added. "You needn't purse up your mouth, Miss Puss! Your aunt the same as told me you were engaged the morning she went away. I'd bring him to terms, if I were you! I was glad to see you flirt with Charley Thorne the other night. I think it touched my Lord Kenneth."

Milly felt bitterly glad—yes, wickedly glad—with that dreadful exultation which we have at the success of a plan that wounds what we love, while it stings our own souls. He should feel, feel to the core of his heart, that she was not a baby to be punished and sent into a corner. So people noticed his conduct; no wonder! But she would beat him at his own game.

And there Mrs. Lawrence sat, inventing things, giving a signification to speeches that never was meant, yet not intending any harm; stirring Milly up, as she would have expressed it, for her own amusement, by way of a little amends for the disappointment of having to tell Paul that she had failed in their scheme. She did not even think that she was guilty of wickedness! I declare I sometimes half believe that the sins which will drag us down to hell are those very exploits which we regard so complacently, never ranking them among our sins at all.

"Well, Milly, I shall say no more," she exclaimed at last. "Put up with Halford's conduct, if you choose. Meekness is interesting; but, thank Heaven, I have a will of my own"—beautifully oblivious of the fact that she was blown hither and thither, like a tuft of down, by the wind of any body's breath who took the trouble to influence her. "Why, when I was your age, I would have done any thing for an evening's sport! Your aunt would never find it out; but let the matter rest. Do as you please, of course. I stand by Paul Andrews; I always shall! When a man begins to go down in the world there is some merit in keeping to your friendship, and I shall do it. I can remember, when we were all three young, Eliza Remsen was pleased enough if he paid her attention, though now you say she would not think his house fit for you to set your foot in."

"No, I did not say that—"

"Oh, I'm not particular about words; that was what you meant."

She let fly a few more shafts at Halford and Mrs. Marchmont, and went her way. But, in spite of Milly's determination—stupid obstinacy, Minerva called it—that lady said to Andrews,

"Keep a place at table. I shouldn't wonder in the least if I brought her at the last moment."

The things which had been said rankled in Milly's mind, and made her more angry with Halford; but the possibility of going to the dinner did not occur to her.

It was the very day of the party. Mrs. Lawrence had given up her lingering hope; Paul Andrews had resigned himself to the failure of his plot for annoying the man who had overwhelmed him with civil contempt, and to the endurance, where Milly was concerned, of the smart which the most hardened animal suffers at the knowledge that some innocent creature shrinks from him.

Milly wanted to see Halford; a change had come over her. Had he appeared at the moment she would have forgotten his sins, and been remorseful over her own errors and shortcomings. She wrote him a note, and gave the man-servant directions to take it to Mr. Halford's hotel. Now Cæsar inherited a full share of the indolence so bounteously bestowed upon the children of Ethiopia, and, feeling no desire for a walk this morning, gave the note to a Bismarck-tinted friend of his, who had dropped in to pay him a visit, and must pass Halford's lodgings on his way home. Fascinating Hannibal took the letter, and promised faithfully to leave it; but he chanced to meet a salmon-hued lady of his acquaintance on the road, and was beguiled into a promenade, and the note in consequence was forgotten.

Milly waited and waited. The day was passing; no answer—no message. She rang the bell to inquire if the note had been sent. A maid-servant hurried off to ask Cæsar, and came back with the positive assurance that he had dispatched it without delay. Still Halford did not make his appearance. Milly had leisure to pass through a thousand changes of feeling. She cried from disappointment; she grew angry; she excused him, only to bestow increased blame a moment later; then she cried again, and after those last tears felt harder and more resentful. If he had even answered her note, offering any excuse whatever for his refusal of her request, she could have forgiven him; but to be treated with this utter show of indifference was more than Milly could bear.

It was late in the day when Mrs. Lawrence's carriage stopped at the door, and the servant came up to say that Mrs. Lawrence wanted her to go and drive, only she was to make haste. Milly did not wait to reflect that she was in no mood to endure any body's society. She threw on her bonnet and mantle, and ran down stairs.

"Actually here!" exclaimed her friend as she appeared at the door. "Milly, you are an angel not to have kept me waiting."

Milly laughed discordantly; the color rushed over her cheeks; she stepped into the carriage, and off they drove. Mrs. Lawrence talked about the dinner—regretted that she could not have Milly with her; but the girl was too busy with her thoughts to pay much attention to the remarks or her own answers. They took a few turns about the Park, then Mrs. Lawrence complained of feeling cold, and they turned homeward down Fifth Avenue.

"I want to stop at Mrs. Delancy's a moment," Mrs. Lawrence said. "I'll not make a call. It's just to ask about a servant who used to live with her."

Milly declined going into the house, so her friend left her in the carriage, and went upon her errand. Milly sat idly looking through one of the windows, watching the gay equipages dash past, thinking how contented every body appeared, and wondering why the change in her life, which had promised such happiness, should have brought her this great trouble—wondering, fretting, and bemoaning her wretchedness, without having the least idea that her own actions could have mended matters.

Suddenly down the avenue passed two persons on horseback, riding fast, talking and laughing gayly. These were Mrs. Marchmont and Kenneth Halford. One glance she had, and they were gone; and there Milly sat, her blood turning to ice about her heart, and her head reeling till the long rows of houses seemed to totter, as if about to fall in one common ruin.

Do you know what it is to be frantically, insanely jealous? To go so mad that, for the time, you would sell body and soul to be avenged—to do something that should destroy yourself, here and hereafter, that the false one might have eternally to regret the misery as of his causing? If you do not, pray to God to keep you from such phrensy and the calamities you may bring down under its influence.

Milly sat with her hands clenched in her muff, her teeth set, and her eyes blazing with a light that had never before shone in them, her whole mind lost in a whirl of fierce emotion which shook her every nerve. Back came the widow, and they drove away through the gathering twilight, Mrs. Lawrence rattling on about some wonderful story she had heard during her visit, till at length Milly interrupted her by exclaiming, suddenly,

"I will go with you to this dinner!"

"Oh, you darling girl; I am so glad! Now you are behaving sensibly! Your aunt will never know it."

Little cared Milly, at that moment, if the whole world knew of it. What were any consequences that might arise to her? Kenneth Halford should be made to feel—that was all she thought of; the worse the place, the greater the wound to his pride! Go? Why, she would have gone, she thought, if the fiend had guarded the door, and claimed her soul for his forfeit!

"You shall have a charming evening," pursued Mrs. Lawrence. "Do wear the blue dress and silver ornaments you wore last at my house."

"I shall go," repeated Milly, in the same defiant tone—"I shall go."

They reached the corner of the street where Mrs. Remsen lived.

"Let me out here," said Milly; "I'll walk home."

"It's only a step—you'd better drive."

"No, no; I want to walk—I must walk," returned Milly.

"I shall call for you at half-past seven, precisely," said Mrs. Lawrence. "Now, pray look your sweetest. How lucky that Maud went with her mother! You'll have no one to prevent you."

Milly was out of the carriage before it fairly stopped, and hurried along without a parting word.

"I do think she must be mad," said Mrs. Lawrence to herself. "What has come over her, to look like that? She must have seen or heard something of Halford that has made her horribly angry. Well, I don't care what it is—she's going with me! Mr. Paul Andrews, the sooner you send me that lovely cabinet the better. I have kept my word. I do so hate to be beaten!"

She drove on in the best possible spirits, debating with herself as to which particular salon should enshrine her long-wished-for treasure, and laughing as she thought of Kenneth Halford's fury when he heard of Milly at this dinner; and he would quickly hear of it. Dick Faulkner would take care of that.

Of any evil consequences to Milly, beyond a lecture or a lover's quarrel, soon made up, she never dreamed. She only looked at the mischief and amusement, and was as happy as a boy over a pocketful of stolen apples.

Milly got into the house and up to her room. She took no time to think. Think, indeed! You might almost as well have asked red-hot lava to pause for reflection as her dizzy mind.

It was already late, so she dressed herself, looking more lovely than she had ever done in her life. This culmination of the excitement of the past weeks into this fever had done its work. She was lovely; but not like the dreaming, romantic Milly of so brief a time back. To one who understood what made the change, there would have been something piteous in the eager face with its flashing eyes, the scarlet spots on either cheek, and the defiant smile on the lips which had so lately been tender and tremulous.

Half-past seven came very soon. The carriage was at the door. Mrs. Lawrence came into the house, to be certain that Milly was dressed to please her, and, as the girl ran down stairs with her white cloak on her arm, could not refrain from exclaiming, aloud,

"You were always pretty," she cried, enthusiastically; "but to-night you are positively beautiful!"

Milly jested and laughed, and the false excitement supported her until it was too late to retreat or think. She was in Paul Andrews's drawing-room; he was holding her hand, looking into her face with his languid eyes, and uttering fulsome compliments.

Then her reason came back. She realized the full insanity of her step, saw clearly what she had done. She looked about at the people; men whom she met at large balls—two or three known to her by sight as reckless and dissipated; women, with several of whom she had never been allowed to be on speaking terms; others, with whom she acknowledged acquaintance, protected as they were by their husband's names; and every body looked a little curiously at her, as if wondering by what odd chance she was there.

Milly's rage and jealousy could not keep up to their white-heat any longer. She was glad to creep into a chair, and do her best to prevent her teeth chattering, from the chill which shook her, unable to talk to those who approached, transformed at once into so commonplace a girl that Paul Andrews regarded her in disgust. He would have been ready to throttle Mrs. Lawrence for swindling him out of his cabinet, only he consoled himself by recollecting that at least her presence in his house would punish Halford.

Nor did Milly improve after the party was seated at the table. The color would not come back to her cheeks, nor the light to her eyes. The jests at which the others laughed only puzzled her; or, if she dimly understood, they filled her with horror. She was seated near Andrews; but, after trying to talk with her, and receiving only monosyllables in reply, he gave up the task in a rage, wondering what people saw in the washed-out little thing to admire, and thinking that Helen James, if somewhat passée, was worth a dozen like her.

It seemed to Milly that they remained a lifetime at table. It was all like a bad dream. The noise, the laughter, the quantity of wine the men drank, the freedom of the women's talk—the whole affair was insupportable. Toward the close of the dinner, Dick Faulkner made his appearance, and there was much chatter over his excuses for not coming in earlier.

"I think Andrews said supper," he averred; and it was evident that he had been drinking freely. Then he saw Milly, and called out with his usual insolent familiarity, though she scarcely knew him,

"Ah, Miss Crofton, delighted to see you here. Mrs. Lawrence is showing you a little life, eh?" Then he recollected his wife's gossip about the engagement between Milly and Halford, and added, "I say, Paul, where's the book-man—Halford, you know?"

"Not invited," returned Andrews, curtly.

"Nor Mrs. Marchmont?"

"She—she couldn't come."

"Does Halford's name naturally suggest hers?" somebody asked.

"Oh yes," returned Dick, with an evil laugh;

for the intimacy between the two had caused him almost as much annoyance as it had Milly.

"Here's her health — a bumper to Alice Marchmont!"

It was so plain that he was partially intoxicated that the women made a move to leave the table. Milly thought she must die before she could get out of the room. When they returned to the *salon*, Milly begged Mrs. Lawrence to let her go home; but her friend would not listen to it.

"What nonsense! after coming," she said. "I can't imagine what ails you to-night; you don't look or act like yourself."

"I don't feel like myself, either," replied Milly, with a quivering lip. The excitement which had given her a false courage was gone, and she never felt more like a burst of babyish tears in her whole life. "I do so want to go," she pleaded.

"Oh, wait a while!" said Mrs. Lawrence, longing to doze in peace till the men appeared. "You can't go yet; it would look so odd. Paul would be vexed, and scold me."

So Milly took refuge in a corner, and occupied herself, as shy young ladies do, by turning over a volume of engravings, and none of the women paid any attention to her beyond a contemptuous assent to Paul Andrews's dictum that she was a poor, washed-out thing, and not worth the talk her coming out in society had caused.

After a while her retreat was invaded by Dick Faulkner, and then Milly decided that she must die outright. He sat down by her and began to talk pleasantly enough. The extra wine he had drank since the ladies left the room had removed the apparent traces of having too deeply indulged; but he was affected by it in a certain way. Quietly as he talked, he could not keep from touching on subjects and throwing out hints which he would have avoided at another moment.

"Is Mrs. Marchmont a friend of yours?" he asked.

"I know her — meet her very frequently," Milly replied, wishing only that he would take himself off.

"You mean you don't like her. I've watched you both this last fortnight! I'm fond of studying people. You hate her, Miss Crofton."

Milly was not too much subdued to look offended, but remained silent.

"You'll not own it," he continued; "but all the same, you can't deny — yes, you hate Alice Marchmont."

"If I did, Mr. Faulkner, I really can not see that the fact could interest you enough to repay discussion."

"It might; wait a bit! I'm not sure, but I hate her myself, at least —"

Here he became conscious that his tongue threatened to stray into disclosures in regard to his private sentiments, and stopped.

"I must ask Mrs. Lawrence to let me go home," Milly said. "I am tired."

"Just a moment. I want to say something to you," pursued Dick, wondering how he could manage to annoy Alice Marchmont by letting her suppose that he had given Milly a dangerous hint about her affairs. "I say, the bewitching widow has been worrying you a great deal of late."

"You must excuse my listening," said Milly, in a trembling voice, which she tried in vain to render firm and dignified.

"Now, you'd better — you'll be glad after," urged he; and, as he had placed himself in front of the taboret where she sat, it was impossible for her to rise until he moved. "They say you are engaged to Kenneth Halford; but she sees him oftener than you do."

Milly had tried to get out of her seat, as he spoke those first words, but the conclusion of his sentence made her sink back.

"Please to let me go away," she said, faintly.

"In a second. No matter what my reasons are for warning you, I do —"

"I don't want any warnings!" Milly broke in.

"I think I must give you a spell that will leave her powerless to harm you — petrify the white witch, eh? as the princess does in the legend."

Milly did not try to interrupt him now.

"Where was I? Oh! the first time she annoys you, just whisper in her ear — mind you do it skilfully — 'Dick Faulkner says "the Ides of March" have come, but not gone.'"

He moved away, and allowed her to escape. She hurried back to Mrs. Lawrence's side, and again pleaded to go home. Paul Andrews happening to overhear her request, said,

"I am sorry you so soon repent having honored my house with your presence, Miss Crofton."

Of course, she had to set matters straight, but succeeded very indifferently.

"I am too stupid even to be polite," she added, beginning to laugh, for fear she should cry; and Andrews did not contradict her assertion.

"Nobody will go these two hours," said her silly friend; "and I promised to play a game of whist."

"You needn't go. The carriage is here; only let them take me and come back for you," whispered Milly. "I can't stay — I'm ill."

She looked so, in truth. Mrs. Lawrence began to grow alarmed, and eager to escape further responsibility.

"Well," she said, "if you will go, you will! Paul, tell them to order the carriage. Miss Crofton is going."

Milly got away. Mrs. Lawrence accompanied her, kissed her at the head of the stairs, and called her a foolish child; but Milly could only think of the happiness of escaping.

"It's a dead loss," Andrews said to his relative, as she returned to the drawing-room. "Your little friend is the most consummate idiot I ever saw in my life! I hope your house will burn the day you get the cabinet."

The instant Milly reached home she rushed

up stairs and flung herself on the bed. All she had gained by the step, which in her frenzy she fancied would be so great a triumph over Halford, was an intense headache and an intolerable fear of her aunt's discovering her adventure. She had not even the pleasurable excitement which might have lent an interest to her freak. There had been no pleasure, no success. She had not appeared a sort of drawing-room meteor to Paul Andrews and his guests. She had sat among them, pale and stupid as an overgrown school-girl, suffering from shyness and too much plum-cake.

Verily, Milly's taste of stolen fruits was not sweet! The apples of Sodom had turned to ashes on her lips.

She lay on her bed, and shook and shivered, and could only get warm as she remembered Andrews's false smile, or the echo of some of those horrid jests haunted her. Then she seemed burning up with shame, and fairly wished the floor might open and let her away down into the dark, and hide her forever from her fear and humiliation. When that crisis passed, she could remember Dick Faulkner's words, and there appeared more meaning in them than had struck her at the time.

"I am glad I went," she thought, in a quick reaction of resentment; "glad—glad! Every body knows that he is false to me. I knew it before, only I tried not to believe it. But I'll tell her. If he knows something that can frighten her, she shall think he has told me. I'm not likely to forget his words! I wish it was day. I wish I stood face to face with them both. Oh, I shall go mad!"

So Milly battled with her demons, and yielded to the fierce dictates of her jealousy and her rage, till it fairly seemed as if weeks must have elapsed in that vigil, the pure, girlish face looked so worn and seamed with misery and passion.

While she struggled the night through in her pain, Alice Marchmont held a watch darker and sterner than this of a young girl's heart troubles. It was almost dawn before she finished a letter many times interrupted, two or three copies impatiently torn, but the task always resumed; and at last it was done.

Then the restless march was resumed, fright and despair tugged at her soul as they had so often done before, and the quiet seemed full of voices that mocked coldly at her agony, and repeated the story of her shame. Thus she wore the darkness out, and saw the dawn break chill and gray, then crept to her bed, not so much to sleep as to shut out the hateful light which she could have prayed never to see again.

CHAPTER XXVI.

TWO LETTERS.

AFTER that unquiet vigil, and the heavy, unrefreshing sleep which followed, Alice Marchmont appeared down stairs at her usual hour in the morning, determined in nothing to vary from her ordinary habits during these dreadful days, as though holding fast to such trifles was the one gleam of security in her awful suspense. Some way, when she forced herself to go on in the accustomed routine, there were moments in which she could almost persuade herself, even now, that her fears could not all be real, since nothing in her daily life was changed.

Miss Portman was already out on a shopping expedition, from a sense of duty, with some country friends; so Alice had the freedom of the library, and was at liberty to be idle and dull, without having to answer troublesome questions. The unrestraint did not last long, however, for the servant came to say that Kenneth Halford wished to speak with her, and Mrs. Marchmont roused herself from her apathetic reverie, remembering that she had a sharper scrutiny to baffle than the observation of her timid, easily satisfied relative.

"This is a fearfully early visit," he said, as he entered; "so I beg your pardon in the commencement."

"It is almost noon," she replied; "so your excuse is a polite way of telling me that I am a lazy woman—a bit of revenge, I suppose, for my having won yesterday's race. The gallop did me a world of good. I mean to ride every morning."

In spite of his feeling it necessary to excuse his appearance at this hour, he had already stopped at Mrs. Remsen's house to inquire after Milly; for the not seeing her on the previous day had given him time somewhat to forget the numerous annoyances she had caused him of late. But Milly had gone with one of the little children to the dentist's, so he could only go into the nearest florist's, and scribble an affectionate note, to be sent with choice flowers—a note telling her that he should be too much occupied to return, but he would see her that night at Mrs. Lawrence's reception. Then he walked on to Mrs. Marchmont's, for there was something which he felt he ought to say to her, though the necessity was any thing but agreeable.

The two talked the ordinary commonplaces of conversation for a few moments; but he was a man who liked to get an unpleasant thing off his mind as quickly as possible, so he took advantage of a break in the talk to observe,

"Perhaps you will think my errand here an impertinent one; but I could not resist coming."

Naturally her first thought was that he had learned the truth; she was always expecting somebody to overwhelm her with it. Not even a servant could enter the room hastily in these days without giving her a sensation of terror. She became languidly composed at once. Her ability to endure still, shaken and unnerved as she was, had something wonderful in it.

"What an appalling commencement!" said she, in her most indolent voice. "You would pique my curiosity, if I had any left."

"We are such very old friends that I thought

I might take the liberty," he continued, rather hesitatingly.

"Tell me what you want to, and excuse yourself afterward," she said, her tone growing suddenly impatient, though she looked as unmoved as ever.

"A friend of mine—a business man—told me last evening that there were vague reports in circulation about your affairs—"

"Do you mean business affairs?" she interrupted.

"Yes, of course. Now, as I knew that you were negotiating with the South-western Company for the sale of your Virginia lands, it occurred to me as possible that the stories might have a malicious origin—that is, might be the work of some persons who wanted to prevent the sale, either because they had coal-lands in the same neighborhood, or—".

"The sale was effected several days ago. I have received the first payment," she broke in again, utterly incapable of listening to his explanation, which in his slight embarrassment he made tedious, as people always do when afraid of saying a wrong word.

"Then I disquieted myself needlessly," he replied, "and I am very glad of it. I congratulate you on your success."

"Thanks; success is invariably so pleasant," she said, bitterly. "But you have roused my curiosity, though I just denied possessing any. Tell me exactly what your friend said."

"It was only a vague story. I could not make much out of it," he answered, evasively, wishing heartily that he had held his tongue, or, at least, been sensible enough to ask outright if she had sold her lands, instead of repeating the gossip.

"You can tell me what he said," she insisted, with a flash of the imperiousness which had grown upon her of late. "From whom did he say the report came?" She knew what the answer would be, and dreaded to hear it, yet, when he hesitated, could not help asking more sternly, "Who originated the report, Mr. Halford?"

"I believe it was Mr. Faulkner. At least, it was he who repeated the gossip in my friend's hearing."

She did not stir; not a line of her face altered.

"I want to hear the whole conversation, word for word," she said, slowly.

"Why, it was little more than a hint that the company had better be careful. It struck me as meant to cast some doubt on your titles. It is of no consequence since the sale is effected."

"Where did it take place? when?"

"Two or three days ago—more than that, I believe; but I only heard of it yesterday. It's not worth thinking about now, though! I presume some disappointed land-owner invented it," he replied, careful only to answer the last clause of her question.

"I asked you where."

"Upon my word, I—"

"I have a reason for wishing to know, Mr. Halford. I beg you to tell me the place where the conversation occurred, and, as near as possible, the words used by Mr Faulkner."

He could not help mentally comparing the wayward, pretty imperiousness of Alice Berners in the old days with the overbearing haughtiness which this woman at times displayed, thinking, as he had often done, how sad it was that life should have changed her so utterly.

"It was in a room of a café near Wall Street —a place where the brokers go a great deal. Faulkner was there lunching with a couple of men; they had just struck one of their grand coups, and were having a Champagne-breakfast after—"

"And having drank too much, were talking about the women of their acquaintance; I understand! Don't hesitate. I am a good many years past the possibility of being shocked by the way in which bad men talk. What was said about me?"

"I am sorry I mentioned the subject—"

"I said that I did not want excuses!"

Her haughtiness would have been insufferable, only, guarded as her face was, he read something there which filled him with pity.

"I only meant to add that, having done so, it was better to tell you just what occurred. Not very dreadful, after all."

"Not when one has lived long enough to know what men are. I beg your pardon."

"My friend was lunching at the next table. The first thing he heard was some chatter—"

"The words, if you please."

"These," he replied, a little out of patience: "One of Faulkner's companions said, 'So the fascinating widow is trying to sell her lands; they say she is rather pushed.' The second man asked, 'Who says so? I don't believe it.'"

"And he—Faulkner?"

"He had evidently been drinking too much—"

"He said—"

"'I believe it, and I know it! I'd advise anybody who means to take Mrs. Marchmont's note or buy lands of her to make sure of the indorsement on the titles.'"

"Was that all?"

"Every word. My friend said the two began to chaff Faulkner, to tell him that probably you had snubbed him, and he changed the conversation, apparently discovering that he had said more than he intended."

"I thank you for coming," she said; "it was very kind of you."

"Very useless, under the circumstances."

"No matter. Oh, this world, this disgusting world, where a man like that is allowed to go about staining women's names by the mere taking of them on his lips!"

"Certainly, had there been the least reason, you have friends enough who would call him to account," he said.

"No, no; nothing so bad as that could happen—the surest way to ruin a woman that ever men invented! Oh! you would not—promise me, no matter what you heard—you would not do that!"

"There will be no necessity; he will never dare."

"Oh, there is nothing he would not dare!" she cried, recklessly, and as soon as the words were spoken knew she had revealed the fact that for some reason she feared this man.

"What do you mean?" Halford asked, eagerly.

"Only that he is a brute and a coward," she answered, her voice once more disdainful and quiet.

"We are very old friends, Mrs. Marchmont. I wish I might say to you all that is in my mind."

For the first time it occurred to him to connect the troubles which he felt certain oppressed her with Faulkner.

"It could do no good," she said; "but I am grateful for your kindness."

She turned away her head, but, quickly as she moved, he caught the expression of her face. This sympathy had shaken her out of that unnatural self-control. He thought, if he lived a hundred years, he could never forget her countenance as it looked then, with its dilated eyes and the features fixed in the awful whiteness of wrath and despair.

"You suffer!" he exclaimed. "Is there nothing I can do? Can you think of no way in which I can serve you?"

She turned back at the sound of his voice, drew her hand across her forehead, and looked at him with a strange ghost of a smile upon her lips, past caring what he thought; past caring how fully she betrayed her wretchedness, in the intense longing which had come over her for some human sympathy in the darkness.

"Again I thank you," she said, in a cold, grating voice; "you have done all that you can in making the offer. No human being could help me further, and I think Heaven will not."

It seemed heartless to remain silent; but what could he say? It was impossible to intrude upon her secrets, whatever they might be —to ask the slightest question as to the cause of her distress; yet it was dreadful to leave her alone in a misery so deep that even faith in the Divine mercy had deserted her.

After a little she spoke again:

"I believe that sounded wicked; I did not mean it so. It was weak, too, and that is almost more unpardonable. I am bold and self-reliant enough"—she had nearly said, desperate—"but sometimes I am forced to remember that I am only a woman."

"If you would let me speak; if I could venture to without appearing downright insolent!"

"I should not think you so; but there is nothing more to be said. See, I have not tried to hide from you that I suffer—it is a great deal for me to confess. I could not do it to any body else! Only forget it; don't let me ever see the consciousness in your face."

"If it is about business—if you would only tell me."

"It is not."

She had begun to tell a lie; she would not do it. She was weary of her burden of dissimulation. It was enough to bear the stain of guilt, the awful memory which placed her in the rank of men and women outside the pale of humanity; she would no longer add to that the petty falsehoods wherewith the weakest of her sex shielded their little sins.

"Impossible, was what I meant to say—impossible!"

The tone, the look, told him that, whatever her trouble might be, she had regarded it on every side, and knew that an iron door shut between her and any hope of assistance. He comprehended that at this instant it was neither pride nor fear which kept her silent, nothing but the utter impossibility of any aid availing.

"I am deeply grieved," he said, touched to the heart. "I know that sounds very poor; but it is all I can say."

"It is a great deal," she replied, with that same phantom of a smile still upon her lips. "There is no other human being who has seen enough even to say so much."

He saw that she was wholly unfit for further conversation, and rose to go.

"I can't bear to leave you like this," he said; "but I believe it is the kindest thing I can do."

"Yes, the very kindest. You know I am used to bearing my burden alone."

It was the more painful to witness her wretchedness, and remember that she had the whole world at her feet, and she with some secret weighing on her soul which shut out any possibility of peace.

He returned quickly to her side, saying,

"If there should arise a moment when I could help you—"

"I would ask your assistance—yes; but there never will. I don't know what you must think, Kenneth; I don't much care! When you entered this room I did not believe any thing could ever make me admit to a human creature that I suffered."

"But you are not sorry that I know?"

"I am glad—glad! Don't be troubled; don't think about me! How kind and good you are! And you are happy—tell me that you are?"

He forgot the annoyances and doubts of the past weeks, or, rather, they seemed as nothing in the presence of her misery, and Milly's image rose before him like a vision of rest.

"Yes," he answered; "I have more contentment than I deserve."

"Not more; and I am glad! When you see me again I shall be like myself, and you can forget. Better so."

He went away, and many times during the morning, busy as he was, he remembered and pitied her, yet could not help contrasting her with Milly, and feeling a certain exultation in the midst of his thankfulness, that his choice had fallen upon his childish, unworldly young betrothed instead of this woman, weighed down in the midst of her splendor by some secret which she must guard alone. He thought no evil of her, as many men would have done. Whatever her faults might be, he knew that she was pure enough even to be Milly's friend. He could only account for her misery by supposing one of two causes. He had always believed that she had some unfortunate attachment since the day when his sense of honor led him to offer her his hand, though he had been forced to acknowledge that it could not be for any man whom he ever saw near her now. Besides this, he feared that she was in terrible business embarrassments; perhaps Faulkner had deluded her into one of his brilliant schemes, and she found herself surrounded by difficulties, even cramped for money, which would be fearful to her. But he got no nearer the truth than that in his fancies, and gladly as he would have aided her, he felt that he could not offer moneyed assistance. It would appear an insult. So he thought a great deal about her as the day wore on, but more about Milly. He had been a little hard of late; he had expected too much of this pretty child. He should see her to-night; he would change back to the old manner at once; pet her into the cheerfulness and amiability formerly her chief charm. He had been wrong, possibly. He must not train and develop her too rapidly; he would be very patient henceforth with his flower, even at the sacrifice of his own tastes and comfort. He wished that the evening were come; he was wild to see her again, and he smiled at his boyish impatience, but felt glad that he was capable of it.

After he had gone, Alice Marchmont sat by the window where he left her, staring at the blue sky, with a face such as an old painter might have given to a lost spirit gazing up through the blackness of purgatory toward the light of the far-off, unattainable heavens.

At last she drew from her dress the letter which she had written the previous night, tore it slowly into fragments, went to the hearth, and flung them into the flames.

"Burn," she thought; "oh, I wouldn't care if it was your soul or mine!"

She walked up and down the room in one of the eager marches in which nowadays she so often tried to tire herself, then after a while sat down at a table and began to write. She must send some message to Faulkner; she could wait no longer. But it would have been madness to forward the epistle she had consigned to the flames. There must not be a line or word which the whole world could not see; yet she found it difficult to write, making several commencements, tearing them up, even flinging aside her pen often, as if half decided to let matters take their course. But it was finished at length—a simple request in the third person, that Mr. Faulkner would have the goodness to

call upon her at his earliest convenience upon a matter of business.

Once written, a spasm of mad anxiety came over her; she folded and sealed in great haste, rang the bell, and ordered the man to send it to Mr. Faulkner's office—he was sure to be there at that hour—and see that the person waited for an answer.

It was a full hour and a half before the messenger returned, an eternity in the mood which had taken possession of her. Ferguson, the model of an English servant, appeared at last; but, before he left her to read the note he brought, had to explain that the delay was not the fault of the boy in buttons who had taken it. Mr. Faulkner was not at his office, and the small emissary had been obliged to return up town to the gentleman's private dwelling. Having satisfied his conscience by justifying the small boy, he bowed himself out, and Mrs. Marchmont was free to open her letter.

"I am so grieved," wrote the insolent wretch, without preface of any sort, "to disappoint the most charming woman in the world; but I can not come this morning. I was just getting into the carriage to drive to the railway when your note reached me. I have come into the house to write my excuses, and say how grieved I am that I must defer the happiness of an interview —a happiness of which I have been so long deprived. But I am forced to leave town on business, and shall not return until Sunday. However, I shall meet you that evening; for I know you are invited to Mrs. Granger's dinner. We can have a little conversation, and arrange any time that suits you best for me to come to your house. My time is always at your disposal; and I am, as ever, the most devoted of your slaves, DICK FAULKNER."

She tore it with passionate fury, as she would have torn his black heart at that moment if it had been within her reach!

Four whole days to wait—almost five—for it was only Wednesday now. Oh, those days!

The man-servant appeared with another note, one of John Worthington's pleasant epistles. How the sight of his signature at the bottom of the page burned her aching eyes! He wrote, begging her not to forget that he had changed his weekly dinner-party to this night. It had always been her habit to come to him once a fortnight, but it was an age, owing to her unpardonably long stay in Washington, since he had seen her at his table.

She could not go—she would not! She had borne so much that she could not trust her fortitude as she did at first. Sit by John Worthington's side to-night, meet his kindly smile; no, it was beyond her power of endurance! She wrote, telling him that she should be unable to come. She had promised Mrs. Lawrence, without fail, to be at her reception, and could not break her word, as she had treated the little woman shamefully all winter.

"That would seem no reason to refuse your dinner," she wrote, "only I promised you weeks ago not to be so dissipated any more. Therefore, I can only go to one place in the same evening. You see what it is to make wise laws; the fulfillment of them is sure to fall unpleasantly on yourself. I hope you will miss me terribly, and that your party will appear as stupid to you as mine is certain to do to, yours faithfully, JOHN WORTHINGTON."

That was the signature she had written! She saw it as she began to fold up the sheet. The bewildering agony caused by the sight of his name had so confused her faculties that she had actually put his signature to her note, in his writing, too! She had a brief season of enacting insanity, the poor soul! then the letter was destroyed, burned, and another written. She was so nervous and afraid now that three separate times, after sealing and directing it, she tore the note out of the envelope, to be certain that there was no treacherous mistake. Even after the letter was gone she fell to thinking about it, and was ready to send after the messenger, rush to the house herself and get possession of it before Worthington returned home, lest there should be some betrayal of her secret in its pages.

So the day dragged by; it seemed more endless and horrible to Alice than any of its predecessors. Then she remembered that she had said the same of each in turn since the night which shut her out forever from the possibility of innocence or peace.

CHAPTER XXVII.

"THE IDES OF MARCH."

THE next morning Mrs. Remsen and Maud returned, and Milly was obliged to exercise a little self-control. Miss Maud was more tiresome than usual, for she wanted to relate a romantic episode which had befallen her during her absence. Unluckily, Milly soon discovered from Maud's contradictions that one portion or the other of the story must be a figment of the imagination. She was ill-natured enough to point out the discrepancies, and Maud flew into a passion. After lavishing a few flowers of rhetoric upon her cousin, she departed to visit her sister, Mrs. Ramsay, who would listen with less critical acumen than Milly displayed.

Later there came a brief note from Kenneth Halford. He could not call, because there was another wearisome meeting of a learned society in which he was interested; but he would see her that evening at Mrs. Lawrence's. Not a word in reference to the request she had written him the morning previous; no reason for not having come to the house.

"He does not condescend to excuse himself," Milly thought. "My letter was not worth a mention."

This slight was almost more unpardonable than all which had gone before, and Milly a hundred times inwardly vowed that she would

never forgive him, and brought her passion up to fever heat again by the persistency with which she fastened upon that resolve. Let him go back to his old love; let him do what he pleased with his life, so that he left her in peace!

It was a dark day, indeed. Aunt Eliza herself was not in her usually equable mood, naturally enough, after having traveled all night, and Milly's manner was not calculated to soothe her. Mrs. Remsen asserted that she had hurried back expressly on Milly's account; but Milly, in her misanthropy, her new unbelief in every thing and every body, told herself that if her aunt had not been as crazy for amusement as a girl of sixteen she would not have returned; very ungrateful on the young woman's part, and she knew it, and was more irritable with her relative on account of the knowledge.

Milly's dress for the evening was not finished. Milly boldly declared that she did not care whether she went or staid at home, and Mrs. Remsen was divided between wrath and astonishment. She forced Milly to work, and sat down to assist, for a good deal of the girl's finery had to be arranged by their own hands, stylish and French as it always looked. It had been too late in the season for her aunt to afford her the extravagance of a new gown, though she was engaged to a rich man; so there was serious business in hiding a silk already worn under some wonderful combination of ribbons and tulle.

"I thought you would have had it done days ago," said Mrs. Remsen. "The idea of leaving it till the last minute!"

"I hate the sight of it," returned Milly. "I wish there were no such things as balls. I'd rather not go."

"Of course you must go," said Mrs. Remsen. "I never saw a girl like you; the wind is not more changeable! What on earth ails you lately, Milly?"

"Nothing," said Milly; "only I hate parties."

She ripped the trimming off the silk skirt with incautious haste, tore the fresh tulle which was to cover it, and altogether made such havoc that, but for Aunt Eliza's patience and skill, the gown would have been a dismal failure.

"I could shake that girl with pleasure," thought Mrs. Remsen, but restrained her rising temper. Milly was soon to be rich and independent; too severe a lecture would not be proper under the circumstances.

The evening came at last, and they were on their way to Mrs. Lawrence's, with Milly, out of her passion and bitterness, wishing that she were driving to her own funeral instead of a ball.

They had not been long in the house before Mrs. Marchmont appeared in a costume which so lighted up her pale beauty that it seemed to have increased from the winter's dissipations, the late suppers, the interminable German co-

10

tillions, which had worn the freshness out of so many faces, youthful and blooming when the season began. Since her last effort to soften Milly, Mrs. Marchmont paid very little attention to her during the few times they had met. She was growing into the habit of looking over Milly's head, and ignoring her girlish airs of state and dignity; not that Alice really cared about her manner, except from considering it an impertinence.

To-night Milly vowed that she would not in any way notice the woman, even if Mrs. Marchmont addressed her outright. She neither cared how it looked nor what people thought; she would not do it, and there was an end.

As ill luck would have it, not ten minutes after Milly formed that resolution, her furbelows caught in a stand of plants while dancing at the end of the room, and her dress would have been absolutely ruined had not Mrs. Marchmont chanced to be near. She darted forward, and extricated Milly, who was only giving fierce tugs which threatened utter annihilation to her draperies, while her partner made matters worse by his assistance, with the awkwardness common to the male sex in the presence of such disasters. The skirt was loosened before Milly had time to see who had aided her. She turned, exclaiming, "I am so much obliged—" saw that it was Mrs. Marchmont, and left her sentence unfinished, while her face changed so quickly that a mole could have discovered she would rather have had body and soul torn into fragments than be indebted to this woman for her release.

Alice perceived it plainly, smiled down at her from her superior height with a careless contempt which few of her sex could have equaled, and said, in her most indifferent voice,

"Pray don't thank me, Miss Crofton. I did it for the sake of the flutings; I can't bear to see a pretty dress ruined."

Then she swept Milly an overwhelming courtesy, and was gone.

Between shame at her own rudeness, rage at the lady's cool scorn, and various other contending emotions, Milly stood speechless. But it was necessary to remedy the misfortune to her attire, so she asked Charley Thorne to take her up stairs, that she might find some one to mend her puffs and flounces. She could hardly stand still while the maid was setting her to rights, and lamenting the accident, and congratulating her that it did not show in the least where it was pinned.

"Thanks," Milly said, impatiently; "any way will do. Oh, I don't care how it looks!"

She turned into the hall, took Charley's arm again, and went down stairs. The first sight that met her eyes was Kenneth Halford dancing with her enemy. He had just arrived, and Mrs. Marchmont wickedly took possession of him at once. When the galop was over, he came to Milly as she stood leaning against a pillar at the upper end of the great drawing-room, while Thorne had gone in search of a

glass of water at her request, for her throat seemed on fire.

"At last!" exclaimed Halford, the unavoidable separation of the past few days having left him forgetful of every thing except his love. "Oh, my dearest Milly, it has been an age since I saw you!"

She turned upon him in a kind of suppressed fury.

"How dare you speak to me?" she said. "Don't come near me again to-night!"

It was very absurd, I know, but, considering all that she had undergone, perfectly natural, and it was just as natural that Halford, entirely ignorant of her cause for indignation—a real cause this time, since she had every reason to suppose that he had received her note—should walk away without reply.

Mrs. Marchmont was punishing her cruelly for her rudeness; Halford was punishing her from a determination that she should feel what it was to give him grave offense; and after that he and Alice were led on by that spirit of coquetry which seizes most people under the influence of a mood like theirs. They danced, they talked, they were as careless of appearances as two people are when the man is furious against some one whom he loves, and the woman a soured, imbittered creature who has rushed forth for an evening's excitement to escape the horrible spectres which haunt her solitude.

Just as it began at a ball, so it ended. In the very chamber, the tiny, half-lighted boudoir, away from the noise and glare of the ball-room, where Kenneth Halford had held Milly to his breast, and lifted her by his whispers into a new world—in that very spot, the beautiful realm which had been tottering for days, as if shaken by an earthquake, fell into fragments at Milly's feet, and crushed her heart under its ruins.

Milly had borne her torture until she could endure no further; she had danced and flirted with Charley Thorne, almost unconscious what she did or said, and at last she must have a few moments to herself. She ran up stairs, and got into the first empty room she could find, saw with a shudder that she had entered the boudoir, but would not retreat. It was added wretchedness to stand there and recall the events of that night which looked so far off—only a few weeks distant—but seeming whole years away, and Milly forced the fresh agony mercilessly upon her soul.

She stood shrouded among the window-curtains, completely concealed from view, when into the boudoir came Kenneth Halford and Mrs. Marchmont. They were laughing and talking, saying all manner of ridiculous things which both knew meant nothing whatever; for each understood the other too well not to perceive that this gayety rose from bitterness and trouble.

They were speaking of the past, the days when Alice Berners had been a dreaming, happy girl; and before Milly could regain self-possession enough to make her presence known, she caught words which, to her distorted senses, shook the very ground from under her feet,

"Never to love as he had loved then—"

Milly heard that broken sentence from Halford's lips; the rest was uttered in French, too rapidly for her to understand; but she had no need to hear more. It was enough, surely it was enough!

Then she saw Halford raise Mrs. Marchmont's gloved hand — that slender, beautiful hand—and touch it with his lips. Sparks of fire danced before Milly's aching eyes; a whole volume of passionate utterance could not have meant more to her jealous fancy. Before she could carry into execution her idea of confronting them, Mrs. Marchmont uttered some laughing ejaculation, and Halford passed out of the boudoir as she turned to leave by a door that led into the dressing-room.

She walked so close to Milly that the girl felt the touch of her garments, and shrank back with a faint exclamation of horror, as if something noxious, deadly, had brushed against her.

Mrs. Marchmont caught the sound, and looked back. Milly's quick movement had disarranged the curtains so that she was visible.

"Is that you, little Miss Milly?" the lady asked, laughingly, and with perfect composure. "I did not see you."

The tone, the epithet, what seemed to the girl a wicked triumph in the dark eyes—all helped to render her more insane.

"It was natural that you should not," she answered, in a voice so sharp that, even through her rage and bewilderment, the tone struck her own ear as strangely as if some evil spirit had hissed the words from between her parched lips.

The voice was so full of insulting significance that Mrs. Marchmont could not resist saying,

"You place a more modest and proper estimate on yourself than I should have expected, dear Miss Milly."

"Have the goodness not to speak my name," she exclaimed. "I don't wish to hear it from your lips."

Mrs. Marchmont laughed; the scene appeared so ridiculous, Milly's manner so exaggerated, that she could not remain serious.

"Not tired of your name already?" she asked, while Milly shook with a new spasm of fury at the sound of that cruel merriment. "Ah, you see, you girls of to-day live so rapidly!"

"At least, we have a sufficiently bad example in the women old enough to know better," retorted Milly.

"You should take warning from it, child! Don't you understand that we good-naturedly make light-houses of ourselves to show you the way you ought to go? But, all the same, it is very naughty of you to remind me of my immense age." And she laughed again.

"You laugh—you dare to laugh!" Milly muttered, while her white teeth, set hard like a vise, showed through her parted lips.

"Verily, mademoiselle, I have no great dread of so doing," replied Alice, quietly. "But permit me to ask the meaning of this little private ball-room tragedy? I am out in my points from not having an idea of the part I am expected to play."

"You are always ready to act any part that is treacherous and false," cried Milly, too mad by this time to attempt the slightest restraint or care if she made herself ridiculous.

Mrs. Marchmont had wholly forgotten the scene of a few moments before; had been so busy with her own thoughts that she hardly noticed Halford's kissing her hand; but she remembered it now, and knew that Milly must have witnessed the whole.

"Ah!" said she, with malicious emphasis, "you had not just entered the room."

"I was here when you came," answered Milly, defiantly.

"And you staid?"

"I staid."

"That is," returned Alice, "you remained quiet—listening."

The retort was cruel, but Milly's unlady-like manner provoked it. She was sorry in an instant.

"Not listening," Milly said; "I had no wish to hear a word; but I saw—"

She broke off abruptly, suddenly recalled to a sense of the way in which she was exposing her misery.

"Truly, you saw!" cried Alice, mockingly. "How shocking! Pray, don't compromise me; that would be very heartless."

Back to Milly's mind rushed the words Dick Faulkner had spoken, and she cried,

"If I'd wished I could have done that before."

There was such meaning in her voice that Mrs. Marchmont stared in wonder and dread.

"May I ask the solution of these mysteries?" she asked, coldly, without a trace of her inward emotion apparent in features or manner.

"It would be very easily given," replied Milly, laughing in her turn.

"Really? Then perhaps you would be kind enough to offer it, though I fear you mistake in supposing it can possess the slightest interest for me," Alice said.

The playful contempt with which she still spoke angered her listener more than the harshest words could have done, because it seemed to denote that she was a rude, unreasonable child, not to be treated with a show even of seriousness.

"I make mistakes less often than you think, Mrs. Marchmont," returned Milly.

"You are more fortunate, then, than the rest of our sex. I congratulate you on your wisdom and prudence."

Her sneers were what Milly could least endure. She turned to move away and end the interview; perhaps she would have obeyed the impulse had not Alice laughed again. Milly confronted her suddenly, saying,

"Would you like to hear a message that was given me last night?"

"Well, that would depend," drawled Alice. "Now it is a message—the interest grows! But—one thing—are you sure it was meant to be repeated for my benefit? I never care to hear what was only intended for other people's ears."

"It was for you, and from Mr. Faulkner."

Alice Marchmont retreated a step, and stood looking full at her with fiery eyes.

"A valuable acquaintance for a young lady!" said she.

"He is your acquaintance, not mine; but he gave me the message."

"The mystery grows deeper," returned Alice, slowly; but now a tremor ran through the scornful voice, and Milly caught it, and was so unwomanly in her passion that she rejoiced in having at last pierced the haughty woman's armor.

"Would you like me to explain? Are you as anxious as you were a moment since?"

"Whenever you can sufficiently come down from histrionics to do so rationally," answered Alice, clutching desperately at the self-control which threatened to escape her.

"I fancy I can at least make myself intelligible," sneered this transformed Milly, who might have been startled to see the passion-lined face with which she confronted her enemy.

"It would be somewhat more interesting than this theatrical display, though I do full justice to your dramatic talent," said Alice.

"You shall have your way, then—"

"Oh yes! by all means—the message," interrupted Mrs. Marchmont, while her heart beat almost to suffocation at the idea that any hint of her story had come into the possession of this girl, who had unexpectedly changed from childish thoughtlessness into a woman's implacability. "Very good, of you to take so much trouble for a person you seem to hate so energetically," she continued, trying for any careless words which should give her an instant's breathing space to call up her strength before this blow, whatever it might be, should strike her.

"I did not seek the office—it was forced upon me. I had no desire to occupy myself with you or your secrets."

"Secrets now! Why, you talk like an astrologer. Are you sure you have not dreamed the whole matter?"

"You shall judge of that for yourself."

"Oh, I don't believe you will ever give me the opportunity! I have been trying to urge the oracle into speech for the last five minutes," said Alice.

"Mr. Faulkner bids you remember that the Ides of March have come, but not gone," returned Milly, slowly.

Mrs. Marchmont stood motionless: not a muscle quivered; her eyes never wandered from Milly's face; despair and agony worse than death tore at her soul, but she was prepared; and there was no show of emotion, save the hard ring of her voice, as she said,

"Was that all?"

"All I was to tell you," replied Milly. "Enough, too, I fancy."

"We shall see that later," Alice said. "You must have seen Mr. Faulkner in one of his fits of intoxication—a singular time for a young lady to converse with him; certainly, it was not in your aunt's presence."

"You want to find out if any body else knows. There does not. I don't want to talk to you any more."

She turned abruptly away, and Mrs. Marchmont passed into the dressing-room, closing the door behind her. As Milly sank into a seat, she heard Halford's voice saying,

"I have looked for you everywhere! Your aunt's head ached so fearfully that she has gone home, leaving you to the care of Mrs. Ramsay. May I come in? Are you vexed yet?"

She was standing in the centre of the room before he finished speaking. She said, in a husky tone,

"Come in—yes, I want you! I have something to say, and you must hear me. I set you free. You are a bad, false man, and from this night I will never speak to you again!"

"Milly!" he exclaimed.

"Don't call me by that name. Don't let me hear it again."

"What ails you?" he asked. "Are you mad, child?"

"Yes—child!" she repeated, with such bitterness that all the suffering of the past weeks seemed to burst out in the tone. "That is what you thought me—a child!"

He caught her hands, and held them fast in spite of her struggles.

"Don't look so," he said; "be quiet, Milly! What is the matter?"

"Let me go—don't touch me—don't come near me!"

He was so startled by her emotion, and his dread of its effect upon her, that there was no room in his mind for anger.

"I love you," he said, roused into an earnestness which had never warmed his voice before. "You know that I love you, dearest child!"

She forced herself away from him, and leaned against a table, panting for breath.

"You loved me as you would a child," she said; "and I tell you I am a woman strong to love, strong to hate, and I hate you; hate you with a force my love never had; hate you for the knowledge you have brought to me; hate you for the woman's experience which has taken away my youth; hate you for what you are—for what you have made me!"

"Milly, Milly!" he could only exclaim, stunned by this passionate utterance, this outburst of fiery strength from the creature who had been his sunbeam, his blossom.

The real nature, which happiness might have developed slowly into perfection, had sprung to sudden maturity, warped and distorted under the suffering of the past weeks, and the madness of the past hour. Milly's childish innocence, Milly's May-day were gone forever.

"What has changed you like this?" he demanded. "What has happened? Tell me—explain."

"Explain?" she repeated. "I was here in this room. I saw and heard you."

"You are wrong," he said. "I see what you think; but you are mistaken. I love you, Milly, I love you!"

"You don't love me—you don't know me! If you ever cared, it was because you thought me a child. I am a woman, and a bitter one!"

Her passion revolted him. He began to grow angry.

"You act like a crazy creature," he said. "Speak sensibly; explain what you want."

"Go out of this room," she answered, "and as you go, remember that you pass out of my life forever. Go!"

His mood changed, his anger subsided. There was a depth, a fearful reality in her manner and words which he had not at first comprehended. He could not lose her like this. There was a revelation of character he had little expected. Could this bitter, unyielding woman be the child whom he had played with and sought to punish into obedience?

"Only listen to me, Milly!"

"There is no need; I tell you I saw and heard."

"But you are mistaken. Let me explain—"

"Oh, stop!" she interrupted, with a gesture of absolute abhorrence. "There has been falsehood enough, deceit enough! I don't know why you trifled with me, out of your pitiful man's vanity; but don't attempt it any more."

"How can you venture to accuse me of falsehood?" he asked. "By what right do you suspect me of treachery? I tell you that what you saw and heard can be easily explained."

"I want no explanation. I will hear none."

"Then you are madder than I thought."

"Not mad now; coming to my senses. I have been mad. Oh, I don't care for to-night—that was only the proof! But these weeks of wretchedness—the misery you have made me endure! I don't forgive these. I never will!"

"And have I had nothing to endure, Milly?" he asked, controlling himself from the very sight of her agitation. "Have I had nothing to complain of?"

"Nothing," she retorted; "nothing."

"Do you call your caprices, your ill-temper nothing?"

"There has been only what you brought on us both. You goaded me into my caprices and ill-temper."

Had she been jealous from the first of Alice Marchmont? Jealous, and concealed it as long as possible, so that her annoying ways, her perversity, had been outbursts from that silent well of trouble, instead, as he had fancied, a pretext to indulge her willfulness. His temper was naturally hasty, but he had much more self-control than Milly, and these thoughts enabled him to reason and plead with her.

"Perhaps I have been wrong," he said; "but it was unintentional. I beg you to believe that."

These were words which Kenneth Halford had never expected to speak to his blossom, a concession which might have led to good results had it come earlier; for it meant a good deal, when one considered his character and the patronizing nature of his affection for Milly. But it was too late. At this moment the avowal seemed a fresh insult.

"If I have been wrong," she answered, "I am not sorry! If I have made you feel, I am glad. It was very little I could do to repay the suffering you brought upon me."

"Why were you silent, why—"

"You deceived me from the first."

"Say what you will, Milly, you know I loved you."

"Admitting that you did, it was as a child—a baby. I tell you again that is what I can not pardon. You see your mistake now. I am no child, but a woman. You must know that you can not care for me."

"I do, Milly—indeed, I do!"

"To say that with your kiss warm on that woman's hand—your old love. Oh, she is fit to be! I tell you that your affection is an insult to a good, honorable girl. I will never hear of it again."

"This is too much!" he said. "No man could be expected to endure such language, such unwomanly taunts."

"If I am unwomanly, it is your fault. You are to blame for every thing—every thing!"

Milly was thinking as she spoke of that dinner at Paul Andrews's house, divided between shame and a desire to fling the story down upon him, to prove that she could be as reckless as he, and cared as little for consequences when thus driven out of herself.

Just then Adelaide Ramsay came into the room. Seeing them both so visibly agitated, she hurried forward, saying,

"I don't wonder you are furious, Mr. Halford. I never heard of any thing so atrocious in my life! Many a man would break with her outright, and nobody could blame him. What mamma will say, I can't imagine. You may thank your stars, Miss Milly, that she has gone home with a headache."

The pair gazed at her while she poured forth this harangue with wonderful rapidity, gazed, divided between surprise and indignation.

"You needn't look like that, Milly," pursued Adelaide. "I am your cousin, and have a right to speak. The pity is that you were always too headstrong to listen to me as you ought."

"If Miss Milly is as much at a loss as I am

to discover Mrs. Ramsay's meaning, she must be puzzled, indeed," said Halford, with his most magnificently freezing air.

"Oh, that won't do for me! It may answer for the world; but with me!" cried Adelaide, shaking her head until the flowers and butterflies and bows and false hair and miracles of all sorts which crowned her apex threatened to desert her utterly. "And I side with you, Mr. Halford. I promise you that—entirely."

Halford looked at her, more and more mystified; but Milly understood now to what her cousin alluded. The story of the dinner had already spread abroad, and she supposed they were quarreling over Milly's escapade.

"Go away, Adelaide," Milly said; "I don't want you here. We were not talking of what you thought. Go away."

"I know you were talking of it," she replied, "and can see that Mr. Halford is furious, and so will mamma be, and I shall tell her—and the things people will say!"

"Tell what you like and whom you like," said Milly, with a haughty gesture of dismissal which Adelaide did not regard.

"You are bold enough about it! To go to a dinner at Paul Andrews's house—good heavens! Indeed I shall tell mamma! Why, you will be ruined if it gets out!"

Kenneth Halford had been sufficiently agitated before, but now he turned pale as death. He never looked at Milly; he evinced no sign of anger; he only said to Adelaide, in a low, quiet voice,

"We were not speaking of that affair. Mrs. Ramsay will confer a great favor on me by not mentioning it either to her mother or any one else."

Mistress Adelaide sailed out of the room in a towering passion with them both, but feeling very uncomfortable under Halford's open contempt, and conscious that her spite against Milly had led her into an exceedingly rude action. Whatever her sentiments might be, or her behavior among her relations, before the world in general she liked to appear a lady. She was gone, and Halford turned on Milly.

"You went to Paul Andrews's dinner?"

"Yes," she replied, defiantly. "Where I go or what I do is no affair of yours, Mr. Halford. I have already told you so."

"No wonder Mrs. Ramsay was beside herself," he said, ignoring the latter part of her speech. "To go to that man's house—"

"And that I went was your fault, too," interrupted Milly. "You would not even answer my note. I was not worth so much attention. You could not spare the time from that woman."

"What note?"

"The one I wrote you yesterday; probably you have forgotten."

"I received no note from you yesterday, Milly."

Milly laughed her unbelief of the assertion. Oh, such a bitter, harsh laugh to hear from lips so young as hers!

"I don't know what you mean, Milly."

"You did not even have an appointment with Mrs. Marchmont?" sneered Milly.

"I was out on horseback and met her; I rode home with her. I had no note from you."

He began reproaches for her rashness in going to the dinner; Milly replied with renewed anger and scorn, and so they went on until words passed between them which could not be forgotten or forgiven. Milly upbraided him with having made a secret of his former engagement, broke their own so decidedly that there was nothing for him but to submit. At last she cried out,

"Go away—go! I hate and loathe you more than ever! You are perjured every way!"

Kenneth Halford flung back some last angry words, and went from her.

Milly dared not stand there, dared not think; all her energies were bent in an insane determination to hide what she suffered. Down into the ball-room she hastened; some one asked her to dance. She was whirling through a waltz, she was laughing and talking as wildly as Mrs. Marchmont herself, her eyes were blazing, her cheeks scarlet; those who knew her best looked on in wonder; men crowded about. She was a new creature, and they could only marvel at the change.

Adelaide tormented her to go, threatened to leave her; but Milly never heeded. It was almost daybreak when she consented to leave, laughing and coquetting to the very door with the men who hovered about her. Then forth from the last ball of the season Milly Crofton passed, leaving her youth behind forever.

The latest sight she beheld was Halford bending over her foe—the latest sound she remembered hearing, that woman's mocking voice!

She was at home. As she reached her aunt's door, Mrs. Remsen came out in her dressing-gown, demanding the reason of her late return; but Milly would not speak—she could not. She rushed on to her chamber, tore off her cloak, then her overstrained nerves gave way, and at length a merciful insensibility put an end to her sufferings for the time.

CHAPTER XXVIII.

THE MORNING AFTER.

MILLY must have lain a long time on the floor in a swoon, for when she came to herself the daylight was streaming broad and full through the curtains; the fire had died out entirely, and she was so chilled and weak that at first she could neither rise nor comprehend what had happened.

Then all came slowly back the terrible memory of the past night! Milly dragged herself to her bed, and lay down—lay there for hours—not sleeping, not even thinking connectedly—a wild whirl in her brain; but with the stern unforgivingness strong in her mind. At last she heard some one knocking at her door. It was a servant, sent by Mrs. Remsen to know if she was coming down. Milly began to realize that life must go on again. She could not remain there in her solitary anguish; she must go forth and meet her aunt, give explanations of all that had happened, listen to blame and reproaches, and live and act like other ordinary mortals. She threw off her crushed ball-dress and managed to get into a morning-gown, but did not leave her chamber.

Then Mrs. Remsen came up; she was very angry at Milly's staying so long behind her at the ball; had been frightened by her appearance when she ran past her on her return; still more angry and alarmed as she thought the matter over and became convinced that something very strange and unpleasant had occurred. Up stairs she marched, and knocked loudly at Milly's door; but there was no response.

"Open the door, Milly!" she exclaimed. "I insist on coming in."

Milly hesitated a little, then allowed her aunt to enter. As well now as ever, she said to herself. The scene and the contest must come; let her get them over, and be done. She did not notice her aunt's look of astonishment, listened passively while she broke into a torrent of exclamations and inquiries, and insisted upon an explanation of this mysterious conduct. Milly sat down, calm from the exhaustion which follows such fearful excitement, but so determined that her aunt's anger had slight place in her thoughts.

"Are you ill, Milly?"

"No," returned Milly, wearily.

It was such an effort to speak! If she could only be left quite alone; not compelled to see the face of any human being; allowed to wear out in utter solitude the first hours of the anguish which had come upon her!

"You look dreadfully ill," pursued Mrs. Remsen; "you are as white as a ghost, and your eyes look as if you had not closed them during the night."

There was no need of answer. Milly sat dumb.

Mrs. Remsen's anxiety at her appearance was merged in curiosity to know what had happened, and a sudden dread that by some folly Milly had endangered her whole future.

"If you are not ill," she said, with no great amount of tenderness in her voice, "will you tell me what is the matter?"

"I am very tired, aunt," replied Milly, resolutely. "I wish you would not make me talk this morning."

"This is too ridiculous!" exclaimed Mrs. Remsen, beginning to feel very indignant. "I insist upon an explanation. Milly, what has happened to you?"

She was silent. How could she put her misery into language to that woman standing so coldly before her? How could she cry out that her heart was broken? The whole world, the beautiful world where she had been wandering, laid in ruins at her feet, with every sweet hope, every youthful joy crushed under them!

"Will you tell, now?" urged her aunt.

Milly tried to speak. There was a suffocating sensation in her throat which kept the words back; the only sound she could make would be a groan; and, even in that early stage of her trouble, Milly had strength of soul enough to be determined on hiding the full depth of her suffering.

"Have you quarreled with Kenneth Halford?" asked her aunt. "I suppose that is the trouble—I thought so last night. You are a very foolish girl; but there is one consolation, lover's quarrels are easily remedied."

She spoke lightly, forcing herself to believe that Milly's pain was only caused by youthful exaggeration of some very trifling difficulty, which would be set at rest before the day ended.

"Just tell me what you quarreled about; for you did quarrel with Mr. Halford, didn't you?" she continued. "It seems very dreadful to you, I have no doubt; but you may be quite sure that a few words will set matters straight, and you will be even happier than before."

"Set matters straight! Be happier than before!" Milly could have repeated the assurance in an insane shriek. There she sat, struggling with her trouble—a trouble that had transformed her suddenly from girl to woman, and must blast her whole youth; and this worldly-minded aunt, unable to see the change in her, stood talking as if she were still a child, to be coaxed and fondled back to good behavior.

Milly heard her aunt's voice again, but it sounded faint and as if it came from a great distance. The very objects about the room, so familiar and treasured, looked strange to her, as if the whole aspect of the apartment had altered during the night.

"Now tell me all about it, Milly, like a dear, good girl," Mrs. Remsen was saying. "I promise that every thing shall be set right. You shall not be called upon to make concessions or do any of those things girls think so very humiliating; every thing shall be arranged. Only tell me."

Milly did not speak; the idea of putting her misery into words was a new torture, and it would be still worse to tell the story of her lover's treachery, to describe the scene she had witnessed, to go over the gradual growth of her doubts till they had culminated the previous night. And her aunt would spare her nothing; Milly was sure of that. She would insist on a full and explicit account, regardless of the girl's pain; so Milly sat there silent, not stubborn, but because it was so hard to begin the sickening tale.

"Now, don't be obstinate, Milly; it is only foolish, and I give you the credit of not being like girls in general. What did you and Mr. Halford quarrel about? Don't say you have not quarreled, for I am sure of it."

She seated herself beside Milly on her sofa,

and remembering all that depended upon this marriage, not only for Milly, but herself, she grew more gentle in her desire to bring her niece into a conciliatory frame of mind; but Milly shrank from her, could not bear her touch, nor any one near her just then, and she turned away.

"I declare, Milly, one would think you were acting a play!" said her aunt, growing angry again. "I don't suppose you have been struck dumb or are quite out of your senses. I beg you will not be ridiculous."

These words did Milly good; they gave her strength. No, her suffering must not be made despicable. She would be like herself, or, if not that, perfectly calm. Let her aunt question; each inquiry was like pressing a hot iron upon her wounds; but she must grow accustomed to endurance. If the story must be told, as well now as ever. So when her aunt said again,

"Will you tell me what is the matter between you and Mr. Halford?"

She answered in a sharp, strained voice,

"I shall not marry Mr. Halford. I have told him this; I no longer love him."

She closed her lips firmly, and sat looking in her aunt's face, utterly indifferent to the incredulity and wrath which she read there.

"Not marry Kenneth Halford?" cried Mrs. Remsen. "Oh, you must have gone mad—quite mad!"

"I am not mad, Aunt Remsen," returned Milly. "I know very well what I am saying: I shall not marry Mr. Halford."

"And you have told him so?"

"I have told him so." Still in the same quiet voice.

Mrs. Remsen leaned back aghast; the affair began to appear more serious than she had expected; still she could not believe that the difficulty was beyond remedy. Of course Milly's declaration went for nothing. Young women frequently made such resolves, when angry, for the express purpose of being teased into breaking them. Mrs. Remsen would be cool. She had an idea that Milly could be abominably obstinate, if thoroughly aroused; she would be cool. She must get to the bottom of the matter without delay.

"At least, you can give some reason for this extraordinary determination, I suppose?"

If it were possible Milly's white face grew whiter when her aunt's question obliged her to think of the reason she must give for her conduct: the words she had heard Kenneth Halford speak to Mrs. Marchmont—the words—the kiss upon her hand!

Mrs. Remsen looked at her in amazement. She knew that it was not in Milly's nature to betray deep feeling easily. She had no girlish fondness of moaning for the edification of her friends on every plausible occasion, and wearing her sorrows painted upon her countenance. This made her aunt wonder; unable to understand the mingled storm of pain and indignant scorn which swept across her features while she recalled the scene of the previous evening as it was impressed upon her excited mind.

"Don't look like that, Milly!" Mrs. Remsen exclaimed, not knowing in the least what to think of the girl in this new phase of character. It was not in her disposition to open her arms and bid her niece come and rest therein like a stricken deer. Moreover, she felt instinctively that Milly would have preferred the coolest contempt to such an effusion of pity and tenderness.

"What horrible thing can Kenneth Halford have done that you should look like this?"

"He has done what I never can—never will forgive! If I believed my heart weak enough to pardon him and receive him again, I would tear it from my bosom with my own hands!"

Could this be Milly, uttering these wild threats with such passion? No wonder Mrs. Remsen asked herself this question, as Kenneth Halford had done on the preceding night. If it was Milly, it certainly was not the same creature who had been treated as a child, supposed to have no thoughts or feelings beyond those common to girls of her age—not the Milly who, a month ago, just one little month, had been so loving, so confiding, with her heart so full of sunshine, her eyes so glad with content. No, never that Milly any more. She was gone—dead in this sudden wreck of hope and trust. The creature who had taken her place was a woman, bitter, and even defiant, with a knowledge of evil forced upon her of which the other Milly had been entirely innocent.

A perception of this change came over Mrs. Remsen's mind. She began to see with what and whom she had to deal. There must be something very black at the bottom of all this; but it should be cleared up, set right. Fortune, position, a successful future could not be flung aside for any reason that the heart alone might dictate. The bare possibility of a disaster and failure roused Mrs. Remsen to extreme anger.

"You certainly are crazy, Milly," she said. "This is some fancy you have taken, some wild fit of anger at a small offense—"

"Fancy!" interrupted Milly, while two scarlet spots began to blaze in the whiteness of her cheeks. "You will have me speak, you will make me put my shame into words—shame for one of my age to have the knowledge of sin forced upon her!"

"What, for Heaven's sake? He could have done nothing so terrible as your words would imply! You don't know what you are saying, you can't know."

"If you had seen your husband bending over another woman, kissing her, speaking words of love in her ear, would you have known what it meant?" cried Milly, in a sharp, frightened tone. "Let me alone, aunt; don't ask me questions—I shall not answer. It is bad enough to know this without being forced to put it into words. Let me alone, I say."

Mrs. Remsen turned away, utterly bewildered. She could not trust herself to speak for the moment. She was sorry for Milly, but furious with her, with Halford, every one, because this sudden barrier had come between her and the fulfillment of her wishes.

"It is that Mrs. Marchmont!" she exclaimed, wrathfully, after a long silence which Milly could not break.

"You see!" exclaimed Milly. "You had noticed; you knew that he loved her; you knew—"

"I knew nothing of the kind," retorted her aunt; "I don't believe it now. She is an abominable flirt, and the best of men will humor such a woman."

"Humor!" repeated Milly.

"Yes," continued Mrs. Remsen; "it's their way, I suppose, because she is so beautiful. I don't pretend to defend the thing, but all men will do it. I have no idea that there was any thing wrong in what you saw or heard—just ridiculous gallantry and coquetry. The truth is, you have been behaving as badly as possible to Mr. Halford for several weeks. You were jealous of Alice Marchmont all the time, and I was sure of it. If you had but spoken one word to him, it might all have been set right."

"Would you have had me beg and implore him to be true?" cried Milly. "Am I a dog to be petted when he chooses, and sent into a corner when he grows weary of me? Oh, Aunt Remsen, you don't know me! I am no longer a child; I am indeed a woman, to feel with all a woman's passion, and hate with all her strength."

This was a new sort of talk in Mrs. Remsen's experience of young ladies; and she was at a loss what to do or how to receive it. She did what most women would have done under these aggravating circumstances—grew more angry, and commenced the detail of her own personal wrongs and injuries arising out of the affair.

"After all the pains I have taken," she said, "to be treated in this way! I have been a good mother to you, Milly; I have brought you up with every care, kept Maud out of society on your account, and now you behave in this unheard-of manner."

"Would you have me marry him?" demanded Milly, with a flash of indignation in her eyes.

"Girls can't break engagements with impunity," urged Mrs. Remsen, evasively.

"If I had been his wife, I would have left him," said Milly. "There are many things I could bear patiently—neglect or ill-treatment; but when one whom I have loved shows me that I have deceived myself, that his heart is not mine, there is no power strong enough to keep me with him—my love is dead."

"There are other things to be thought of in marriage besides love," returned Mrs. Remsen.

"I know you believe so; I told you in the beginning, aunt, that I did not care for other considerations. You laughed at me, and thought it a girlish folly; but I meant it.

If I marry a man, I must respect and love him. Since my engagement I have seen all these things still more clearly. I do not love Mr. Halford; I do not respect him; I consider him false and despicable! I can not marry him—I will not!"

"What am I to do? I can't give you another such winter. I am embarrassed as it is; and, after all, you are not my daughter, though I have been so fond of you. Oh, you mad, crazy girl!"

"I don't care to go again into society, aunt. I will help you all I can. Send away the governess. I'll teach the children; I'll sew; I'll do any thing—any thing!"

"Do be sensible, then, and look at matters in the usual way," replied Mrs. Remsen, not yet despairing of bringing her niece to reason, or, more strictly speaking, unable to cease urging her arguments, even after they were thoroughly exhausted. "I don't at all understand the affair yet; no one could, I should think. Do pray explain—"

"Have a little mercy, Aunt Eliza! Can't you see how you hurt me?"

"It's very well to have such sensitive feelings," cried Mrs. Remsen, anger getting the upper hand again; "but they are more natural in a novel than in real life. I'd rather see a young lady show docility and obedience, be a little more ready to rely upon the advice of friends, than turn like a serpent to sting the bosom that has warmed her."

Mrs. Remsen was slightly indulging in high tragedy, too; but as hers sprang from disappointed worldliness, it was rather ridiculous; while Milly's, however exaggerated, had the dignity which only real suffering gives to such expressions.

"I've no wish to make you unhappy, Aunt Remsen," she said. "I am very grateful to you for your goodness; but don't reproach me for what is no fault of mine."

"It is your fault, I tell you, Milly! For a long time you have irritated Kenneth Halford in every way—"

"He tortured me," broke in Milly, roused to passionate self-exculpation; "he stung and wronged me; he followed that woman about, and left me."

"Did you expect to keep him fastened to your chatelaine like a gold breloque?" asked Mrs. Remsen, sarcastically, interrupting in her turn, as even ladies will when excited.

"I expected him to love me as he had promised," answered Milly, resolutely. "I expected him to keep his vow in deed and in thought. As well be actually false to me as allow his mind to stray."

"You are absurdly and insanely jealous," said her aunt. "That is exactly what ails you."

"Not now," replied Milly, bitterly. "One must love to be jealous, and Kenneth Halford has killed my love with that one blow."

Mrs. Remsen fairly ground her teeth. I am

sure she must have regretted not being a man;
a little hearty plain-talk would have been such
a relief, and a sort of safeguard against breaking a blood-vessel, which she really thought she
must do.

"I don't believe," she almost shrieked; "no,
I don't believe out of a mad-house so crazy a
creature was ever seen! I thought you had
common sense, and here you show yourself the
most doleful fool that ever worried a woman's
life out. I'd like to put a straight-jacket on
you, and send you up to Bloomingdale! I
would, indeed. I verily believe it would be
the proper place for you."

"Send me, if you like, Aunt Eliza; I'll go
there or anywhere you please."

"Now, don't play the martyr," groaned Mrs.
Remsen. "For Heaven's sake, don't add that
to all the rest, unless you wish to make me as
crazy as you are."

"Perhaps I had better go away," pursued
Milly, catching at the idea with a feeling of relief. "It might be better for all of us."

"And where in the name of goodness would
you go?"

"I don't know; I think I don't care. I
could teach children—"

"For pity's sake do be quiet! I shall certainly go out of my senses! My niece a governess; it would be a pretty story to tell, wouldn't
it? Do you wish to ruin us all utterly, have
people call me the most cruel woman that ever
lived, and see Maud's prospects completely destroyed?"

"Then what can I do, Aunt Remsen? Only
suggest something that will prevent my being a
burden to you, and I will obey."

"There is but one thing to be done; a bat
could see it plainly," retorted Mrs. Remsen, as
if deciding upon young women's futures was
the ordinary occupation of the mysterious beast
she mentioned.

"Tell me; only tell me," begged Milly,
wearily.

"Let me send for Kenneth Halford, and get
a frank, full explanation of this affair."

"Never—never!" cried Milly. "Any thing
but that!"

"Of course, I knew you would say so! Any
thing except the only thing that can be
done."

"There is no explanation possible."

"Now, Milly Crofton, that is just romantic
nonsense, nothing more. Listen to me! You
will have to live in the world, not in a novel.
You will have to do as other women do, put up
with such kind of trouble. Romance is all very
well, and love is all very well; but they are
rank nonsense when carried too far. Neither
of them endures beyond five-and-twenty. When
a woman marries, she should look at the future.
As she grows old, she wants position and money; without these, all the love that ever poet
dreamed of becomes the most utterly worthless
drug that it is possible to imagine."

Milly was listening, grown so quiet that Mrs.

Remsen thought her words were beginning to
have an effect.

"Go on," said Milly, when her aunt paused
for breath, speaking with a calmness that would
have sounded ominous had the lady been sufficiently composed to notice it.

"So I say, when a girl has found these things
as you did, let her take no notice of the gilding
wears off her romance; let her trust to her woman's tact to keep a certain hold upon the man
she marries; in short, let her take the benefits
Heaven offers, and not demand impossibilities."

She ceased, overcome by her own eloquence,
and Milly, looking intently in her face, asked,

"You think I have no reason to feel hurt
and outraged?"

"I don't say that; it's aggravating to see
one's lover devoted to another woman; but
they will all of them do it! I am sure Mr.
Halford only wanted to punish your caprices.
Talk quietly with him."

"No, Aunt Eliza, I can not blind myself.
He knew this Mrs. Marchmont long ago; he
loved her! He was pleased with her girlish-
ness, and engaged himself to me thoughtlessly.
Then this woman resumed all her old power
over him."

"I don't believe a word of it all!"

There was no logic in the assertion, but it
was the best Mrs. Remsen could do under the
circumstances. Flat denial was the only ground
left for her to take.

"Aunt Remsen, if there were no other reason, I would not marry him now that I know
he thought me a child; loved me only as he
might some pretty plaything."

"Time enough after you are married to show
him that you are not," urged Mrs. Remsen.

"Oh no; for I should only bring untold misery on myself. I could not be patient when
I saw that he considered me incapable of sharing his loftiest feelings, his deepest secrets. I
should weary him with my anger and my importunities. Every week would separate us
more widely."

Where, in Heaven's name, had this child
learned such arguments? Mrs. Remsen stared
at her with something of the feeling a person
might have if a pet song-bird, that had been
content with its lumps of sugar and its gilded
cage, suddenly transformed itself into a mountain eagle, beating against the bars of its prison,
struggling fiercely with every thing which op-
posed its flight, and betraying in every movement the uncontrollable spirit of its race.

"I say," continued Milly, "that, putting all
else aside, this view of the case would be enough
to make me break my engagement."

Mrs. Remsen groaned again.

"Aunt Eliza, I have only been childish and
thoughtless because I was happy. My love
seems to have changed me entirely, and roused
deep feeling and keen perception that I did not
know I possessed. Suffering has made me so
much older, that it seems out of my power to go
back to my girlish carelessness."

Mrs. Remsen sat up in her chair, and gurgled in her throat in the vain effort to speak, and stared aghast and helpless.

"I can remember my mother; I know now what she suffered? She married a man older than herself, who regarded her as a child, and could never be made to understand that as the years went on her intellect widened to the fullness of his. He sought companionship among women of the world, and crushed her by his unrecognition of her claims, until she drooped, faded, and dropped into her grave, glad to be at rest."

Mrs. Remsen was silent, a little awed, and much softened. Her love for that sister, so early dead, had been the purest, the least selfish feeling of her whole life.

"I should not do that," Milly went on, her voice hardening and her face growing stern; "I could not allow myself to be crushed without a struggle. In time I should surely come to hate the man who, from pride and blind conceit, refused me my true place in his heart. I should become capable of any act which might wound and teach him that the creature he had looked down upon and petted like an infant was able to sting his very soul and ruin the life in which he thought she made so small a part—a thing pleasant to have, like flowers or music, but, like them, to be put aside whenever it should suit his lordly will."

Mrs. Remsen was still dazed; but she must say something. Her experience, her worldly wisdom would not allow themselves to be completely silenced by this strange creature that Milly had come to be.

"You should say all that to Kenneth Halford," she began; but Milly went on, almost without a pause.

"I say it to him! If he could not see it, better to part. Since he loved only a child, it was not I whom he loved, for I am one no longer. He wanted a plaything; he must look elsewhere. Let him buy one with his wealth and position. My heart is beyond his purchase."

"I tell you, Milly, these feelings will pass out of his mind," urged her aunt; "he will love and respect you after this."

"You forget the rest," replied Milly; "or, rather, you will not remember; but I can not forget! He has put a gulf between my heart and his that he could never cross."

"Your jealousy again."

"Call it what you please."

"Just follies that torment you."

"Think so, if you will, you can not persuade me. I saw them together—I heard his words. I can not go over all these things again. It would be of no use."

She began to tremble again, and leaned wearily back in her seat; she had not tasted food that day, and after her long fainting fit and terrible excitement she was thoroughly exhausted. It was more plainly visible now, in contrast to her recent passion and firmness.

"You are ill, Milly. Oh, you will kill yourself!"

Milly shook her head.

"No, Aunt Remsen; people can't die so easily. I used to think a great trouble would kill suddenly; but now I believe it must take years and years, when one is so young and strong as I."

She looked too pale and haggard, now that the color which excitement had brought to her face began to die out, to be scolded much more.

Mrs. Remsen sat puzzling her brain as to what could possibly be suggested further as at all likely to have influence upon the girl; but she could only go over the old arguments dressed in a little different fashion, and they proved as ineffective as before. At last Milly cried out, in a voice which fairly frightened her,

"Let me alone, Aunt Remsen; let me alone, I beg!"

And there was no opportunity to scold or argue more just then, for, as she spoke, Milly fainted entirely away. Mrs. Remsen was a sensible woman, so, instead of shrieking for help, she managed to lift her to the bed, and worked over her until she recovered consciousness again. Mrs. Remsen had a horror of scenes, thought them positively vulgar. People who have no great degree of feeling are much given to that opinion. Any thing which thoroughly arouses them from their selfish comfort is so tiresome and *mauvais genre*.

But, with all her foibles, Mrs. Remsen was kind-hearted, as I have said; and just then her irritation and disappointment were forgotten in anxiety, and she did every thing that could be of use in the gentlest and most womanly way.

Milly turned her face from the light, and closed her eyes as if she were going to sleep—a mere artifice to induce her aunt to leave her.

"You can rest now," said Mrs. Remsen, "and be quite restored when you wake;" and she kissed her, as women do kiss each other—touching the face to be so honored with the tip of the nose—and went out of the room.

Milly was so fortunate as to lie on her bed all the morning unmolested, her aunt having told Maud and the servants that she was ill with a nervous headache, and on no account to be disturbed. Maud, at least, was not likely to intrude upon her, under such circumstances; for that young lady was as much out of her element in a sick-room as a useless creature could well be. Mrs. Remsen took a little time to deliberate, and then she sat down and wrote a note to Kenneth Halford.

She commenced thus:

"MY DEAR FRIEND,—Our little girl is quite ill—"

Then she hesitated. She had much womanly delicacy in her composition; she could not appeal to his sympathy by exposing Milly's weakness. She reflected a little longer, and, after much trouble and many erasures, wrote and dispatched the following:

"DEAR MR. HALFORD,—I wish you would come and see me as soon as you receive this. You and I are old friends, and can afford to talk openly with one another; and I am sure you feel that in any thing I might say I should have your happiness, and that of our fanciful little Milly, very closely at heart.

"So come and talk with me, and let this light cloud be swept away by our mutual endeavors before it grows darker; come, with your usual kind frankness, and be certain that you will find me now, as ever, your very sincere friend,   ELIZA REMSEN."

Mrs. Remsen felt a sense of relief when her missive was gone; at least, she had done something, and that is always a comfort when one has been at a loss. Halford would at once obey her summons; of that she felt certain, and the more she reflected the more confident she became that every thing would end well. Her spirits returned, her distress and irritation passed away. Several times she stole up to Milly's room on tiptoe and looked in. The girl's face was buried in her pillow, she seemed to be sleeping quietly, and with each visit Mrs. Remsen felt her hopes revive. But only too soon the final blow overthrew them utterly. As she was descending from one of these expeditions she met Cæsar, the man-servant, with a letter in his hand.

"For madam," he said, with one of his grand bows. "The individiole did not wait for no answer."

Mrs. Remsen glanced at the superscription. It was in Halford's hand, and she went into the little reception-room to read it.

"All will be arranged now," she thought, as she tore open the envelope in haste. "I am very glad I wrote."

She unfolded the note, glanced at the date, and with a start and an exclamation of mingled wrath and dismay, hurriedly read the contents. This was Kenneth Halford's answer

"Steamer *Laura*, 12 M.

"DEAR MADAM,—Your note has just been brought to me; the date above will explain my hurried reply. I am leaving for South America. The task of explanation remains with your niece, who last night brought our engagement so decidedly to an end that my own self-respect renders it impossible to me to employ any means—if such were in my power—to change her determination.

"I wish you and yours every happiness, and trust that the years which will probably elapse before my return may not wear from your mind all kindly recollections of

"KENNETH HALFORD."

Mrs. Remsen read the letter twice, as if she found it difficult to understand the contents, crushed it in her hands as dramatically as an actress could have done, and between rage and disappointment came near a fainting fit herself.

"Gone to South America!" was all she could utter, in a voice that would have done justice to Queen Constance's famous speech, for the first time conscious of her own utter helplessness. He had put it beyond her power to do any thing now. "Gone to South America! Two mad people together, and I am to bear the consequences of their folly!"

Yes, Kenneth Halford had gone. In his anger with Milly, his sorrow at having lost his beautiful hope of peace, his bitterness toward himself and fate, he had gone.

CHAPTER XXIX.

HORTENSE'S WISDOM.

LIKE most people disappointed of their plans, Mrs. Remsen had not magnanimity enough to bear her mortification and Milly's conduct with any degree of patience. She sat holding Kenneth Halford's letter in her hand, as yet too confused and angry to see her way. Before she had composed her mind beyond the desire to go up to Milly and overwhelm her with fresh reproaches, Adelaide Ramsay hurried into the room, having seized the earliest opportunity to acquaint her mother with the affair of the dinner-party, in spite of Halford's prohibition.

Mrs. Remsen was looking so white and amazed that Adelaide knew something extraordinary must have occurred; she glanced at the note in her mother's hand, recognized Halford's writing, and jumped at a conclusion in a flash.

"Has he broken with her?" she demanded, breathlessly. "I don't blame him in the least; any man would have done the same. I only wonder you have patience with her, to lose a match like that; but she deserves it all and more."

Mrs. Remsen only leaned back in her chair, and stared at Mrs. Ramsay without reply. It was evident that people had conspired to drive her out of her senses! What was this which she did not know—what further mystery was at the bottom of Milly's conduct and Halford's departure?

"I don't wonder you look as if you had fallen from the clouds, mamma," pursued Adelaide. "I never heard any thing so horrid in my life, never! But what does he say? Let me see his letter."

Mrs. Remsen allowed her to take the epistle, and sat steadying her dizzy head upon her hand while Mrs. Ramsay perused it.

"Gone to South America—actually gone! Well, Miss Milly has concluded her affairs finely! 'Leave the explanation to your niece,'" she read aloud, "'who has brought our engagement so decidedly to an end.' Oh! that's all nonsense, you know. But it's very good-natured in him to allow her the credit of breaking it, I am sure; but he really did it himself, any man would; and so proud as Kenneth Halford has always been—"

"In Heaven's name, Adelaide, tell me what you are talking of?" broke in Mrs. Remsen. "Milly has nearly crazed me this morning, and you now seem determined to finish the work."

"What have I done, mamma? You don't expect me to take her part! I think Halford is right; he ought to throw her over; she quite deserved it."

"I don't know what you mean," groaned Mrs. Remsen. "Milly broke the engagement herself, and it is the maddest thing ever a girl did."

"Now, that is the sheerest nonsense," said Adelaide, with her usual respectful candor. "Of course, one must say so. It is the only loop-hole of escape for her."

"I declare I think I shall go mad, among you all," cried her mother. "Do talk connectedly, Adelaide, and explain yourself."

"Why, mamma, I think your brain is turned. I'm sure I spoke plainly enough. It was the quarrel about the dinner that made him do it. I came to tell you, but it seems Milly has already confessed it herself."

"Dinner!" repeated Mrs. Remsen. "What dinner, Adelaide?"

"Then you don't know—she didn't tell you?"

"Tell me what? Heavens and earth! Adelaide, what is it?"

Mrs. Ramsay at last perceived that her news had not been forestalled, and she burst forth with the energy peculiar to people when able to impart unpleasant tidings in regard to some one whom they heartily dislike.

"Day before yesterday Milly went to a dinner given at Paul Andrews's. Halford discovered it, and this has caused the trouble between them."

Mrs. Remsen rose from her chair and sank back in it again; she could only repeat in a choked voice,

"A dinner-party at Paul Andrews's house!"

"Yes, mamma; Mrs. Lawrence took her there, and Milly did it on purpose to vex Halford, who has a mortal horror of the man. She ought to be shut up in a convent; there's nothing bad enough to do to her! Now you understand it all. Of course, Halford has broken with her."

Mrs. Remsen's first impulse was to fly in search of Milly with some undefined idea of putting an end at once to that young lady; but she controlled herself, and made Adelaide relate such particulars as she could vouch for. It was difficult to keep Mrs. Ramsay's imagination down to a plain statement of facts, as she had a marked talent for embroidery. She ended her story with the interview she had personally interrupted at the ball, in describing which she was able to employ her most gorgeous colors, and her mother could not demand authority.

"I always insisted to you that she was the worst girl in the world; I hope you are satisfied of it now!" she added, by way of conclu-

sion. "The idea of indulging her as you have, of leaving her in Mrs. Lawrence's charge during your absence! I thought you must be mad at the time."

Mrs. Remsen was not a worm to endure even the slightest trampling meekly; no, even though it was the most humiliating hour of her life.

"You would never see after her," she said. "You are almost as much to be blamed as Milly."

"There, mamma, you needn't attempt a word of that sort; I am married now, and my days for being lectured are over! I don't like Milly; I never did; and I wasn't going to bother myself with her. She has ruined the best chance she will ever have, and I wash my hands of her and her affairs."

"What will people say?" moaned Mrs. Remsen.

"Say she deserves it," said Mrs. Ramsay, viciously.

"Adelaide," urged her mother, "for all our sakes we must declare that she broke the engagement. Halford's letter is proof of that."

"Oh! say whatever you please; I've no objection to repeat it; but people will believe what they choose. I've done; I shall not say another word against her, only I don't pity her in the least."

"Pity her!" cried Mrs. Remsen. "I ought to put her in a strait-jacket!"

"A very good idea, mamma. Now I must leave you. Where is Maud? I want to see her a moment about that worsted-work; I suppose she has been too lazy to finish it."

She took herself and her finery out of the room, dismissing all thoughts of Milly's troubles in her own particular affairs, and leaving her mother to her reflections.

After a few moments Mrs. Remsen rose and went up stairs, determined to "have it out" with Milly. But when she reached the chamber she found the girl really asleep, and looking so pale and ill that the aunt could not find it in her heart to obey her first impulse and waken her. She could not help being sorry for the child, in spite of her anger, so she turned away. Out of sight of Milly's worn young face, her wrath returned, and a restless night did not leave her in a more placable mood.

At noon the next day Milly had not appeared, and Mrs. Remsen went out to make visits without having seen her. During her absence she learned, to her horror, that Milly's escapade was quite well known, and Halford was said to have left her in consequence. There was no doubt that these ill-natured reports would hurt her fearfully; and any hope of seeing her safely married and out of the way grew fainter with each visit in Mrs. Remsen's mind. She made the best she could of the affair. To those who knew of the engagement she avowed that Milly had dissolved it, and even showed Halford's letter to a favored few; but people are not easily led to believe that which they would rather not, and the world seems often to prefer thinking the worst. Mrs. Remsen hastened to confront Mrs. Lawrence; she must give herself that small spark of satisfaction. I suppose few women ever received from one of their own sex a more dreadful "wigging" than that rattle-brained lady caught at the hands of Eliza Remsen. To make matters worse, Mrs. Lawrence was as impulsively warm-hearted as she was thoughtless. She had only taken Milly to the dinner for "the fun of the thing," and was truly grieved to hear that it had been the means of bringing such trouble upon her.

"I never was so sorry," she said over and over again. "If ever I can make it up to little Milly, I will; indeed I will!"

"If you will please leave her to me in future, and have no further care for her, it is all I ask of you," retorted Mrs. Remsen, finally.

Mrs. Lawrence was not angry; she continued her remorseful apologies and malapropos suggestions until Mrs. Remsen departed in a state of subdued fury. Indeed, the kind-hearted widow went about doing battle valiantly for Milly, declaring point-blank that she had never been at the dinner; and when this did not answer, she averred that the child went with her, not knowing whose the dinner was, and hurried off as soon after she discovered the truth as civility would permit. She affirmed, moreover, that Halford had flirted so outrageously with Alice Marchmont that Milly could no longer endure it. I am bound to say that in her desire to screen her favorite she tried to blacken poor Mrs. Marchmont's character unmercifully, and committed numberless sins in the way of untruths. She brought on a fierce enmity between herself and Paul Andrews, and did so fight like an amiable dragon, right and left, in Milly's cause, that she really softened somewhat the reports; but Mrs. Remsen did not forgive her any the more.

When people have really done one an injury, it is only tantalizing to find them sorry and ready to atone; one would rather they remained stoical and indifferent, so that there should be no drawback to nourishing a genuine hatred and applying the objurgatory Psalms to their cases when one reads the Bible.

But, while Mrs. Lawrence was going about on her errand of penitence, Mrs. Remsen had descended upon Milly almost as belligerent as the Assyrian of old, and there was no kind angel to protect the poor, foolish child.

"I never expected to be so stunned and shocked in my life—never!" cried Mrs. Remsen. "I could not at first believe it; I can hardly do so now! To do a thing like that—a young girl! Why, Milly Crofton, I should think you would expect some horrible judgment to follow such conduct!"

"I am very sorry I went, Aunt Remsen, for your sake," said Milly; "but I had suffered so much, and when he neglected my note in order to go out with that woman, I did not care what I did. I only wanted to hurt and offend him most."

"But you have hurt yourself more!"

"After all, a great many people go to Mr. Andrews's dinners. Oh, I don't care what they say!" said Milly, growing desperate.

"No wonder Mr. Halford broke the engagement—"

"Oh, Aunt Remsen, I told you he did not! I did that myself before Adelaide came in; he knew nothing of the dinner until she told him—paid very little attention to it then."

"But this thing ought of itself to have made you try to effect a reconciliation, for your own sake."

"Never, Aunt Remsen; not if I were actually to be disgraced! People must say and think what they please, pity or blame me, believe that he left me or not. I would not be reconciled to this man if he came to kneel at my feet and implore it."

"No more stage effects, I beg," returned Mrs. Remsen. "There is no danger of your ever seeing him again; a prouder creature does not live than Kenneth Halford—"

"And my pride is equal to his; I will stoop no quicker than he would."

"Milly, I will not have you talk so—it is abominable! At least, you might appear sorry."

"I can not act a lie; and my love has gone out forever," said poor Milly, believing what she said. "You would not have borne it any more patiently than I did; no woman could have done so."

"You know very little of what women are obliged to endure."

"That is when it is too late to find a remedy," replied Milly. "A wife may be forced to bear such ignominy, to hold fast her heart to keep it from bursting, and still smile patiently before the world. I was able to break my bonds and end my pain."

"You talk like an idiot!" exclaimed the exasperated Mrs. Remsen. "It is useless to say more to you."

"If you will only leave me to myself, I shall be so very thankful."

"That is very well, now that you have done all the mischief you possibly can. If you had the smallest particle of gratitude or decent feeling in your composition, you would remember the trouble this brings upon me."

"I do remember, Aunt Eliza, and I am indeed sorry for it; but I can not help that now."

"Such a future!" groaned her aunt. "I thought you were going to be so happy! I was very fond and so proud of you; I loved you because you were so like your mother; and now—that you should treat me in this way!"

"I couldn't help it, Aunt Remsen; indeed, I couldn't help it," pleaded Milly.

"What am I to do?" pursued Mrs. Remsen, once more growing eloquent upon the subject of her own personal grievances. "Maud can't be kept back any longer; it wouldn't be fair; she would never submit to it, and I can't take you both out next year. It's quite out of the question."

"Oh, Aunt Eliza, I don't wish to go anywhere again. I have told you that, and I will teach the children."

"Now, that is nonsense. You know I can not let you do such a thing. You know I would not; it only sounds more foolish and ungrateful than the rest."

"I did not mean it so, indeed, Aunt Eliza," said poor Milly.

"And I had hoped so much from you," Mrs. Remsen quavered, not heeding Milly's words. "Mr. Halford could have placed Bob in the Naval School. I could have bought that house I wanted on my own terms, with him in the family. Oh, Milly, I think you are the most atrocious girl I ever heard of!"

As she thought of her wrongs anger was uppermost again, and she scolded until she raised a corresponding tempest in weary Milly's mind at last.

"Let me go away; send me away," she sobbed. "I can not stay here. I can not bear such scenes. You will kill me! I shall go out of my senses if you do not let me alone!"

Then the passion in each feminine breast broke into hysterical sobs, and finally both wept themselves into tolerable composure. It was altogether the best thing which could have happened; Mrs. Remsen could talk no more, and Milly was left to weep herself to sleep—the only lullaby she was likely to find at present.

Of course, this conversation was only the beginning of many similar scenes, before they had learned to look the matter full in the face and call up a little resignation. It was well for Milly that her cousins were so hard upon her, as Mrs. Remsen was forced at last to defend her a little; and this fact kept matters from reaching their extreme limit of endurance between Milly and her aunt.

Maud would have been a perfect little wasp if she had dared; indeed, she never failed to tease Milly when she found a safe opportunity. Adelaide Ramsay "cast Milly off," as she had pompously declared she should do; but, as she had always been as indifferent and cold as possible, the additional ill-nature was not sufficiently apparent to be painful. As for Hortense, the intellectual daughter of the family, she descended sufficiently from the elevation of her missions and ologies to be fearfully shocked; but her mind was so filled with the sufferings of missionaries in the South Sea Islands, and the probable appearance and tastes of the inhabitants (if any such existed) of the regions about the North Pole, that she could not be expected to dwell upon Milly's poor little troubles.

She came to the house during the first excitement, saw Milly, and deluged her with wisdom and advice; but under all her learned follies she had a more tender heart than either of her sisters, and did not reproach her with so much cruelty.

"It all comes of your having an undisciplined mind," she said. "Oh, Milly, I told you long ago that you ought to undertake a course of mental philosophy, or even geology or conchology, or at least something really to develop your reasoning powers."

"Never mind, Hortense," replied Milly, honestly grateful for such good-nature; "I can study now."

Mrs. Maynard rushed into a long dissertation, in which she proved satisfactorily to herself that the world could never revolve properly in its orbit until women should be differently educated. Then she branched off in modest praise of her own mental qualifications, reached the fertile subject of her grand occupations, and the thorough manner in which she was fulfilling her destiny, and ended with this climax, "If I were you, Milly, I would be a missionary!"

Mrs. Remsen entered the room in time to catch these last words, and, her patience in these days being mere thread-paper, she exclaimed,

"I declare, Hortense, I almost think you are a greater idiot than Milly herself!"

Hortense smiled in lofty compassion. She could not be ruffled, because her wisdom was deemed folly by those who were too ignorant or too shallow-minded to comprehend its depth.

"Mamma," she said, grandly, "you never did understand me; but I am not to blame for that. You may call my life folly; you may consider the approval of such men as Professor Driver and Doctor Brazen not worth having, but I can not agree with you. In his day Galileo was regarded as a madman and—"

"Oh, Hortense!" broke in her mother, giving herself an exasperated shake.

"One moment, mamma, then I have done! Where was I? These constant interruptions render connected thought impossible. Oh! I repeat what I said, for I did not make the assertion without due reflection; if I were Milly, I would become a missionary."

"She is about as fit for it as her white kitten is to become a bishop," returned Mrs. Remsen. "Milly has thwarted her own destiny! She was meant to be rich—a woman of the world—"

"Oh, mamma!" sighed Hortense, interrupting in her turn, while Milly leaned back in her chair and felt contemptuous of both. "Do you believe there is no higher destiny than being a butterfly, thinking only of dress and trivial amusements, of the attractions of wealth and the enervating weaknesses in which most women pass their lives?"

"Hortense," said her mother, "I don't mean to argue. I am quite willing to admit that in your case the learned and high-minded style succeeded admirably. But it strikes me that, in spite of your wisdom, you were not unwilling to marry a rich man; that you think as much of dress as we frivolous women; and enjoy your wise dinners and stilted reunions in quite as dissipated a fashion as we do balls and operas, besides taking your fair share of them, too."

Hortense smiled benignly—a smile meant to express the wide difference between their conduct and her habit of varying the important duties of life by lighter pursuits at convenient seasons.

"If Milly were like Angelone Davidson, she might lecture."

Mrs. Remsen shrieked.

"Only a prejudice on your part, mamma," interposed Hortense, equably.

"I beg you won't go on talking of it, at all events," shivered Mrs. Remsen.

Hortense smoothed her ruffles, smiled complacently, and meditated an overflowing of eloquence; but concluded that it would not be worth the trouble, considering her audience, and continued,

"If it had pleased Heaven to make her a woman of genius, she might write something, or paint."

"It did not," said Mrs. Remsen, "and I thank Heaven for it. She has given me trouble enough as it is; goodness knows what might have happened if she had been troubled with soul-pinings and aspirations."

"She is, indeed, happier. The children of genius suffer anguish of which the world little dreams;" and Hortense sighed as if she had a soul as full of poetry and pangs as Sappho herself.

"There is only one thing for Milly to do," said her aunt; "let her write to Mr. Halford; let her say—"

"Aunt Remsen," interposed Milly, "it is perfectly useless to go over all that again. I have told you I would never do it; I had much rather die!"

"Oh, Milly, your obstinacy will kill me!" cried Mrs. Remsen. "I can not endure this much longer."

"Mamma," said Hortense, assuming the attitude she affected when about to get off something particularly brilliant, "in some respects Milly is right—woman's dignity must be maintained! I am sorry for her in many ways; but I say frankly, suffering is good for her; bitterness is a tonic. Let Milly be brave, press her thorn of suffering to heart, go on unflinchingly, and out of the darkness and trouble will come consolation and wisdom!"

Milly had a dim idea that Charlotte Brontë had said the same in a better way, but she held her peace.

Mrs. Remsen was goaded beyond endurance, and exclaimed, "If you can not do better, Hortense, than uphold Milly in her wickedness, you had better be silent."

"I do not uphold her, mamma; I blame her; but I pity her, too, because I see so plainly the causes which have brought this affliction upon her," continued Mrs. Maynard, waving her hand in the air, as she careered, well-mounted, upon her oratorical hobby. "Women's minds are not properly developed, women's souls not thoroughly roused from the chaotic—"

"Hortense," snapped her mother, dismounting her with cruel haste, "you may as well stop talking, for I can not understand one word you're saying."

Hortense sighed and frowned ominously, then decided to smile again from the height of her superiority, and shook out her flounces preparing to depart.

"It seems my advice can not aid you," she said, with an accent of serene pity for their weakness. "Professor Driver says he would rather have my opinion on certain subjects than that of most of the scientific men in America; but—well—neither you nor Milly is Professor Driver."

Milly thought of the professor's crooked nose that seemed always trying to go round a corner before him, and congratulated herself upon the fact her cousin had stated.

"Oh, Hortense," said Mrs. Remsen, unable to keep the peace; "you are a pretty woman, and you have really a fair share of brain; but your 'ologies and the flattery you receive are quite turning your head, and destroying your common sense."

"Mamma, Jean Paul Richter says—"

"I don't at all care what he says. The opinion of a musty old Dutchman isn't going to help me out of my troubles."

"Oh, mamma, if we could only learn to receive troubles aright! The crushed grape yields the wine—"

"But I am not a crushed grape; don't talk nonsense."

Milly couldn't help an actual laugh. It was many days since she had felt in the mood to laugh.

"You may find laughing matter in this affair, but I don't," said her aunt, adopting the injured tone.

"Mamma," said Hortense, "you are so worldly."

"I suppose I was intended to be so, or I should have been sent somewhere else to live! It is easy for you to preach—not a care in the world, plenty of money, and even your household affairs troubling you no more than if such things did not exist."

"Do you think my mind is to be brought down to a level like that?" demanded Hortense, vehemently. "Do you suppose I would fold up my talents in table-cloths, and wear out my brain consulting about what I should eat?"

"Nevertheless, you seem to enjoy your good dinners quite as much as any one."

"I could dine off the simplest fare," returned Hortense, "provided I had intellectual intelligences to share it."

"But you would not have them," retorted her mother. "They take good care to carry their intellectuality where nice dinners are to be found."

Hortense held up her hands in holy horror

of such heretical opinions, and as she did so her eye caught a new bracelet she wore.

"Isn't it pretty?" she said, extending her arm toward Milly. "It was the only one in that pattern that Tiffany had."

Milly thought bitterly, "They would talk of themselves and their petty affairs if I was lying here dead! Hortense is kinder than the other girls, but even she has no more heart than one of her big books; and Aunt Eliza is killing me with her uncertain tempers—one moment pitying, the next abusing me for my ingratitude."

"Adelaide will be horribly vexed," said Mrs. Remsen. "She told me about the same bracelet yesterday, and said she had almost teased Mr. Ramsay into buying it for her."

Hortense smiled complacently. In spite of her lofty aims, she was woman enough thoroughly to enjoy the delight of possessing a thing some one else had been eager to procure.

"I think little of such trifles," she observed, with superb indifference. "If I had to wheedle and tease as Adelaide does to obtain them, I should go without."

"Perhaps," added Mrs. Remsen, doubtfully.

"If she would only go away," thought Milly. "I shall hate them all soon. If I were only quite alone—away in a Western forest, where no human being could reach me!"

But the Western forest was not accessible; she was obliged to remain quiet, and receive Hortense's parting words of counsel.

"You ought not to sit down idly and grieve," she began; but Milly flashed out at once. Any thing like pity she could not endure.

"I am not grieving; I have nothing to grieve over. Be good enough to understand that perfectly, Hortense."

"Nothing to grieve over?" cried her aunt. "Oh, you are a wicked girl—and the trouble you have given me—the pain and the disappointments!"

"I did not mean that, Aunt Remsen; I am sure you know what I intended to say quite well. I am sorry to disappoint you, heartily sorry; but I have no other trouble to grieve over."

"Then you really did break the engagement?" asked Hortense.

"Yes, and I should do it again with the same reason."

Mrs. Remsen leaned back in her chair and emitted the most dolorous groan to which she had yet given vent. She had become an adept in the art during these past few days, but this latest effort was such a triumph that it quite startled her listeners.

"Why, Adelaide said Mr. Halford did it," returned Hortense, as soon as she had sufficiently recovered from the effects of her mother's moan to speak again.

"Adelaide is a chattering magpie," cried Mrs. Remsen, roused to speech again. "Things are quite bad enough. She needn't try to disgrace Milly by spreading such reports."

"Oh! she only told me; she will be careful before the world, but among ourselves—"

"Among ourselves the matter need not be discussed," interrupted Milly, with the new firmness and decision she had gained of late. "I beg you to understand, once for all, Hortense, that I broke my engagement with Mr. Halford because I found I did not love him. I never wish to hear his name mentioned again."

"This is the way she goes on," said Mrs. Remsen, disconsolately; "it is enough to drive me distracted."

"But, mamma, if she found that a youthful fancy had deceived her, it was wise to pause in time."

"I shall go to my own room," replied Mrs. Remsen. "I will not hear such language applied to the subject. If you choose to encourage Mildred in her wickedness—"

"I don't, mamma; you misunderstand me. Regarded from a worldly point of view—and one of the worst features of the life and education of the present age is the fact that we must often be, to a certain extent, worldly—Milly has done a very unwise thing."

"I do not want advice, Hortense. My aunt is the only person to whom I should look for it."

"And much attention you pay to it, after it is given," said Mrs. Remsen.

Hortense did not allow her equanimity to be disturbed by Milly's hasty words; she only looked pityingly at them both, thinking what weak creatures they were, and how differently she would behave in the place of either.

"You comprehend me as little as my mother does, Milly," said Hortense, with her loftiest air. "I could say nothing sadder. But I must go now; I have to attend a meeting of the Shirt-sewers' Union and see the Committee on the Hayti Fund, and Professor Drivler dines with us. Oh, Milly! and Mrs. Tonguay, too. If you could only hear her talk, it would do you a world of good."

Milly found herself shuddering at the bare idea.

"I don't wish to hear any one talk just now," she said. "My head is aching fearfully."

"And my heart aches, too," added her aunt, in her very saddest voice. "I do think I am the most unfortunate woman in the world. What your dear mother would say to you if she were alive, I can not imagine."

Milly remembered how that mother had suffered, and became softened by the thought of the sympathy she would have had for this distress, till a wish rose in her mind to be quietly at rest by that mother's side under the green turf, far away from the bustle and weariness of this life.

"Well," said Hortense, "it seems I can say nothing to aid either of you. Mine would be a life thrown away, indeed, if my opinion were of as little importance everywhere as it seems to be here."

11

"Now, Hortense, don't talk nonsense," interposed her mother.

"Oh, mamma, it is indeed so! I can see it plainly. Not that I am angry; I only think how astonished Professor Drivler and others of my friends would be if they saw it. But good-bye to you both. Come and see me very soon."

She gave her mother a dutiful kiss, and Milly a patronizing tap upon the shoulder, smiling grand commiseration of their folly in not seeking and using her advice. Before she reached the foot of the stairs, Mrs. Remsen remembered something that she wished particularly to say to her daughter, and hurried out; so Milly was left to a little quiet, a thing she most longed for and greatly needed.

CHAPTER XXX.

DESPERATE.

It was Saturday at last. Alice Marchmont had remained shut up in her room for two days, so that no report of Milly's broken engagement or Halford's departure had reached her, as Miss Portman was always glad to stay at home, and had taken advantage of her cousin's indisposition to close the doors against visitors, and live as solitary and unsociably as an ancient nun.

This morning Mrs. Marchmont decided to go to Milly. At least, she had a right to demand from the girl how much Dick Faulkner had revealed in regard to her affairs. No matter how Milly behaved, she could not be in a worse position, and she desired before the next night's meeting with Faulkner to know exactly where she stood, so far as the babblings of his wicked tongue were concerned.

She drove to Mrs. Remsen's house, and sent in her card to that lady herself, tolerably certain that if she asked for Miss Crofton she would be denied admittance. Mrs. Remsen was not at home, but Miss Maud happened to be in the reception-room, and gave orders that the visitor should be shown in. She had an envious admiration for Mrs. Marchmont's beauty and grace, and as she seldom had an opportunity of seeing her, determined to have that satisfaction now.

So Alice entered and was very gracious, according to her habit with young girls, and Maud, bold as brass, began to explain that her mamma was out, and that she, Maud, would never be forgiven if she did not detain Mrs. Marchmont till the mother's return.

Mrs. Marchmont was very willing to be detained—at least, for a while—and though she had only seen Maud a few times had sufficiently guaged her mental calibre to know how to flatter her into a complacent mood. That result gained, Alice said, sweetly,

"My visit was partly for your cousin, Miss Crofton. I wanted to see you all. Is she in?"

"Oh, yes," Maud answered, volubly, "she's up in her room—been playing invalid since Mrs. Lawrence's ball."

"Indeed! Not seriously indisposed, I trust."

"Bless me! no," returned the magpie; "just one of her fancies. I suppose she's sorry, now it is too late."

Alice was too busy with her own reflections to notice the girl's words, and only said,

"Would you be kind enough to let her know that I am here?"

"To be sure," said Maud; "but I don't believe she will come down. She stays in her room, and acts as if she was possessed."

She rang the bell, and sent up Mrs. Marchmont's message; presently back came the answer. Miss Crofton was particularly engaged, and could see no one.

"Just like her," pronounced Maud; "but I'll tell mamma how rudely she behaves—ill-natured thing!"

"But you," said Mrs. Marchmont, with her blandest manner and her sweetest smile, "are so kind and frank that I am sure you will do me the favor to say to your cousin that I wish particularly to see her. I have a reason."

"Of course," said Maud, instantly devoured by a rampant curiosity. "What shall I tell her you want?"

"She might be vexed if I did not tell her first," urged Alice, gently.

Maud had to go away unsatisfied, and having after a good deal of difficulty obtained admission to Milly's room, delivered the message.

"I shall not see her," cried Milly, to whom the visit seemed a crowning insult.

"Then I'll ask her to tell me," said Maud, anxious to have her curiosity gratified.

"You will attend to your own affairs, if you please," returned Milly.

"It is my affair," said Maud, in a passion at once. "You need not try to treat me like that any longer. You'll never be married now."

"Have the goodness to go away," was the only answer Milly made.

"I'll go and tell Mrs. Marchmont you say you'll not see her."

"If you add that I will not, now or ever, I shall be much obliged," returned Milly.

Down stairs flew Maud and repeated what Milly had said, adding a rapid account of her cousin's late misdemeanors, including the story of the broken engagement, which Maud vowed was Halford's work because Milly went to Paul Andrews's dinner. Mrs. Marchmont was shocked and pained, but the reason Maud gave prevented her blaming herself for any share in the catastrophe. She got away from the girl's chatter, and hurried out of the house, having gained nothing by the step, as she bitterly thought, except to afford that heartless Milly a fresh triumph. The creature would believe that she had been frightened into an attempt to sue for mercy.

The day got by—the evening. She went to the opera, in spite of Miss Portman's expostulations; and that lady drove her nearly wild the whole evening by her sighs and head-shakings, and her assurances to every body who entered the box that Mrs. Marchmont ought to be at home and in bed. But Alice bore it; she bore the next day's suspense, too; bore seeing Miss Portman depart for church, and the recollection of all which kept herself from joining in the services she had once so dearly prized.

Alice Marchmont went to Mrs. Granger's dinner, and found, just as she expected, several of the leaders of the fast set which she had grown to abhor in the depths of her heart. Dick Faulkner's wife was there, indulging in her little attempts at stinging with sugared words; and, yes, there was Dick himself—Alice saw him bowing to her; and though she had been so anxious to discover what his first look would reveal, it told her very little.

He did not offer to approach her; he looked much as usual, she thought, only paler and more insolent, so that she was sure he had been off on some carouse, such as people said had become frequent with him of late. The half-hour of waiting was nearly over before he came near her. Mr. Lewis had just left her to speak with some new-comer; she could feel Dick Faulkner's approach, and shuddered as if some noxious reptile were crawling toward her.

"I was so sorry not to be able to go to you the day your note reached me," he said. "If you knew what a pleasure it was to me to see even a line of your writing once more!"

She just regarded him with a glance of surprise and disgust which sent the blood to his face.

"You do not believe me?" he persisted.

"I did not listen to what you said," she replied. "There is only one subject upon which I propose to converse with you."

He turned away without another word, just giving her one look out of his black eyes which was absolutely like a flash of fire.

Dinner was announced. Mr. Lewis came to take her in. It seemed to Alice Marchmont that they were walking over a mine which was ready to explode, and that she had no power to save herself—as like a nightmare as if she had been actually in the midst of a horrid dream. She was very gay, though, after the dinner fairly commenced; indeed, she could not tell what demon possessed her, but she could not resist saying the most stinging things to each and every one in turn, and especially tormenting Dick Faulkner. All the while she felt that he was capable of suddenly crying the truth about her in the ears of the charming assembly.

He persisted in talking to her; he was seated nearly opposite, and she could see that he drank even more wine than usual. She would have been glad of any excuse for getting away from his neighborhood; if she could only faint, as she had done a few weeks before! But, no, her nerves seemed braced as they had not been during all these months, and she could not resist daring the danger in every way.

I once heard a man describe being on a railway-engine and seeing a train shoot round a curve toward them, the engineer trying vainly to slacken the speed; he knew that an instantaneous death menaced him, yet he could only stand there and stare at it coming nearer and nearer—utterly incapable of any effort to save himself, if such had been possible—could only stand and stare, while it seemed like some hideous dream, and through the suspense in which every faculty was centred flashed broken thoughts and sudden memories of half a lifetime gone by. I can think of nothing that forms so fit a comparison for Alice Marchmont's state of mind.

She was watching the danger; she knew it came nearer and nearer, yet, through her own reckless talk, through the idle laughter and conversation which went on about her, all manner of things, trifling and grave, events of her past existence would arise.

She could remember a wood where, as a child, she had found wonderful flowers — the variegated blossoms in Mrs. Granger's coiffure recalled them; she could see the lofty pine-trees and her little child-phantom so plainly. Some trivial game with a playmate; a sunny June morning long ago, with Kenneth Halford coming over the lawn to the house, and her old self watching him through the Venetian blinds. Any thing, every thing that was utterly removed from the present; and always she could catch the flash in Dick Faulkner's eyes, observant of her wherever he looked, with whomsoever he talked, and knew that the danger was coming more and more near.

They were discussing a late English novel, a story of a woman's guilty secret ending in discovery, ruin to herself, and disgrace to those connected with her; an adventuress, who had made for herself a place and retained it safely, until out of her own past rose the ruin which overwhelmed her.

"The best part of the book is, that it is true to nature," exclaimed Dick Faulkner, suddenly, as the rest were leaving the subject.

Every one was the more astonished because literature was not his forte, and he had been drinking much Champagne while the volume was under consideration.

"Mr. Faulkner means to astonish us by appearing in a new character," Alice could not avoid saying; "a criticism of a novel. Really, Mr. Faulkner, we shall expect to discover that you have been all this while a genius in disguise, writing the cleverest reviews and hearing us admire them."

"I thought you disliked novels, Mr. Faulkner," said the hostess.

"But I do read them occasionally, though I think Mrs. Marchmont considers me a dunce," he said, with his wickedest smile at Alice.

"Oh no! At least, I never thought that," she retorted, laughing, but with emphasis.

"At all events," continued he, "I read this book; and I must insist that it is natural."

"Ah, very well," said Alice, mockingly; "I retire from the contest. Mr. Faulkner's opinion is doubtless founded upon his choice of acquaintance among the sex, and ought to be as convincing as a veritable argument."

"I think it natural," he went on, in a dogged manner, "because I once knew of a case which was a parallel, at least."

"Let us hear it," cried Mrs. Granger. "I dote upon true stories. You are sure it is true?"

"Perfectly sure," he said. "That would be its sole merit in my way of telling; I can only give the bare details, and Mrs. Marchmont already laughs at me for getting out of my line."

Such an evil smile! did the others notice?

"I promise not to laugh," she said, "oh, most modest *raconteur*; but at the same time I reserve to myself the privilege of doubt if the story is about a woman. You masculines are never correct in your judgments of us."

"I don't judge. This is the story—the man told me who knew. A lady, a great lady, as the novels would say, courted and spoiled by the world, found herself getting dreadfully into debt—"

"Oh, it's a vile slander," interrupted Mrs. Granger. "We won't hear him, will we, Mrs. Marchmont?"

"Yes; we shall want to know how to act when we get into debt," she answered.

She leaned back in her chair, her fingers trifling with a bunch of grapes, and her eyes turned full upon Dick Faulkner's face with a calm smile.

"She must have been a Frenchwoman," said Mr. Lewis. "Wasn't she a Frenchwoman, Faulkner?"

"Oh yes, say a Frenchwoman, if you like," he answered; "shall we, Mrs. Marchmont?"

"Call her the Queen of Sheba, if you will; but please do tell us what she did."

It was coming! At least, suspense was over; that seemed, strange as it sounds, a little comfort.

"She had to pay a sum of money."

"Well," said Mrs. Granger, "she sold her jewels?"

"No!"

"Got married?" suggested some one.

"No, that wasn't in her line. Make a guess, Mrs. Marchmont."

She held up the cluster of grapes in a pretty way, and said, carelessly, never once taking her eyes from his face, and making him feel their power through all his rage and the recklessness caused by wine, "I shall not guess; I'll wait and pronounce a verdict."

"She committed a forgery!"

The women cried out in horror.

"An utter libel!" exclaimed Mrs. Granger.

"Really, Dick," said his wife, "you will never succeed as a *conteur* if you can't keep nearer to the probabilities."

"She committed a forgery!" repeated he.

The cluster of grapes had not fallen from Alice Marchmont's white fingers; she had not stirred, not even seemed to breathe.

"Was she found out?" asked some one.

"Else I should not have heard it, I suppose," said Faulkner. "Yes; a man found it out—a man who had loved her, and whom she had treated in a most outrageous manner."

"What did he do?" inquired a half-dozen voices at once.

Dick Faulkner looked again at the graceful figure opposite—the white hand held the grapes, the eyes regarded him still, the lids just a little drawn over the dilated pupils; but the whole attitude of careless elegance unchanged.

"What do you suppose he did, Mrs. Marchmont?"

"That would depend on the man," said she, speaking without apparent effort. "Was he a gentleman or a villain?"

"Oh, do tell us what he did!" implored the other women.

Alice looked at him still. For the life of him he could not finish; his story was falling flat enough, from the utter impossibility of rousing the slightest show of emotion in her face.

"Perhaps he paid her debts," said Mr. Lewis, "by way of being heroic."

"I don't know what he did," said Faulkner, drinking off his glass of Champagne. "I only wanted to show you that there was nothing improbable in describing a woman of position as doing all sorts of out-of-the-way things."

There was a general chorus of indignation at his attempt at a story, and by the time this was ended the ladies rose from the table.

"I have been learning billiards, Sophy," Mrs. Granger said to Mrs. Faulkner as they ascended to the drawing-room.

"Oh, let us go and play!" she answered. "Those tiresome men will stay down there for an hour, and it is so stupid for us four, all women."

"Shall we go?" asked Mrs. Granger.

"Go, you two, and take Miss James for umpire," said Alice. "I want to go to sleep in the bay-window. I'm tired."

"You haven't looked well for a month past," said Mrs. Granger; not that she had thought of it before that minute.

"Nonsense; I am quite well. Go and play your billiards."

So the three went down the stairs again, the billiard-table being on the dining-room floor, and Alice went on up into the great salon that she so disliked, with its collection of gilded fripperies, and thought that it looked to-night more than ever like an upholsterer's shop.

She had not long to wait. She knew Dick Faulkner would follow her, and she had scarcely seated herself when he came in. He walked straight toward her sofa, and sat down by her side.

"The other ladies are playing at billiards,"

said she, with a little yawn, spreading out her robes between them.

"I know they are; that is the reason that I came up."

"Hadn't you better join them?" she asked, sweetly. "I told them I was going to sleep, and I am nearly so now."

"What did you think of my story?" he asked.

She was fanning herself negligently, as if making an effort to keep awake.

"Frankly," said she, "it was not a success. Either the audience was not sympathetic, or you were not in the vein for story-telling."

"What would they have done, do you suppose, if they could know it was the truth, as you and I did?"

The fan dropped from her hand, and as it hung to her wrist by the silken cord, it rattled against the side of her sofa under the sudden nervous trembling which seized her. The next thing she knew this man had both her hands in his, was holding them in a close, painful grasp, and saying, in a rapid, suppressed voice,

"I love you, Alice—I love you! Don't be so hard—you shall hear me now! Never mind the note; don't think about it! Oh, Alice Marchmont, I'd give my soul for just one smile! Only love me, do try to love me!"

She made one effort and freed her hands, so sick and faint, with a blinding spasm of indignation and outraged womanhood upon her, at his touch.

"One word more," she said, starting to her feet, and speaking in a voice of icy coldness, "and I will summon your wife!"

"Call the whole world," he exclaimed, with a burning, beseeching look. "I'm not ashamed of loving you! I'm sick of this farce of respectability! Call—ah, you don't dare!"

"Continue, and you shall find that I dare any thing—"

"Don't put me in a rage," he interrupted. "You have driven me nearly desperate during these weeks; you can't go further! I swore you should not escape me. Don't make me talk to you like this! Let me tell you I love you as no man ever loved—"

With the remembrance of all she had done to escape this wretch, to be obliged to suffer the contamination of such words!

She made a step toward the bell.

"Take care," said he. "Call, and it will then be too late; you will make me so furious that I shall speak what can't be taken back!"

"There is nothing more you can say to harm me! Great Heaven!" she cried, "if there were, don't you know I'd hear it sooner than such words! If I were drowning, and only your hand could save me, do you think I would be degraded by its clasp?"

"The hand that has held a pen to sign a forged name can't easily be damaged," said he, with a sneering laugh. "There, it's out now! You want war—and you shall have it! You won't let me love you? Then you shall give up to my hate."

She sank back into her seat.

"Yes, that's better," said he.

"I am waiting for an explanation of your words," she said, with forced calmness. "You will be pleased to state distinctly what you mean."

"What is the use of this?" he exclaimed. "No trouble need come to you; I have sworn that! But there's no good in keeping up this pretense of bravado. I'd sell my soul for you."

She turned her back on him in silence.

"Better not," he half whispered. "Remember the note—it's a nice signature—looks well —John Worthington!"

With one last superhuman effort at self-control she faced him again.

"Exactly," she said; "the note with his indorsement upon it. I am ready to pay you the money."

He laughed scornfully.

"There's not money enough in Wall Street to buy it," he said; "so there's no good to talk of that."

"It is mine; you are bound to give it up!"

He laughed again. Nothing could save her! she must go over the precipice—after all, after all!

"We shall see what John Worthington will say to your writing his name on the back of the little paper," he said.

"I think he is quite able, Mr. Faulkner, to manage his own affairs. Is there any thing extraordinary in his obliging as old a friend as I am in that way, if I had chanced to need?"

"Yes; for I heard him say he had never done such a thing for any human being, and never would."

"He is a thorough gentleman, incapable of compromising a woman by talking about her affairs."

"Will you say that he indorsed this note?"

"I will not talk further with you on any subject, Mr. Faulkner. You first insult me with your love—your love—— Great Heaven! that you should dare to misuse such a word!"

"Go on, now. I would not stop you if I could."

"After that, you accuse me of forgery!"

"As I will do to-morrow to John Worthington."

"And John Worthington will have your heart's blood in return. Nonsense, Mr. Faulkner, I am not to be terrified into listening to your offers of affection. Is that the only way in which you have been able to bring any woman near to you? I am of a different make, believe me."

"At all events, I shall ruin you," he went on, as if she had not spoken.

"And I say it is not in your power. Since you can't avenge, you had better take your money."

"I mean to have both," he answered.

"The next time you take the liberty of supposing a lady to have committed a crime, go differently to work, if you wish to terrify her," she said, struggling still, vain as she knew the effort to be.

"It came to me in a flash," he went on, still paying no attention to her words. "You may believe I was waiting till something should happen to put you in my power! When I saw that note in old Hermans's desk, it was all plain to me. He told me in the beginning you had given one—"

"After you had told him the amount, and by your falsehoods made him believe that I had confided in you."

"Just as you please. At least, I found out that to pay me off you had given the note; it flashed across my mind then—the story you and John Worthington were telling last summer about your learning to copy his writing—bah! It was as transparent as day!"

"Have you nearly finished, Mr. Faulkner? All this is very tiresome."

Again, as she stood there in her scornful beauty, though trembling in every limb with terror and despair, the gust of passion swept over him, and he cried out, "Only let me love you; give me one gentle word—a smile; you know I am your slave—"

"Not if it were to save my life—my soul!" she broke in, with a gesture of loathing.

"Then to-morrow I go to John Worthington; he shall know it. I'll take Hermans with me. Don't suppose me a fool; of course he'll hold his tongue, but I can let the world know, and how do you think he will like that? You, that live to be admired and respected! Bah! my revenge will be more complete than if I saw you in prison!"

She was wringing her clasped hands, struggling for breath; he had touched the right chord at last.

"Take in the newspapers, Mrs. Marchmont," he continued; "I promise you there shall be paragraphs worth your reading. Then, if you like, prosecute the editors, and when the case comes on see if John Worthington is able to swear that he indorsed that little bill."

She heard doors open and close on the floor below, the click of billiard-balls, the voices of men and women as the former left the dining-room to overlook the ladies' game. They were not yet coming up—no hope, no help possible.

His voice again took that pleading tone worse to bear than his threats and unmanliness.

"Alice! Alice! only think! It isn't too late; let us forget every thing! Go away with me—let me take you to Italy! I'll make your life like a dream of happiness!"

She turned and fled. At this instant he heard a step on the stairs, and thought that had frightened her. He followed her, whispering, "I'll come to you to-morrow; think of it. You may save yourself yet."

She got up into the dressing-room; she did not faint; she had only one thought—to get out of the house, beyond the sight of that man, the sound of his voice. She must not faint or

go mad there; and yet truly it seemed to her that the final crisis had arrived; her reason was in danger. She drank some water, and wet her forehead with the icy drops; she groped about, blind and dizzy, feeling for the bell-rope; reached it at last, and rang. She had got into a chair when Mrs. Granger's maid came.

"Order me a carriage, please," she said; "I am not well, and must go home."

"Oh, Mrs. Marchmont, you do look so white!" the girl exclaimed, and she was voluble in offers of assistance and exclamations of distress, before Alice could speak again; for Mrs. Marchmont was the admiration of the domestics, on account of her kind ways and words, wherever she went; and Mrs. Granger's French-woman in particular cited her as "the one properly dressed lady in America."

"Shall you have the salts? Is it like an *evanouissement?* I go to call madame—"

"No, no!" said Alice; "don't disturb her. It is nothing but fatigue. I want to get home; just call me a carriage."

"But madame's has this instant arrived; it waits."

"Then find my wraps—yes, that is all. Thank you!"

She ran away, with the kind creature's expostulations in her ears.

"Tell Mrs. Granger I was so unwell I had to go home, and would not disturb her," she had sense enough to say, remembering, even then, that her conduct would need some excuse. There was no one in the drawing-rooms as she hurried past the doors, no one in the hall below, and she left the house unobserved. She sprang into her brougham, and, as the man was closing the door, said,

"Drive to Mr. Worthington's; go quickly!"

She allowed herself no time to think. The order had been given without any actual volition on her part. She had not meant to go there. She had not even been thinking. She covered her face in her wraps, and cowered down in the seat till the carriage stopped. The man ran up the steps and rang. She saw the door open, got out of the brougham into the hall. The housekeeper came into the hall, and said,

"Oh! Mrs. Marchmont, you have driven round for Miss Portman. They are not back yet. Indeed, I think Miss Constance was to take her home."

"At all events, I will wait. I want—is Mr. Worthington in?"

"He's in his study, ma'am."

"I will go to him," she said, and went on through the hall. As she reached the study door, it opened. Mr. Worthington had heard the voices.

"Mrs. Marchmont!" he exclaimed; "and Constance has not come yet."

He caught sight of her face, never staid to utter another word, but led the way into the room and closed the door. She covered her face with her trembling hands.

"Shut the door, John Worthington," she said, hoarsely. "Shut it close!"

A fearful premonition of trouble came over him as he looked at her standing there like the ghost of her former self.

"In Heaven's name, Alice, what has happened?" he exclaimed.

"Do you remember your promise?" she gasped, uncovering her haggard features, "to be my friend—to forgive—"

"Alice! Alice! always!"

"Then the time has come! God help me! John Worthington, I have no hope of help even from you!"

As Alice Marchmont spoke these words, she tottered back and forth, and seemed about to fall. Mr. Worthington started forward, but she would not let him support her.

"Don't touch me," she cried, "don't touch me! You are a good man—an honest man. You should not touch one like me!"

"Alice! Alice! are you mad?" he asked. "Sit down—you are falling!"

"No, I must not. Mad? I don't know. Perhaps this is the last time we shall ever stand face to face. Did I ask you to forgive me? I can't expect that; you will hate me!"

He thought she must be raving; he tried to take her cold hands and put her in a chair. She retreated from him, only crying again, "Don't! don't touch me! I came here to tell you. Let me do it, quick! Oh, my sin! Oh, my God, John Worthington, my shame!"

He made a step backward, putting out his hand as if to check her revelation, his face as white as her own.

"I'll not believe it!" he cried. "If an angel from heaven told me you were guilty, I'd not believe it. You are mad, Alice—you must be mad!"

"I think I have been mad," she moaned. "I do think that, though it is no excuse."

He sat down in the chair which he had pushed toward her; the great drops of perspiration stood on his forehead.

"Tell me your trouble," he said, in a slow, difficult voice; "tell me."

She flung up her arms with an appealing gesture, and sank on her knees at his feet.

"Don't, Alice!" he pleaded. "I can't bear this. I can't see you humiliated."

"The only place for me, the fittest place," she said, "except the prisons where such women as I have been sent! I forged your name, John Worthington!"

She tried hard to keep back the hysterical spasm, fought against it bravely; but it would have its way. She struggled there at his feet in tortures pitiable to witness. He had not spoken; she felt him raise her in his arms and carry her to a sofa. He brought water, and after a time she could swallow a few drops. He bathed her forehead gently, and soon she was able to speak.

"You will think I am making a scene," she said, brokenly, "to enlist your sympathy—"

"Hush! hush!" he interrupted, finding words at last. "Don't say such things to me! I am thanking the Merciful Father that it is not the old story—the sin I should have expected from another woman's lips!"

"He pities me!" she sobbed—a dry, choking sob, more painful than tears. "I don't deserve it, I don't deserve it! Oh, you don't understand, you don't know what I said! I have forged your name."

"And did I not promise you that there should be nothing which I would not do for you?" he said. "Surely I can let you use my name. Only be calm, be quiet, and tell me every thing. The worst is over for you now—nothing shall touch you."

"Oh, nothing could be so horrible as what I have endured! If I could have asked God's help, as you did just now, this would not have come to me! I have been so wicked in my pride. I have forgotten every thing in my mad vanity, or I should not have been left to fall into this fearful sin."

"A sin, Alice, for which your bitter remorse is atonement—your confession ample amends."

"Oh no, no; I should never have made the confession if escape had been possible—there is no help! But I have suffered, oh, I have suffered! Such days and nights, John Worthington! if I could tell you the half! No wonder I have grown pale and old in these weeks; and there is gray in my hair, John! Oh, it seems as if I had lived an eternity since that fearful day!"

"My poor child! Poor little Alice!"

She could not see the movement he made as if he would have taken her in his arms, and shielded her against his heart even, from every painful memory. She had buried her face in the cushions at the sound of his tender words, and cried out,

"Don't speak so to me; you'll kill me with your kindness! I can't bear it!"

He sat down by her side, smoothing her hair gently with his hand, but not speaking till the sobs were checked again, and she lay quiet.

"When you can, you shall tell me all about it," he said. "I would not ask you to say another word, only that it will be better for you to tell me, and then I am quite sure I can arrange every thing."

"I can tell you," she answered, sitting upright, and trying to look in his face. The emotion she saw there, and above all the yearning pity, so overwhelmed her with remorse that she could only fall at his feet once more, crying,

"Forgive me! only say you forgive me! But don't speak so kindly, don't look like that! If you do, I think I must die here."

The tears rained down. For weeks she had been able to shed none, but now it seemed as if she would weep her very life away. He let her cry. He knew how near madness she must have been, and that nothing could help her so much as those tears. He did not attempt to raise her. She sat there at his feet, shedding those blessed tears, and at last she heard his voice, saying softly,

"*Hear my prayer, O Lord! and let my crying come unto thee. Hide not thy face from me in the time of my trouble; incline thine ear unto me and hear me. Yea, like as a father pitieth his own children, even so the Lord is merciful.*"

The blessed words from the dear Liturgy, which had once been so familiar to her. Even her tears slowly ceased, and it seemed to Alice Marchmont as if God had sent one of his pitying angels to whisper these assurances in her agony. They sat in silence for a little, then she said, in a quiet voice,

"I can tell you now—all the miserable story."

She sat there at his feet and told it, concealing nothing, and beginning further back than the time when I took up the record of her life. She told him of the old, old days of her girlhood, when they had separated her from all that would have made her girlish happiness. She told him of the lonely years with a husband who had not been as tender as he ought of the young creature he had taken to his keeping, for she had not deceived him; when he had married her, he knew that she had no heart to give him. She kept back no detail of her wicked extravagance during the ensuing years, when she had been dazzled by her newly-regained liberty and the adulation of the world; while in her ignorance and folly it had seemed to her that her fortune was inexhaustible—without the slightest thought she had spent the thousands lying ready for investment at the time of her husband's death.

Dick Faulkner's connection with her life; her allowing him to win money for her; her debts and troubles, and the harassing sense of degradation; her permitting him to keep on, because each week she believed his promises, and that she was about to realize a sufficiency to pay him and all her other debts. She kept nothing back. She made no effort to excuse herself; she did not think that excuse was possible. But it was a blessed comfort to sit there, at his feet, and tell the whole; to feel that she had no longer to bear her guilt in secret; that, whatever might come, she had done all she could to atone; and now, whatever he decided upon she was anxious to do.

"I want you to tell me," she said; "and I'll do it. I can't thank you for your kindness, but oh! John Worthington, you are a good man; and when you meet my father in the other world—the father who died when I was an innocent little girl—he'll thank you for your kindness to me."

"Don't talk of thanks, Alice; there's no such word between you and me—you—"

"Because you pity me so," she exclaimed, "you feel so now; but oh! to-morrow and to-morrow, and for all times to come! You'll think then—how can you help it? not harshly, I know; but you'll always remember! You wouldn't like to see me near Constance; then you would think of it. I must go away; I can

not look at the face of any human being I have ever known. Ah, how lonely! John Worthington, if only people could know in advance the bitterness of sin, they would keep their hearts right by prayer—if only they could know!"

"Alice, I can't hear you talk like this! Child, the Saviour forgave all penitent sinners. Repentance brings a sure forgiveness; and a sin forgiven is swept away forever out of the soul, only as its memory keeps the heart full of thankfulness to Him who died for us."

"You are so good—so good! You don't despise me as I do myself?"

"My child, what right have I to despise a penitence that the Highest of all finds acceptable?"

So many years since she had heard such words, or thought such feelings possible!

"You must not talk any more to-night," he said; "you must have absolute quiet, and leave this matter to me. Will you stay here, or will you go home?"

"Oh, let me go home—let me go now before Constance comes! I can not, must not see her!"

"You shall go home. Don't look so frightened; you are worn out."

"It comes over me anew," she sighed, "each time I think. Yes, let me go home."

"And don't think about this any more; think of nothing to-night but rest. These weeks are gone—dead; there is nothing needed but that man's silence and the note, and both are easy to have. His manner of obtaining it has placed him in our power."

"Oh, does it? Can you get it?" she asked, remembering once more the dreaded world's scorn, which she had nearly forgotten in John Worthington's forgiveness. "You'll send me word? Oh, I remember—he said he should come to-morrow. Don't let him come to-morrow; I can't bear it!"

"There is no danger of his troubling you again at any time. I have your authority, and shall prevent it. I shall see you to-morrow morning, and meantime you will try to rest?"

He wrapped her up tenderly, and said,

"I shall tell Constance you waited—no one will think there was any special reason for your visit."

"You think of every thing!"

"All I want is to think of something to give you a night's sleep."

"And I haven't had one in so long—so long! Oh, those nights!"

"Don't think of them; all that is ended now, and you can rest," he said. "Come, now; I will put you in your carriage."

She hesitated a little.

"What is it, Alice?"

"Oh, I can not say it! I haven't any words—"

"It doesn't need saying, Alice."

As he put his hand on hers to draw it through his arm, she bent her head and pressed her lips on it with a feeling of such pure devotion as she had never felt for any human being since the day when she could recollect her father's pardon for some childish fault. She felt his strong frame quiver in every nerve, but he did not speak.

They went through the hall in silence, and he placed her in the carriage.

"Good-night, now," he said. "You promise me to rest and sleep?"

"Yes, and I think I can, too. I owe it to you; whatever peace my life may ever find, I shall owe to you."

She was driven away, back to the home she had left with such a frightful sensation of having in the world no place of refuge. She entered it now with the feeling of one who had seen an earthquake suddenly yawn before his feet, and when he seemed about to be overwhelmed in the darkness the chasm closed, and the stars came out in the heaven above.

That night a merciful slumber without dreams locked her senses, so long stranger to them, and gave her new strength to meet the waking and the new day which must come.

CHAPTER XXXI.

CÆSAR'S CONFESSION.

So these first days dragged by for Milly. There were useless discussions between herself and her aunt, endless reproaches and complaints, which threatened to end in destroying all affection between the two.

Milly was determined to be brave and show no wound. She saw every one who visited at the house, and forced herself to appear the same as usual. She laughed and talked so gayly, and played her part so well, that the world went away completely puzzled, and almost inclined to believe that she had had matters her own way where Kenneth Halford was concerned. But the reaction when she was once more alone was terrible. It was well for her that spring had come and the festivities of winter were nearly over, and people busy preparing to get away from town, or the strain upon her nerves would have broken her down completely. As it was, they were worn to the most acutely sensitive state; the sudden opening of a door made her spring from her chair; a loud voice would give her a headache which lasted for hours. She was obliged to see Mrs. Lawrence; for, notwithstanding Mrs. Remsen's lecture, the little woman was so conscience-stricken about Milly that she actually made her way into her presence one day when she had met the belligerent aunt in the street, and knew she might enter the house in comparative safety.

"Oh, Milly, little Milly!" she exclaimed, beginning to cry at once, "I am so sorry; I never meant you any harm, believe me. I just thought it fun, and I have quarreled with Paul Andrews, and I've told every one you didn't go; and if you did, it was without knowing

whose dinner it was; and I wish my feet had been cut off before I did it;" and here she broke down, and Milly had to comfort her—it was the first sincere sympathy the poor child had met with.

"Dear Mrs. Lawrence, you have done nothing; I don't care about these ill-natured reports."

"Yes, but I've ruined your happiness; your engagement is broken off."

"But not on that account. It was all my own doing. Mr. Halford did not even know of the dinner until afterward."

Mrs. Lawrence brightened wonderfully, and very soon was offering protestations of friendship for the future without stint.

"I wish you would be my guest at Newport this summer for a nice long visit; I'm sure your aunt must be horrid cross just now. Won't you promise, dear?"

But Milly had no desire for gayety; moreover, she would not have chosen to trust herself to Mrs. Lawrence's care, even if her aunt would be willing—a thing not probable.

"If ever I can help you, dearest little Milly, you may be sure I will. I declare, if I should die before you are married, I'll leave you all the money I can will away from my husband's relatives—see if I don't!"

Milly assured her that she much preferred her continuing to live, and made her laugh at the droll speeches under which she was learning to conceal her suffering.

"I do wish you would come and see me; but I don't suppose your aunt would let you," said Mrs. Lawrence.

"No, I suppose not," Milly said, frankly.

"Well, I can't blame her. Of course, she is furious about your losing such a chance, and blames every body concerned; but you are not angry with me, little Milly; you are sure you are not?"

"Indeed I am not, dear Mrs. Lawrence; I think you are as kind-hearted as it is possible to be, and I like you very much."

"You are a little darling!" cried she. "I just wish you were my own niece; you should break as many engagements as you pleased; you would be so nice to have always near one."

Milly thought of her own temper and bitter feelings of late, and was heartily ashamed to be the recipient of so much praise; but Mrs. Lawrence would not hear a word to gainsay her own opinion.

"I like you so much more than any young lady I ever knew," she said. "If you should ever need a friend, do promise to come to me. I suppose I must go now. If your Aunt Remsen found me with you she would be furious; but I was quite determined to see you."

"And you must go away feeling that you have never done me any harm," said Milly.

"That will be a great comfort, and you really don't look unhappy. People think me frivolous and silly; but I do love you, and can understand you. I used to be a different sort of woman once—indeed I did!" She sighed, and the tears came into her eyes; tears for some faded romance in her younger days; but she was too cheerful really to repine.

"The Lord knows when I shall see you again," she said. "I am going down to the Island soon, my dear. Keep up your courage, and remember what I have said."

She kissed Milly a dozen times, repeating every sort of extravagant proffer, and went away greatly relieved in her kind heart and mind. Then, before many days foolish young Charley Thorne must needs present himself to Milly, and, after many pretexts and transparent evasions, pour out his tender story.

"Oh, Miss Milly, it wasn't for any of these things that I came—you know it wasn't! I love you so—I have always loved you! I was broken-hearted when I heard you were engaged to Mr. Halford; but they say you have sent him off. Miss Milly, I came to ask you to care for me a little—to marry me, and let me try to make you happy."

Milly was overcome with remorse when she remembered how, in her recklessness and anger with another, she had led this young man on to love her, forgetting that it might be sad and earnest to him.

"I am so sorry, oh! so sorry," she faltered. He looked in her face and saw the sympathy there, but nothing more. He was not brilliant or deep, but he really loved her in his boyish, impetuous way, and his love made him clear-sighted enough to understand now that he had no hope.

"You mean you can't care for me," he said. "I know what being sorry means! Oh, Miss Milly, don't you think you ever could?"

"Never, Charley, never, I'm quite sure; but I wouldn't have grieved you for the world."

"Never mind all that," said he, bravely, "only I did so hope; I couldn't help it, you know. For all they said you were engaged, you were so kind and pleasant that I was fool enough to think perhaps you did like me a little, and had been drawn into that other affair against your wishes."

He said this without having the least idea how his words reproached Milly, making her see her coquetry in an entirely new light—as an absolute sin against that other young heart.

"I wish you could feel differently about it, Milly; I'm rich, you know, and I'd try so hard to make you happy."

"Don't, Charley; please don't."

"I won't say another word if it pains you, Milly. What makes you look so sad and changed? People say you are gayer than ever since Halford went away, but I can see you are not at all the same."

His love gifted the foolish fellow with new perceptions; he could feel that he beheld another Milly sitting there, very unlike the girl with whom he had danced and made merry, though he could not have explained his thought.

"I'll tell you, what, Milly," he exclaimed,

suddenly. "If that fellow Halford has treated you ill, I'll follow him to the ends of the earth and punch his head. I always did hate him."

He looked eager to be dispatched on the journey at once, and Milly hastened to set his mind at rest.

"No one has treated me ill, dear Charley; but I have behaved shamefully to you, and I ask your pardon for it."

"Now, don't," he stammered. "You'll have me making a fool of myself in a minute, and I mustn't do that. Oh, Milly, I wish you could love me! I'm twenty-one now; my fortune is all my own, and I know if you don't marry me I shall get into no end of scrapes, and perhaps ruin myself."

"Don't say so, Charley, for that would make me very unhappy."

"Would it—would it, really now?"

"Indeed, indeed it would!"

"Then I'll do no such thing. I'll be as steady as a light-house. I'll not spree, even if the fellows do call me a muff," cried Charley, bravely. "I wish I only had a regularly good head-piece—I'd—I'd do something so grand and magnificent that you'd be glad to love me. But I'm good for nothing," sighed honest Charley, "unless it's at getting up tableaux and playing billiards, and they're no good, you know. A fellow can't go about making a picture of himself, or being like that French chap—what's-his-name—that'll send a billiard-ball clear round a corner and bring it back to pocket."

Milly looked at him and listened; he seemed so very young, years and years younger than herself in her experience and distress; and she envied him his youth and freshness, even his folly.

"And you are sure you couldn't care for me?" persisted Charley.

"Only as a sister might, Charley; in that way I care a great deal for you, and always shall."

"Yes, that's nice," said Charley, doubtfully. "It's what women always say to the men they won't marry. Oh dear! I'm sure I don't know what to do with my life—it's an awful bore, you know! You see I have been building a sort of chateau—what-do-you-call-it?—I never could remember the French word; and now its tumbled about my ears, and I stand like—the fellow among the ruins of Carthage, you know," said Charley, with dramatic effect, recalling the simile from some long-forgotten school-book.

"But you will try and get over it soon, Charley, and find out how much better it is for you, and cease to care for me in that way."

"Maybe so," said Charley, ruefully; "so does a fellow get over the toothache, but it hurts deucedly while it lasts."

Here was Charley Thorne attempting comparisons and being imaginative; but Milly was too sick at heart to smile at his oddities or blunders. She had to send him away convinced at last; but when it came to parting he grew desperate, and nearly blubbered.

"I never thought I should wish to use my new revolver except for fun," sighed he; "but I'd like to, now."

He was so dismally in earnest, that Milly's self-reproaches and sorrow for his pain would not permit her to get impatient with the poor boy.

"Well," cried he at last, "I must say good-bye! You've made my life a blank, Miss Milly, but it isn't your fault! I feel just like the man in Tennyson, you know—

'Oh, my Amy, mine no more—
Oh, the barren, barren moor-land!
Oh, the dreary, dreary shore!'

Only I don't think you're false or shallow, you know; but I'm sure Broadway and the Avenue will be a desert to me now, and the Park a deal more lonesome than any moor-land."

He got as far as the door, but had to come back; it was all cruelly serious with him, and he was suffering to the full extent of his capacity. He kissed Milly's hands, quoted more Tennyson, slapped his forehead as he had seen Edwin Booth do in a play, and then he flung himself out of the room.

As ill-luck would have it, he met Mrs. Remsen in the hall, and as keeping his emotions secret was not an art in which Charley excelled, he was fain to tell her his troubles, and his determination of doing something desperate, before Milly had begged him not.

Mrs. Remsen was seized with an idea. Why should not Milly take possession of this silly boy and his half-million, and bring him up reasonably? Plenty of girls would have accepted him thankfully. If Milly only would do so, everything might be arranged, and Mrs. Remsen's anxieties at rest. She contented herself with telling Charley that young women often changed their minds, and that he must not consider all at an end and lose courage. "Faint heart never won fair lady."

"That's what the play says. Mary Gannon used to do the boy so well in it," said Charley; "but I don't know about it. Milly might do exactly what she pleased with me; I'd never cross her—such a pony-carriage as she should have! I wouldn't even let the dogs into the house if it bothered her;" and after this concession Charley felt that masculine devotion could go no further.

"I am sure you would be a kind husband," Mrs. Remsen said, determined, under the influence of her new idea, not to see that he was a fool.

Charley was flattered by the praise, and took himself off less burdened with black despair, though he went along the street muttering,

"I feel like Mariana in the 'Moated Grange,' by Jove!

'She only said, "My life is dreary;
He cometh not," she said;
She said, "I am aweary, aweary,
I would that I were dead!"'

That's it, for all she wasn't a fellow; it just expresses it."

He thought of numberless self-pitying and pathetic bits of poetry, and went resolutely home to be miserable over his woes, in spite of meeting Jack Norris and Harry Colville, and other choice spirits of his own calibre, who tried to lure him into Phelan's for billiards, or Delmonico's for luncheon.

Charley Thorne shook them off impatiently. Billiards, he said, were "a drug;" food was "disgusting." Even the sight of a wonderful little black-and-tan dog Jack Norris had gave him no pleasure, and Harry Colville's stunning trowsers and gorgeous scarf failed to awaken envy in his soul.

"There's a gulf between me and them," said Charley to himself, as he trudged through Union Square; "a gulf they can't bridge over, except with Byron's 'Bridge of Sighs,' by Jupiter! I know just how those chaps used to feel when they went over it. I shall go out of town; maybe I'd better go back to Europe; that's what the fellows always do in English novels—rush over to the 'Continent.' I wonder why the rest of Europe isn't the Continent as well as Paris, for it's always just going to Paris they mean by it. Oh dear, I'm very wretched! If I was to go and see those terrier-pups to-day; but I sha'n't; I've no heart for anything now. There goes Tom Sora; and it's Lydia Mason walking with him, and they look so happy—Oh I hate them—I hate the whole world; I wish I was dead!"

Charley banged his hat down over his eyes, and strode home, as miserable in his own way as more rational and broader-minded people are in theirs.

Mrs. Remsen was at the same time advising Milly to marry Charley Thorne, and Milly was so outraged that she seemed to have reached the crowning moment of her humiliation and misery.

"I begin to believe, Aunt Remsen, that you would sell me, body and soul," she said. "I marry that boy, that baby without an idea in his head!"

"But he is so rich; he would be very kind; he is good looking, and of good family. Many a girl would be glad enough to get him."

"Let them take him, I beg."

"I never saw a girl throw away her life and prospects as you do! You would not marry Halford, a man of mind and brain; you won't marry Charley Thorne, because he is a fool. In Heaven's name, what would you wish to have?"

"I wish for nothing, Aunt Remsen, except to be left alone."

"You'll not have offers of marriage every day! I never knew so lucky a girl, or one who so recklessly rejected her chances."

"Aunt Eliza, would you like to see me marry Charley Thorne? Answer honestly."

"I know twenty girls who would be only too rejoiced to do it," she answered, evasively.

"I have not a feeling in common with him;

he could no more share my thoughts than I could understand Hebrew."

"Oh! if you are going to talk like Hortense, I have done. Having genius, and soul, and inward yearnings for congeniality, and Heaven knows what other nonsense, may be all very well for a young lady with a fortune; but when she has hardly a penny of her own, I call such things downright wicked, and if they don't bring a judgment on your head I shall wonder."

Mrs. Remsen reproached Milly bitterly; but I suppose she would have been sorry to see her sacrificed in this way. At the moment, all she could think of seemed to be the madness of deliberately throwing away a half-million of money.

"You could be married at once," she said; "and that would put an end to all the stories about you. Charley would take you to Europe immediately. Why, he would be a perfect slave to any whim of yours."

"And the sin, Aunt Remsen—the wickedness of marrying a man whom I could not love nor even respect, whose weakness I must indeed despise. You say nothing of these."

"And you, you think nothing of repaying my long years of affection with ingratitude, of the wickedness of making one a skeleton with anxiety about your future. You don't think of these things in this moment of delicacy and religious scruples."

This series of excitements, following in such rapid succession, was killing little Milly. She wrung her hands, and burst into a torrent of despairing tears that frightened Mrs. Remsen, who knew better than any one how terribly her nerves had been tried.

"I shall say no more," she continued, "though I don't know how we are to get on this summer; I feel as poor as a church-mouse. What I can afford must be spent upon Maud, and we must economize."

"I want nothing, Aunt Remsen—nothing but rest."

"As for keeping the governess, I think it a useless expense this summer," pursued Mrs. Remsen. "What with some money I have lost, and all that I have spent upon your winter, so certain was I of your doing well, that I feel quite penniless for the present."

"I will teach the children, do any thing for them, as I have told you. Let me go down into the country; I shall be so glad to get away. I can take the children, and that will be an economy. You will be able to go with Maud to a watering-place."

"I am in a nice state of mind for society," sighed Mrs. Remsen; "you have so dispirited me. How can I tell that Maud will not behave in the same way—fly in the face of Heaven just as her good luck is all accomplished and ready to accept?"

Milly might have added that she hoped that Maud would not have all her hopes blighted when they looked most blooming, her faith in human nature, her trust in life, almost her belief in the goodness of God, shaken to its foundation by a blow from the very hand which had promised to make existence brighter and more beautiful. But she had grown shy of giving utterance to her feelings, even before her aunt. So Milly remained silent.

"Perhaps you think Maud's future of little consequence," said Mrs. Remsen.

"Indeed, Aunt Remsen, I was thinking a great deal about it, and hoping that it might be bright and pleasant."

"There shall be no more nonsense," said her aunt, forcibly; "on this I am determined. I have learned to my cost what romance and poetical feelings lead to."

Milly shivered at her aunt's harsh tone; Mrs. Remsen had imagination enough to understand Milly somewhat; but, after all, when one is vexed and disappointed it is very difficult to be generous, and one is prone to lose respect for romance and poetry when they stand in the way of getting one's youthful charges successfully settled in the world.

The time that Mrs. Remsen had named for leaving town was the first week in May, and it arrived at last, although to Milly it had seemed that the day would never come. Matters had been more definitely arranged between aunt and niece, and the actual dislike which seemed at one time imminent was gradually passing from their minds. Milly had promised to be governess to the little girls, and Rob was to be sent to boarding-school. No more holiday life for Milly; she felt she must be useful, since she had so lamentably failed in the ornamental part, and wished to make all the amends in her power.

Maud was horribly disappointed and disagreeable when she was made aware of the plans in contemplation for the summer, and she rebelled with an explosion of wrath, as loud as she dared make it in her mother's presence, mingled with premonitions of the avalanche of reproach which would fall on Milly's devoted head at the first convenient opportunity.

"Go into the country now, and to stay, and at that horrid poky place I have always so hated!" cried the young lady. "And you promised me that I should go to Newport; you know you did, mamma!"

"But you wouldn't care to go there before August?"

"I shall die of stupidity in the country, I know I shall," moaned Maud. "Not a soul to speak to that one cares about—oh dear! oh dear!"

Just then she was seized with a brilliant thought. Adelaide was good-natured to her, when it did not interfere with her own comfort, and Mr. Ramsay was always so. Maud felt confident that, if she bemoaned her fate in his hearing with sufficient clamor to penetrate the abstraction in which he passed the time out of business hours, he would bid Adelaide snatch her from the impending fate. So, when the process of packing for the journey commenced, Miss Maud arrayed herself and departed to her brother-in-law's mansion, looking like Niobe, just before the process of petrifying that damp and unhappy female. She was so fortunate as to find Mr. Ramsay at home, as she expected, for it was near the dinner hour; and what was equally satisfactory, her sister Adelaide was in an unusually good humor, as she had coaxed her husband into giving her a lovely brooch and ear-rings that day.

"I have come to dinner," announced Miss Maud; "and I am as miserable as I can possibly be."

Mr. Ramsay came out of his brown study, and nodded pleasantly, as he had only heard the first part of her announcement, relapsing immediately into abstraction.

"Great bear!" thought Maud; "I'd like to pinch you into a little feeling!"

Adelaide displayed her jewelry for Maud, and she was forced to admire it in spite of the bitterness in her soul, for fear of the consequences; but she took the earliest occasion to begin the recital of her wrongs, and Adelaide grew more amiable than ever, after roundly abusing poor little Milly.

"I'd rather die, Adelaide, than be buried in the country. I think mamma is downright cruel, and, as for Milly, I quite begin to hate her."

"She's horribly aggravating," returned Mrs. Ramsay; "it's all her fault, I'm sure, and I wonder mamma has any patience with her."

"If you were in my place you would go perfectly wild," pursued Maud. "Oh, I don't know what I shall do!"

She fretted and complained, occasionally glancing toward Mr. Ramsay; but his thoughts were full of some Western railway stock that had risen astonishingly in the market that morning, and he did not even remember that she was in the room. At last Maud began to weep; she bubbled and trickled like a mountain brook, and distressed Adelaide, because such noisy grief interfered with her comfort; but the desired effect was at length attained. Mr. Ramsay heard, came out of his meditations, and exclaimed,

"Heyday, pussy, what in the world is the matter?"

Maud only sobbed the louder, and Adelaide said,

"She's in despair at having to go down to the country place; and mamma is so discouraged by Milly's horrid conduct that she has no spirits left for any thing else."

"You don't want to go into the country, pussy?" said Mr. Ramsay, kindly.

"Oh, it's horrid!" sobbed Maud; "it's enough to kill any one."

"Well, well, don't cry so; you'll spoil your pretty eyes! Stay with us; Adelaide can take you to Saratoga, and then you can go with her to Newport, too. Don't cry!"

Maud was in an ecstasy of delight; this was better than she had dared even to hope. Adelaide, being softened by Maud's judicious admiration of herself and her new jewels, and animated by a desire to punish Milly by the contrast, entered into the scheme with sufficient satisfaction. Maud went home in delight, and informed her mother of her good fortune, and Mrs. Remsen was almost as glad as her daughter at the turn affairs had taken.

"I shall go to Adelaide at once," said Maud. "I can do no good here, can I, mamma?"

"None in the least," Mrs. Remsen replied, truthfully enough. "You had better get your trunks packed, and go to-morrow. I can arrange with Adelaide to get you any thing else you may need."

So Maud escaped the discomforts and disagreeables of the last days one spends in a house under such circumstances. It would have been a shadow upon that gentle young person's happiness if she could have known how much Milly was relieved by her departure, and with what satisfaction she looked forward to the quiet of the country, undisturbed by her cousin's uncongenial presence; but Maud, feeling sure that Milly must be wretched over the contrast to her good luck and anticipated summer of content, departed in the full tide of bliss.

Mrs. Remsen, Milly, and the children went down into the country; but, before their departure, a revelation was made to Milly, which somewhat softened the fierce anger and sense of injury that had helped her to keep up a show of courage.

Cæsar, the coffee-colored, was going, as he always did in the summer, to coin gold at a watering-place, and lord it as head waiter over more humble and deeper-tinged companions in labor. The evening before his departure he asked for an interview with Milly. Cæsar's dark-hued conscience had awakened; he knew very well what had happened to Milly, as servants always do know the troubles in the family, and Cæsar took remorse to himself in the affair of the note which his young mistress had given him, and which had lain for so many days forgotten in the recesses of Julius Hannibal's treacherous pocket, that the two ebony idiots decided that it was of no use whatever then to deliver it. Cæsar could not make up his mind to leave the house without confessing his guilt, for he cherished a chivalrous devotion for Milly; but he put off his revelation, like a wise creature, until the moment when it could do no possible good. He told his story with the grandiloquence peculiar to his race, beginning with,

"I little 'spected Miss Milly, that annoyings could ever reach you from any resource where I was connected, but I trusted to friendship, and friendship has proved a Gorgorious knot, which I had to cut distinctively."

Cæsar wrote for an Ethiopian paper, and was a poet much admired among the select circles in colored society where he moved. In consequence of this turn of mind, his conversation was often so flowery and ornate, to say nothing of its peculiarity, that it was difficult to discover his precise meaning, a difficulty not quite unheard of, however, in the case of other poets. But he soon made himself clear enough for Milly's comprehension by producing the unfortunate note, wrapped in tissue-paper and tied with a pink ribbon, as he had laid it carefully aside after its recovery; and he bowed before Milly, as he presented it, with a contrite air which would have made the fortune of a "negro minstrel," if it could only have been reproduced in its perfection.

Milly had no thought of reproving him — where would be the good of doing so now? She took the billet, told Cæsar that it was not of the slightest importance, and thanked him for his honesty, though it had come somewhat too late.

——————◆——————

CHAPTER XXXII.

OVERREACHING HIMSELF.

SEVERAL days elapsed before John Worthington could see Faulkner, for business had called him out of town. During this time Worthington did not go to Mrs. Marchmont. He knew that his presence would only be a pain until he could tell her that the matter was definitely arranged. He wrote her a kind letter, begging her to feel no uneasiness, and she rested upon that assurance. At length he grew tired of the waiting himself—at least, he could not bear the idea of her suffering this suspense any longer. She received another note—he had gone to Washington in search of the man.

Dick Faulkner's schemes at this juncture had led him further than he contemplated, and he was at the capital, hoping to gain private information as to the way certain bills before Congress would turn, in order that he might strike some grand *coup* in stocks, and relieve himself from his present embarrassment—the first check which he had met since he commenced his bold operations. Worthington was in a position to do him great harm in the opinions of the honorable members and senators whom he wished to reach; and his arrival, and the fact that Mrs. Marchmont had actually revealed the whole truth, was an unexpected blow.

There was a private meeting between the two men; and, before it ended, John Worthington gave the coward a secret to guard on his own account, for he shook him until he was black in the face; and probably, since the days of his boyhood, Dick Faulkner had never received so thorough a chastisement. It grew out of his venturing to sneer at Mrs. Marchmont when irritated by Worthington's cool assumption of a right to claim the note.

"You couldn't swear it was yours; you couldn't deny, if it came to a trial, that the woman was a forger," he said.

"There is no possibility that any such question should arise," Mr. Worthington answered, with ominous composure. "There may be a trial, but it will be against you. Mrs. Marchmont gave a promissory note to the man Hermans, with my indorsement on the back—"

"A forged indorsement!" broke in Dick.

"When she went to take it up," pursued Worthington, more quietly than ever, "she found that you had stolen it."

"I paid the money."

"Exactly; but you represented yourself as her agent—exhibited a letter which Hermans will swear you said was written by her the day before, to give you the authority for action. Miss Portman will swear that this letter was written months previous, and referred to an entirely different business. The case is a very clear one, Mr. Faulkner; I shall have the pleasure of conducting it myself."

Dick Faulkner began to have the look of a feline animal driven into a corner.

"Also, in connection with that case there will be brought up another," continued John Worthington. "Since your arrival here, you and your agents have been guilty of an attempt at bribery of certain members of Congress for the furtherance of a bill you want carried through."

"I never offered a penny to one of them."

"I am aware of that; but promises to secure them a share in your gains, and an offer to make your word good in advance, constitute bribery just the same."

Faulkner attempted to bluster, but the effort was so signal a failure that he recognized its absurdity, and said, sullenly,

"Well, what do you want?"

"To take up the note with my name on the back, which you obtained under false pretenses, and give you my check for the amount."

Faulkner pulled the bill out of his pocket, received the check in exchange, and might have escaped further humiliation had he been able to restrain his tongue.

"You've got the whip-hand of me," said he, with a malicious grin. "You're about the shrewdest man I ever met, John Worthington, I'll own that! But there are some things you can't set right. You can't make my lady an honest woman; you can't hinder the fact that every time you look at her you will remember she's a forger; you can't prevent her knowing you think it, or help her forget that she came near being my—"

He never finished that sentence. Then it was that he found himself clutched in Worthington's nervous arms, and, though a strong man himself, lifted bodily like a child, and flung on the floor in the struggle. I am happy to add that John Worthington also so far forgot his habitual control as to apply the toe of his boot vigorously to the prostrate form. An account of a duel would have been more dramatic, but not so pleasurable to narrate, nor so sore a punishment to the dastardly wretch.

The morning after this occurrence, Alice

Marchmont sat waiting for her visitor almost with such feelings as men of old must have waited for the coming of the angels who sometimes visited them. I think the comparison is not too strong, nor do I mean to be irreverent. It was the very thought in her mind. Could there remain a hope that her repentance would prove effectual had the feeling been less?

He had saved her—this man whom she had been afraid to trust—saved her, and given her back to life. She could see, too, that her sin was not so much against him as against her own soul; but it was only now that she saw this. During those weeks of blind anguish, her chief dread was in losing the respect and admiration of those about her, and, worst, the idea that exposure would deprive her of his esteem and friendship. It was horrible enough to be flung down from her place in the world—to become the theme of gossip and execration; but to live without him was more terrible.

Now she was willing to accept her humiliation; she had not been brave enough to confess her folly and obtain his aid; she had elected to commit the sin, and must endure the expiation.

She wondered, as she sat there, what life would be to her henceforth. She could not take it up from the spot where this great trouble had made the break. In all time to come, existence must be very different to her from any thing which had gone before. But nothing was clear to her mind as yet; nothing beyond the thankfulness, the penitence, the desire to be set right.

So occupied was she with her reflections that John Worthington entered the room before she was aware, and saw her face as it looked in her solitude—very pale still, but with the restlessness and anxiety, the repression and fear quite gone out of it—a purer, sweeter face than it had been in years. She did not rise; she was feeble, as if after a long illness. She put out her hands in silence; he took them in his own, and held them in that firm, gentle grasp which gave her a sense of such protection.

"It is all arranged," he said; "I must repeat what I wrote, so that we may be done with the subject forever."

"And you went after him—you saw him!"

"Understand me," he said; "it is all over."

"All over!" She whispered the words as a man might the sentence of his reprieve coming when he was in sight of the scaffold.

"Arranged without his even having the privilege of an evil thought, Alice; but I told no untruths."

"No, no; I am sure of that."

"So it is over, and there is a whole new life before you."

He sat down by her, and she looked at him with the trust and confidence which, before these troublous times, had offered so beautiful a contrast to her capricious moods with others.

"And that is what I want to know about," she said. "I want to have a new life. I think

for a time I must go away. It will be better for me. I can't explain what I mean. I sha'n't go just because I am ashamed to meet you and know what must be in your thoughts; I would try to bear that—?

She had spoken more and more slowly—could get no further.

"Shall I show you one way to a new life?" he asked.

"Yes; you will help me."

She did not notice that his face had grown a little pale, and that his hand trembled as it rested on her chair.

"Will you be my wife, Alice?" he asked, softly.

She looked at him for an instant, doubtful whether she could have heard aright.

"Will you be my wife?" he continued, "and let me shield you even from every sad thought?"

She never dreamed of the secret which had lain in his heart for years. She could not imagine that the offer came from any other motive than his intense sympathy, his great goodness. He was not content to have saved her; he was so anxious to restore her to her own self-respect that he asked her to become his wife, hoping thus to make her feel that she had not lost her claims to esteem. He would marry her, and guard her happiness so carefully that never, by word or look, would he betray what he suffered in remembering her past. But she could not accept the sacrifice. It would be a sin blacker than her great crime. Yet she must not let him perceive that she recognized it as a sacrifice, because then he would overpower her by his arguments, and she was so weak that she might yield—all the weaker that her heart yearned toward him as it had never done toward any other man. She reached these conclusions with her usual rapidity, tired as she was, and, when he attempted to continue, said, quickly,

"Please don't say any more—not a word. I can not listen! Don't make me seem harsh and ungrateful—I can't listen."

The answer fell like a stroke of doom, and crushed the vague hope which had been growing in his mind during these last days. His old supposition had been correct; she cared for some one else. All he could do now was to spare her pain; hide his trouble, bury the long-treasured secret more deeply in his soul, let her believe that no sentiment stronger than sympathy had prompted his speech.

"Since it pains you, Alice," he said, in an unfaltering voice, "I will never speak of this again—never. You shall forget that I have mentioned it, or remember it only to know how entirely you can trust my friendship."

"I do know! I can't thank you. Oh, I am dumb—but I feel it—God bless you!"

She was so much shaken and disturbed that he rose and went away at once. That night he received a long letter from her, and two days after the gay world was astonished by the news that she had sailed for Europe.

So they parted; and close as each had been to reading the other's secret, no perception of the truth struck either heart.

CHAPTER XXXIII.

BEARING HER BURDEN.

MILLY and her aunt went away into the country, accompanied by the children—away to a little place which was Milly's sole possession, and where they had been in the habit of spending a few months of retirement almost every summer, in order to be able to afford the expenses of the winter.

Mrs. Remsen spoke vaguely of their "place" as a little nest, where she sought rest and domestic felicity; and although these were not the reasons which took her there, it was a spot in which one might have been well content, if in a mood to enjoy the quiet loveliness of the surroundings. The house was not far from a village that seemed always wrapped in a Rip Van Winkle sleep, with its small, vine-covered dwellings, its pretty church and school, and all the appurtenances that go to make up a well-regulated hamlet; not forgetting its shop, where the farmers' wives from the vicinity brought their butter and eggs to sell, taking in exchange all manner of bright-colored finery, to delight the eyes of their daughters; and the quaint old inn, where the same set of seedy loungers gradually grew more and more dilapidated as the years went by.

The cottage was small; but it had a wide hall, a pretty parlor, with white draperied windows, and a book and music room on one side, with shady bay-windows, besides a great vine-covered porch. It had a smooth, sloping lawn in front, a lovely pine wood at the back, and one might have played the misanthrope in such quarters with tolerable resignation. The view from the porch was quietly lovely, with a little river—a tributary of the Hudson—in the middle distance, cultivated fields and bits of woodland on either side, and a range of blue-tinted hills closing in the distance far away, beautiful and mysterious as distant hills must always be.

Mrs. Remsen pronounced herself fond of the country, but her idea of enjoying it thoroughly was to have an immense house and constant flocks of visitors, so that she never accepted the months at her hermitage save as a stern necessity. It had always been pleasant enough here to Milly, though sometimes rather dull. In her youthful heedlessness, she had not enjoyed to its full extent the peace which Nature brings if we only seek her faithfully, and now she had lost the power to do so.

There they established themselves, and prepared to pass the summer; and what a summer—what a dreadful summer to Milly in every way! She wondered how she lived through it; but though the bloom wore out of her cheeks and the light out of her eyes, her health would not quite fail. Her aunt had, in a great measure, ceased her allusions to the past, but there was winter between their hearts, and each blamed the other that it was so; and both were right, and both were wrong. Milly kept to the strict letter of their agreement, but it was in the spirit which would make one rush into martyrdom. She taught the children even, and she brought them on well; but the duties that might have been made so pleasant were nearly unendurable, and she almost hated herself and her charge sometimes. The children were quick to understand this, and they complained of Milly's indifference; then Aunt Eliza found fault in a frigid, conscientious way worse than her old petulance, and Milly was impatient or sullen, and every thing was as bad as it could be. I wish I could say that my poor Milly bore her woes in either a heroic or an angelic manner; but she was only a very woman, suddenly come out of her childhood, and so she could but be natural.

The spring dragged heavily on into summer; the summer deepened to its prime, but brought no change, no hope of peace to Milly, or relief to her aunt. Maud was having a success at Newport with her sister. This was Mrs. Remsen's only consolation; and she could not forbear reading bits from her letters to Milly, and irritating her by hints of what she herself might have been enjoying, until the poor girl was white and shivering with pain.

Her aunt thought her wholly to blame now. She must have driven Halford away by her caprices and bad temper. But, in truth, he was more in fault than Milly, as men past their first youth always are when they want to marry a wife because she is young and childish, and then get impatient with the faults growing out of the very qualities they had desired, and forget that a girl who is capable of real, earnest love is also capable of being gently led into a noble womanhood. They were all wrong—just as we often are in this world; but Milly's trouble was hardest to bear, because it was her first. As we grow older, we know that, however dark is the night, it must surely pass at length, if it be only into a gray quiet like an autumn afternoon.

In first suffering we do not understand this. The first clouding of the sky, the first obscuring of all beauty in life, is much more terrible than when later we have grown somewhat accustomed to seeing our flowers fade, and our suns go down. Ah! no matter what may come afterward—misery, ruin, even disgrace—there is nothing so overwhelming as the first swoop of affliction upon the entirely undisciplined heart.

So they all struggled on after their different ways; Kenneth Halford looking back into the past from his foreign wanderings, with a keen regret that deepened daily as he found how difficult it was to take a new interest in life; Aunt Eliza disgusted with young people generally; and Milly so rebellious that sorrow worked no good in her nature.

She chafed most because she could not with one wrench tear out the past from her heart. She did not know that the pain from the scar of a healed wound is sometimes more insupportable, with its dull aching, than the keenness of the first agony. Twenty times each day she might say to herself that she scorned the memory of this man who had wronged her—hated herself—the whole world; but then she raged inwardly because she could not deny that she was intensely and entirely miserable. She was in that state of mind when even sensible people do the most senseless things—sit on the wet grass—stare at the moon at unholy hours—eat and drink dreadful things at impossible seasons, or not eat at all; and when the physical system refuses longer to bear this ill-treatment, added to the incessant hen-pecking of the soul, and gives way and perishes, friends talk of their having died of a broken heart, or some such malady of which rational human beings have no business whatever to die.

Poor Milly, with her changed face, her mournful eyes, and her dark, gloomy thoughts! She had no faith left in mankind; she grew cynical, and discovered falsehood in the most trivial action; could see no justice in heaven or on earth. You who have left the freshness of your youth far behind you can perfectly understand the different stages of suffering through which she passed. These were the seasons when her crushed pride rose and helped her to loathe the recollection of her brief dream; then days and days when she could summon neither pride nor hatred—could only crouch down under the sharpness of her suffering, like a wounded deer dying in its thicket. Then would follow periods almost of mental vacuity, when she seemed only to vegetate; though all the time, through her apathy, she could feel the dull ache of her trouble like a bodily pain that is deadened by laudanum—the days were so long and dreary, the nights seemed endless. Either she had not energy enough to stir except as her duties compelled her, or else she rushed forth to walk mile after mile, until she actually sunk down from physical prostration; but whether she was shut up in the house tortured by her own reflections, or wearing her strength out by overfatigue, the pain never would leave her heart.

To some persons this may seem very silly, but it is dreadfully true, notwithstanding. It is terrible for the young to suffer, and Milly's was real suffering. It was no false sentiment, no romance from which she could recover, and be then all the stronger and wiser. Hers had been the love that comes but once to the heart, and which deforms and distorts the mind, or develops it to its fullest beauty, according as one bears the happiness or trouble which it brings; and Milly had not yet learned to bear hers wisely.

A brief visit from Hortense was the only break in the monotony. She was on her way, with a party of wise people, to visit the Mammoth Cave, and other marvels of nature sufficiently grand to interest such lofty minds. She stopped at the cottage for a few days, having arranged to rejoin her companions in a city farther west, where they were to tarry for a time, in order that one of the professors might illuminate the region by a course of his scientific lectures.

Mrs. Remsen was divided between the pleasure of having some one to whom she could talk freely, and annoyance at the extreme trouble such a guest would bring to the small domestic staff; and Milly comforted herself by the remembrance that it might have been worse if Adelaide Ramsay had chosen to come. Hortense was in the full tide of a flood of botany and geology, and quite determined to turn these few days to account, that she might astonish her intellectual companions when she should rejoin them. If she had chanced to be in a poetical mood, she would have expatiated upon the loveliness of nature, the glory of the hills, the poetry of the flowers; but, in her present mania, she only saw in the hills and rocks materials to be chipped with a little hammer she carried in her pocket, and she made cruel havoc among all the blossoms within her reach to get at their hearts and their anatomy, and called them divers learned and unpleasant sounding names, which seemed adding insult to injury. She dragged Milly about with her on her expeditions; and while Hortense pounded at the rocks, convinced that every hard and particularly ugly stone contained some wonderful mineral, or depopulated the gardens and fields of flowers and mosses, Milly sat perfectly unconscious of the stream of eloquence and wisdom poured out in her hearing, gazing always at the blue hills in the distance with a weary longing and unrest.

Hortense, like many people with great minds, always declared that she never cared about what she ate; but her little requirements in this way nearly drove the servants crazy, and irritated Mrs. Remsen exceedingly; while Milly was obliged to spend half her days sewing up rips and torn places in their visitors' gowns, for she had no idea of making a guy of herself in stout ugly garments, even if she were strong-minded and given to ologies.

"I could pass my whole life here," Hortense said, again and again, with enthusiasm. "Here one could study in quiet, and feel one's mind expand undisturbed."

"I am sure you quite grumbled when you were a girl and obliged to come here," retorted Mrs. Remsen one day, when she was not in a mood to listen with patience to her daughter's raptures. Hortense did not choose to notice the remark.

"But, alas!" she went on, "there is so much else that it is one's duty to do. I take my hours of study usually from my time for repose; I must live in the bustle of the world because I can do the most good there."

Mrs. Remsen quietly left the room; her stock

12

of patience grew daily more threadbare; and when Hortense began wildly galloping her hobby it was better to retreat. Milly was sitting in the open window; the morning lessons were over, and she had some needle-work in her lap; but her hands were idle, her eyes fixed on the distant hills.

"Milly," said Hortense, "I see a great change in you."

"I am in perfect health," returned Milly, impatiently. "Now don't begin to fancy there is any thing the matter with me."

"You mistake," explained Hortense; "I meant a change in your mind; I see an altered soul look out of your eyes."

"Oh, Hortense, I can't feel either poetical or metaphysical, I warn you."

"You ought to turn all your trouble to a proper use—"

"I have no trouble," interrupted Milly. "Two or three times you have talked to me as if I were a broken-hearted Letitia Landon; please to understand that I am nothing of the sort."

"Milly, Milly, don't grow hard and commonplace!"

"Oh, but I quite wish to," said Milly; "it is the only way to go comfortably through the world."

"Occupy your mind," cried Hortense; "study—think—enlarge your soul and your intellect."

"That is all very well for you who have not a care in the world. If you were to teach those children, I fancy you would be quite tired enough each day without attempting learned studies."

"Don't mention your petty cares," said Mrs. Pierson with scorn. "Look at my life. Do I ever have an hour to myself? I attend to my hospitals, my schools, and my societies, but I also find time for intellectual improvement."

"Well, I don't care about it," returned Milly, shortly.

Hortense lifted her hands in horror.

"I knew Maud was an idiot, and Adelaide not much better," she exclaimed; "but I did think that, under all your girlish frivolity, there was a soul which would sooner or later rouse itself."

"I am sorry to disappoint you, Hortense; I dare say I am an idiot, too; but what difference does it make?"

"Difference!" sighed Hortense; "think! oh, think! Life is forever; we pass from one cycle of existence to another; we grow higher, and nobler, and purer! Let us begin here the work of wisdom that must go on through the endless cycles of Eternity!"

"That is the worst of it," said Milly, in a dreary voice; "forever!"

"What do you mean, Milly?"

"Forever, you know; you said it. It's hard enough to live this life, but to think that there will never be an end—that we must live on and on. Oh, I would rather have been a stone!"

"Are you a heathen, Milly?" questioned Hortense, looking at her quite aghast.

"I wish I was," said Milly; "they have a Juggernaut that kills one; ours rolls and crushes us, and leaves us still alive."

"It is wicked, Milly, to say such things. You might as well be an atheist as to talk like that!"

But Milly was in one of those moods when neither religious teachings nor good example can keep us from indulging in useless, impious thought, and Hortense possessed no eloquence which could bring her out of that state of mind.

"I don't see that it matters much whether we are wicked or good," said Milly. "We have nothing but trouble all the same."

"But trouble is good for the soul," pursued Hortense, grandly. "It makes it grow and widen. Used aright, it is a magic wand that opens for us the doors which lead into the very heart of Nature's mysteries."

Milly listened to Mrs. Pierson's mixed metaphors with intense irritation, not to say disgust. It was easy enough for her to talk—this woman who had never known a real trouble — whose queer, old, learned husband was her slave—whose whole life was sunshiny and pleasant.

"She's a greater fool than the other two," thought Milly, "though she does speak five languages, reads Arabic, and knows Humboldt by heart. Her learning has only made her more shallow."

"Suffering!" pursued Hortense. "Why, Milly, it is grand to suffer."

"I'm sure you know nothing about it," retorted Milly. "Keep to your books and your sciences, Hortense — you are quite at home there; but when it comes to trouble, you are no more competent to speak than I am to teach Sanscrit."

Hortense was stupefied with amazement at the idea of there being any subject upon which she could not speak like one inspired.

"Milly," said she, compassionately, "you are growing cynical and ill-natured; you used to be a perfect little sunbeam; I don't know you any more."

Milly felt the old choking in her throat, and caught up her work and began sewing industriously.

"I suppose it is the precursor of old-maidism," she answered, trying to laugh, and feeling sorry that she had snubbed Hortense, who was at all events kind, and always good-natured.

"Do you mean to be an old maid?" inquired her cousin, here taking another tack at once.

"Yes, very likely."

"Why don't you become a Sister of Charity?" cried Hortense, with enthusiasm. "You have no taste for books; you could never adopt one of the learned professions; but you could give up your life to duty, and go about like a ministering angel among poor humanity."

"I don't think I care enough about humanity to wish to help it much," replied Milly, stitching away industriously.

"You are an enigma," said Hortense; "I will own it, you puzzle even me!"

"If I puzzle you more than I do myself, I am astonished," thought Milly, as she worked on.

Hortense was silent for a few moments, pulling a number of flowers in pieces and strewing their leaves upon the carpet. Like many persons troubled with a love for hobbies of all sorts, she was not always tidy in the pursuit. Just now her mania was quite distressing; the carpets never were clean, and one stumbled over bits of rock and fossils in all sorts of places where they had no business. She looked at Milly as if she had been some species of remarkable flower that she could neither classify nor comprehend, and this state of mind was very unusual with Mrs. Pierson, priding herself as she did upon her ability to read character.

"You would be an interesting study, Milly," said she, presently, in a meditative way. "I wish Mrs. Tonguay could be with you for a time. Mental peculiarities are quite her forte."

"Do you think me like a musty old botany book, that any one may peep into at will?" said she; "or that I can be chipped at, and so made to reveal myself, as you do the rocks, by the aid of any body's hammer?"

"Don't be violent, Milly; always restrain yourself in discussion. Dear me, how odd you have grown!"

Milly threw down her work and passed out on the lawn, repeating Hortense's words to herself. Odd, indeed—strangest of all, to herself—and the worse thing was, that nothing would ever bring her old self back, nothing could ever set the crooked life straight.

"Nothing!" said Milly, again and again; "nothing!"

She looked up at the clear summer sky, with its masses of fleecy white clouds sailing away toward the zenith, afar off to the misty hills, and her very soul sickened within her. The light wind stirred the maple boughs, and shook fragrance from the hearts of the blossoming flowers; the sun shone golden and soft; the day was balmy and beautiful; but there was no power in the brightness which could warm Milly's heart, no spell in the calmness of the afternoon that could quiet her wounds. Very soon the children came out and espied her, and made multifarious requests, with which she complied, but there was no pleasure in it; she had no happiness as of old in gratifying them, only the determination to do her duty, and in the most uncompromising way.

"Cousin Milly," said little Dora, suddenly, when the wrinkle in her little French costume had been set smooth, "why don't you act as if you loved me any more?"

"What a foolish question!" said Milly.

"No it isn't, cousin! Last winter you used to play with us, and come into the nursery to show us how beautiful you were in your ball-dresses, and we loved you ever so; but now you never play with us, and you never tell us fairy stories. Why don't you?"

The words came at a moment when they touched Milly. She leaned her head on the child's flaxen curls and wept piteously; tears which did her more good than any she had shed for a long time, seeming to wash away a little of the bitterness from her soul.

"Don't cry, Cousin Milly," pleaded Dora, frightened at this unexpected response to her childish expostulations. "I didn't mean any thing; please don't cry; don't."

"Let me cry, Dora dear; it does me good."

This was incomprehensible to the little one, in whose mind tears were associated with ill-learned lessons or offense to mamma, or some other enormity of like nature; but, with the odd intelligence of her age able to sympathize with that emotion which she could not comprehend, she just remained holding fast to Milly's hand, and never uttering a word.

The tempest passed; Milly wiped away the scalding drops, kissed Dora, and said,

"You mustn't tell any one how foolish I have been, Dora dear."

"Indeed I won't never tell nobody," returned the child, becoming all negatives in her earnest asseveration. "But oh, Milly," with her eyes like saucers, "have you been bad?"

"No one is any too good," returned Milly, evasively. "But I liked to cry, dear; it has made me feel better."

"I'm awfully glad of that; but it's very queer," said Dora, looking puzzled. "But I'll not tell; and Milly, I won't bother you so much any more, now that I know you are so sorry about something."

The little one ran off to join her sister, and Milly walked about the lawn and garden until she had sufficiently regained her composure to be presentable before her aunt and cousin. But when she entered the house, she found Mrs. Remsen nodding over a novel, and Hortense deep in one of Professor Drivler's printed lectures, and neither noticed her.

"I need not have feared they would see there was any thing the matter," thought Milly. "Unless I chanced to die before their eyes, they would never discover there was any thing wrong with me."

Hortense's visit came to an end, and she proceeded on her journey in high spirits, leaving the house very quiet after the rustle of her silken trains, and the incessant rat-tat of her geological hammer had died out of it.

Then came more letters from Maud and a few from Adelaide. They were enjoying Newport to the fullest extent, and Maud described herself as creating a marked sensation. Indeed Adelaide wrote that she found Maud quite the belle of the season—of course, meaning the unmarried belle; for Mrs. Ramsay could not make up her mind to believe that girls were ever so much admired as their wedded sisters. Mrs. Remsen was willing to remain buried until winter, in order to give Maud a brilliant season; but the seclusion so foreign to her tastes did not tend to make her a more amiable companion, and she could not forbear occasional little flings at Milly for being there, buried alive, teaching the children, when she might have been displaying bridal paraphernalia, to the envy of every feminine heart at Newport or elsewhere.

Oh, those bright, golden days, how long they seemed to Milly! Worse a thousand times than clouds and tempests would have been, she thought she could have found something responsive in the howl of the blast or the fury of a tornado; but the drowsy, indolent quiet of those long summer days nearly drove her wild.

"And this must go on," she thought, "for weeks, months, years—as long as I shall live! My youth has gone from me, my power of enjoyment has gone. There is nothing left but the bare husks of life. I feel as if I were journeying over a straight road, under a gray November sky; not a turn, not a hillock, not a tree to rest under; only an endless stretch of white road, and the dust getting into my eyes, and I growing always more weary and more faint. And one can not die! Suffering doesn't kill. I know I am looking different—older, and paler, and I feel always so tired; but nothing really ails me; my health doesn't fail; I shall be obliged to live on. I wonder I did not kill myself at first. It would have been wicked, I suppose; but could the punishment have been any worse than that I endure here? Never to have any end, never to be any different, if I live to be an old, old woman! What will become of me at last? When Aunt Remsen dies, I shall be quite alone in the world. I could teach then; there would be nobody's pride to save; the girls would not mind if only I was never a trouble to them. It would be better than being quiet, with nothing to do but feel this ache at my heart—day and night—day and night." Such were often Milly's thoughts while the glad summer wore on, and still there came no relief.

CHAPTER XXXIV

MRS. LAWRENCE'S PROMISE.

SEPTEMBER had come; the sky wore its golden haze; the hills grew softer and more beautiful, and the quiet of the season somewhat soothed Milly's unrest.

About this time Mrs. Remsen was seized with a violent rheumatic fever, from the effects of a drenching which would have upset the stoutest hydropathist that ever shivered under a bath of ice-water in December, and very ill she was. Never was illness more fortunate, in one respect—I mean in the effect it had upon our faulty Milly. She began with the intention of being a martyr; she took entire charge of the sick-room; she watched day and night; and, before Aunt Eliza left her bed, Milly was doing her duty from far different motives than those which had actuated her in the outset.

Sitting in that darkened chamber, Milly found ample time for retrospection, and was forced to regard her conduct and her suffering in their true light. The hardness and bitterness left her soul, and the discipline to which she was obliged to submit did her a world of good. At first Milly had not much leisure to reflect—her aunt was too ill, peevish and exacting also, as the most patient people are under that dreadful malady, and Milly had to exert all her energies in the task which devolved upon her. But when the sick woman ceased to endure constant pain, could sleep a good deal by night and day, then, in her silent watches, came Milly's time for thought, which she could neither drive away nor turn a shade from its proper hue.

She was able, at length, to see that she had poorly deserved the short-lived happiness vouchsafed her; able to understand that her undisciplined nature had not been capable of any real and permanent content. She could see, too, how suffering might work good to mind and heart, instead of imbittering the whole nature, as she had allowed it to imbitter hers; so that, if continued, her cynical speeches and lack of faith would render her insupportable to all with whom she came in contact.

Mrs. Remsen could sit up, permitted the children to enter her room, and recovered a portion of her former energy. Her old tenderness for Milly revived, she was so like the dead sister who had been fondly loved. Of course Mrs. Remsen was often peevish and unreasonable, and Milly had many relapses into her mental distempers; but she had character enough to struggle on, now that she saw the light. Her very sorrow grew different; she suffered, and her poor young heart ached wearily; but she began to discover that, because one hope failed, she had no right to cry out that the whole world was barren. Naturally, she rather went to the opposite extreme for a while, and was overstrict with herself—it is so difficult to preserve a happy medium in dealing with one's own peculiarities.

She found leisure for a long walk each day; Mrs. Remsen saw how much she enjoyed it, and would not permit her to forego the gratification, and the solitary rambles helped her greatly. She observed and felt the beautiful as she had never before done; each change in the soft skies, each new aspect of loveliness was caught by her, and she looked out toward the glorious hills with an increasing serenity very unlike the wicked impatience of the previous months.

I am not transforming her into a heroine or an angel; she was sadly human still, and full of faults; but, trying to do right, people are helped in the effort. It was difficult to be composed under trifles when she was solacing her mind with dreams of great sacrifices; pin-pricks are hard to endure serenely. The children would be careless about their lessons; Aunt Eliza would moan when her tea had too much or too little sugar in it; the kitchen staff would be stupid and provoking; and as many days were spoiled completely as ever an acolyte ruined *plats* while acquiring the sacred mysteries of the culinary art. But Milly persevered; sometimes, just as she thought herself advancing promisingly, back she slipped; she would hurt herself severely, and have to lie on the thorns and weep a little; but she always picked herself up and trudged gallantly on, gradually learning life's lessons—going slowly but surely toward the light.

One day, in particular, Mrs. Remsen was extremely cross—as you or I would have been with a shoulder that creaked like a rusty hinge when we tried to use it, and a trip-hammer beating furiously in the left temple. The servants had to be set in order, the children wanted twenty things at once, and each of the twenty something they had no business to require, and they all the more clamorous on that account. But Milly bore it splendidly — saved herself from the least slip, and held fast to her patience. When quiet was restored, Aunt Eliza's shoulder comfortable, and her head induced to leave off its trip-hammer performance under Milly's skillful manipulations, Mrs. Remsen lay looking at her in silence for a long time.

"Milly," she said at length, "you are not like the same girl."

Milly seized the thread of her aunt's reflections and smiled.

"I hope not," she answered; "there was need of a change."

"I never saw a better nurse. Oh, Milly, you have been your mother over again since I was ill!"

Milly did not burst into tears, or throw herself on her knees before her aunt with a long-winded apostrophe of thankfulness. She continued her work, and tried to keep her voice quiet, as she said,

"Then you must love me once more for her sake."

"I have always loved you, even when I was most angry," Mrs. Remsen replied. "I can see where I was wrong, but I loved you as well as one of my own children all the time; I want you to believe that."

"I do believe it, aunt, and it makes me happy," Milly said. "I have been a very foolish, ungrateful girl in many things; in others I have been unfortunate—"

"Yes, Milly," her aunt interrupted, softly; "I ought to have recollected that."

"I want you to try and forget my faults," Milly went on, "and I will try to forget my little troubles; then we shall do very well."

Mrs. Remsen could not help thinking what good fortune Milly deserved, and her thoughts reverted to the hopes of the past.

"Oh, Milly," she said; "if only things had not ended as they did!"

"Don't, aunt, please! I don't want to talk or think of what has gone by. Let it be a sealed book between us. It will be better every way."

Mrs. Remsen was silent again for a while. She watched Milly's face, from which the weariness and discontent had faded, leaving it changed and womanly. She felt, more keenly than she often allowed herself to feel, that life held something for the young beyond dress and gayety, something higher than the mere hope of wealth and station. Then, too, she began to think that Milly might get over her trouble in time, that she might find a new object to love, and all the happiness and good fortune come which Mrs. Remsen wished her.

"Milly," she said, "we will go away from here before long. My dividends are coming up again, and I shall be able to draw a sum that will make us very comfortable, and we'll have a pleasant winter."

"I am very comfortable here, I give you my word."

"But you can't go on living like this; I don't wish to turn you into a governess or seamstress! It's not natural for a girl to stay shut like a hermit in a cave."

Milly laughed more like her old self than she had done in a long time.

"But, aunty, this house is not a bit like a cave, and I like to sew. I have learned to like teaching the children, too. I think I am bringing them on very well—don't you?"

"Indeed you are; much better than that stupid Miss Lane ever could or would. But you are young; you must have pleasures suitable to your age—change, society."

Milly shuddered to recall her brief career; it had been very delightful; but oh, the black, dreadful end! She could not care longer for the world, because there was no aim back of its charms; it would be sadly hollow and blank to her lacking that. How could she sigh for crowds, when she could no longer go among them to watch for one dear face? How could she join in the old dances, remembering the season when a beloved arm supported her—sit and listen to the familiar operas and plays, when there was no one treasured friend to whom she could turn for sympathy and appreciation.

"I want a quiet life, aunt," she said. "You gave me my butterfly season, and I soiled my wings terribly, and flew in the very face of the wind. It would not be just to Maud or the younger ones, who will soon take her place, for me to wear out the last of my youth in amusement, and put you to an expense which ought to be reserved for them."

And Mrs. Remsen thought what a dear, wise girl she had grown; indeed, she could not permit her, with her heightened beauty and her new mental attractions, to sink into a household drudge for the sake of her other charges.

"But, Milly," she began, "you may marry."

"Aunty, don't talk about that; I shall never marry. I don't mean to be foolish or romantic, but I know, I know that I couldn't love any man—again."

She checked Mrs. Remsen by a sign when she would have expostulated, and went on:

"Aunt, I feel as you did after Uncle George died. Don't make me say any thing more. I have buried my love; I could not build a new palace over its grave. I don't wish to talk about these things, or think of them, further than is unavoidable; but it is better for us to understand each other thoroughly."

Mrs. Remsen did not speak, but in that moment she acknowledged the true force and womanliness of Milly's nature.

"You are not angry, aunt?"

"No; but it pains me to think of your living solitary and sad, when you would know so well how to use happiness."

"I have it, aunt; at least, I am not unhappy—the rest will come in time."

"Yes, yes; we will trust to time," Mrs. Remsen said.

Milly smiled, comprehending what was in her thoughts, but not anxious to pursue the subject.

After this conversation, the understanding between the two was perfect; and, as Mrs. Remsen's health improved, the days passed so pleasantly that the restless, active woman quite enjoyed her period of convalescence. She was sometimes anxious about Maud, but she hoped for the best, and trusted to Adelaide's letters that every thing was going as well with the young lady as if she were there to watch; and with each week Milly's companionship grew more dear, and Milly's example produced its effect upon her habits and range of thought.

It was October—beautiful, gorgeous October. They were expecting letters from Maud, now at Mr. Ramsay's country-seat, and the morning passed without bringing them, though the postmaster had faithfully promised to send his boy if any arrived, and Milly had tempted the youth himself by offering pleasant inducements in the way of sixpences.

Mrs. Remsen felt confident there were letters at the office, and Milly was beset by an odd restlessness, as if expecting news herself, though certain there was none to come. So, when the early dinner-hour went by, and the afternoon wore on without bringing the small boy, Milly set out for the village. She was still haunted by her vague expectation when she reached the place. The old postmaster put on his spectacles, admitted that he thought he had letters, entered into a lengthy speculation as to the cause of "George Washington's" delay, and, when Milly's patience was entirely exhausted, began slowly turning over the piles of letters, and at last counted her down three with as much reluctance as if he had been a philanthropist called upon to help some one in secret. Milly looked at the envelopes — all for Mrs. Remsen: one in Maud's young-lady hand, the other from the lawyer, and the third evidently a business letter likewise. Milly turned homeward with an actual feeling of disappointment, and then laughed at herself for her folly; she had not the slightest reason to expect a letter from any quarter. It was only a return of her

old restless ways. She walked on briskly, because she knew her aunt would be anxious, and forgot her own causeless disappointment in the pleasure which lighted up Mrs. Remsen's face as the letters were laid in her lap.

"An actual mail-bag," said Aunt Eliza, with true feminine delight. "Oh, this is from Maud; now let us see what she says."

She skimmed the epistle in her eagerness, then read portions aloud for Milly's benefit. It was full of glowing accounts of picnics, garden-parties, petitions for new costumes, appeals for money, hints of significant attentions, and a long paragraph about Charley Thorne.

"He is very devoted to me, mamma, and I can't think he ever cared a straw about Milly—it was just one of your fancies. He sings duets with me, and he reads Tennyson aloud of a morning, while I work on Addie's chair-coverings. I'd rather he read a jolly magazine story, of course, but it's very nice of him."

"I hope you are not jealous, Milly," said Mrs. Remsen.

"Not in the least, I assure you. He is the best-hearted young fellow in the world; and if he likes Maud, and she him, it will be a good thing for both."

"We shall see," said Mrs. Remsen, complacently. "At all events, every thing seems to go on well with her. But oh what an extravagant puss she is, and Adelaide encourages her in it. They have no idea of having old dresses made over into new. You are a genius in that way, my dear."

"A proof that I must be meant for narrow means; but Maud hates such things."

"Here's Mr. Whiting's letter," said Mrs. Remsen; "it's only about those railway bonds, I see."

She took up a third letter, glanced at the superscription, and turned the epistle over to look at the seal. "I don't know this writing," said she; "who can it be from? It's postmarked New York; why, who can it be from?"

Milly laughed outright at her aunt sitting there and perplexing herself as people love to do over an unknown chirography.

"Suppose you should open it," she suggested.

Mrs. Remsen looked as if the thought had not occurred to her, but, after another instant's contemplation, followed Milly's advice. She tore open the envelope, and out fell an inclosure. Mrs. Remsen glanced at it, and exclaimed, "Why, Milly, it's a letter for you!"

Milly took it, wondering a little after the fashion for which she had laughed at her aunt, till it was Mrs. Remsen's turn to cry out.

"For mercy's sake, open it, you silly child! You'll never find out the contents by staring at the address," quite oblivious of her own perplexed staring while she thought the epistle was intended for herself.

Milly opened the letter and began to read, then glanced up in astonishment, almost fright.

"What is it, Milly?" exclaimed her aunt, still nervous enough, from her recent illness, to be easily alarmed. "There's no bad news—nothing about the girls?"

Milly shook her head, finished the page, and sat an instant, pale and startled, regardless of her aunt's continued inquiries; then she buried her head on the arm of the sofa and sobbed heartily.

"Milly, Milly, what is it, child?" cried Mrs. Remsen, now absolutely frightened. "Is it bad news?"

"Oh, good news—good news; and I don't deserve it," sobbed Milly. "Only read this, Aunt Remsen."

Mrs. Remsen grasped the epistle and devoured the contents in surprise, mingled with other feelings, as she read. Mrs. Lawrence had died suddenly, but at the last she had not forgotten the careless promise she made to Milly. She had left her all the property that was in her control; and this letter was from her lawyer, to announce the fact to Milly that she was now mistress of some two hundred thousand dollars, or its equivalent, in all sorts of safe investments.

It would be difficult to describe the feelings of the pair in the first moments of this good fortune, they were so bewildered; but soon they were mingling their tears; and to Mrs. Remsen's credit be it said, that her emotions were as full of pure, unadulterated gratitude as Milly's own.

"Poor Mrs. Lawrence!" the girl said, regretfully; "and I have scarcely thought of her all the summer!"

"My dear, she was so much older than you."

"She did not forget; she said she should do this."

"When—what do you mean?"

Milly had to explain about the visit she had received from Mrs. Lawrence, in her penitence, the previous spring, and Mrs. Remsen said,

"Poor dear woman! I am glad I had already forgiven her, and was sorry I scolded her."

"She was not to blame."

"It's all over, anyway. Dead, and left you all this money—poor Minerva! And that silly Maud never to mention her death, though it seems she died at her country place, and it's not more than ten miles from Mr. Ramsay's."

She took up the letter again, and found a half-page which she had overlooked; and there, edged in between a description of Adelaide's new croquet costume and the account of a picnic, was the mention—

"Oh, I forgot to tell you—Mrs. Lawrence is dead—erysipelas or something. Addie and I did not go to the funeral for fear of infection; besides, that day we had a grand croquet-match, and her house was so far off that Addie said she could not count as a neighbor."

Mrs. Remsen threw down the epistle in disgust. They went over the lawyer's letter again for such brief particulars as it contained, and Milly could only remember how kind the dead woman had been, and wonder at the hardness and unbelief of human nature in which she had

herself so long indulged. Mrs. Remsen did not jar upon her thoughts by any worldly calculations; indeed, while waiting the next two days for the further details promised by the man of business, they could only dwell on Mrs. Lawrence's invariable goodness; and Aunt Eliza said, over and over,

"Poor Minerva, I am so glad I forgave her! We were old school-friends, and I never was really cross to her but that once."

It would be preposterous to say that Milly felt any poignant sorrow, and it was right and natural that, after that season of regret, she should turn to her changed prospects, only not forgetting to feel thankful in this new prosperity.

"I have not deserved it, aunt," she said; "oh, I have not deserved it."

"No one more," Mrs. Remsen answered; "and I am sure you will use it wisely."

"I will try," Milly said, humbly; "and you must help me."

That night, as she sat alone in her room thinking of all which had happened, Milly could not combat the profound depression which stole over her. What could wealth do now? It could not give back her lost youth; it could not restore the love gone from her, or warm into a second blossoming the hopes which clung, sere and dead, about her heart. Those were dark hours, but she was helped through them, and, when morning came, could again remember that, if this change in her life might not restore its brightness, at least it could be made a blessing to others.

Mrs. Remsen began to hold long consultations with her; and if Milly had been her own daughter she could not have found her more ready to appropriate this fortune to the general good.

"You see, aunt," she said, "it just furthers my plan of living with you after the others are gone. When the little ones grow up and marry, you and I will cling together, and grow old and comfortable."

Aunt Eliza smiled at the prospect; indeed, she could afford to wear her most benignant smile in these days; for the share which Milly appropriated to her use out of this new income would make her independent of all pecuniary cares. Milly was too generous to have a tinge of the mean pride in regard to money which is possessed even by so many persons who give freely; she only remembered how much she owed her aunt, and was anxious to show her gratitude.

"I think," she said, "that I should like to enlarge this house, and always spend the summers here. We could make the place lovely."

"Oh, very easily, and at a moderate expense," replied Mrs. Remsen, who had a mania for building and altering. "I think it an excellent idea. I am fond of the old house."

She commenced at once, in fancy, to throw out wings and put in bay-windows, and was exceedingly provoked at an interruption by the children just as she was arranging an extensive conservatory.

"You never leave Milly a moment's peace," she said, as the small ones gathered about their cousin, each with half a dozen petitions.

"But Milly likes it," they pleaded; "don't you, Milly?"

And Milly assured them that she did.

She sent Maud a present to buy ball-dresses, which caused that young lady almost to forget her envy of Milly's good fortune in the contemplation of the numerous benefits likely to accrue to herself therefrom. Adelaide wrote that Milly must be very happy to have an opportunity of showing her gratitude to them all, but added that she believed in gratitude only when she saw some tangible proofs of its existence. She hinted sweetly that she did not expect to see such evidences in Milly's case, and, if they were displayed, should believe that they only rose from a fear of people's considering her an utter monster if she acted otherwise.

Then Hortense sent an epistle full of good-natured congratulation on the first page, branching off into endless sentences of sesquipedalian words, in which she proved that Milly knew nothing about the value or uses of money, and demonstrating with equal force what she ought to do under the direction of those capable of guiding her. Hortense's plan, as well as Milly could understand it, seemed to be for her to found an establishment, and become the head of a sort of modified nunnery, with a hospital attached. Milly laughed heartily over the characteristic letters of her cousins, and Adelaide would have been disgusted to perceive that her malevolence failed to wound, and Hortense shocked that Milly could laugh at opinions shared by the whole intellectual coterie, Professor Driver and Doctor Brazen included. The next news was that pretty Constance Worthington had met her fate, and was to be married immediately. She begged Milly to come to her, and of course she departed. The Crittendons were at Mr. Worthington's country-seat, and they proposed to Milly to go back with them to Europe. Mrs. Remsen decided to remain in America until spring, then she would put Rob at West Point, and follow Milly with her daughters. She felt convinced that, if she did not take Maud out of Charley Thorne's reach, he would succumb before the winter was over, and she wanted that restless young lady settled in life.

So, in the late autumn, Milly sailed once more for the storied lands of the Old World, and the new existence began.

CHAPTER XXXV.

IN A HIGHLAND GLEN.

THE winter passed quietly and pleasantly to Milly, in the Italian cities which they sought; and if she did not find happiness, at least it was a season very different from the darkness of the previous months.

When spring came, her friends took her back to England to meet her aunt, who arrived with the younger members of her brood. Maud had passed out of her hands; as usual, Mrs. Remsen's scheme had proved a success, and she rested on her laurels like a victorious general. Charley Thorne had yielded to destiny, and Maud was his wife. Milly thought it probable they would get on well enough, and Charley go comfortably on toward a corpulent middle age, submitting easily to Maud's rule, caring less and less about Tennyson, and forgetting his inner nature in the attractions of good dinners and such other sweetness of existence as might be offered.

When summer came, Mrs. Remsen and Milly established the little girls in a quiet English village, under the care of their governess—a woman whom a friendship of years had proved worthy of trust—and wandered away into the beautiful scenery of the Highlands. The hotel where they stopped to rest for a fortnight was situated near the edge of one of the loveliest of the Scottish lakes, and not far off was the most picturesque little hamlet imaginable.

It is too near the close of my story to rave about scenery, so I shall only tell you that they settled down there and enjoyed the bright days to the full; and to Milly it was like new life and strength to breathe the fresh air of the mountains.

She spent her days out-of-doors; and there was no glen so hidden that she did not explore its recesses, no moor so steep that she did not climb it to watch the landscape spread out like a picture below. Very rapidly mind and body grew invigorated and thoroughly healthy. She was worlds away from the fanciful girl who had known that brief season of happiness, as far removed from the impatient creature who had struggled with such blind restlessness under the thralldom of a first great sorrow.

One day she had rambled a long distance up among the hills, had passed so many twists and windings between the rocks, and through such a variety of mossy glens, that she was really unable to tell which way led to the hotel. She mounted still higher, in the hope of attaining some point of view which would give her a sight of the village, or at least some landmark whereby she could direct her course. She came only upon a lofty water-fall with which she had not yet made acquaintance, and it seemed to her more peculiarly lovely than those she had before visited. In front of her rose a perpendicular mass of rock to a great height, completely covered with green moss and delicate, feathery ferns, over which a stream of water swept in a broad, thin sheet, like a fine embroidered lace veil flung over the emerald tints, and fell into a moss-lined basin just at her feet. The thick moss smothered the noise of the falling water, so that it foamed into the basin with a bell-like murmur so musical that it seemed to Milly to be singing some exquisite melody.

She stood there some moments, looking and listening, then moved on toward a projecting ledge, and found that she was not alone in the enchanting place. A lady was seated there, her head turned away; she moved at the sound of a stone which Milly's foot dislodged—looked up, and Milly saw that it was of all people in the world the one she least wished to meet—Alice Marchmont.

The girl felt her heart cease beating for an instant; it was like coming face to face with an evil destiny that had taken human shape to mock her with the fearful fruition of its work. She could neither move nor breathe for several instants; could only stand looking full in the woman's countenance with a sensation of absolute dread.

At the first glance Alice's short sight prevented her recognizing Milly, in the strength and beauty the face had gained out of her suffering and repentance—the face she had known as so childishly pretty. Seeing her gaze returned with that perplexed expression one wears when trying to recall a countenance, Milly felt that she was unrecognized; if she could only get away before the creature had time to remember or address her! But the very movement to obey her thoughts—so quick and impulsive—brought to Mrs. Marchmont's mind the excitable girl of the old days, and she knew her at once.

"Miss Crofton!" she exclaimed. "Surely it is Miss Crofton—not some trick my eyes are playing me!"

When Milly heard Alice Marchmont's voice, her first impulse was to hasten on without a word; but Alice came toward her holding out her hand with as much friendliness as if their last meeting had no place in her mind.

"So it really is you," she said, laughing. "How you do stare! But no wonder; the idea of our meeting in this out-of-the-way place! I am not quite certain yet that it is not your double; do speak, and tell me you are not a ghost."

The same ringing laugh that had so vexed Milly's heart in the days gone by, the same low, indolent voice, which gave such a peculiar charm to every word. What a torrent of recollections surged up and shook her very soul on hearing the sound!

Men under such unpleasant circumstances are slow to think and act, unless in a case where a fellow-man is concerned, and there is a shadow of pretext for knocking him down; but women's thoughts come and go like flashes of lightning. This woman should not perceive that she had power to move her in any way—should not be able to exult in the idea that Milly had never recovered from the effects of the blow dealt by her hand. But Alice's intention was very different; she had long since forgiven Milly's cruelty, and had sometimes feared that she might unconsciously have had a share in bringing about the trouble between her and Halford.

"It is Mrs. Marchmont," Milly said, with delightful indifference. "No wonder you are surprised to see me—I less so! The place is so lovely that I am not astonished to see a fairy, or any other beautiful creature, appear."

"Ah! you have found voice—you are not a spirit," returned Mrs. Marchmont; "and what a pretty greeting you give me; please shake hands."

But Milly was busy arranging her dress; it had been looped over a blue petticoat, and some of the festoons had obligingly given way.

"I would with pleasure," said she, laughing as gayly as Alice herself; "but you see my hands are both occupied. Imagine that American greeting done and over."

She did this so very well that any other woman might have been deceived; but Alice saw that Milly still hated her.

"The little unforgiving monster!" thought Mrs. Marchmont; "what did I ever do to her? But how lovely she has grown! what in the world has changed her so? There's a soul looking out of those eyes that has been newly wakened. I must really find out what it all means; who would have dreamed it?"

"You are too busy with your dress, or too indifferent to be surprised," said she; "but I can't forego my woman's privilege. How came you here? indeed, where did you come from? Do tell me."

"Up the hill—from the village; and I have torn my prettiest petticoat," replied Milly, laughing again.

Mrs. Marchmont began to be vexed; but she enjoyed a bit of high comedy well performed, and could not help laughing too.

"You vexatious creature," cried she; "how came you in the village, then, since one must question categorically?"

"Oh dear, yes—I beg your pardon—think of my being so stupid as not to understand! I really believe the air of these quiet places dulls one's wit."

Alice had an internal conviction that Milly's, so far from being dulled, had been decidedly sharpened by the air or some other unknown cause. She had been the recipient of coolness and raillery quite long enough; perhaps she had better warn this young woman that the dullness of the country had not yet deprived her of her old, dangerous weapons.

"So odd a place to meet you," said she; "of course it must be a bridal journey. Only lovers or misanthropes would come to so quiet a place. Am I to congratulate you?"

"Only on the pleasure of meeting yourself," she said, not flinching under the thrust which renched a wound that Alice, ignorant of her own share in Milly's trouble, did not dream of touching.

"It is I who am to be congratulated, my dear young lady," said Alice, in her most languid way.

"Or else pitied," said Milly.

"How so, I beg?"

"Since you say the place could only be sought by lovers or misanthropes," returned Milly, following up her success.

"*Pas mal*," said Alice, laughing again. "Oh, well, every one knows that I am a misanthrope; but a charming young blossom like yourself can not urge such a plea."

"Oh, I came with my aunt," replied Milly; "so the being in love or misanthropic will fall to her charge."

"How comfortable and convenient to have an aunt," said Alice, with the slightest perceptible sneer; "I wish I had one."

"Yes," drawled Milly, with a whole volume of meaning in her distinct and deliberate utterance; "I dare say you would often have found one a great convenience."

Alice Marchmont remembered on the instant Maud's story of the dinner-party; the best of women in such an encounter will be wicked toward each other.

"Yes," she said, meditatively; "but observation has shown me that they are not always a sufficient shield for young women to hide behind."

"Indeed?" answered Milly. "Oh, I know nothing about that; but I am quite willing to take your experience for it. I have never had occasion to hide behind any one."

"No," said Mrs. Marchmont, in a tone of voice so nicely balanced between a doubtful assent and an interrogatory that a man would have believed it the former; but the blood tingled in Milly's veins, for she knew very well which was intended, and felt the full force of the taunt.

"I am so grateful for your warm confirmation of my words," said Milly, sweetly.

"And the gratitude of a dear girl like yourself is such a charming thing to have," said Alice, with equal sweetness.

The foils had clashed and glanced off equally; it was scarcely worth while to continue the encounter on that ground.

"What lovely views there are from these hills. I must have been wandering miles," was Mrs. Marchmont's next remark, moving nearer to the edge of the cliff. Milly assented, and for a few moments they did enthusiastic admiration of the scenery in mutual accord.

"It must be getting late," said Milly, suddenly, glancing at her watch. "Why, it is after sunset!" she added, in dismay. "And I fancy we are a long way from the village. Indeed I don't quite know where we are; I was climbing the hill hoping to get a look out, when I came upon you."

"I was in the same predicament," said Alice. "I tried several paths, but each one seemed to lead me further astray than the one before it; I am very fortunate to have met you."

She knew that would vex Milly, and it did so.

"Fortunate, provided I can help you out of your difficulty, but I am not certain that I shall be able to do so."

"*Ciel!*" cried Mrs. Marchmont. "Well, *ma belle*, we shall at least have the consolation of being lost together."

"You will make me unwilling to find the way home if you remind me of that pleasure," said Milly.

"Ah!" said the other, "but we shall go together, too."

"Not if I can help it," thought Milly; "I'll put her in the right path, and leave her; she makes me feel too wicked!" But she did not express her reflection in words or voice. "I only hope we may be able to find the way," she said, pleasantly. "I will go on to the extreme top of the cliff; very likely I can see the village from there. Don't follow me, for if I slipped I should throw you backward."

Mrs. Marchmont stood quietly near the water-fall watching Milly as she ran up the stony path with a rapid step, her stay in this place having made her quite a mountaineer. She reached the top, and Alice saw her look eagerly about, then try several paths, and finally sit down on a mossy rock to rest, thoroughly fatigued by her unusual walk. Presently she descended, stepping slowly down over the rocks with what to most people might have passed for caution in descending the rugged way; but Alice, with her quick perceptions, interpreted the hesitation more correctly; she knew that Milly could hardly endure being obliged to rejoin her.

"What a dreadful disposition she must have!" thought Alice. "One would have supposed she might have forgotten her dislike of me in all these months."

Just then she heard Milly speaking as she drew near the fall. "I can see no sign of the village," she said; "it is very odd where we can be."

"Perhaps the place is enchanted, and the genii are angry because we have come," returned Alice, trying to laugh, but feeling greatly disturbed by Milly's words, for she had just discovered that she was thoroughly exhausted.

"The worst of it is," continued Milly, "there's a heavy cloud coming over that mountain—mist or rain, or both; so we must hasten in some direction."

Mrs. Marchmont rose to her feet at once.

"You have no idea which path would lead us least astray?" she asked.

"Not the slightest," replied Milly, with composure. "Whether we had better go down the way I came up, or go to the top of the cliff and ascend on the other side—the village must lie in one direction or the other."

"How re-assuring!" responded her companion.

"Yes; we can have the satisfaction of believing ourselves right until the last moment."

"Thank you, but I don't like the idea of last moments! *Eh bien*; which path do you propose to take?"

"I am as much at a loss as you can be. I have taken so many turns, and climbed so many hills, that I can not tell the right hand from the left."

Alice began to laugh again from sheer fatigue and nervousness.

"We shall have to imitate the school-boy," said she, picking up a little flat stone. "See—I toss this in the air; if the gray side comes uppermost, we go back by the way you came; if the yellow, we try fate on the other side of the cliff."

"Very well; but I warn you the path seemed very steep as I looked down at it."

Mrs. Marchmont shrugged her shoulders indifferently.

"One—two; now for luck or fate!"

She tossed the little stone in the air. As it fell, both leaned over it. The yellow side was uppermost.

"We are doomed to try the cliff," said she. "I confess to being very superstitious. I wouldn't tempt destiny by going the other way for the world."

She spoke half in jest, half in earnest. But Milly herself had the same little superstitious feeling in favor of following the decision of their oracle, such as it was, a feeling every body has had in moments of perplexity, though admitting its folly.

"So be it," she said. "We had better go at once; either it is growing dusk, or that cloud is coming very fast."

They clambered up the ascent, Milly somewhat burdened with a plaid which she had brought on her arm to make a comfortable seat, and Alice so weary that even the excitement of knowing they were lost could not make her forget her intense fatigue. But of all persons in the world, each felt that her companion was the last to whom she would admit either weariness or fear; so they climbed on, laughing and jesting, and being as witty and clever for each other's benefit as if they had been in a ballroom, with a crowd of men to listen to and appreciate their bon mots. They were at the top of the cliff, and stopped an instant to get breath and look out for some sign of the village.

Away in the west were broad streaks of dark red, half covered with smoky flecks; but the mist and rain, coming up from the south, had rushed so rapidly between, that it was like gazing out over a gray sea, and in the dim light the path at their feet looked fearfully precipitous and uncertain. Alice Marchmont gave one glance, and then started back a little.

"Are you afraid?" asked Milly, with polite contempt in her voice.

"Not in the least; my head was dizzy for a moment. It is over."

"Come, then, I'll go first."

"No, indeed; as the elder, that is my privilege."

Be helped out of an unpleasantness or danger, as it might chance to be, by Mrs. Marchmont? No; Milly felt that she could not, even

if the consequence of leading the way were a fall from the height and a broken back. She started down the suspicion of a pathway without another word, and Alice followed, with a careless laugh on her lips. Two woodsmen could not have shown less appearance of timidity, and certainly would have displayed more caution than these women, animated by feelings of cordial dislike on the one side, and repulsion on the other, caused by a consciousness of that dislike.

Down they hastened. The descent, which, under ordinary circumstances, would have been rather difficult than dangerous, was now somewhat perilous; for the red light died rapidly out of the sky, and the mist surged on toward them, some drops of chilly rain already beginning to fall, as a precursor of the storm which was close at hand. They had passed the steepest part of the way, and were apparently approaching a number of glens similar to those on the other side of the hills, and the sound of water-falls were again audible.

"Can you see out at all?" Mrs. Marchmont asked.

"Not in the least. I thought when we got here I should be able to form some idea of our whereabouts."

"But you can't?"

"No more than if we were in the moon."

Alice began to laugh, made a misstep, caught at a shrub for support; but the twigs gave way in her hand, and she fell to the ground, unable to repress one sharp cry of pain. Milly was some distance in advance, peering about among the shadows, but she heard the exclamation, and called,

"You did not fall? You're not hurt?"

There was no answer. She hastened back to the spot, and found Mrs. Marchmont nearly fainting, but trying to rise to her feet.

"Oh, are you hurt?" Milly asked, her anxiety roused at once.

"I think not; I can't tell till I'm up—very awkward of me—thank you," as Milly aided her.

But the instant she tried to stand the pain forced a groan from her, and she would have fallen again if Milly had not held her firmly.

"What is it? Where are you hurt?"

"My foot—"

"You have sprained your ankle?"

"I don't think it is; the pain is in my foot. Let me sit down a moment; perhaps I have only bruised it against a stone."

Milly forgot her dislike to the woman—the wrongs she had received at her hands—every thing except her suffering, and that she could see was excessive, by the whiteness of Mrs. Marchmont's lips, and the nervous contraction of her hands. Carefully as she could have touched a sister, Milly seated her on a convenient bank and supported her in her arms.

"I think the pain will pass in a moment," said Alice, trying to keep her voice from trembling. "Don't let me tire you; I can sit up."

"Lean against the tree, and let me loosen your boot-lacing," Milly said, for she saw that the pain did not decrease.

In spite of her hasty deprecation, Milly knelt and unlaced the dainty kid *bottine.*

"Ah, that is easier; perhaps if I draw it partly off for a little it will get better."

Milly attempted to do so, but Alice fairly shrieked—then exclaimed, as Milly stopped, in a fright,

"I do beg your pardon; I didn't think I was such a baby. Let it alone—I can walk—I must walk."

She struggled to her feet, tried to take a step, and fell backward.

"I can't do it," she said, the horrible pain sending a deathly faintness over her. "I must have broken some bone in my foot."

"Let me get your shoe and stocking off, and—"

"No, no; it would do no good! See, now; you must not mind me; just leave me here, and make your way down to the village."

"Indeed I will do no such thing!"

"You must reach it in time; you can send some one back for me."

"I can not leave you alone, Mrs. Marchmont—indeed I will not; so we'll not discuss it further."

"Then I must walk, if it kills me."

"You must do no such thing," returned Milly, firmly, restraining her as she tried to rise.

"It would be much wiser for you to go on and leave me," said Alice. "I should be perfectly safe."

"I'm not quite such a brute," exclaimed Milly.

"Indeed you are only too kind," returned Alice, warmly. "But you see, it can do no good to stay; I'm not afraid; besides, you would be sure to find help somewhere."

"I might find myself in the deep woods at the foot of the mountain as likely as anywhere."

"Honestly, would you rather stay?"

"Honestly! I don't know which way to turn."

"Well, certainly, there's no use filling the neighborhood with lost and distressed females; we may as well stay together if you are so good as to wish it, and—"

A severer twinge checked further words for the moment.

"I must find a more comfortable place for you," Milly said, "and get your boot off. Wait a moment."

She ran a little farther down the descent, and found herself in a sheltered glen; in the dim light she could see a water-fall dashing across the rocks, not far off a group of trees, under which last she spread her plaid, and then hurried back. In spite of Mrs. Marchmont's expostulations, Milly half carried, half led her to the place. Supported by Milly, she managed to get at last to the trees, and then sank on the plaid almost unconscious. Milly held her in her arms until the faintness had somewhat passed, too much frightened to remember any thing except that she was a woman, and needed help.

"What a miserable idiot I am!" cried Alice, recovering; "I dare say the hurt is nothing."

"I'm not so sure of that," Milly answered. "Let me try to find out what is wrong."

Milly drew off the boot and stocking as tenderly as possible, and examined the dainty white foot; Alice had displaced one of the little bones in the instep. Milly knew at once what was the matter, for young Rob, with the usual ill luck of boys at vacation-time, had met with a similar accident the preceding summer. She explained the nature of the hurt, saying,

"If you will let me, I am quite sure I can push the bone into its place, and bandage it as I saw the doctor do. There will be very little pain after."

"Oh, I should be so glad! Can I walk then?"

"Ah, that I can't promise. Rob was not allowed to attempt it for more than a week!"

"Fancy a week's sojourn here!" cried Alice.

Milly did not waste more words; she tore their handkerchiefs in strips, took the wounded foot in her hands, and easily pushed back the bone, the operation being slight enough to any one gifted with common sense and a keen faculty of observation. Then she bound it deftly with her impromptu bandages, wet them thoroughly, and finally folded Mrs. Marchmont tenderly in the plaid.

Alice had not uttered a word during the operation, which was painful enough, as I can aver from experience; but when it was over the relief was so great that she breathed a long sigh of positive content.

"Is that better?" asked Milly.

"It is like coming out of purgatory! How good you are to me—and how skillfully you did it!"

"Luckily I was obliged to watch the doctor. Rob would not sit still unless I held him fast in my arms."

"I am sure any surgeon would have hurt me much more—men are so awkward."

The pain was now sufficiently gone for them to consider their situation, and there was certainly nothing for it but to stay where they were. Mrs. Marchmont announced that she had a packet of biscuits in her pocket, and Milly had some fruit and a drinking-cup in the little velvet sachel which she always took with her in her walks to carry a book in. It was evident, as the rain had not continued, that the most unpleasant thing which could happen would be to suffer with cold.

"If you had not been unlucky enough to meet me," said Alice, "you would be safe at home long before this."

"No, indeed; I should only be lost somewhere else, and quite alone—at least I am very glad we are together."

"Do you really mean it?"

"I do; I am in earnest now; I would not say it else."

"Then I thank you heartily, and may be as glad as I wish to be that you met me, since you are not sorry."

"The storm has passed by," said Milly; "there will be no rain; perhaps the mist will go before the moon rises."

"If we were only men, we should carry plenty of matches for our odious pipes, and could have a fire."

"Are you cold?"

"Not at all—I am so wrapped up; but I'm afraid you are. Do take part of the plaid."

"Not yet; I'm warm enough. We have chanced on a bed of heather, where the sun has been lying all day, and my feet are as warm as possible."

"How absurd it all seems," said Alice; and they both began to laugh, which did them good.

By this time they discovered that they were hungry, and Mrs. Marchmont's paper of biscuits and Milly's forgotten fruit became treasures.

"It is better than the choicest supper at the Trois Frères," Alice declared. "By-the-way, when did you come abroad?"

"Last autumn," Milly answered.

"A friend wrote me that you were here, and that you are an heiress in these days. I congratulate you."

"You are very good."

"People may moralize as much as they please; money is a nice thing to have! So your friend Constance Worthington is married. I hope she is happy. Dear me—one forgets so—your aunt was very ill just before you left America."

"Yes—very ill."

"So the voyage was partly on her account?"

"No; she only came over this spring. I was with Mr. and Mrs. Crittendon until then."

"Nice people—very. You must have enjoyed these months greatly."

"I have; we were very quiet all winter, but I liked that."

"At your age?"

"One sometimes feels in that mood after taking care of a sick person," Milly answered, dryly.

"Ah! yes. I should think that might be. But I know very little about illness—I have been such a useless creature. I never was with any sick person except my husband," she added, in a softer voice, "and he only lived a very short time."

Alice said no more. Straightway Milly's thoughts rushed into the future. This woman would yet marry Mr. Halford! Well, and what was either of them to her? At present she had only to reflect that she was beside a human being who had need of her assistance. On the morrow they would separate, and each go her way—Mrs. Marchmont to wait for Halford, herself to take life as it came to her with what patience she might. She was recalled from these quickly flashing thoughts by Alice's voice repeating, meditatively,

"No, I knew nothing about illness until my husband's death."

"I am sorry if it was a great grief to you," Milly said, and never remembered how strangely the words would sound until they were spoken.

"It was not a grief to me in itself," Alice said, quietly "but it was a very solemn season. It made me think and reflect as I had never done before."

She said nothing else, and Milly did not choose to ask her what she meant. The conversation was assuming a serious tone not agreeable to her; she had no desire to learn any thing in regard to Alice's state of mind or feelings, and certainly no intention of betraying her own.

"The mist is passing away," she said, after a short pause; "the stars are beginning to come out; we shall have moonlight presently."

She rose and began to walk about the little glen in the gloom. Alice had not noticed her words, but her moving roused her from the reverie into which she had fallen.

"I am sure you are cold," said she.

"Indeed, no; I am impatient to see the moonlight. It will make the water-fall look very lovely, I am sure."

"How it sings!" said Alice; "I always envy running water; it seems to be so happy."

Presently the sky lightened; the tops of the cliffs and trees became tinged with streaks of pale, uncertain radiance that gradually brightened and grew silvery, till at last the moon sailed slowly up over the fleecy clouds. The rays streamed broad and full on the sparkling cascade, and turned the little glen into a fairy bower to which the lingering masses of mist made tinted hangings that were too lovely to be described by any words.

Mrs. Marchmont uttered an exclamation of extreme delight, and then was still, entranced by the loveliness of the scene. She glanced toward Milly; the girl was standing in front of the cascade, leaning carelessly against a tall tree, the moonlight resting full upon her face and upturned eyes, transfiguring them to that almost unearthly beauty which only moonlight can give. Alice bent forward, watching her curiously. Was this the creature she had left a spoiled, capricious child—this woman with the solemn eyes, and a strange, self-controlled expression on the beautiful mouth—the whole face changed into a lofty type of loveliness, which showed that not only had the soul developed into full power, but some terrible and bravely conquered suffering had smitten youthful and childish follies from her heart?

Had the separation from Kenneth Halford done this? Great Heaven, this girl had loved him, then—really loved! Alice seldom gave any one of her sex credit for the ability to love; but when she did, she pitied and admired her beyond measure. A great sympathy for Milly filled her soul, deepened by a sensation of absolute awe at the expression of her face in the white glory of the moonbeams.

"Milly!" she called, suddenly.

"Are you suffering again?" asked Milly, as she came toward her, startled by the tone.

"No, no; I beg your pardon. This odd adventure makes me silly and fanciful. You looked so like a lovely spirit, as you stood there, that I almost expected to see you float away."

"Ah, you have such a fund of pretty fancies and compliments," Milly answered, coldly.

"I did not mean to compliment; I was just speaking my thoughts—one doesn't often; but surely in this place it is very pardonable to be surprised into it."

"I suppose so."

"Are you angry because I called you by your first name?"

"I did not notice it."

"It was odd I should have done it; but I used to hear you called so very often."

Milly felt a hot flush of anger pass over her —the allusion was to Kenneth Halford. How dared this woman make even the most distant reference to his name!

"Let me wet the bandage again," she said, in the most commonplace tone.

"It is not necessary; my foot is perfectly easy, and I am as warm as possible. You will freeze, I am sure, if you walk about. Come, wrap yourself in the plaid, and let us watch the moonlight together."

"I'm not cold, and so very wide awake that I could not keep myself quiet," Milly replied.

With these thoughts again roused in her mind, she could not go near Mrs. Marchmont; her only chance of regaining composure was in getting back to ordinary topics of conversation while she walked about.

"Please do come," begged Alice, "else I shall think you still hate me too much."

"But since I am not cold—"

"Ah, but I am sure you must be; I implore you to come! Well, if you won't, I'll get up and throw your plaid away," exclaimed she, with a pretty willfulness.

There was nothing for it but to make a scene which would render herself ridiculous, and be downright cruelty under the circumstances, or to comply with Mrs. Marchmont's wish. So Milly sat down beside her, and Alice wrapped the plaid carefully about her, leaving her hand to rest caressingly on Milly's shoulder, and the touch of those slender fingers sent a chill to Milly's very soul.

"Ah, you are shivering even now!" exclaimed Alice. "You will catch cold and be ill, and all by my fault. Oh, I bring bad luck to every one who comes near me!"

"I don't think you will bring any bad luck to me," replied Milly, steadily, "in this instance."

"I hope you don't believe I wish to in any instance," said she, catching the last words. "I hope you don't," she repeated, when Milly did not speak.

"I hope not, certainly," she answered, trying to laugh; "but since you say you are so unfortunate to your friends, perhaps it is lucky for me that we are not likely to meet, if ever we get out of this wood."

"What an odd idea! Not meet? What can you mean?"

Milly had said more than she intended.

"I mean nothing—like most people. I should have said not soon, or often."

"Oh, that would pain me to believe," cried Alice, impulsively. "I'm such an absurdity; it seems to me as if we had been ever such a long time here together, and had grown well acquainted."

She was trying her fascinations, thought Milly, bitterly; but Alice Marchmont was quite powerless to deceive her.

"Are you laughing at me?" Alice asked.

"Oh no. I accept your last words as I do your other pretty speeches; they are very pleasant to hear."

"But you don't believe? That is downright unkind. I did not think you could be so hard-hearted! I wish I had not let you bind up my foot. I think I would rather have been left quite alone in the wood to-night than be indebted to a person who can think meanly of me."

She spoke so warmly that Milly was really touched. She relented sufficiently to believe that Mrs. Marchmont was sincere for the moment; but there was no reason why she should be deceived by so ephemeral a feeling, even if the lady was.

"There is no cause for gratitude," she said, cordially enough. "I shall think you are feverish, and be frightened if you are so easily agitated."

"Are you always calmness personified?" asked Mrs. Marchmont, smiling again. "Well, I am impulsive, as you see, even after all the discipline life has brought me; and there is one thing above all in which I think I shall never change—if I am to love any one I do it without warning, and I think I must love you in spite of yourself."

"Even if I had hostile intentions, I should in that case be obliged to throw down my arms. You are so entirely invincible, you know."

"You are mocking, and I am sure you have some strong dislike for me. Why is it? You do dislike me, don't you?"

Milly was silent; the truth was too rude to tell, and she was not willing, even for civility, to stoop to falsehood.

"You seem quite to hate me," persisted Alice.

"Not at this moment," replied Milly.

"Come, that is better than nothing—a long step gained. I'll be wise, and not ask more questions."

"How did you happen to find this quiet village?" said Milly, wishing to change the subject of conversation.

"The village that I can not find, you mean?

Oh, I was tired, and bored with well-known places and people, and I chanced to hear some one rave about this lake and the water-falls; so the next morning I set off in search of them."

"You reached here to-day?"

"Yes; but how did you know?"

"I did not—at least, that it was you. A servant told mine of another lady who had arrived, wondering I suppose, to see strangers so late in the season."

"So we are positively living under the same roof?"

"When we get back to it, if ever we do."

"Oh, they'll hunt us up," said Alice, with her usual *insouciance*. "Your aunt is sure to be frightened, and send to look you up, and my old servant will go quite mad."

"Poor aunty! I declare it was wicked of me to forget her anxiety."

"We are the heroines; it is for the others to be anxious. What time is it now?"

Milly looked at her watch; it was almost midnight.

"I did not think it was so late," said Mrs. Marchmont.

"Hark!" said Milly, starting up. "There are voices!"

They listened—the cries were repeated, and Milly shouted as loudly as she could in return. It was not long before the landlord and his party came down the cliff path, and Alice ungratefully whispered to her companion,

"I'm rather sorry they found us. I was very comfortable, and we should have got acquainted if they had only left us to play babes in the wood till morning."

As she spoke the words she looked up, and by the glare of the lanterns which shut out the moonlight she saw John Worthington's face.

CHAPTER XXXVI.

MADE CLEAR.

MILLY found her aunt in a state of great alarm, and almost inclined to be hysterical over her restoration, until she forgot the intention in her wonderment at learning who had been the girl's companion in this untoward adventure.

"Alice Marchmont!" she exclaimed. "Why I never heard the like! They told me there was another lady out, but they said it was a Mrs. Marsham. What on earth did you say or do?"

"We laughed," said Milly; "then she broke her foot; then I mended it; then we lay down in my plaid and talked trash; then the people found us. But who do you think headed the scouting-party?"

"I don't know; I am past surprise."

"Mr. Worthington. He told me he reached here just as the excitement about us was at its height; and oh! he hurt his arm coming back, to complete the romance."

"It is exactly like a romance," cried Mrs. Remsen.

"Oh, very like," returned Milly, yawning. "But I shall go and see Mrs. Marchmont, then get to bed, and finish the romance in the morning."

It had all come about naturally enough, romantic as it appeared to Mrs. Remsen. Alice Marchmont had been wandering about the Continent since her hasty departure from America, and had lately come over to England. She was seized with a desire to visit the Highlands once more, and, as Miss Portman detested mountain scenery, had left her at peace near London, and wandered off with no guardianship but that of her maid and man.

For several months past, John Worthington had received no letters from her; it had grown difficult for her to write in the old, calm, friendly way. He became too anxious to endure longer her silence; he set sail for Albion. He found Miss Portman, learned the direction her relative had taken, and started in pursuit. He followed her from one place to another, and reached the hotel only a few hours after her arrival.

The next day Mrs. Marchmont was unable to leave her bed. She had caught a severe cold; and this, added to the sprain, made her really ill, though it seemed to Milly that she was suffering more from mental agitation than physical pain.

John Worthington heard of her state from the physician, and did not attempt to see her, but he lay in wait for Milly, and fairly startled her by his manner and eager questions.

"Beg her to admit me as soon as she is able," he urged.

Milly went back to Mrs. Marchmont and repeated the message; but there was no reply. Alice turned her head on her pillow, so that her face was hidden, and did not speak for a long time. Milly might have thought that she slept save for the spasmodic quivering of her hands at intervals, and the choked sobs which occasionally shook her frame, but the girl was too wise to worry her charge by a single question. Alice grew so much worse after the physician paid his afternoon visit that she needed constant care; and finding her maid more helpless than a frightened partridge, Milly could not leave the room.

It was strange enough to sit by that bed, watching the woman whom she believed had willfully and wickedly worked her so much harm; to recall her own dislike, and their last meeting; but this was no time to indulge in unkind feelings, nor was there in her thoughts any Pharisaical idea of heaping coals of fire on her enemy's head.

As night came on, Alice's fever increased so much that she was slightly delirious. However, the doctor had prepared Milly for this; so she was not alarmed.

Between sleeping and waking, Alice talked disconnectedly of people and things concerning which Milly was ignorant—of trivial and long-forgotten matters, as well as those nearer. Sometimes she seemed frightened, oppressed by danger—once she called out Worthington's name, and uttered appealing words. Then she roused herself with an effort, and said,

"How good you are—how kind and tender! Wasn't I talking great nonsense?"

But the struggle to keep awake and sensible was too great for her wearied nerves, and she dozed again, complaining that she was so tired —so tired! She journeyed over stony roads; she was out of breath climbing steep hills; she was, through all, full of grief at her inability to explain something, and begged for Milly's little warm hand to hold in hers, because without it she was so lonely.

At length she fell sound asleep, and Milly sat regarding the beautiful face, afraid to move lest she should disturb her, and thinking what a strange chance it was that had brought them together under such circumstances. Milly was no wiser than the rest of us, and said chance, when, if she had stopped to reflect, she knew there was no such thing—no space for it in the grand plan of human existence.

The next morning Mrs. Marchmont was better, but, by the physician's orders, she remained in bed; indeed, after one rebellious attempt to leave it, she resigned herself to the necessity of obedience without further complaint.

The day wore on, and Milly scarcely left her. Toward evening she went down stairs for a few moments, to give Mr. Worthington more explicit tidings than she had been able to send, and he handed her a letter for Mrs. Marchmont.

"It is shameful to keep you a prisoner here," Alice said, as she returned to the chamber; "but I do so hate staying alone!"

"I could not leave you to your servant; I am glad to stay," Milly answered.

"Have you seen Mr. Worthington?" Alice asked, after a pause.

"Yes; his arm is better. I could relieve his anxiety about you, too."

"He was anxious—my good old John!"

"I have something to give you when you are well enough to read it," Milly added.

Alice stretched out her hand, and Milly put Worthington's letter into it and busied herself at the other side of the room, while Mrs. Marchmont read the epistle. For a long time she lay quiet. It was growing dusk now; Milly could not see her face, but she thought that Alice was weeping. At last Milly heard her call her name in a steady voice.

"What is it?" she asked, going toward the bed. "Shall I help you to move?"

"No," Alice answered. "Sit down by me —I want to talk to you."

"Shall I ring for a lamp?"

"Not yet, please; I like the twilight. You're sure you don't mind staying with me?"

"I like to stay; do believe it."

"Dear Milly—I may call you Milly?"

"If it pleases you," Milly said, softened in spite of herself, and wondering if she could possibly have misjudged this woman throughout—wondered, too, if she had as much exaggerated the wrong done her as she had Mrs. Marchmont's share in it.

"Do you remember our last meeting in America, Milly?" Alice asked, suddenly. "Weren't you a little hard on me then?"

"Very hard; I have many times since been sorry; but I was so hard and wicked in those days."

"My poor Milly," returned Alice, tenderly; "were you suffering too?"

This was an admission Milly could not bring herself to utter; she remained silent. Presently Alice spoke again.

"I am thinking about your goodness to me. I haven't had much tenderness shown me in my life, Milly. Oh! those days I was speaking of—how I suffered; my pride has become more tamed than yours—I don't mind owning it. Do you know who was very good to me then, though he had no idea what caused my trouble? Shall I tell you who it was?"

"Of course, if you like," Milly answered, slowly.

"It was Kenneth Halford."

Alice felt the hand which she had taken grow cold and begin to quiver, but she held it fast.

"Don't draw away, Milly; be quiet, child! I want to talk to you about him."

"And I don't care to hear," Milly replied, steadily.

"Because you don't believe with me that he was kind and true?"

"Partly that," said Milly, her voice growing a little hard. "But perhaps you knew him better than I did."

"Oh, Milly! And you once promised to be his wife?"

Milly snatched away her hand with an impulse to rise and leave the room, but Alice clung to her.

"You must not go, Milly! You will forgive me if my question sounded cruel; indeed I did not mean to be."

"Then we will talk of something else," Milly said, decidedly.

"We must speak of this; I implore you to let me!" Alice cried. "It is not curiosity, oh, believe that; but I must know what separated you and Kenneth Halford."

"I can imagine no reason why—"

"Hush, Milly! It is for my soul's peace! I had sometimes feared that I— Oh! now, what John Worthington writes—"

"Mr. Worthington can know nothing about the matter," interrupted Milly. "If you insist upon an answer, it is easily given."

"Tell me, Milly; do tell me!"

"His arrogance and my girlish caprices, his misunderstanding of my character and my lack of faith in him. Reasons enough for us to separate, since they proved there could be no real love between us."

"No, Milly, no; I am sure he loved you."

"Don't say another word, Mrs. Marchmont," said Milly, sternly. "If we are to speak or meet again, this subject must be at an end between us!"

"Then you still dislike me so much that you will not talk frankly. Perhaps I might be able to explain away your harsh judgment of me;" and she drew Milly to her, placed her hand on the unwilling head, turned the face toward her own, and looked pleadingly in the blue eyes. "How could you answer me like that?" she asked.

"No other subject could make me do so," said Milly, somewhat softened.

"Because—because you love him?" whispered Alice.

"Is it probable?" returned Milly, with the bitter laugh which had of late been unfamiliar to her lips. "Do you think I belong to the order of women who can love on after falsehood and deceit? I think there is not so much of the spaniel in my nature!"

"Kenneth Halford never intentionally deceived a human being; I know him to be incapable of it," said Alice, warmly.

Then came back to Milly the thought which had occurred to her that night in the glen—Alice loved him, and would marry him! Now she must not shrink from his name if it should wring her heart to listen.

"I know what I say," pursued Alice; "you may trust me, Milly; I am sure of it."

"Indeed, Mrs. Marchmont, its truth or falsity can have no interest for me," Milly answered, calmly. "Mr. Halford has passed completely out of my life and thoughts."

"Oh, Milly! When Kenneth Halford loved you so dearly—you believe that he loved you?" Alice asked.

"No," said Milly, coldly; "I am sure that he did not. He was a man tired of the world, and considering me a child, he fancied me for a time; but when he found that I could think and feel, even if I could not reason, and that I was horribly ill-tempered and exacting, he was glad to let me go."

"Did he say all this?"

"He was not likely to say it, Mrs. Marchmont, but I was quick to understand. Young as I was, you can not suppose that I was an utter idiot, without perception or imagination."

"On the contrary, I fancy both were only too excitable," replied Mrs. Marchmont. "So you sent Mr. Halford away?"

"Out of my life at least; yes."

"I only heard the incomprehensible story your little cousin told me the day I tried to see you," said Alice; "but I knew you must have broken the engagement; he was not a man to do that, although you did torment him."

"Perhaps he complained to you," said Milly, her eyes flashing.

"No, Milly," said Alice, gently, "you could not think so. I found it out for myself, but not long before he went away, and I have had no news of him since."

Milly found herself wondering at this; perhaps Alice loved him without return. Milly softened into a kinder mood.

"Nor have I," said she; "so we have reached the conclusion of the episode; and now we can talk of something else."

"Not quite yet, dear Milly. I must understand why you disliked me so much. Tell me why you broke your engagement, Milly."

This question brought back too plainly the night when she had parted with Halford—the kiss she had seen him press on Alice's hand—the broken words she had heard him speak.

"I think we had better end here," said she, slowly.

"What made you start, dearest Milly? You say you don't love him?"

"I was thinking of you, rather than of him," Milly said, forcing herself to speak calmly. "I was thinking how odd that we two should be here together, and that you should ask me this question."

"Now tell me what you mean, Milly."

"At all events, I did not mean to say that."

"But you have said it; you must explain. Child, I have reason to think that I had a share in your trouble. You vexed me often, and I fancied that you liked Halford, and wanted to tease you. Can you forgive such meanness?"

"Easily—now."

"After I was certain of your engagement, I did not want to do any harm; but I thought it only a kindness to you both to teach you to be less impulsive and exacting. It was very wicked of me. I did not know you."

"But this—"

"Wait, Milly! John Worthington's letter has shown me the truth. He tells me that Halford, in one of his letters, told him that you were annoyed by our friendship. Worthington wrote me this now, that I might try to set right any wrong I had done. Oh, let me try, Milly! If you will show me your whole heart, I shall believe that you have ceased to think harshly of me; and I, too, need a little tenderness, Milly, oh, so much! What did I do?"

"There is no need to go back over the past," Milly said; "it is dead and gone—let it rest! I don't dislike you now."

"You must tell me what share I had in your trouble."

"I was jealous, if you will know," cried Milly; "he tormented me, I hated you bitterly, but I blamed him none the less."

"But he loved you, Milly, child! He loved you."

Milly's penitent regret died out under fresh anger at these words.

"Hush!" she said, harshly. "You say you wish me to believe you; don't make it quite impossible. He loved you, Alice Marchmont, and you knew that he did."

Her soul was full of bitterness. The old be-

lief in Alice's falsity came back so strongly
that she longed to get away. She rose to leave
the room, but Alice clung to her, saying, vehemently,

"You are wrong, child; he was good and
true; he did not love me."

"Oh, madam!" cried Milly, indignantly,
"what can you gain by trying to cheat me
now? That night at the ball—that last night,
when I saw him kiss your hand, I heard him
say—" She broke off with a shudder, and
turned proudly aside, but Alice held her hands
fast.

"Try to believe me, Milly," she pleaded;
"let me tell you how it was."

"You were free to love him," went on Milly. "The treachery was on his side—treacherous to both, since he was my betrothed husband
when he spoke those words of love to you."

"He never did—there is your error. Give
me a moment, child, and I can explain all this.
I understand now—I remember that night—"

"Then we need talk no more."

"It is for that very reason you must listen;
you were mistaken. Milly, don't refuse to hear
what may bring back peace to you."

Milly made a violent effort, and conquered
her passion. Alice held her hands, looking up
into her face, her lovely eyes misty with tears,
and Milly's heart believed, in spite of pride.

"Go on," she said. "I will hear you."

"Kenneth Halford and I were friends; we
had been nothing else since my girlhood. He
knew all my life's story, more of my early
wretchedness than any other person, and it
made a strong tie between us. You are listening, Milly, and believing?"

"Yes, yes—go on," said Milly, with her face
averted.

"I liked you," pursued Alice; "you were
so very pretty—like a flower or a picture. I
did not know you really cared for him. At last
it was rumored that you were engaged. I
thought he would have told me if it were true.
You grew dreadfully rude to me, and I vexed
you in return; but I had not the most distant
idea of destroying your future peace."

"Go on," said Milly, softly.

"You were capricious with Mr. Halford.
You made him think that he had been mistaken in you, that you were jealous and tyran-
nical, and that your love could never bring him
the rest and peace he craved, perhaps too self-
ishly. Do you see this?"

"I have no wish to exculpate myself. I did
wrong; but at least I was true! I loved him,
and he—"

"Wait, Milly, I am coming to that—that last
night. You did behave badly; he was hurt,
and angry; and I was in such a reckless mood
—if you could know what I was living through
—Milly, I was like the man who had a sword
suspended over his head by a hair, and knew
that the blow might fall at any moment!"

Milly drew both the shaking hands into hers
with a sudden pity, and held them fast.

"We were standing in that little room; he
had told me of his engagement to you, and his
fears that he had been mistaken in your character. I answered that I thought you a child;
but since it was youth and innocence that he
coveted, he must be content. I told him he
was wrong not to show you more of his true
self, and teach you to come up where he stood,
if he really loved you. 'I do love her,' he
said; 'she is my last hope of happiness;' and,
Milly, I am sure he meant it."

Milly listened breathlessly now.

"Then he began talking all sorts of nonsense
and bitter misanthropy. He said at last that
he was a greater fool than he had thought;
that he had never believed he could be so weak
as to love as he did; then broke off, laughing,
ashamed, I suppose, that I should see how much
he suffered, said something about my being a
sweet comforter, and, just out of a man's foolish gallantry, kissed my hand, and hurried away.
A moment after, I saw you in the room. I can
see how it all appeared to you, Milly; but now,
surely, you believe me—say that you do."

"Yes," answered Milly; "I can not doubt
you."

"Then you forgive me, too, dear, my share
in your suffering?"

"Wait, Alice, till I can think. It is I, you
know, who need forgiveness."

"And are you satisfied now—you are at
rest; you exonerate Kenneth Halford from any
charge of deceit?"

"Entirely, dear friend; I see it all clearly
now."

"And you are glad again—you hope?"

There was no responsive pressure to the hand
which held Milly's. Alice looked in her face
in surprise.

"What is it?" she urged; "what is it you
are thinking of now?"

"I thank Heaven that I have not loved a
man unworthy," Milly answered, drying a few
quiet tears. "I am full of remorse for the bitterness I cherished in my heart during those
black days, grateful to God that I have since
tried to be less wicked; for if this news had
come to me in their midst, I should have been
overpowered by shame at my sin against the
Father in losing hope and faith."

"And that is all, Milly?"

"That is all! Glad to know you thoroughly; for I love you now, dear Mrs. Marchmont,
and always shall."

"And I love you, too, and want you to be
happy."

"I shall grow so, if I try to fulfill my duties.
You know there is no other real happiness."

"But there is another happiness, dear child;
and it is not too late to find it."

"Hush! Alice."

"Does not the confirmation of his truth
bring back your old love, your old hopes,
Milly?"

"No, Alice; I feel that the past is irrevoca-
ble."

"Not to you—not to you, with nothing to blot out but the remembrance of a lover's quarrel."

"Oh, Alice! Kenneth Halford and I are separated forever; and it is better so," Milly said, her voice breaking a little. "He never loved me as I really was—he loved his own ideal. He was wrong to patronize and look down upon me, and—and I was outraged by perceiving it. It was not wholly the foolish jealousy of a girl. I had always the feeling of a woman who is slighted and underrated."

"But every thing would be so different now."

"Not in the least, believe me. He wanted a child's love—to be looked up to and worshiped quite blindly, and without question. I am not that child. The man who loves me will and must respect me, too, and feel that there is no depth in his soul I could not reach, no aspiration that I am unfit to share."

"How firm and stern you are! I thought you were only influenced by your belief in his falsehood."

"Now that doubt is quite past, the other causes which must sooner or later have separated us do not lose their importance."

"But when I tell you that he did so love you—"

"Don't mock me with the word, dear friend; you and I know what love really is. There are many girls content to remain children all their lives, to take only a vicarious interest in the things which occupy their husband's hearts and minds; you do not think me such a one?"

"No, Milly, you are not, indeed."

"And since it was such a wife Kenneth Halford wanted, he could never really love me. By this time he will have forgotten his dream. I had not passed deep enough into his life to be long regretted."

"I can not believe that, Milly."

"Well, if he regrets me, it is as one misses a favorite flower, a bird, any trifle with which one amused the leisure hours of his life."

"If he could see you as you really are."

"You forget that it would be the strongest reason of all for not loving me. I am not a child, and it is a child he longs for, not a woman. Would you have me call him back, if it were possible, to be disappointed anew? No, I am sure you would not. My life is tranquil; leave it me."

Alice urged her no further; she only sighed,

"It is so dreary to be quite alone; life is sometimes so heavy."

"Perhaps not in time, dear Alice; I believe not."

"Ah! you can hope it. I am older than you. I have had a trouble more sharp; but it seems to me that life is very dark, without one strong and tender friend. Ah me! But go you to bed; I needn't keep you up listening to my wailings."

They talked for a while longer. Alice persuaded her to relate every circumstance connected with the broken engagement; then she sent her away, insisting that she could sleep if left alone.

She spent the night almost as wakefully as she had done so many others, but at least it held one means of relief. She wrote a long letter to Kenneth Halford, and, when it was finished, she murmured to herself,

"At all events, I can do so much; thank God for that!"

CHAPTER XXXVII.

INTO THE LIGHT.

THE next day Milly found Mrs. Marchmont suffering less physical pain, but she knew the instant she looked in her face that no sleep had visited the hollow, mournful eyes during the whole night.

Alice talked, and tried to be herself, keeping so resolutely away from any serious subject that it was not until nearly night that Milly could induce her to listen to Mr. Worthington's urgent requests for admission.

"I must see him," Alice said; "I have just been trying to put it off. I am such a coward."

Several times she had uttered vague hints of the sort, but Milly could demand no explanations.

"He is very anxious about you," she said. "I think he suffers a good deal, too, with his arm."

"Oh yes, he was hurt; I forgot it—selfish wretch! Go and tell him to come up, Milly. To-morrow I'll see your aunt, too. I am ashamed to have behaved so ill."

Milly assisted her to rise and dress, established her in an easy-chair, and went in search of Mr. Worthington, beginning to perceive that there was a deeper feeling hidden in both hearts than the old friendship which she had believed the tie that bound them.

He came into the room, and Alice's last effort at self-control gave way; she could only bury her face in her hands and weep silently. He sat down, soothed her back to quiet by his gentle words, and at last she could look up and talk connectedly, and try to thank him for his goodness.

"But you have not told me why you ceased writing," he said, after they had talked for a long time.

The color flickered across her cheeks as she answered, with an attempt at her old playfulness,

"You can't expect me to have grown quite free from caprices in little more than a year."

"Was it because I wrote something that I ought not?" he asked. "Were you afraid I would trouble you with my foolish wishes? You should have remembered that I had promised never to do so again."

"No, no; not that!" she replied, faltering. "I knew that was not likely to happen; it was the impulse of a moment; even an angel's pity could not—"

"Alice, Alice!" he interrupted, "you know what made me speak—you must know."

"Yes," she said, "and I did full justice to your goodness! You pitied me so; but I couldn't let your pity make you forget. I couldn't be any man's wife, least of all yours."

"I never thought to tell you my story," he said, "but I must; then, if you bid me, I will go away. Alice, I have loved you all these years! I never spoke, for fear it should break up our pleasant friendship; but I loved you as passionately, as devotedly as ever woman was loved."

"You loved me!" she said, almost in a frightened voice. "You loved me!"

"Always—with the full strength of my heart. When that trouble came, I loved you more fondly than ever I thought; every day since you have grown closer and closer to my soul. Perhaps I oughtn't to say this. I don't mean to trouble you."

"Oh, John Worthington, John Worthington, it isn't that! But how could you love me? how could you care for me?"

"I suppose nobody ever was able to answer that question, Alice; but I do love you—the one love of my life. I love you so truly that even if you can never care for me I will not trouble you by my pain."

"You have been an angel to me!" she said, brokenly. "No one was ever like you. All these years you have been my ideal of everything that was noble and good."

"Alice! Alice! do you know what you are saying? Do you know what hope you are giving me?"

"Ought I?" she asked, simply as a child. "Do you tell me what is right, John Worthington."

"Try to love me, Alice; to understand how boundless my affection is for you—how lonely the rest of my life must be if we separate again. Could you try, Alice?"

She hid her face in her hands, but he heard her voice, low and firm now,

"I think I must have loved you all the while; but this last year taught me plainly. I missed you so! oh, I missed you so!"

John Worthington folded her in his arms, with the thankful content of a man who has found the realization of a life's fondest wish, and she wept her tears of gratitude upon his shoulder.

For a time neither of them could talk much, but it was easier at length; and then there was so much to say, that Milly, waiting in her chamber, grew a little impatient of the long interview. All the evening they sat together, and Alice thought that she must have passed into another world. Every thing was settled for her; she had no need to make decisions, to weary herself with fears or doubts. She put her trust in his assurances, and was at rest.

Mrs. Remsen and Milly were to be induced to accompany them to Edinburgh. Miss Portman would join them there.

"Then I shall have you fast," he said; "my wife, my own wife!"

"Not so soon; I am not fit. Wait till you are sure I mean to be worthy—oh, John!"

But the strong arm was drawing her closer again.

"I want my happiness," he pleaded; "I can't afford to wait any longer; this dreadful year of loneliness is enough. Alice, my darling, for you and me the past is dead; between you and the merciful Father it will be a bond to bring you closer to Him."

He would have it so, and she had nothing more to urge. It was so sweet to rest upon his decision, and know that it must be right.

In less than four weeks the news of the marriage reached America; and though people in general thought it sufficiently extraordinary, they were obliged to admit the suitability of the match.

After the departure of the newly-wedded pair, Mrs. Remsen and Milly lingered in the neighborhood of that most picturesque of cities, sending for Miss Gorham and the children to join them.

September came, and on one of its loveliest evenings Kenneth Halford opened the gate of the pretty cottage where Milly and her aunt had made their home for a time. He had been a very unhappy man during his wanderings, finding that his love for Milly was a deeper-seated sentiment than he had himself recognized. He learned to think of her, not as the spoiled child whom he had wished to direct, and by whom he was to be blindly worshiped, but as the true woman into which he saw his love might have developed her. Then Alice Marchmont's letter reached him, and he hastened away to try if life might not yet win peace and rest.

Milly had been out among the woods and fields. Toward sunset she reached the grove which crowned the hill back of the house, and sat down on a rustic bench to watch the crimson and white clouds sweep up the west. Sitting there in the gathering brightness, Milly's thoughts went back to the old days, and the dream which had beautified her youth—thinking sadly, as she seldom now allowed herself to do, of all that might have been, of the fulfillment of hope which might have reached her had she been more patient, more ready to leave her destiny in higher hands.

Milly had learned to be content, satisfied to pluck the little flowers which grow up in our daily paths, but which most of us crush unconsciously under our feet, while staring away into the future and the unattainable. Milly knew that, with no great love to brighten existence, her life, regarded by itself, must appear a little faded, a little solitary; but she was trying not to live for herself, not to dignify selfishness by some poetical name; therefore she was able to endure the lack of warmth and coloring, and look bravely forward along the appointed path.

And while she thought, and sternly told herself that she had a great deal to be thankful for, some one came quickly up the hill from the cottage. She raised her eyes at the sound of footsteps, and there Kenneth Halford stood before her, his hands stretched out in eager welcome, his voice calling,

"Milly! Milly!"

She could not rise or speak; the meeting was so unexpected that his presence seemed scarcely real.

"Won't you speak to me, Milly? Won't you at least say that you are glad to see me?"

He caught her hands, and held them fast while he poured out the story of his contrition and suffering.

"I have come to ask your pardon, Milly; will you grant it? As soon as we were parted I saw how blind and mad I had been! I did think you a child, Milly; but I loved you with all my heart. I could see when too late how my man's arrogance had made me hard and cruel. I knew that it was I who had been wrong; I longed so for your forgiveness; shall I have it, Milly?"

"If you felt like that, think what my feelings were," Milly answered, when she could reply. "I have learned how falsely I suspected you, how wicked I was. Oh, you can never forgive that!"

"Mrs. Marchmont wrote me the whole story, Milly; I don't wonder you doubted me. You are not to blame; it was all my fault—my selfishness that caused the whole trouble. Can you forgive me?"

"As entirely as you have forgiven me."

"Can you trust me with your heart again?" he urged. "Can you love me once more, Milly?"

She turned her face away, but her voice was steady, almost solemn, as she answered,

"I never ceased to love you, Kenneth—not for a day or an hour."

It was the old, old story, which is always beautiful, always new—the story of love and reconciliation—the true love which knows upon what it is built, and has learned to treasure its blessings aright.

"To think that I have wasted so many months of our lives," Halford said, after they had talked deep into the twilight. "We might

have been happy all this dismal season, which seems a century to look back on."

Milly shook her head and smiled.

"No, Kenneth, we should not have been happy; the trouble must have come. We began wrong; I was too ignorant, too undisciplined, for peace to have been possible."

But he could only see his own error, and lament his own blindness and folly.

"I think I am humbled now, Milly. I know that all that is purest and best in my life must come from you—that all my great joys must depend upon you, every care be lightened by your sympathy. I know that I am honored by your love; the sole reason I can believe there is any good left in me is because you are able to care for me."

"Oh, Kenneth!"

Milly's voice was so sweet as she uttered the name which he had not heard since he left her, to wander among careless strangers; Milly's eyes so beautiful, as she raised them to his face with her whole soul shining from their depths, that he could only fold her to his heart again, and let the common world drift out of sight, leaving them alone in their glorified Eden—just them alone.

They were married at once. There is nothing more to tell.

Two winters afterward, Mrs. Remsen gave a grand party in honor of their return home. Adelaide Ramsay was there, looking like a peripatetic jewelry shop; Hortense, talking right and left to whoever would listen, about some wonderful theory in regard to a man's having three separate souls; and Charley Thorne, seeming contented enough with Maud by his side.

John Worthington and his wife were there, too, and it seemed to Alice that, as she leaned on her husband's arm, and gazed at Milly's radiant face, the last troubled memory swept away forever into the oblivion of the past.

Dick Faulkner had already disappeared from the haunts which once knew him, had almost faded out of the recollections of those who called themselves his friends. In the financial ruin which overtook him, he would have fared still worse, had not his wife received from the woman he had so cruelly tormented, a check, signed, like the note for which Alice Marchmont periled her soul, with John Worthington's name.

THE END.

HARPER'S LIBRARY OF SELECT NOVELS.

Mailing Notice.—HARPER & BROTHERS *will send their Books by Mail, postage free, to any part of the United States, on receipt of the Price.*

MISCELLANEOUS POPULAR NOVELS

PUBLISHED BY HARPER & BROTHERS, NEW YORK.

Harper & Brothers publish, in addition to others, including their *Library of Select Novels,* the following Miscellaneous Popular Works of Fiction:

(For full titles, see Harper's Catalogue.)

DICKENS'S NOVELS, Harper's Household Edition. Illustrated.
   Oliver Twist. 8vo, Cloth, $1 00; Paper, 50 cents.
   Martin Chuzzlewit. 8vo, Cloth, $1 50; Paper, $1 00.
   The Old Curiosity Shop. 8vo, Cloth, $1 25; Paper, 75 cents.
   David Copperfield. 8vo, Cloth, $1 50; Paper, $1 00.
   Dombey and Son. 8vo, Cloth, $1 50; Paper, $1 00.
   Nicholas Nickleby. 8vo, Cloth, $1 50; Paper, $1 00.
   Bleak House. 8vo, Cloth, $1 50; Paper, $1 00.
   Pickwick Papers. 8vo, Cloth, $1 50; Paper, $1 00.
   Little Dorrit. 8vo, Cloth, $1 50; Paper, $1 00.
   To be followed by the Author's other novels.
COLLINS'S* Armadale. Illustrations. 8vo, Paper, $1 00.
   Man and Wife. Illustrations. 8vo, Paper, $1 00.
   Moonstone. Illustrations. 8vo, Paper, $1 00.
   No Name. Illustrations. 8vo, Paper, $1 00.
   Poor Miss Finch. Illustrations. 8vo, Paper, $1 00.
   Woman in White. Illustrations. 8vo, Paper, $1 00.
COLLINS'S NOVELS: ILLUSTRATED LIBRARY EDITION, 12mo, per vol. $1 50.
   Armadale.—Basil.—Hide-and-Seek.—Man and Wife.—No Name.—Poor Miss Finch—The Dead Secret.—The Moonstone.—The New Magdalen.—The Woman in White.—Queen of Hearts.
BENEDICT'S My Daughter Elinor. 8vo, Cloth, $1 75; Paper, $1 25.
   Miss Dorothy's Charge. 8vo, Cloth, $1 50; Paper, $1 00.
   Miss Van Kortland. 8vo, Cloth, $1 50; Paper, $1 00.
BLACKWELL'S The Island Neighbors. Illustrated. 8vo, Paper, 75 cents.
BRADDON'S (M. E.)* Birds of Prey. Illustrations. 8vo, Paper, 75 cents.
   Bound to John Company. Ill's. 8vo, Paper, 75 cts.
BROOKS'S Silver Cord. Ill's. 8vo, Cloth, $2 00.
   Sooner or Later. Illustrations. 8vo, Cloth, $2 00; Paper, $1 50.
   The Gordian Knot. 8vo, Paper, 50 cents.
CHURCH'S (Mrs. Ross)* Prey of the Gods. 8vo, Paper, 50 cents.

BRONTE Novels.
   Jane Eyre. By Currer Bell (Charlotte Brontë). 12mo, Cloth, $1 50.
   Shirley. By Currer Bell. 12mo, Cloth, $1 50.
   Villette. By Currer Bell. 12mo, Cloth, $1 50.
   The Professor. By Currer Bell. 12mo, Cloth, $1 50.
   Tenant of Wildfell Hall. By Acton Bell (Anna Brontë). 12mo, Cloth, $1 50.
   Wuthering Heights. By Ellis Bell (Emily Brontë). 12mo, Cloth, $1 50.
BULWER'S (Sir E. B. Lytton)* My Novel. 8vo, Paper, $1 50; Library Edition, 2 vols., 12mo, Cloth, $2 50.
   What will He Do with It? 8vo, Paper, $1 50; Cloth, $2 00.
   The Caxtons. 8vo, Paper, 75 cents; Library Edition, 12mo, Cloth, $1 25.
   Leila. 12mo, Cloth, $1 00.
   Godolphin. 12mo, Cloth, $1 50.
   Kenelm Chillingly. 12mo, Cloth, $1 25.
   A Strange Story. 12mo, Cloth, $1 25.
   Parisians. 12mo, Cloth, $1 50; 8vo, Cloth, $1 00.
BULWER'S (Robert—"Owen Meredith") The Ring of Amasis. 12mo, Cloth, $1 50.
DE MILLE'S Cord and Creese. Illustrations. 8vo, Cloth, $1 25; Paper, 75 cents.
   The American Baron. Illustrations. 8vo, Cloth, $1 50; Paper, $1 00.
   The Cryptogram. Illustrations. 8vo, Cloth, $2 00; Paper, $1 50.
   The Dodge Club. Illustrations. 8vo, Cloth, $1 25; Paper, 75 cents.
DE WITT'S (Madame) A French Country Family. Illustrations. 12mo, Cloth, $1 50.
   Motherless. Illustrations. 12mo, Cloth, $1 50.
FARJEON'S (B. L.)* Blade-o'-Grass. Illustrations. 8vo, Paper, 25 cents.
   Bread-and-Cheese and Kisses. Illustrations. 8vo, Paper, 35 cents.
   London's Heart. Illustrations. 8vo, Cloth, $1 50; Paper, $1 00.
   Golden Grain. Illustrations. 8vo, Paper, 35 cents.

* For other Novels by the same author, see *Library of Select Novels.*

CHARLES READE'S Terrible Temptation. Illustrations. 8vo, Paper, 30 cents; 12mo, Cloth, 75 cents.
  Hard Cash. Illustrations. 8vo, Paper, 50 cents.
  Griffith Gaunt. Ill's. 8vo, Paper, 25 cents.
  It is Never Too Late to Mend. 8vo, Paper, 50 cts.
  Love Me Little, Love Me Long. 8vo, Paper, 50 cents. 12mo, Cloth, $1 50.
  Foul Play. 8vo, Paper, 25 cents.
  White Lies. 8vo, Paper, 50 cents.
  Peg Woffington and Other Tales. 8vo, Paper, 50 cents.
  Put Yourself in His Place. Illustrations. 8vo, Paper, 75 cents; Cloth, $1 25; 12mo, Cloth, $1 00.
  The Cloister and the Hearth. 8vo, Paper, 50 cents.
  The Wandering Heir. Ill's. 8vo, Paper, 25 cents.
CURTIS'S (G. W.) Trumps. Ill's. 12mo, Cloth, $2 00.
EDGEWORTH'S Novels. 10 vols. 12mo, Cloth, $1 50 per vol.
  Frank. 2 vols., 18mo, Cloth, $1 50.
  Harry and Lucy. 2 vols., 12mo, Cloth, $3 00.
  Moral Tales. 2 vols., 18mo, Cloth, $1 50.
  Popular Tales. 2 vols., 18mo, Cloth, $1 50.
  Rosamond. Illustrations. 12mo, Cloth, $1 50.
EDWARDS'S (Amelia B.)* Debenham's Vow. Illustrations. 8vo, Paper, 75 cents.
ELIOT'S (George) Adam Bede. Illustrations. 12mo, Cloth, $1 00.
  Middlemarch. 2 vols., 12mo, Cloth, $1 75 per vol.
  The Mill on the Floss. Ill's. 12mo, Cloth, $1 00.
  Felix Holt, the Radical. Ill's. 12mo, Cloth, $1 00.
  Romola. Illustrations. 12mo, Cloth, $1 00.
  Scenes of Clerical Life and Silas Marner. Illustrated. 12mo, Cloth, $1 00.
GASKELL'S (Mrs.)* Cranford. 12mo, Cloth, $1 25.
  Moorland Cottage. 18mo, Cloth, 75 cents.
  Right at Last, &c. 12mo, Cloth, $1 50.
  Wives and Daughters. Illustrations. 8vo, Cloth, $2 00; Paper, $1 50.
JAMES'S* The Club Book. 12mo, Cloth, $1 50.
  De L'Orme. 12mo, Cloth, $1 50.
  Gentleman of the Old School. 12mo, Cloth, $1 50.
  The Gipsy. 12mo, Cloth, $1 50.
  Henry of Guise. 12mo, Cloth, $1 50.
  Henry Masterton. 12mo, Cloth, $1 50.
  The Jacquerie. 12mo, Cloth, $1 50.
  Morley Ernstein. 12mo, Cloth, $1 50.
  One in a Thousand. 12mo, Cloth, $1 50.
  Philip Augustus. 12mo, Cloth, $1 50.
  Attila. 12mo, Cloth, $1 50.
  Corse de Lion. 12mo, Cloth, $1 50.
  The Ancient Régime. 12mo, Cloth, $1 50.
  The Man at Arms. 12mo, Cloth, $1 50.
  Charles Tyrrel. 12mo, Cloth, $1 50.
  The Robber. 12mo, Cloth, $1 50.
  Richelieu. 12mo, Cloth, $1 50.
  The Huguenot. 12mo, Cloth, $1 50.
  The King's Highway. 12mo, Cloth, $1 50.
  The String of Pearls. 12mo, Cloth, $1 25.
  Mary of Burgundy. 12mo, Cloth, $1 50.
  Darnley. 12mo, Cloth, $1 50.
  John Marston Hall. 12mo, Cloth, $1 50.
  The Desultory Man. 12mo, Cloth, $1 50.
JEAFFRESON'S* Isabel. 12mo, Cloth, $1 50.
  Not Dead Yet. 8vo, Cloth, $1 75; Paper, $1 25.
KINGSLEY'S Alton Locke. 12mo, Cloth, $1 50.
  Yeast: a Problem. 12mo, Cloth, $1 50.
KINGSLEY'S (Henry)* Stretton. 8vo, Paper, 40 cts.
LAWRENCE'S (Geo. A.)* Guy Livingstone. 12mo, Cloth, $1 50.
  Breaking a Butterfly. 8vo, Paper, 35 cents.
LEE'S (Holme)* Kathie Brande. 12mo, Cloth, $1 50.
  Sylvan Holt's Daughter. 12mo, Cloth, $1 50.
LEVER'S* Luttrell of Arran. 8vo, Cloth, $1 50; Paper, $1 00.
  Tony Butler. 8vo, Cloth, $1 50; Paper, $1 00.
  Lord Kilgobbin. Illustrations. 8vo, Cloth, $1 50; Paper, $1 00.
McCARTHY'S* My Enemy's Daughter. Illustrated. 8vo, Paper, 75 cents.
MACDONALD'S* Annals of a Quiet Neighborhood. 12mo, Cloth, $1 75.
MELVILLE'S Mardi. 2 vols., 12mo, Cloth, $3 00.
  Moby-Dick. 12mo, Cloth, $1 75.
  Omoo. 12mo, Cloth, $1 50.
  Pierre. 12mo, Cloth, $1 50.
  Redburn. 12mo, Cloth, $1 50.
  Typee. 12mo, Cloth, $1 50.
  Whitejacket. 12mo, Cloth, $1 50.

MULOCK'S (Miss)* A Brave Lady. Illustrated. 8vo, Cloth, $1 50; Paper, $1 00; 12mo, Cloth, $1 50.
  Hannah. Illustrated. 8vo, Paper, 50 cents; 12mo, Cloth, $1 50.
  The Woman's Kingdom. Illustrated. 8vo, Cloth, $1 50; Paper, $1 00; 12mo, Cloth, $1 50.
  A Life for a Life. 12mo, Cloth, $1 50.
  Christian's Mistake. 12mo, Cloth, $1 50.
  A Noble Life. 12mo, Cloth, $1 50.
  John Halifax, Gentleman. 12mo, Cloth, $1 50.
  The Unkind Word and Other Stories. 12mo, Cloth, $1 50.
  Two Marriages. 12mo, Cloth, $1 50.
  Olive. 12mo, Cloth, $1 50.
  Ogilvies. 12mo, Cloth, $1 50.
  Head of the Family. Trumps. 12mo, Cloth, $1 50.
  Mistress and Maid. 12mo, Cloth, $1 50.
  Agatha's Husband. 12mo, Cloth, $1 50.
MORE'S (Hannah) Complete Works. 1 vol., 8vo, Sheep, $3 00.
MY Husband's Crime. Illustrated. 8vo, Paper, 75 cts.
OLIPHANT'S (Mrs.)* Chronicles of Carlingford. 8vo, Cloth, $1 75; Paper, $1 25.
  Last of the Mortimers. 12mo, Cloth, $1 50.
  Laird of Norlaw. 12mo, Cloth, $1 50.
  Lucy Crofton. 12mo, Cloth, $1 50.
  Perpetual Curate. 8vo, Cloth, $1 50; Paper, $1 00.
  A Son of the Soil. 8vo, Cloth, $1 50; Paper, $1 00.
RECOLLECTIONS of Eton. Illustrations. 8vo, Paper, 50 cents.
ROBINSON'S (F. W.)* For Her Sake. Illustrations. 8vo, Paper, 75 cents.
  Christie's Faith. 12mo, Cloth, $1 75.
  Little Kate Kirby. Illustrated. 8vo, Paper, 75 cts.
SEDGWICK'S (Miss) Hope Leslie. 2 vols., 12mo, Cloth, $3 00.
  Live and Let Live. 18mo, Cloth, 75 cents.
  Married or Single? 2 vols., 12mo, Cloth, $3 00.
  Means and Ends. 18mo, Cloth, 75 cents.
  Poor Rich Man and Rich Poor Man. 18mo, Cloth, 75 cents.
  Stories for Young Persons. 18mo, Cloth, 75 cents.
  Tales of Glauber Spa. 12mo, Cloth, $1 50.
  Wilton Harvey and Other Tales. 18mo, Cloth, 75 cents.
SEDGWICK'S (Mrs.) Walter Thornley. 12mo, Cloth, $1 50.
SHERWOOD'S (Mrs.) Works. Illustrations. 16 vols., 12mo, Cloth, $1 50 per vol.
  Henry Milner. 2 vols., 12mo, Cloth, $3 00.
  Lady of the Manor. 4 vols., 12mo, Cloth, $6 00.
  Roxobel. 3 vols., 18mo, Cloth, $2 25.
THACKERAY'S (W. M.) Novels:
  Vanity Fair. 32 Illustrations. 8vo, Paper, 50 cts.
  Pendennis. 179 Illustrations. 8vo, Paper, 75 cts.
  The Virginians. 150 Illustrations. 8vo, Paper, 75 cts.
  The Newcomes. 162 Illustrations. 8vo, Paper, 75 cents.
  The Adventures of Philip. Portrait of Author and 64 Illustrations. 8vo, Paper, 50 cents.
  Henry Esmond and Lovel the Widower. 12 Illustrations. 8vo, Paper, 50 cents.
TOM BROWN'S School Days. By an Old Boy. Illustrations. 8vo, Paper, 50 cents.
TOM BROWN at Oxford. Ill's. 8vo, Paper, 75 cents.
TROLLOPE'S (Anthony)* Bertrams. 12mo, Cloth, $1 50.
  The Golden Lion of Granpere. Illustrated. 8vo, Paper, 75 cents.
  The Eustace Diamonds. 8vo, Cloth, $1 75; Paper, $1 25.
  Can You Forgive Her? 8vo, Cloth, $2 00; Paper, $1 50.
  Castle Richmond. 12mo, Cloth, $1 50.
  Doctor Thorne. 12mo, Cloth, $1 50.
  Framley Parsonage. Ill's. 12mo, Cloth, $1 75.
  He Knew He was Right. 8vo, Cloth, $1 50; Paper, $1 00.
  Last Chronicle of Barset. 8vo, Cloth, $2 00; Paper, $1 50.
  Phineas Finn. 8vo, Cloth, $1 75; Paper, $1 25.
  Orley Farm. Ill's. 8vo, Cloth, $2 00; Paper, $1 50.
  Ralph the Heir. Illustrations. 8vo, Cloth, $1 75; Paper, $1 25.
  Small House at Allington. Ill's. 8vo, Cloth, $2 00.
  Three Clerks. 12mo, Cloth, $1 50.
  Vicar of Bullhampton. Illustrations. 8vo, Cloth, $1 75; Paper, $1 25.
TROLLOPE'S (T. A.)* Lindisfarn Chase. 8vo, Cloth, $2 00; Paper, $1 50.
  Diamond Cut Diamond. 12mo, Cloth, $1 25.

* For other Novels by the same author, see *Harper's Library of Select Novels.*

APRIL BOOK-LIST.

☞ HARPER & BROTHERS *will send any of the following books by mail, postage prepaid, to any part of the United States, on receipt of the price.*

☞ HARPER'S CATALOGUE *and* HARPER'S TRADE-LIST *will be sent by mail on receipt of Six Cents.*

Vincent's Land of the White Elephant.

The Land of the White Elephant: Sights and Scenes in Southeastern Asia. A Personal Narrative of Travel and Adventure in Farther India, embracing the Countries of Burma, Siam, Cambodia, and Cochin-China (1871-2). By FRANK VINCENT, Jr. Magnificently illustrated with Map, Plans, and numerous Woodcuts. Crown 8vo, Cloth, $3 50.

"This new work of Oriental travel and adventure presents fresh, accurate, and original information about Farther India and its people. It is not padded with historical, political, ethnographical, or geographical matter obtained at second-hand from books, but is a record of the author's own travels and observations. The chapters which treat of Burma and Cambodia, including full descriptions of their kings and courts, and of Cochin-China, carry the reader through entirely untrodden fields; while the chapters relating to Siam, besides a complete account of Bangkok, the king, and palace, contain a very interesting narrative of a long journey made through the heart of the kingdom, and a carefully written, popular description, now for the first time published, of the magnificent ruins of Angkor, on its eastern frontier. The work is splendidly illustrated with engravings, maps, and plans, and is in all respects one of the most interesting and valuable books of Eastern travel ever given to the public."

———

Farther India is still more or less a sealed book to most of us, and one could not desire a more pleasant tutor in fresh geographical lore than our author. He won our heart at once by plunging *in medias res*, instead of devoting a chapter to the outward voyage; and he tells us sensibly and intelligently, in a natural and unaffected style, what he saw and heard.—*John Bull*, London.

"The Land of the White Elephant," by Mr. Vincent, is another instance of the superiority of your countrymen over ours in the writing of books of travel, as a general rule. For directness, for saying what he has to say straight off, and beginning at the really interesting and important portion of his travels at once, instead of reiterating old descriptions which every one has read a score of times, Mr. Frank Vincent is almost unique, and his book a model. It is rendered additionally interesting by the extraordinary changes which are taking place in Siam, that remote and wonderful land now making strides toward the adoption of Western civilization more energetic than those of the "Land of the Rising Sun" itself.—*London correspondence of the N. Y. Herald.*

The work presents us with a personal narrative of travel and adventure in Farther India, embracing the countries of Burma, Siam, Cambodia, and Cochin-China. Mr. Vincent is an American gentleman, and his travels took place in the years 1871-2, so that his volume has the great advantage of reflecting the actual existing state of these lands.—*Daily News*, London.

This is in many respects a model book of travel. For once a traveler eschews any thing like book-making, and, although Mr. Vincent visited India and China, Ceylon and Japan, he limits his narrative to lands that are far less familiar to us. The route he describes in his volume led him up the Irrawaddy to independent Burma; thence, returning to Rangoon, he made the circuit of the Malay Peninsula, and, after a visit to the kingdom of Siam, made his way through Cambodia to the French settlements in Cochin-China. The volume is profusely and excellently illustrated, and convenient maps add to its value. Mr. Vincent gives a plain but pleasant account of all that struck him as best worth noting. * * * In many ways the journey was extremely interesting, and, what is more to our present purpose, it was a journey extremely interesting to read about. * * * The whole of his book is worth reading, as giving the latest observations of an intelligent traveler over countries that are rapidly changing their characteristics.—*Pall Mall Gazette*, London.

We are inclined to assign to this book a place of foremost interest among the travel books of the year. The architectural and sculptural plates alone add immensely to its value.—*Examiner*, London.

A not unwelcome addition to our knowledge of the Indo-Chinese peninsulas. It is written in a clear and unaffected style. It is descriptive of forests, lakes, rivers, capitals, and ruins. It shows the author to be possessed of some of the qualities indispensable to successful exploration—energy, endurance of heat, fatigue, and petty annoyances, good humor, quickness of observation, and intelligence. Its value is enhanced by two or three maps throwing light on some disputed points of geography, as well as by many excellent engravings which place before us the pagodas with their wonderful tracery and the reigning monarchs in their robes of State.—*Saturday Review*, London.

Evangelical Alliance Conference, 1873.

History, Essays, Orations, and Other Documents of the Sixth General Conference of the Evangelical Alliance, held in New York, October 2–12, 1873. Edited by Rev. PHILIP SCHAFF, D.D,. and Rev. S. IRENÆUS PRIME, D.D. With Portraits of Rev. Messrs. Pronier, Carrasco, and Cook, recently deceased. 8vo, Cloth, nearly 800 pages, $6 00.

About one hundred men, from various parts of the world, eminent for learning, ability, and worth, holding high rank in theology, philosophy, science, and literature, men of genius, power, and fame, were carefully selected, and invited to prepare themselves, by months and years of study, for the discussion of themes of immediate and vital importance. They were chosen, as the men of thought and purpose best fitted to produce Treatises which should exhibit, in the most thorough and exhaustive form, the TRUTH, as sustained by the Holy Scripture and the most advanced and enlightened human reason. The results of this concentrated thought and labor are embodied in this volume. Rarely has a volume issued from the press which

contained a more varied and extensive array of talent and experience.

The vital topics of Evangelical Theology, the delicate relations of Science and Religion, the difficult subjects of practical Benevolence, Philanthropy, and Reform are here discussed by clear, sound, and experienced minds. Pulpit orators, of renown and recognized position, have contributed to this volume their best productions.

It is, in short, a library of Christian thought and learning—the latest expression of master-minds upon the important topics that are now moving the Christian world—and should be read by all who would be educated in the thought of the age.

Motley's Life and Death of John of Barneveld.

Life and Death of John of Barneveld, Advocate of Holland. With a View of the Primary Causes and Movements of "The Thirty Years' War." By JOHN LOTHROP MOTLEY, D.C.L., Author of "The Rise of the Dutch Republic," "History of the United Netherlands," &c. With Illustrations. In Two Volumes. 8vo, Cloth. *(In Press.)*

Victor Hugo's Ninety-Three.

Ninety-Three. A Novel. By VICTOR HUGO, Author of "Toilers of the Sea," "Les Misérables," &c. Translated by FRANK LEE BENEDICT. 12mo, Cloth, $1 75 ; 8vo, Paper, 75 cents.

Tyng on a Christian Pastor.

The Office and Duty of a Christian Pastor. By STEPHEN H. TYNG, D.D., Rector of St. George's Church in the City of New York. Published at the request of the Students and Faculty of the School of Theology in the Boston University. 12mo, Cloth, $1 50. *(Nearly Ready.)*

Colonel Dacre.

Colonel Dacre. A Novel. By the Author of "Caste," &c. 8vo, Paper, 50 cents.

There is much that is attractive both in Colonel Dacre and the simple-hearted girl whom he honors with his love.—*Athenæum, London.*

Colonel Dacre is a gentleman throughout, which character is somewhat rare in modern novels.—*Pall Mall Gazette.*

Field's Memories of Many Men and of Some Women.

Memories of Many Men and of Some Women : being Personal Recollections of Emperors, Kings, Queens, Princes, Presidents, Statesmen, Authors, and Artists, at Home and Abroad, during the last Thirty Years. By MAUNSELL B. FIELD. 12mo, Cloth, $2 00.

Abounds in anecdotes, and the personal sketches of eminent characters are so cleverly drawn that we have the originals before us.—*Philadelphia Press.*

He has written a pleasant volume of personal gossip, detailing in a frank, unpretending way a host of interesting anecdotes of all sorts of people. * * * A very entertaining volume.—*N. Y. World.*

The book is very cleverly executed, and is entertaining in no ordinary degree. * * * He has preserved plenty of anecdotes which embody much that is pithy and pungent about them.—*Boston Saturday Evening Gazette.*

Possibly other Americans have had as good opportunities and made as much of them as Mr. Field, but few have taken the trouble to publish theirs in a book.—*Boston Daily Advertiser.*

One of the most interesting books of the season.—*St. Louis Dispatch.*

Mr. Field, in jotting down these recollections, has not endeavored to write history, or even biography, but just gossip. It is gossip, nevertheless, so bright and entertaining, and affording so vivid a view of the informal domestic or social life of the persons concerned, that it is more interesting than elaborate biography could have been.—*Boston Journal.*

Mr. Field's anecdotes are bright and clear; are told with a facile pen and an appreciation of the "point" which at once entails the interest of the reader. * * * Sprightly and spirited.—*N. Y. Commercial Advertiser.*

A chatty book of anecdotes and reminiscences. It has something to say about almost every man prominent in political circles, both in this country and in Europe, during the last quarter of a century.—*Phila. Evening Bulletin.*

It is a volume of unusual interest, amusing, instructive, and companionable.—*St. Louis Times.*

Bulwer's The Parisians.

The Parisians. A Novel. By EDWARD BULWER, Lord Lytton, Author of "The Coming Race," "Kenelm Chillingly," "A Strange Story," "The Caxtons," "My Novel," &c., &c. With Illustrations by SYDNEY HALL. 12mo, Cloth, $1 50; 8vo, Paper, $1 00.

* * * Lord Lytton was as much a dramatist as a novelist, and his plots were always carefully woven. Down to the very last chapter of "The Parisians" our interest is skillfully kept not alive but glowing. * * * In a word, "The Parisians" is its author's ripest work. Lytton's aftermath is in many ways a richer crop than his spring yielded. Graces of style, acquired by long labor, have grown into a second nature. * * * We have the last novel of a novelist who, conscious of the lapse of time, is consciously writing for posterity. Many will read it often; none need regret to have carefully read it once.—*Athenæum*, London.

It is one of the most characteristic and remarkable of its author's works. The book is characteristic in the fact that we find in it some of the more obvious points that distinguish Bulwer purely as a novelist. There is the carefully conceived and elaborately involved, but always artistically arranged and developed plot, in which this writer surpassed all his contemporaries. There are characters, like Graham Vane and Victor de Mauleon, which so bear the stamp of his mind that one could hardly be misled into doubting their parentage. There are ripened fruits of that spirit of observation that long since passed out of its crude stage. Nearly the whole panorama of French life which it furnishes may be said to be of this stamp. The Marquis de Rochebriant, Frederic Lemercier, Raoul and Enguerrand de Vandemar, Louvier, Savarin, Gustave Rameau, are all strong types of character, and together put France in her recent era more perfectly before the reader than she has ever been presented by any writer with whom we are familiar, in any form. * * * The book is a credit both to the heart and the head of Bulwer in the declining years of his life, and is an admirable legacy of the ripest stage of his mind. The two posthumous productions of his pen, "Kenelm Chillingly" and "The Parisians," are scarcely inferior in interest as novels to any thing he wrote, and in acuteness of observation, wisdom and purity of reflection, and almost perfect polish of literary style, they surpass all his previous works. The close of his career is crowned with its noblest offering. * * * It pictures Paris before its fall. We see in it Louis Napoleon upon the throne. We find in it the secret of the strength that made this the splendid and dazzling point of power that it presented to the world for years before it toppled and fell; and we see, also, the causes, both in social life and in public profligacy, that were surely undermining this apparently impregnable prosperity. These were never so graphically analyzed and laid bare. * * * Few things in literature are finer than the description of the social condition of France which made her so easy a prey, in spite of the bravery and the pride of her people.—*Boston Saturday Evening Gazette.*

That "The Parisians," though incomplete, is the greatest production of Lord Lytton's pen, will, we think, be the general verdict. It has greater breadth of plan, a larger scope, and is informed with a higher and more matured philosophical spirit than any of his other works. * * * Every one who takes up the book is lured on from page to page by a fascination which never relaxes its hold upon the mind. We follow, with increasing interest, the fortunes of the various characters of the story, because we insensibly become interested in them, as we do in living characters. At every step we feel the charm of the author's style, of his incisive wit, of his keen, clear observation. The volume abounds in brilliant sayings, as well as profound ones. The author never allows himself or any of his characters to inflict dullness on the reader, and whether speaking in his own person or through another, avoids the fatal error of prosing. There are chapters and books in "The Parisians" on which the reader dwells with special pleasure, and to which every one will turn back with delight for a reperusal; but there is none which he will feel inclined to skip in the hurry to get on with the story.—*Boston Journal.*

The author has set before himself the task of painting French society in Paris in the last days of the Second Empire, and he has accomplished this task, foreigner as he was, with a skill which a born Frenchman might well envy. As an historical fiction "The Parisians" stands higher than "Rienzi" or the "Last Days of Pompeii." It is a satire in the sense that it remorselessly depicts the follies and crimes of the imperialist regime, and is a far abler satire than the "New Timon." It is more brilliant in its epigrammatic wit than "Pelham," and smoother in the flow of its narrative than "Kenelm Chillingly." * * * It will always be treated by students of literature with the respect due to a brilliant and exceptionably able novel.—*N. Y. World.*

On every page of "The Parisians" we find evidences of the painstaking, thorough preparation for his task which distinguishes all the works of Lord Lytton. * * * "The Parisians" is a rare and noteworthy instance of the successful artistic use of contemporary history for the purposes of fiction. * * * His aim was to portray, through the living medium of fiction, the social and political condition of France at the close of the second empire, and we hazard the statement that no future historian will give a more faithful or more graphic picture of the France and the Paris of '69 and '70 than is to be found in the pages of this novel. * * * The reader who takes it up will not willingly lay it down until the last page is reached, and he will rise from its perusal with the conviction that it is a work worthy of a place by the side of "The Caxtons" and "My Novel." —*N. Y. Evening Post.*

Sara Coleridge's Memoir and Letters.

Memoir and Letters of Sara Coleridge. Edited by her Daughter. With Two Portraits on Steel. Crown 8vo, Cloth, $2 50.

This is a very choice contribution to the literature of its class; not surpassed in literary interest or intellectual power by any female correspondence that we possess. It is, moreover, a valuable addition to the literature which has gathered round the names of the Lake poets. We are again admitted within the charmed circle of which Southey, Wordsworth, and Coleridge are the presiding deities.—*British Quarterly Review.*

This charming volume forms an acceptable record and presents an adequate image of a mind of singular beauty and no inconsiderable power.—*Examiner*, London.

This charming work. * * * We can hardly conceive an intelligent reader for whom the work will not have a charm, as telling genuinely and naturally the life, the daily thoughts, and hopes, and occupations of a noble woman of a high order of mind, and as mirroring a pure heart. Her letter-writing is thoroughly unaffected; there is never straining for effect.—*Athenæum*, London.

* * * The records of the life of a singularly gifted, intellectual, and accomplished woman—one whose memory is a benefaction to the race.—*N. Y. Times.*

Baird's Annual Record.

Annual Record of Science and Industry for 1873. Prepared by Prof. SPENCER F. BAIRD, Ass't-Secretary of the Smithsonian Institution. With the Assistance of some of the most eminent men of Science in the United States. Large 12mo, over 800 pages, Cloth, $2 00. (*Just Ready.*)

Uniform in style and price with the volumes for 1871 and 1872. The Three Volumes sent to one address, postage paid, on receipt of $5 00.

The Heart of Africa. By Schweinfurth.

The Heart of Africa; or, Three Years' Travels and Adventures in the Unexplored Regions of the Centre of Africa. From 1868 to 1871. By Dr. GEORG SCHWEINFURTH. Translated by ELLEN E. FREWER. With an Introduction by WINWOOD READE. Illustrated by about 130 Woodcuts from Drawings made by the Author, with Two Maps. 2 vols., 8vo. (*In Press.*)

"Traveling, not in the footsteps of Sir Samuel Baker, but in a westerly direction, Dr. Schweinfurth reached the neighborhood of Baker's Lake, and, passing through the country of the Niam-Niam, he remained for some months in the hitherto unknown kingdom of Monbuttoo. In a geographical sense, his book will contribute in an important degree to the solution of the Nile problem; and ethnologically it will tend to set at rest the disputed question as to the existence of a dwarf race in Central Africa. Dr. Schweinfurth is an accomplished draughtsman, and his work is elaborately illustrated from his own drawings."

Tristram's Land of Moab.

The Land of Moab: The Result of Travels and Discoveries on the East Side of the Dead Sea and the Jordan. By H. B. TRISTRAM, M.A., LL.D., F.R.S., Hon. Canon of Durham. With a Chapter on the Persian Palace of Mashita, by JAS. FERGUSON, F.R.S. With Map and Illustrations. Crown 8vo, Cloth, $2 50.

Dr. Tristram's account of his visit to the Land of Moab will be welcomed by all who have longed to know something more of a country so intimately connected with the history of the Israelites. Pleasantly written and well illustrated, the narrative sustains its interest throughout, and gives a vivid picture of the present condition of the country.—*Athenæum*, London.

The volume has all the interest of a drama, and will be a rich feast to the reader who comes to its perusal with the eagerness all Christians feel in those countries which were the scene of all the events and most of the prophecies recorded in Holy Writ. It is written, too, in the choice language Canon Tristram knows so well how to use. Altogether this book is one delightful to read, and full of information.—*The Presbyterian.*

Lottie Darling. By John Cordy Jeaffreson.

Lottie Darling. A Novel. By JOHN CORDY JEAFFRESON, Author of "Isabel," "Not Dead Yet," "Live it Down," "Olive Blake's Good Work," &c. 8vo, Paper, 75 cents.

"Lottie Darling" contains some delicious love passages and original and striking sketches of character. The plot is one of powerful interest.—*Graphic*, London. A story of healthy tone, and readable throughout.—*Examiner*, London. In "Lottie Darling," Mr. Jeaffreson has achieved a triumph. It is a capital novel, as sparkling as it is original, as powerful as it is amusing. It is healthy in tone, interesting from beginning to end, and contains sketches of life and character unusually vivid and well drawn.—*Morning Post*, London. This story is well told. It opens up a phase of life hitherto untouched by any novelist.—*Daily News*, London.

Pet. A Book for Children.

Pet; or, Pastimes and Penalties. By H. R. HAWEIS, Author of "Music and Morals." With 50 Illustrations. 12mo, Cloth, $1 50.

Prettily written and sure to interest children. The illustrations are very good.—*Pall Mall Gazette*, London. Evidently the work of a writer who is at heart a boy yet, and gains from this fact a freshness and truth.—*Hour*, London. "Pet," the dearest little heroine who ever graced a story book. * * * "Pet" will win the hearts of all readers, whether they are fathers and mothers or their boys and girls.—*Athenæum*, London. A charming little volume.—*Daily News*, London.

The Blue Ribbon.

The Blue Ribbon. A Novel. By the Author of "St. Olave's," "Jeanie's Quiet Life," "Meta's Faith," &c. 8vo, Paper, 50 cents.

An admirable story. The character of the heroine is original and skillfully worked out, and an interest is cast around her which never flags. The sketches of society in a cathedral city are very vivid and amusing.—*Morning Post*, London. The very best work the author has yet given us. It is strong in its plot, which is admirably worked out, and careful in discrimination and portraiture of character. It is one of the best novels of the season.—*English Independent*, London. The reader will be both pleased and interested in this story. It abounds in picturesque, healthy dialogue, touches of pathos and quiet good sense, which will surely make it popular.—*Standard*, London. An unquestionably interesting story. We like "The Blue Ribbon" very much.—*Spectator*, London.

Among our Sailors.

By J. GREY JEWELL, M.D., late United States Consul, Singapore. With an Appendix containing Extracts from the Laws and Consular Regulations Governing the United States Merchant Service. 12mo, Cloth, $1 50.

Mr. Jewell was for some years United States Consul at Singapore, and in that station he had an opportunity to note the abuses of the American merchant marine. His book is mainly to call attention to the injustice with which officers and men are treated, in the hope that legislation and philanthropic effort will correct the abuses of which he complains. As a whole it is an excellent work, and will unquestionably do good in the way intended.—*N. Y. World.*

An exceedingly intelligent, instructive, and entertaining work. Every page in the volume is freighted with telling revelations of the sea. No space is wasted with idle rhetoric. Similar narratives have been published in fragmentary style in the current news of the day for many years, but no other effort within our recollection has been made to bring the facts together in a form calculated to constitute a thrilling and powerful appeal, such as we have before us now. "Among our Sailors" is a deserving book, and it will be more talked about among the classes to which it addresses itself than any work that has reached them in many years.—*Brooklyn Eagle.*

It is very seldom that we meet with a book which is more useful, and withal more interesting, than this. The condition of our sailors, the hardships, often

amounting to cruelties and oppressions, which they undergo, the relations subsisting between ordinary seamen and a ship's officers, form an important chapter in the life of one of the most valuable sections of the people. The peculiar circumstances that surround the life of a sailor, his ignorance of the means of obtaining redress, and the short time that he usually remains on shore, deprive him of the opportunity, afforded to most other persons, of submitting his grievances openly to the world. Dr. Jewell has, therefore, done a good work in taking up a cause which, for these and other reasons, has too long been left unnoticed. It is a work which, so far as we are aware, has never before been attempted in this country; but it has fallen, at last, into efficient hands, and the result is a book that should be read by every one who has the interests of the American mercantile marine at heart. A long practical experience has given Dr. Jewell ample qualification for the duty he has undertaken; and while, by a clear explanation of the laws, some of which he has either in whole or in part added, he has furnished a valuable manual for the sea-faring community, he has also, by the vivid narrative of facts and the accumulation of much minute detail, supplied a most interesting book to the general reader.—*N. Y. Times.*

"Ship Ahoy!"

A Yarn in Thirty-six Cable Lengths. Illustrated by WALLIS MACKAY and FREDERICK WADDY. 8vo, Paper, 40 cents.

"This capital sea-story grew out of the popular agitation aroused in England by Mr. Plimsoll's startling *exposé* of the abuse of sending unseaworthy and overloaded ships to sea, so heavily insured that their loss would be profitable to the owners and shippers. The adventures which make up the narrative of 'Ship Ahoy!' have their parallels in actual experience, but

with them is interwoven a romantic love-story which awakens the reader's sympathy and maintains his interest to the close. 'Ship Ahoy!' forms an excellent pendant to Dr. Jewell's work, 'Among our Sailors,' recently published, in which public attention is called to many flagrant abuses to which American sailors are subjected."

Twelve Miles from a Lemon. By Gail Hamilton.

Twelve Miles from a Lemon : Social and Domestic Sketches. By GAIL HAMILTON, Author of "Woman's Worth and Worthlessness," "Little Folk Life," &c. 12mo, Cloth, $1 50.

The title of this volume is explained by the familiar story of Sydney Smith, who described his living in Yorkshire as being so out of the way that it was actually "twelve miles from a lemon," and consequently a like distance from all the other elements of punch and civilization. Miss Dodge apparently lives at much the same distance from Boston, and regarding Boston and lemons as synonyms of civilization, she has written a volume of sprightly little essays and sketches relating for the most part to the humors and infelicities of suburban life. In many respects it is the most entertaining of her numerous books. It is simply a volume of brilliant, witty, and audacious gossip, touching upon countless topics, and perpetually moving the reader to pleased or sardonic mirth.—*World, N. Y.*

It is written in the curt, crisp, self-assertive, and somewhat aggressive style in which the author is fond of propounding her theories and fancies.—*Herald, N.Y.*

The book is not only readable, but it will be read : its clever treatment of the petty trivialities of everyday life, and its outbreak from these into the broader atmosphere of right and wrong, alike commend it to the everyday reader.—*Evening Mail, N.Y.*

This is a light, airy, and pleasant book, containing some hard hits at the foibles, mistakes, pretensions, and extravagances of the times.—*Episcopalian, Phila.*

Gail Hamilton is one of those writers who are never dull. Her manner may be considered jerky and fantastic, but there is always point in her sallies, and a vast amount of good mother wit.—*Inter-Ocean, Chicago.*

Through Fire and Water.

Through Fire and Water. A Tale of City Life. By FREDERICK TALBOT. Illustrated. 8vo, Paper, 25 cents.

Trollope's Phineas Redux.

Phineas Redux. A Novel. By ANTHONY TROLLOPE, Author of "The Warden," "Barchester Towers," "Phineas Finn," "Orley Farm," "The Small House at Allington," &c. Illustrated. 8vo, Paper, $1 25 ; Cloth, $1 75.

A Princess of Thule. By Wm. Black.

A Princess of Thule. A Novel. By WILLIAM BLACK, Author of "Love cr Marriage?" "Kilmeny," "The Strange Adventures of a Phaeton," &c., &c. 8vo, Paper, 75 cents.

We have at least one nearly perfect novel. * * * His beautiful, his almost perfect story. * * * There is a mingling of humor of the raciest, with pathos most true, simple, and dignified.—*Spectator*, London.

This is not the first time that our author has shown himself capable of describing a fascinating woman; and the excellent descriptions of natural beauty, the thorough mastery of local peculiarities, the truth and accuracy with which the local dialect and modes of thought are reproduced. * * * Those who like novels of character will be amply gratified. Complete individuality distinguishes all concerned.—*Athenæum*, London.

It is not of many novels it can be said they are good from the title to the end, but this may be fairly remarked of Mr. Black's last work, to which he has given so happily descriptive a title. Mr. Black never relies for effect upon violent means. He contrives by delicate, subtle, but sure touches to win the interest of his readers, and to retain it till the last volume is laid down with reluctance. The characters of Sheila and her father, Mackenzie, ought to have an enduring and recognized existence in fiction. * * * The "Princess of Thule" is altogether a remarkable novel; it will add to the reputation which Mr. Black has already made by his sincere and undeviating loyalty to the best principles of the art in which he excels.—*Globe*, London.

If Mr. Black had written no other novel than this, he would have made himself a high place in the republic of literature. It is witty, humorous, pathetic, and throughout artistic.—*Scotsman*.

It is quite refreshing to take up such a work of fiction. It is no exaggeration to say that the story exercises a sort of fascination over the reader from the first chapter to the last, and this by no fantastic spell, but by the charm of the purest, truest, and most healthy sentiment.—*Daily Telegraph*, London.

We do not remember to have read any where of a more wholly fascinating heroine than Sheila.—*Court Circular*, London.

A novel which is both romantic and natural, which has much feeling without any touch of mawkishness, which goes deep into character without any suggestion of painful analysis—this is a rare gem to find among the *débris* of current literature, and this, or nearly this, Mr. Black has given us in the "Princess of Thule." * * * His success, which is undoubtedly great, is due to a careful study and competent knowledge of character, to a style which is free from blemish, and to a power of graphic description which is but very seldom met with.—*Saturday Review*, London.

It is full of fine character-rendering, with the all-brightening thread of humor glimmering out now and then. * * * A work of singular power and delicacy.—*British Quarterly Review*.

Christlieb on the Methods of Counteracting Infidelity.

The Best Methods of Counteracting Modern Infidelity. A Paper read before the General Conference of the Evangelical Alliance, New York, October 6, 1873. By THEODOR CHRISTLIEB, Ph.D., D.D., Professor of Theology and University Preacher at Bonn, Prussia. 12mo, Flexible Cloth, 75 cents.

The public will not soon forget the powerful impression made during the recent sessions of the Evangelical Alliance, by Dr. Christlieb, whose paper on "The Best Methods of Counteracting Modern Infidelity" was read before the Alliance.—*Christian Union*.

This paper of Dr. Christlieb's is regarded as the ablest and best presented before the Evangelical Alliance, and it has elevated him at once to the front rank of Evangelical divines of the present age.—*Lutheran Observer*.

Diamond Cut Diamond.

A Story of Tuscan Life. By T. ADOLPHUS TROLLOPE, Author of "Lindisfarn Chase," "A Siren," "Durnton Abbey," &c. 12mo, Cloth, $1 25.

Many novels have been written of the people of this country, and "Diamond Cut Diamond" is among the best of them. * * * The plot is symmetrical, and the story is smoothly and pleasantly told.—*N. Y. World*.

It reveals an interesting picture of social life in Italy, and is very cleverly written.—*Lutheran Observer*.

This is a tragic story of priestly interference in the private affairs of domestic life—a thoughtful and well-written story. Mr. Trollope is a fine writer.—*Presbyterian*.

It is picturesque and extremely natural.—*Universalist*.

The style is clear, and the descriptions entertaining.—*The Christian Advocate*, Pittsburgh.

This well-told story.—*The Episcopalian*.

We unhesitatingly place it among the highest of its class. Its plan is not a complicated one. Its characters are few enough almost to be counted upon the fingers of one hand. But for symmetry, attentiveness to detail, careful finish, and general effect, we bestow upon it our warmest praise. * * * There is to our eye something exquisite in the fullness of contour, sharpness of outline, and richness of color with which it has been wrought by the writer. * * * It is, in a true sense, a work of art.—*The Congregationalist*.

The plot is happily conceived, and is worked out with great ability.—*New Bedford Standard*.

The Bazar Book of Health.

The Dwelling, the Nursery, the Bedroom, the Dining-Room, the Parlor, the Library, the Kitchen, the Sick-Room. 16mo, Cloth, $1 00. (Uniform with the "BAZAR BOOK OF DECORUM," Price $1 00.)

Trollope's Harry Heathcote of Gangoil.

Harry Heathcote of Gangoil: A Tale of Australian Bush-Life. By ANTHONY TROLLOPE Author of "The Warden," "Barchester Towers," "Orley Farm," "The Small House at Allington," "The Eustace Diamonds," &c., &c. Illustrated. 8vo, Paper, 25 cents.

www.ingramcontent.com/pod-product-compliance
Lightning Source LLC
Chambersburg PA
CBHW020618030726
47497CB00007B/2303

www.ingramcontent.com/pod-product-compliance
Lightning Source LLC
Chambersburg PA
CBHW020617030726
47497CB00007B/2293